Django Wexler graduated Carnegie Mellon University in Pittsburgh with degrees in creative writing and computer science, and worked for the university in artificial intelligence research. ntually he migrated to Microsoft and Seattle, where he now vith two cats and a teetering mountain of books. When not ing Shadow Campaigns, he wrangles computers, paints tiny rs, and plays games of all sorts.

www.djangowex

@DjangoWe

Praise for Django

An extremely strong debut, flintlock fantasy at its best ... there's a new military fiction cowboy in town and his name is Django'
Nick Sharps, *SF Signal*

'The coolest fantasy story you'll read this week'
i09

'an excellent book'
SFX

I absolutely loved it. Wexler balances the actions of his very human characters with just the right amount of imaginative "magic" to keep me wanting more'
Taylor Anderson, bestselling author of the *Destroyerman* series

xler has produced something unusual in the fantasy line, a setting reminiscent of the early Victorian period, out e bleeding edge of Empire, a world of dust and bayonets muskets... and magic. The characters are fascinating and all of them have secrets ... I read it at a gulp and look

S

THE THOUSAND NAMES

Book One of the Shadow Campaigns

DJANGO WEXLER

DEL REY

1 3 5 7 9 10 8 6 4 2

First published in the US in 2013 by ROC, part of the Penguin Group
Penguin Group (USA) Inc.,
Published in the UK in 2013 by Del Rey, an imprint of Ebury Publishing
A Random House Group Company
This edition published in 2014

The Random House Group Limited Reg. No. 954009

Addresses for companies within the Random House Group can be found at:
www.randomhouse.co.uk

A CIP catalogue record for this book is
available from the British Library

The Random House Group Limited supports The Forest Stewardship
Council® (FSC®), the leading international forest-certification organisation.
Our books carrying the FSC label are printed on FSC® -certified paper.
FSC is the only forest-certification scheme supported by the
leading environmental organisations, including Greenpeace.
Our paper procurement policy can be found at:
www.randomhouse.co.uk/environment

Printed and bound by CPI Group (UK) Ltd, Croydon, CR0 4YY

ISBN 9780091950606

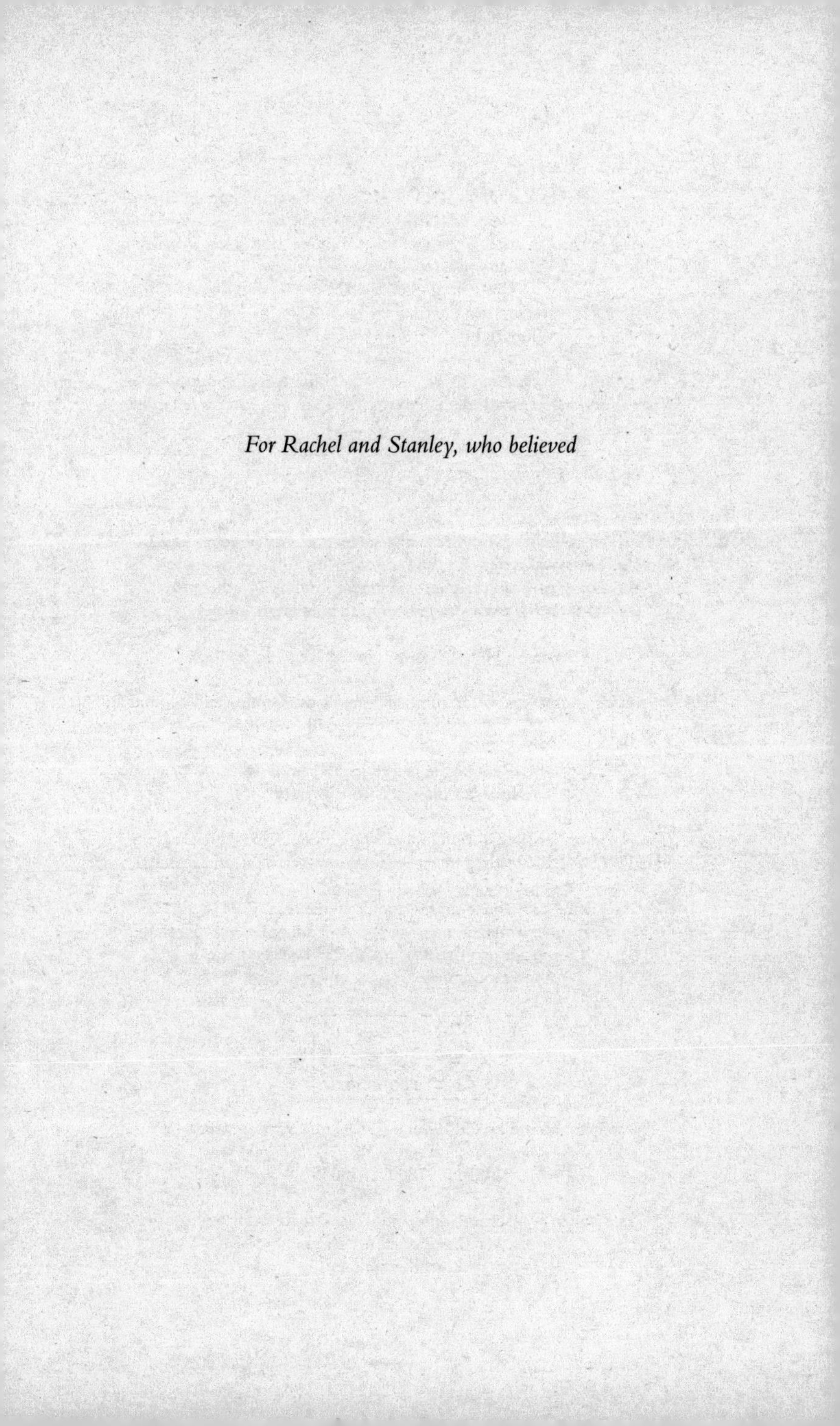

For Rachel and Stanley, who believed

ACKNOWLEDGMENTS

I have a lot of people to thank, so let me get right to it, in roughly chronological order.

This is not, in any sense, a historical novel. At best it was *inspired* by history, in the loosest Hollywood sense of the word. But it began with my interest in history, and the inspiration for that is almost entirely traceable to a series of late-night conversations with Neal Altman and Konstantin Koptev (among others) after sessions of CMU's Vermillion Anime Club.

Neal's impromptu mini-lectures sparked an interest that has turned into a lifelong hobby. Later, he got me into historical war-gaming and introduced me to the equally knowledgeable Jim Naughton. The two of them happily lent me stacks of reading material, and from that (as usual) everything else followed. So many thanks to Neal, Jim, and everyone else who pushed lead in Jim's basement. Keep rolling sixes, guys.

I read many wonderful histories, but a few stand out as particularly inspiring. David G. Chandler's *The Campaigns of Napoleon* probably led in as straight a line to *The Thousand Names* as anything did. He manages to make real events as thrilling to read about as anything in fiction, and it leaves me in awe. When I started working on the larger context of the series, Simon Schama's *Citizens* provided a similar service. Those two, and all the other hardworking historians who don't get to just make this stuff up like I do, have my everlasting gratitude.

In more recent history, I have been assisted at every turn by any number of talented and sympathetic individuals:

Dr. John Baer helped me through a very difficult time, and without him I'm not sure this book would ever have reached its first draft.

Elisabeth Fracalossi did yeoman's work as the alpha reader, getting the chapters hot off the presses and helping me through the rough patches. Knowing that at least *one* person is waiting for you to finish is invaluable.

My awesome beta readers provided wonderful feedback at every stage. In no particular order, thanks to Prentice Clark, Janelle Stanley, Carl Meister, Amanda Davis, Dan Blandford, and Lu Huan.

I never used to understand why, in their acknowledgments, authors always sound so pathetically grateful to their agents. Now I understand: they have magical powers. Seth Fishman's wizardry is particularly strong, and it's increasingly clear that signing on with him is probably the best single decision I ever made.

Alongside Seth was the great team at the Gernert Company—Rebecca Gardner, Will Roberts, and Andy Kifer—and Caspian Dennis at Abner Stein in the UK. My deepest thanks to all.

Last chronologically, but in no other sense, there are my editors, Jessica Wade at Roc and Michael Rowley at Del Rey UK. Their help made this book immeasurably better, and they managed the difficult trick of coediting wonderfully. My thanks as well to the talented teams at both publishers, who don't get to put their names on the book but who make sure that every little bit of it shines.

Finally, to the ghost of a certain *petit caporal*, I can only offer my sincere apologies.

THE THOUSAND NAMES

N
Khandar
The Demon Sea
Fort Valor (Sarhatep)
The Coast Road
The Lesser Desol
Legend
Battle
Desert
Town
Road
Fortress
Bridge
Miles
0
10
20
Map by Cortney Skinner

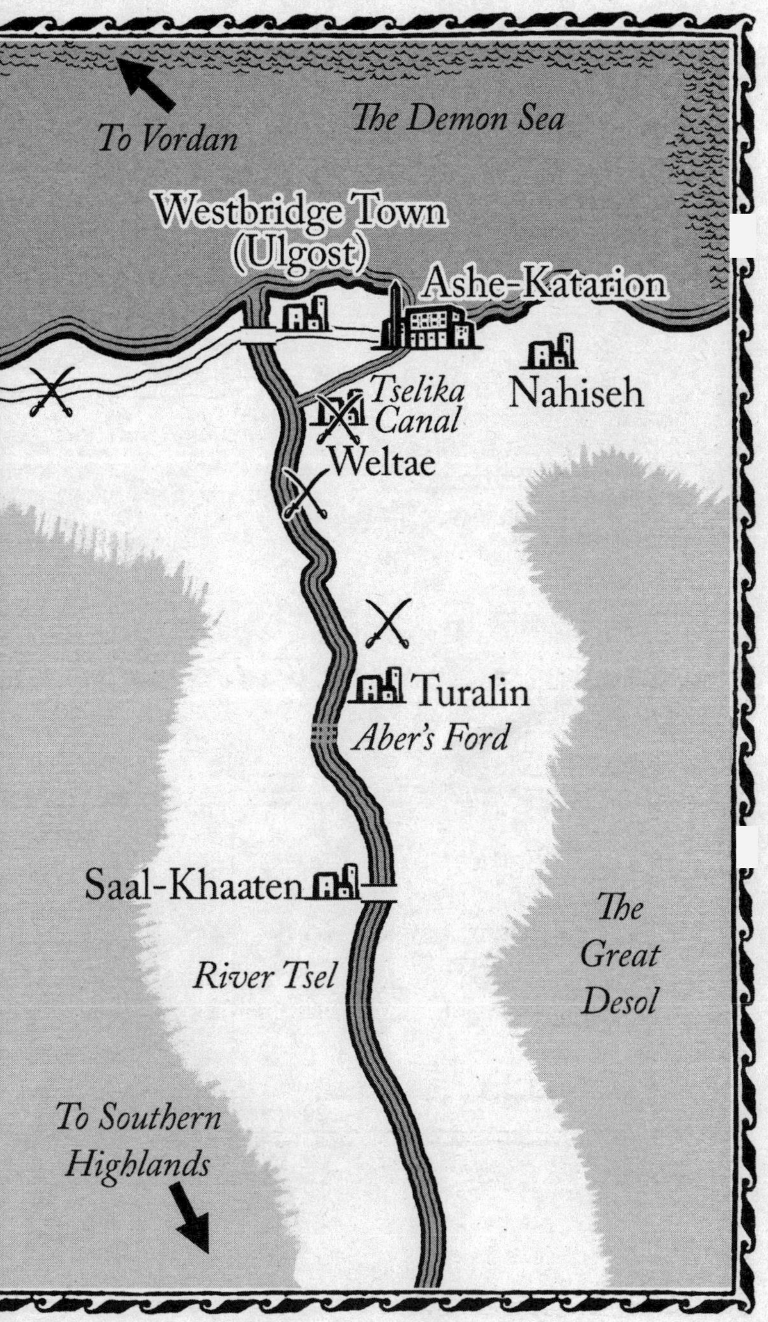
To Vordan
The Demon Sea
Westbridge Town
(Ulgost)
Ashe-Katarion
Nahiseh
Tselika
Canal
Weltae
Turalin
Aber's Ford
Saal-Khaaten
The
Great
Desol
River Tsel
To Southern
Highlands

PROLOGUE

JAFFA

The new supreme rulers of Khandar met in the old common room of the Justices, the cudgel-bearing peacekeepers and constabulary who were now the closest thing the city of Ashe-Katarion had to a civil authority. It was a gloomy space, buried deep in the city's ancient gatehouse. Jaffa-dan-Iln, as Grand Justice, was the nominal host of the gathering, and he'd done his best to straighten up, removing decades of accumulated rubbish, packs of cards, dice, and misplaced papers. There was no way to hide the marks and patches on the carpets, though, or the plain sandstone walls, devoid of decoration except where some bored Justice had carved them with a belt knife. The table was cheap wood layered with stains, and the chairs were a mismatched set dragged from every room of the gatehouse. Jaffa had rearranged the bookcases and other furniture to at least conceal the more obscene bits of graffiti.

The chime of a bell on the stairs heralded the arrival of the first visitor. General Khtoba entered the room cautiously, as though advancing on an enemy position. He wore his uniform—dun trousers and jacket over a white undershirt, the jacket fringed with gold at the shoulders as befitted his rank. A crimson triangle, open on top like a squat *V*, had been hastily sewn over his heart to represent the fires of the Redemption. At his side was a sword so filigreed with gold and silver that it sparkled as he moved. Behind him came two other officers of the Auxiliaries, similarly uniformed but less impressively accoutred.

The general looked over the room with barely concealed distaste, selected the least tatty chair, and sat, offering Jaffa only a grunt of recognition. His officers took seats flanking him, as though they expected trouble.

"Welcome, General," Jaffa said. "Would you care for any refreshment?"

The general scowled. He had a face made for scowls, with bushy eyebrows and lips shadowed by a broad, drooping mustache. When he spoke, gold gleamed on his teeth.

"No," he said. "I would care to get this over with. Where are the damned priests?"

The bell downstairs rang again, as if to answer this minor blasphemy. There was the sound of a considerable party on the steps, and then the priests of the Seraphic Council entered, all in a gaggle.

Jaffa had grown up knowing what a priest looked like—either an old man, bearded and fat, in gaudy green and purple robes, or else a woman demurely shrouded in silks. This new kind, these hard-eyed young men in spare black wraps, made him uncomfortable. There were no women among their number, demure or otherwise. Their leader was a younger man with close-cropped hair and a scar under one eye who took a seat at the table opposite the general. His flock remained standing behind him.

"I am Yatchik-dan-Rahksa," he said. "Appointed by the Divine Hand to lead the Swords of Heaven and oversee the final cleansing of foreign taint from our land."

The name meant "Angel of Victory," which Jaffa supposed was appropriate enough. The Divine Hand himself had started the fashion for taking the names of angels when he'd called himself Vale-dan-Rahksa, the Angel of Vengeance. At the rate the Council was expanding, there would soon be a serious shortage of angels.

Jaffa wondered what would happen when they ran out of manly, intimidating names and were reduced to naming themselves after the Angel of Sisterly Affection or the Angel of Small Crafts.

Khtoba bristled. "That cleansing should have begun weeks ago. The cursed Vordanai were like a fruit in our hands, ripe for the plucking, but they were permitted to escape. Now the task of evicting them will cost many of the faithful their lives."

"The truly faithful are always prepared to lay down their lives for the Redemption," the priest said. "But I think you overestimate the difficulty, General."

"Overestimate?" Khtoba frowned. "Perhaps you'd like to try scaling the walls of Sarhatep without the help of my guns, then."

Yatchik smiled beatifically. "Walls are no obstacle to the will of Heaven."

"So the servants of Heaven have discovered how to fly?"

"Sirs," Jaffa said. "Before we begin, I should remind you that our council is not yet complete."

"Oh, of course," the general drawled. "Let us wait to see what a bunch of boy-fucking horse thieves have to say."

"The gods value all their children," Yatchik said. "And glory comes to all who serve the Redemption."

The bell rang a third time before Khtoba could respond. The last member of the council made no noise on the stairs, and entered the chamber with only the slightest whisper of silk. He was dressed in black from head to foot, loose-fitting robes cinched at the waist, wrists, and ankles in the Desoltai style, with a black silk scarf wound around his head. His face was invisible behind his famous mask, a simple oval of brushed steel with two square holes for eyes.

This was Malik-dan-Belial, the Steel Ghost, chieftain of the desert tribes. He had risen to prominence long before the beginning of the Redemption. The Ghost's Desoltai raiders had been a thorn in the side of the prince and the Vordanai for years, and the Ghost himself was the hero of a hundred stories told in hushed whispers. It was said that he *had* no face, only an inky void behind the steel mask, and that he'd traded his very identity to a demon for the ability to see the future.

No one rose as he entered, so it fell to Jaffa to greet him. He got up from his seat and bowed.

"Malik," Jaffa said. The Ghost had never claimed another name or title. "Welcome. Please, take your seat."

"Yes, welcome," said Yatchik. "We were discussing plans for the final destruction of the Vordanai. Perhaps you might care to add your opinion?"

"It is too late," said the Ghost. His voice rasped like silk over steel, harsh with the heavy accent of the desert. "The *raschem* fleet has arrived, with transports and ships of war."

"I've heard nothing of this," Khtoba said. "Where did you get this information?"

The Ghost fixed the general with his blank, faceless gaze. "The ships came into sight yesterday evening."

Khtoba sat tight-lipped. The Steel Ghost had always displayed a remarkable ability to know more than he should. It was just possible that a man on a fast horse, with a string of remounts, could have covered the hundred miles between Sarhatep and the city along the coast road, but Khtoba's own men had undoubtedly been watching that road and presumably they'd seen nothing. That meant either that some Desoltai messenger had accomplished the same feat cross-country, over the scrubland and desert of the Lesser Desol, or that the Steel Ghost really did have some magic at his command.

"We'll need to confirm that," the general said. "If what you say is true, my couriers should bring the news by tomorrow."

"Even still," Yatchik said, "we know nothing of their intentions. They may mean to take the prudent course and return to their own lands."

Khtoba bared his teeth. "In which case we've lost our chance for vengeance on the foreigners and their Exopterai dogs."

"That the Redemption is accomplished is enough," said the priest. "We need spill no more blood than necessary."

Jaffa had seen the charnel pits in the great square in front of the Palace. Presumably, Yatchik would say that *those* deaths had been necessary.

"They will not leave our shores," the Ghost said. General and holy man both turned to look at him. "The transports are unloading. Men, guns, stores in great quantity."

"How many men?" Khtoba snapped, his earlier reluctance to accept the Desoltai's information forgotten.

"Three thousand, perhaps four."

The general snorted. "What can they hope to accomplish with so small a force? Can they be mad enough to believe they will defeat the Redemption? My Auxiliaries alone outnumber them."

The Ghost shrugged.

"Perhaps they mean to simply hold Sarhatep," Yatchik said. "If so, they are welcome to it. There is nothing of value so far down the coast."

"They cannot be allowed to retain a foothold," Khtoba said. "We must soak the sand in Vordanai blood and pack a ship full of their heads to send back to their king. He must understand the folly of sending armies against us."

"Then," Yatchik said, soft as a snake, "will you march against them?"

Khtoba froze. Jaffa saw the trap. The general was more afraid of the priests than of the foreigners. If he marched his strength away from the city and weakened himself in battle, there was no guarantee he would find a friendly welcome on his return.

"My friends," Jaffa said, "the city is restless. Not all have accepted the Redemption. It may be that the *raschem* will simply wait, and if they do, I suggest that we do the same."

"Yes," said Khtoba. "My men are needed to keep order."

In truth, the drunken soldiers of the Auxiliaries were more of a detriment to public order than a help in keeping the peace, but Jaffa knew better than to say so. Yatchik smiled.

"In that case, General, you are in accord with my own views."

Khtoba grunted, conceding the point. Jaffa turned to the Ghost.

"Can we rely on you to keep us informed as to the foreigners' movements?"

Malik-dan-Belial inclined his masked head slightly. "However," he said, "I do not believe they will stay at Sarhatep."

"Why?" said the general, anxious to be done with this council.

"Among the thousands, there is one who possesses true power. An *abh-naathem*. Such people do not cross the oceans to no purpose."

Khtoba snorted. "So the Vordanai have sent us a wizard, then? We'll see if his spells make him proof against cannonballs."

"The power of the gods will overcome any *raschem* magic," Yatchik said. "Those who trust in the Redemption need have no fear of spells or demons."

The Ghost only shrugged again.

Stripped of his painted cloak and staff of office, the Grand Justice passed into the slums of Ashe-Katarion as the sun sank toward the horizon. He wore the garb of a common trader, a plain brown wrap belted with a rope, and a heavy cudgel swung from his hip.

There were parts of the city to which the writ of the prince's Justices had never extended, except in name, and this was one of them. Once there had been an informal accord between those who enforced the law and those who flouted it. The criminals kept their operations quiet and orderly, and made certain that the bodies found floating down the river never belonged to anyone wealthy or important. In return, the Justices turned a blind eye to their activities.

That peace had gone by the board with the coming of the Redemption, along with all the other unwritten rules that made the ancient city work. Some of the slums had practically emptied as the desperate poor flocked to the Redeemers' banners. Others had become armed camps, with raids and counterraids leaving corpses that lay in the street for days to be torn by packs of feral dogs.

Jaffa therefore kept one hand on his cudgel, and shot hard looks at the unwashed children who watched him from doors and alleyways. The few adults he saw were hurrying along, eyes down, intent on their own errands. This slum, known for reasons understood only by historians as the Hanging Garden, was one of those that had seen the greatest concentration of Redeemer fervor. The dwellings of those who had left to follow the holy flame had been rapidly colonized by the city's enormous population of vagrant youths, always in search of someplace to sleep where they wouldn't be bothered by thieves, pimps, or Justices.

Along with the squatters had come others who wished to hide from Ashe-Katarion's new rulers. Jaffa turned off the main street, a hard-packed dirt road pocked with occasional half-buried paving stones, and into a narrow alley. This ran on for some time, twisting and turning, and eventually opened out into an irregular courtyard.

Here, some of Ashe-Katarion's ancient architecture had survived the attentions of the years and the insatiable demand for cut stone. A broad fountain stood in the center, dusty dry now, watched over by a weathered stone god with arms spread in an attitude of benediction. Erosion had blurred his features until he was unrecognizable. Uneven flagstones still floored the rest of the yard, with hard, wiry grass pushing up through the cracks between them.

It was here, in this hidden yard, that the last true servants of the gods waited. Jaffa approached the wicker chair set beside the fountain and fell to his knees, head lowered.

"Welcome, child." The figure in the chair was cloaked and hooded, despite the spring heat, and her hands were swathed in white bandages. Her voice was desiccated, cracked and dry, like the very voice of the desert.

"Holy Mother," Jaffa said, keeping his eyes on the broken flagstones, "I have news from the council."

"You bring more than news, it seems." There was a dusty sound from the cloaked woman that might have been a laugh. "Onvidaer, bring me our guest."

There was a startled squeak from behind Jaffa, and the shuffling of sandals. The Grand Justice remained in his attitude of obeisance, sweat beading on his face. "I am sorry beyond words, Mother. I did not think—"

"Rise, child," the cloaked woman said. "No harm has been done. Now let us see what fish our net has caught."

Jaffa got to his feet and turned, weak with relief. Standing behind him was a young woman of fifteen or sixteen, scrawny and stick-limbed. Her skin was smudged with the filth of the slums, and she wore only torn trousers and a dirty vest. Her hair hung in thick, greasy clumps.

Onvidaer had one hand on the girl's upper arm, holding her still without apparent effort. He was a young man, only a few years older than his prisoner, but lean and well muscled, with the copper-gray skin of the Desoltai. He wore nothing but a loincloth, showing broad shoulders and a muscular chest to good effect, and his face was round, almost cherubic. His other hand held a thin-bladed dagger.

"She followed Jaffa," he announced. "For some time before he came here. But she has reported to no one."

"Such a ragged little alley cat," rasped the woman in the chair. "But what house does she belong to, I wonder?"

"No one," the girl said. Her eyes were full of defiance. "I've done nothing, I swear it. I never followed him."

"Now, now," the woman said. "Cool your anger. Were I in your position, I might do better to beg for mercy."

"I don't know who you are, or . . . or anything!"

"We will find out the truth of that soon enough." The hood turned. "Summon Akataer."

A huge shadow detached itself from the wall behind the old woman, resolving into an enormous, hairless man in leather breeches and straps. He gave an assenting grunt and wandered out through the rear of the square, where empty doorways gaped into long-deserted apartments.

"Now, child," the old woman said. "Who sent you here?"

"No one sent me!" she said, jerking at Onvidaer's grip. "And I'm not a child."

"All men are children of the gods," the old woman said, not unkindly. "And all women, too, even little alley cats. The gods cherish all their children."

"Just let me go." There was desperation in the girl's voice, and Jaffa had to harden his heart. "Please. I won't tell anyone anything—"

She stopped as the huge man returned, accompanied by a skinny boy of eleven or twelve years in a white wrap. The boy was as bald as his giant companion, with solemn features and bright blue eyes. He bowed to the old woman, nodded politely to Jaffa, and turned his eyes to the girl.

"We will find out what she knows," said the old woman. "Onvidaer."

The girl threw a wild glance at the knife. "Please. You don't have to hurt me. I don't know anything—I swear—"

"Hurt you?" The old woman gave another paper-dry laugh. "Poor child. We aren't going to hurt you."

Jaffa saw the sudden hope bloom in the girl's eyes. At just that moment, Onvidaer moved with the speed of a striking snake, raising her wrist above her head and sliding the long, thin dagger into her left side beneath the armpit. It went in smooth as silk, finding the gap between her ribs. The girl gave a single jerk, eyes gone very wide, and then her legs buckled. She hung from the young man's grip on her wrist like a broken puppet. Her head lolled forward, greasy hair swinging in front of her face.

"I have no desire to cause anyone *pain*," said the old woman. "Onvidaer is extremely skilled."

Jaffa closed his eyes for a moment, running through the words of a prayer. Once, such a thing would have sickened him. Once, he had even sought to bring the prince's justice to Mother and all who served her, to break the secret temples and bring their obscenities to light. Now, having seen the men who had risen in her place, he had bound himself to her service. Now he was able to look on the death of an urchin girl without much more than a tremor. There had been so many deaths, after all. And one lesson the Redeemers had taught to Ashe-Katarion at painful length was that there were worse things in life than a quick ending.

Mother crooked a bony finger. "Now, Akataer."

The boy nodded. Onvidaer gathered the girl's other arm above her shoulders, so she hung with her knees just brushing the flagstones. Akataer put one hand under her lolling head and lifted it, looking solemnly into her blind, staring eyes and brushing back her hair. Then he leaned in, with the quiet concentration of a craftsman at work, and gently kissed her. His tongue pushed past her slack lips. There was a long, silent moment.

When he was finished, he put one hand on the side of her face and pulled open the lid of one rapidly filming eye until it gaped in ludicrous surprise. Again the boy leaned close, this time extending his tongue through his teeth, and ever so carefully he touched the tip of it to the corpse's eye. He repeated the procedure with the other eye, then stepped back and muttered a few words under his breath.

In the depths of the girl's pupils, something took shape. Her body swayed, as though Onvidaer had shaken it gently. Her eyes closed of their own accord, slowly, then flickered open. In place of white, irises, and pupils, they were now filled from edge to edge with green fire. Her lips shifted, and a wisp of smoke curled upward from the corner of her mouth.

The old woman grunted, satisfied. She gestured Akataer to her side and patted him proprietarily on the head with a white-wrapped claw. Then she directed her attention to the thing that had been the urchin girl.

"Now," she said, "we shall have some answers."

"This is Mother," said Akataer, in a high, clear voice. "I charge you to answer her questions, and speak truthfully."

The corpse shifted again, drooling another skein of smoke. The glowing green eyes were unblinking.

"You followed Jaffa here," the old woman said, gesturing at him. "This man."

There was a long pause. When the corpse spoke, more smoke escaped, as though it had been holding in a draw from a pipe. It curled through the girl's hair and hung oddly still in the air above her. Her voice was a drawn-out hiss, like a hot coal plunged in a water bucket.

"Yesssssss . . ."

Jaffa swallowed hard. He'd been half hoping Mother was wrong, though that meant the girl would have died for nothing. Small chance there, though. Mother was never wrong.

"And who bade you follow him? Who are your masters?"

Another pause, as though the dead thing were considering.

". . . Orlanko . . . ," she said eventually, reluctantly. ". . . Concordaaaaaat . . ."

"The foreigners," the old woman said. She made a hawking sound, as though she would spit but didn't have the juice. "And what were the *raschem* looking for?"

". . . Names . . ." The corpse groaned. ". . . Must . . . have . . . the Names . . ."

She wriggled in Onvidaer's grasp, and the green flared brighter. Akataer glanced anxiously at the old woman, who waved one hand as though bored by the proceedings.

"Dismiss her," she said.

The boy nodded gratefully and muttered another few words. All at once, the corpse slumped, green fires dying away. The girl's eye sockets were a charred ruin, and the stench of burned flesh wafted across the yard.

"You have done well, Akataer," the old woman said. "Return to your chambers. Onvidaer, dispose of that."

Jaffa frowned. "Mother, I don't understand. What did she mean, 'the names'? Our names?"

"It is not necessary for you to understand, child," the old woman said. "Put the business from your mind, and tell me what occurred on the council."

Jaffa remembered Khtoba's sarcastic aside at the prospect of Vordanai sorcery, and wondered if the general would be quite so flippant had he been in attendance here. Would a cannonball kill Mother? Jaffa, looking at her frail, wrapped form, decided that he thought not.

He cleared his throat and began, summarizing the talk and giving his impressions. The old woman listened attentively, interrupting only once, when Jaffa was speaking of Yatchik-dan-Rahksa.

"He said nothing of Feor?" she asked.

Jaffa shook his head. "No, Mother. She must still be a prisoner, or else . . ."

"She is not dead," the old woman said. "I would have felt her passing. No, they hold her still. Go on."

When he had finished, there was a long silence. The old woman's hands, loose ends of the wraps fluttering, were never still. They sat in her lap, fingers entangled like eels, tugging here and there at the bindings as though they pained her.

"An *abh-naathem*," she said. "There is a warning there, though that puffed-up fool Khtoba and the upstarts who usurp the names of angels are too deaf to hear. The Desoltai remember the old magics."

Jaffa remained silent. It was not his place to offer an opinion.

"Child," the old woman said, "I want the truth from you, now, not what you think will please me."

"Yes, Mother." Jaffa bowed his head.

"Will the Vordanai retake the city?"

He looked up, taken aback. "Mother—I am no soldier. I cannot—"

"As best you can tell," she said, her ragged voice almost gentle. "Is it possible?"

Another pause.

"The Redeemers have assembled a vast host," Jaffa said, thinking aloud. "But they are poorly trained, and armed only with faith. Khtoba's Auxiliaries are better, but . . ."

There was a smile in the old woman's voice. "You distrust Khtoba."

"The man would sell his own mother for a thimbleful of power," Jaffa said. "As for the Steel Ghost and his Desoltai, they will do as they see fit, and who can say what that will be?" He shrugged. "If I were the Vordanai captain, I would not attempt it. But if the gods smile on him and frown on us—yes, it is possible."

The old woman nodded thoughtfully.

"I will give you a message to carry," she said. "You must conceal it from Khtoba and the Council, of course. But I think it is time that I met this Steel Ghost."

Part One

Chapter One

WINTER

Four soldiers sat atop the ancient sandstone walls of a fortress on the sun-blasted Khandarai coast.

That they were soldiers was apparent only by the muskets that leaned against the parapet, as they had long ago discarded anything resembling a uniform. They wore trousers that, on close inspection, might once have been a deep royal blue, but the relentless sun had faded them to a pale lavender. Their jackets, piled in a heap near the ladder, were of a variety of cuts, colors, and origins, and had been repaired so often they were more patch than original fabric.

They lounged, with that unique, lazy insolence that only soldiers of long experience can affect, and watched the shore to the south, where something in the nature of a spectacle was unfolding. The bay was full of ships, broad-beamed, clumsy-looking transports with furled sails, wallowing visibly even in the mild sea. Out beyond them was a pair of frigates, narrow and sharklike by comparison, their muddy red Borelgai pennants snapping in the wind as though to taunt the Vordanai on the shore.

If it was a taunt, it was lost on the men on the walls, whose attention was elsewhere. The deep-drafted transports didn't dare approach the shore too closely, so the water between them and the rocky beach was aswarm with small craft, a motley collection of ship's boats and local fishing vessels. Every one was packed to the rails with soldiers in blue. They ran into the shallows far enough to let their passengers swing over the side into the surf, then turned about to make another relay. The men in blue splashed the last few yards to dry land and collapsed, lying about in clumps beside neatly stacked boxes of provisions and equipment.

"Those poor, stupid bastards," said the first soldier, whose name was Buck. He was a broad-shouldered, barrel-chested man, with sandy hair and a tuft on his chin that made him look like a brigand. "Best part of a month in one of those things, eatin' hard biscuit and pukin' it up again, and when you finally get there they tell you you've got to turn around and go home."

"You think?" said the second soldier, who was called Will. He was considerably smaller than Buck, and his unweathered skin marked him as a relative newcomer to Khandar. "I'm not looking forward to another ride myself."

"I fucking well am," said the third soldier, who was called—for no reason readily apparent—Peg. He was a wiry man, whose face was almost lost in a vast and wild expanse of beard and mustache. His mouth worked continually at a wad of sweetgrass, pausing occasionally to spit over the wall. "I'd spend a year on a fucking ship if it would get me shot of this fucking place."

"Who says we're going home?" Will said. "Maybe this new colonel's come to stay."

"Don't be a fool," Peg said. "Even colonels can count noses, and it doesn't take much counting to see that hanging around here means ending up over a bonfire with a sharp stake up the arse."

"Besides," Buck said, "the prince is going to make him head right back to Vordan. He can't wait to get to spending all that gold he stole."

"I suppose," said Will. He watched the men unloading and scratched the side of his nose. "What're you going to do when you get back?"

"Sausages," said Buck promptly. "A whole damn sack full of sausages. An' eggs, and a beefsteak. The hell with these grayskins and their sheep. If I never see another sheep, it'll be too soon."

"There's always goat," Peg said.

"You can't eat goat," Buck said. "It ain't natural. If God had wanted us to eat goat, he wouldn't've made it taste like shit." He looked over his shoulder. "What about you, Peg? What're you gonna do?"

"Dunno." Peg shrugged, spat, and scratched his beard. "Go home and fuck m' wife, I expect."

"You're married?" Will said, surprised.

"He was when he left," Buck said. "I keep tellin' you, Peg, she ain't gonna wait for you. It's been seven years—you got to be reasonable. Besides, she's probably fat and wrinkled by now."

"Get a new wife, then," Peg said, "an' fuck her instead."

Out in the bay, an officer in full dress uniform missed a tricky step into one of the small boats and went over the side and into the water. There was a chorus of harsh laughter from the trio on the wall as the man was fished out, dripping wet, and pulled aboard like a bale of cotton.

When this small excitement had died away, Buck's eyes took on a vicious gleam. Raising his voice, he said, "Hey, Saint. What're you gonna do when you get back to Vordan?"

The fourth soldier, at whom this comment was directed, sat against the rampart some distance from the other three. He made no reply, not that Buck had expected one.

Peg said, "Prob'ly go rushin' to the nearest church to confess his sins to the Lord."

"Almighty Karis, forgive me," Buck said, miming prayer. "Someone threw a cup of whiskey at me, and I might have gotten some on my tongue!"

"I dropped a hammer on my foot and said, 'Damn!'" Peg added.

"I looked at a girl," Buck suggested, "and she smiled at me, and it made me feel all funny."

"Oh, and I shot a bunch of grayskins," Peg said.

"Nah," said Buck, "heathens don't count. But for that *other* stuff you're going to hell for sure."

"Hear that, Saint?" said Peg. "You're goin' to wish you'd enjoyed yourself while you had the chance."

The fourth soldier still did not deign to respond. Peg snorted.

"Why do you call him Saint, anyway?" said Will.

"'Cause he's in training to be one," Buck said. "He don't drink, he don't swear, and he sure as hell don't fuck. Not even grayskins, which hardly counts, like I said."

"What I heard," Peg said, taking care to be loud enough that the fourth soldier would overhear, "is that he caught the black creep on his first day here, an' after a month his cock dropped off."

The trio were silent for a moment, considering this.

"Well, hell," said Buck. "If that happened to me I guess I'd be drinking and swearing for all I was worth."

"Maybe it already happened to you," Peg shot back immediately. "How the hell would you know?"

This was familiar territory, and they lapsed into bickering with the ease of long familiarity. The fourth soldier gave a little sigh and shifted his musket into his lap.

His name was Winter, and in many ways he was different from the other three. For one thing, he was younger and more slightly built, his cheeks still unsullied by whiskers. He wore his battered blue coat, despite the heat, and a thick cotton shirt underneath it. And he sat with one hand resting on the butt of his weapon, as though at any moment he expected to have to stand to attention.

Most important, "he" was, in fact, a girl, although this would not be apparent to any but the most insistent observer.

It was certainly unknown to the other three soldiers, and for that matter to everyone else in the fort, not to mention the roll keepers and bean counters a thousand miles across the sea at the Ministry of War. The Vordanai Royal Army not being in the habit of employing women, aside from those hired for short intervals by individual soldiers on an informal basis, Winter had been forced to conceal the fact of her gender since she enlisted. That had been some time ago, and she'd gotten quite good at it, although admittedly fooling the likes of Buck and Peg was not exactly world-class chicanery.

Winter had grown up in the Royal Benevolent Home for Wayward Youth, known to its inmates as Mrs. Wilmore's Prison for Young Ladies, or simply the Prison. Her departure from this institution had been unauthorized, to say the least, which meant that of all the soldiers in the fort, Winter was probably the only one who was of two minds about the fleet's arrival. Everyone in camp agreed that the new colonel would have no choice but to set sail for home before the army of fanatics arrived. It was, as Buck had mentioned, certainly better than being roasted on a spit, which was the fate the Redeemers had promised to the foreigners they called "corpses" to mock their pale skin. But Winter couldn't shake the feeling that somehow, three years later and a thousand miles away, Mrs. Wilmore would be waiting with her severe bonnet and her willow switch as soon as she stepped off the dock.

The scrape of boots on the ladder announced the arrival of a newcomer, and the four soldiers grabbed their muskets and arranged themselves to look a little more alert. They relaxed when they recognized the moon-shaped face of Corporal Tuft, flushed and sweating freely.

"Hey, Corp'ral," said Buck, laying his weapon aside again. "You fancy a look?"

"Don't be a moron," Tuft said, panting. "You think I would come all the way up here just to look at a bunch of recruits learning to swim? *Fuck.*" He doubled over, trying to catch his breath, the back of his jacket failing to cover his considerable girth. "I swear that fuckin' wall gets higher every time I have to climb it."

"What are you going to do when you get back to Vordan, Corp'ral?" Buck said.

"Fuck Peg's wife," Tuft snapped. He turned away from the trio to face Winter. "Ihernglass, get over here."

Winter cursed silently and levered herself to her feet. Tuft wasn't a bad sort for a corporal, but he sounded irritated.

"Yes, Corporal?" she said. Behind Tuft, Peg made a rude gesture, which provoked silent laughter from the other two.

"Cap'n wants to see you," Tuft said. "But Davis wants to see you first, so I'd hurry up if I was you. He's down in the yard."

"Right away, Corporal," said Winter, swallowing another curse. She slung her musket over her shoulder and took hold of the ladder, her feet finding the rungs with the ease of long practice. She seemed to draw more than her share of wall duty, which was undoubtedly another little gift from the senior sergeant. Nothing was too petty for Davis.

The fortress—Fort Valor, as some Vordanai cartographer had named it, apparently not in jest—was a small medieval affair, little more than a five-sided wall with two-story stone towers at the corners. Whatever other buildings had filled it in antiquity had long since fallen to bits, leaving a large open space in which the Vordanai had raised their tents. The best spots were those right against one of the walls, which got some shade most of the day. The "yard" was the unoccupied ground in the center, an expanse of dry, packed earth that would have been ideal for drills and reviews if the Colonials had bothered with such things.

Winter found Davis waiting near the edge of the row of tents, watching idly as two soldiers, stripped to the waist, settled some minor argument with their fists. A ring of onlookers cheered the pair indiscriminately.

"Sir!" Winter went to attention, saluted, and held it until Davis deigned to turn around. "You wanted to see me, sir?"

"Ah, yes." The sergeant's voice was a basso rumble, apparently produced somewhere deep in his prodigious gut. Davis would have seemed fatter if he wasn't so tall. As it was, he loomed. He was also, as Winter had had good occasion to find out, venal, petty, cruel, stupid as an ox in most respects but not without a certain vicious cunning when the situation arose. *In other words, the perfect sergeant.*

"Ihernglass." He smiled, showing blackened teeth. "You heard that the captain has requested your presence?"

"Yes, sir." Winter hesitated. "Do you know—"

"I suspect I had something to do with that. There was just one thing I wanted to make clear to you before you went."

"Sir?" Winter wondered what Davis had gotten her into this time. The big man had made her torment a personal project ever since she'd been transferred to his company, against his wishes, more than a year before.

"The captain will tell you that your sergeant recommended you for your sterling qualities, skill and bravery and so forth. You may find yourself thinking that old Sergeant Davis isn't such a bad fellow after all. That deep down, under all the bile and bluster, he harbored a soft spot for you. That all his taunts and jibes were well intentioned, weren't they? To toughen you up, body and soul." The sergeant's smile widened. "I want you to know, right now, that that's bullshit. The captain asked me to recommend men with good records for a special detail, and I've been around enough officers to know what *that* means. You'll be sent off on some idiot suicide mission, and if that's got to happen to any man in my company I wanted to be sure it was you. Hopefully, it means I will finally, finally be rid of you."

"Sir," Winter said woodenly.

"I find I develop a certain rough affection for most men under my command as the years wear on," Davis mused. "Even the ugly ones. Even Peg, if you can believe it. I sometimes wonder why you have been such an exception. I knew I didn't like the look of you the first day we met, and I still don't. Do you have any idea why that might be?"

"Couldn't say, sir."

"I think it's because, deep down, you think you're better than the rest of us. Most men lose that conviction after a while. You, on the other hand, never seem to tire of having your face rubbed in the mud."

"Yes, sir." Winter had long ago found that the quickest, not to say the safest, method of getting away from an audience with Davis was simply to agree with everything the sergeant said.

"Oh, well. I had some lovely duty on the latrines lined up for you." Davis gave a huge, rolling shrug. "But instead you get to find out what lunacy Captain d'Ivoire has dreamed up. No doubt it will be a glorious death. I just want you to remember, when some Redeemer is carving chunks out of you for his cookpot, that you're there because old Sergeant Davis couldn't stand the sight of you. Is that understood?"

"Understood, sir," Winter said.

"Very well. You are dismissed."

He turned back to the fight, which was nearly over, one man having wrapped his arm around his rival's neck while he pounded him repeatedly in the face with his free hand. Winter trudged past them, headed for the corner tower that served as regimental headquarters.

Her gut churned. It would be good to be away from Davis. There was no doubt about that. While they'd been in their usual camp near the Khandarai capital of Ashe-Katarion, the big sergeant's torments had been bearable. Discipline had been lax. Winter had been able to spend long periods away from the camp, and Davis and the others had had their drinking, gambling, and whoring to distract them. Then the Redemption had come. The prince had fled the capital like a whipped dog, and the Colonials had followed. Since then, through the long weeks of waiting at Fort Valor, things had gotten much worse. Cooped up inside the ancient walls, Winter had nowhere to escape, and Davis used her to vent his irritation at being denied his favorite pursuits.

On the other hand, Winter had learned to parse officer-speak, too. A "special detail" definitely sounded bad.

There was a guard at the open doorway to the building, but he only nodded at Winter as she entered. The captain's office was just inside, marked by the smiling staff lieutenant who waited by the door. Winter recognized him. Everyone in the regiment knew Fitzhugh Warus. His brother, Ben Warus, had been colonel of the Colonials until he'd taken a bullet through the skull during a hell-for-leather chase after some bandits upriver. Fitz had been widely expected to leave for home after that, since everyone knew he was only here for his brother's sake. Inexplicably, he'd remained, employing his easy smile and flawless memory on behalf of the new acting commander.

Winter always felt a bit uncomfortable in his presence. She had small use for officers of any description, much less officers who smiled all the time. At least when she was being shouted at, she knew where she stood.

She stopped in front of him and saluted. "Ranker Ihernglass, reporting as ordered, sir."

"Come in," said Fitz. "The captain is expecting you."

Winter followed him inside. The captain's "office" had more than likely been someone's bedroom back when Fort Valor was an actual functioning fortress. Like every other part of the place, they'd found it stripped to the bare rock when they arrived. Captain d'Ivoire had made a kind of low desk out of half the bed of a broken cart propped on a pair of heavy trunks, and he sat on a spare bedroll.

This desk was strewn with paper of two distinct sorts. Most of it was the yellow-brown Khandarai rag paper the Colonials had used for years, recycled endlessly by enterprising vendors who rescued scraps from trash heaps and scraped the ink off, over and over, until the sheet was as thin as tissue. Amidst these, like bits of polished marble in a sand heap, were several pages of honest-to-Karis Vordanai stationery, crisp as though they had just come off the mills, bleached blindingly white with creases like razors. They were obviously orders from the fleet. Winter itched to know what they contained, but they were all carefully folded to shield them from prying eyes.

The captain himself was working on another sheet, a list of names, wearing an irritable expression. He was a broad-shouldered man in his middle thirties, face browned and prematurely wrinkled like that of anyone else who spent too much time in the unforgiving Khandarai sun. He kept his dark hair short and his beard, just starting to show slashes of gray, trimmed close to his jaw. Winter liked him as well as she liked any officer, which wasn't much.

He looked up at her, grunted, and made a mark on his list. "Sit down, Ranker."

Winter sat cross-legged on the floor across the desk from him. She felt Fitz hovering over her shoulder. Her instincts were screaming that this was a trap, and she had to remind herself firmly that making a break for it was not an option.

It felt as though the captain wanted her to open the conversation, but she knew better than to try. Finally he grunted again and fumbled around under the desk, coming up with a little linen bag. He tossed it on the desk in front of her, where it clanked.

"For you," he said. When she hesitated, he gestured impatiently. "Go on."

Winter worked her finger through the drawstring and tipped out the contents. They were two copper pins, each bearing three brass pips. They were intended for the shoulders of her uniform; the insignia of a senior sergeant.

There was a long silence.

"This has to be a joke," Winter blurted, and then hastily added, "sir."

"I wish it was," the captain said, either oblivious to or intending the implied insult. "Put them on."

Winter regarded the copper pins as though they were poisonous insects. "Sir, I must respectfully decline this offer."

"Too bad it isn't an offer, or even a request," the captain snapped. "It's an *order*. Put the damn things on."

She slammed her hand on the desk, just missing the dangerously upturned point of one of the pins, and shook her head violently. "I—"

Her throat rebelled, closing so tight she had to fight for breath. The captain watched her, not angry but with a sort of bemused curiosity. After a few moments, he coughed.

"Technically," he said, "I could have you thrown in the stockade for that. Only we haven't got a stockade, and then I'd just have to find another damned sergeant. So let me explain." He sorted through the papers and came up with one of the crisp sheets. "Aboard those transports are enough soldiers to bring this regiment up to book strength. That's nearly three thousand men. As soon as they dock, I get this *instruction*"—he gave the word a nasty spin—"from the new colonel, telling me that he hasn't brought any junior officers and he wants me to provide people who are 'familiar with the natives and the terrain.' Never mind that I haven't got enough for my own companies. So I've got to come up with thirty-six sergeants, without stripping the other companies *completely* bare, and that means field promotions."

Winter nodded, her chest still tight. The captain made a vague gesture in the air.

"So I ask around for men who might be able to do the job. Your Sergeant Davis picked you. Your record is"—his lip quirked—"a bit odd, but good. And here we are."

The sergeant would be apoplectic if he knew she was being promoted, rather than sent on a dangerous foray into enemy territory. For a moment Winter reconsidered her objection. It would be worth it, almost, just to watch his face turn tomato red. To make Buck and Tuft salute *her*. But—

"Sir," she protested, "with all due respect to yourself and Sergeant Davis, I don't think this is a good decision. I don't know *how* to be a sergeant."

"It can't be difficult," the captain said, "or else sergeants couldn't do it." He sat back a little, as though waiting for a smile, but Winter kept her face rigid. He sighed. "Would it reassure you if I said that all the new companies have their own lieutenants? I doubt that your duties will involve as much . . . initiative as Sergeant Davis' do."

Shortage of lieutenants was a perennial problem in the Colonials. The primary purpose of the regiment, it sometimes seemed, was as a dumping ground for those who had irretrievably fucked up their Royal Army careers but hadn't quite gone far enough to be cashiered or worse. Lieutenants—who, by and large, came from good families and were young enough to still make a life outside the service—would usually resign rather than accept the posting. Most companies were run by their sergeants, of which the regiment always had a sufficiency.

It *was* reassuring, slightly, but it did little to address her primary objection. She'd spent three years doing all she could to avoid contact with her fellow soldiers, most of whom were vicious brutes in any event. To now get up in front of a hundred and twenty of them and *tell them what to do*—the thought made her want to curl into a ball and never emerge.

"Sir," she said, her voice a little thick, "I still think—"

Captain d'Ivoire's patience ran out. "Your objections are noted, Sergeant," he snapped. "Now put the damn pins on."

With a shaking hand, Winter took the pins and fumbled with her coat. Being nonregulation, it lacked the usual shoulder straps, and after watching for a moment the captain sighed.

"All right," he said. "Just take them and go. You have the evening to say your good-byes. We're breaking the new men out into companies tomorrow morning, so be on the field when you hear the call." He cast about on the table, found a bit of rag paper, and scribbled something on it. "Take this to Rhodes and tell him you need a new jacket. And *try* to look as respectable as possible. God knows this regiment looks shabby enough."

"Yes, sir." Pocketing the pins, Winter got to her feet. The captain made a shooing gesture, and Fitz appeared at her side to escort her to the door.

When they were in the corridor, he favored her with another smile.

"Congratulations, Sergeant."

Winter nodded silently and wandered back out into the sun.

Chapter Two

MARCUS

Senior Captain Marcus d'Ivoire sat at his makeshift wooden desk and contemplated damnation.

The Church said—or Elleusis Ligamenti said, but since he was a saint it amounted to the same thing—that if, after death, the tally of your sins outweighed your piety, you were condemned to a personal hell. There you suffered a punishment that matched both your worst fears and the nature of your iniquities, as devised by a deity with a particularly vicious sense of irony. In his own case, Marcus didn't imagine the Almighty would have to think very hard. He had a strong suspicion that he would find his hell unpleasantly familiar.

Paperwork. A mountain, a torrent of paper, a stack of things to read and sign that never shrank or ended. And, lurking behind, on, and around every sheet, the looming anxiety that while *this* one was just the latrine-digging rota, the *next* one might be important. Really, critically important, the kind of thing that would make future historians shake their heads and say, "If only d'Ivoire had read that report, all those lives might have been spared." Marcus was starting to wonder if perhaps he'd died after all and hadn't noticed, and whether he could apply for time off in a neighboring hell. Spending a few millennia being violated by demons with red-hot pokers was beginning to sound like a nice change of pace.

What made it worse was that he didn't *have* to do it. He could say, "Fitz, take care of all this, would you?" and the young lieutenant would. He'd smile while he was doing it! All that stood in the way was Marcus' own stubborn pride and, again, the fear that somewhere in the sea of paper was something absolutely vital that he was going to miss.

Fitz returned from escorting another newly frocked sergeant out of the office. Marcus leaned back, stretching his long legs under the desk and feeling his shoulders pop. His right hand burned dully, and his thumb was developing a blister.

"Tell me that was the last one," he said.

"That was the last one," Fitz said obediently.

"But you're just saying that because I told you to say it."

"No," the lieutenant said, "that was really the last one. Just in time, too. Signal from the fleet says the colonel's coming ashore."

"Thank God."

One year ago, before Ben Warus had gone chasing one bandit too many, Marcus would have said he wanted to command the regiment. But that had been in another lifetime, when Khandar was just a sleepy dead-end post and the most the Colonials had been required to do was stand beside the prince on formal occasions to demonstrate the eternal friendship between the Vermillion Throne and the House of Orboan. Before a gang of priests and madmen—more or less synonymous, in Marcus' opinion—had stirred up the populace with the idea that they would be better off without either one.

Since then, Khandar had become a very unpleasant place for anyone wearing a blue uniform, and Marcus had been living right at the edge of collapse, his mouth dry and his stomach awash in bile. There was something surreal about the idea that in a few minutes he was going to become a *subordinate* again. Hand over the command of the regiment to some total stranger, his responsibilities reduced to carrying out whatever orders he was given. It was an unbelievably attractive thought. The new man might screw things up, of course—he probably would, if Marcus' experience with colonels was any guide—but whatever happened, up to and including the entire regiment being massacred by screaming Redeemer fanatics, it would not be his, Marcus', fault. He'd be able to turn up for heavenly judgment and say, "Well, you can't blame me. I had orders!"

He wondered if that carried any weight with the Almighty. It was something to tell the Ministry of War and the Concordat, at any rate, and that was probably more important. Of the two, the Almighty was a good deal less frightening. The Lord, in his infinite mercy, might forgive a soldier who strayed from the path, but the Last Duke certainly would not.

Fitz was saying something, which Marcus had missed entirely. His sleep lately was not what it ought to have been.

"What was that?" he said.

The lieutenant, well aware of his chief's condition, repeated himself patiently. "I said that the troops are almost all ashore. No cavalry, which is a pity, but he's brought us at least two batteries. Captain Kaanos is sending the companies up the bluff road one at a time."

"Will there be room for everybody inside the walls?"

Fitz nodded. "I wouldn't want to stand a siege, but we'll be all right for a few days."

This last was something of a joke. Fort Valor itself was a joke, actually. Like a strong lock on a flimsy door, it was effective only as long as the intruder remained polite. It had been built in the days when the most dangerous threat to a fortress was a catapult, or maybe a battering ram. Its walls were high and unsloping, built of hard native limestone that would crumble like a soft cheese once the iron cannonballs started in on it. They wouldn't even need a siege train—you could take the place with a battery of field guns, especially since there was no way for the defenders to emplace their artillery to shoot back.

Fortunately, no siege seemed to be in the offing. The Vordanai regiment had scuttled away from Ashe-Katarion, the prince's former capital, and as long as they looked like they were leaving, the Redeemers had been content to watch them go. Still, Marcus had bitten his fingernails to the quick during the weeks of waiting for the fleet to arrive.

"Well," Marcus said, "I suppose we'd better go meet him."

The lieutenant gave a delicate cough. Marcus had been with him long enough to recognize Fitz-speak for "You're about to do something very stupid and/or embarrassing, sir." He cast about the room, then down at himself, and got it. He was not, technically, in uniform—his shirt and trousers were close to regulation blue, but both were of Khandarai make, the cheap Vordanai standard issue having faded or torn long ago. He sighed.

"Dress blues?" he said.

"It would certainly be customary, sir."

"Right." Marcus got to his feet, wincing as cramped muscles protested. "I'll go change. You keep watch—if the colonel gets here, stall him."

"Yes, sir."

If only, Marcus thought, watching the lieutenant glide out, *I could just leave this colonel entirely to Fitz.* The young man seemed to have a knack for that sort of thing.

The dress uniform included a dress sword, which Marcus hadn't worn since his graduation from the War College. The weight on one hip made him feel lopsided, and the sheath sticking out behind him was a serious threat to anyone standing nearby when he forgot about it and turned around quickly. After five years at the bottom of a trunk, the uniform itself seemed *bluer* than he remembered. He'd also run a comb through his hair, for the look of the thing, and scrubbed perfunctorily at his face with a tag end of soap.

"Why, Senior Captain," Adrecht said, coming through the tent flap. "How dapper. You should dress up more often."

Marcus lost his grip on one of the dress uniform's myriad brass buttons and swore. Adrecht laughed.

"If you want to make yourself useful," Marcus growled, "you might help me."

"Of course, sir," Adrecht said. "Anything to be of service."

References to Marcus' rank or seniority from Captain Adrecht Roston were invariably mocking. He had been at the War College with Marcus, and was the "junior" by a total of seven minutes, that being the length of time that had separated the calling of the names "d'Ivoire" and "Roston" at the graduation ceremony. It had been something of a joke between them until Ben Warus had died, when that seven minutes meant that—to Adrecht's considerable relief—command of the Colonials settled on Marcus' shoulders instead of his.

Adrecht was a tall man, with a hawk nose and a thin, clean-shaven face. Since his graduation from the War College, he'd worn his dark curls fashionably loose. Keen, intelligent blue eyes and a slight curve of lip gave the impression that he was forever on the edge of a sarcastic smirk.

He commanded the Fourth Battalion, at the opposite end of the marching order from Marcus' First. He and his fellow battalion commanders, Val and Mor, along with the late Ben Warus and his brother, had been Marcus' official family ever since he'd arrived in Khandar. The only family, in fact, that he had left.

Marcus stood uncomfortably while Adrecht's deft fingers worked the buttons and straightened his collar. Looking over the top of his friend's head, he said, "Did you have some reason to be here? Or were you just eager to see me embarrass myself?"

"Please. Like that's such a rarity." Adrecht stepped back, admiring his handiwork, and gave a satisfied nod. "I take it from the getup that you're off to meet the colonel?"

"I am," Marcus said, trying not to show how much he wasn't looking forward to it.

"No time for a celebratory drink?" Adrecht opened his coat enough to show the neck of a squat brown bottle. "I've been saving something for the occasion."

"I doubt the colonel would appreciate it if I turned up stumbling drunk," Marcus said. "With my luck I'd probably be sick all over him."

"From one cup?"

"With you, it's never just one cup." Marcus tugged at his too-tight collar and sat down to turn his attention to his boots. There was a clatter as his scabbard knocked over an empty tin plate and banged against the camp bed, and he winced. "What have we got to celebrate, anyway?"

Adrecht blinked. "What? Just our escape from this sandy purgatory, that's all. This time next week, we'll be heading home."

"So you suppose." Marcus pulled at a stubborn boot.

"It's not just me. I heard Val say the same thing to Give-Em-Hell. Even the rankers are saying it."

"Val doesn't get to decide," Marcus said. "Nor does Give-Em-Hell, or the rankers. That would be the colonel's prerogative."

"Come on," Adrecht said. "You send them a report that the grayskins have got some new priests, who aren't too fond of us and have a nasty habit of burning people alive, and by the way they outnumber us a couple of hundred to one and the prince is getting shirty. So they send us a couple of thousand men and a new colonel, who no doubt thinks he's in for a little light despotism, burning down some villages and teaching a gang of peasants who's boss, that sort of thing. Then he *gets* here and finds out that the aforementioned priests have rounded up an army of thirty thousand men, the militia that *we* trained and armed has gone over to the enemy lock, stock, and barrel, and the prince has decided he'd rather make the best of a bad job and take the money and run. What do you think he's going to do?"

"You're making the assumption that he has an ounce of sense," Marcus said, pulling his laces tight. "Most of the colonels I met back at the College were not too well endowed in that department."

"Or any another," Adrecht said. "But not even that lot would—"

"Maybe." Marcus got to his feet. "I'll go and see, shall I? Do you want to come?"

Adrecht shook his head. "I'd better go and make sure my boys are ready. The bastard will probably want a review. They usually do."

Marcus nodded, looked at himself in the mirror again, and paused. "Adrecht?"

"Hmm?"

"If we *do* get to go home, what are you going to do?"

"What do you mean?"

"If I recall, a certain count told you that if you ever came within a thousand miles of his daughter again, he would tie you to a cannon and drop you in the Vor."

"Oh." Adrecht gave a weak smile. "I'm sure he's forgotten all about that by now."

Marcus, feeling prickly and uncomfortable, stood beside Fitz at the edge of the bluff and watched the last few companies toiling up the road. The path switchbacked as it climbed the few hundred feet from the landing to the top of the cliff. The column of climbing men looked like a twisted blue serpent, winding its way up only to be devoured by the gaping maw of the fort's open gate beside him. There seemed to be no end to them.

The men themselves were a surprise, too. To Marcus' eyes they seemed unnaturally pale—he understood, suddenly, why the Khandarai slang for Vordanai was "corpses." Compared to the leather-skinned veterans of the Colonials, these men looked like something you'd fish off the bottom of a pond.

And they were so *young*. Service in the Colonials was usually a reward for an ill-spent military career. Apart from the odd loony who volunteered for Khandarai service, even the rankers tended to be well into their second decade. Marcus doubted that most of the "men" marching up the road had seen eighteen, let alone twenty, given their peach-fuzz chins and awkward teenage frames. They didn't know how to march properly, either, so the column was more like a trudging mass of refugees than an army on the move. All in all, Marcus decided, it was not a sight calculated to impress any enemies who might be watching.

He had no doubt they *were* watching, too. The Colonials had made no effort to patrol the hills around the fort, and while the rebel commanders might believe the Vordanai were on the verge of departing for good, they weren't so foolish as to take it on faith. Every scrubby hill and ravine could hide a dozen Desoltai riders. The desert tribesmen could vanish on bare rock, horses and all, if they put their minds to it.

In the rear of the column, far below, a lonely figure struggled after the last of the marching companies under the burden of two heavy valises. He wore a long dark robe, which made him look a bit like a penny-opera version of a Priest of the Black. But since the Obsidian Order—perennial of cheap dramas and bogeymen of children's stories—had been extinct for more than a century, Marcus guessed this poor bastard was just a manservant hauling his master's kit up the mountain. One of the sinister inquisitors of old would hardly carry his own bags, anyway. He wondered idly what was so important that it couldn't be brought up in the oxcarts with the rest of the baggage.

His eyes scanned idly over the fleet, waiting for the colonel himself to emerge with his escort. He would be a nobleman, of course. The price of a colonel's commission was high, but there was more to it than money. While the Ministry of War might have been forced to concede over the past hundred years that there were commoners who could site guns and file papers as well as any peer, it had quietly but firmly drawn the line at having anyone of low birth in actual *command*. Leading a regiment was the ancient prerogative of the nobility, and so it would remain.

Even Ben Warus had been nobility of a sort, a younger son of an old family that had stashed him in the army as a sinecure. That he'd been a decent fellow for all that had been nothing short of a miracle. Going purely by the odds, this new colonel was more likely to be akin to the ones Marcus had known at the War College: ignorant, arrogant, and contemptuous of advice from those beneath him. He only hoped the man wasn't *too* abrasive, or else someone was likely to take a swing at him and be court-martialed for his trouble. The Colonials had grown slack and informal under Ben's indulgent command.

The servant with the bags had reached the last switchback, but there was still no flurry of activity from the ships that would indicate the emergence of an officer of rank. More boats were landing, but they carried only supplies and baggage, and the laboring men down at the dock were beginning to load the carts with crates of hardtack, boxes of cartridges, and empty water barrels. Marcus glanced at Fitz.

"The colonel did say he was coming up, didn't he?"

"That was the message from the fleet," the lieutenant said. "Perhaps he's been delayed?"

"I'm not going to stand out here all day waiting," Marcus growled. Even in the shade, he was sweating freely.

He waited for the porter in black to approach, only to see him stop twenty yards away, set down both valises, and squat on his heels at the edge of the dusty path. Before Marcus could wonder at this, the man leaned forward and gave an excited cry.

Balls of the Beast, he's stepped on something horrible. Khandar was home to a wide variety of things that crawled, slithered, or buzzed. Nearly all of them were vicious, and most were poisonous. It would be a poor start to a professional relationship if Marcus had to report to the colonel that his manservant had died of a snakebite. He hurried down the path, Fitz trailing behind him. The man in black popped back to his feet like a jack-in-the-box, one arm extended, holding something yellow and green that writhed furiously. Marcus pulled up short.

"A genuine Branded Whiptail," the man said, apparently to himself. He was young, probably younger than Marcus, with a thin face and high cheekbones. "You know, I'd seen Cognest's illustrations, but I never really believed what he said about the colors. The specimens he sent back were so *drab*, but this—well, look at it!"

He stepped forward and thrust the thing in Marcus' face. Only years of army discipline prevented Marcus from leaping backward. The little scorpion was smaller than his palm, but brilliantly colored, irregular stripes of bright green crisscrossing its dun yellow carapace. The man held it by the tail with thumb and forefinger, just below the stinger, and despite the animal's frantic efforts it was unable to pull itself up far enough to get its claws into his flesh. It twisted and snapped at the air in impotent rage.

It dawned on Marcus that some response was expected of him.

"It's very nice," he said cautiously. "But I would put it down, if I were you. It might be dangerous." Truth be told, Marcus couldn't have distinguished a Branded Whiptail from horse droppings unless it bit him on the ankle, but that didn't mean he wouldn't give both a wide berth.

"Oh, it's absolutely deadly," the man said, wiggling his fingers so the little thing shook. "A grain or two of venom will put a man into nervous shock in less than a minute." He watched Marcus' carefully neutral expression and added, "Of course, this must all be old hat to you by now. I'm sorry to get so worked up right off the bat. What must you think of me?"

"It's nothing," Marcus said. "Listen, I'm Captain d'Ivoire, and I got a message—"

"Of course you are!" the man said. "Senior Captain Marcus d'Ivoire, of the First Battalion. I'm honored." He extended his hand for Marcus to shake. "I'm Janus. Most pleased to meet you."

There was a long pause. The extended hand still held the frantically struggling scorpion, which left Marcus at something of a loss. Finally Janus followed his gaze down, laughed, and spun on his heel. He walked to the edge of the path and dropped the little thing amidst the stones. Then, wiping his hand on his black robe, he returned to Marcus.

"Sorry about that," he said. "Let me try again." He re-offered his hand. "Janus."

"Marcus," Marcus said, shaking.

"If you could conduct me to the fortress, I would be most grateful," Janus said. "I just have a few things I need to get stowed away."

"Actually," Marcus said, "I was hoping you could tell me where the colonel might be. He sent a message." Marcus looked over his shoulder at Fitz for support.

Janus appeared perplexed. Then, looking down at himself, inspiration appeared to dawn. He gave a polite cough.

"I suppose I should have been clearer," he said. "Count Colonel Janus bet Vhalnich Mieran, at your service."

There was a long, strained silence. It felt like the moment just after you'd done something monumentally stupid—bashing your thumb with a hammer, for example—and just before the pain came flooding in. A quiet moment, in which there seemed to be all the time in the world to contemplate the destruction you'd wrought.

Marcus decided to take the bull by the horns. He stepped smartly back, coming to stiff attention, and ripped off a salute that would have made his instructors at the War College proud. His voice rose to a parade-ground bark.

"Sir! My apologies, sir!"

"No apology necessary, Captain," Janus said mildly. "You couldn't have known."

"Sir! Thank you, sir!"

They matched stares for another long moment.

"We had better get the formalities over with," Janus said. He fished in his breast pocket and produced a crisply folded page, which he handed to Marcus. "Senior Captain d'Ivoire, as ordered by the Ministry of War in the name of horses and all, I am hereby assuming command of the First Colonial Infantry Regiment."

Marcus unbent sufficiently to take the note. It said, with the usual Ministry circumlocutions, that Count Colonel Janus bet Vhalnich Mieran was directed to assume command of the First Colonial Regiment and employ it, "as far as practicable," to suppress the rebellion and protect the interests of the Kingdom of Vordan and her citizens. At the bottom was affixed the seal of the Ministry, sky blue wax impressed with the image of a diving eagle. He handed it stiffly back to Janus.

"Sir," he said. "You have the command!"

Another salute, which the colonel returned. And that was it—with those few words command of the Colonials and all the attendant responsibilities were removed from Marcus' shoulders. He took what felt like the first breath of air he'd had in the weeks since the rebellion.

"And with that done," Janus said, tucking the paper away, "I hope you'll do me the favor of relaxing a little. That stiff posture is bad for the spine."

The parade-ground rigidity was already producing an ache across Marcus' shoulders. He gratefully complied.

"Thank you, sir. Welcome to the Colonials." He waved Fitz forward. "This is Lieutenant Fitzhugh Warus, my aide."

Fitz saluted smartly, as comfortable with strict military decorum as Marcus was awkward with it. Janus nodded acknowledgment.

"Lieutenant," he said. "You're the younger brother of the late Colonel Warus, are you not?"

"Yes, sir," Fitz said.

"My condolences on your loss, then. Your brother was a brave man."

"Thank you, sir."

That was fair enough, Marcus thought. Maybe not terribly bright, or honest, but *brave*, certainly. He was surprised Janus knew anything about him, though. For all the attention the Colonials had received from the Ministry of War before the rebellion, Khandar might as well have been on the moon. *Perhaps he's just being polite.*

"If you'll wait a moment, sir, I'll have someone carry your things," Marcus said. "We have rooms prepared for you inside."

"I'll carry them myself, if it's all the same to you," the colonel said. "Just show me the way."

"As you wish. Shall I order some food brought in as well? You must be tired."

"No need," Janus said. "My man is accompanying the rest of my baggage, and he can handle all the arrangements of that nature. Besides, it seems incumbent on me to pay a call on His Grace as soon as possible, don't you think?"

"His Grace?" Marcus was puzzled for a moment. "You mean the prince?" It had been so long since he'd given the exiled ruler any serious thought that he'd almost forgotten the man was with them.

"Of course. It's for his sake I'm here, after all."

Marcus quashed a frown. Janus was likely to be disappointed when he came face-to-face with the ruler of Khandar, but that was not for him to worry about it. *All I need to do now,* he reminded himself, *is obey orders.*

"Yes, sir. I'll get someone to show you to his chambers."

"I'd appreciate it if you'd accompany me, Captain." Janus flashed a smile. "I may need your expertise."

If so, we're in it pretty damned deep. Nevertheless, Marcus saluted. "Certainly, sir!"

Once they were under the shade of the fortress walls, the colonel doffed his flowing black robe, which turned out to be a thin silk affair sheer enough to be folded up like a pocket handkerchief. Marcus hurriedly summoned a nearby soldier to collect it and instructed him to take it to the colonel's quarters. The astonished man was too startled to salute properly, but Janus acknowledged him with a cheerful nod.

Under the robe, the colonel wore an ordinary uniform. It was as crisp and unfaded as Marcus' dress blues, but without any of the gilt or ornamentation Marcus might have expected from a senior officer. Only a pair of Vordanai eagles on his shoulders, silver with flashing jade eyes, marked his rank.

Janus himself was mostly unremarkable, aside from his relative youth and his striking eyes, which were a luminous gray color and somehow a size too large for his face. His dark hair was cut and combed in precise military style, which made Marcus uncomfortably aware that his own was getting out of control.

The prince's apartments were on the other side of the fortress. His entourage had insisted that they have one of the corner towers to themselves, so Marcus had given them the northwest tower, which faced the ocean and was unlikely to be needed for any defense. The huge silk banner that the prince had hauled all the way from Ashe-Katarion snapped from an upper story: a gray eagle on a white field, half concealed behind a rearing red scorpion.

The tower itself was protected by the Heavenly Guard, but Marcus had placed his own sentries at a polite distance, reliable men from the First Battalion. The last thing he needed was an altercation, and he also wanted to discourage any covert investigation of the prince's things. A dozen sealed wagons had accompanied the royal court on the retreat, and camp rumor said they'd been filled with as much of the Vermillion Throne's relics and treasury as the prince had been able to lay hands on.

Marcus' sentries saluted and stepped aside at his approach, but the pair of Khandarai flanking the door were more obstinate. Marcus had to bite his lip to keep from smiling at their earnest scowls. No doubt the Heavenly Guard had once been a fearsome fighting force, but that time was long past. More-recent princes had filled the ranks with aging sycophants, and these two presented a typical example. Both were gray-haired, and the one on the left had rolls of fat threatening to burst around the edges of his gilded breastplate. The spears they bore were elaborately worked with gold and silver wire.

One of them banged the butt of his weapon on the flagstones as the two officers approached and barked a challenge in Khandarai. Marcus turned to Janus and translated. "He wants to know who we are."

A smile flickered across the colonel's face, there for an instant and gone again, like heat lightning.

"Tell him the new colonel begs an audience with the Chosen of Heaven," he said.

Marcus made a sour face, but translated dutifully. His Khandarai was rough and ready, and his accent was atrocious, but the guard understood him well enough. He and his companion stepped apart and gestured the two Vordanai through the doorway.

The first floor of the tower was a single large room. When they'd arrived it had been empty, like the rest of the fortress. Now the floor was strewn with overlapping carpets, and veils of hanging silk obscured the dirty stones. Incense burned in gilded braziers, lest the nose of the Chosen of Heaven detect an odor he did not approve of. A small table was set with silver bowls of water and fruit, in case he should be hungry or thirsty.

Under the attempt at opulence, the seams were showing. The

fruit on the table was dried and old-looking, and all the veils couldn't hide the squat, utilitarian proportions of the chamber. Most damning of all, only a half dozen or so Khandarai danced attendance on the man who had once commanded the attention of thousands. A pair of young women of no obvious function lounged at the bottom of the throne, another pair wielded fans in a vain attempt to move the stifling air about, and a plump-faced man bustled up, all smiles, as Janus and Marcus approached.

The throne itself was not the actual Vermillion Throne. That hallowed seat, a marble-and-gilt monstrosity that would have half filled this room, was back in the Palace at Ashe-Katarion, no doubt being warmed by the holy bottom of some Redeemer. The servants had done their best here with carved wood and red paint, but the result was still more a chair than a throne, and Marcus thought it looked uncomfortable.

On it sat Prince Exopter, the Chosen of Heaven, Supreme Ruler of Khandar and the Two Desols. He cut the traditional figure. His own hair was cropped short beneath an elaborate painted wig that to Marcus' eyes resembled a gaggle of snakes having an orgy, and his gray-skinned face was slathered in white and red makeup so thick that it was practically a mask. Gems and gold glittered everywhere—on his fingers, at his ears, at his throat—and the purple silk drape he wore was fastened with a diamond brooch, while seed pearls clattered gently on the fringes.

Marcus wondered if the colonel would be overawed. *I doubt it. He's a count himself, after all.* Technically, a count might not beat a prince in the hierarchy of nobility, but the humblest peer of Vordan considered himself far superior to any Grand Pooh-Bah from abroad, no matter what lofty title the foreigner might affect.

As they entered, Janus glanced around with an expression of polite but distant interest. The round-faced man, sweating freely, bowed low in front of the pair of them.

"Welcome," he said, in accented but passable Vordanai. "I am

Razzan-dan-Xopta, minister to His Grace. The Chosen of Heaven bids you to approach his magnificence."

The prince, his face unreadable under the caked-on makeup, said something in Khandarai. He sounded bored.

"His Grace welcomes you as well," the minister translated. "He is most pleased that you have obeyed his summons."

This was the part that Marcus had been dreading. While he could understand most of the natives, the denizens of the royal court spoke a formal dialect that bordered on a separate language. He couldn't catch more than one word in four, not even enough to be certain that Razzan was providing an accurate translation.

He leaned close to Janus and whispered, "The prince may be under the impression that the only reason you were sent is because he asked them to—"

Janus held up a hand for silence, thought for a moment, and said, "Give His Grace my greetings. I have the honor to be Count Colonel Janus bet Vhalnich Mieran, commanding the First Colonial Infantry. I believe His Grace already knows Senior Captain d'Ivoire."

Razzan rendered that, and listened to the response. "His Grace is most gratified that his valued friend Farus the Eighth would send him so worthy an individual."

Janus bowed again. "I will do my utmost to live up to His Grace's expectations."

The prince's lip twisted, and he rattled off something that sounded unhappy. Razzan hesitated a moment, then said, "His Grace is curious regarding the whereabouts of the rest of his fleet."

The colonel's expression never flickered. "The ships are all arrived, and anchored in the bay."

Exopter spoke again, at some length.

"His Grace wonders if perhaps there has been some error in translation." Razzan licked his lips. "Only thirteen vessels are currently in the bay, he understands."

"That is correct."

"But that is insufficient. His Grace's summons to his most beneficent ally King Farus the Eighth specifically instructed him to send one hundred thousand men. Thirteen ships could never carry so many."

Marcus almost choked on a laugh. A hundred thousand men would be most of the Royal Army, and it would take every ship on the coast to carry them. Razzan was feigning incomprehension, but the royal eyes were watchful.

"The ships have brought sufficient replacements to bring the First Colonials to full strength," Janus said. "Along with ammunition, supplies, and other necessaries."

Exopter snapped something. Razzan said, "Are these men of the First Colonials demons, then? Does each fight with the strength of ten men? Are they impervious to bullets?"

No hint of a smile crossed Janus' expression, but Marcus could hear the amusement in his voice. "They are brave and skilled, but I must admit that they are only men."

"Then His Grace would like to know how you plan to go about regaining his kingdom with a single regiment." Razzan said it politely, and looked apologetic, but there was a gleam in the prince's eyes, as though he'd just delivered a killing stroke. "Or, perhaps, you plan no such thing? Perhaps our friend the king has abandoned his sworn duties?"

"His Majesty would never dream of it," Janus said. "As for regaining your kingdom, you may rest assured that the matter has my full attention."

The prince drawled a response, and Razzan turned pale. Before he could muster a suitably watered-down translation, Janus rattled off a string of court Khandarai so perfect that the obsequious minister gaped. Even the prince was taken aback, eyes widening under the painted mask. Marcus blinked.

"If that's all," Janus continued in Vordanai, "then I will take my leave. Please thank His Grace for his time."

He turned on his heel and stalked out of the room, the pair of Heavenly Guards parting before him. Marcus hurried to keep pace, feeling like a boy running at the heels of an older brother. He waited until they were well clear of the tower to speak.

"I didn't know you spoke the language, sir." He tried to keep his tone neutral, but it still felt uncomfortably accusatory.

"I speak seven languages," Janus said absently. "In addition to the usual Vordanai, Noreldrai, and Hamveltai, I have made a particular study of Borelgai, Murnskai, Vheedai, and Khandarai." He shrugged. "Though I will admit I needed to brush up on the more formal usages. I found the time aboard ship most conducive to study, as there was so little else to occupy the mind."

"That's . . . very impressive."

Janus shook his head and seemed to come back to himself. "I'm sorry. I didn't mean to boast."

"Not at all, sir."

"If we're to work together, Captain, it is important that we be honest to ourselves and one another about our capacities. I'm sorry if I caught you off guard."

"It just surprised me, sir." Marcus hesitated. "What did the prince say to you? I can follow most Khandarai, but not that formal stuff."

Janus' lip quirked. "He said that my full attention didn't amount to much, considering that the king had sent the dregs of his officer corps."

"Dregs" was a fair description of the Colonials, but that hit a little close to home. Marcus winced. "And what did you say to him?"

"I told him that since he was coming to us as a beggar, dregs were the best that he should expect." The quick smile again. "I suppose that was not . . . diplomatic of me."

"After he insulted His Majesty, it's only understandable," Marcus said loyally. "But . . ."

Janus noticed the hesitation and cocked his head, birdlike. "What is it? You may always speak freely with me, Captain, provided we are alone."

He took a deep breath. "Do you really intend to try to recapture Khandar, sir? Most of the men are expecting to get right back aboard the transports and sail home."

There was a long silence. Janus regarded Marcus thoughtfully, his gray eyes glittering. There was something extraordinary about those eyes, Marcus thought. They seemed to look *through* you, past all the trappings and courtesies and even through flesh and blood until they got at your very essence. If there really was a Beast of Judgment, it would have that sort of stare.

"And what are you expecting, Captain?" Janus said softly.

"I—" Marcus stopped, sensing a trap. "I wouldn't venture to anticipate your plans, sir."

"But what would your opinion be?" Janus leaned closer. "What would you do, if the command was yours?"

Turn tail and never look back. Marcus shook his head slowly. "According to the last reports before we retreated, the Redeemer army at Ashe-Katarion was nearly twenty thousand strong. It will be larger by now. Then there's General Khtoba"—he wanted to spit at the sound of the name—"and his Auxiliaries, six battalions worth of Vordanai-trained and Vordanai-armed soldiers. And ever since this Steel Ghost whipped up the Desoltai and threw in their lot with the priests . . ." He spread his hands. "If we're up to full strength, we'll have nearly four thousand men."

"A bit more," Janus interrupted, "with the attached cavalry and artillery."

"A bit more than four thousand," Marcus agreed. "Against—call it thirty thousand. Six to one against us, and that's only counting soldiers in the field. Practically the whole population of Ashe-Katarion wanted to see the back of the prince by the time the Redeemers had gotten them fired up."

"Six to one," Janus said. "Those are long odds."

"Long odds," Marcus said. "I'm not saying my men aren't up to a fight, sir. If we had another brigade, a few more guns, maybe a regiment of cuirassiers, I wouldn't hesitate. But long odds are long odds."

Janus gave a slow nod. Then, as though reaching a decision, he grinned.

"Would you care to take your dinner with me, Captain? I suppose I owe you an explanation."

Before dinner there were a few hours of daylight remaining. That meant more paperwork. There was no way around it; the ledgers and files of the Colonials had gotten woefully out of date during Ben Warus' tenure, in spite of Fitz' clandestine efforts to clean up his brother's messes, and Marcus had hardly had time to make a start on the backlog. Now, with upward of two thousand new recruits needing to be added to the rolls and dozens of rank amateurs for sergeants and lieutenants, the ocean of bureaucratic requirements threatened to close over his head.

Marcus was not a man to admit defeat easily, though, and he spent the rest of the day puzzling through arcane forms and adding his signature where required. He barely noticed when Fitz ghosted in and left a steaming cup by his elbow. When he reached out for it and took a sip, though, the taste made him look up.

"Tea?" he said. "Real tea? Have you been holding out on us, Lieutenant?"

The young man smiled. "From the fleet, sir. Compliments of the colonel, as a matter of fact."

Marcus pursed his lips and blew across the top of the mug, then took a longer swallow. The delicate flavor worked like some sorcerer's incantation, flinging him across the miles and years to a safer time. For a moment he was back at the War College at Grent, letting a steaming mug cool by his elbow as he worked his way through another dense text on tactical theory and half listened to Adrecht prattle about the latest campus gossip. He closed his eyes.

The Khandarai drank coffee—a rare delicacy in Vordan, but so cheap here that you could buy the raw beans for pennies to the bushel. They liked it dark and sludgy, and heavily spiced. It was a taste Marcus had managed to acquire over the years, and it certainly packed a kick that would keep you up for half the night, but still . . .

He breathed out, feeling at least fractionally more at peace. "Thank you, Fitz."

"My pleasure, sir."

Marcus opened his eyes. "Speaking of the colonel . . ."

"Yes, sir?"

"It appears he'll be requiring my services, at least part of the time. I'll be relying on you to take care of the First."

Properly speaking, Marcus should have had at least two more field lieutenants to whom he could delegate command authority in his absence so that his staff lieutenant could concentrate on staff work. As it was, though, Fitz wore all the hats, sometimes simultaneously.

"Of course, sir. No need to worry on that score." He hesitated. "If I may, sir . . ."

Marcus sipped at the tea and waved a hand. "Hmm?"

"What's your impression of the colonel?"

"He's . . ." Marcus paused, thinking. "He's very clever."

Fitz frowned. "Clever" was not a good thing in the lexicon of the common soldier. Clever officers came up with elaborate plans that backfired at just the wrong moment and got you killed.

"He's a count," Marcus went on, "but he doesn't stand on privilege. Likable, I suppose, but there's something"—he thought of those eyes, gray and judging—"something a little *odd*. I don't know." He shrugged. "I've just met the man myself."

"Has he given you any indication what he plans to do?"

Before Marcus could reply, there was a knock at the outer door.

Fitz hurried off to answer it, and Marcus turned back to the papers in front of him, trying to bully his eyes into focus. He took a long drink and let it sit on his tongue, warm and bitter.

A cough made him look up again and swallow hurriedly. Fitz stood at the inner doorway. His expression was as officially blank as usual, but the barest hint of an arched eyebrow indicated that something strange was afoot.

"There's someone to see you," the lieutenant said. "A Miss Jennifer Alhundt."

Marcus was taken aback. "Really?"

"Yes, sir."

"Show her in, I suppose." Marcus straightened up and tugged at his collar, peripherally aware of the sweaty patches that were beginning to show through his dress blues.

The woman was pale, even for a Vordanai. She had the look of someone who'd spent too much time indoors, an impression enhanced by watery eyes behind silver-rimmed spectacles. Her hair was long and dark, tied back in a severe braid. She wore a thin brown coat over a shapeless cotton blouse and brown trousers. When Marcus had left Vordan, a well-bred woman wearing trousers would have been, if not a scandal, at least the occasion for much comment. He wondered idly if all the noble ladies had traded their frilly dresses for boyish leggings since then. Stranger things had happened in the world of high fashion.

He got to his feet as she entered, and sketched a bow, which she returned awkwardly. Her spectacles threatened to fall off, and she caught them automatically and pushed them back up her nose with a well-practiced motion.

"Welcome, Miss Alhundt. I'm Captain Marcus d'Ivoire. Will you sit down?" He paused, suddenly painfully aware that he had just asked a lady to squat on the bare floor. He coughed to cover his embarrassment. "Fitz, fetch a cushion for Miss Alhundt, would you?"

"Thank you," she said. "I'll be fine."

They settled themselves on opposite sides of Marcus' crude desk, and she peered at him through thick lenses in the manner of a naturalist studying some surprising insect. Marcus was still trying to work out a polite way to ask what the hell she was doing here when she said, "I expect you're wondering what I'm doing here."

He shrugged, and waved desperately at Fitz, who bustled off. "Would you like some tea?"

"Please," she said. "I came in with the fleet, of course. I'm on assignment."

"What sort of assignment?"

"His Grace was instructed by His Majesty to gather an independent perspective on events in Khandar."

Marcus froze. "His Grace?"

"His Grace, Duke Orlanko," she clarified. "I'm with the Ministry of Information."

Fitz appeared with the tea, which saved Marcus from having to think of an immediate response to that. Miss Alhundt accepted the mug from the lieutenant, sipped, and resumed staring at Marcus.

"The Ministry of Information," Marcus said eventually. "May I ask in what . . . capacity?"

"Only a poor scholar, I'm afraid." She gave a tight little smile. "I know our reputation, Captain, but I assure you that His Grace employs many more scribes than he does spies and assassins."

Miss Alhundt certainly didn't look like a spy or assassin. She had the air of someone more comfortable with books than people. But everyone in Vordan knew about the all-seeing eye and long reach of Duke Orlanko's Concordat.

"And you mentioned a royal order?" he said, buying time.

She nodded. "His Majesty was concerned that the reports we'd been receiving from Khandar might be . . . inadequate. In view of our expanded commitment and the situation here, he thought it expedient to try to get a disinterested view of how things stand. That isn't easy to do through military channels."

"Fair enough, I suppose." Marcus shifted uncomfortably. "So what is it that you need from me?"

"I just thought I would introduce myself." She favored him with a smile, showing pretty white teeth. "I'm afraid my experience in the field is rather limited, and I'm sure I'll be relying a great deal on you and the other officers for your opinions."

"I thought you were supposed to get an unbiased view of things."

"I will present your views along with my own opinions," Miss Alhundt said. "That way, His Majesty and His Grace will have all the available information. Things have certainly been confused lately."

Marcus could imagine that. He'd written only one hasty report during the retreat, and it was unlikely that even that had reached the capital by now. *His Grace must be groping in the dark. No wonder he sent some of his own people along. But her?*

"I'll do whatever I can," he said. "You understand, though, that this is now Colonel Vhalnich's command. My opinions may not count for very much anymore."

"I'll be speaking to the colonel, too, of course," she said briskly. "I take it you've met him?"

"I received him this afternoon."

"Would you care to offer your impression?"

"I wouldn't," Marcus said. Gossiping with Fitz was one thing, but talking about a senior officer to a civilian was deeply taboo, even if that civilian *didn't* work for the secret police.

"Fair enough," Miss Alhundt said, still smiling. "I understand." Abruptly, she held her hand out across the table. "I do hope we can be friends, Captain d'Ivoire."

Marcus shook awkwardly, again at a loss. Miss Alhundt sipped, handed her teacup to Fitz, and got to her feet.

"And now, I imagine you have work to do," she said. "I'll see you soon, I'm sure."

Once the young woman had swept back out the door, Marcus looked up at his aide. "Do I have work to do?"

"Yes," Fitz said. "But first you're having dinner with the colonel, remember?"

The door to Janus' quarters opened at Marcus' approach, revealing a liveried servant with a haughty expression. Marcus, caught off guard, sketched a slight bow, and received a nod in return.

"I'm Captain d'Ivoire," he said. "The colonel's expecting me."

"Of course, sir." The manservant, a pinch-faced man with a shock of white hair who couldn't have been younger than fifty, gave Marcus a somewhat deeper nod and a disapproving stare. "Come in."

"Ah, Captain!" called Janus from inside. "Augustin, you can get dinner started."

"Yes, sir." The manservant bowed again, deeply, and withdrew.

"Augustin has been with my family since he was a boy," Janus confided as the man bustled away. "He thinks of it as his mission in life to maintain the dignity of my station. Don't let him bother you."

Somewhat to Marcus' surprise, the largest and outermost chamber of the little suite had been converted into a passable imitation of a dining room. The walls were still bare rock and there were no carpets on the floor, of course, but a table big enough for six had appeared, complete with chairs, napkins, and cutlery. Even plates—Marcus hadn't seen real china since he'd arrived in Khandar. He wondered whether the colonel planned to carry it all into the field.

"Take a seat, Captain! Take off your jacket, if you like." Janus was in his shirtsleeves, his blue coat tossed carelessly on top of a trunk in one corner. "You may have gathered that I don't stand on ceremony." When he saw Marcus still hesitating in the doorway, he commanded, "Sit! I'll be back in a moment. I need to sort something out."

He bustled off through the flimsy curtain that divided the dining room from the rest of the suite. Marcus, somewhat uncertainly, took one of the chairs and settled into it. It was a more complex affair then it appeared at first glance, with a canvas seat and back, and was surprisingly comfortable. After a bit of investigation Marcus decided the thing could be folded up for transport.

His curiosity piqued, he picked up his plate. The lack of heft told him it wasn't porcelain after all; it felt more like tin. He rapped it with his fingernail.

"A special alloy," the colonel said, from the doorway. "And the glaze is an interesting design. It has nearly the look of proper china, doesn't it? But it's practically impossible to scratch." He shook his head. "The food won't be much, I'm afraid. Augustin is a wizard, but there's only so much that can be done with salt beef and hard bread."

Marcus, whose last meal had been a thin mutton soup from a wooden bowl, shrugged.

"Once we've had some time to settle in, I hope that you'll introduce me to the local delicacies," the colonel went on.

"When we left Ashe-Katarion," Marcus said, "the thing to eat was roasted *imhalyt* beetles in the shell. Under the right conditions they can grow to be eight inches long, and the meat is supposedly delightful."

Janus didn't bat an eye. "It sounds . . . fascinating. Did you spend a great deal of time with the locals?"

"Before the Redeemers, we had reasonably good relations," Marcus said, considering. "On the whole I wouldn't say they loved us, of course, but I had friends in the city. There was a little place by the harbor that sold *arphalta*—that's a sort of clam—and I used to spend my free evenings there. The damn things are hard to get open unless you know the trick, but the meat is sweet as candy."

Marcus paused, wondering suddenly if the little *arphalta* shop was still there or if it had been consigned to the flames by the

Redeemers. Wondering, for that matter, how many of his friends might have shared a similar fate.

"I wish I'd been here," the colonel said. "It's a fascinating culture, and I'd have loved to have explored it in peace. I imagine any further interactions will be somewhat—strained."

"Quite probably," Marcus deadpanned.

Augustin came back in with a silver tureen of thick red soup and a pair of bowls. He placed and poured with all the noiseless elegance of the ancient retainer, then went back to the kitchen for glasses and a bottle of wine. He presented the latter to Janus for approval.

"Yes, that will do," Janus told him. Glancing at Marcus, he said, "You have no objection to Hamveltai *flaghaelan*, I hope?"

Marcus, whose appreciation of wine began and ended with what color it was, nodded uncertainly.

"Augustin was quite upset with me when I didn't allow him to bring half the cellar," Janus said. "I kept telling him that we were unlikely to require a Bere Nefeit '79 while on campaign, but he was most insistent."

"One never knows what may expected of one," Augustin said. He poured deftly. "A gentleman must always be prepared to entertain guests in the manner of a gentleman."

"Yes, yes." Janus took up his glass and raised it. "To the king's health!"

"The king's health," Marcus echoed, and sipped. It was good, truthfully, though after years of Khandarai rotgut it felt like drinking fruit juice. He was more interested in the soup—if the ingredients were salt beef and hard bread, they had certainly been well concealed. Before he realized it he had cleaned the bowl and found himself looking around for more.

"Another helping for the captain," Janus said.

"Thank you, sir," Marcus said. He cleared his throat. "You'd best know, I had a visitor this afternoon—"

"Our Miss Alhundt? Yes, I thought you might."

"She . . ." Marcus paused, looking at Augustin. Janus caught his expression.

"You may trust in Augustin's discretion. I certainly do. However, if it makes you more comfortable—Augustin, would you leave us for a few minutes?"

"Certainly, sir." The manservant bowed. "I will be outside if my lord requires anything."

He ghosted out. *He should get together with Fitz,* Marcus thought. Both men had obviously mastered the art of noiseless movement in order to sneak up on their superiors.

"You were saying something about Miss Alhundt?"

"Ah, yes, sir." Marcus shook his head. "She works for the Ministry of Information. I suppose you know that."

"I do indeed," Janus said. "What did you think of her?"

"Personally?" Marcus shrugged. "We didn't talk long enough to form much of an opinion. A bit stuffy, perhaps. Harmless."

The corner of Janus' lip twitched. "Harmless in her person, perhaps. How much do you know about the political situation back home?"

Politics. Marcus fought back a surge of panic. "Almost nothing, sir. We don't even get the gossip until it's six months stale."

"I won't bore you with the details of plots and counterplots. Suffice it to say that for some time now His Majesty's government has been divided into two factions. One—call them the 'peace' party—favors a greater accommodation with the Borelgai and Emperor of Murnsk, and particularly with the Sworn Church of Elysium. The other side would prefer an aggressive policy toward both. Precisely who belongs to which faction is never entirely clear, but the leader of the peace party has for some time been His Grace Duke Orlanko." Janus cocked his head. "You've heard of him at least, I trust?"

"The Last Duke," Marcus said. "Minister of Information."

"Indeed. It was the ascendancy of the war party that brought us the War of the Princes, which ended so disastrously at Vansfeldt."

"You don't need to remind me of *that*," Marcus said. "I was there."

He'd been on his tour as a lieutenant, supervising a supply company well short of any action. He'd been close enough to catch the distant flash and grumble of the guns, though, and to be caught up in the panicked rout that followed.

Janus nodded. "After the treaty was signed, the peace party found its rule nearly uncontested. The death of Prince Dominic had robbed the war party of its leader, and the king was too debilitated by grief and illness to interfere. Orlanko forged closer ties than ever to the Borelgai and the Church. As the king's sicknesses have become more frequent, Orlanko's power has increased. If His Majesty were to die—Lord forbid, of course—Princess Raesinia might take the throne, but Orlanko would rule, to the extent that he does not already."

"All right," Marcus said uncertainly. "What does that have to do with Khandar? I would have thought we'd be the last thing on his mind."

"Indeed. When the Minister of War suggested a Khandarai expedition, everyone expected Orlanko to oppose it. Instead, he not only threw his own weight behind it, but demanded that one of his people be sent along as an official observer."

"Why?"

Janus smiled. "I have spent most of the past few months trying to figure that out. One possibility is that he guessed that I would be chosen for the command. The Duke and I are . . . not on good terms. He may think that we are doomed to either bloody failure or ignominious retreat, and in either case he could use the fallout to destroy me."

Marcus, somewhat alarmed by the casual reference to "bloody failure," kept his expression carefully neutral. "But you don't think that's it."

"I don't. It's too roundabout, even for a compulsive schemer like Orlanko. No doubt my downfall would be gratifying, but there's something here that he wants." Janus pursed his lips. "Or something that *someone* wants. It may be that Orlanko is merely an errand boy for his friends in the Sworn Church. There have been a great many clerical comings and goings from the Ministry of Information lately."

"What would the Sworn Church want from Khandar?"

"Who knows?" Janus shrugged, but his eyes were hooded. "It could be anything. They still believe in demons up in Elysium."

"It doesn't seem very clever of Orlanko to put his agent out where everyone can see her," Marcus said. "I can have a couple of men tail her, if you like."

"Thank you, Captain, but don't bother. As I said, I suspect she's harmless in her person. The real agents are no doubt salted amongst our new recruits."

Marcus hadn't thought about that. All those new men, and how was he supposed to know which to trust? He felt a sudden, irrational stab of rage at Janus. *What the hell have you brought down on my regiment?*

After a moment he said, "Why tell me all this, sir?"

"I take it you're not accustomed to senior officers speaking plainly?" Janus chuckled. "No, don't answer that. I'm trying to be honest with you, Captain, because I need your help. You know the country, you know the Khandarai, and most important, you know the Colonials. I'm not foolish enough to think I can do this without you and your fellow officers."

Marcus' back straightened involuntarily. "I will perform my duty to the best of my ability, sir. As will the others."

"I need more than obedience. I need a partner, of sorts. With the Redeemers in front of us and Orlanko behind, I need someone I can trust."

"What makes you think you can trust me?"

"I've read your file, Captain," Janus said. "I know you better than you might think."

There was a long pause.

"What is it that you intend to do?" Marcus asked eventually.

"Whether he intended it or not, Orlanko has backed me into a corner. My orders require me to suppress the rebellion, but no one at the Ministry of War understood how badly out of hand things had gotten here. The only way out is to fight the campaign and win, while keeping one eye on Miss Alhundt and whatever friends she may have brought with her."

Marcus considered for a moment. "May I ask something, sir?"

"Of course."

"I don't fancy the idea of my men being used as pawns in this game between you and the Duke. I want . . ." Marcus hesitated. "I would like your word, as an officer, that you really think this can be done. I'm not interested in helping you die gloriously." *Or doing so on your behalf.*

He'd been worried that Janus would take offense, but the colonel gave another quick smile. "Of course, Captain. You can have my word as an officer, a count, or in whatever other capacity you'd like."

"As an officer will be sufficient," Marcus said, fighting a grin. "I never did place much trust in nobility."

CHAPTER THREE

WINTER

Winter returned from breakfast to find all of her worldly possessions smashed into the dirt.

Someone had taken down her tent, folding it neatly around the poles in accordance with regulations. Before they could do this, they'd had to dump everything out of it, and from the look of things there had been a fair bit of stomping back and forth to make sure her belongings were ground to bits against the parched earth of the courtyard.

Davis was nowhere in evidence, of course, but she could see Peg sitting in front of his own tent, a little way down the row, looking on with a sly smile. No doubt he was hoping to see her scrabbling in the wreckage to rescue what she could, and Winter decided abruptly that she wasn't going to oblige him. Her worldly possessions didn't amount to much, anyway. She'd had to leave almost everything behind in the retreat—her pillows, sheets, and other comforts, her private tent, the little hoard of Khandarai books she'd gathered while studying the language. The only things left were a few mementos and curios she'd picked up in Ashe-Katarion, and she wasn't going to grub on her knees in front of Peg for those.

Instead she turned on her heel without a word and went in search of her new company. This was not an easy task, as the encampment had nearly tripled in size overnight. The new soldiers were marked out by the solid blue of their still-creased tents, but since they outnumbered the old Colonials three to one, that alone wasn't a great deal of help. Winter ended up collaring a staff lieutenant and asking directions to the First Battalion, Seventh Company, which the harassed young man provided with bad grace.

Walking through the neat rows of tents, fresh from some Vordanai factory and laid out in perfect accord with the instructions in the *Regulations*, Winter couldn't help feeling out of place. Despite the addition of a new jacket, her uniform was a long way from perfect, and she felt like the pips on her shoulder drew every eye. She returned the curious stares.

Children, she thought. *This is an army of children.*

The men she saw eating breakfast or chatting in little groups in front of their tents looked more like kids playing dress-up than like proper soldiers. Their uniforms were too neat, with every bit of seam and trim still in place. Most of the faces she saw were as little in need of a razor as her own.

The tents of the Seventh Company were marked by a stenciled sign tied to a post. Otherwise, there was nothing to distinguish them from the surrounding sea of humanity. Winter had never felt like she was part of an *army* until now—the Colonials had been more like a tribe, small enough that you had at least a nodding acquaintance with anyone you were likely to meet. Now she understood a little of what some of the older men talked about, having served with real armies on the continent. The sheer busyness of the camp felt oppressive.

She shook her head, wandering down the row of tents. A wave of whispers and stares preceded her. When it reached a small knot about midway down, a trio of soldiers broke away and hurried over, planting themselves stiffly at attention in her path. When she stopped, they gave a simultaneous salute, and she had to clench her fist to keep herself from automatically saluting back.

Instead, she nodded, noting the single copper pip on each shoulder. That made these three corporals, half of the six that were standard complement for an army company. For a long moment, they stood in silence, before it dawned on Winter that it was up to her to make the next move. She cleared her throat.

"Ah . . . thank you, Corporal. Corporals."

"Sir!" said the young man in the middle. He was short, no taller than Winter, and with lank brown hair and the pasty skin of someone who'd spent too much time indoors. Despite his rigid bearing, he looked as though he was about sixteen.

"I'm Winter Ihernglass." There was a formula for this, somewhere, but she'd be damned if she could remember what it was, so she went on as best she could. "Senior Sergeant Winter Ihernglass. I've been assigned to this company. I think." She looked around, suddenly nervous. "This is First Battalion Seventh Company, isn't it?"

"Sir, yes, sir!" the corporal barked. "Welcome, sir!"

"And you are . . . ?"

The young man was practically vibrating with pride. "Senior Corporal Robert Forester, sir! And this is Corporal James Folsom, and Corporal Drake Graff. Welcome to the Seventh Company, sir!"

"You said that already," Winter said. "But thank you."

The corporal seemed to deflate a little. "Yes, sir." Then he brightened. "Would you like to proceed to your tent, sir, or do you want to review the men immediately?"

"Reviewing is the lieutenant's job, I think," Winter said. "We have got a lieutenant, haven't we?"

"Yes, sir! Lieutenant Anton d'Vries, sir! I understand he's still with the other officers, sir!"

"Well, he can handle the reviewing." She eyed the other two corporals, who seemed a little embarrassed by their comrade's enthusiasm. "Just show me to the tent, if you would."

"Sir, yes, sir!"

The corporal about-faced, so stiff it made Winter's joints ache just to watch, and started down the row of tents. Winter and the other two followed.

"Corporal Forester?"

"Yes, sir?"

"You may relax a little, if it would make you more comfortable."

"Sir, yes, sir!" The boy shot her a grin over his shoulder. "In that case, sir, please feel free to call me Bobby. Everyone else does."

They arrived at a tent, identical to all the rest in its factory-fresh neatness, whose flap was pinned back to reveal the interior. There was only one bedroll, Winter was glad to see, along with a knee-high portable writing desk and a regulation knapsack. In the Ashe-Katarion days, Winter had gotten out of sharing a tent by buying an extra with her own money. Since the retreat, she'd been sleeping beside two soldiers of Davis' company, which clearly made them as unhappy as it made her uncomfortable. She'd been dreading a similar arrangement in her new unit, but apparently a sergeant rated a tent to himself. *Maybe there's something to being promoted after all.*

Winter went inside with the others. She and Bobby barely had to bow their heads, but Corporal Folsom, a tall, broad-shouldered man with blond hair and a drooping mustache, had to bend practically double, and once inside he squatted on his haunches to avoid brushing the ceiling. Winter sat down on the bedroll and let out a long breath. There was another awkward silence.

"Would the sergeant like me to send someone to fetch his baggage?" Bobby suggested.

"Ah, no," Winter said. "I haven't got any, actually. Had to leave everything else behind in the retreat. In fact, I'd be grateful if you could have someone run down to army stores. I'm going to need more shirts, trousers"—she looked down at herself—"practically everything, really."

Bobby straightened to attention even further, if that was possible. "Sir, yes, sir! I'll attend to it at once!"

"And a sewing kit," Winter added. She'd grown practiced at making certain surreptitious alterations to her shirts to help conceal the shape underneath, although in that respect it helped that she didn't have *that* much to conceal.

Bobby saluted, drillbook-perfect, and hurried out of the tent as though his life depended on it. Winter looked from one corporal to the other in the embarrassed silence that followed.

"Corporal . . . Graff, was it?" she said.

"Yessir," Graff said. "I have to apologize for Bobby, sir. He's a good lad, but . . . keen, you know? I imagine he'll grow out of it."

"I imagine so," Winter said. "Are you three the only corporals in the company?"

"Yessir. Should be three more, but we didn't have any others who'd admit to meeting the requirements."

"Requirements?"

"Reading and writing, sir. And there's a test on regulations. Bobby volunteered, I was a corp'ral already, and we talked Jim here into it." He shrugged. "Now that we're in the field, maybe the lieutenant will tap some more men for the job."

Winter nodded. "What's the lieutenant like?"

"Couldn't say, sir," Graff said. "Haven't met the man."

"But—"

"He only joined the comp'ny just before we set sail," the corporal explained. "Officers were on a separate ship, of course. And he hasn't stopped by yet."

"I see," Winter said. "And how many men have we got?"

Graff looked suddenly worried. "A hundred and twenty, sir," he said slowly, as though explaining to an idiot. "That's a company's worth."

Winter thought about telling him that none of the old companies in the Colonials had more than eighty, and some many fewer, but decided against it. Instead she turned to the third corporal, who hadn't yet spoken.

"You're Corporal Folsom, then?"

The big man nodded.

"Have you been with the army long?"

He shook his head. Winter, in the face of such implacable silence, looked to Graff for support. He shrugged.

"Jim doesn't talk much," he said.

"I can see that."

Bobby returned, ducking through the open flap with a leather portfolio under one arm. He straightened up and saluted, again, then presented the portfolio to Winter with the air of someone offering a sacrament. Winter regarded him blankly.

"Reports, sir," the corporal said. "Daily sick lists, equipment, and infractions. I've been keeping them since we left the depot."

"Ah." Winter tried to smile as she took the portfolio. "I'll be sure to look through them carefully."

"Yes, sir! And once you've signed your approval, I'll forward them to the lieutenant, sir!"

"I've got to sign them all? Why?"

"Daily reports are only provisional until approved by a senior sergeant, sir. There's also the company accounts in there, sir. They've got to be tallied and brought up to date with the reports."

"You can't do that, either?"

Bobby looked shocked. "Corporals are not permitted to view the company accounts, sir!"

Winter regarded the folder in her hand as though it were some new and particularly poisonous species of scorpion. The Colonials, as far as she knew, had managed without the formality of paper accounts. Admittedly, they'd managed rather *badly*, all things considered, with equipment constantly in short supply and pay so far in arrears that the men joked that if they'd been allowed to collect interest they'd own the kingdom by now. Apparently things were to be different from now on. She allowed herself a moment of pleasure at the thought of Davis, a pencil between his fat fingers, trying to puzzle his way through a book of accounts.

"All right," Winter said. "I'll take care of it."

"Thank you, sir! And I've forwarded your request to the quartermasters, sir!"

"Right."

The three men looked at her. Winter stared back. After a moment Graff cleared his throat.

"Is there anything else you need from us at this time, sir?"

"What?" Winter shook her head. "Ah. No. No, that will be all, Corporal. Corporals. Thank you." She felt, vaguely, that something more was expected of her. "I look forward to working with all of you."

Bobby saluted again, his whole body vibrating with attentiveness. Graff gave a nod, and Folsom said nothing.

> *13th of May, 1208 YHG. One hundred thirteen present, six sick, one suspended. Ranker Gabriel Sims assessed 1b 6p for loss of cap (blown overboard). Ranker Arcturo d'Venn judged in violation of Regulations Ch. 6 Part III Para 2b, Behavior Likely to Incite Disorder. Sentence: Confinement, 2 days. Ranker Falrad Inker judged in violation of Regulations Ch. 6 Part II Para 3a, Excessive Drunkenness. Sentence: Hard Labor in service of Captain Belson, 1 day.*
>
> *14th of May, 1208 YHG. On hundred fourteen present, four sick, two suspended. Ranker George Tanner assessed 4p for damage to civilian property (ship's rope). Ranker—*

Winter closed her eyes and massaged her temples, which had started to throb alarmingly. Bobby's handwriting was not helping—it had the careful precision of someone who'd practiced under a tutor's switch, but he wrote so small the words all ran together. No doubt the corporal had been motivated by a sincere desire not to consume too much of the king's paper.

She leaned back from the miniature desk, hearing something pop in her back, and looked at the discouragingly large stack that remained. Fatigue settled on her like a heavy blanket, payment for the keyed-up nervousness she'd been feeling ever since her interview with the captain. She crawled over to the bedroll and flopped onto it facedown.

This could almost work. She shied away from the thought, as though even to contemplate it invited disaster. *I could live with this.*

So far, her secret seemed safe. And being a sergeant had definite advantages: the privacy of her own tent, and a certain automatic distance from the rankers. If a stack of account books was the worst she had to deal with, then it was undeniable that Captain d'Ivoire had done her a favor.

The remaining unknown was the company lieutenant—she'd already forgotten the man's name—and what his attitude might be. Even there, though, signs were encouraging. The less time he spent with the men, the better, as far as Winter was concerned.

For the first time in weeks she allowed herself to contemplate the future with something other than a sense of dread. The fleet had been dispatched weeks ago, in response to reports of rebel strength that were themselves weeks out of date. Even rankers like Buck and Peg could see that it was fruitless to remain here now that the Redeemers had taken the capital. "Fort" Valor was a joke, a death trap. It might be a few days until the new colonel resigned himself to the situation, but soon enough they'd all be packed aboard ship and set a course for home.

The voyage itself loomed large in Winter's apprehensions, but that was only a discomfort to be endured, like so many others. And then . . .

The Colonials will get some awful posting. They were more or less a penal regiment, after all. *Far away from the city, maybe up north, keeping the king's sheep safe from Murnskai raiders.* Either way, they would be a long way from Mrs. Wilmore's, and anyone who might connect a boyish sergeant with the ragged girl who'd made her escape from that institution.

Winter closed her eyes. *Honestly, I'm sure they've forgotten all about me.*

"Sergeant?"

Winter surfaced from a dream of cavernous, echoing halls and a pair of haunting green eyes. For one confused moment, she was convinced she was back at Mrs. Wilmore's Prison for Young Ladies, and that Khandar and everything that had come after that was the dream.

"Sergeant? Sergeant Ihernglass?"

Winter opened her eyes.

Bobby stood by the open tent flap, looking embarrassed. Beyond him was the gray darkness of early evening, broken by the flickering, reflected light of campfires. Winter slowly sat up, feeling her cheeks redden. She coughed.

"Y-yes? What is it, Corporal?"

"Sorry, sir," Bobby said. "I didn't mean to wake you."

"It's all right." Winter yawned. "It's been a long day, that's all."

"Yes, sir. For all of us, sir." The boy hesitated. "Dinner's on outside, sir. Would you care to join us?"

Winter felt a sudden complaint from her stomach—she hadn't had anything to eat since breakfast. But she shook her head.

"I'm not sure that would be . . . appropriate."

"Then I'll bring you something, sir, as soon as it's ready," Bobby said.

"Thank you, Corporal," Winter said, with real gratitude. "In the meantime I suppose I'd better get back to this paperwork."

The corporal saluted and left, letting the tent flap fall closed behind him. Winter rubbed her cheeks, trying to massage some life into them, and then her temples, to discourage the headache she still felt looming.

From outside, there came the low buzz of voices in conversation, punctuated by the sound of laughter. She wondered, idly, how much of it was at her expense. Nothing new there, of course.

She pulled herself over to the desk and tried to focus on the accounts ledger, but the figures swam across her vision. Rubbing her eyes with the heels of her palms, she caught a sudden flash of green. *A pair of green eyes, and a half smile.*

Her fingers curled through her hair. *Why now, Jane? Three years . . .* Fingernails tightened on her scalp, to the point of pain, hands tightening to claws. *What more do you want from me?*

With some difficulty, Winter forced her hands into her lap and sat back. Her heart thumped a fast tattoo, matched by answering pulses in her temples.

Red hair, dark and slick as oil, slipping through my fingers . . .

Can you be haunted by someone who isn't dead?

There was a rap at the tent pole. Winter opened her eyes and took a long, shaky breath.

"It's me, sir. Bobby."

"Come in."

The corporal entered cautiously, obviously determined not to embarrass his sergeant again. He carried a platter with a steaming tin bowl, which filled the tent with the smell of spiced mutton, and a couple of hardtack crackers. Winter took it from him, set it on the desk on top of the accounts, and attacked it with genuine enthusiasm. The retreat had wreaked havoc with the army's supply trains, and the quality of food had seriously declined since their Ashe-Katarion days. The new officers had obviously put things back in order. The mutton was in a sort of soup, not quite a proper stew, and the hardtack absorbed the juices and softened to something approaching an edible consistency.

It wasn't until she was mostly finished that she noticed the folded slip of paper on the platter beside the food. Catching her expression, Bobby gave a polite cough.

"It's a message for you, sir. We had a courier just now from the lieutenant." He paused, torn between curiosity and propriety. He obviously hadn't risked a peek.

Winter nodded and picked up the paper, breaking the blobby wax seal. The contents were short and to the point, although the scribbled signature was illegible. Winter read the note again, just in case she'd gotten something badly wrong.

"Sir?" Bobby prompted, watching her face.

Winter cleared her throat. "We're ordered to strike tents at first light tomorrow, and be ready to march by ten o'clock. Can you inform the men?"

"Yessir!" Bobby said, saluting. He turned, obviously pleased with this responsibility, and left the tent.

Ready to march? Winter gratefully let this new worry banish both the account book and her memories. *Where? Down to the fleet?* That was possible, of course, although she'd have thought the ships would need longer to replenish their supplies. *But if not there, then where? Against the Redeemers?* She allowed herself a smile. She couldn't believe even a colonel would be mad enough to try *that.*

MARCUS

Marcus awoke to the groans and curses of the First Battalion soldiers as their lieutenants rousted them from their tents. He dressed hurriedly, had a brief conference with Fitz, then went in search of Janus.

He found the colonel waiting by the gate, watching the men break camp. Aside from his horse, which stood quietly with all the well-bred dignity befitting Vordan's finest, he was alone. All around the courtyard, tents were coming down and stacked arms were being reclaimed by their owners. The First Battalion, entitled to the place of honor at the head of the march, was already starting to form up.

The regiment, Marcus thought, resembled a snake. At rest it was coiled tightly around itself, forming a more-or-less orderly camp with lines of tents, horses, and artillery parks. The work of picking up all the accoutrements would go on for some time, even as the head of the column started out. Each battalion had its assigned tasks in making or breaking camp, depending on its place in the order. The First would march out, dragging the Second after it, and so on, until the snake was fully extended and crawling down the road.

It was the tail that worried him. The Preacher's guns could keep up, more or less, but on the retreat the ox-drawn supply carts had ended up strung out over miles of rough track, straggling in well after dark. Now, Marcus looked at the route ahead and imagined every rock hiding a Desoltai scout, and every defile a gang of Redeemer fanatics.

The sound of hooves from behind him took a moment to penetrate his gloom. Janus glanced back and said, "Ah. I believe this is our chief of cavalry. Captain, would you be so kind as to provide an introduction?"

"Of course, sir." Marcus waited while the horseman dismounted, spurs jingling. "Colonel, may I present Captain Henry Stokes? Captain, this is Count Colonel Janus bet Vhalnich Mieran."

"Sir!" The captain saluted, with his usual ferocity. Henry—that was what Marcus called him to his face, although he was more commonly known to officers and men alike by the nickname "Give-Em-Hell"—was a short, bandy-legged man with a pigeon chest and a peacock's disposition. His weapons were always brightly polished, and Marcus didn't doubt that he'd given them an extra rubdown today. He wore an expression of fierce concentration.

A major contributor to Henry's inferiority complex, in addition to his height, was that the Colonials hardly *had* any cavalry. Members of that branch of the service were generally wealthier and better connected than those in the infantry, and thus less prone to—or at least more able to get out of—the kind of official disapproval that got a man sent to Khandar. To add insult to injury, the great Vordanai stallions and geldings so beloved of the horsemen fared poorly in the arid climate, so by now most of the captain's hundred or so troopers were mounted on smaller, sturdier Khandarai breeds.

"Captain," Janus said. "I regret that we have not had the chance to meet before now. Matters have, unfortunately, been busy."

"Sir!" Henry was practically vibrating with excitement. "Think nothing of it, sir! Just glad to be on the march again, sir!"

"Indeed. I'm afraid there is a great deal of hard work ahead for you and your men."

"Sir!" The cavalryman's chest was so puffed up he looked in danger of leaving the ground. "Just point the way, sir, and we'll give 'em hell!"

Janus coughed. "I'm sure you will. At the moment, however, I require them to serve in a more reconnaissance-oriented capacity."

Henry deflated a little. "Yessir."

"You're to range ahead of the advance, make sure the road is clear, and report on any potential opposition." Janus had obviously picked up on some of the captain's attitude, because he added, "That's *report*, not engage. And make sure your men travel in groups. I understand the Desoltai delight in ambushes."

Henry looked sour. That was light cavalry work, and Marcus knew his heart was in the cut-and-slash of the cuirassiers. He saluted anyway.

"If anyone's out there, sir, we'll find them."

"Excellent. Once you've gone fifteen miles, or thereabouts, detail some men to start laying out a campsite."

"Yessir!" Henry turned and remounted. Janus watched him ride away.

"He seems a most . . . enthusiastic officer," the colonel said, once the captain was out of earshot.

"Yes, sir," Marcus said. "Very keen."

"I must say, a little more cavalry would be a comfort." Janus sighed. "Ah, well. We must work with what we're given."

"Yes, sir."

Janus shot him a penetrating glance. "You seem dissatisfied, Captain."

"No, sir," Marcus said stiffly. "Just a little bit anxious, sir. That matter we discussed last night."

"Ah." Janus shrugged. "If it helps relieve your mind, we're hardly likely to run into any opposition this far out. Any raid they could mount would have only nuisance value."

Marcus nodded. In the courtyard, the march had begun, and the snake was uncoiling and on the move. Standing beside the colonel, Marcus was forced to see his men through an outsider's eyes, and the perspective made him wince.

It was easy to see, even at a distance, the distinction between the recruits the Colonel had brought with him and what everyone already called the "Old Colonials." Rather than break up existing companies, Janus had simply installed the new men as additional units onto the regiment's four battalions. The old companies, being lower-numbered, led the way on the march, which meant that the long blue snake appeared to be suffering from some sort of skin disease that started from the head. The Old Colonials had done their best, digging long-forgotten blue jackets out of trunks or wheedling them from the quartermasters, but their shirts and trousers didn't match, and everything was ragged and worn. Here and there a flash of color marked a man who'd refused to give up some treasured bit of silk.

The recruits, by contrast, were an unrelieved mass of blue, broken by the sparkling steel and brass of polished weapons. They marched in the vertebrae-shattering, knee-smashing style dictated by the *Manual of Arms*, rather than the world-weary slouch of veteran soldiers. Even their packs were all identical, tied up with the bedroll behind the neck, just so. The Old Colonials looked more like a pack of beggars, with clothes tied around their heads to keep off the sun and extra waterskins dangling from their belts.

Before too long, the tramp of thousands of pairs of boots raised such a cloud of dust that the men were nearly obscured. Marcus derived a slight satisfaction from the knowledge that all those bright blue uniforms and all that flashing steel wouldn't be quite so pristine by day's end. The leaders of the march—Marcus' own First Battalion—had already passed through the gate and up the road, and the companies of the Second were forming up. The sound of drums came through faintly, under the rumble of thousands of footsteps.

"Musicians," Janus said, apropos of nothing in particular.

"Sir?"

"I knew I had forgotten something. One always does, when leaving on a long journey." He smiled at Marcus. "The Colonials lack a regimental band, do they not?"

"No, sir. I mean, yes, sir, we don't have one. I suppose it's hard to earn yourself a tour in Khandar as a musician. We make do with the battalion drummers."

"Music can have a fine effect on troops on the march. De Troyes wrote that, in his experiments, merely including bands reduced straggling by up to thirty percent, and that he was able to extend the daily distance by almost a mile." He trailed off, looking thoughtful. Marcus cleared his throat.

"Hadn't we better mount up, sir?"

"Yes," Janus said, shaking his head. "Don't mind me, Captain. Sometimes I find myself . . . distracted."

"Of course, sir."

Chapter Four

MARCUS

Rank, Marcus thought, *has its privileges.* And in an army on the march, any little bit of comfort was to be savored.

In this case, the privilege was having someone else to erect his tent. It had been carried with the rest of the First Battalion baggage and put up for him at the center of the area allotted to his men. No doubt Fitz had supervised the furnishings, such as they were—camp bed, folding desk, a pair of trunks, and the leather portfolios full of paperwork.

Marcus sat down heavily on the camp bed, keeping his boots well clear so as not to dirty the sheets. He stared dully at his boot-laces, trying to remember how they functioned.

Fifteen miles. Not so far, in the scheme of things. Scarcely a journey to notice, in a well-sprung carriage, and certainly nothing a good horseman should complain of. Marcus was many things, but a good horseman was not one of them, and he ached from thighs to shoulders.

He could not even blame his mount, since he'd chosen her himself. He had purchased the mare a year or so earlier, after making a search of the Ashe-Katarion markets for the calmest, most stolid, least demanding mount that could be had. The sort of horse frail old ladies rode to church, or whatever it was that Khandarai old ladies did. He'd named her Meadow, on the theory that this might help.

And it had, in a way. Meadow was as unflappable an animal as had ever been bred, which meant that Marcus had to confront the fact that his frequent equine misadventures were solely the result of his lackluster horsemanship. The upshot was that up to now Meadow had led an extremely comfortable life and was hardly ever called upon to do any actual work, while Marcus walked or rode on carts whenever he could and saddled up only when it was absolutely unavoidable.

But senior officers were *expected* to ride while on the march. And not just in a straight line, either, but up and down the column, watching for problems and encouraging the men when their spirits flagged. Janus had set the example here, eschewing his black sun cape for full dress uniform to let the men get a good look at him. Marcus, perforce, had to follow, with the result that it felt like he'd ridden closer to thirty miles than fifteen.

For all that, the men in the ranks had it worse. Fifteen miles was a good day's walk under the best of conditions, but it was hellish with a full pack and the Khandarai sun blazing down. The Old Colonials, toughened by years of trudging through the heat, had grumbled and produced all manner of unorthodox headgear to keep off the vicious rays. The recruits, feeling they had something to prove, had shuffled gamely in their veteran comrades' wake and dropped like flies from exhaustion and heatstroke. Give-Em-Hell's cavalry were even now ranging back along the route of march, gathering up the stricken and delivering them to the regimental surgeon to be given a cold compress and a jot of whiskey.

Fifteen miles. Damn the man. It was Janus who'd insisted on the pace. *At least the Redeemers had the courtesy to start their revolution in April instead of August.* Even in spring, in spite of the coastal breezes, the Khandarai heat was trying. By high summer, the coast would be baking, and the inland desert would become a bone-dry furnace. *Be thankful for small graces.*

A rap at the tent pole made Marcus raise his head. That would be Fitz, ideally with dinner. He shifted, gingerly, to a sitting position and said, "Come in."

Fitz entered, but not alone. Val was as dusty and sweat-stained as Marcus, but didn't look half as exhausted. An aristocrat's son, Captain Valiant Solwen had learned to ride about the time he'd learned to walk, and no doubt considered the day's journey merely a bracing jaunt. He was short and broad-shouldered, giving him an almost apish appearance when not on horseback. His looks were not improved by a ruddy face that hinted at his ability to consume truly heroic amounts of alcohol. He adorned his upper lip with a pencil-thin mustache, which he claimed gave him a rakish air, and he spent an inordinate amount of time maintaining it. In Marcus' opinion it made him look like a penny-opera villain.

"I'm sorry," Val said, with a half smile. "I didn't realize you were going to bed straightaway."

"Just resting my eyes," Marcus muttered. He turned to Fitz. "Have they got dinner going yet?"

"Yessir," the lieutenant said.

"Mutton again, I suppose?"

"More than likely, sir." Khandar was rich in sheep, if little else. "Shall I fetch you something?"

"Please. Val, will you join me?"

"I suppose so," Val said, without enthusiasm.

Marcus swung his legs down and unlaced his riding boots, letting his feet emerge with an almost audible creaking as his bones flexed back into shape. He stood up in his socks and winced.

"Always meant to get new boots," he said. "A hundred boot makers in Ashe-Katarion, there's got to be one who can get it right. Kept putting it off, though, and now here we are." He grinned at Val. "There's a lesson in that, I think."

" 'Make sure you've got decent boots, because you never know when a pack of bloodthirsty priests are going to take over the place'? Doesn't sound very widely applicable."

"More like, 'Don't put things off too long, because you may never get a chance at them.'" Marcus went to one of his trunks, flipped it open, and rooted amongst his assorted rags until he found what he wanted. He held the bottle up to the lamp. The wax seal over the cap was still intact, and amber liquid glistened seductively inside the lumpy glass. Bits of green stuff floated on the surface. Herbs, Marcus hoped. "I've been saving this one. Damned if I know why. Scared to drink it, maybe." He held the bottle out to Val. "Join me?"

"Gladly," Val said. While Marcus hunted for his tin cups, Val added, "Adrecht has the same idea, I think. He's convinced that we're all going to die, so he's drinking his way through that liquor chest of his."

"Serve him right if he falls off his horse and hits his head," Marcus said.

"Small chance of that. Last I heard, his head already hurt so badly he was riding in a wagon and cursing every bump in the road."

Marcus laughed and came up with the cups. He broke the seal, poured, and offered one to Val, who took it gratefully.

"To Colonel Vhalnich!" Val proclaimed. "Even if he is mad."

He emptied his cup and made a sour face. Marcus only sipped from his. The sensation on his tongue made him think Val had the right idea after all. He frowned.

"Mad?"

"What else, marching us out here like this?" Val leaned forward. "That's what I came to ask you. You've been spending a lot of time with him. Has he let you in on the big secret?"

Marcus thought for a moment of Miss Alhundt and Janus' feud with the Last Duke. "I'm not sure what you mean."

"The plan!" Val gestured violently with the cup, spraying a few drops of liquor against the tent wall. "He can't be planning to just march up to Ashe-Katarion and knock on the gates, can he? You know as well as I do what'd happen next. The Redeemers have a goddamned *army* in the city. What are we supposed to do against that with one regiment?"

"I know," Marcus said, downing the rest of his drink in one brutal swallow.

"But does *he*? In other words, is he ignorant, stupid, or deluded?"

"He knows," Marcus said. Then, echoing his words to Fitz, "He's clever."

"Clever! Clever's the worst. God save us from clever colonels." Val shook his head. "Have you talked to Mor?"

"Not recently."

"He's not happy."

"I can imagine." Captain Morwen Kaanos was irascible at the best of times, which these hardly were. And his dislike of anything related to the nobility was well-known. He and Val had a long-simmering feud on the subject, based on nothing more than Val's being a distant cousin to some peer or other. Janus was an actual *count*, and taking his orders was certain to send the captain of the Third Battalion into a rage.

"He's not the only one," Val said quietly. "I've been hearing a lot of talk, Marcus."

Silently, Marcus proffered the bottle. Val gave it an evaluative look, then sighed and refilled both cups. He looked suspiciously into the depths of his drink.

"What are the green bits?" he said.

"Herbs," Marcus said. "What kind of talk?"

"Commonsense talk," Val said. "Which is what worries me. Talk like, we should have shipped out from Fort Valor. Talk that there's thirty thousand screaming savages who like to cook and eat anybody with pale skin, and that if they want Khandar so badly they're welcome to the damned place. Talk that maybe it would be best to take a quick hike to the rear, 'cause there's no sense getting killed just so some damned count can play soldier. It's going to be a run for the boats in the end, so why not get a head start?"

Marcus frowned, looked at his cup, and set it carefully aside. "You think anybody's serious?" The Colonials were famous grumblers—it was practically the regimental sport—but . . .

"Not yet," Val said. "But it's days before we get to the city, even at this pace. The recruits seem to be game, but I'm not sure how long that'll last. They're awfully green. Did you know that most of them didn't finish their time in depot? Some of them didn't have *any*. I talked to a whole company today who said they'd marched straight from the recruiting station to the ships."

That was disturbing, too, partly because it reminded Marcus how little time he'd spent with his own men. Janus seemed determined to make him into a kind of aide-de-camp, and had been monopolizing his time.

"They'll toughen up quickly," he said aloud. "Khandar has that effect on people. It certainly did on me."

"Tough is one thing," Val said. "It doesn't do much good if they don't know how to handle their muskets or form a line."

Marcus sighed. "What do you want me to do about it?"

Val looked perplexed. "Talk to him, of course."

"Talk?" It took Marcus a moment to get that. "To the colonel?"

"He spends more time with you than anyone in the regiment," Val said. "I don't think he's given me more than the time of day. So it's on you to tell him what we need. I don't understand what the goddamned hurry is, but we need to cut down the marches and get these men drilling. Even a few days could make a big difference."

"Easy enough to say," Marcus said. "I don't think he'll listen to me."

"If he doesn't, we're all in the shit," Val said. "Half the supply train is *still* trying to catch up, and this 'road' is a joke. If we do another few days like this, we'll be on short rations, and if you think the men are grumbling *now* . . ."

Fitz reappeared, bearing two bowls of the ubiquitous dump-everything-in-a-pot-and-boil-it meal known affectionately as "army soup." Marcus glared at it, but Val took the proffered spoon and dug in with a will.

"I'll try," Marcus said. "That's all I can promise."

Val shrugged, too busy eating to reply.

Standing outside Janus' tent, as torches and fires flared throughout the camp and the reds of the sunset gave way to darkness, Marcus realized he had no idea how to begin.

There was certainly no procedure for it in army etiquette. Captains didn't offer unsolicited advice to colonels, much less issue warnings or present demands. They might occasionally give their opinion, when asked, but directions started from the top and flowed downward. That was the point of the chain of command, after all. A colonel was supposed to know what he was doing.

All the relief that he'd felt when Janus had taken command had vanished. Marcus stood, one hand raised to knock at the tent pole, and dithered.

How would Fitz do it? The lieutenant never openly contradicted his captain, but he had his ways of making it known when he thought Marcus was making a bad decision. A glance, a cough, a "Yes, *sir*" with just the right tone of voice—the meaning always came across as clearly as if he'd shouted. But he, Marcus, wasn't Fitz; he didn't have the boy's carefully calibrated manners. *Or half his brains, for that matter.* Besides, he and Janus had been together for only a day or so. It had taken Marcus years to learn the ins and outs of Fitz's little hints.

He had still not reached a decision when the tent flap opened and Augustin emerged. The old servant bowed ever so slightly and cleared his throat.

"His lordship instructs me to say that if you're only going to stand there, you might as well come inside," he said, with a touch more dryness than was really necessary. Marcus instinctively bristled, but fought the reaction down.

"Thank you," he said, with as frosty a tone as he could manage. "I shall."

He followed the manservant through the tent flap. From Augustin's manner, Marcus half expected that the man had worked some magic to transform the standard army-issue tent into a feudal palace, complete with ancient oil paintings and suits of medieval armor.

Instead, he found a tent much like his own, if somewhat neater and better organized. A simple bedroll was still stowed in one corner, a set of trunks in another. The colonel sat on a cushion in front of a wide wooden table, divided into quarters and cunningly hinged so it could be stowed away for transport. Beside him sat another trunk, this one full of books. Marcus couldn't read the titles in the dim light, but they all had the same dark green leather binding, and fit as neatly inside the little case as if it had been designed for them. It probably had, Marcus reflected. Janus had certainly come prepared to his army career.

"Captain," he said, looking up from a stack of loose pages. "Have a seat. I assume this is not a social call?"

"No, sir." Marcus debated remaining on his feet, but decided there was nothing to be gained from it. He took the cushion opposite Janus. "I wondered if I might have a word."

"Of course." Janus slid the papers aside and steepled his fingers. "What's on your mind?"

Marcus glanced uncomfortably at Augustin, who had discreetly faded into the background. Janus looked up at the manservant.

"Augustin, would you be so good as to make the captain a cup of tea?" he said.

With another sour look at Marcus, Augustin bowed and ghosted out.

"You really must learn to ignore him," Janus said. "I assure you that his discretion is impeccable. But, if it makes you more comfortable . . ." He spread his hands.

"Thank you, sir." Marcus cleared his throat. "I—that is—I'm not sure how to begin."

"You have some advice for me," Janus said.

Marcus blinked. "How did you know that?"

"You'd hardly dither so over a report or some minor matter, would you?" Janus gave a disarming smile, gray eyes shining in the lamplight. "I *did* ask for your assistance, Captain. So long as we're in private, you may always consider yourself at liberty to speak your mind. I can't promise I will always follow your counsel, but I'll certainly listen."

"Thank you, sir." He took a deep breath. "Then I respectfully suggest that the marches be shortened, and that we institute some sort of regimental drill."

There was a moment of silence. Janus, leaning back, cocked his head as though considering the matter from a new angle. Finally he said, "And why do you say that?"

"Fifteen miles a day . . ." Marcus paused. "It's not that the men aren't capable, sir, but the wagons won't make it. Our supplies—"

Janus waved a hand. "There'll be time for the supply train to catch up, never fear. It's more important that the troops accustom themselves to hard marching. Soon enough we'll have need of it."

Marcus sat back, feeling defeated. Janus, watching him, burst out laughing.

"Sir?" Marcus said uncertainly.

"I'm sorry," the colonel said, still chuckling. "It's my own fault, I think. I'm not yet used to what you might call the military context. Captain, if you disagree with me, I encourage you to say so. I'm not Karis speaking the Law."

"You're a colonel," Marcus pointed out. *And a count besides.* "It's not my place—"

"I intend to take advantage of your judgment and expertise.

That means you must be more than a dumb recipient of my lordly wisdom. So long as the enemy are not actually before us, I expect you to correct me if I say anything foolish."

"Yes, sir," Marcus said. He'd forgotten how useful that phrase was—it could mean anything you wanted it to mean.

"So—you're not really worried about the supply train, are you?"

"Sir . . ." Marcus paused again, then gave an inward shrug. "There's been talk. The men aren't happy—well, that's nothing new—but they don't think we can win. They're saying that you're just out for glory, or that you're mad, and if we come up against the Redeemers . . ." He shook his head. "I haven't spent much time with the recruits, sir, but the Old Colonials feel . . . fragile. They'll march, for now, but one hard rap and they'll fly all to pieces."

Janus said nothing. His smile had gone, replaced by a thoughtful expression, but there was still a touch of humor at the corners of his eyes. Encouraged, Marcus went on.

"Val—Captain Solwen, that is—came to me this afternoon. He said some of the new men never even made it to depot, and none of them had the full training course."

"That's true," Janus said. "The Ministry was unwilling to send an experienced regiment to Khandar, so it was decided to bring the Colonials up to strength by throwing together the scraps from the depots and the backcountry recruiters."

"Then I'm not sure hard marching is what they need. They might get where they need to be, but will they fight when you need them to?"

"Just because they're untrained doesn't mean they're cowards." Janus frowned. "I was hoping the veterans would provide some unofficial instruction."

"From what I've seen, sir, the two groups don't seem to mix much. And the recruits need to practice formations most of all. That's not something you can do on your own time."

The colonel tapped one finger on the table. "Nevertheless," he said, "time is of the essence. If we delay . . ." He appeared to be speaking half to himself, and didn't wait for an answer. "I will think on it. Thank you, Captain."

"Sir—"

"You've made your point." Janus smiled again, but only briefly. "Now I need to consider." The tent flap rustled, and the colonel looked up. "Ah, and here's Augustin with your tea!"

Though he knew Give-Em-Hell's men had swept the route of march, Marcus found his eyes drawn to every obstacle that might hide some kind of ambush. It made for uncomfortable riding, all the more so because Janus seemed oblivious to any sense of danger. With the sun barely past the overhead, the heat was at its worst, and Marcus had to keep wiping sweat from his eyes with the back of his sleeve. Meadow plodded placidly beneath him, unperturbed.

Behind him, the regiment trudged onward, four thousand men in blue uniforms that by now had a healthy coating of the ubiquitous brown dust. To the left, the land fell away gradually to the sea, and on the right rose a line of dry, rocky hills. In between was a strip of ground bearing what the Khandarai laughably called a road, which amounted to a pair of wagon ruts and a path worn through the scattered scrub weeds. The only virtue the track had was that it kept the men from getting lost. Hundreds had dropped out, from heat or exhaustion, and would have to straggle in as best they could after the main body finally reached camp.

And if there's a Desoltai ambush over the next rise . . . The Redeemers were the principal enemy, but it was the desert nomads Marcus feared the most. The Desoltai had never been comfortable with Vordanai hegemony, and they'd thrown in with the rebels at the first opportunity. They lived out in the Great Desol, where the more cautious Khandarai feared to go, and practiced both horsemanship and marksmanship in endless raids against one another and the surrounding towns.

And now they have a leader. The Steel Ghost, a subject of endless rumor, was supposed to have committed a dozen atrocities already, and to possess fell powers besides. But the man's personal characteristics were less worrisome than the fact that the Desoltai were united, and committed to ridding their land of foreigners.

It wouldn't take much. A hundred horsemen would cut us to pieces. The infantry might be able to form square, eventually, but the wagons and guns would be so much meat for the butchers. *And with Give-Em-Hell out scouting, we wouldn't be able to chase them off.*

He looked at Janus, who rode with the unconcerned air of a man without a care in the world, moving with a natural grace in his saddle. Marcus scowled.

The hell of it was, the colonel was probably right. He would get away with it today—the odds of the Desoltai being so far west were small. And he'd get away with it tomorrow, and the next day, until one day he didn't. Then it would be too late. *But try explaining that to him.*

He glanced over his shoulder at the drummers, three of whom walked beside the sweltering column. Each battalion had its own, stationed around the colors, and in theory signals could be relayed from one to the next, allowing orders to pass all the way down the extended line of march without the need for galloping messengers. This worked well enough on the drill field, Marcus knew, but in the field of battle only the simplest commands would get through. "March," say, or "halt."

Or "form square." Marcus stiffened as the idea struck him. Just for a moment, he allowed himself to think of the possible consequences. Janus would be furious, of course, and as a count he might have influence at court in addition to his pull in the Ministry. He could . . .

. . . What? Ship me to Khandar? Marcus reined up, and Meadow came to a halt. After a few moments the drummers drew level.

"Sir?" one of them said, a heavyset, red-bearded man named

Polt. His cheeks were slick with a sheen of sweat, and he looked about ready to drop. "Is it time to call a rest?"

Janus had proscribed rest and water breaks every two hours, but there was some time yet before the next. Marcus looked at Polt's eager face and smiled.

"We're having a drill. Beat emergency square," he said.

"Sir, I— What?" He scanned the horizon frantically for signs of approaching enemies. "Really?"

"Yes, really. Do it now."

"But—" He caught Marcus' expression and decided not to argue. Instead he turned on his heel and addressed the two drummer "boys." In a normal regiment, these would be promising young sub-officers, but no one promising was sent to Khandar. These two looked like they were older than Marcus.

"Emergency square!" Polt bellowed, veins standing out on his neck. "Now!"

The three carried their drums strapped to their backs, where an ordinary soldier would have his pack. They scooted them round and let them fall flat, the straps holding them at waist level, and retrieved their heavy wooden sticks. Tentatively at first, but with increasing volume, they pounded out a basic rhythm. *Boom*, pause, *boom*, pause, *boom boom boom*—a simple signal for a vital command that might have to be executed on a moment's notice, with no more warning than a sentry's scream.

At the sound of the drums, the men at the head of the column halted. Those behind took some time to react, so the whole column closed up a little, but the regiment was still dreadfully strung out. There were no neatly dressed ranks on the march. Men walked in little clusters, vaguely divided by company, with their sergeants and lieutenants more concerned with chivying slackers than keeping order. They were expecting the command to halt for rest, and some few even took the opportunity to sit down in the road.

It was a few moments before the battalion drums picked up the signal, but once they did, it echoed up and down the whole column. The effect was everything that Marcus had hoped for—or, more precisely, dreaded. The Old Colonials knew what the signal meant, but had only a foggy idea of what they were supposed to do; the recruits mostly didn't understand, but they knew *something* was up by the panicky looks. Their officers, the lieutenants Janus had brought with him, were split about evenly between the two camps. Marcus heard a few shouts of "Square! Form square!" but for the most part these were submerged in the babble.

The long march column contracted as the men instinctively bunched up, forming a blob around the battalion color bearers and the drums. From where he was sitting, Marcus had a good view of the First and Second Battalions, and he was pleased to see that the First, at least, was slowly coming into some kind of shape. That was Fitz at work—he had a brief glimpse of the lieutenant grabbing an officer several years his senior by the arm and shoving him in the right direction. The blob gradually opened out in the center and became a ring, whose sides straightened as sweating lieutenants and sergeants shouted their men into something like a line. Bayonets came out of their sheaths, and there was a chorus of swearing as the recruits tried to fit theirs with suddenly awkward fingers.

The *Manual of Arms* said that a battalion in column of companies should be able to form square within two minutes of the order being given. A battalion on the march was allotted a bit more time, five minutes considered the standard. It was at least fifteen before the First Battalion emerged into something recognizable as a formation—a hollow rectangular block, each side three ranks deep, with fixed bayonets bristling like a hedge of steel points from every face.

Nor was the First the worst offender. Val had screamed the Second into shape, and Marcus didn't have a good view of the Third, but before long a stream of running, shouting men came up the road from the rear. Marcus thought they were from the supply train, fleeing a supposed enemy attack, until he saw the uniforms and the desperate, shouting officers and realized they were the men of the Fourth Battalion. Apparently all attempts to bring order there had failed, and the men had decided their only chance was to seek shelter in the steadier squares. A few shoving matches resulted, and Marcus winced, hoping that no bayonets would come into it. The last thing he needed was for his demonstration to cause actual casualties.

Next up the road came a dozen guns, pulled at a brisk trot by sturdy Khandarai horses, and accompanied by a double column of gawking artillerymen. Marcus had to grin at that. *At least the Preacher knows how to keep his men in order.* An infantryman of the Fourth, seeing the approaching cannon, decided he would be safer in amongst them, while a sword-waving lieutenant ran after him to a volley of curses and protests from the gunners.

All it needs is a fat captain with his pants around his ankles chasing a skinny blonde with a tuba going oompah-oompah, *and we'd have a perfect music-hall farce.* Marcus jerked Meadow's reins and turned back toward Janus, steeling himself for the colonel's reaction.

Janus was staring at the disorderly scene below. It took Marcus a moment to realize he was *laughing*, inaudible in the din. When he saw Marcus approaching, he turned on him with a faint but unmistakable smile.

"Sir!" Marcus barked, trying to make himself heard. Janus brought his horse alongside and clapped him on the shoulder.

"Point taken, Captain," he said. "Your point is very much taken." He shook his head ruefully. "Once everyone gets sorted out, you may order a halt for the day. We start drill in the morning."

A halt was inevitable in any event, as it took most of the rest of the day to get the troops back into something approximating order and untangle the panicked supply trains. Marcus winced when Fitz presented him with the final bill—forty-six men with scrapes and bruises, four horses so badly injured they'd had to be put down, and one wagon that had cracked an axle when its driver had driven it into a ditch. It could have been worse, though. The losses of matériel could be replaced or repaired, and he was relieved to hear that no one had been seriously hurt. *And who knows how many lives saved, down the road.* As the sun was setting, Marcus headed back to his tent with a cautious sense of optimism.

He was nearly there when a meaty hand descended on his shoulder. He started, spun to face his assailant, and found himself staring into a wild tangle of hair that failed to conceal a mocking smile.

"What's the matter, Senior Captain? You seem a little jumpy."

Captain Morwen Kaanos, of the Third Battalion, was a tall, heavyset man with weathered, tanned skin that spoke of years in Khandar. Between a thick goatee, bristly muttonchops, and an unkempt mustache, his face was almost invisible. His eyebrows were bushy as well, giving him the look of a wild man, hermit, or possibly the scruffier class of saint. The hand he'd clapped on Marcus' shoulder was big enough to be called a paw, and the hair on the back of it was practically fur.

"It's been a long day," Marcus said, irritated by his own reaction. "And I was hoping to get off my feet for a minute."

"Don't let me stop you," Mor said, in his heavy mountain accent. "Mind if I poke my head in, though? We wants a word."

Marcus gave an inward sigh, but nodded. The two of them practically filled the little tent. Marcus sat heavily on his bedroll and started unlacing his boots, while Mor stood by the flap, arms folded across his chest.

"I hear," he said, "that we got you to thank for the mess this afternoon."

"Where did you hear that?"

Mor tapped his nose, then shrugged. "Ain't no big secret. Polt's been telling the story since he put down his drum. Prob'ly 'cause half the Old Colonials seemed inclined to blame it on him."

"They're angry, are they?" Marcus worried at a knot that seemed to have become inextricably glued tight with sweat and Khandarai dust.

"Some are. You didn't make them look good back there."

"*I* didn't make them look bad, either. I've seen a pack of wild dogs form a better square."

"Hell, your boys in the First weren't too quick about it," Mor snapped. "Don't try to pin this—"

"It's on no one," Marcus said. The knot came free, and he slid his foot out of the boot with a sigh of relief. "It's a gang of half-trained recruits and a bunch of old grumblers who've had it too soft for too long. What do you expect?"

"What *did* you expect? Why'd you do it? Don't tell me you saw some old goatherd on a pony and shat your pants."

"I did it," Marcus said grimly, "because I knew what would happen, but His Lordship didn't believe me."

"Ah." Mor uncrossed his arms. "Suddenly it all makes sense."

Marcus frowned. Mor was always happy to suspect the worst of senior officers, particularly noble officers. As a general rule, the Colonials didn't dwell on the stories of how they'd ended up in exile, or ask about the disgraces of others, but Mor's tale was well-known: he'd illegally dueled a nobleman, he said, over the attentions of a young woman, and had accidentally killed the man. Whether that was true or not, he certainly harbored an inveterate hatred of nobility and privilege.

"He's not bad," Marcus said. "I think we can work with him. He just needed a little lesson on what's possible and what isn't. If he thinks he's going to take this lot into battle after a week of forced marches . . ."

"Battle?" Mor said. "You think it'll come to that?"

"Probably. We aren't marching all this way for our health."

"Last time I checked, there were a hell of a lot more of them than there are of us. Has anybody told His Lordship?"

"I told him myself," Marcus said. "Fighting isn't just about counting noses, though."

"Let's hope you're right about that. Though I'd lay ten to one we come scampering back down this road before the month is out."

"Either way," Marcus said, starting on the other boot, "it's not our problem."

"True. Our problem is currently sprawled in a supply wagon, making a solid try at drowning himself in wine."

Marcus swore softly. "Adrecht."

"Adrecht. You saw the way his men behaved today?"

Marcus nodded. Adrecht's Fourth Battalion hadn't even managed to stay together, let alone form square. "Where was he?"

"Search me, but he wasn't with them. Lieutenant Orta said he rode off around midday and never came back."

"Saints and martyrs," Marcus cursed. "Is he *trying* to get himself brought up on charges?"

"Last I talked to him, he was convinced we were all going to end up on Redeemer spikes, so I'm not sure he cares anymore." Mor gave Marcus a careful look. "What do you want to do?"

Marcus heard the question under the question. *Do we cover for him*, he translated, *and try to snap him out of it? Or ignore it and let the colonel deal with him?* He suspected he knew what Mor's opinion was. Mor had never had much use for the mercurial, unreliable captain of the Fourth.

"What do you think of this . . . Orta, was it?"

Mor shrugged. "He seems competent enough. A little hesitant to cuss an' shove when he needs to, though. The new lieutenants your colonel gave us are a bunch of spoiled-rotten assholes, and they like to talk back."

Marcus wondered if Fitz had the same problem and hadn't

mentioned it. Somehow he doubted it. Fitz had a way of getting what he wanted, though he never raised his voice.

"Right. Have you got a sergeant with a big mouth you'd be willing to part with for a while?"

Mor laughed. "You can have your pick of a dozen."

"Send one or two of them over to Orta, and tell him to work on getting the Fourth into shape. Hopefully that will buy us enough time to have a word with Adrecht."

"I suppose that's fair enough. It's going to have to be you that talks to him, though. He's never paid me much mind, and I doubt he'll start now."

Marcus nodded. "I'll wait until morning. Hopefully he'll have dried out a bit by then."

"Either that or he'll still be sleeping it off." Mor sighed. "I hope he appreciates this."

"I'm sure you're not likely to let him forget."

The big man laughed. "Bet your ass."

By rights, it ought to have been easy to get to sleep. The day had left Marcus near exhaustion, though more from anxious fretting than physical exertion. On the way back to his tent the only thing he'd been able to think about was collapsing into bed, but now that he was actually there sleep refused to come. He felt alert, even twitchy. If someone had tapped his shoulder he might have jumped a foot. Lying on his side, he could feel the *thump-thump* of his pulse, fast enough to march to.

After an hour, he dragged himself up with a silent curse, slipped his boots on without tying the laces, and staggered outside. The sky was a blaze of stars, dimmed only slightly by the torches and fires that still burned amidst the rows of tents. The moon hung huge and horned just above the western horizon, washing the labyrinth of blue canvas in a ghostly light.

When he started out, Marcus had the notion of taking a walk to convince his body to let him rest, but by the time he passed the last row of tents his steps had acquired more purpose. Beyond where the camp ended, across a few hundred yards of scrub, a line of torches marked the ring of sentries.

Sentries carried loaded weapons, and on a night like this they were bound to be jumpy. Marcus stopped a good fifty yards from the line, cupped his hands to his mouth, and shouted, "Sentry, ho! Friends approaching!"

The torch waggled in response. Marcus crossed the remaining distance at a brisk walk and found a young man with a musket resting on his shoulder and a torch in one hand. The shadows made everyone seem pale and hollow-eyed, but from the deep blue of his uniform Marcus could tell he was a recruit. He straightened up when he saw the captain's bars on Marcus' shoulder and tried to figure out how to salute with a torch in one hand and a musket butt in the other.

"No need, Ranker," Marcus said. "I'm just taking a quick look at the lines. What's your name?"

"Ranker Ipsar Sutton, sir!" He tried to salute again and nearly singed his forehead. "First Battalion, Fifth Company, sir!"

"One of mine," Marcus said. "I'm Captain d'Ivoire."

"I know, sir!" the young man said proudly. "I saw you at the drill this afternoon."

Drill, Marcus thought, *is one way to put it.* "How long is your shift, Ranker Sutton?"

"Another three hours, sir!" He gestured with the torch. "Nothing to see so far, sir!"

"It does us good knowing you're out here," Marcus said. "I for one couldn't sleep otherwise."

"Yes, sir!" Sutton stood up even straighter. "Thank you, sir!"

"Keep up the good work." Marcus patted him genially on the shoulder and walked on, into the darkness.

He went along the line of sentries, meeting each man in turn and exchanging a few words of greeting. They were all recruits

—apparently this section of the perimeter was held by the Fifth and Sixth companies—and to man they seemed distressingly keen. Getting a word from him seemed to cheer them up immeasurably, and by the time he turned back to his tent Marcus felt like he'd actually done some good.

It would have been different with the Old Colonials. Familiarity bred contempt, of course, and after the long years in the camp near Ashe-Katarion even the rankers had come to treat officers with a genial disregard. It might have been different if Ben Warus had been the sort of colonel to take offense at insubordinate conduct, but he'd always been an easygoing type, and the others took their cues from him. Seeing the straight postures and bright young faces of the recruits reminded Marcus of his last year at the War College, drilling squads of sweating underclassmen out on the Long Field.

That was what the army was supposed to be like. Not . . . this. He'd long ago resigned himself to the fact that Khandar wasn't much of a post. It certainly wasn't what he'd envisioned when he'd started at the College. But that had been *before*, when he'd still cared about his career and his standing in the world, before he'd volunteered for service at the edge of the world with the hope that it would let him outrun his ghosts. He'd done his best to enjoy the soft life of a sinecure and not to dwell on the past. Then, during the retreat, he'd been too busy to think. But now, with his comfortable routine broken—

"Good evening, Captain," said a woman's voice from the darkness. Such women as were with the regiment—laundresses, cooks, and whores, those who'd been brave enough to accompany the column when it had marched—would be on the other side of camp, with the supply train. That left a field of one, so Marcus hazarded a guess.

"You must have eyes like a cat, Miss Alhundt."

"Good night vision is essential in my line of work." She materialized out of the darkness.

"For peeking in people's windows?"

"For poking through dusty old shelves," she said, toying with her glasses. She pushed them up her nose and looked down at him through the lenses. "You wouldn't believe the mess back at the Ministry vaults. There are some rooms where we don't dare risk open flames."

"Couldn't have that. You might set fire to everyone's secrets."

"Secrets are not really my business, Captain. There's so much to know that isn't hidden at all."

"Fair enough," Marcus said.

"What about you?" she said. "Are you out spying on your subordinates? Or is this a surprise inspection?"

"Just checking over the arrangements," Marcus said.

"Very diligent of you," Miss Alhundt said. "I understand we also have you to thank for that . . . exercise this afternoon."

Marcus shifted uncomfortably. "What about it?"

"Did you intend to embarrass Colonel Vhalnich? Or merely to delay his progress?"

"Neither. It was a—a demonstration. I wanted to make a point."

"The point that the Colonials are woefully unprepared."

That was it precisely, of course, but he didn't want to say so. Marcus shook his head in silence.

"Do you mind if I ask why?" Miss Alhundt said.

"I'm not sure why you're so interested."

She cocked her head, one finger touching the bridge of her glasses. Beneath the spectacles, the severe hairstyle, and the mannish clothes, he guessed she was actually quite pretty.

"Because I'm curious about you, Captain," she said finally. "You are something of an enigma."

"I don't see why that should be. I'm just a soldier."

"A soldier who honestly volunteered to serve in Khandar. An *officer*. That makes you one of exactly two."

Marcus snorted. "Really? Who's the other fool?"

"Colonel Vhalnich, of course."

"But—" Marcus bit back his response. Jen smiled.

"He's talked to you about me, then," she said. "It's all right. I won't insult you by asking to tell me what he said. I'm going to guess it was something like, 'She's here because that villain Orlanko is up to something.' "

"*Is* that why you're here?"

"After a fashion." She leaned closer and lowered her voice. "The colonel has a reputation for eccentricity. He also has powerful friends at court. They worked hard to get him this assignment."

Janus hadn't mentioned *that*. Marcus considered for a moment. "Why?"

"His Grace would very much like to know." She tapped her nose. "Therefore, here I am."

"I see."

She cocked her head. "I don't suppose you have any light to shed on the subject?"

Marcus stiffened. "I don't."

"I thought not." She straightened up. "Just remember, Captain, that when all is said and done, we're all on the same side here. I want to serve the king and Vordan just as much as you or the colonel."

"I'm sure you do," Marcus said. "And right now, the best way I can serve is to get some sleep. I understand that the colonel wants us to start drilling after the march tomorrow."

"Of course, Captain. Don't let me keep you from your bed."

"Adrecht!" Marcus called, knocking at the tent post. "Get up!"

If the soldiers of the Fourth Battalion found anything unusual in the sight of the senior captain storming down to their commander's tent before dawn, they didn't say anything about it. The sky was lightening in the east, and in the First Battalion camp the men would already be up and about, breaking down their gear and getting it stowed on wagons in preparation for the day's march. As rearguard, the Fourth Battalion had a bit more time to wait, though in Marcus' opinion the extra sleep didn't make up for having to eat the dust of the whole column all day.

Adrecht's tent was not the usual faded blue army issue, peaked in the center and barely tall enough for Marcus to stand erect. It was silk, to start with, and much larger, with four foundation posts, while the army tents had only two. Once, it had been elaborately decorated with frilled hangings, ropes of colorful cloth, and colored-glass lanterns that threw fanciful patterns against the fabric—years in Ashe-Katarion had given Adrecht time to exercise his talent for acquiring the trappings of luxury. Now all of that was gone, the fine fabrics either packed in trunks or abandoned in haste on the retreat to Fort Valor.

And a good thing, too. If they'd had to set up Adrecht's whole palace every night, they would never have outrun the Redeemers, however halfhearted the pursuit had been. Marcus knocked again, hard enough to sting his knuckles. "Adrecht!"

"Marcus?" The voice sounded muffled, and not just from the thin silk walls. "'S that you?"

"I'm coming in," Marcus announced, and slipped past the tent flap. The broad interior was unlit, and the weak morning light did little to relieve the gloom. Marcus blinked until his eyes adjusted, then spotted a lantern hanging from one of the tent poles. He rummaged in his pockets until he produced a match, then lit the lamp and hung it up again. Its swinging sent the shadows to arcing wildly.

Adrecht groaned and held up one hand to block out the light. "Good God," he said, raising his head from the silk cushion where it rested. "What do you think you're doing? It's much too late for this kind of nonsense."

"It's early, not late," Marcus said. There was another lamp on the other side of the tent, and he lit it as well.

"When did you turn so pedantic?" Adrecht groped with one hand until he came up with a heavy gold pocket watch, which he clicked open. "See? It's two in the morning. What kind of time is that to be waking me up?"

"It's dawn," Marcus said.

"Is it?" Adrecht blinked at him. "You're sure?"

"Most of us can tell by looking."

"Well, that's a relief." He shook the gold watch, then snapped the cover shut. "My watch has stopped. I thought I was just drunk."

"You *were* drunk."

That was a guess, Marcus had to admit, but an educated one. By the light of the lamps he could see that there were several empty bottles strewn across the rug-covered floor of the tent. A trunk in one corner held three rows of cotton-padded compartments, suitable for transporting fine liquors. More than half the slots were empty. Another pair of trunks, tumbled haphazardly between the tent poles, spilled a mess of clothes, books, and papers that looked as though it had been thoroughly rummaged.

There was little else, not even a bedroll. Adrecht had gotten rid of the uncomfortable army-issue camp furniture at the first opportunity, replacing it with fine hand-carved pieces purchased in Ashe-Katarion. Marcus had forced him to leave it all behind when they'd fled, lest some gilt-encrusted armoire take up wagon space needed for food. *That* argument had led to a week of strained relations.

"It's really dawn?" Adrecht said again, looking up with eyes filmed by a gathering hangover.

"Yes," Marcus snapped. "Get up."

With some effort, Adrecht managed to lever himself into a sitting position, legs crossed in front of him. His fine white linen trousers were stained purple where he'd spilled something across them. He looked down mournfully at the splotch, then up at Marcus.

"I need a drink," he proclaimed. "You want a drink?"

"Water," Marcus said. "Do you have any water around here?"

"Water!" Adrecht made a double circle over his heart with one hand, the ancient Church ward against evil. "Don't say that so loud. God may hear you and strike you down. Water!" He snorted. "I made good progress last night, but if I recall there was a little something left in the purple bottle . . ." He fumbled with a bottle, which glugged the last few swallows of its contents into the carpet. Adrecht shrugged and tossed it aside. "Oh, well. There's still a few more."

Marcus located a carafe of lukewarm water and handed it over. Despite his protests, Adrecht drank greedily, without bothering to locate a cup. He swirled the final mouthful around, then swallowed it thoughtfully.

"I don't remember drinking any gun oil," he said. "But now my mouth seems to be coated with the stuff. Are the lads playing pranks, do you think?"

"Adrecht . . ." Marcus looked for somewhere to sit, but after a survey of the rancid carpet he decided against it. He squatted instead. "Adrecht, where were you yesterday?"

"Yesterday?" He blinked slowly. "Yesterday . . . yesterday . . ."

"Drinking somewhere?"

"Oh, yes. One of the quartermasters invited me to spend the march in his wagon, since I offered to share my spirits with him. Great fellow, absolutely wonderful. He—I can't recall his name, actually, but he was kindness itself."

"You were at it all day?"

"Not *all* day. I wouldn't call it *all* day. Just . . . you know . . ." He shrugged. "So what?"

"You should have been with your men."

"Why? For moral support? They know what they're supposed to do. It's just marching, after all."

"When I called for emergency square—"

Adrecht snorted. "Why would you do a damfool thing like that?"

"If there'd been an attack, we might all have been killed."

"If there'd been an attack . . . ," Adrecht said mockingly. "Come off it, Marcus. Sit down and have a drink with me."

"Damn it, Adrecht," Marcus said. "What in hell is wrong with you?"

There was a long pause while Marcus tried to regain control of his temper. Adrecht was a good officer and a good friend. He was smart enough, God knew—at the War College his help had gotten Marcus through a half dozen examinations. And in the field he was personally brave almost to a fault. He was prone to black moods, however, and a bad one could last for weeks, especially when it was exacerbated by drink.

"I should think that would be obvious," Adrecht said. He staggered to his feet, using one of the tent poles to aid him, and started toward the liquor chest. Marcus moved to intercept him, and Adrecht leaned back and glared at him with exaggerated irritation.

"I'm trying," he said, "to become a monk. Obviously. The Preacher has finally convinced me that the time of the Beast is upon us. Only I have to get rid of all my worldly possessions first, d'you see? You gave me a good head start"—he narrowed his eyes—"but there was still the liquor to think of. Not really fair to tip it out, I thought. So I'm working my way through the lot. Once I'm done, then"—he clapped his hands—"it's off to the monastery with me."

"It's going to be off to the Vendre with you," Marcus shot back. "And in irons. We have a new colonel, if you haven't noticed. If you keep this up, sooner or later—"

"Please, Marcus," Adrecht said with a chuckle. "The Vendre? Really? You don't believe that, do you?"

"You'd be lucky to get the Vendre. More likely it'd be a firing squad. Dereliction of duty—"

"I'd be happy to die by an honest Vordanai bullet," Adrecht said. "At least if I'm allowed to get drunk off my ass beforehand. It'll make me better off than the rest of you." He shook his head. "Come on, Marcus. Do you honestly think any of us are going home, in irons or otherwise? The Redeemers don't exchange prisoners; they eat them."

"We're not prisoners yet," Marcus said.

"We might as well be. Or has the colonel explained his secret plan to you? I'm curious to hear it."

Marcus shifted uncomfortably. "The colonel doesn't explain his plans to me. But he's not just marching off to be a brave sacrifice for king and country, if that's what you mean."

Adrecht snorted. "We ought to have gotten right back aboard those ships. This is a death march, and most of the men know it. Can you blame them if they're not responding well?"

"The other battalions still obeyed orders." *Eventually.*

"I always did have more than my share of smart ones." Adrecht caught Marcus' expression and sighed. "Marcus—"

"I'm trying to help you," Marcus said. "If you're not up to the job anymore, best say so now."

"Oh, very clever, Doctor-Professor d'Ivoire. Play on Captain Roston's pride, maybe that'll get him back into the firing line."

"Damn it—"

"All right, all right!" Adrecht held up a hand. "I'll be at the drills. That's what you want to hear, isn't it?" He shook his head again. "Though it's a hell of a thing to force a man to spend his last few days on earth sweating and shouting orders."

It's really bad this time. He's already given up. There was something bright and brittle in Adrecht's eyes, as if a dark, cynical humor was the only thing keeping him on his feet. The only time Marcus had ever seen him like this was five years ago, when he'd first got word he was shipping out to Khandar. *Saints. Maybe Mor was right. If this Lieutenant Orta is any good, maybe we* should *keep him in charge.*

That would mean getting rid of Adrecht, though. Unless Janus could be persuaded to accept his resignation, the only way for a captain to leave his company was in disgrace. *He'd never do it.* And Marcus owed him whatever help he could manage.

"Well?" Adrecht said. "Was there anything else, Senior Captain?"

"No." Marcus turned to leave, but paused at the tent flap. "I really am trying to help, you know."

"Oh?" Adrecht snapped. "Why?"

Sometimes I have no idea. Marcus shook his head and slipped out.

CHAPTER FIVE

WINTER

The day was typical for spring in Khandar—that was to say, merely unbearably hot, rather than actually lethal as the summer heat might have been. The sun was a physical presence, a weight pressing down on the shoulders. It blasted any exposed skin and left uniforms soaked and heavy with sweat. Even after three years, it could catch Winter by surprise. The men in the ranks had it worse—for one thing, they didn't have the luxury of officer's caps—and some them were already swaying on their feet. Winter hoped d'Vries would call a halt before anyone actually collapsed.

She'd nearly collapsed on that first day's march. The hundred miles or so from Ashe-Katarion to Fort Valor was the longest trek the Colonials had ever undertaken, and before that, Winter's experience with marching had been limited to a few parades in honor of Prince Exopter.

On the retreat, they'd covered the distance in a fortnight, and they'd been accompanied by so many wagons the soldiers hadn't even carried their own weapons. The return journey was apparently going to be much faster. None of the recruits had seemed surprised when they received orders for a *fifteen*-mile march, carrying not only muskets but full packs, but Winter had nearly groaned aloud. She'd made it, barely, but the pains in her legs and shoulders afterward had been an uncomfortable throwback to her days at Mrs. Wilmore's. The old woman had firmly believed that backbreaking labor was a cure for immorality.

The second day's march had been cut short by the fiasco of an alarm, and the poor performance of the troops had apparently made an impression on someone. The officers had announced that the third day's march would be only five miles, and that they'd be in their new camp by noon. By this time Winter had rediscovered the muscles in her legs and found them not *too* badly decayed from the old days, and she was beginning to think she could handle this after all.

She should have known better. God only ever answered her prayers when He was plotting something worse. The word had come down that the remainder of the day would be reserved for drill. The recruits accepted this as a matter of course, but the Old Colonials swore and grumbled.

The announcement had brought the lieutenant back from his usual position at the head of the column. Apparently eating dust alongside his men didn't fit his mental picture of an officer's duties, but putting them through snappy evolutions on the drill field did. Winter had seen him only a couple of times over the past few days, and it was only now that she had the chance to make a detailed inspection.

Lieutenant Anton d'Vries wore a tailored blue uniform as regulation-perfect as any of those sported by his soldiers. He was a small, wiry man, with dark eyes and a pouting mouth under a luxuriant mustache. His hair was carefully combed and stiffened with powder in what was presumably the latest fashion from Vordan, though the effect was rather ruined by the regulation officer's cap. He wore a sword, the leather of the scabbard still polished and shining, and carried a thin walking stick that whistled through the air when he pointed with it. Winter flinched every time he stood beside her, in fear of an accidental blow to the side of the head.

Drill, she had discovered, was worse than marching. When the column had been in motion, at least they'd had the feeling of *accomplishing* something, even if it was only sweeping another few miles underfoot. They'd been allowed to fill their canteens when they passed a stream, and to talk or even sing as they walked. Most of all, no one had been judging them. The only measure of success was whether you staggered into camp before nightfall.

Now the hundred and twenty men of the Seventh Company stood in a solid block, three men deep and forty across. Each was accoutered just so—cartridge box on the left hip, doubled straps across the chest with sheathed bayonet, musket held against the right side with fingers curled around the butt in a nerve-deadening position. They were required to wait, under d'Vries' narrowed, sunken eyes, until he ordered them to move.

Winter stood in front of them, facing the center of the company, beside the lieutenant. Her task was to relay his orders to the troops, and make certain they were obeyed. *Not an enviable position.* Not only did she have d'Vries' special attention, but she could feel the dull resentment of every man in the company. Sweat trickled down her face and soaked her hair, and every inch of skin seemed to be itching at once. They had been at it for two hours so far.

D'Vries tapped his stick against his leg and watched his men with a haughty distaste. He cleared his throat and looked back and forth along the triple line with an undisguised scowl.

"Right," he said. "We will try that again. *On* the signal, *right* oblique, *double* pace!"

He spoke in a conversational tone. Winter had to repeat those orders loud enough to carry to the ends of the line. Her throat was already ragged, but she summoned up the energy. It came out as more of a croak, but d'Vries didn't appear to notice.

The company drummers struck up the double pace, heartbeat-fast. The line shuffled into motion, and almost immediately it became obvious that little progress had been made.

Long ago, in what felt like a different lifetime, Winter had been a girl younger than any one of the rankers. All she'd known of the military life was the stories she'd read of great battles, in which unflinching men marched precisely through their evolutions while their ranks were torn by ball and shot. Since her unorthodox method of self-recruitment had prevented her from spending the weeks in depot where the men presumably learned such stoicism, she'd done her best to make up for it, acquiring a copy of the *Manual of Arms* and the *Regulations and Drill of the Royal Army of Vordan* and working hard to memorize both. The knowledge had turned out to be almost useless, of course, but some of it remained with her years later.

Consequently, she knew what was *supposed* to happen. At the first beat of the drum, each man would take a step with his right foot, placing it exactly one standard pace—thirty-six inches, according to some hallowed measuring stick in the bowels of the Ministry of War—in front of the other. The next step would be on the next drumbeat, and so on, so that the company moved forward in perfect order, each man remaining stationary with respect to his fellows.

This would be hard enough, but d'Vries had called for an *oblique* advance, which meant that with each pace forward every man was supposed to move a half pace sideways, producing a sort of diagonal sidle. From the faces of the soldiers, Winter was sure that many of them hadn't understood this, or at any rate didn't remember until it was too late.

The result was about what Winter expected. Some men started with their left foot instead of their right, which meant they bumped into the man beside them. Others forgot to move obliquely, with similar results. Still others stepped too far, or not far enough, and then trying to maintain their place lost the beat of the drum and fell out of step. Two men in the rear rank somehow entangled the straps of their packs and collapsed in the dust when they tried to move in opposite directions, thrashing like a couple of inverted turtles.

Within twenty yards the neat three-rank block had dissolved

into a blob of red-faced, shoving men. When Winter called for a halt and the drummer stopped playing, they stumbled a few more steps from sheer inertia, then scrambled to push their way back into the correct files. It was a full five minutes before some semblance of order had returned.

Thus it had gone every previous time as well, and d'Vries' lips had tightened with each successive failure. Now his patience was apparently exhausted. He turned to Winter, cold with anger.

"Sergeant!" he snapped.

Winter saluted. "Yessir!"

"I've seen enough. I want you to keep these fellows at it"—he raised his voice—"until they get it right or they damn well drop dead on the field! Do you understand me?"

"Ah, yessir."

The lieutenant's lip quivered. "Right," he managed, and stalked off, walking stick snapping out to flick impudent bits of gravel from his path. Winter watched him go, feeling the pounding of the sun on her shoulders, and tried to figure out what she was supposed to do next.

Her eyes found Bobby in the first rank. The boy was red-faced, from either embarrassment or the sun, and he was visibly trembling with fatigue. Winter had been in Khandar for two years, as d'Vries had not, and she knew that dropping dead in the field was far from simply a rhetorical possibility. Too much more of this and the heat-stroke cases would overflow the infirmary.

She looked across the dusty scrap of land that was serving as the regimental drill field. It was scrub plain, like all the land they'd marched over. Occasional rocks or knots of tough, wiry grass broke the monotony of endless parched earth. The only color came from a tiny stream meandering through on its way to the sea, which winked and sparkled in the middle distance. A dozen companies were currently occupied in various exercises, being put through their separate paces according to the whims of their officers. Winter watched one lieutenant berating his men as though they were disobedient mules, and inspiration struck.

"Right," she said, turning on her heel. Raising her already ragged voice, she managed, "Company, quarter-*right*!"

The men, who'd been watching her with some apprehension, gave a kind of collective sigh and straightened up again as best they could. They turned in place through ninety degrees, which converted a block of men forty long and three deep into a column three wide and forty long. Winter stalked over to what was now the front, drummers hurrying behind her.

"On my signal," she said, "march pace, forward. Align on me. March!"

The drums started again, slower this time, and the column shuffled into motion. Without the distraction of trying to move sideways, and with only three men per rank to contend with, the march wasn't terrible. Winter walked in front of the first rank, who adjusted slightly to stay behind her, letting her steer the long column like a snake.

She found what she wanted, a hundred yards away. Another company, in the usual three-rank line, was practicing the *Manual of Arms* while a sergeant barked orders. A lieutenant stood beside them, looking bored. Their backs were to her and her men.

Winter led the column in that direction, glancing over her shoulder occasionally to make sure her company was still in good order. There was a moment's hesitation as they closed with the other company. She took the opportunity to step sideways, out of their path, and shout, "Forward! Charge pace!"

The drums thrilled faster. The men in the front ranks, when it became clear what they'd been ordered to do, went to it with surprising gusto. No one in the other company noticed until it was far too late. There were a couple of startled squawks, and then the long column collided with the rear of the line at a dead run. Winter's men bowled through, knocking the others sprawling, until someone in the opposing company started fighting back. A punch was thrown, somewhere in the press, and a moment later the whole of the two companies was a mass of fistfights and roughhousing, going at it with all the sudden energy of discipline released.

Winter, standing at the edge of the melee with the horrified drummers behind her, looked over her handiwork with a satisfied expression. The lieutenant of the other company, a fat man with a scraggly beard, bore down on her while his sergeants tried in vain to restore order. Winter saluted and forced her face to assume a blank expression.

"*What* in all the *hells* do you think you're doing?" the lieutenant said, vibrating with anger.

"Sorry, sir. Following orders, sir!"

"Whose orders?"

"Lieutenant d'Vries, sir! Said to keep the men at it. Didn't mean to run into you, sir!"

The lieutenant eyed her, uncertain of what attitude to take. He settled on contempt. Winter struggled to maintain her facade of amiable idiocy.

"Well, you'd better sort this out," he said. "If your damned men aren't out of my company and off this drill field in five minutes, the captain will hear of it, do you understand?"

"Yes, sir!" Winter spun back toward the mess she'd created. "Corporal Forester!"

The boy had extracted himself after the initial rush, wriggling eel-like to the edge of the press, and was looking on nervously. At the sound of Winter's voice, he whirled and snapped to attention.

"Let's get these men off the drill field!" She gestured at the lieutenant behind her. "Right away, he says!"

She could tell he was having trouble suppressing a smile, too, as understanding dawned. "Yes, *sir*!"

The brief punch-up seemed to have dissipated all the exhaustion of the previous few hours, and the men streamed off the field in a raucous crowd, laughing and shouting to one another. The carnival atmosphere continued once they were back at the camp. Someone produced a handball from somewhere, and soon two impromptu teams were scrimmaging up and down the line of tents, while spectators laughed and cheered from the sidelines.

Winter couldn't see where they found the energy. The release of tension had left her feeling shaky and drained, and she wanted nothing so much as a few hours of oblivion. Under the exhaustion was a dull sense of dread. Her little ruse, which had seemed so clever in the moment she'd thought of it, now felt ridiculously transparent. D'Vries wouldn't care if she'd had contradictory orders or not—he would only see that his demand had not been obeyed, and she'd bear the brunt of his anger. He'd bust her back down to ranker, send her back to Davis.

She pushed her way into the cooler semidarkness of her tent. On the little desk sat the papers—long marches had left her little time to work on settling the accounts, so an intimidating stack still remained. She knew she should address them, but at the moment the thought of picking up the pen made her feel ill.

Instead she slumped onto the bedroll, and stretched out, not even bothering to take off her boots. *Surely I'm tired enough now. If I just close my eyes for a moment . . .*

Warm, soft lips on hers, fingers running along the small of her back, the heat of a body pressed against her. Jane's hair, dark red and soft as sin, spilling down over Winter's bare shoulder like a velvet curtain. A brief flash of her eyes, as green as emeralds.

Jane pulled away from the embrace, stepping back. She was naked, the most beautiful thing Winter had ever seen.

"You have to get away," Jane said. "Not just away from the Prison. Away from all of it. Away from everyone who wants to tie you up and take you back . . ."

Winter could say nothing. Her throat felt thick.

Jane raised one hand. A dagger glittered, flashing silver. "Take the knife," she said, as though instructing a friend on how to carve a roast. "Put the point of it about here"—she raised her head and put the tip of the dagger on her throat, just under her chin—"and press in, upward, as hard as you can."

"Jane!" Winter's scream sounded distant in her own ears.

The knife slid in, smooth as silk. Jane's emerald eyes were very wide. She opened her mouth, but no words emerged, only a tide of thick, sticky blood.

Winter jerked awake, pulse pounding in her temples, ears full of screams in the dark. They took a long time to fade. She lay perfectly still, feeling the ache in her limbs and staring at the blue fabric of the tent.

Can you be haunted by someone who isn't dead?

There was a rap at the tent post. Winter sat up, pathetically eager for a distraction.

"Who's there?"

"It's me," said Bobby from outside. Winter glanced guiltily at the stack of reports, but it was too late to do anything about them now.

"Come in."

The boy ducked inside. He was rubbing one hand with the other, and Winter could see a bruise blossoming along his knuckles. She felt a brief pang of sympathy.

"Sorry about that," Winter said.

"About what?" When she indicated his hand, he smiled broadly. "Oh, this? It's nothing, sir. One of the men of Third Company was inconsiderate enough to obstruct my fist with his jaw. I'm fairly sure he got the worst of it." Bobby looked suddenly uncomfortable. "That was all right, wasn't it, sir? A corporal is not permitted to involve himself in brawling with the rankers, but under the circumstances—"

"It's fine," Winter said. "I take full responsibility. Was anyone badly hurt?"

"Two of the men had to carry Ranker Ibliss back from the field, sir."

"Oh, dear. Will he be all right?"

"I think so." Bobby coughed. "Apparently he suffered a blow to an unfortunate area."

Winter looked quizzical.

"Kicked in the nadgers, sir. Probably not on purpose. You know how it is."

"I see. I hope Third Company isn't going to hold a grudge."

"Better if they do, sir!" Bobby was smiling again. "The captain of my depot battalion used to encourage fighting between the companies. A good rivalry helps knit the unit together, he always said."

"How long were you in depot?" Winter asked.

"A month. Should have been six weeks, but I was transferred out ahead of time for this expedition. Still, I count myself lucky."

"Why?"

"I *had* a month," Bobby said. "Some of the rankers got much less. A few had none at all, straight from the recruiting station to the ships."

"No wonder they can barely march," Winter muttered. "Does the lieutenant know this?"

"He should, sir. He has all the files."

That didn't mean he'd read them, or that he cared. Winter mulled that over.

"I meant to thank you, sir," Bobby said.

"For that?" Winter said. "It was just a trick."

"A clever trick, though. The men will be grateful."

"Just wait until d'Vries screams his head off tomorrow. That gratitude may be short-lived." Winter sighed. "Sorry. I'm not in the best of moods. Did you need to see me for some reason?"

"Just to say that, sir. And to ask if you wanted your dinner brought in."

"I suppose." Winter looked at the little tent, with the desk full of daily reports and the bed haunted by unpleasant memories. Bobby seemed to read her mind.

"You're welcome to eat with us, sir."

Winter made a face. "I wouldn't want to put anybody off."

"You wouldn't—"

"Oh, come on. You must know how it is. You can't have the same kind of talk when the sergeant is listening in." That was how it had always been in Davis' company, anyway, although Winter had rarely been a part of the conversation.

"Come and join us," Bobby said. "I think you'll feel better for a little talk, sir."

Winter chuckled. "Only if you promise to stop calling me 'sir,' Bobby."

"Yessir!" Bobby snapped to attention, eyes shining, and Winter couldn't help but laugh.

Dinner was cooking when they emerged. In theory, the company was subdivided into six sections of twenty men, each led by a corporal. These units were more commonly called "pots," since the main feature of each one was the iron cookpot in which the communal meals were brewed. In the Seventh, the boundaries between the pots were apparently pretty fluid, and all six vessels were gathered around a common fire. The men ate from whichever they liked and sat where they wanted, on the ground, on rocks, or on empty boxes of supplies. Mostly they gathered in circles, talking, laughing, and playing at dice or cards.

Bobby led Winter to one such circle, where she recognized Corporal Folsom among seven or eight other men. They opened up obligingly to make a space on a makeshift bench of hardtack crates, and someone handed Winter a bowl full of the steaming broth that was the standard evening meal when time and supplies allowed. Chunks of mutton floated in it, and the surface was slick and shiny with grease. Winter accepted a cracker of hardtack from another man and let it absorb the juice until it was soft and sodden, then gobbled it down. She hadn't realized she was so hungry.

At first Winter's fears seemed to be justified. The men had been talking and laughing until she arrived, but under the eyes of their sergeant they ate in awkward silence. Bobby called for a round of introductions, which produced a half dozen names that Winter promptly forgot. Then another silence fell, more uncomfortable than the first.

It was Corporal Folsom, oddly, who provided the first crack in the wall. He broke his usual quiet to comment, apropos of nothing, "Didn't realize there'd be so many streams here. They always told me Khandar was a desert."

Bobby seized eagerly on this scrap of conversation. "I heard the same thing. When you read about it, it's always sand dunes and camels. I haven't even seen a camel yet."

"This is the wet part," Winter offered. "We're only a dozen miles from the coast, so it gets a little rain now and then. And we're coming up on the Tsel valley. If you walked twenty or thirty miles south, you'd be in the Lesser Desol, and there'd be no water for days in any direction."

"What about camels?" said one of the soldiers, whose name was either George or Gerry.

"No camels," Winter said. "Not here. Camels aren't native to Khandar, actually. The Desoltai use them, but they live out in the Great Desol, to the east of the Tsel."

"Are they the ones who wear steel masks all the time?" said another man.

Winter laughed. "Not all of them, just their leader. He calls himself Malik-dan-Belial, which means 'Steel Ghost.' Nobody knows what he really looks like."

"Seems like a pretty cowardly way to go about to me," another soldier said. "What about this city we're marching toward, Ashe-Katarion? Is it as big as Vordan?"

"Not even close. Barely a town, really."

"Any chance of getting a decent drink?" someone said, and there was a round of laughter.

Winter smiled. "There was the last time I was there, but that was before the Redeemers turned up. A bunch of crazy priests. Apparently they don't like drinking, or good food, or anything that's any fun."

There was a snigger. "Sounds just like our lot, then."

"Maybe in a Sworn Church," someone else offered. "In depot the Free Chaplain could drink half a squad under the table."

They went on in that vein, and bit by bit the tension melted away. Most of the men were taller than Winter, so as often as not she was looking *up* into their broad, well-scrubbed faces, but for all that she suddenly felt how much older she actually was. There wasn't a man in the circle older than eighteen. They were all *boys*, barely off their farms or away from the Vordan City tenements, and underneath their smiles and bravado there was a nervous core that Winter recognized.

And *she* was the one they looked to for reassurance. She was the one who knew how things worked, here in Khandar and in the army. It was simultaneously touching and terrifying, bringing with it the full realization of what they expected of her. When they got to the subject of how she'd extracted them from drill that morning, none of them thanked her, as Bobby had. They seemed to consider it a matter of course, part of the duties of a sergeant, to stand between the rankers and the insanities of the higher echelons. There were quite a few japes at the expense of d'Vries. The first was offered hesitantly, but when Winter laughed as loud as the rest of them, that hurdle fell away as well.

"So what about this Colonel Vhalnich?" said the one Winter

was almost certain now was George. He was a large young man with mousy hair and freckles. "The talk says he's mad."

"He must have done something horrible, to get this command," said Nathan. He was short and bespectacled, and considered himself something of an expert on matters military.

"I heard he volunteered," said one of the others, whose name Winter still hadn't caught.

"Then he must be mad," George said.

"What do you think, Sergeant?" Nathan said.

Winter shrugged uncomfortably. "I've never met the colonel, but Captain d'Ivoire is an Old Colonial. He won't let this Vhalnich do anything too crazy."

"So where the hell are we marching, then?" George said.

Opinions differed on that point. Nathan was certain that the Redeemers would flee for the hills as soon as it became clear that the Vordanai were in earnest. George continued to insist that Colonel Vhalnich was going to get them all killed, although he seemed curiously unconcerned by the prospect. Bobby said that they were merely providing an escort for the prince, who would negotiate with the rebels until they reached a settlement. But it was Folsom who provided the most thoughtful answer. When the big corporal cleared his throat, the circle fell silent.

"I figure," he said, "Colonel Vhalnich's got to show that he *tried*, doesn't he? He can't just take us all back home to Vordan. He's got to fight at least once, or else the ministers will have a fit. That's where we're going." He shrugged. "That's what I figure, anyway."

After that, they got back on the subject of Lieutenant d'Vries, and Winter took the opportunity to excuse herself. She tapped Bobby on the shoulder as she stood, and the boy looked up at her.

"Can I have a word?" Winter said.

They walked away from the little circle. The sun had gone down and the sky was darkening fast, already purple-gray. Winter stared upward pensively, where the stars were beginning to glitter.

To someone raised in the smoky, torch-lit warrens of Vordan City, the nights of Khandar had been a revelation. Instead of the occasional twinkle, the stars marched across the sky in their uncounted thousands, and when the moon rose it seemed clear enough that she could reach out and touch it.

It had been a long time since she'd noticed the night sky like that. But it occurred to her that Bobby and the other recruits would only just have seen it for the first time. She wondered if any of them had spent a night staring up slack-jawed in wonder, as she had.

She wanted to thank the corporal for dragging her out of her tent, but she couldn't think of a way to begin. When she glanced at Bobby's face, shadowed as it was in the fading light, it was clear that the boy understood. Winter gave a grateful sigh.

"I had an idea," she said, "while we were talking. It might get us into trouble, though."

"Let's hear it," Bobby said cheerfully.

"The key is going to be timing." Winter chewed her lip thoughtfully. "We'll need to spread the word tonight, so we can get everyone rounded up quick once the march ends tomorrow . . ."

"Load!"

Winter had dispensed with the drumbeat that the regulations prescribed. It was essential for drillbook perfection that every soldier perform the twenty-six numbered movements from the *Manual of Arms* in unison, synchronized to the beat of the drum, but in practice she found that it only confused the men. Instead she walked up and down in front of the triple line, letting her footsteps serve as cadence.

The rankers, already grimed with sweat, struggled with their weapons. Winter sympathized. Loading was a complicated process. First you took your paper cartridge, filled with premeasured powder and the lead musket ball, and tore it in half with your teeth, holding the ball end in your mouth and keeping the end with the powder in your hand. Then you opened the lock, tipped a little powder into the pan, and closed it again. The rest of the powder went down the barrel, which required you to ground the butt of the weapon and hold it against your boot. The cartridge scraps went in with it, for good luck. Finally, you spat the musket ball and the rest of the cartridge into the barrel, grabbed the iron ramrod from the rings that held it slung under the weapon, and jammed the whole mess home with two or three good strokes.

There wasn't enough extra powder to practice loading, so the company was going through the steps in mime. Once the ramrods had rattled back into their rings, each man again brought his musket to the ready position, held at his side with the left hand curled around the butt. Some took longer than others. Winter, counting heartbeats, estimated it was half a minute or more before the whole company was ready. She clicked her tongue.

"Level!" she shouted, walking aside to clear the theoretical line of fire. Every man raised his musket to his shoulder and pulled back the hammer. Here and there she heard a quiet curse as someone fumbled the maneuver or a musket barrel whacked against the side of a neighbor's head. Only the front two ranks readied their weapons, while the third waited. The barrels protruded like bristles on a porcupine, all along the company line.

Winter waited a few more heartbeats, then raised her voice again. "Fire!"

Eighty fingers tightened on triggers. On each weapon, the lock slid open and the flint snapped down, raising sparks where it scraped against the steel. Without powder, there was no sound but the rapid series of clicks. Winter strode back in front of them.

"Load!" And they began again.

They'd been at it for an hour already. The march had ended at noon, and with Winter's encouragement the Seventh Company had hurried through the business of setting up tents and making camp and then rushed out to the drill field well before Lieutenant d'Vries had arrived. They'd been the first ones there. Winter had gone over what she expected of them, some basics from the *Manual of Arms* and a few things that weren't in the drillbook at all. If they were going to have to drill, it might as well be *useful* drill.

Some of the men groaned when she'd explained her approach, but she saw relief on a great many faces. Bobby had said some of them hadn't even made it to the depot before they'd been summoned up, and others had had only a few days or weeks of what was supposed to be a month and half of basic training. Even the grumblers had to admit it made a nice change from endless failures at esoteric skills like double-pace oblique marching.

Midway through the loading, while they were fumbling with their rammers, Winter turned to face them and shouted, "Square!"

This had been new to even those who had had their full time in depot, since the drillbook never mentioned company squares, but she'd coached them through it and they'd gotten the idea after a few repetitions. The whole company immediately broke off loading, and the edges of the line—ten files from either side—about-faced and stepped toward the rear. They filed in behind the first three ranks, so that the line had been halved in length and doubled in width.

Once they were in place, each man drew his bayonet from its leather sheath. These blades, ten inches of wickedly pointed steel, locked onto a lug beside the barrel of the musket with a twist, converting the weapon into something approximating a spear. This done, the first rank knelt, and the second rank leveled their muskets over the heads of the first at an angle. The three files on the edges of the line turned through ninety degrees to face outward instead of forward and back.

It was smartly done, at least this time. The result wasn't a proper square—more of a rectangle, Winter noted pedantically—but it was easy to form, and the hedgehog of gleaming bayonets looked like a formidable obstacle. The third rank kept at their loading, awkwardly now as they tried to avoid cutting themselves on their own bayonets, and when they had finished they leveled their weapons. The hope was that the combination of fire and steel would prove an impregnable barrier to enemy cavalry.

Winter let them hold it for a few moments, then called, "Re-form!" The square melted back into a line, with considerably more confusion and disorder than it had shown going the other way. She made a mental note to work through that a few more times.

By now the drill field was filling up, and Winter's men had gotten a few curious looks from other officers. She'd ignored them, reserving her attention for her men, but she'd positioned them so that she'd have a good view of the path back to camp. When she saw Lieutenant d'Vries approaching, with his powdered hair and his walking stick, she stopped and leaned close to Bobby.

"Take them up to the end of the field and back, would you?" Winter said. "I'll have a word with the lieutenant."

"Right," the corporal said, practically glowing with the joy of responsibility. He stepped out of the ranks and gestured to the drummers, who had been squatting in the dirt, unneeded until now. "Company, guide center, ordinary pace, forward *march*!"

The drums took up the funeral thump of the standard walking pace, and the Seventh Company set off in reasonably good order. Winter remained behind, waiting at attention for d'Vries. The young officer watched bemusedly as his soldiers marched away, then gave Winter his full attention.

"What," he said, "is going on here?"

Winter saluted. "Remedial drill, *sir*!"

D'Vries' lips moved silently as he worked that out. "Remedial drill?"

"Yessir."

"I received a report from Lieutenant Anders," d'Vries said. "He was most displeased—"

"Yessir!" Winter cut him off. "Disgraceful behavior, sir! I take full responsibility, sir!"

"You'd damn well better," the lieutenant said, rallying a little. "And now—"

"The men were clearly in need of a little discipline, sir!"

"Yes," d'Vries said suspiciously. "Discipline is important. But my drills—"

"They're not worthy of your attention, sir!" Winter barked. "Bunch of shirkers, sir. But I'll soon have them whipped into shape!"

"Whipped into shape," d'Vries repeated. He obviously liked the sound of that. He glanced up the field, where Bobby had just reversed the line and started marching it back toward them. "They certainly deserve a little whipping."

"As I said, sir, I take full responsibility. Discipline will be restored, sir!"

There was a moment of silence. D'Vries ran his hand along his mustache a few times and decided that, on the balance, he approved.

"Right," he said, his voice regaining confidence. "Remedial drill. Well done, Sergeant. I expect to see good results."

"You'll get them, sir!"

"Keep them at it, keep them at it." He knocked a dirt clod about with his walking stick. "I'll leave you to it, then."

"Sir! You may rely on me, sir!"

"Indeed."

D'Vries turned away, looking a little lost but not altogether unhappy. Bobby arrived beside Winter, signaling the drummers to halt, and Winter favored the corporal with a smile.

"You got rid of him?"

"For the moment," Winter said. "Nothing confuses an officer like violently agreeing with him."

She'd learned that from Davis, whose barked affirmations had brought more than one superior nearly to tears. The big sergeant had nearly always gotten his own way, orders or no orders. It pained Winter to think that she'd actually learned something useful from the man, but she supposed she was in no place to complain.

She sighed. "At some point we're going to have to practice the damned oblique marching. D'Vries will want to see that we can do it properly. We've probably got a few days' grace, though, and I'd rather spend the time on something worthwhile."

Winter said this with more confidence than she actually felt. For all that she'd been with the Colonials for two years, she had never participated in an actual *battle*. Her combat experience was limited to marching, parading, and exchanging a few shots with bandits or raiders who invariably fled or surrendered rather than fight it out. For the most part, she was marching blind, but she didn't dare let on to Bobby.

"Yessir," the corporal said. Then, a bit diffidently, "I wasn't aware that forming company square was a standard evolution, sir."

"It's not," Winter said. Normally squares were formed by battalion, a thousand men at a time. "But the old colonel once told me that as long as you've got four men left, you ought to be able to form square. Given what happened the other day, I thought we would practice it a bit."

"Fair enough, sir." Bobby looked at the men behind her, who were taking advantage of the brief respite to drink from their canteens or fan themselves against the heat. "Shall we get them back to it, sir?"

Winter nodded.

That evening, Bobby and Graff taught Winter to play cards. It was a traditional soldier's entertainment, but due to her self-enforced isolation Winter had never learned. When she'd mentioned this, the others had responded with disbelief, and then nothing would do but that they get together a game immediately.

Graff dragged the other two corporals and a couple of soldiers together, while dinner bubbled in the pots, and launched at once into an explanation so complicated that Winter didn't understand more than one word in three. It didn't help that Graff mixed his exposition of the rules with lengthy asides about strategy, or that the game he'd chosen apparently had more exceptions and special cases than army regulations did.

"Right, so say he shows a three," Graff said, oblivious to his audience's puzzlement. "Or two threes, or two fours, but not two fives, because then he might be working on a turtle. Now you've got to either challenge, double, play, or pass. You're not going to want to challenge, because even if you win all you get is his buy, and with threes against nines you've got no better than sixty-forty. If you double, then you both draw another card, and he's hoping for at least a king so he can threaten an axe, while you want to see more like a six or seven, but not a five, because of the turtle. So say you do. You both throw in another buy—"

He tossed a coin from his own pile into the pot, then took one from the small pile in front of Winter and did likewise. Winter caught Bobby's eye across the circle. The boy shrugged and gave a wry smile.

"Oh, ho!" said a booming voice from over her shoulder. "Gambling, is it? The Holy Karis isn't going to like that, Saint. He's not going to like that at all! See, I let you out of my sight for half a minute and you're already sliding down the dark path."

Winter's heart froze in her chest, and for a moment she couldn't breathe. The others around the circle were all looking at her, and she forced herself to turn and confront the shadow looming up behind her.

"Sergeant Davis," Winter said stiffly.

The huge man laughed. "Good evening, *Sergeant* Ihernglass."

He rounded the little circle, dark eyes never leaving her face. Buck and Peg stood behind him, trailing the big sergeant like dogs. When he was across from her, he pushed his way forward and sat down cross-legged. The soldiers on either side spread out hurriedly to make room.

"I just thought I'd come by," he announced, "to see how our Saint is getting on. I'm sure he's told you all about me. Good old Sergeant Davis, and all that. Taught him everything he knows."

"Welcome to the Seventh, Sergeant Davis!" Bobby said eagerly.

Davis ignored him. "So how *are* you getting on, Saint?"

The past week seemed to roll away. Davis, flanked by Buck and Peg with their nasty grins, filled the world. He had been a constant in her life for more than a year. Without him pushing down on her, the past few days, she'd felt safe enough to unfold a little. Now here he was again, to mash her flat.

"Fine," she muttered. "Good."

"You should have seen what he did yesterday!" Bobby burbled, oblivious to the tension. "Lieutenant d'Vries had told us—"

"Oh, we've got all kinds of funny stories about our Saint," Davis said softly. "Remember that time we all went to the inn, and we all clubbed together to buy him a whore?"

"*I* remember," Buck said. "God, that was a beautiful girl. Standing there wearing not a stitch when we opened the door to his room, and he looks at me, and I said, 'Go on, friend, all for you!' "

"Then he sends her away," Peg said. "What a damned waste. And Buck says, 'Bloody martyrs, Saint, have you even *got* a cock?' "

Davis just smiled. Winter could well remember what had happened next. Buck, so drunk he could barely stand, had followed his words with a grab for her crotch, presumably to check. When she'd stepped out of the way, Peg had grabbed her from behind. In the ensuing scuffle, she'd kicked Buck in the face and bitten the back of Peg's hand.

The sergeant had administered "justice." He couldn't sanction fighting amongst the company, he said, and ruled that Winter had to stand and receive two blows for the ones that she'd given. In the interest of fairness, he himself would deliver them. The first punch, to her face, had nearly broken her nose; the second, in the gut, had left her curled and retching on the floor. The rest of them had looked on, laughing.

Involuntarily, Winter's hand went to her cheek, where the massive bruise had blossomed. Davis saw the movement, and his smile twitched wider.

"D'you think, *Sergeant*, that we could have a word in private?" Davis said. "Man to man. For old times' sake?"

Winter, anxious to get away from the curious looks of her new company, nodded jerkily. The three Old Colonials rose. She led them back toward her tent, away from the pots and the fires, and into the narrow alley between two canvas walls.

"Sergeant," Davis said. "You, a sergeant. Fucking martyrs, this army is really gone to shit, isn't it?"

"I didn't want it," Winter said. "I told the captain—"

"I thought I was sending you out for a suicide mission," Davis interrupted, "and the captain makes you a sergeant. How the hell did you pull *that* one off?"

"Prob'ly sucked his cock," Peg said.

"Saint does have a pretty little mouth," Buck mused. "Practically like a girl's."

"Was that it, Saint?" Davis said. "You engage in a little persuasion? Thought you could put one over on old Sergeant Davis? Hell, that's not so bad, a little cock-sucking for a double promotion. Should have let him fuck your arse—then you might have made lieutenant, and I'd have to salute *you*. Wouldn't that be a hell of a thing?"

"What do you want?" Winter managed.

"What do I want?" Davis echoed. "God, I'm not sure. I suppose I want an army where little pieces of shit like you aren't promoted over the heads of better men, to where you can get people killed. But I'm not likely to get it, am I?" He shrugged his massive shoulders. "How about this? You go to the captain and tell him you're done being a sergeant. It's too much for you. You can't handle it. Suck him off again if you have to. Then you can come on back to old Sergeant Davis. Won't you like that?"

"He wouldn't let me." Winter felt her hands curl into fists. "I *tried* to tell him no, but he wouldn't—"

"What, because you were too good to be a sergeant?" Davis leaned close to her, until she could smell the foul rotted-meat stink of his breath. "Fucking Saint. You're just too good for this world, aren't you?"

"Maybe we ought to, you know, help him along," Buck prompted.

Davis smiled. Winter saw, suddenly, that he was going to hit her. She tensed, ready to dodge, but Buck and Peg were on either side of her, boxing her in.

"Sergeant?"

It was Bobby's voice. Davis froze. Winter looked cautiously over her shoulder. The boy stood at the end of the little alley, framed by the firelight.

"We're still talking," Davis rumbled. "Piss off."

"The thing is," Bobby said, advancing, "we were in the middle of a game, and we can't go on without the sergeant. So if you wouldn't mind having your chat in the morning?"

Buck stepped in front of Bobby. The Old Colonial had at least a foot and fifty pounds on the boy. He loomed.

"Sarge said piss off," he growled. "We're busy."

"But—"

Buck put one hand on each of Bobby's shoulders, pressing hard. The boy's legs buckled, and he fell involuntarily to his knees.

"Listen, kid," Buck said. "Just crawl back out of here, and you won't get hurt."

Winter caught Bobby's eye. *Go!* She tried to communicate the message, but apparently it didn't get across. The boy smiled and flicked his eyes upward.

"'Scuse me," said a deep voice, behind Davis. Corporal Folsom stepped forward and smiled at Winter.

Davis half turned, his face twisted in rage, and then paused as he reassessed the situation. He was a big man, used to commanding respect by physical presence alone, but Folsom was nearly as tall as he was. Moreover, Davis' bulk was layered with fat, the product of years of soft living in Ashe-Katarion. The corporal had a laborer's build, corded with muscle. There was something in his stance that spoke of a familiarity with violence—he stood on the balls of his feet, ready to move.

Peg turned to face him, too, and there was a moment of dangerous silence. Winter wanted to scream, or run, or do *something*. She wanted Corporal Folsom to push Davis' fat face through the back of his skull, but at the same time the thought terrified her. Standing up to Davis led to pain: that lesson had sunk into her very bones. Better to avoid notice. But there was no avoiding notice now.

A clatter of boots behind Bobby broke the pause. Corporal Graff turned the corner, puffing a little, and behind him came a half dozen brawny soldiers. Davis reached a decision. He straightened up, and his face twisted into a parody of a smile.

"My, you do take your games seriously," he said, slapping Peg jovially on the shoulder. "Well, I suppose the sergeant and I had more or less finished our business." He grinned down at Winter, eyes flashing murderous fire. "Now you take care, Saint. We wouldn't want anything to happen to you, would we? Don't go stepping on any scorpions."

"Stepping on a scorpion" was the standard cover story for any intra-regimental violence. When some poor bastard was so bruised and bleeding he couldn't make roll call, his fellows would report that he'd stepped on a scorpion.

Bobby gave a bright, guileless smile. "Don't worry, Sergeant. We'll take good care of him."

"S'right," Folsom said, from behind Davis. "Don't worry."

"Well, that certainly makes me feel better." Davis clapped his hands, gruesomely cheerful. "Come on, lads. Let's leave the Saint and his new company to their dinner."

Buck seemed eager to go. Peg was more reluctant, glaring acidly at Folsom, but at a glance from Davis he turned away. The soldiers behind Graff parted to let the three Old Colonials through. After a moment, Winter heard Davis' booming laughter.

"Sergeant?" Bobby said, closer at hand. "Are you all right?"

"Fine," Winter said automatically. Her breath still came fast, and her heart pounded. Her gut felt twisted into knots.

"You look like you need to lie down for a bit." Bobby stepped beside her. "Let me help you—"

At the brush of the boy's fingers, Winter pushed him away, too violently. It was a conditioned reflex, and she regretted it immediately. The expression on Bobby's face was like she'd kicked a puppy. She swallowed hard and straightened, fighting for self-control.

"It's all right," she said. "I'm fine. I just need to rest a bit." She looked around. "Go back to dinner, the rest of you."

The soldiers behind Graff stood aside as she passed by them to slip into her tent. She sat on the camp bed, not bothering to light the lamp, and hugged her stomach. The muscles there were taut in memory of the impact of Davis' meaty fist.

Someone knocked at the tent pole. "It's Graff."

Winter didn't want to see him, or anyone else, but that would be a poor way to show gratitude. "Come in."

The corporal entered, looking a little embarrassed. Winter looked up at him curiously.

He coughed. "I wanted to say that I'm sorry," he said. "For interfering. I thought it prudent, but it was a liberty, and you'd be well within your rights to be angry."

Winter shook her head dumbly.

"Jim was worried about you," Graff explained. "He sees more

than he lets on most of the time. There were three of them and just you, and we thought, well, that's hardly fair. So I ran over and rounded up a few of the lads who looked like they'd been in a fight or two."

"Thank you," Winter managed.

Graff relaxed. "Thing is," he said, "I've seen the type before. These backwoods sergeants are the worst—present company excluded, of course. They get a tiny bit of authority and they turn into little tin gods. Even worse when they're big bastards like this Davis." He shrugged. "Well, you don't have to worry about him. That lot are all cowards at heart. Show them a strong front, and they'll just scurry along."

Winter shook her head. She *knew* Davis. He was a brute and a bully, and quite possibly he was a coward, but he also had overweening pride and a vicious cunning. Show him a strong front, and he'd find some way around it, some way to strike when you weren't watching.

"I can't do this," Winter said quietly.

"Do what?"

"Any of this." She waved a hand. "How am I supposed to be a sergeant? I don't have the first idea what I'm doing, and now Davis . . ." She shook her head, her throat thick. "I can't do it."

"You're doing a first-rate job so far," Graff said. "I've served under much worse, let me tell you."

"But what am I supposed to do now?"

"Come back out and have dinner, for starters. You'll feel better for a hot meal."

Winter nodded slowly. Before she could rise, there was another rap at the tent pole, rapid and frantic.

"What?" Graff barked.

"It's Bobby," came the reply. "You've got to come out and see this!"

*

A squadron of cavalry had returned, walking down the aisle that separated the Seventh Company's tents from those of the neighboring units. Winter recognized Give-Em-Hell at their head, looking as puffed up and proud as a rooster. A dozen of his men followed behind him in a loose square. In the center were four men on foot, and it was these that were the center of attention.

Most of the recruits had probably never *seen* a Khandarai, unless one had rowed the boat by which they'd come ashore. The natives were shorter than Vordanai, with dark hair and gray-brown skin. This last varied; they were called "grayskins," and Winter had arrived expecting everyone to be the color of gunmetal, but in Ashe-Katarion she'd seen everything from the pale ash coloring of the nobility to the brown-black faces of the Desoltai, burned crisp by the desert sun.

These particular Khandarai were about average in that respect. They looked skinny and poorly fed, and they were dressed in fraying, baggy white cloth, painted all over with V shapes in red and yellow.

"Who are they?" Bobby asked, standing beside her.

"Not farmers, that's for certain," Graff said. "Look, they've got ammunition pouches."

"Redeemers," Winter said. She remembered that sigil all too clearly. "The triangles are supposed to look like flames."

"What are they doing out here?" Bobby said. "I thought all the Redeemers were at the city."

"Scouts," Graff said grimly. Winter nodded.

Bobby looked from one to the other, confused. "What's that mean?"

"It means that out there somewhere"—Graff pointed east—"there's an army."

"It means we're going to have a fight before long," Winter said. Staring at the sullen fanatics, she could almost forget about Davis after all.

PART TWO

JAFFA

"So, General," said Yatchik-dan-Rahksa. "We see the true shape of your courage at last."

Khtoba's frozen face cooled another few degrees. "Courage?" He looked as though he wanted to spit. "Arrogant pup. Fight a few battles yourself before you speak to me of courage."

"And how am I to do that, if I heed your counsel?" the priest replied. "You would have us cower here, praying the hammer does not fall on our heads!"

"*You* may pray as you like," the general said. "If you had studied the art of war as you've studied the teachings of the Divine Hand, you would know there is such a thing as *strategy*. We are strongly placed here, and there is nothing between Ashe-Katarion and the Vordanai but flyspeck villages and miles of worthless desert. Let them make the march. At the end of it, we'll be that much stronger, and they that much weaker."

"Are you so certain of that?" Yatchik said. "Already the people mutter that we fear to face the foreigners. Wait another few weeks and even the devoted may lose heart. *Action* is what is required." He sniffed. "Besides, what need do we have of strategy? We have the blessing of Heaven. *And* we have the numbers."

"Numbers," Khtoba said, "aren't everything."

Jaffa sat, watching them go after each other like a couple of angry cats. They had been at it for some hours, circling around to side topics before returning again and again to the main issue. The Vordanai army had left its tumbledown fortress at Sarhatep and was advancing up the coast road. The Steel Ghost had told them as much, and Khtoba's scouts had belatedly confirmed it. Yatchik was all for a general advance to meet and crush the foreigners where they stood, but the general was more cautious.

The real issue went unspoken. The authority of the Divine Hand rested on the violent sanction of the Swords of Heaven, the Redeemer host now nearly twenty-five thousand strong, gathered in the plain around the city. But that host could not sustain itself indefinitely, not without starving the people it was intended to protect. At some point the Hand would need to make the transition from revolutionary to ruler, to disband the army and restore a semblance of normal life to the city, but he didn't dare to do so with the Vordanai still in the field.

Khtoba, on the other hand, had everything to gain by waiting. The Auxiliaries, smaller and better disciplined than the peasant horde, drew their supplies from well-stocked and -guarded depots. They were also the only claim to power Khtoba had, and he was loath to risk them. A defeat, or even a costly victory, might leave his ranks so depleted that one of his rivals would gobble him up.

And the Steel Ghost? Jaffa glanced at the silent figure in black, and wondered. He hadn't said more than a few words during the whole affair. Jaffa had delivered Mother's message to him, but he'd given no sign of his answer.

At this rate, nothing would be accomplished. Jaffa thought on his instructions from Mother and decided it was time to break the deadlock.

"My friends," he said, interrupting their sniping, "might I make a humble suggestion?"

All eyes turned on him, Yatchik's large and liquid, Khtoba's piggy and red. The Ghost's, of course, were unreadable behind his mask.

"The foreigners are a threat to the Redemption," Jaffa said. "Perhaps even the greatest threat. But they are not the *only* threat. There are still followers of the prince hiding in the city, or gone to ground in the outskirts. Bandits and raiders multiply like locusts."

Khtoba shot a glance at the Ghost. The Desoltai had always been the most feared, and certainly the most effective, of the "bandits and raiders." For all that they were now allies of the Redemption, there was no love lost between the Auxiliaries and the nomads.

"So," the general said, "you agree, then, that we must remain here."

"Some of us must," Jaffa replied, before Yatchik could object. "But we must also consider what the enemy may do. Suppose they decide to wait where they are indefinitely."

"Exactly!" the priest said.

"Therefore," Jaffa said, "I suggest that the Auxiliaries remain here to defend the city, while the army of the Redemption marches forth to lay waste to the invaders."

Both men looked at him for a long moment, then exploded at once.

"Of all the foolish—"

"You can't—"

"The Grand Justice speaks wisely," rasped the Steel Ghost, in a whisper that somehow cut through the chatter. Jaffa rallied a bit at this unexpected support.

"To confront the enemy with less than your whole strength is folly," Yatchik said. "Even *I* know that much of your 'art of war.'"

"True," Jaffa said, "but, as you say, we have the numbers. Surely the faithful will not be defeated by heathens?"

The priest was silent for a moment. "It's not a matter of victory or defeat. Or course we will be victorious. But how many will need to lay down their lives? If General Khtoba's assistance could reduce the suffering among the devout—"

Khtoba snorted. "Now whose courage is in question?"

He was smiling like the cat that had eaten the canary, and small wonder. Jaffa could see the scenario playing itself out in the general's mind. With the Redeemer army away from the city, he would have the only reliable body of men. The Divine Hand could be put under proper control, and sooner or later the general would have the throne he'd always coveted. Yatchik could see it, too, of course, but Jaffa had one more card to play.

"And," he said, "we know that the prince—may his name be cursed—rides with the *raschem*. Surely the glory of his capture is a goal worth the risk?"

Yatchik's eyes lit up. It was common knowledge that Prince Exopter had fled the Palace with most of his treasury and wagons full of valuables, all the loot his dynasty had extracted over centuries of tyranny. It was not the glory that attracted the priest, but the gold. Whoever brought that wealth back to the Redemption would find his star on the rise. Now it was Khtoba's turn to sputter.

"Now, see here—," he began.

Jaffa sat back and left them to it. He thought they would agree in the end, but as long as they did *something* it would make no difference. He hoped fervently that the Redeemers and the foreigners would annihilate one another, although there seemed small chance of that. As Yatchik said, the Khandarai had the numbers. Even if they lost two-for-one, the tiny Vordanai force would be extinguished long before the Swords of Heaven.

He saw the Steel Ghost looking at him—at least, the mask was turned in his direction, though the eyes behind it were still invisible. When he had caught his gaze, the Desoltai chieftain dipped his head in a slight nod.

Jaffa nodded back. Mother would get the meeting she wanted after all.

FEOR

Feor sat with her head in her hands, eyes closed, trying to block out the screams. She kept returning to the day the temples fell, the day her fellow holy orphans had died beneath the swords of the vicious new priests. No matter how many times she went over it, nothing would change, not for her and not for Aran or Mahl or any of the others. But she couldn't seem to stop herself from remembering, over and over.

She'd been treated well enough. A few bruises from Gaedra's massive hands were nothing. She remembered the look in Aran's eyes, the dawning terror an instant before the eunuch's club dashed his brains to paste against the wall.

The flap of her tent rustled. She could tell it was him without looking up. The huge man didn't seem to have bathed since that awful day, and he gave off a sour stench.

"Get up. Yatchik wants you."

Feor raised her head, but apparently too slowly for Gaedra's taste. He grabbed her forearm and jerked her painfully to her feet, then forced her to stand on her toes as he straightened to his full height. Her shoulder burned.

"I said get up, little whore. Dirty slut. Worthless cunt."

A deep rage smoldered in Gaedra. He had been a servant of the temple, like her, but the eunuch had betrayed his sacred trust and opened the doors to the Redeemers. Even that had not slaked his thirst for vengeance, and he took his anger out on her, abusing her as much as his limited vocabulary would allow. Yatchik-dan-Rahksa had not, as yet, permitted him to go any further.

She bit down a gasp and managed to say, "And what would you know about such matters?"

The eunuch roared and spun, slinging her through the tent flap and out into the camp. She hit the ground with her aching shoulder and rolled, breathless with pain. Gaedra stalked after her, and she scrambled back to her feet before he could grab her again.

"When Yatchik speaks, you obey." He smiled. "Or not obey. Perhaps then Yatchik will see how useless you are. And after that . . ."

Feor straightened her robes, sniffed, and turned in the direction of Yatchik's tent. Gaedra hurried along at her heels, but when they arrived at the priest's plain black dwelling, the eunuch hung back. Feor ducked through the flap and went inside alone. Yatchik-dan-Rahksa sat on a cushion in the semidarkness, studying a leather map unrolled on the dirt floor. He shot her a questioning look.

"Feor. You know what I need from you. Have you reconsidered?"

"You understand nothing," she told him, for what seemed like the hundredth time. "Even if there is an *abh-naathem* among the *raschem* army—"

"There is," Yatchik interrupted.

He was right about that, although she refused to admit it aloud. For several days now she had been able to feel the dull presence of the foreign sorcerer, lurking off to the west like the sun just passing below the horizon. There was power there, more power than she'd ever felt before. More, even, than she felt from Mother or Onvi.

"Even if there is," she repeated, "and even if I wished to help you, I could not."

"You are a *naathem*," he said. "Your magic can defend us from his."

"You speak of 'magic' as though you knew something of it," Feor scoffed. "I tell you again, you do not understand. My *naath* cannot do what you ask."

"I do not have time to understand." Yatchik stood, his thin frame unfolding to its full height. His head brushed the cloth ceiling, and Feor had to look up to see his serious eyes. "Tomorrow the faithful take their vengeance on the *raschem*. Whatever fate they suffer will be your fate also. If I were you, I would be more careful how I speak."

"I know you would," Feor said. "But that is because you have never truly had faith."

CHAPTER SIX

WINTER

It figured, of course, that after all the drill their first assignment would be something they'd never practiced.

Moving inland from the coast, the land rose irregularly in a series of low rills, roughly perpendicular to the road the Colonials were marching along. Colonel Vhalnich was worried about these ridges, as well he might be. Even Winter, no student of strategy, could see that any cannon emplaced here would have a formidable field of fire. Companies had been broken out, therefore, to advance up the high ground, make sure it was clear of scouts or sharpshooters, and "if possible, make contact with and ascertain the location of the enemy."

Winter wondered whether Colonel Vhalnich—or Captain d'Ivoire, who'd actually issued the order—had really thought about the last part of it. Lieutenant d'Vries had certainly taken it to heart. As a result, the Seventh Company was currently splashing through a stream between the ridge flanking the road and the next hilltop, getting farther and farther from the main body. Winter had been growing correspondingly more and more nervous, until she finally felt she had to say *something*.

D'Vries was mounted, which made him hard to approach. Winter patted the flank of his horse, a beautiful dapple gray that was obviously suffering badly in the Khandarai heat, and tried to attract the lieutenant's attention.

"Sir?" When this had no effect, she resorted to the slightly humiliating expedient of tugging at the tail of his coat, like an anxious child accosting a busy parent. "Sir, could I have a word?"

"Eh?" D'Vries looked down. He was in his element at last, riding boldly at the head of his company, resplendent in his bright blue-and-gold. A sword with a silver-filigreed sheath hung at his belt. Even his spurs gleamed with polish. "What is it, Sergeant?"

"I wondered—," Winter began, but d'Vries interrupted.

"Speak up, man!"

Winter cursed silently, then said, "I wondered, sir, if perhaps we've come far enough."

"Far enough?" He looked down at her disdainfully. "We haven't found anything!"

"Yes, sir," Winter said. "But we were ordered to hold the ridge—"

"And to make contact with the enemy!" the lieutenant said.

She gave a quiet sigh. He'd said the same thing at the outset. "But, sir, if we're attacked—"

He barked a laugh. "Then my men will have to show their mettle!"

Winter felt lost. She wanted to explain that mettle wasn't the issue—if they located a substantial force of the enemy, a mere hundred and twenty men weren't likely to be able to make much of a stand, however valorous they were. But d'Vries would only laugh and call her a coward.

"In any case," he said, "this is my first assignment, and I've been ordered to locate the enemy. I do not intend to return as a failure!"

That there were a dozen companies with similar orders, up and down the line of march, had apparently made no impression on him. Winter saluted and turned away, feeling the day's heat throbbing against the back of her neck and soaking her uniform in sweat. Her breasts ached where she'd bound them too tightly; she'd had only a few hours with the sewing kit, and hadn't gotten the measure quite right on her replacement undershirts. Her skin itched where it rubbed against the soaked cotton.

Most of the men were suffering equally, if in different ways. A few days of drill had helped, but it took longer than that to truly become accustomed to the hellish sun. As they passed the stream, they took the opportunity to drink, refill their canteens, and splash water on their faces. The little brook was brackish and warm, but it was pleasant even so.

They were advancing in loose order, not the shoulder-to-shoulder line they'd practiced on the drill field. The men took advantage of the laxer discipline to talk and joke with one another as they trudged across the bottom of the valley and started up the opposite height. They didn't seem worried. Winter flinched at each burst of laugher, but she was the only one.

She kicked savagely at a dry puff bush as she passed, and it exploded satisfactorily into a thousand drifting seed pods. The hell of it was, more than likely nothing would come of all her nerves. So far none of the scouts had sighted anything more than distant horsemen, who turned and fled at the first approach of anything in blue. Give-Em-Hell's cavalry ranged out ahead of the column, covering the most likely approaches of an enemy force. These reconnaissances were just a precaution. *But, of course, try telling that to d'Vries.*

Bobby drifted over to her. The boy was plainly exhausted, sweat running down his face in rivulets, but he struggled gamely onward under the weight of pack and musket. He even managed a smile.

"Aren't—aren't—" He labored for a moment to catch his breath. "Aren't we getting a bit far out?"

Winter snorted. "D'Vries thinks the colonel has ordered him personally to chase down the entire enemy army."

"He'll get a dressing-down from Captain d'Ivoire, I bet."

"Maybe." Winter shrugged. "Captain d'Ivoire's a busy man."

"Think he'll call a halt when we get to the top of the next ridge?"

"God Almighty, I hope so." Winter looked at the perspiring troops now struggling up the slope. "Otherwise we won't even need to run into the Redeemers. The sun's bad enough."

Bobby nodded wearily. They walked on in silence, picking their way around occasional screes of loose rock or clumps of hardy shrubs and grass. This ridge was taller than the one that ran along the road, and Winter imagined it would afford quite a view. She hoped that d'Vries would be satisfied with taking a look from the top.

There was a surprised shriek from her right, followed by a burst of laughter.

"Sarge! I think something bit Cooper!"

More laughter. Winter left Bobby's side and hurried over to a small group of soldiers, acutely aware that getting bit by something in Khandar was no laughing matter. In the city she'd known a Khandarai trapper who'd claimed there were a hundred and seven varieties of snakes in the Lesser Desol, and at least a dozen kinds of scorpions. Each was dangerous in its own particular way.

On inspection, however, Cooper turned out merely to have stepped in a prickerbush, whose barbed thorns had snagged his trousers and drawn angry red scratches down his leg. Winter got the lad disentangled, much to the amusement of his companions.

As she straightened up, there were shouts from above, at the top of the ridge. Winter thought at first that another man had had an encounter with local wildlife, but from the volume it sounded as though the whole company had stumbled into a nest of snakes. Above it she heard the high, shrill voice of the lieutenant.

"Back! Go back!"

He came into sight over the top of the ridge, his terrified horse moving far too fast already, blood spotting the animal's flanks where he'd kicked it viciously with his spurs. A few soldiers followed, picking their way down the rocky slope as fast as their legs would carry them.

Winter spat a curse that would have given Mrs. Wilmore an apoplectic fit on the spot. She forced her weary legs to move, sprinting the last dozen yards to the crest of the ridge, and found most of the Seventh Company still gathered there. The thin line had contracted to a tight bunch as the soldiers instinctively huddled together.

The top of the high ridge afforded an excellent view. Over her shoulder, Winter could see the ocean, though the coast road and the Vordanai army were blocked by the lower ridge behind them. Ahead of her, to the south, the furrowed land stretched on and on until it flattened out into the sandy wastes of the Lesser Desol.

The objects of the soldiers' attention were closer at hand, however. Off to the east, the coast road became visible again as it swung inland to avoid some obstacle, and there a vast host had gathered. It looked more like a camp than an army, with tents and crude banners showing the crimson flame of the Redeemers on a black field. Men milled around, reduced to ants by the distance, and there was no mistaking the flash of the sun from polished steel blades.

Spreading south and east from the camp was an apparently endless tide of horsemen. They rode in small groups of twenty or thirty, and there were more groups than Winter could count, covering the valley at the foot of the ridge. They were shabby-looking men, un-uniformed and mounted on scrawny beasts liberated from their lives as cart horses or field animals, but they screamed and drew swords when they saw Vordanai blue against the horizon. Priests in black wraps egged them on, screaming loudest of all and waving the riders forward.

The lieutenant was still shouting, barely audible over the shrieks of the Redeemers.

"Back! Back to the column!"

The closest groups were only minutes away. The slope would slow them, but not enough. Winter cursed again. She hurried to the mass of men on the ridge, only to find it melting away before she got there. The soldiers, momentarily transfixed by the sight, had recovered their wits, and one by one they were making the same decision as d'Vries had. There were only a few dozen left when she arrived, Bobby and the other two corporals among them.

Winter grabbed Bobby's shoulder. The boy looked up at her, eyes wide.

"Wh-wh-what—"

"Back down the hill," Winter said. "But *stop at the stream*. Understand that? Get everyone you can to stop at the stream."

"We have to get back to the column," Bobby gabbled. "We'll be killed—oh, saints and martyrs—"

"We'll never make it," Winter said. "Too far. If we run they'll cut us down. We have to stand them off!"

She glanced up at the other two corporals for support. Graff looked dubious, but Folsom nodded grimly. He took off down the hill at a run, bellowing at the top of his lungs.

"The stream! Halt at the stream!"

"Help me," Winter said to Graff, and started grabbing men by the arm and pulling them away from the crest. Mesmerized by the sight of their own deaths approaching at a gallop, at first they refused to move. Winter turned them about by brute force, shouted in their ears to form up at the stream, and pushed them so they stumbled down the slope. Graff followed her example. By the time the pair of them were the only ones remaining, the first of the Redeemer horsemen were already climbing the ridge.

Winter spun at a piercing, inhuman shriek. D'Vries had tried to get even more speed from his mount, in spite of the rocky, broken ground, and the gray had put a foot wrong. The animal went down and rolled, screaming its terror, and the lieutenant was thrown free. Both came to rest near the bottom of the slope. The horse tried to rise, but immediately went down again, one foreleg refusing to bear its weight. D'Vries, miraculously unhurt, took one look at it and continued his run on foot, splashing across the muddy stream in his enameled leather boots and starting up the opposite slope.

Folsom's shouts were having some effect. The long-legged corporal had reached the bottom before most of the men, and he waved his musket in the air while he called on them to form. Some gathered around him, although no formation was evident, and those still coming down the slope headed for the crowd that was growing in the creek bed. Others, mostly those already past the stream, kept running after the lieutenant.

"Come on," Winter said to Graff, and ran. Turning away from the horsemen was hard, and keeping herself from stumbling in the first dozen yards was harder. The small of her back itched, expecting a musket ball or a rider's saber. When the ground leveled out enough that she could risk turning her head, she found she'd made better time than she'd thought. The first of the Redeemers were just cresting the rise, whooping and shouting at the sight of the Vordanai soldiers running for their lives. They wouldn't be able to gallop down without the risk of ending up like d'Vries.

She spotted Folsom in the crowd of nervous men, some of whom looked ready to take off running again. Winter cupped her hands to shout as she ran.

"Square! Make them form square!"

She covered the rest of the distance at a dead sprint, Graff behind her, his stubby arms pumping. Folsom was already at work, shoving the uncomprehending men into line. He'd managed to force the knot of men into a hollow oval, but it was open at the back, where the men were spreading out along the creek bed. Winter pulled up short, gasping for breath.

"Fix—fix—" She coughed, mastered her lungs by sheer force

of will, and managed, "Fix bayonets. Two ranks. Don't shoot till they close. Graff!"

The wiry corporal was beside her, hands on his knees. "Yes?" he replied, coughing.

"Straighten them out. Hold fire. You understand?"

She caught his eye, and he nodded. Winter ran around the face of the oval, toward where the line dissolved into an amorphous mass. Bobby was at the edge, still shouting at the men who were climbing the opposite slope behind the lieutenant. Winter grabbed the boy's hand.

"Listen. Bobby, listen to me!" Winter gestured up to where the riders were picking their way through the rocks, only minutes from contact. "We need a rear face to this formation. Otherwise they'll just go around and take us from behind, you understand?" She became aware that the men nearby were listening, too, and raised her voice. "Form up! Double line! We have to guard their backs"—she waved at the men at the front of the square, now in a recognizable line—"and they'll guard ours! Form up *now*!"

Bobby raised his voice as well, high and girlish with barely mastered fear. The men started to form, pushing and shoving, and on the inside of the square Folsom started taking them by the shoulders and jamming them into the right positions. As the formation came together, the nerves of the recruits seemed to steady. It was agony to look *away* from the oncoming horsemen, as the back face of the square was obliged to do, but under Winter's prodding they stopped staring over their shoulders and concentrated on their weapons. Bayonets came out of their sheaths, and each man fixed the triangular steel blade to the lug just below his musket barrel. Folsom still bellowed from inside the square.

"Hold fire until my command! Any man who fires without my command is getting cracked over the head!"

It was strange to hear the big corporal speak so freely, as though danger had finally loosened his tongue. Graff was at work on the right face of the square, and Winter went to the left, but the men didn't require much steadying. Some critical threshold had been passed, and the Seventh Company had gone from a fleeing mob back to an organized body of soldiery.

The sudden clap of a gunshot cut through the shouts of the men, and Winter saw a wisp of smoke rising from the ridge. The rider who'd fired lowered a stubby carbine and drew his sword. Other shots followed. Every bang and flash was accompanied by a collective swaying of the men in the square, each man individually attempting to dodge.

"Hold fire!" Folsom screamed. "Hold your fire, by Karis the Savior, or you'll wish you had!"

The line of horsemen directly opposite the square slowed their descent, but those beyond it on either side swept forward with wild cries. Free of the rocky ridge, they spurred their horses to a gallop, starting up the smaller rill beyond. D'Vries had made it halfway to the top, with the men who'd fled straggling behind him, but the horsemen easily caught up to them. Some of the men turned to face their pursuers, and there was a ragged chorus of shots and a billow of smoke. Winter saw a couple of horses go down. Then the riders were on them, shouting and slashing with their sabers or jabbing with long spears. The last Winter saw of Lieutenant d'Vries was a brief glimpse of glittering gold and silver as four men closed in around him.

Other men were cut down as they ran, or spitted on the spears. Some tried to fight, blocking the sabers with the barrels of their muskets, but the clang of steel on steel invariably drew the attention of another horseman, who cut down the unfortunate soldier from behind.

Directly above, on the crest of the high ridge, a party of Redeemers was forming. They'd been quick to sweep around the sides of the square, giving it a wide berth to stay out of easy musket range, but none of them had yet challenged it directly. Here and there a carbine or even a pistol cracked, but at that distance the riders had little chance of hitting even the tight-packed ranks of the Vordanai formation. Winter could see one of the black-wrapped priests screaming at the top of his lungs, and the scattered horsemen gathered into larger groups. Many continued on, over the low ridge behind which the Vordanai main column waited.

A group was forming on the other side of the square as well, and smaller units circled around the sides, like predators eyeing prey for a hint of weakness. Winter realized, belatedly, that she was *outside* the protective wall of bayonets. She looked around quickly to make sure she was the last one still standing beyond the line, then stepped sideways between two of the musket barrels that protruded like spears. The men shuffled aside to let her in, then closed behind her like a curtain.

Corporal Folsom stood in the center of the tiny clear area inside. The faces of the square were only ten men wide, so the interior was about twenty-five feet across, bisected by the creek bed and the muddy, trampled ground around it. The corporal saluted, as though nothing unusual had happened.

"Where's Bobby and Graff?" Winter said. Folsom pointed to where the two of them stood side by side in the rear rank, and Winter pulled them out. Bobby looked white-faced and terrified, knuckles standing out bloodless as he clutched the barrel of his musket. Graff, grizzled and bearded, was harder to read, but Winter thought even he was looking a little gray. She did her best to appear unconcerned.

"Right," she said. "We each take a face. Hold fire until twenty-five yards, and then only one rank. Second rank holds fire until point-blank. You understand?" She caught Bobby's eye. Graff was a veteran, and Folsom seemed to know what he was about, but the boy looked rattled. "Senior Corporal Forester, do you understand?"

"Yessir," Bobby said automatically. He blinked, and some life returned to his face. "Hold fire till twenty-five—"

"Right. And whatever you do, don't let them step back an inch. No horse alive will charge a row of bayonets, but if they waver—"

The priest on the hill cut her off. He sang a single high note, close to a howl, breathtaking in its pitch and purity. It would have been almost beautiful if Winter hadn't recognized it—the Redeemers in the city had given the same cry before they set light to the pyres of heretics. The riders answered with a roar, and there was a sudden thunder of hooves as they started forward. Winter couldn't begin to estimate their numbers—hundreds at least—

"Go!" she told the corporals, and ran to the south face, directly opposite where the priest had gathered the largest band of the enemy. Her voice rose to a hoarse shout, scraping her throat raw. "Hold fire! First rank, kneel and ready to fire *on my order.* Second rank, hold fire. Hold!"

The horsemen started out slowly, picking their way down rough ground at the top of the hill, then gaining speed as the slope flattened out. The distance closed rapidly. Seventy yards, sixty, fifty—

A musket cracked to her right, followed quickly by a couple of others as trigger fingers tightened in sympathy.

"Hold your *fucking* fire!" Winter screamed, and heard the corporals echoing the call. Bobby's voice was high and tremulous, while Folsom's bass shouts carried over the thunder of hooves.

Answering cracks came from the advancing mob. More carbines, and the range was shorter. Most of the shots went wide, but just in front of Winter a man grunted as if in surprise and slumped forward. From behind her, she heard a shriek.

Thirty yards. The riders had to close in to match the narrow face of the square, until they were riding boot to boot and five-deep. Spears and sabers waved in the air, and gray-skinned faces twisted in fury. The red flame of the Redemption adorned every breast. Twenty-five yards.

"First rank, *fire*!" Winter screamed, echoed moments later by the three corporals.

For an instant all four sides of the square were fringed in fire, the yellow-pink glare of muzzle flashes, followed by a billow of smoke. With the enemy packed so tightly, they could scarcely miss, and every ball seemed to find either a horse or a rider. Men dropped from their saddles as though swatted by invisible giants, and horses screamed and collapsed, spilling their riders onto the unforgiving earth. Every horse that went down took two or three others with it, until they formed a pile of terrified, thrashing animals and screaming riders. Those behind broke to the left or right, avoiding the obstacle, or if they were particularly brave urged their mounts into a jump. Staggered and broken, the charge closed nonetheless.

"Second rank on my command!" Winter shouted, unsure whether anyone but the men right beside her could hear over the tumult. "First rank, *hold steady*!"

She heard Folsom's bellow, and a snatch of Bobby's voice excoriating his troops with words a lad his age ought not to have known. The riders were so close now that the whole world beyond the blue square seemed to be filled with horses and shouting men.

The front rank of Vordanai had knelt to allow the second rank a clear field of fire, and set the butts of their muskets against the dirt. Their bayonets presented an unbroken line of razor-edged steel points to the oncoming riders, and if the men were foolish enough to want to hit that obstacle at a gallop, the horses were not. They shied away, swinging to either side in order to avoid contact with the bayonets, only to collide with the attackers against the other faces of the square who were doing the same. Other riders reined up and managed to bring their animals to a halt just outside the line, but they, too, had to work quickly to avoid collision with those coming on behind them.

In an instant the wave of screaming riders had become a melee of shoving men and rearing horses. Those closest to the square slashed down at the points of the bayonets, trying to bat them aside. Somewhere a pistol cracked, and a man in the rear rank of Winter's side of the square toppled backward, hands clawing at the red ruin of his face. His cry was inaudible amidst the tumult.

"Second rank, *fire*!"

She wasn't sure if the men heard her or simply could wait no longer. Forty muskets cracked, the sound like a bludgeon against her ears, and lurid smoke wreathed the whole scene. The effect on the horsemen was fearful. At that range, the ball from a musket would pass through flesh and bone like wet tissue paper, with enough energy to come out the other side and kill again. Horses screamed and collapsed, all around the line, and men were shouting and cursing at one another. There were more cracks, either late firing or enemy weapons.

"First rank, hold steady! Second rank, *load*!"

If they had been able to press forward, the Redeemers might have broken the square. With the bayonets of the second rank withdrawn so they could hurry through the drill of stuffing powder and ball down their barrels, the first rank stood momentarily alone, a thin line of steel. But the volley had torn horrid gaps in the mob of attackers, and those that remained were having difficulty controlling their mounts, much less pressing forward over the still-thrashing bodies of those that had fallen. On the edges, a few were already shying away.

Half a minute—*Too slow,* Winter thought—and the second rank's weapons swung back into line. More of the riders started to turn away.

"Second rank, *fire*!"

Another volley ripped out, more ragged than the first, but nearly as effective. Suddenly the horsemen were fleeing, riding away from the square with the same desperate speed with which they'd charged. A ragged, spontaneous cheer erupted from the Vordanai as their enemies fanned out and away. Winter's voice cut through it like a knife.

"First rank, *load*. Second rank, *steady*!"

Through the shredded wisps of smoke, she could see the black-clad priest still waiting at the top of the ridge, with a considerable body of men around him. The first wave was rapidly dispersing in all directions, but some of them turned their horses about when they'd regained a safe distance. Others kept going, despite the shouts of their comrades. Outside the square, screams rose from the field of broken men and animals.

When the first rank had finished loading and reestablished the line of bayonets, Winter told the second rank to load and took a moment to look behind her. All the faces of the square were intact—as she'd known they had to be, or else some rider's saber would have taken her from behind—and she could see the three corporals echoing her orders. Here and there a Vordanai soldier had slumped over in place, and his comrades had closed ranks around him. A few others, not as badly hurt, had walked or crawled to the center of the square. She saw one man, with an almost mechanical calm, tearing strips from his smoke-grimed undershirt to wrap around the bloody ruin of his left hand.

The cry of the Redeemer priest—that high note, incongruously pure—drew her attention back to the ridge. With the survivors of the first attack out of the way, the black-wrapped cleric urged his own mount down the hill, and the men gathered around him followed. They kicked their horses to a reckless speed, and more than one stumbled and fell amid the rocks and wreckage, but the rest came on.

"Hold fire!" Winter shouted. "The same damn thing again—just hold until they close—"

At twenty-five yards, the first rank exploded into flames, and men fell up and down the charging line. There were fewer of them, and being more loosely packed they suffered less than the first wave had. The survivors, including the priest, urged their mounts into a gallop and pushed on over the corpse-strewn ground.

Winter watched the priest with fascination. He was unarmed, practically standing in his stirrups and holding the reins with both hands. His high-pitched song had given way to a shriek, and his face was screwed up in ecstasy or hatred. By fervor or superior horsemanship, he'd outdistanced all of his companions.

"Second rank," Winter shouted, "*fire*!"

A half dozen muskets had drawn a bead on the man in black, and they all cracked together. The priest had nearly reached the line, and he urged his animal into a final leap to clear the barricade of dead or dying horses that lay in front of the square. In midair he seemed almost to explode, bits of black wrap blowing outward in sprays of blood. A bullet found his horse as well, and the beast's front legs collapsed when it landed just in front of the square. It was traveling too fast to be stopped so easily, though. The horse twisted and rolled, nervelessly, and collided with the wall of bayonets.

In dying, the animal had achieved what the living riders could not. It slammed into the men in the square, knocking their bayonets aside or trapping them in its flesh. Three more riders followed close behind it, having evaded the volley and threaded the obstacles, and they charged into the gap.

One soldier, knocked down by the corpse of the priest's mount, found a horse riding directly over him. He thrust his bayonet point upward and rolled aside as the animal collapsed with a shower of blood. The rider on the left found another man jabbing at him and leaned forward to aim a cut at the soldier's hand. His attacker rolled backward with a cry and a spray of gore.

The third horseman, hefting a spear, came directly at Winter.

Her first instinct, to get out of the path of the charging animal, saved her life. The horseman reined up beside her and thrust, but she threw herself aside just in time. He circled, fending off an outthrust bayonet, and came at her again. This time she had to roll as he passed, and fetched up against the corpse of a young man in blue, hands still clenched around his musket. She snatched the weapon, swung it clumsily to point at the rider, and started fumbling with the cock. The pan clicked open, letting the priming charge trickle out into her face.

Winter spat, tasting the salt of the powder, and blinked a few grains from her eyes in time see the spear coming down at her. Abandoning any attempt to fire the musket, she blocked the swing with the barrel and thrust the bayonet back at him. The Redeemer shouted when the point scored on his arm, and dropped his weapon. He wheeled away just in time for the rider who'd been unhorsed to charge her, screaming. Winter scrabbled away, leveling the musket like a spear, but the man kicked the barrel with his booted foot and it jolted from her hand.

Something flashed past her, dressed in blue. Bobby charged with all his weight behind his bayonet, like a medieval lancer. It caught the man high in the chest and sank in until the barrel was flush with his skin. The Redeemer toppled, dragging the musket from the boy's grasp. Bobby sank to his knees beside the corpse, but a half dozen soldiers swarmed past him and Winter. Dimly, she saw them butcher the wounded horseman like a hog, then move on to close the gap opened by the dying horse. Around the outside of the square, the rest of the late priest's companions were shying away, and at that moment another volley boomed out, pressing them into full flight.

Winter's heart hammered so fast she was certain it was about to explode. She searched her body for pain, and discovered with mounting disbelief that she seemed to be relatively intact. Another volley exploded all around her, chasing the fleeing Khandarai, but her battle-numbed ears barely registered it. She rolled over and crawled to where Bobby sat staring into space in the direction the Khandarai had come from.

"Bobby!" Winter said, her own voice distant and ringing in her ears. "Corporal! Are you all right?"

Bobby looked at her quizzically, as though she were speaking in a foreign tongue, and then blinked and seemed to recover himself a little.

"Fine," he said. "I'm fine."

Winter staggered to her feet. The square was intact, the first rank of men kneeling grim-faced with leveled bayonets while the second rank busily loaded yet another volley. Beyond that, she could see nothing. The smoke had piled up around the company like a fog bank, and even the sun was only an unseen presence overhead.

She heard a couple of cracks, distant gunshots, but they sounded a long way off. Before long, even the drumming of hooves on dry earth had faded like departing rain. A light breeze coming down the valley started to shred the smoke, and snatches of blue sky became visible.

The second rank had loaded and leveled. Winter saw Graff and Folsom looking at her for orders. Bobby was still immobile on the ground.

"First rank, load," Winter croaked. She turned in place, wishing she could see. Beyond that smoke, the Redeemers could be waiting, re-forming for another assault—

But they were not. By the time all the company's muskets were reloaded and ready, the dense bank of smoke was drifting into tatters, and the valley floor became visible. For as far as the eye could see in any direction, it was empty. The Redeemer cavalry had moved on, the vast bulk of the horsemen simply sweeping around the tiny square and on toward the main Vordanai column. In the immediate vicinity of the Seventh Company, the ground was littered with shattered, screaming horses, wounded men, and corpses. On the slope of the northern ridge, patches of blue marked where Vordanai soldiers had been cut down as they ran. Some of them moved feebly, but most were still.

Winter stared in dumb disbelief. She felt someone move to her side, and looked up to see Graff, his bearded face twisted into a parody of a smile.

"Well, that seems to be over." He scratched the side of his nose. "What the hell do we do now?"

Chapter Seven

MARCUS

The Colonials went through the evolution from march column into square with considerably more expertise than they'd shown a few days before, though they were still too slow for Marcus' taste. From above, they would have looked like a chain of four diamonds strung out along the road, points aligned with one another so that the faces of the squares could shoot without risking friendly fire. The Third and Fourth battalion squares, at the back of the column, had formed around the artillery and the vulnerable supply train, while Give-Em-Hell's cavalry were gathering nearby.

The diminutive cavalry captain himself rode over to where Marcus, Janus, Fitz, and the regimental color party waited by the First Battalion square. He reined up and, his eyes gleaming, ripped off a tight salute to the colonel.

"Give me leave to charge them, sir," he said, his pigeon chest swollen with pride. "I'll clear that ridge in a flash."

Janus raised a polite eyebrow. "You don't think you're at too much of a numerical disadvantage?"

"Each man in blue is worth a dozen of those cowardly goat-fuckers," the captain said.

Marcus winced at this, but Janus was unperturbed.

"Indeed. Though, if our scouts are even marginally trustworthy, they would outnumber you roughly thirty to one. Possibly more."

"But they won't be ready for it!"

The colonel shook his head sadly, as though he would have loved nothing better in the world than to let the captain off his leash.

"I'm afraid the cavalry has too important a part to play in today's battle to risk it at this stage, Captain. Keep your men close. You're to shelter inside the Second Battalion square, understand?"

"But—" Give-Em-Hell caught Janus' eye, and somewhat to Marcus' astonishment he subsided. "Yes, sir. As you say." He put his heels to his horse and rode toward where his men waited, near the front of the column.

Marcus leaned toward his commander. "I apologize for Captain Stokes, sir. He's a good cavalryman, just a touch overeager."

"Eagerness has virtues all its own, Captain." Janus shrugged. "There is a place for every man, whatever his talent or temperament. Captain Stokes will have his turn." He looked up at the ridge. "I can't imagine what they're up to. If they take much longer, I shall have to order up some artillery to hurry them along."

The hilltop was dark with enemy horsemen gathering around a dozen black-clad priests who chose that moment to break into their sweet, high song. They all hit subtly different notes, and the result was a ringing harmony that echoed down from the ridge with a weird, unearthly beauty. Marcus felt his jaw tighten, but when he looked at Janus he saw that the colonel was sitting with his eyes closed, absorbing the melody. He opened them again only when the keening was answered by a roar that seemed to come from thousands of throats.

"Do Khandarai priests always sing like that before they enter battle?" Janus asked.

Marcus shrugged. "I don't think so, sir. As far as I'm aware, it's a Redeemer thing."

"Hmm." Janus looked thoughtful. "Pity."

"Perhaps we ought to take shelter, sir?"

Janus examined his hand for a moment, flicked a bit of grit from under one fingernail, then looked up again at where the enemy horsemen were beginning to pour over the ridge. "Very well. Let's find a safe vantage."

The interior of the First Battalion's square was a bare patch of trampled earth seventy yards or so to a side. Behind the triple ranks that formed the edge stood the lieutenants, one to each company, while the sergeants prowled back and forth. All around him, men loaded their weapons and fixed their bayonets.

Janus had produced a spyglass, a fearsomely expensive-looking thing in brass and blond wood. His horse's height let him peer over the heads of the men around him, and he shook his head regretfully.

"A mob. Nothing more than a mob."

Marcus watched the horsemen thundering down from the ridge. Without the aid of a glass, most of what he could see was the dust raised by their passage. The priests were still at the front, waving the others forward, and he could see a few of the "soldiers," ragged men with improvised weapons, riding scrawny horses.

"A *big* mob," he said. "From what the scouts said, there have to be three or four thousand of them."

"Four thousand or forty, it makes no difference," Janus said. "A charge like that will never break a solid square." He gave Marcus a smile, his big gray eyes unreadable. "Assuming our men are up to it, of course. If not, things will become exciting very quickly."

"They're up to it, sir." Marcus put a certainty into his voice that he didn't feel.

"We'll soon see."

Marcus watched the approach of the riders impatiently. There was nothing for him to *do*, not now. The lieutenants would give the orders to load and fire, and they knew their business—or if they didn't, it was too late to teach them. The gleaming line of bayonets shifted slightly as the men on the sides of the square turned in place to face the oncoming tide. Marcus felt oddly detached as the huge cloud of dust glided toward them, like the leading edge of a sandstorm.

"Level!" The shout, from a dozen throats at once, brought Marcus back to reality. The horsemen were only sixty yards away, coming on at the gallop, and their shouts filled the air. Fifty yards, then forty—

He never heard the order to fire, only a single musket's *crack* followed by a roar that spread along the formation like a blaze catching in dry tinder. Two sides of the square flashed and boiled with smoke. He could see a few horses fall, but most of the effect was hidden by the dust. The first rank of soldiers knelt, bayonets braced in the dirt, while the third rank began to reload. The second had reserved their fire, the points of their blades projecting between the men of the first.

The last Marcus could truly *see* of the battle was the riders splitting against the point of the square, flowing around it like water breaking around a rock. Unable to charge home, they ended up riding along the faces of the formation, slashing impotently at the ranked bayonets. The second rank fired, and more horses went down. Then the dust of the riders' charge mingled with the smoke to obscure his view entirely. He could hear the calls of the sergeants, to load and fire, but the organized crash of volleys was gone now. Each man fired at fleeting targets, or at no target at all, flinging his lead into the gritty fog and trusting that some Redeemer would stop it. Muzzle flashes from outside the square showed here and there through the murk, but few of the riders had pistols or carbines. Those that did seldom got a second chance to use them—the unmistakable glare of a shot instantly drew a dozen answering blasts from the faces of the square.

The other squares were fighting, too. Marcus could hear the thunder of their fire, but for all he could see they might as well have been on the face of the moon. He glanced across at Janus. The colonel sat, reins held lightly in his hands, his eyes closed in contemplation. The expression on his face was utterly relaxed, lips curved in a slight smile. It made Marcus look away, uncomfortable, as though he'd walked in on his superior doing something private and sordid.

It went on that way, and on and on and on, longer than Marcus would have believed possible. Out in the smoke, the riders circled, rode past, formed and charged, but all invisibly. Men fell on the faces of the square and were dragged into the center—here one who'd lost the fingers of one hand to a saber, there a boy with his elbow shattered by a carbine's bullet. One by one the square filled with these unfortunates. The toll on the Redeemers was worse, far worse. Marcus knew it had to be, but the only evidence was the shouts of men and the screaming of horses. He began to feel as though there was no end to the men out there, as though his own soldiers would be picked off, one by one, until only he and Janus remained, alone in the fog—

The colonel opened his eyes, and his smile broadened.

"Well," he said, "that would appear to be that."

It was a few moments longer before Marcus realized he had the truth of it. The sound of hoofbeats on hard earth was fading, and the cracks of muskets sputtered out like a dying fire. The screams of the wounded, human and animal, seemed to rise in volume now that they were the only sounds on the field. Slowly, the fog of smoke and dust began to dissipate, prodded by the sea breeze.

Janus flipped his reins abruptly, and his horse trotted toward the edge of the square. A lieutenant hastily pushed his men aside to make way. Marcus followed. Their mounts picked a careful path through the dead and dying men who littered the ground around the square until they had fought clear of the dusty murk and emerged into bright sunshine. Marcus was astonished to see how little the sun had progressed. He would have sworn they'd been fighting for hours.

All around them, the enemy were fleeing, toiling up the slope or galloping east and west along the coast road. None of them even paused for a look at the two horsemen in blue.

"Well," Janus said, "it seems the men are up to it." He expressed no particular emotion at this, as though it were merely another piece of data in an interesting experiment. He stared into the distance for a moment, then turned to Marcus. "Order the regiment back into column. We'll march clear of the field, rest a quarter of an hour, then continue down the road."

"Sir?" The men would be exhausted. Marcus himself was quivering with released tension. A quarter of an hour didn't seem like nearly enough.

"We're not finished yet, Captain. You heard the scouts' report. The enemy infantry awaits us."

"Might it not be better to withdraw, then?" Marcus asked. "We could take a strong position to the west—"

"No," Janus said. "We must press our advantage."

Marcus was a little dubious that they *had* an advantage. By all accounts, the Redeemer host was at least twenty thousand strong, outnumbering the Vordanai army five to one. True, they were mostly peasants and fanatics recruited by the hysterical appeals of Redeemer priests, but twenty thousand men was still twenty thousand men.

"What about the casualties?" he said.

Janus pursed his lips. "Detail a company to care for our wounded. The dead can wait until nightfall, as can the business of gathering prisoners."

"Yes, sir." That sat poorly as well. The men wouldn't like not being able to stop to bury their fallen comrades, although Marcus was dubious that they'd be able to bury *anyone* in the sun-scorched, iron-hard earth.

But orders were orders. Marcus rode in search of Fitz.

★

A vast cloud of dust marked the Redeemer army, rising above the coast road like a grounded thunderhead. A similar plume trailed the Vordanai column, leaving the rearmost battalion and the drivers in the train spitting grit. Marcus glanced sidelong at Janus, who was riding as carefree as if he were off to the theater.

"Sir," Marcus said after a while, in case the colonel hadn't noticed the looming cloud.

"Captain," Janus said, "I'm aware that we have not reached the stage in our relationship where I have your full trust, but I hope you're prepared to believe that I'm not actually *blind*." He pointed a short way ahead. "There's a bit of a ridge there, and the road veers slightly north. Not much, but every bit helps."

After another few minutes, the colonel reined up, and Marcus stopped beside him. Fitz, in his role as aide-de-camp, was still trailing at a respectful distance. To Marcus' eye, there wasn't much to distinguish this barren patch of roadway from what they'd been riding along all day, but Janus seemed satisfied.

"This will do," he said. "Draw up, all four battalions in line. Tell Captain Stokes to take the flanks, but that he's not to go riding off without my express orders. And find me Captain Vahkerson, if you would."

Marcus nodded, still fighting the sour feeling in the pit of his stomach, and started dictating orders to Fitz. Before long the dust was everywhere, and with it the clatter and shouts of men getting into formation. The battalions went through the evolution from columns into long, three-deep lines with the usual hesitation and confusion, and Marcus winced every time a sergeant cut loose with an angry tirade. If Janus noticed or cared about the poor performance, however, he didn't show it.

Captain Vahkerson—the Preacher to all the Old Colonials—turned up, on foot and covered head to toe in dust. He saluted grimly.

"Lord's blessings be on you, sir," he said, doffing his peaked artilleryman's cap. He was a rail-thin man, with long, wiry arms patched with ancient powder burns. His hair was thinning from the top, as if in natural imitation of a monk's tonsure, but he maintained his ferocious beard and whiskers. A Church double circle, wrought in brass, hung around his neck and flashed when it caught the sun.

"And you, Captain," Janus said solemnly. "Bring up your guns. Half batteries on the flank and the outer intervals. Leave the center to me."

"Yessir," the Preacher said. "We should have a nice field of fire once the dust clears."

"As to that," Janus said, "you're to hold fire until the infantry opens. Load with double case and wait for my order, you understand?"

"Sir?" The captain frowned, then caught Janus' expression. "As you say, sir. I'll see to it."

Janus nodded, and glanced at Marcus as the artillerist hurried off. Marcus had been trying to keep his expression neutral, but Janus seemed to see through him without apparent effort. "You don't approve, Captain?"

"Just a thought, sir. A few rounds at five hundred yards might serve to break their momentum a bit."

"It would indeed. But is that really what we want?" Janus favored him with a tight-lipped smile. "Trust, Marcus. You'll see."

"Yes, sir." He caught sight of a familiar figure moving toward the front. "Excuse me for a moment."

Miss Alhundt was an awkward rider, Marcus was surprised to see, possibly even as bad as he was. He guided Meadow alongside her small Khandarai mount. She was in her usual brown coat and trousers, with her braid coiled and pinned at the back of her neck. Her spectacles were covered in bits of grit and dust, and she rubbed at them ineffectually with the back of one hand.

"Miss Alhundt," Marcus said, "what exactly do you think you're doing?"

"Observing," she said. "His Grace commanded me to be an observer, and to do that I must observe, don't you think?"

"You can observe from the rear. The firing line is no place for a—" He almost said "woman," but sensed this would not go far toward convincing her. "—a civilian."

"From the rear I wouldn't be able to see. I'm not averse to danger, Captain."

"This isn't the opera," Marcus snapped. "Men are going to be *dying* here in a few minutes."

She nodded, unimpressed.

"Besides," he said, "if our line breaks—"

"I would be safer in the rear?" She raised an eyebrow. "That seems unlikely, unless you think the Redeemers would neglect to pillage the supply train. In fact, a position near the front makes it more likely that I would be killed outright in the event of a serious defeat, which frankly I would find preferable to the alternative."

"But—"

"It's all right, Captain," Janus said from behind him. "I asked Miss Alhundt to attend us."

Marcus turned in his saddle. "*You* asked her?"

"Of course." He gave a thin smile. "I would not want the Minister of Information to think I had anything to conceal."

Miss Alhundt's expression turned stubborn, and she seemed about to argue, but he cut her off.

"Miss Alhundt, you have just come from the wagon train, I believe?"

She nodded, disconcerted. "Yes. Why?"

"Did you happen to note what His Grace Prince Exopter was doing?"

Her lips twitched. "Hiding, last I saw. He disappeared into that giant wagon of his around the time the Redeemer cavalry attacked, and hasn't come out since."

"I see. A pity." Janus glanced at Marcus. "I invited His Grace to witness this as well, you see. I think it will prove an interesting lesson."

I wish I had half his confidence. Marcus looked back at the still-forming line. The Preacher had unlimbered his guns in the gaps between battalions, and some of his men were leading the teams back to a safe distance, while the rest started loading. Each round of case shot looked a bit like a battered tin bucket, closed at both ends, and the ammunition rattled and clanged as the gunners forced it down the barrels.

As the troops came into position and lapsed into stillness, all eyes were to the east, where the cloud of dust rising above the enemy host loomed larger every minute. Here and there, when a breeze cleared a patch, it was possible to see them—a seething mass of brown and black covering the narrow plain from the shore to the north to the edge of the southern ridge.

There seemed to be no end to the Khandarai army. If it really deserved the name "army." On the whole, Marcus thought not. It seemed to be more of a mob—no units, not even an attempt at organization, just a huge sea of humanity pressing forward in the desire to get to grips with the foe. Here and there he could pick out Redeemer priests, wrapped head to heel in black, walking backward in front of their flock so they could continue their harangues.

The "soldiers" of this force would have been almost laughable in any other context. They were the sweepings of Ashe-Katarion, the poor fools who dwelt in the gutters and tenements, summoned to war by the priests' promises of retribution in this world and rewards in the next. Each was armed with whatever he had had to hand. There were swords and spears, a few muskets and blunderbusses, but also hoes, picks, and cudgels.

But there were so *many* of them. Twenty thousand, the reports had said; Marcus had no way to count them, but they seemed to go on forever. The flat ground around the road was fairly narrow, only a mile or so from the sea to the hills, and the Khandarai covered it like a swarm of locusts. Their charge would swamp the thin Vordanai line, and even if it didn't, the flanks were vulnerable. It would be easy for the Redeemers to circle around the edges and take the line of blue from the rear.

We were fools to leave the fort, Marcus thought. The ancient sandstone walls might have been useless against a modern army, but they certainly would have sufficed against this mob. Now, in the open, the Redeemers could bring their numbers to bear.

The leading edge of the host had advanced to within long cannon range. Some of them obviously knew it, and a shiver seemed to go through the whole force as individuals paused, tensed, waiting for the distant puffs of smoke and the scream of cannonballs. When it didn't come, they pressed onward, driven forward by those behind them.

Closer, and closer still. When it became obvious that no fire was forthcoming from the Vordanai line, the Khandarai began to howl, and the priests sent up their weird, high-pitched cry. The swarm surged forward.

Janus had a pair of lieutenants by his side to act as runners, and he summoned them with a crook of his finger.

"I will give the order to fire myself," he said. "Make sure that's understood. Any man who shoots beforehand will have a great deal to answer for."

The young men scampered off. Marcus watched them go, then turned back to the approaching horde. They were in easy cannon range now. The Preacher's guns ought to have been pounding them, cannonballs snatching great gaps in those tight-packed ranks, carrying men away by the dozen. It might not have been enough—Marcus wasn't sure if anything would be enough—but it would be something. But Janus had ordered them loaded with double case, two rounds of tight-packed musket balls in thin metal shells, converting each piece into something like a giant shotgun. At close range, the effect would be fearful, but the wasted opportunity for fire made Marcus wince.

The priests were ahead of the wave of men, urging them on with their song and their example. There was a slight slope up toward the Vordanai position, but the attackers slowed only a little. The front ranks, composed of those men most eager for blood, were a solid line of bristling steel of every description.

Marcus spared a glance for his own men. The triple-ranked battalions stood, still as statues, muskets already loaded and at the ready. Here and there, Marcus saw a man turn to look anxiously over his shoulder, as though to make sure the road was still open behind them in case a hasty flight became necessary. The sergeants, prowling behind the ranks, raised a shout if any man looked for too long.

Steady, Marcus decided, but only for the moment. Mor wasn't the only one who'd worked out the odds. The Old Colonials hadn't survived in Khandar by fighting unwinnable battles. As for the recruits, Marcus could remember the balance of pride and terror he'd felt the first time he'd gone into action. The pride would hold them for a while, but if that balance tipped toward terror they'd break badly. When that happened, the whole line would give way at once.

The colonel looked at the approaching enemy, gray eyes shining, nothing on his face but serene confidence. He seemed almost a different man here on the battlefield, as though some madness had taken hold of him. Val had told him that camp gossip said the colonel was insane. Marcus hadn't paid it any mind, since soldiers said the same of practically every officer who made a decision they didn't agree with. Now, though, looking at the gleam in those huge eyes—

He glanced at Miss Alhundt, and found her looking at Janus as well. When she turned to Marcus, their gazes met, and a spark of understanding leapt between them. *She sees it, too*. Marcus was filled with a sudden terror—if he really *was* mad, it was too late, too late to do anything but run—

The cries of the Redeemers drew his eyes forward again. They'd started their sprint too early, Marcus could see, a common mistake among green troops. It was easy to misjudge distances, and the men were always eager to start running. Now they were slowing to a trot or a walk, clumping up as the wave behind them pressed on. Here and there, knots of men hesitated, intimidated by the wall of silent Vordanai uniforms and the sight of the waiting guns. But the majority came on, to two hundred yards, legs pumping as they pushed themselves back into a run. One hundred.

Fire! Marcus wanted to scream. They'd get in two volleys, if they were lucky. The cannon would take a frightful toll. *Fire!* But he held silent.

The screams turned triumphant. The leading edge of the horde spread out as men broke into a dead sprint, weapons flailing. They had barely forty feet of ground to cover. Even placid Meadow shied at the cries, and Miss Alhundt's horse shifted nervously backward, though Janus kept his mount under expert control. The Vordanai line hadn't even fixed bayonets—it was going to be slaughter—

Marcus turned desperately to the colonel, only to find Janus looking back at him. His gray eyes were sparkling, and a hint of a smile played at the corner of his mouth.

"Fire," he said.

"Fire!" Marcus roared.

He was drowned out by the crash of muskets. What resulted was not the blast of a single volley, but a rapid, rising thunder as the firing spread from the center of the line to the flanks, like flame racing along a fuse. Half a second after it had begun, Marcus heard the deep *crump* of the guns speaking as one.

Double canister at ten yards. Oh, saints and martyrs. Even in the midst of shock and terror, Marcus had a moment to feel pity for the charging men. The bucket-like case shot would disintegrate when the main charge went off, carrying its load of half-inch balls outward like a giant load of buckshot. Those balls retained enough force to kill at five hundred yards; from thirty feet, they would hit like the hammer of God.

For a moment, between the blinding flash of musketry and the billowing smoke, he could see nothing. As the roar died away, it took the bloodthirsty shrieks of the Redeemers with it, and a moment of shocked silence seemed to fall across both armies. Then, as though on command, the wails of the wounded rose like the screams of the hosts of hell.

The volley had gone through the Redeemer host like a reaper's scythe through wheat. Corpses lay three-, four-, five-deep in front of the Vordanai line, mixed with wounded men and here and there a few who had come through miraculously unscathed. In front of the guns, there were no such fortunates, and not even any corpses recognizable as such. Pieces lay scattered like dismembered dolls, legs and arms and shattered skulls, men who had been hit by a dozen balls and torn to shreds. For an instant the field of fire of each piece was clearly visible, a giant cone of fallen men spreading back through the horde as though swept by a giant broom, while those to either side stood stunned into insensibility.

In deference to the shouts of their officers, the blue-clad soldiers did not stop to admire their handiwork. Ramrods rattled as the triple line reloaded. They were still slow, and a quick man might have been able to sprint through the field of corpses and reach them, but none of the Khandarai even tried. In less than a minute musketry started to roll again, not all at once but unit by unit as lieutenants called for fire. The pall of smoke was stabbed again and again by yellow-pink fire, and Marcus could hear more screams.

Something had been hanging in the balance, some equilibrium between the stunned immobility of the Khandarai survivors and the pressure of the still-eager men behind them, shielded from the fire by distance and the bodies of their comrades. The second volley tipped the balance, and men started to run. Some were fleeing, some running toward their tormentors. Some, unable to breast the current of men behind them, ran sideways along the ranks of Vordanai like ducks in a shooting gallery. When the third volley exploded, those few who'd tried to reach the blue line went down with it. One by one, the guns spat a second discharge of lethal projectiles. The Preacher aimed at the thickest points in the crowd, where those trying to flee met those coming up from behind, and the fire cut them down in clumps.

Then there were no more men trying to close, or even pressing forward from the rear. The whole vast host was in flight, panic spreading from man to man like a plague, until even those who hadn't gotten close enough to taste the smoke were throwing down their weapons to speed their flight. Only the black-clad priests tried to stem the rout, and few listened to their entreaties. One cluster sent up their high-pitched song yet again, and it moved something in their followers. A knot of men started to gather around them, accreting more as these brave few grabbed their comrades bodily and turned them back to face their foes. It lasted until the Preacher took notice. One of the guns growled, sending a storm of metal in their direction. Priests and men were blasted to bloody ruin, and the rout resumed.

The colonel turned back to Marcus. His smile was gone, but his eyes still sparkled.

"The men are to fix bayonets and advance. Keep the pressure on. They may make a stand around their camp." Then he did smile, slightly. "Oh, and a message to Captain Stokes. Tell him the leash is slipped. Tell him"—Janus paused—"tell him to give them hell."

Even a half mile down the road, leaving the scene of the slaughter behind, the plain was still dotted with corpses. Some wounded men had made it this far before their legs gave out. Others had been cut down by Give-Em-Hell's pursuing horsemen. Janus had instructed that quarter was to be offered to those who asked for it, but thus far few had, preferring to trust to their legs rather than the mercies of the foreigners.

Marcus rode slowly, feeling dazed. What had seemed like an eternity while it was happening now felt like a flash, an instantaneous transition. A few minutes separated certain doom from total victory. The men had seemed to take it in stride, setting off after the Khandarai with a chorus of cheers and yells, but Marcus was having more difficulty.

He couldn't have known. It nagged at him like a broken tooth, best avoided but unavoidable. *He* couldn't *have known.* There had been a moment, just a moment, after the first volley had slammed out. A matter of thirty seconds or so, when *nothing* had protected the Vordanai line, not even bayonets. *If they'd pushed the charge home, that line would have shattered like glass. Every man for himself, and damn the consequences.* Marcus was certain that he himself had been only an instant from putting the spurs to Meadow and riding for it. Perhaps that was what rankled.

It hadn't worked out that way, of course. *But he* couldn't *have known they'd break. Not for certain.* Janus had tossed the dice, and they'd come up sixes, but the thought of what might have been made Marcus' stomach roil.

Even worse, he didn't know *why.* Why hold fire for so long? Why deploy to meet that giant horde at all? He wanted to march up to the colonel and demand an explanation, but that simply wasn't done. Colonels were under no obligation to explain their battle plans to subordinates.

If he was overconfident before this, now there'll be no stopping him. Marcus thought of the strange light in those gray eyes and shivered. "He couldn't have known." *But he acted as though he had.*

"You seem troubled, Captain."

Marcus hadn't realized he'd spoken aloud, or that Miss Alhundt had been riding alongside him. He looked up into her dirty spectacles and managed a sickly grin.

"Apologies, Miss Alhundt. I didn't see you there."

She waved a hand. "You were preoccupied. I merely wondered with what."

"Tired," Marcus said. "Just tired."

That was true enough. The nervous energy had gone out of him like water out of a bath when the plug was pulled, leaving him feeling unutterably empty. He wanted nothing more than to find a bed and sleep, for all that it was only midafternoon. But he couldn't—not yet. There was more work to be done. Messengers had already carried his orders to the troops, telling them to re-form at the edges of the Redeemer camp and set guards while details of picked men rounded up the prisoners. He wanted no wanton violence toward civilians, and in this at least Janus had agreed with him. The tedious, grisly business of tending the wounded and burying the dead would last long into the evening as it was.

Miss Alhundt's horse stepped daintily over a dead man in the road, lying on his face with his back slashed open by a cavalry saber.

"I must admit I had a moment of doubt when the Redeemers came so close. It seemed risky." She caught his eye. "But I'm not a military expert."

Marcus' lip twitched. He said nothing, but he was sure she could read everything she needed in his expression.

"And yet," she went on, "this is certainly a victory. Even His Grace can have no cause for complaint."

Enough is enough. "What are you getting at, Miss Alhundt? What do you want from me?"

"I want to know where your loyalty lies."

"Where it always has," Marcus growled. "With king, country, and the chain of command."

"In that order?"

"I'm not going to play word games with you."

"It's not a game, Captain. I need your help."

Just for a moment, Marcus thought he saw something genuine

in her expression. The coy, clever smile was still in place, but there was something in her eyes. It was the look of someone treading water over an infinite abyss. Then she turned away.

"What's that?" she said.

"What?"

"That." She pointed with one hand. "The smoke. Has there been more fighting, do you think?"

Marcus lifted his eyes. Beyond the next bend in the road, a column of smoke was rising. It wasn't the gray-white color of powder smoke, which in any event tended to hug the ground like fog. This was the thick black smoke of burning wood and canvas, burning wagons and stores and blankets—

"Brass Balls of the Beast," Marcus snarled, kicking Meadow to a trot. "What the hell have they gotten into?"

CHAPTER EIGHT

WINTER

Winter hiked wearily back toward the ravine where she'd left what remained of her company. The immediate aftermath of the Redeemer's attack had been a desperate scramble to rescue what wounded they could and then run for the nearest cover. They'd ended up in a wind-carved defile through the high ridge, narrow enough at both ends to be easily defended. Only then had Winter felt secure enough to give most of the company a rest, while she and Bobby picked a cautious path up the empty hillside to find out what had happened.

When they returned, Graff shouted the men awake. Most of the survivors had dropped wherever they'd halted, sprawled across the narrow floor of the ravine like a blanket of corpses. But the corporal's yell produced a miraculous resurrection, and as Bobby related the good news the buzz of conversation spread, punctuated by whoops and hollers. Winter pushed her way through the jubilant throng and found Graff.

"Good to see you back safe, Sergeant," he said.

"Thanks." She jerked her head in Bobby's direction. "You've heard?"

"I'm not sure I believe it."

"We had the whole story from a couple of Give-Em-Hell's

outriders," Winter said. "From the top of the hill you can see the Redeemer camp burning."

"Nice to get good news for once," Graff said.

"Better than the alternative," Winter agreed. "But we've still got a bit of a walk ahead of us, and it'd be best to make it before dark. How many of the wounded need to be carried?"

The corporal counted on grubby fingers. "Fox . . . Inimin . . . Gaff . . . Regult . . ." He looked up. "Four, I think."

"What about Eiderson?" Winter wasn't good with names, but she was starting to remember a few. Eiderson was a big, blond man with a sarcastic manner, prone to sneers, but he'd screamed loudest of all when they'd carried him from the battlefield with a carbine ball through the thigh.

"He died," Graff said quietly. "An hour or so back."

"Oh." Winter felt guilty that this news didn't affect her more. "Four, then. Eight men to carry them, and four more just in case. Bobby and I will stay with them. Can you take the rest of the men ahead?"

Graff frowned. "There could still be Redeemers about. Best to stick together."

She shook her head. "The outriders said we're in the clear. The more men we get back to a camp by nightfall, the less worried I'll be."

"As you say, Sergeant," Graff said. "Take Folsom as well, then. I can ride herd on the others."

Winter glanced up at the sun. It had touched the horizon, and lurking under the still-stifling heat she could feel the chill of the desert night, waiting to pounce.

They rigged stretchers for the four wounded men out of muskets and torn jackets, and fashioned makeshift torches from scraps and scrub grass for when night fell. Graff set off first, with the balance of the company, promising he'd send riders to escort them the rest of the way once he reached the regiment. Winter and her small party left the ravine just after sunset, picking their way down the center of the valley where the land was flattest. The wounded men whimpered and moaned, and any false step that jolted them produced heartrending screams.

At first the stretcher bearers and their escorts kept up a lively chatter, Bobby among them, though Folsom had reverted to his usual silence and walked silently at Winter's shoulder. As twilight deepened from red to purple, though, the gathering darkness smothered conversation like a shroud. The four unburdened men lit their torches, which gave enough light to place their feet by, but no more. They filled the valley with flickering, dancing shadows, decorating every rock with a long black streamer.

A column of smoke was visible, rising from burning Redeemer stores and blotting out a chunk of the darkening sky. Winter directed them toward it, which was the direction the valley ran in any case. She'd intended to skirt the base of the conflagration once she arrived, but at ground level it was more of a cloud than a bonfire, with no clear edges. They were in the Khandarai camp, or the remains of it, before they realized it.

There was actually very little to mark it as a camp of any sort. There were no neat lines of tents, as in the Vordanai encampments. Bedrolls and sheets were scattered at random, interspersed with crude lean-tos of linen and sticks. Amidst these were all the detritus of an army on the march—weapons, spare or broken, sacks of meal or fruit, bones and offal from butchered animals, bits of clothing left behind for the final march into battle.

Most of what would burn had been blackened by fire, and here and there fitful embers still smoldered, sending up choking black smoke. Before long, full dark arrived, and the circle of light cast by the torches defined the limit of their vision. They walked in silence, objects coming into view a few paces ahead and falling into oblivion after they'd passed, like floating wreckage flowing around a ship under sail.

Winter barely noticed the first body, blackened and charred by flame, curled into a ball amidst the crisped ruins of a bedroll. Only the skull marked it as something that had once been human. The next, though, was a ragged man coated crimson from a dozen wounds in the back, lying facedown in the dirt. Past him was a man with a spear still in his hand, the side of his head shot away by a musket ball. From then on, as they entered the center of the camp, they encountered more and more corpses, until they all had to tread carefully to avoid crushing stiff, outflung fingers or stumbling over twisted limbs.

There were women, too, Winter realized with a start. Some, dressed in rags and curled around the wounds that had killed them, were indistinguishable from the men, but this far into the camp any resistance had apparently collapsed, and the victors had found time for a bit of sport. They passed one body naked and spread-eagled, her throat cut in a ragged red half circle like a broad grin. Elsewhere the torchlight revealed the pale buttocks of three women laid facedown in a row, robes hiked up to their armpits. A gray-bearded old man lay nearby, killed by a single shot to the chest.

It went on, and on, and on. Winter wanted to scream, but she didn't dare. Inside the smoke cloud, she had no way to navigate, so all she could do was lead her men on a straight course and pray they'd come through it eventually. She watched the faces of the men in the flickering light. Folsom, behind her, might have been carved of stone, but Bobby's eyes were wide as saucers. The boy had dropped back when they found the first corpse, and with each successive discovery he pressed closer to her side. Winter reached out and found his hand with hers, tentatively. She wasn't sure if the gesture was unmanly, but Bobby twined his fingers through hers, and gripped tight.

She felt an odd need to explain, to make excuses. *It's war. This is what it's always been like. After a battle, when their blood is up, men will do things they'd never consider otherwise.* But her throat was too tight to speak, and the burning camp had the heavy, unbreakable silence of a cathedral.

Winter wondered how much of the devastation had been wrought by the Old Colonials and how much by the recruits. She had a depressing feeling that she knew the answer. Old Colonel Warus had taken a dim view of rape and pillage when it was committed under his eye, but he hadn't troubled to extend that eye very far. And when a village had been suspected of harboring bandits or rebels . . .

They were not the only ones in the camp, though no living person strayed into the circle of firelight. Other torches moved here and there, bobbing among the slowly dying flames like distant will-o'-the-wisps. Alone, or in groups of two or three, they picked their way through the ruins. In search of plunder, presumably, though there was little of value that Winter could see. She could hear them at times, too, rough voices calling to one another over the crackle and spit of the flames.

It seemed they'd been walking for hours in silence, and even the cries of the four wounded men were muffled. When Winter heard a low, agonized groan, she assumed it came from her party, but it was followed by a hiss and a muffled curse. She stopped, and held her palm up to halt the others.

Bobby's hand tightened convulsively, then slipped free.

"What is it, sir?" the boy said.

"I heard something," Winter said. "Someone's alive, near here."

The soldiers looked at each other. One of them, a sandy-haired youth holding one end of a stretcher, spoke up.

"Are you sure?" he said.

"I heard it, too," Folsom rumbled, and pointed. "Over that way."

The soldier glanced at his companions, then shrugged. "So what? It's got to be a grayskin."

"It could be one of ours," Winter lied. The curse she'd heard had been in Khandarai. "We can't just leave him." She surveyed their faces and came to a quick decision. "You keep on. The camp can't be much farther. If we can find him, Corporals Forester and Folsom will help me bring him in."

The man nodded. Another soldier kindled an extra torch and handed it to Folsom. The stretcher bearers and their escort trooped off, leaving Winter and the two corporals alone.

Bobby made a visible effort to control himself, shifting his musket from one hand to the other and shaking out stiff fingers where he'd gripped it too tightly. He took several long breaths and then turned to Winter, determination written in his face. Winter found her respect for him increasing. He was obviously scared, even terrified, and equally obviously determined not to let it prevent him from doing as he was ordered. Folsom, as usual, was impassive.

"Right," she said. "Let's go."

They walked in the direction of the sound, past torn blankets and smoking piles of rubbish. Corpses were everywhere, sprawled in attitudes of fear and flight where they'd been cut down by their pursuers. Winter forced herself to look around, searching for movement. Bobby cupped his hands to his mouth and shouted a greeting, but it produced no reply, and he didn't repeat it.

Then Winter caught a flicker of motion. She pointed.

"There!"

There was an overturned wagon, a dead horse still tangled in the traces. Someone crouched behind it, a dark shadow against the dull red light from distant fires. Winter stepped forward, hands spread, trying to look nonthreatening.

"Hello?" she said, then tried again in Khandarai. *"Keipho?"*

She half expected whoever it was to flee. She certainly did not expect the enormous shadow that rose up from behind the broken wagon, eyes glowing with reflected torchlight. It roared like a bull, a deep, animal sound with no human language in it, and charged.

It was a man, she could see, tall and thick-limbed, shirtless, with a hairy white belly that strained at his belt. His face was wild with rage, and in his hands was a curved sword half as long as Winter was tall. He vaulted the dead horse in a single stride, weapon held above his head.

From Winter's right came a *bang* that shattered the stillness like a rock through a pane of glass. Smoke billowed from Bobby's musket, but the boy had pulled the trigger before getting the weapon level, and the ball whined off into the night. The giant barely broke his stride, headed straight for Winter, his blade raised for a two-handed downward cut that would have chopped her in half.

Folsom stepped into his path, bulling forward underneath the stroke so that the pommel of the sword glanced off his shoulder. The corporal had let his musket fall, but he still held the torch in his left hand, and he pressed it against the giant's back. The big man roared, and his knee came up and buried itself in Folsom's stomach. Folsom gave a grunt and staggered backward, and the Khandarai came around with a backhand slap that lifted him off his feet and sent him sprawling in the dust.

Winter dove for the musket Folsom had dropped, rolled, and brought it to her shoulder as she came up. The Khandarai had his sword raised once more, this time to decapitate the fallen corporal, and Winter had the whole of his broad back as a target. She pulled back the hammer, hoped like hell the jostling hadn't spilled the powder in the pan, and pulled the trigger.

The *bang* of the weapon sounded sweet in her ear, and even the mule kick against her shoulder was reassuring. She saw dust fly from the giant where she'd hit him, and he went suddenly still, sword held high. The ball had gone in near the small of his back, and she could see blood begin to spurt, but he gave no sign of pain. Instead he turned, slowly, revealing a matching hole in his gut. His sword still raised, he took first one step toward Winter, then another.

Die, Winter begged, half a prayer. *Die, please just die!* But he came on, blood gouting down the curve of his belly in regular pulses. She raised the musket in a halfhearted attempt to block his downward blow, knowing he could easily hammer the weapon aside.

Another *bang* from behind her, and the huge man sprouted another gaping red wound, this time high on his chest. He staggered like a drunk, grounding the point of his sword as though he meant to lean on it. Then finally, mercifully, he toppled, with one last roar that was more like a moan. The impact of his collapse seemed to shake the ground, and for a long moment Winter couldn't look away, fearing that he would once again clamber to his feet. When she finally managed to look over her shoulder, she saw Bobby standing with a leveled musket, smoke rising from the lock and barrel.

Folsom groaned, and the sound seemed to break the spell. Winter rolled over and managed to get to her knees, and Bobby let his weapon fall and hurried to her side.

"Sergeant!" he said. "Sir! Are you all right?"

"Fine," Winter said, when she had the breath. "He didn't touch me. Check on Folsom."

But the big corporal was already getting to his feet. The left side of his face was blotchy and smeared with blood from a few small cuts, but he waved away Bobby's offered hand and went to Winter's side. Together, the two of them hoisted her to her feet and helped her remain there, in spite of some unsteadiness around the knees.

"What?" Bobby said. "What in the name of all the saints was that?"

"Goddamned monster," Folsom muttered.

"He was a *fin-katar*," Winter said. Her own voice sounded distant through the blood rushing in her ears.

The two of them looked at her. "A what?" Bobby said.

"A *fin-katar*," Winter repeated. "It means 'a divine shield.' They're kind of a holy order. The personal guards of the Khandarai priesthood." She frowned. "The *old* priests. Not the Redeemers."

Folsom frowned. "How d'you know?"

"Look at the size of him," Winter said. "They all look like that. The priests do something to them."

The big corporal made the sign of the double circle over his heart. "Sorcery."

"I've heard it said," Winter said. "Or some trick with powders and potions. Someone once told me the *fin-katar* eat only poison pear and drink only scorpion venom." Her brain felt like it was slowly starting to work again. "What the hell was he doing *here*, though?"

"Plenty of priests with this army, looked like," Bobby said.

"The Redeemers hate the old priesthood," Winter said. "They blame them for leading the people astray in the first place."

Folsom shook his head. "Infidels."

Winter hadn't known the big man was particularly pious, but then she knew little enough about him. Or any of them, for that matter.

"You can't tell me *that* was what we heard moaning," Bobby said, eyeing the enormous corpse.

"No." As her heart calmed, weariness seeped back into Winter's limbs. She found that she'd suddenly lost her taste for her mission of mercy. "But maybe we ought to go back. God only knows who else is hiding somewhere around here."

Folsom nodded fervently. His cheek was already purpling into what promised to be a hideous bruise. Bobby looked less certain, though.

"It sounded like it came from somewhere close," the boy said. "Maybe—"

Another voice, thin and papery, like the whisper of a ghost. "Please. I'm here."

Bobby looked around, startled, and Folsom grabbed for one of the muskets. The words, Winter realized after a moment, had been in Khandarai. Neither of the corporals understood the plea as such. She waved them hurriedly to silence and spoke aloud in the same language.

"Where? Where are you?"

"Wagon . . ." The voice was faint. "Please . . ."

Winter looked at the overturned wagon. It was big and solidly constructed, really too much for a single horse. There was a space under it, where the walls held the bed off the ground. The front was blocked by the driver's box, but the back was open where the tailgate had been knocked away.

"Are you underneath?" Winter said, still in Khandarai. "You can come out. We won't hurt you, I swear." The voice sounded young, and probably female.

"Can't," it said. "Stuck." There was a long pause, and then a muffled scream. When it came again, the voice was thick. "I can't . . ."

"Hold on."

Winter went to the wagon, intending to circle to the open tailgate and peer underneath. Halfway there, though, she saw the pale shape of a hand, palm up. Whoever was under the wagon had been caught when it overturned, one arm pinned to the dirt by one of the wooden walls. *No wonder she can't move.* The flesh of the forearm was angry red and purple where the board pressed against it.

"Folsom!" Winter said. "Can you shift this?"

The big corporal approached, looking speculative, and circled around to the rear, where he could get a grip on the bed. He gave it a tentative pull and grimaced.

"Not much," he said. "We'd need a couple more men to flip it."

"Just lift it a little," Winter said. "Only for a minute."

By now he'd seen the hand, and he nodded grimly. He squatted, put both hands under the bed, and straightened up with a grunt. The wagon came up with him, wheels spinning slowly.

The girl screamed, high and piercing. Winter took one look at her outflung arm, which had an extra bend above the elbow where the wagon had been resting, and knelt down to grab her by the legs instead. She scrabbled for a moment in the semidarkness under the wagon, uncomfortably aware of the weight that would crash down on her back if Folsom's strength failed him, until she managed to get a grip and pull. The girl slid free, but her broken arm shifted, and she gave another shriek right in Winter's ear. Bobby grabbed her shoulders as they emerged and pulled her away from the wagon, and Folsom let the weight fall back to earth with a crash.

"Are you all right?" Winter asked in Khandarai. She got no response, and when she leaned closer she could see that the girl's eyes showed only the whites. Her gray skin seemed unnaturally pale.

"Dead?" Bobby asked.

Winter shook her head. The girl's chest moved, breath coming shallow and fast.

"Passed out, I think. Her arm's broken." At first glance, there didn't seem to be any other wounds. "We'll have to carry her."

"Carry her where?" Bobby said.

"Back to camp," Winter said. "And—"

"To a regimental surgeon?" Bobby said.

That brought Winter up short. If the officers were turning a blind eye to rape and murder, she doubted the surgeons would have much time for an injured grayskin.

"Back to my tent, then," Winter said. She wondered if someone had set up their tents, or if they'd all been written off for dead.

"Someone will see," Bobby said. "What are you going to tell them?"

There was a long pause while Winter chewed her lip.

"Wrap her in a blanket," Folsom said, dusting off his hands. "Another wounded man carried into camp. Nobody'll notice."

Winter looked down at the unconscious girl. She had a heart-shaped face, gray skin dusted with soot, and long, dark hair that was a mass of dirt and tangles. She wore only a simple gray robe, cinched at the waist with a wispy cord belt. Winter guessed she was younger than Bobby.

"We'll try it," she said. "And then I'll think of something."

Getting the girl into camp was easier than Winter had dared hope. The Colonials had raised their tents upwind of the burning Redeemer camp, within easy distance of the little brook as it emerged from the valley and ran into the sea. The city of blue canvas was the same shape and size as ever, as though nothing had happened, and the sentries only looked them over briefly and then waved them through.

The Seventh Company's tents had indeed been erected along with the rest. Winter saw no one as she and the two corporals threaded their way to her own dwelling. It was after full dark, and if the rest of the men were as exhausted as she was, they were no doubt sound asleep. The need to collapse was almost overwhelming, but she held it off for the moment.

Folsom let the girl down on Winter's pallet. Her eyes were tightly closed now, and Winter couldn't tell if she was awake or not. A soft moan escaped her lips as her broken arm touched the ground.

"That needs tending," Folsom said.

Winter, finally sitting, was wondering if her legs would actually drop off. She gave a weak nod.

"Fetch . . ." She paused. Someone in the company had set broken arms before, surely, but inquiring openly would give the game away. "Bobby, fetch Graff. You'll probably have to wake him." The gruff corporal was a veteran. Doubtless he'd dealt with this sort of thing before.

"Right," Bobby said. The boy's eyes were bright with exhaustion, but he went nonetheless.

Folsom grunted and left the tent as well, returning a few moments later with a cracker of hardtack and a block of Khandarai cheese in one hand and a canteen in the other. These he offered to Winter, who took them gratefully. She'd had nothing to eat since morning but a few crumbs gobbled in haste in the ravine, and even dry the hardtack was welcome. The cheese was a touch overripe, but she sliced and devoured it anyway, and washed it down with the lukewarm water.

Graff pushed his way in, rubbing sleepy eyes, with Bobby behind him.

"Glad to see you made it, Sergeant," he said, "but I don't see—" He stopped when he saw the girl on the pallet. "Who's this, then?"

"We picked her up in the camp," Winter said quietly. "Her arm's broken. Can you do anything for her?"

Graff looked from Winter's face to Bobby's, uncertain. Then he shrugged.

"I'm no cutter, but I could wrap a splint. Did it break the skin?"

"Not that I saw," Winter said.

"Should be all right, then," he said. "It's not likely to fester, anyway. I'll need some clean cloth, and a length of board."

Bobby left again to fetch the supplies, and Graff went to the pallet to examine the girl. He nodded approvingly.

"Looks like a nice clean break," he said. Then, glancing at the tent flap, he lowered his voice. "Sergeant, are you sure you know what you're doing?"

"No," Winter said truthfully. "But you saw the camp, didn't you?"

Graff shifted uncomfortably. "It's war."

"We heard her calling, and . . ." Winter shrugged. "I couldn't just leave her there."

The corporal was silent for a long moment. "Fair enough," he said, after a while. "The colonel said that we're staying camped here for at least another day, for the sake of the wounded. Hopefully she'll be well enough that we can turn her loose by the time we march."

"Thank you, Graff."

He colored slightly under his beard. "Not my place to question the sergeant's decisions."

Winter laughed, and Graff smiled.

"'Sides," he said gruffly, "it's us that should be thanking you. Every man of us. Even if most of those out there don't know it, I do. If you'd let them keep running, we'd all have ended up on spits."

Winter was taken aback. "I—it was just the right thing to do. You could have seen that as well as I did."

"Should have," Graff said. "But it was you that did it."

She nodded awkwardly. The conversation was interrupted when Bobby returned, bearing a selection of boards and a spare sheet ripped into strips. Graff took these implements and set to work, rolling the girl onto her back and gently stretching her arm out along the pallet. Her eyelids flickered, and she moaned again.

"Folsom, hold her down," Graff said. "Can't have her shifting about on us. Sergeant, she's going to scream . . ."

Winter cast about, found one of her discarded socks, and wadded it up. Murmuring apologies, she pushed it into the girl's slack mouth. Graff nodded and began his work. The flesh of the broken arm moved sickeningly under his fingers, and Winter had to look away. The girl's jaw tightened on the sock, as though she wanted to bite through it, but she gave no sound. After a few moments, the procedure was done, and Graff was winding her arm round with linen.

"That should hold it," he said. "If she starts to show fever, we'll have to unwrap it and take a look. If it's festered after all, then the arm will have to come off." He caught Winter's eye. "And don't look to me for *that*."

Winter nodded. "Thanks again."

"It's nothing." He tied the linen off and got to his feet. "Now, if the sergeant will excuse me, I'll be going back to bed."

"Go," Winter said. "All of you. Get some sleep."

"What about her?" Bobby said. "Someone should watch her. What if she wakes up?"

"Hopefully she'll have enough sense to stay quiet," Winter said.

"Or she'll slit your throat," Graff said. "She's a grayskin, after all's said and done."

Winter gave a tired shrug. "If you find me with my throat slit in the morning, you'll know what's happened."

The three corporals grumbled a bit more, but in the end they left. Winter gathered the sheet and pillow from her bedroll to soften the hard earth, and stretched out. It was lumpy and uncomfortable, but she was asleep the instant her eyes closed.

Jane sat beside Winter on a long bench, watching Mrs. Wilmore lecture on the nature of charity.

Winter was afraid to turn her head. There were proctors prowling about, with sharp eyes and vicious switches. But she could catch glimpses of Jane out of the corner of her eye, red hair falling around her face like a curtain of dark crimson silk. She could *smell* her, even under the deep, earthy scent they all carried from working in the Prison gardens.

She could feel Jane's hand on her knee, thumb rubbing tiny circles through coarse fabric. Inch by inch, the hand ventured higher, fingers exploring her thigh like mariners venturing into uncharted waters. Her skin pebbled into goose bumps, and her throat was tight. She wanted to tell Jane to stop, certain that at any moment she would hear the whistle of a proctor's stick. And she also wanted to grab Jane by the shoulders, press her close—

"You still have it?" Jane said. Her fingers slid farther upward, Winter's skirt bunching around them.

Winter risked turning her head, but Jane wasn't looking at her. Her eyes were hidden by the fall of her hair.

"Do I have what?" Winter whispered.

"The knife," Jane said, too loud. "You have to bring the knife—"

Light, filtered gray-blue through canvas. It took Winter a moment to remember where she was—not back in the Prison, nor back in the ravine, with Khandarai horsemen all around, but safe in her tent in the midst of the Colonial camp.

And not alone. She sat up from her improvised bed and immediately regretted it. Her body felt like a solid mass of aches and bruises, and the sweat and grime of the previous day had dried into a crust on her skin. She leaned forward, clutching her head, and groped for a canteen. The water was tepid, but it cut through the dust in her mouth.

The Khandarai girl lay on the bedroll beside her. She was exactly where they'd left her the night before, and so still it was a moment before Winter realized that she was awake. Her eyes tracked Winter, but other than that she didn't move a muscle. It reminded Winter of a rabbit, paralyzed by the glare of a stalking fox. Winter cleared her throat and spoke in Khandarai.

"It's all right," she said. "We're not going to hurt you."

The girl seemed to unfreeze a little, but made no reply.

"How do you feel?" Winter indicated her own left arm. "Does it hurt badly?"

"Where am I?" the girl said.

Her speech had an almost musical lilt, and Winter was suddenly painfully aware of the grating inadequacy of her Khandarai pronunciation. She'd picked the language up in bits and pieces from books, once she'd taught herself to read the flowing Khandarai script, and she'd practiced in bars and on the street. Unconsciously, she'd adopted the accent, which meant that she sounded distinctly lower-class to Khandarai ears.

"In our camp," Winter said. "This is my tent."

"Camp," the girl said. "The *raschem* camp."

Raschem was "bodies" or "corpses," Khandarai slang for Vordanai and other pale-skinned foreigners. Winter nodded.

The girl suddenly fixed her with a long stare. Her eyes were the peculiar purple-gray common among the Khandarai, which foreigners often found unsettling.

"Why?" she said. "Why did you bring me here?"

"We found you in . . . the burned camp." Winter groped for the words. "We did not want to leave you to die. Do you remember?"

"Remember?" The girl raised her broken, splinted arm. "I am not likely to forget. But I do not understand. Your soldiers were killing everyone. Taking the women first, and then—" Her gray skin paled. "Have you brought me to—"

"No," Winter said hastily. "Nothing like that. I swear."

"Then why?" The purple eyes were mistrustful.

Winter felt like she couldn't muster a sufficient explanation in her native language, let alone pick her way through it in Khandarai. She changed the subject.

"My name is Winter," she said. "Winter-dan-Ihernglass, you would say." She mustered the politest language she had. "May I know yours?"

"Feor," the girl said. Catching Winter's expression—Khandarai invariably went by both given and family names—she added, "Just Feor. I am a mistress of the gods. We give up our other names." She looked warily around the tent. "May I have some water?"

Winter handed the canteen across wordlessly, and Feor took it in her good hand and drank deeply, letting the last drops fall on her tongue. She licked her lips, catlike, and set it carefully aside.

"I'll get some more," Winter said. "And some food. You must be hungry."

When she started to rise, the girl held up a hand. "Wait."

Obediently, Winter stopped and sat down again. Feor fixed her with that peculiar gaze.

"I am your prisoner?"

Winter shook her head. "Not a prisoner. Not really. We just wanted to help you."

"Then I can leave as I please?"

"No!" Winter sighed. "If you go out into the camp, someone really will take you prisoner. Or just kill you, or—"

Realization dawned on the girl's face. "They don't know. The others, they don't know that you've brought me here."

"Only a few. People I trust." And how had *that* come to be? Winter reflected. She'd known the three corporals for only a few days. Battle worked strange magic sometimes. "We'll figure something out, I promise. But for now you have to stay here."

Feor nodded gravely. "As you say." She put her head on one side. "When you . . . found me, was there a man nearby? A large man, with no hair."

Her face gave no indication of her feelings on the matter. Winter debated briefly.

"Yes," she said eventually. "He's dead."

"Dead," Feor repeated. "Dead. That is good."

Winter stared at her. *A mistress of the gods*, she'd said. A priestess. But a priestess of the old ways—the Redeemer priests were all men, and their faith preached that the leadership of the priestesses of the old temples had been the first step on the path to corruption. Winter had heard them shouting that message on street corners in Ashe-Katarion often enough, before the Redemption had grown into a revolution.

So what was this girl doing in the middle of a Redeemer army? Winter shook her head.

"I'll get us something to eat," she said. Feor gave another grave nod. There was something terribly solemn about her. *Not that she has much reason to smile.*

Outside the tent, the camp looked little different from any of the others they'd pitched on the road from Fort Valor. The same rows of blue tents, the same stands of stacked muskets. Only wisps of dark smoke rising to the west gave any hint of what had happened the day before. *That, and the fact that some of these tents are empty.*

The sun was already high overhead, and the men were up and about. Some tended their weapons, sharpening bayonets or cleaning the powder and grime from musket barrels, while others diced, played cards, or just sat in circles trading stories of the day before. When they caught sight of Winter, they straightened up and saluted. She waved them back to what they had been doing and went in search of Bobby.

She didn't have to look far. The young corporal arrived at a run, hurrying down the line of tents, and practically ran into her. Winter took a hurried step back as Bobby stopped, drew up, and gave a crisp salute. The boy's uniform was clean, and his skin looked freshly scrubbed, though traces of black powder smoke still darkened his sandy hair.

"Good morning, sir!"

"Morning," Winter said. She leaned close and lowered her voice to a whisper. "Do you think you could find some food and water that I could bring back to my tent?"

"Of course!" Bobby smiled. "Wait here, sir."

He dashed off, leaving Winter alone in the midst of her company. She became aware, bit by bit, that the men were watching her. She turned in a slow circle, as though inspecting them, but inside she was baffled. They seemed to want something from her, but Winter was damned if she knew what.

"Er," she said, and a dozen conversations suddenly died. More distant sounds cut through the sudden silence. Shouts, the whinny of horses, wagons creaking. An army camp was never truly quiet, but it seemed as though a great sucking void had sprung up, centered on her. Winter felt the muscles of her throat trying to close in panic. She coughed.

"Hell of a job, yesterday," she said. "All of you. Well done."

A shout rose from a dozen throats at once, any words lost in the roar. All the rest quickly joined in, and for a minute the cheering drowned out all other sound. Winter raised her hands, and it gradually died. Her cheeks were pink.

"Thanks," she said. The cheers immediately resumed. She was rescued by the appearance of Bobby, carrying a pair of canteens and a sack. The corporal was grinning broadly. Winter took him by the shoulder and marched him at an undignified pace back toward her tent.

When the cheers had once again died away, Winter leaned close.

"Did you put them up to that?"

The boy shook his head. "No need, sir. They're not stupid. They know what happened yesterday."

"And they're *cheering*?" Winter didn't feel much like cheering herself. A little under a third of the men under her command had not come back from their first assignment.

"They're alive, aren't they?" Bobby flashed his grin at her. "If we'd followed d'Vries when he ran, we'd all be dead by now. You were the one who got them to make a stand." He coughed delicately. "I think it helps that d'Vries got what was coming to him. Not that you heard me say so, sir."

Contempt dripped from Bobby's voice at this last. It was true, Winter reflected. Soldiers had odd feelings toward their officers. A man could be a bully, like Davis, or a drunkard, like Captain Roston of the Fourth, or a tantrum-throwing martinet, and retain the affection of at least some of those who served under him. But the one thing that no soldier could abide was cowardice. Even Winter, who was an odd sort of soldier at best, found she felt only a cold disregard for the lieutenant who had fled at the first sight of the enemy.

"I didn't . . ." Her voice trailed off. "It was only what needed to be done. Anyone could have seen that."

"But you did." Bobby shrugged, then lowered his voice. "How's our patient?"

"Awake and talking," Winter said. "I've been trying to explain the situation to her."

"What exactly *is* the situation, sir?"

Winter grimaced. "Damned if I know."

Feor tore into the bread and cheese hungrily, only slightly impaired by having only one arm to work with. Bobby watched her intently, until Winter gave him a sidelong glance.

"You've never seen a Khandarai up close, have you?"

"No, sir. Except for yesterday, of course." He hesitated. "Can she understand us?"

"I don't think so." Winter switched to Khandarai. "Feor?"

The girl looked up, mouth full of bread.

"Do you speak Vordanai at all? Our language?"

She shook her head, and went back to eating. Winter passed that along to Bobby.

"You're pretty good with their language," the corporal said.

"I've been here for two years," Winter said.

It wasn't really an explanation—many of the Old Colonials had picked up no more of Khandarai than they needed to order in a tavern or a brothel, but Winter had tried hard to learn the language as she explored the city. Under the current circumstances, though, she thought that her—hobby, call it—might seem vaguely disloyal.

Feor finished the last of the bread, drank from the canteen, and gave a little sigh. Then, as though seeing Bobby for the first time, she sat up a little straighter and resumed her austere expression.

"Thank you," she said.

Winter translated, then said to Feor, "He doesn't speak your language."

She nodded, eyes a little distant, as though pondering something.

"Listen—," Winter began, but the girl raised a hand.

"Let me have a moment, if you would," she said, and took a deep breath. "I am not a fool, Winter-dan-Iherngláss. Or at least I like to think not. I understand what you have done for me. I do not"—her mouth quirked—"I do not *quite* understand why, but my ignorance of your reasons does not diminish the fact that you saved my life, and apparently not to simply make me your slave or your whore." She bowed, first to Winter and then to Bobby, so deep that her forehead nearly touched the ground. "I thank you, both of you."

Winter nodded awkwardly. "She's grateful," she said in response to Bobby's questioning look.

"And as you have given me this gift," the girl went on, "I will not throw it away. Tell me what you need me to do, and I will do it. I trust that, if you meant me harm, you have already had ample opportunity to accomplish it."

Winter gave another nod. She felt a small knot of worry dissolve. If the girl had been stupid, or obstinate, the chances would have been high that she'd not only get herself discovered but that Winter and the others might be punished in the bargain.

"I'm still figuring this out myself," Winter said. "I hope that we can find somewhere safe and let you go, but it may take some time."

Feor inclined her head. "If that is the gods' will."

"If you don't mind, may I ask you a question?"

The girl nodded.

"What were you doing with that army?" Winter shifted awkwardly. "You do not seem like one of"—she fumbled for the Khandarai words—"the men of the Redemption."

Feor laughed. It was the first expression of humor that Winter had seen out of her, and it transformed the severe angles of her face. Her eyes sparkled.

"No," the girl said. "I am not. I was there as a prisoner of Yatchik-dan-Rahksa."

"The . . ." Winter's lips moved silently. "The angel of vengeance?"

"The—" She said another couple of words that Winter didn't know. Seeing the incomprehension, Feor went on. "The high priests of the Redeemers take the names of angels. This one was the leader of the army of the Faithful."

"Why would he bring you along?"

"Because he is ignorant. He thinks—thought—that I would have the power to counter the magic of your leader."

Now it was Winter's turn to laugh. "Our colonel isn't a wizard, at least not that I know of." "Wizard" didn't quite translate properly, but Feor seemed to catch the gist. She shook her head.

"There is a man of power among your army. Malik-dan-Belial warned us, and this close even I can feel it. Yatchik's ignorance was in thinking I would be able to defend him against such a man. What power I have is not of that sort."

"Power? As a mistress of the gods, you mean?" Winter shifted uneasily. The subject of religion made her uncomfortable.

"No." Feor's face went distant again. When she spoke, it was slow and careful, as though speaking was difficult. "I am a *naathem*."

Winter paused. She'd encountered the word before, but a proper translation had always eluded her. The Khandarai seemed to use it to mean "wizard" or "sorcerer," although not quite in the Vordanai sense and without the connotation of evil those words carried to Vordanai ears. Literally it meant "one who has read." But even among Khandarai, *naathem* were the domain of myths or fairy tales. No one she'd ever spoken with had claimed to have met one, any more than a modern Vordanai would have personally seen a demon or a sorcerer.

Bobby, in the silence that followed, looked curiously at Winter. "What did she say?"

"She's a priestess," Winter said. "But not one of the Redeemers. They brought her along because they thought that she would defend them against our magic."

The boy laughed. "Our magic?"

"The Redeemers take that sort of thing seriously."

"So she was a prisoner?" He looked curiously at Feor, who looked back with polite incomprehension.

"I think so." She switched back to Khandarai. "Feor, if you could get away from here, where would you go?"

"Back to Mother," she said, without hesitation. "In Ashe-Katarion. She will be looking for me."

Winter sat back. "She wants to go home," she said to Bobby.

"Don't we all," the boy said.

Not all, Winter thought. Aloud, she said, "Hers is a good deal closer than ours. We may be able to manage something."

A knock at the tent pole interrupted them. "It's Graff."

"Come in," Winter said.

Feor gave the older corporal a nod, and he dipped his head uncertainly in return. To Winter he said, "Is she making any sense?"

"To me, anyway." Winter turned to Feor. "This is Corporal Graff. He's the one who set your arm."

The girl raised the bandaged limb. "Tell him he has done an excellent job."

When Winter repeated that, Graff laughed, and colored a little under his beard. "It wasn't anything difficult, just a little break." He smiled at Feor, then turned to Winter. "Got a message. The colonel wants to see you."

Winter's good mood, always a little fragile, evaporated at once. "What? Why?"

"Didn't say."

"You don't think—" Her eyes flicked to the Khandarai girl.

"No, I doubt it. Anyway, he said 'at your earliest convenience,' which means 'right goddamned now,' so you'd better go."

"Right." Winter scrambled to her feet, then looked down at herself. She felt as though she ought to change clothes, but there was no way to manage it with the three of them in the tent. She desperately wanted a bath as well, but that was out of the question. Hygiene was one of the hardest parts of maintaining her secret, at least since the regiment had left Ashe-Katarion. Fortunately, the prevailing standard was not high.

"Keep an eye on her until I get back," she said to Bobby. Then, to Feor, "I need to go. Stay here, and if you need anything, try to show Bobby."

The girl nodded, purple eyes imperturbable. Winter glanced at her one more time, then slipped outside.

"Senior Sergeant Winter Ihernglass, reporting as directed, sir!"

She held the salute until the captain waved it away. The colonel's tent was hardly bigger than her own, though much better organized. A few trunks packed against the canvas walls presumably contained his necessities. In the center was a low folding table and a portable writing desk with pens, ink, and drying sand in securely fashioned containers. The officers sat on cushions, Khandarai style, Captain d'Ivoire on her right and Lieutenant Warus on the left.

At the head of the table sat the colonel. He was not what she had been expecting. Younger, for a start, and thin-featured and delicate instead of stocky and gruff, as so many of these senior officers seemed to be. His long fingers were constantly in motion, twining, untwining, steepling or tapping something. Deep gray eyes regarded her thoughtfully, as though weighing what they saw in the balance. She had the unpleasant feeling that she would be found wanting.

"I apologize for my condition, sir," she said. "After we returned to camp, I needed to rest, and I received your order shortly after waking."

The colonel smiled, and something in his eyes glittered. "Do not fret about it, Sergeant. Under the circumstances . . ."

Captain d'Ivoire cleared his throat. "We've heard from some of the men of your company, but I just want to make sure we have things accurately. You were ordered to scout the ridge parallel to our line of march?"

She nodded, her chest tight.

"The late Lieutenant d'Vries led the company down that ridge, across the valley, and up the next rise," he said.

"He was eager to make contact with the enemy, sir."

"Did you advise him to this course of action?"

She straightened slightly. "No, sir. I advised against it."

"On what grounds?"

"That we would be too far from the column to fall back should we encounter the enemy in strength, sir."

He nodded. "Then, at the top of the ridge, you saw the enemy cavalry approaching. The company"—the captain glanced at a paper on the table— " 'ran for it like a bunch of rabbits,' as one of your men put it."

"They were startled, sir. The enemy were . . . numerous."

The colonel's lip quirked slightly at the understatement, but he said nothing. Captain d'Ivoire went on.

"What was Lieutenant d'Vries' response at this juncture?"

"He . . ." Winter paused. Criticizing one senior officer in front of another was simply Not Done. For one thing, officers tended to club together, so the most likely result would be some kind of subtle retribution. But he *had* asked. She sought for a positive interpretation of the facts. "The lieutenant started to ride at once for the main column. I imagine he was eager to alert you to the presence of the enemy."

Another slight smile from the colonel, and something like a smothered laugh from Fitz Warus. Captain d'Ivoire's face remained composed.

"At which point you took command of the company and ordered them to form square at the bottom of the valley."

"Yes, sir."

"Which they proceeded to do, in spite of the fact that company squares are not a formation in our drillbook."

"We had . . . a little practice, sir."

"And then you held off the attack of, what, three thousand enemy horsemen?" The captain looked at Fitz.

"At least three thousand," the lieutenant said.

"Most of them just rode by," Winter said. "Only a few hundred actually stopped to attack us, sir."

"I see." D'Ivoire turned to the colonel. "There you have it, sir."

"Indeed I do," the colonel said. "The only pity is that the lieutenant's unfortunate demise has robbed me of the chance to castigate him for his incompetence. All that remains is to acknowledge *your* accomplishment, Sergeant."

Winter blinked. "Sir?"

"You rescued your company from an impossible situation, and brought them safely back to the column when your officer broke and ran. That *is* an accomplishment, I would say."

"Sir," Winter said stiffly, "thirty-eight men of the Seventh Company are dead."

Colonel and captain looked at one another, then back to her. The colonel gave a slow nod.

"Nevertheless," he said, "things could have been much worse, and that deserves recognition. You are hereby brevetted to lieutenant, for the duration of the campaign, with the Ministry of War to review and approve a full promotion following the conclusion of hostilities. You'll remain in command of the Seventh Company, as you have demonstrated such aptitude for it."

"Yes, sir." That didn't seem quite sufficient. Winter licked her lips and looked from one officer to the other. "Thank you, sir."

The colonel waved a hand airily. "Well done, Lieutenant."

"Congratulations." Fitz Warus stood and took her hand amiably. He led her away from the table and out of the tent, talking, but Winter still felt too stunned to reply. Apparently he didn't mind. He left her at the edge of the little group of tents that belonged to the senior officers, with another handshake.

How am I going to tell Bobby? The boy would overreact, and she wasn't sure she could stand it. She shook her head, then remembered Feor.

I wonder if I should have told the colonel. An hour ago, she wouldn't have even considered it, but that was before she'd met the man. He seemed—not friendly, of course, not even *kind*. But fair, possibly, and even-tempered. That was a pleasant change from Colonel Warus, whose rages had been rare but legendary. She had the feeling that he wouldn't fault her for rescuing the girl, and he'd see to it that she wasn't treated badly.

She shook her head. No matter how she parsed it, it felt like a betrayal. Winter smiled crookedly and turned her steps back toward the Seventh Company's tents. *We'll have to deal with this ourselves.*

Chapter Nine

MARCUS

"Adrecht!" Marcus rapped twice at the tent pole. There was no reply, and he frowned. "Adrecht, I'm coming in."

He twitched the flap aside, letting a shaft of sunlight in and momentarily brightening the semidarkness under the translucent canvas. There was a soft sigh and a murmur from the far end.

"Marcus?" Adrecht said. "Is that you?"

"It's me," Marcus said, picking his way carefully among bits of discarded clothing. He blinked the darkness and made out a figure lying on a mat at the other side of the tent. "We need to talk. I—"

He paused. Some of the clothing on the floor couldn't be Adrecht's, unless the Fourth Battalion captain's tastes were stranger than Marcus had given him credit for. He took a step closer and saw that there were two people on the bedroll. The smaller one sat up, letting the sheet fall away from her. She was a Khandarai girl, not more than eighteen or nineteen, with dark eyes and long dark hair. Her small breasts were uncovered, but it didn't appear to concern her.

"Saints and martyrs," Marcus swore. "She had better not be from the Redeemer camp."

"What?" Adrecht sat up suddenly. "No! Honestly, Marcus, what do you take me for?" He brushed the girl's cheek lightly.

"Dali's a camp follower. She's been with us since Ashe-Katarion."

Marcus relaxed a little. Quite a few Khandarai had followed along with the regiment when it had fled the Khandarai capital: those whose livelihood depended on the Vordanai soldiers or who didn't fancy their chances under the new regime. More had come to them while they waited at Fort Valor and on the return march, drawn by the chance to sell their wares, their services, or their bodies to the foreigners.

"Well, tell her she needs to go," he said.

Adrecht gave an exaggerated sigh and said something in Khandarai. He spoke the native language better than Marcus did—better than any of the officers, in fact, except possibly Fitz. The girl laughed and rolled to her feet, stretching ostentatiously in front of Marcus before hunting around on the floor for her clothes. The sight of her body, lithe and trim, forcefully reminded Marcus of how long it had been since he'd enjoyed that particular comfort. He ground his teeth while he waited for her to gather her things and go.

In the meantime, Adrecht had slipped into a pair of trousers and gotten out of bed. When the girl had gone, he turned to Marcus and crossed his arms on his bare chest.

"Well?" he said. "What is it this time? It can't be missing drill; I heard the announcement last night." Janus had given the regiment the day off for recovery, except for those needed on work details.

"It's not that."

"Well?" Adrecht smiled. "Why do you look so gloomy? We won, didn't we?"

The victory seemed to have reinvigorated the Fourth Battalion captain. He almost looked his old self again, albeit still missing his fancy trappings.

"It's not the battle, either," Marcus snapped. "It's what happened afterward. Have you been out to the camp?"

"Oh." Adrecht looked away. "That was . . . unfortunate."

" 'Unfortunate' is not the word I would choose," Marcus said.

"I gave an *order* that the men halt outside the camp and return to their formations. Your men ignored it."

"It wasn't only *my* men," Adrecht protested.

"The Fourth led the way," Marcus said.

There was a long pause. Adrecht shook his head irritably.

"Come on, Marcus. What do you want from them?" He waved his hand. "These aren't saints. They're not even proper soldiers. They're the scum of the earth, and you know it—the sweepings of the army. You can't expect them to behave like a bunch of country gentlemen."

"All I expect is that they obey orders."

"After a battle like that you can't blame them for wanting a little . . . release. You know?" Adrecht laughed weakly. His smile faded when Marcus' fist crashed against the tent pole.

"Damn it," Marcus said. "Listen to me. I'm not here to preach the Wisdoms at you, Adrecht. The colonel is not going to be happy about this. If I were you, I'd get a head start and start handing down some discipline as soon as possible."

"But—," Adrecht sputtered. "What am I supposed to do? Start thrashing rankers at random?"

"Do *something*, or else if we do get back to Ashe-Katarion they'll burn the place down around our ears." Marcus turned on his heel.

Behind him, Adrecht said, "There were some of yours right at the front, you know."

I know, Marcus thought. He could guess which, too—Sergeant Davis and his pack of wolves, for starters. Fitz was already asking questions.

He let the tent flap fall behind him and struck out across the camp, setting a slow pace to give himself time to cool off.

Maybe it doesn't make any difference. He hadn't had a moment alone with Janus since the battle, so he wasn't sure if the colonel was angry or not. Plenty of highborn colonels wouldn't have given a copper bit about the rape and murder of enemy camp followers, especially grayskin infidel camp followers. Marcus thought Janus might be different, but—

It doesn't matter. I'm angry enough for the both of us. He'd spent most of the previous evening leading the work details that had finally cleaned up the Khandarai camp. Every overturned tent seemed to hide some fresh horror, and each one added another coal to the pile smoldering in his gut.

And all for what? So that fool of a prince can get back on his crumbling throne? If it was up to Marcus, he'd have handed the man over to the Redeemers and wished them good fortune.

I shouldn't have taken it out on Adrecht, though. As his temper cooled, he could admit that. The Fourth Battalion had been the worst offenders, but the speed of the Redeemer collapse had caught them all by surprise. It was no wonder the officers had lost control.

On the other hand, he's not the one who has to explain it to the colonel.

Marcus' vague feeling of apprehension came into sharp focus when he approached the drill field and saw the artillery arrayed for review, and the colonel in conversation with some of the men. When he hurried over, though, he found the Preacher all smiles.

". . . bless you, sir. We're honored by your interest," he was saying.

"I notice," Janus said, "that these guns have some fascinating modifications."

He gestured to the six cannon that had been with the Colonials when he'd arrived, which had been given pride of place in the center of the line. Chief among these "modifications" was the addition of passages from scripture, engraved all over the surface from muzzle to base. The Preacher insisted this improved the weapon's accuracy. He had a steady hand, and he'd been able to cram quite a large chunk of the Wisdoms onto each gun.

The Preacher doffed his peaked artilleryman's cap. "Weapons of the Lord, sir," he said. "Weapons of the Lord, every one of them.

Gives them an extra bit of sting against the heathens. This one, I started with Martyrs, and got all the way to—"

"This is a Kravworks '98, isn't it?" Janus interrupted.

The Preacher blinked, fingering the brass Church double circle that hung around his neck. "Yes, sir. All our original twelve-pounders are."

"But you've done something to the touchhole." He leaned closer. "I can't quite see from the outside, but—"

The Preacher gave a broad smile. "You've got a good eye, sir! We had to drill out the originals—"

Noticing Marcus, Janus waved him closer and launched into an explanation. "The Kravworks '98 was a botched job," he said. "Problems with the touchhole, something about the boring. The tests showed that the misfire rate would be nearly twenty percent, so most of the guns got sent abroad, or else—"

"To bottom-of-the-barrel outfits like this one," Marcus finished. That was a familiar story—the Colonials got the worst of everything. Muskets that wouldn't fire, uniforms that fell to pieces, cannons that exploded . . .

"Indeed." Janus caught Marcus' expression. "No offense intended, of course."

"None taken," Marcus said. "I understand that Captain Vahkerson's made the best of it."

"What have you got in there?" Janus said to the Preacher.

"Friction primers," he said. "New Hamveltai design. Works a bit like a match. Had to tweak them a little myself, of course, but we've got the misfires down to one in a hundred shots, and that last shot is usually a failed ignition rather than something dangerous."

"Interesting." The colonel appeared to follow all that, which was more than Marcus himself could say. "But aren't Hamveltai primers a bit hard to come by out here?"

"Ah, as to that, my Lieutenant Archer is a dab hand with chemicals. We managed to puzzle out the recipe with only a few scorched gloves to show for it. By the grace of God, all the raw stuff is easy to get locally, so we've got a ready supply."

"Ingenious." Janus put on a broad smile. "He'll have to give me a demonstration of the process at some point."

"Whenever you like, sir! We'd be honored."

"And I was impressed by your performance," Janus replied. "I hope the new pieces are to your satisfaction?"

"Absolutely, sir. Smooth as butter, the whole lot. The six-pounders are particularly fine."

"I picked them out myself before we set sail," Janus said. "If there's anything you need—"

"Actually, sir," the Preacher said, "I understand we captured a number of mounts and packhorses from the heretics. Some of our teams are already under-strength, and we could do with extras for rotation. If you could see your way . . ."

"Of course." The colonel smiled again. "Not worried about having heretic horses pulling your holy guns?"

"Bless you, sir. I'll soon have 'em on the straight and narrow. I read 'em scripture every night, you see."

Marcus didn't know if that was a joke or not. The Preacher had an odd sense of humor.

Janus chuckled. "Very well, then. Carry on, Captain."

"Sir!" The Preacher saluted. "Thank you, sir!"

Turning away from the guns, Janus motioned for Marcus to follow him. Marcus fell into step, almost unconsciously, slowing his pace to match Janus' shorter strides.

"A good man, Captain Vahkerson," he mused.

"A bit eccentric," Marcus said, "but certainly a good officer."

"He's effective," Janus said. "Give me effective and eccentric over stolid and conventional every time." He eyed Marcus sidelong. "There are those who have called me eccentric as well, you know."

"I can't imagine why, sir."

Janus laughed. When Marcus remained silent, the colonel

glanced at his companion. One look, but from that one brief glimpse of those gray eyes Marcus suddenly felt as though his every thought had been revealed.

"Ah, Captain," Janus said. "I think you are not entirely pleased with me."

"Sir?"

"If there's something you wish to say, I encourage you to say it."

Marcus stiffened. "It's not my place, sir."

"Nonsense. In a crisis, certainly, I expect to be obeyed without question, and I must say you have performed admirably on that front. Afterward, however, you may feel free to berate me however you like. My pride is not easily injured."

Marcus blinked. "Sir?"

"However." Janus held up a hand and looked around at the bustling camp. "Perhaps we should be alone."

Janus' tent was nearby. Augustin let them in, his lined face disapproving as always. Once they were seated on opposite sides of the camp table, Janus sent the servant off to the commissary in search of fresh water. Marcus wondered if this was for his benefit.

"Sir," he ventured, "did we have business to attend to?"

"Of course," Janus said. "But first, I think, the air must be cleared. Whatever you wish to say, please say it."

Marcus took a deep breath and held it for a moment. Criticizing a senior officer to his face went against every tenet of army etiquette, not to mention good sense. But Janus had insisted. He tried to frame the question as politely as possible.

Luck. The colonel had gambled, and it had paid off. *But if he was overconfident before, now he'll be positively dangerous. If I can make him see that . . .*

"When the Redeemer infantry first approached," Marcus said, "why did you order us to hold our fire? We could have done them a great deal of damage in the time it took them to form and charge.

We might even have broken up the attack altogether." Marcus swallowed hard, but persevered. "It seemed . . . unnecessarily risky. Sir."

The colonel was silent for a moment, looking thoughtful. "Risky," he said. "Probably. Certainly. But unnecessary?" He shook his head. "What you need to understand, Captain, is that the answer to every question is not in the tactics manual. You should consider the larger situation."

He waved a hand. "For example, you must always consider the character of the enemy. Truthfully, I did not know this one as well as I might have liked—a Vordanai force, for example, or a Hamveltai one would have been a different matter. But I knew they were green troops who had never faced a field battle. Poorly organized, led with enthusiasm but without discipline."

"I would have thought green troops more likely to be disordered by long-range fire."

"Precisely. Disordered, but not broken. Suppose we had opened on them, and they had retired in confusion before reaching musket range. What would the result have been?"

"A victory," Marcus said.

"And then? What would our next move have been?" Janus raised an eyebrow. "Cannon kill with great efficiency, but not fast enough to make up for our numerical disadvantage. We lack the cavalry strength for an effective pursuit. The Redeemers would have simply retired a short distance and confronted us again, at substantially the same odds. Sooner or later, they would hold together long enough to push a charge home, and then—disaster. Or, if they had a commander with any skill, a flanking movement would have forced us to retreat. In either case, once that vast army had its legs underneath it, things would go hard for us."

Marcus nodded. "We might have fallen back to a defensible position—"

"Then we would have been lost for certain. Nothing hardens

men faster than a siege, and they would have little trouble cutting us off from water and forage. The best we could hope for would be to cut our way back to the fleet." The colonel shook his head. "No, the only chance for *victory* was a complete rout. A single, sudden blow, so hard that they would come apart entirely. For green troops, their first contact with enemy fire is crucial. It sets the character, you might say, of everything that comes afterward. Most of those men will never return to the enemy ranks, or if they do they will only run again. Certainly it will take weeks before they can assemble another force half so large. And, in the meantime, the road to Ashe-Katarion is open."

Marcus sat for a moment in silence, absorbing this.

"Our troops were green as well," he said after a while. "Most of them, anyway. And even the Old Colonials had never fought a battle like this."

"Indeed," Janus said. "I expect this first contact to have a most salutary effect on them."

Luck, Marcus thought. *He risked all our lives on—a hunch? His* impression *of the enemy?* But he couldn't fault Janus' logic. He himself hadn't seen any way to win through against the numbers they'd faced. He'd assumed that, in spite of Janus' talk the night he'd arrived, he planned to make a reasonable effort, prove to his superiors that he was no coward, and then retreat when the situation became untenable.

He really does intend to win. The thought made Marcus shiver.

"Well?" Janus said. "Does that satisfy you, Captain?"

"I'm not sure, sir," Marcus said. "I need to think on it."

"Do so. And feel free to return with further questions." The smile again, there and gone like distant lightning. "It's part of a commanding officer's duty to educate his subordinates."

If that was true, no one had told the other colonels Marcus had served under. *Not that Ben could have taught me much.* He nodded anyway.

"Yes, sir. Now, you said you had business?"

"Indeed," Janus said, without a change in his expression. "I would like you to arrest Captain Adrecht Roston, on the charge of dereliction of duty and others pending investigation."

Marcus stared, feeling as though he'd been punched in the stomach. Janus raised his eyes to the tent flap.

"Ah, Augustin," he said. "Something to eat as well, I think."

"Sir," Marcus began, "I'm not . . ." He stopped, fighting the urge to panic, and cleared his throat. "Are you sure? I'm just not certain that—that this is wise."

"Wise?" Janus raised an eyebrow. "Would you say that Captain Roston is a good battalion commander?"

Marcus almost said, "Of course," automatically—no senior officer could expect an honest answer to a question like that!—but something in those gray eyes made him hesitate.

"Would you say that he has acquitted himself well over the past month?" Janus went on.

Again Marcus was silent. The colonel seemed to take that for a reply.

"Then would you say that he's well liked by his men? That his removal might cause discipline problems?"

Not goddamned likely. There were certainly a few in the Fourth Battalion who would shed a tear at Adrecht's passing, but that would be because they enjoyed the laxity of his discipline, not his company. In Ashe-Katarion he'd practically ignored the rankers, preferring to spend his time with the other officers and a glittering array of Khandarai high society.

"And finally," Janus continued remorselessly, "would you say there are no better men available? Your Lieutenant Fitzhugh Warus, for example, seems to have done exemplary work."

Marcus found his voice at last. "But, sir. Dereliction of duty?"

"He disobeyed a direct order from a superior when his men began looting the Redeemer camp. Or failed to enforce one, which amounts to the same thing. The result was damaging to our cause and our material position. What else would you call it?"

"The men were—are—green, sir. They got out of control—"

"All the more reason to show them that this sort of conduct will not be tolerated." Janus' voice was still pleasant, but Marcus thought he could hear the ring of steel underneath. "A demonstration must be made."

Marcus remembered, uncomfortably, being on the other side of this argument in Adrecht's tent. He nodded slowly.

"I understand that he is your friend," Janus said, letting a little sympathy into his tone. "But you must admit I would be justified."

You don't know him, Marcus wanted to say. Janus hadn't been at the War College with Adrecht, hadn't nursed him through vicious hangovers or watched in mystified envy as he effortlessly charmed young women with his smile and the glitter of his uniform. He hadn't been at Green Springs, where Adrecht and a company of the Fourth had charged across open ground under fire to rescue a half dozen wounded men.

And, of course, he saved my life. Marcus wondered whether *that* had been in Janus' files.

"Sir," Marcus said, "may I make a suggestion?"

"Of course."

"What if I speak to Captain Roston and make it clear that, were he to offer his resignation, you would accept it? That would be . . . kinder."

"I'm afraid not," Janus said. "The effectiveness of the demonstration would be lost." Janus considered. "You may break the news to him, if you like, and ask him to present himself for arrest if you think that would be easier on him. I have no wish to be unnecessarily cruel."

"Thank you, sir," Marcus said hollowly. He saluted. "If you'll excuse me."

*

"All in all," Fitz said, "we got off astonishingly light."

He had to speak up to be heard over the screams. There was a man strapped to the surgeon's board, a mangled arm held in place by a burly orderly while the cutter worked with the bone saw. They'd given the patient a leather-padded stick to bite down on, but apparently he'd lost it. At least his voice drowned the noise of the saw itself, a high-pitched singsong whine that gave Marcus the shivers.

"Counting the scouts," the lieutenant continued, "we have less than a hundred dead or seriously wounded. Another hundred or so that should recover. Given the numbers engaged—"

Marcus nodded as Fitz went on. No one had troubled to count how many Khandarai had died, of course, but it had been a great many. Details were still stripping the field of corpses, stiff and bloated now after a day in the desert sun, and carrying them to the pyres that burned day and night. Gleaners brought back what they could find, but there was little enough. Most of the Redeemer's supplies had burned with their tents.

They walked through the little patch at the edge of the camp that had been designated as the hospital. Open-sided tents shielded the wounded from the sun, and the regimental surgeons bustled back and forth with brisk efficiency. Marcus suspected that much of the activity was for his benefit. As Fitz had said, they'd gotten off lightly. Many of the tents were empty, and of those that were occupied most of the men Marcus could see looked hale enough. Even a minor wound could fester, of course, and a man might lose a limb like the poor bastard back on the table if it got bad enough. *But nevertheless—lightly.*

He still felt a little sick. The worst engagement the Colonials had been in before the Redemption had been the ambush that killed Colonel Warus. They'd lost six men in that fight, and had two so badly injured they'd died later. One more had been invalided home. Nine altogether, and that had been considered a disaster, with the whole regiment in mourning. *And now this.*

That's war, he told himself sternly. The First Colonials had never been a battlefield regiment until now. What fighting they'd done had been bushwhacks and bandit chasing. *I should count myself lucky the men stood up to it.* Indeed, the mood of the camp seemed to have taken a sharp upward turn. The mutters and sour looks had stopped, replaced by smiles and quick, crisp salutes.

"Sir?" Fitz said.

"Hmm?"

"Is something wrong? You seem preoccupied."

"Why do you say that?"

Fitz cleared his throat. "For one thing, sir, we left the camp a few minutes ago. Perhaps we should turn back?"

Marcus looked around. Fitz was right, as always—they'd left the last line of tents and the latrine pits behind, and Marcus had been absently strolling out into open scrub. Twenty yards back, a few confused sentries watched curiously.

"Ah." He looked back at Fitz. "A bit farther, actually."

"Yes, sir," Fitz said, in that way he had that actually meant, *I see that you've gone mad*.

Marcus headed toward a big rock, a boulder half buried in the parched earth with a clump of wiry trees growing from one side. He put his back against it, feeling the warmth, and let out a sigh. Fitz stood in front of him, prim and correct. They were a good sixty yards from camp now. *No chance of being overheard*.

"The colonel," Marcus said, "is going to arrest Adrecht."

Fitz didn't even blink. "On what charge, sir?"

"Dereliction of duty. I talked him into letting me break the news."

"That was very kind of you, sir."

"But now I have to tell him." Marcus grimaced. "I'm not sure I can."

Fitz maintained a diplomatic silence.

"It wasn't really his fault," Marcus said, to no one in particular.

"I mean—partly, of course, but—" He shook his head.

"Perhaps if you spoke to the colonel again, he would accept some lighter form of discipline?"

"No," Marcus said. "He wants to make an example." He hesitated, then added, "He talked about giving you the Fourth."

Fitz' expression didn't change. "I see."

Marcus looked at him curiously. "Do you want a battalion command?"

"It would certainly further my career, sir. However, I would worry about the First in my absence. With you spending so much time with the colonel . . ."

That was true enough. Fitz practically had a battalion command already.

Marcus pushed away from the rock. "I need to talk to the others. Can you track down Val and Mor and have them meet me in my tent around sundown? Make sure you don't let anyone know why."

"Certainly, sir." Fitz saluted.

The walk back to camp felt longer than the walk out had, and the rest of the day seemed to pass only grudgingly. There were account books to sign off on, stores and inventories to approve, sick lists and casualty reports—that was only the top of the stack. Marcus didn't dare wonder what lurked in the bottom layers. By the time he looked up and saw that the horizon had gone crimson, his right hand was stiff and aching, and his fingers were blotchy with spilt ink.

Mor arrived first, red-faced from hours in the sun and in a foul mood. He shrugged out of his uniform coat before Marcus could say a word, tossed it into a corner of the tent, and tugged at his collar.

"They're a bunch of children," he said. "A bunch of spoiled children. Tell them they've done something wrong and they look at you like they're about to cry. I don't know where the colonel dug up this lot."

"The recruits?" Marcus said.

"The *rankers* are fine. It's the lieutenants that are the problem." Mor paced the length of the tent twice, then aimed a kick at his own jacket. "Bunch of stuck-up goddamned paper soldiers. Not one of them had seen any action, and before the battle yesterday they were just about pissing their pants, but now they all think they're Farus the Conqueror come again." Mor shook his head. "Are your lot any better? Want to trade?"

Marcus shook his head, feeling guilty. He barely knew his own company commanders, aside from the Old Colonials. Janus had monopolized the time he ought to have been spending with them.

"Next time we drill I'm going out myself," Mor said. "Make them eat a little dust instead of just wagging their chins. Maybe that will teach them something." He let out a long sigh. "Got anything to drink?"

"Not just now. We've got problems."

"Don't I know it. That's why I asked for a drink." Mor flopped down beside the camp table. "So what's going on?"

"We need— Ah, here he is." Val pushed aside the tent flap and entered, blinking in the lamplight.

"Marcus, Mor," he said politely. "Fitz seemed agitated, so I hurried over."

"Agitated?" Mor said. "He doesn't know the meaning of the word."

"Agitated for Fitz, I mean," Val said.

"Sit down," Marcus said. "We need to talk."

"Now I'm starting to get worried," Mor said with a smile.

"Given the company," Val said, "I think I can guess the subject. It's Adrecht, isn't it?"

"It's Adrecht," Marcus confirmed. "The colonel's not happy with what happened to the Redeemer camp."

"Bah," Mor said. "It's not pretty, I'll grant you, but they got what they deserved."

"Deserved?" Marcus said. "They were running away. There were women—"

"Women who followed an army into battle," Mor said. He waved a hand dismissively. "If they'd stayed in Ashe-Katarion they would have been safe. And nobody *had* to run away. We gave them a chance to surrender."

"That's still no excuse for slaughter," Val said stiffly. "The rules of civilized warfare—"

"Last I checked the goddamned Redeemers were not exactly signatories to the goddamned Convention of '56. They *eat* their prisoners, remember?"

"That's just a rumor," Val said.

"In any case," Marcus cut in loudly, "Adrecht is taking the fall for it. The colonel told me he wants him arrested."

"Arrested?" Val looked incredulous. "For what?"

"Dereliction of duty." Marcus shrugged. "Whether he can make that stick in a court-martial, I have no idea, but Adrecht would spend the rest of the campaign in a cage on just the colonel's say-so."

"Who gets the Fourth?" Mor said.

"Fitz," Marcus said, a sour taste in his mouth. "Or so the colonel implied."

"About time," Mor said.

Val ignored him and turned to Marcus. "What are we going to do?"

"I wanted to see you two first," Marcus said. "We need to decide, together—"

"Decide what?" Mor said. "Sounds like the decision's already made."

"We need to decide if we're going to stand for it," Val said.

"Exactly," Marcus said.

There was a long moment of silence. Mor looked from one to the other, started to chuckle, then trailed off. He sat up abruptly.

"You're serious, aren't you?" he said.

"Adrecht is one of us," Val said. "One of the Colonials. We can't just abandon him."

"He never was worth a damn," Mor said. "And he hasn't lifted a finger since the Redeemers sent us packing. Half the time he's too drunk to walk!"

That hit a bit close to home for Marcus. The answer might be simple for Val, but he was a man of simple loyalties. *Fitz* would *make a better battalion commander than Adrecht. Janus was right about that.* And Adrecht was—well, Adrecht. Marcus had been with the other captains so long that he'd lost sight of them. They were simply part of the landscape, as immovable as the fixed stars. The Colonials without Adrecht would be like waking up without an arm or a leg. But Janus forced him to look with an outsider's perspective, and he had to admit that he didn't like what he saw.

"I can't believe you're talking like this," Mor said. "I know he was at the College with you, Marcus, but—"

"I can't believe you *aren't*," Val snapped. "If it was Marcus or I taking the blame, would that be any different?"

"Of course it would! Adrecht—"

"Got what he deserved?" Marcus suggested.

"Yes," Mor said, though he had the grace to blush slightly.

Mor had never liked Adrecht. Adrecht's feud with Val had reached such epic proportions that it had become a sort of friendship, but between him and Mor there had never been anything but cold politeness. Adrecht's privileged background was the cause, Marcus suspected. The nobility were at the top of Mor's list of hatreds, but as the scion of a wealthy family Adrecht wasn't too far behind.

"He doesn't deserve it," Marcus said. "Not for this. Green troops, in their first real fight—it could have happened to any one of us. His men were just the first ones over the line."

"So what are you suggesting?" Mor said. "You made it sound like the colonel was pretty set on this—do you think you can talk him out of it?"

"If Adrecht is arrested, I'll submit my resignation," Marcus said.

Val nodded slowly. Mor looked from one of them to the other, aghast.

"Do you realize what you're saying?" he said. "This isn't some peacetime infraction. If you refuse to serve during a campaign, the colonel can get you for desertion. Forget spending the march in a cage. He could shoot you on the spot."

Val's face clouded. Evidently he hadn't considered that aspect of the situation. It was one thing to resign as a matter of honor, but quite another to be branded a deserter and shot like a common criminal.

"You were the one who said the Redeemers deserved what they got, Mor," Marcus said. "Can you really let one of your fellow officers be disgraced for letting that happen?"

"If the alternative is being shot, you're damn right I can," Mor said.

"He wouldn't shoot all three of us," Marcus said. "If we stand together—"

"He won't get the chance," Mor said. "I'll have no part of this. I'm sorry, Marcus."

There was a long pause. Marcus looked at Val.

"I . . . ," Val began, then hesitated. "I need to think."

I've lost, Marcus thought. He knew Val too well. In the hot flush of anger and honor besmirched, he would have willingly marched into hell itself, but given a night to reflect, his fears would get the better of him.

He forced a smile and got to his feet. "Well. I think we can leave it there for tonight, then."

"You're not going through with this, are you?" Mor sounded anxious. "For God's sake, Marcus—"

"Good night, Mor. Val."

The two of them left, though not without a few backward

glances. Only a moment after they'd gone, Fitz ghosted in carrying a mug of steaming tea. He presented it without comment.

"Thank you," Marcus said. "That will be all for tonight."

"Sir." Fitz saluted and withdrew.

"Sir," Marcus said. He'd dressed in his best, the formal blues he'd worn to welcome Janus to the regiment, and his salute was parade-ground crisp. Only the darkness around his eyes betrayed any hint of a sleepless night.

If the colonel was similarly troubled, he showed no sign of it. He sat in the blue-shaded half-light of his tent, the folding table assembled and a painted-leather map unrolled across it. Alongside this were a number of paper maps, mostly hasty pencil sketches. He studied these so intently that he didn't even look up at Marcus' greeting, merely waved a hand for the captain to take a seat. Only after a few seconds, when Marcus remained standing, did he raise his head.

"Captain?" he said. "I would value your input, if you don't mind."

"Sir," Marcus said again. He reached into his breast pocket and withdrew a folded slip of paper, which he placed in the center of the map.

"Ah," Janus said. "Is this from Captain Roston?"

Marcus closed his eyes for a moment. "No, sir. From me."

It was the first time that Marcus could recall seeing Janus look surprised. The expression flickered across his face for a split second, only barely visible before iron control slammed back into place. Still, somehow, it was gratifying. *At least he* can *be surprised.* Marcus had half expected to find Janus waiting for him with a court-martial.

The colonel, his expression once more a mask, reached for the note and flicked it open. It wasn't long, just a few lines. A moment later he tossed it aside and looked back up at Marcus.

"Would you care to explain, Captain?"

"Sir. I don't believe it requires—"

"Captain." Janus' voice cracked like a whip.

Marcus swallowed. "The charges against Adr—against Captain Roston. Your original order was relayed to him through me, and I was the officer in overall command. Therefore the failure is mine, as are the consequences. If you required Captain Roston's arrest, I could not in good conscience refrain from submitting my resignation."

"I see." Janus tapped his index finger on the desk. "I assume you're aware that I can reject this?"

"Yes, sir. And I can refuse to recognize your rejection."

"And since we are engaged in an active campaign, that qualifies as desertion," Janus said. "I see." The finger tapped again. "You agreed with me that Captain Roston was not the best man for the job."

"Yes, sir." Marcus hesitated, but there was no going back now. "That doesn't make it right to remove him like this."

Tap, tap, tap. Then, all at once, Janus' face became animated again, as though someone had shone a spotlight on it. "Very well." He pushed the letter back across the table. "You may keep this."

Marcus blinked. "Sir?"

"Getting rid of Captain Roston is not worth losing you in the bargain. You win, Captain." Another flicker, this time a smile. "As usual, it seems."

"Captain Roston—"

"You will convey my displeasure to Captain Roston at the conduct of his men. But unofficially." Janus fixed Marcus with a penetrating stare. "You understand that should the captain fail in his duty again, you will bear the responsibility for it?"

"Yes, sir." Marcus took what seemed like his first breath in hours. "Thank you, sir."

"No thanks are necessary," Janus said. "Now sit. We have plans to go over."

"What—? Now, sir?"

"Time is short," Janus said. "We've wasted far too much on peripheral matters already."

"Yes, sir."

Marcus' mind felt like a clockwork engine thrown suddenly into reverse, gears screeching and stripping. He tried to focus on the map, but it seemed like nothing but a random set of painted splotches.

He did his best not to show his confusion, but hiding his feelings from Janus was apparently beyond his ability. The colonel gave him a cool glance, then waved a hand vaguely.

"A few minutes, on the other hand, will not greatly delay us. I suggest you go and change into your usual uniform. You seem—uncomfortable."

"Yes, sir." Marcus hesitated. "Thank you, sir."

Janus was already bent over the map again, leafing through a stack of scouting reports. Marcus beat a hasty retreat.

Stepping outside, he practically ran into Val. The other captain was approaching at a jog, his uniform sending up a gentle jingling sound like a fool with his cap and bells. He'd embellished it, over the years, with bronze and silver trinkets and embroidery in the Khandarai style. None of them had anticipated needing their dress blues for official Vordanai functions again.

"Marcus," Val said, breathing hard. "I'm sorry. I came as quickly as I could."

"What are you doing here?"

"Have you given it to him already?"

"Given it . . ." Marcus stopped as realization dawned. "You've come to *resign*?"

"Of course!" Val said stoutly, then abruptly looked sheepish. "I admit that Mor nearly had me convinced last night. But this morning I thought—hell—" His blush deepened. "I couldn't stand leaving you in the lurch, and that's that. But it took me a while to get dressed and write the bloody thing out." He fished in his pocket. "Please tell me it'll still do some good."

Marcus smiled. He felt, abruptly, like a weight had fallen from his shoulders, as though he could only now acknowledge the reality of what had happened.

"I don't think the colonel has any need of it," he said. "But it's certainly a great comfort to *me*."

"But . . ."

Marcus clapped him on the shoulder. "Come on. I still need to change."

Half an hour later, back in his regular sun-bleached uniform and fortified by a cup of coffee strongly flavored by a splash of Khandarai liquor, Marcus ducked into the colonel's tent again and snapped another textbook salute. The colonel was in the same attitude as when he'd left, though most of the scouting reports had been converted into pencil notations on the maps.

"Captain," Janus said, "will you actually sit down this time?"

"Gladly, sir." He hesitated. "I must apologize for disturbing your planning earlier—"

The colonel gave an affected sigh. "Think nothing of it. We have more important matters to discuss."

Marcus nodded and sat. The colonel turned the leather map so that it faced him, and tapped a finger on it. It took Marcus a moment to parse—the script was Khandarai, and the mapmaker had used unfamiliar symbols—but once he found the label for Ashe-Katarion, the landscape snapped into place. Janus' finger marked the regiment's current position, roughly thirty-five miles from the city.

"We march tomorrow," Janus said. "The question, of course, is where."

"To the city, presumably," Marcus ventured.

"Indeed. But getting there is going to be a problem. News of our victory has reached them by now, and General Khtoba appears to have bestirred himself at last."

"You think he'll meet us on the road?"

"Unfortunately, I doubt that he'll be quite so bold. No doubt he'll keep to the west bank of the Tsel, and therein lies the difficulty. You see?"

Marcus frowned. He'd never claimed much of a gift for strategy, but the issue here was clear enough. Ashe-Katarion clustered around an inlet called the Old Harbor, repository of the trade that formed the city's lifeblood. In ancient times, the river mouth had been there as well, but the channel had silted over and the mighty Tsel had dug a new path to the sea, some twenty miles to the west of the city. The kings of Khandar had cut a canal south from their city to a bend in the river rather than relocate their temples and palaces to the new outlet.

The result was that the Tsel was squarely between the Colonials and the Khandarai capital. Upstream to the south, the great river wiggled like a snake as it crossed the wide, flat plain, but here at the coast it ran fairly straight. Slow-flowing it might be, but it was nearly a mile wide and presented a formidable obstacle.

There was a bridge a few miles up from the sea, where a pair of rocky islands provided a decent footing. The Vordanai cartographers, in their unimaginative way, had dubbed the triple span Westbridge, and the town that had grown up on both banks Westbridge Town. It was through here that the coast road ran, over the river and down the last few miles into the city.

Marcus had ridden through the town many times, most recently on the retreat from the Redeemers that had ended at Fort Valor. There were no purpose-built defenses, no fortress walls or emplaced artillery, but the place would be a nightmare to take nonetheless. The bridges were narrow, barely wide enough for a pair of wagons to pass one another, and the islands commanded the approaches and provided excellent fields of fire. Troops attempting to cross would have to do so without cover, in the face of every gun the defender could muster, and even if they succeeded in storming the first island they would only have to accomplish the same task twice more. Then, on the far bank, they'd need to hold the bridgehead against whatever counterattack the enemy would have waiting.

"Khtoba's dug in around the bridge," Marcus guessed.

"Like a tick on a dog," Janus said. "With only three battalions, though. He's no fool, and he knows we won't go that way unless we have to." He tapped the map again, upstream of the city. "The other three are here. There's a ford just north of this river bend, good enough to cross if we don't mind getting wet."

A ford sounded hardly better than the bridge. Marcus tried to imagine slogging through a waist-deep river and assaulting the far bank, while the enemy flailed the water with musket and canister. It might be done, if the attackers were determined enough, but the losses would be ghastly.

Janus was watching him with those deep gray eyes, and Marcus decided this was a test. He looked down at the map and searched his memory.

"We might march down the east bank," he said eventually. "There's another bridge here, at Saal-Khaaten, and more fords upstream where the river's narrower."

"Khtoba would follow," the colonel said. "And he has the inside track."

"If we can threaten more than two crossings at once, he'll have to spread himself thinner. He can't cover them all."

Janus gave a slow nod. "It might serve. And then what, once we've crossed?"

"A battle, presumably."

"A head-on fight, and he'll choose the ground," Janus said. "And Khtoba has us three to two."

"The last Redeemer army had us five to one," Marcus said. "I didn't think the odds concerned you."

The colonel waved a hand. "Those were rabble. The numbers didn't concern me because I knew they would never stand up to disciplined fire. They might as well have left three-quarters of those men at home, for all the good they did. But the Auxiliaries are a horse of a different color."

That was true enough. The Auxiliaries comprised six battalions of Khandarai recruited by Prince Exopter and trained by his Vordanai allies. Marcus had taken his turn at the training a time or two, and they'd certainly looked disciplined enough, marching up and down in their brown uniforms. More important, they had Vordanai weapons, including a full complement of artillery. They were supposed to have been a bulwark against rebellion, but no one had counted on the fervor the new religion inspired. The Auxiliaries had gone over to the Redeemers almost to a man, along with their commander.

"On even terms, in open ground, I wouldn't hesitate," Janus said. "But Khtoba is not likely to give us a chance at that. Judging from his actions thus far, I doubt he'd even give battle. More likely he'd fall back behind the canal, or into the city itself, and fight us in the streets. *That* we must avoid at all costs."

Marcus shook his head. "So what, then?"

"The general has given us an opportunity here." He tapped the bridge again, and then the ford. "Two detachments, widely separated, and not much between them but pickets. Where we need to be"—he moved his finger to a point between the two—"is here."

"We'd be surrounded, with no line of retreat," Marcus objected. "Even if we could get there, which we can't, since we can't cross the river."

The colonel grinned like a cat.

It was nearly sundown. Rest—which at the start of the day had seemed like some distant and unreachable oasis—was practically within his reach, and Marcus therefore had a strong inclination not to answer when there was a knock on his tent pole. In theory, it might be important, although short of an impending Khandarai attack Marcus couldn't think of anything that qualified. He compromised by responding with a sort of muffled grunt, in the hopes that the knocker either wouldn't hear him or would give up and go away.

Instead, the visitor spoke. "It's Adrecht."

Damn. "Oh, all right."

Adrecht ducked through the flap. Even in the dim lantern light, there was no mistaking the huge bruise that purpled his cheek and nearly closed one eye. A shallow cut above his eyebrow was dark with scabbed blood.

"Saints and martyrs," Marcus swore. "What happened to you?"

"Mor," Adrecht said, with an exaggerated wince. "Do you mind if I sit?"

Marcus nodded, and Adrecht folded his lanky form up beside the camp table. Marcus waved at his trunk.

"Do you want a drink? I think I've got something . . ."

"No," Adrecht said. His expression was thoughtful. "No, I don't think so."

"So what happened? Mor just jumped you?"

"After a manner of speaking," Adrecht said. "He came into my tent and told me that he'd had it with me, and that Marcus was a better friend than I deserved." He smiled slightly. "With more swearing, of course. Then he picked me up and tossed me into a tent pole. Snapped it in half, as a matter of fact."

"Hell." Marcus' face clouded. "I'll talk to him. I don't care what he thinks, that was out of line—"

"No," Adrecht said. "Not really."

Marcus swore inwardly. He'd hoped to avoid this for a while. "Ah. He told you the whole story, then."

"Most of it. I got the rest out of Val. If you want to keep

something a secret, you ought to think twice before sharing it with those two. Think three times, maybe." Adrecht shook his head. "Why didn't you talk to me?"

"I wanted to keep it quiet."

"Honestly, Marcus."

Watching his friend's expression, Marcus could tell that excuse wouldn't do. He sighed. "I didn't want you to do anything . . . rash."

"Rash? Like turning myself in before you got a chance to resign?"

"Like that, for example."

"Accepting dismissal," Adrecht deadpanned, "rather than risking your being shot for desertion. That would be 'rash.'"

"I suppose so." He frowned, searching for words. It was hard to explain to the others, but he'd never really felt endangered—he had no *reason* to be sure that Janus wouldn't shoot him, or even bring him up on charges, but he felt the certainty nonetheless. "It wasn't really about you. I tried to explain that to the colonel."

"Did he believe it?"

"I'm not sure." Marcus shrugged. "It doesn't really matter."

"I suppose not." Adrecht paused, then said, "Well, if it makes any difference, you were right. I would have been rash."

There was a long, awkward silence. Marcus searched for something to say, but drew a blank, and in the end it was Adrecht who spoke.

"You don't owe me anything, you know. It's been—"

"Eighteen years," Marcus said. "I know."

Another silence. Adrecht sighed.

"What am I supposed to do now?"

"What do you mean?" Marcus said.

"How can I just go back to my battalion now? I know the colonel would rather be rid of me. Mor seems to hate me. And you—" He shook his head. "It seems like I ought to resign, but after what you've been through that would be a bit of a waste, wouldn't it?"

"I don't know." Marcus hadn't thought that far ahead. "Mor will come around eventually. But I think you need to prove the colonel wrong."

"Small chance that I'll get the opportunity. He'll have me guarding the latrines for the rest of the campaign."

"He won't, as it happens." Now it was Marcus' turn to smile. "We're going into action again tomorrow, and you've got a big part in it. Right beside me, in fact."

"Oh." Adrecht didn't sound surprised. "And how did that happen?"

"You volunteered."

"I suspected as much. I'm not going to like this, am I?"

"Probably not," Marcus admitted. "I didn't."

CHAPTER TEN

WINTER

Winter sighed and rubbed her weary eyes. The lantern on her little table had guttered low while she'd been working. She blew it out, added another inch of oil, and wound out more wick, then struck a match and relit it. The sudden flare of light seemed bright as noon in the darkness of her tent.

What I ought to do is sleep. But awake, she could feel the captain's orders for tomorrow staring at her from where she'd tucked them in her coat, and every time she lay down to sleep she found herself faced with accusing green eyes.

Her only solace lay in work, of which there was fortunately a sufficiency. In spite of Winter's intermittent efforts, the company books were still badly out of date. Not only did the various infractions, minor penalties, and daily logs of the march still need to be recorded and approved, but the deaths of nearly a third of the men still needed to be processed. Each of the dead had left behind some pathetic bundle of possessions, all of which Bobby had carefully inventoried and assessed. These would be sold at the first opportunity, and the proceeds forwarded to the dead men's kin along with the army's standard benefits.

The lists made for sad reading. Winter tapped her pen beside a line that read, "One locket or keepsake, brass, containing a miniature of a young woman. Of indifferent quality. 2f 6p." She wondered whether the girl had been a wife, a lover, or merely some object of brotherly affection. Then, frustrated, she tossed the pen aside and leaned back on her elbows. Her eyes, itchy with fatigue and lantern smoke, filled with tears.

"Are you unwell?"

The voice was Feor's—there was hardly anyone else likely to speak to her in Khandarai—but Winter started anyway. The girl was so quiet it was easy to forget that she was there. She lay on her stomach on the extra bedroll Graff had cadged from the quartermasters, reading by the flickering light of Winter's lamp. Aside from the occasional rasp of a turning page, she might have been a queer-looking statue.

"No," Winter said, blinking away the tears. "Well, yes, but not how you mean. I'm tired."

"Your diligence does you credit," Feor said. Sometimes the girl's tone was so solemn that Winter was sure she was joking, but her face never showed any hint of it.

"I'm sorry. I must be keeping you awake."

"It's no trouble. Since I have no duties here, I have time enough to sleep."

With a broken arm, Feor could hardly set up tents, or cook, or clean weapons or uniforms. She spent most of her time bundled in a white robe, trudging along with the quartermasters and the rest of the camp servants. Graff escorted her to Winter's tent when they stopped for the day, and she stayed inside until full dark. Bobby or Folsom brought food in at dinnertime.

Winter had been worried that someone would notice, and undoubtedly many had, but it hadn't attracted the attention she'd feared. The army had started out with a considerable "tail" of servants and camp followers, and had only added to it during the slow progress up the coast road toward Ashe-Katarion. However much the Khandarai might hate their Vordanai oppressors, it seemed as if some of them were not averse to washing those oppressors' clothes, selling them food and wine, or sharing their bedrolls. Not if the price was right. So while it was an open secret that Winter shared her tent with a young woman every night, she was hardly the only one, and the only response from the men had been some wistful grumbling about the privileges of rank.

No doubt Davis and the others were laughing at what their "Saint" was up to. Thankfully, Winter had not run across the sergeant since the battle. If her earlier promotion had angered him, her brevet to lieutenant would drive him to a frenzy. She hoped idly that he'd gotten himself killed somehow, but she doubted she would be so lucky.

"I'm sorry I don't have more for you to read." Winter's inquiries among the servants and camp followers had produced only a couple of slim volumes, mostly myths and tales for children. "You must have seen all that before."

"I consider myself lucky that I was rescued by someone with such a command of our language."

"Most of the Old Colonials speak it, at least a little."

"You have more than a little," Feor said. "You must have made a study of it."

Winter shrugged. "Here and there. There wasn't much else to do while we were in camp."

"In my limited experience, most soldiers seem to be satisfied with drinking, dicing, and whoring. These did not appeal to you?"

"Not especially." Winter cast about, eager to change the subject. "What about you? I suppose you lived on the sacred hill, before the Redemption started?"

Feor nodded. "In a special cloister, with the other *naathem*."

"What was that like? The old priestesses never let any Vordanai so much as set foot on the holy ground."

The girl reflected for a moment. "Orderly," she said. "We live our lives for Mother and the gods. Our days were tightly circumscribed—so much time for prayer, so much for study, so much for chores."

"That sounds familiar," Winter muttered. "Did it bother you, living like that?"

"I knew no other way to live, until the Redemption. We were kept from contact with the unholy."

"What about before you came to the temple? Did you have a family?"

Feor shook her head. "We were all orphans. The word is *sahl-irusk*, sacred children. Those entrusted to the temples in infancy. Mother chooses her *naathem* from among these." She paused, and there was a hint of pain in her eyes. "The last few months have been something of a shock. The Redeemers have brought us . . . chaos."

"And you want to go back?"

"Yes," Feor said. "I must return to Mother."

"Even if she locks you up again?"

"It is for our own protection. *Naathem* are in danger from the unholy world. It would use us, or destroy us."

Winter frowned. "Then why tell me?"

"You saved my life," Feor said. "Lies seemed a poor way to repay you."

Winter nodded. She still wasn't sure what to make of this *naathem* business. Feor seemed ordinary enough, for a priestess. But she clearly believed the title meant something, and Winter had been hesitant to challenge her on it. *Let her have her beliefs, if it makes her happy*. The *naathem* of the stories were monstrous figures, powerful and malicious, but perhaps the priests of the sacred hill meant the term differently.

"I should get some sleep," Winter said. She glanced at her coat, as though she could read the orders through the pocket lining. "Tomorrow is going to be . . . busy."

"Another battle?"

"I hope not. God willing, we'll just get a little wet."

Feor nodded, but thankfully didn't press for details.

"If . . ." Winter coughed. "If something goes wrong, and we're . . . captured, or something like that, you may end up on your own. If you stick with the army, you shouldn't have too much trouble."

"I can wash clothes with the rest, if need be." Feor fixed her with an oddly calm stare. "But you will return."

"Is that a prophecy?"

Another little smile. "No. Just a guess. But hopefully an accurate one."

Winter snorted and blew out the lamp.

If she dreamed, she was too tired to remember any of it. When Bobby came to wake her, an hour before dawn, Winter got out of bed feeling almost refreshed. She dressed in darkness and slipped outside to find the Seventh Company waking up around her, men emerging from their tents grumbling and bleary-eyed. Watching them tighten their belts and take their weapons from where they'd stacked them the night before, Winter felt the first fluttering of the anxiety she'd fought all the previous day.

That anxiety was in full flood by the time the men had formed up and begun the short march to the river. Winter walked at the head of the column, looking over her shoulder every few moments to make certain they were still following. *Why should they follow?* Her stomach roiled. *A week ago I was* Ranker *Winter Ihernglass. Then sergeant. That wasn't so bad. I still just had to follow orders. But now?* The captain had given *her* the assignment, and there would be no one else to blame if it went wrong. *Or if I get my people killed, like d'Vries did.* The lieutenant had been a fool, but . . . *I'm sure he didn't think of himself as an idiot. Who's to say I'm any better?*

The sky was gray with predawn light by the time they reached the river. The Vordanai column had camped a few miles to the west of the Tsel, behind a ridge that would hide their bivouac from any lookouts across the water. They'd left the coast road the day before, behind a strong cavalry screen, and Winter's men trudged across sodden fields and goat tracks to cover the last stretch to the riverbank. The Tsel stretched out before them, looking more like a lake than a river. It was nearly a mile across, milky brown in color, and placid as a millpond.

"Whatever you do," Winter passed the word, "don't drink the water." The warning hardly seemed necessary. After crashing down from the southern highlands and winding its way across the plains, the mighty Tsel was more like an oozing flow of liquid dirt than a proper river. *Not to mention that half of Khandar uses it as a sewer.*

The boats were waiting for them, drawn up on the bank with a guard of a half dozen cavalry troopers. They were a sorry-looking bunch of craft, mostly small fishing skiffs that wouldn't hold more than four or five men, with a couple of shaky-looking rafts and a tub of a barge that looked to have been recently patched and pressed back into service.

"The Auxies aren't stupid," Captain d'Ivoire had explained to her. "They've pulled all the heavy transport over the east bank. But they didn't expect us so soon, so they didn't have time to be thorough. Give-Em-Hell is out there right now, rounding up whatever's left in the fishing villages, and he tells me there's some bits and pieces. Not much, but it should be enough to get your company across, plus a few more men to work the oars. We're volunteering anyone who's ever worked on a boat before."

He'd gone on to explain the strategic situation, pointing here and there on a leather map, but it had rolled over Winter like water off oilcloth. All she'd absorbed was the pertinent facts: *you and your company are going across the river.*

"Right!" she told her men, when they'd gathered around. "Starting putting those boats in the water. Get in a man at a time until it looks like the next man will swamp the thing. Then get down and stay down. I'm not coming back to fish anybody out of the river!"

"But, Sarge, I can't swim!" someone said from the back, and there was a round of laughter. It sounded forced. *They're nervous, too,* Winter realized. Somehow that made her feel a little better.

"Graff," she told the corporal, "you take the barge; that's the biggest. Folsom, one of the rafts. Bobby, stay with me."

The captain's estimate had been accurate, and what was left of the Seventh Company managed to cram aboard the little flotilla, along with the "volunteers" from the rest of the regiment. These rowers were without gear, to keep the load as light as possible, and most of them had stripped their uniforms to the waist in anticipation of a long, hard day's work.

When the last man was aboard, the boats shoved off. Oars flashed, disturbing the smooth brown flow of the river. As the captain had promised, the oarsmen had been chosen from those who knew what they were about, and their progress was steady. The big barge wallowed precipitously low in the water, but with the river so glassy still it hardly seemed a danger.

She'd told the men not to talk once they'd begun to cross. Sound could carry queerly over water, and she was determined not to alert the Auxiliaries until she could no longer avoid it. The morning seemed unnaturally quiet, and every cough or rustle of cloth was audible, even above the creaking of the boats and the steady splash of the oars.

Before long the west bank of the river had dwindled until it was a mere smudge, brown on brown. It was almost like being at sea, with nothing visible but water and a barely distinguishable shoreline. But the sea was never so calm, even on the mildest day. Compared to the gentle rock of the waves, the Tsel felt like something decaying and dead. Even the smell of it was the rich, earthy scent of rot, drifting up from the accumulated silt of a hundred winding miles.

The east bank came into view, so gradually that Winter had to lean forward and squint to be certain. There was a fishing village at this spot on the Auxiliaries' side of the river, a middling-sized place that boasted a long stone quay. Ordinarily it played host to the riverboats that carried grain and produce to satisfy the city's appetite, but General Khtoba had designated it as one of a half dozen spots for his men to store the vessels they'd appropriated from the west bank villages and fisherfolk.

With some relief Winter identified the long, low shapes of the quay and the high-sided barges tied up all around it. It was always good to know that things in the field really were the way the officers had said they'd be, if only because this so rarely turned out to be the case. As they closed, she was further relieved to see no signs of life from the village or evidence of sentries at the riverside. The villagers, no doubt, had fled or been evacuated when the soldiers had arrived.

The quay was so crowded with boats there was no room for her little flotilla to dock. Instead they coasted up beside it, riding next to the enormous grain barges and sleeker fishing skiffs. The shore was a murky mess of mud and cattails, strewn with the skeletons of wrecked boats left there to rot long ago. These obstacles meant they could approach only into the shallows, with the barge bringing up the rear.

Winter waved her hand, and the men piled over the sides, boots sinking in slimy mud and water lapping at their shins. The little boats rocked at the shifting weight, and brown water slopped into the bottoms. Those in the lead waded ashore, raising their knees high to shake off the muck like a troupe of high-kicking dancers. The rest followed. When Winter's turn came, she braced herself and stepped out into the river. Instead of the chill she'd been expecting, the water was as warm as a bath, and her boot sank through a few inches of mud before it met something solid. Something slimy and many-legged brushed against her thigh.

She gave no instructions—this part had all been prearranged. Graff led two dozen men on a broad sweep into the town, to search for and hopefully capture any Auxiliaries who might be on guard.

Winter and Bobby gathered the rest of the company on the shore, assembling on a rough, stony path that ran along the riverbank. The oarsmen swarmed out down the quay, looking for the vessels most likely to suit their purpose.

Graff hadn't returned by the time their leader, a thin-faced corporal Winter didn't recognize, reported back. He kept his voice low, unwilling to break the sepulchral silence.

"We should be able to get a least a dozen of those big barges back for this leg," he said. "Those'll carry a company apiece, easy."

"How many men will you need?" There were too few of the rowers to move the larger boats, so some of the Seventh would have to be drafted as extra hands.

"Call it three dozen."

Winter chewed her lip. That would leave her barely fifty to hold the quay on this side until the boats returned. The captain had been quite specific—they'd need every one of the boats to get the entire regiment and its supply train across. Winter's task would be to make sure the Auxiliaries didn't catch wind of what was going on and wreck the remaining craft before enough men could cross to put them into service.

Things seemed quiet enough, though. She gave a decisive nod and directed the corporal to Bobby, who started telling off men for rowing duty.

The last of the newly crewed barges was just casting off when a pair of shots came from the direction of the village, shockingly loud in the morning quiet. The corporal, aboard the barge, looked back at Winter, but she waved him on and turned to Bobby.

"Corporal Folsom, guard the quay. Corporal Forester, with me." She pointed out another dozen soldiers, and they fell in behind her. They set out into the village at a jog, spurred by another pair of shots that echoed like falling trip-hammers.

The village would barely have qualified as a hamlet in Vordan. It was just a cluster of clay-and-thatch houses, not more than twenty in all, arranged in a rough circle. The occupants were long gone, and the empty doorways gaped at Winter as she passed. Up ahead, against the walls of the last couple of huts, were a dozen men in Vordanai blue. Graff trotted up to meet her, his face grim.

"One of 'em got away. Sorry, sir."

Winter shoved down a sudden thrill of panic. "How many were there?"

"Four. Out a good distance, away from the houses, so we couldn't get close without them seeing. We got as near as we could and tried to bring 'em down, but that was still a long shot."

"Only one escaped?"

"Yessir. We got two, and one whose horse was hit surrendered. They got one of ours, though."

"Who?"

Graff pursed his lips in disapproval at the question, but said, "Jameson. He's dead, sir."

No time for regrets now. "Take me to the man you captured."

Graff nodded and conducted Winter forward. The men Graff had brought with him were still on guard, muskets loaded and at the ready, as though they expected the Khandarai to return any moment. The unfortunate Jameson lay on his face where he had fallen, a bloody hole the size of Winter's fist between his shoulder blades. Winter looked away.

Two Khandarai lay out in the field beyond the village, while a third sat cross-legged under the watchful eyes of a pair of Vordanai. He surveyed his captors with an arrogant air, and, guessing that none of them spoke Khandarai, amused himself by insulting them to their faces.

"You, on the left. If you were not born of the union of a bitch and a goat, then your mother must have been a woman of such surpassing ugliness I wonder that any man would stoop to lay with her." On seeing Winter, he added, "Ah, and here comes the commander, who is evidently a boy of twelve. Drop your pants, sir, and let us see if there is any hair on your cock. Or perhaps you were born without one?"

"Shall I order them to strip you," Winter snapped in Khandarai, "so that we can have a comparison?"

The man sat up a little straighter, but said nothing. Winter shook her head.

"Should I bother asking questions?" she said. "Or should I just tell my men to begin beating you?"

The Khandarai blinked. He was a young man, in the brown and tan uniform of the Auxiliaries. His dark hair was gathered at the back of the neck, in the Khandarai fashion, and his chin was covered with a bristly fuzz that he probably thought of as a beard. By his lack of insignia, he was a ranker—the Auxiliaries used the same ranks as the Royal Army—but he wore an armband of red silk, daubed with the ubiquitous open triangle of the Redemption in black ink.

All in all, aside from the uniform, Winter wouldn't have given him a second glance if she'd passed him in the streets of Ashe-Katarion. She might even have shared a drink with him, if they'd met in a tavern. But now . . .

"I don't know what you're doing here," he said. "But you'd be best advised to surrender when Rahal-dan-Sendor fetches our men. You'll be treated kindly, I assure you."

"How many men in your force? How far away are they?"

He looked at her defiantly. Winter looked over her shoulder at Graff.

"Lay one across his jaw, would you? Then try to look menacing."

"Gladly," the corporal growled.

Winter was still fighting a sick, acid feeling in her gut when she returned, with Graff and Bobby, to the rest of the company.

"I don't know what you said to him," Graff said, "but that was neatly done."

"Sergeant Davis was an excellent tutor," Winter muttered. Her knuckles itched, as though she'd administered the beating herself.

Folsom had the rest of the men loading and checking their weapons. The big corporal stood up and saluted as they approached, and the rankers made to do likewise. Winter waved them back to their task.

"We're going to have guests," she told them. "There's a Khandarai detachment not far from here. Four companies, unless our friend with the black eye was telling stories. We've got maybe twenty minutes before they arrive."

There were a few groans from the men near enough to hear. Winter turned to Bobby.

"How long until the boats get back?"

"It took us nearly an hour to cross, sir." The boy seemed perfectly composed, in spite of the bad news. "It'll probably take the big barges a little longer. Plus they may take some time to get things arranged on the other side. Call it three hours total."

"Captain d'Ivoire will have everything ready the moment they touch bank." That was partly for the soldiers' benefit, but it was also the truth, or so Winter devoutly hoped. She had a lot of faith in Captain d'Ivoire. "So we've got to keep them off the quay for a few hours."

The three corporals nodded. Winter was a little surprised at the lack of protests. She felt as though, in their place, she would have said something like, "That's impossible!" or "We'll all be killed!" Even the rankers seemed more confident than she was. She took a long breath and tried to think.

"Right," she said eventually. "Break into teams of three. Each team takes a hut. One man shooting, two loading. If you haven't got a convenient doorway, knock a hole in the wall. I'll take the first shot myself, so hold fire until you hear it." She raised her voice. "Everyone got that?"

There was a ragged chorus of assent. Winter turned to the three corporals. "Folsom, Graff, get the teams set up around the center of the village. Bobby, you're with me in case I need a runner."

"Yessir!" The boy's eyes were bright. *He's looking forward to this. How can he be looking forward to it?*

"I don't mean to contradict you, sir," Graff said in a low tone, "but what if they don't come in dumb? If I was in charge out there, I'd break out some men to search the houses. If it comes to hand-to-hand, they'll swamp us."

Winter risked a smile. "That's because you're not an educated man, Corporal. Did any of your old commanders do things strictly by the tactics manual?"

He scratched a bearded cheek. "No. At least not for long."

"These Auxiliaries were trained to be model Vordanai soldiers. I should know; we used to have to train them."

"So?"

"So they really *believe* in that tactics manual."

Either the Khandarai had taken longer than Winter had expected to get organized, or else the twenty minutes had merely *felt* like hours. She hoped it was the former.

She and Bobby were crouched in one of the little clay huts. It was nearly empty inside, the inhabitants having carried away everything they could when they left. The only evidence of the occupant's profession was a pile of half-mended net lying against the wall. The building was a simple dirt-floored affair, with a ring of stones in the center for a fire and a single doorway. It now also boasted an impromptu window—a few minutes' work with bayonets had been enough to carve a head-sized hole through the soft clay. It was through this hole that Bobby was keeping watch to the northeast, the direction from which the prisoner had said the Khandarai would come.

When the boy waved her over, Winter's tension ratcheted up another notch. She'd been halfway hoping the Auxie had been lying, out of bravado or a desire to frighten her off. *Apparently not.* Leaning out the doorway, she could see men in the distance, marching across the sodden fields. They were in close order, as though on parade, a wall of brown uniforms and glittering weapons.

At least she couldn't see any guns. That would have spelled the end of any chance of effective resistance—these clay walls would offer little protection from cannonballs, and the Auxiliaries would be happy to blast the huts to pieces and march in over the ruins. *As it is . . .*

She watched for a few tense minutes. Bobby, at the loophole, had a better view than Winter.

"They're doing something," he said. "Changing formation, or—"

"Breaking off." Winter saw it, too. "Damn. They'll send part of the force in and keep the rest as a reserve."

"Should we change the plan?"

"No time now. Just don't shoot until I tell you."

While one group of men stood, staid as cows, out in the fields, the advance force closed in. Winter guessed there were two companies—two hundred forty men, give or take—in a neat column on a half-company front. The leading men passed between the outermost pair of huts, stepping in unison to the steady beat of their drums. She could see a lieutenant in front of the first rank, his drawn sword in his hand.

Winter sent up a silent prayer that her men would remember their instructions, and have the stomach to sit on their hands until the Khandarai got closer. Surprise was a precious thing, and they would get only one chance at it. *Though with another two companies in reserve . . .* She shook off the thought.

Apparently the Almighty was listening. No shots echoed through the village as the Auxiliaries advanced, neat tan boots spattered with mud. The head of the column was nearly level with her hut now, which was most of the way to the waterfront. The rear was just entering the village.

"Think you can hit that lieutenant?" Winter said.

The boy frowned. "That seems a little unsporting, sir."

"Sporting is for handball. Drop him."

The boy nodded and bent to one knee, resting the barrel of his musket on the edge of the loophole. The man Winter had so casually marked for death was barely ten yards away, still oblivious, conducting the march with his shiny sword as if he were in review in front of the palace.

The *crack* of the musket was magnified in the tiny interior of the hut until it sounded like a mountain shattering. Smoke boiled up from the barrel and the lock of Bobby's weapon, obscuring the view through the loophole, but watching from the doorway Winter could see the lieutenant spin and fall.

Almost immediately, shots cracked from all over the village, puffs of smoke rising from doorways and loopholes. The tight column was a difficult target to miss, and a chorus of screams and shouts from the Khandarai attested to the effect of the fire. Bobby grabbed Winter's musket, loaded beforehand, and returned to the loophole. Winter watched a moment longer from the doorway.

As she'd hoped, the ground-in discipline of the Auxiliaries held them in position while their officers tried to make sense of what was happening. With the lieutenant down, some poor sergeant would be shouting orders. In the meantime, the column had halted, the men standing impassively in the face of balls that whistled by or stung like hornets.

That won't last, though. Discipline or not, no soldiers would stand and be slaughtered without replying. The tight ranks of the Khandarai started to break up, individuals or pairs dropping to one knee or turning to find their tormentors. Muskets started to sound from the column, and the zip and whine of balls was soon accompanied by the *pock-pock-pock* of shots hitting clay.

Winter ducked inside, grabbed Bobby's fired musket, and started to reload it. Bobby, having fired his second shot, hit the ground beside her to work on the other weapon. Outside, the fusillade continued. Winter had little doubt the Auxiliaries were getting the worst of it. It would be easy enough to see where the ambushers were firing from, as each loophole and doorway was marked by a cloud of powder smoke. Scoring a hit on the fleeting shapes beyond was another matter.

If they had any sense, they'd have run for it the minute we opened fire. Discipline and the tactics manual triumphed over sense, however. Winter fell into the simple routine—bite the cartridge open, pour in the powder, spit the ball down, and ram the whole thing home. Prime the pan, hand the musket to Bobby, accept a just-fired weapon in return. The barrels grew hotter with each firing, until they scorched her skin when she touched them, but she kept on. Shots hit the house in a steady rain. One or two even broke through the clay. Winter watched, fascinated, as a musket ball smashed through six inches above Bobby's head, caromed weakly off the opposite wall, and rolled to a stop at her feet like a flattened marble.

And then there wasn't another musket to load. The firing died away in fits and starts, but after a minute or so of silence, Winter risked a look out the doorway while Bobby stood vigil at the loophole with a loaded weapon.

The field of battle—if it could be called a battle—was empty except for corpses and a few wounded men, the latter beginning to raise piteous cries. It was hard to get a good sense through the smoke, but there seemed to be a great many corpses, for the most part lying in the neat rows in which they'd stood. Winter emerged from the hut and cupped her hands over her mouth.

"I'm coming out!" she shouted. "Everyone hold fire!"

She could hear a ragged chorus of laughter from the closest buildings. Bobby hurried to fall in behind her, still carrying his weapon, and Winter walked out into the center of the field. Smoke lay as dense as a blanket, drifting only sluggishly in the calm air. The smell of it assaulted her nostrils, an acrid, salty tang with an occasional undercurrent of blood or offal. There was no sign of any upright Khandarai.

Winter turned sharply when a pair of figures loomed through the smoke, but it was only Graff and Folsom. The rest of the company was beginning to emerge. As the realization of what they'd done sank in, here and there they sent up a ragged cheer.

Graff looked over the field of corpses with professional satisfaction. "They won't forget that in a hurry," he said. "Those that got away, anyhow."

Winter gave a weary nod. All the Auxiliaries she could see were either dead or obviously nearly so. The retreating Khandarai had taken the more lightly wounded with them, for which she was grateful. The Colonials could hardly have spared the time to care for them.

"Right," she said, more or less to herself. Then again. "Right. We've probably got a little while before they figure things out. Folsom, collect all our people and find out what we lost. Graff, take a detail and go over the field. The Auxies use the same muskets we do, so gather them all up, along with all the ammunition you can find. If there's anyone out there who looks like they might make it, bring them along. Once that's done, back to the river."

"We're not staying here?" Graff said. "We bloodied their noses—no reason why we can't do it again."

"We can't do it again because they'll be ready for us," Winter said. "Someone out there isn't an utter fool. They won't come in dumb next time. Either they'll break out and come at us in loose order, like they should have in the first place, or else they'll skirt the village entirely and go straight for the boats." She thought for a moment. "More likely the latter. So we fall back to the quay."

"If you don't mind my saying," Graff said quietly, "is that a good idea? We'll have no cover at all. The lads are willing, but we won't last if we have to go volley for volley with four companies."

Winter nodded. "Bobby, you're with me. We're going to see what we can do about that."

"Pull!" Folsom shouted, his deep voice echoing off the barges. "Wait, two, three, *pull*!"

He demonstrated with a massive effort on his own part, muscles standing out in his arms like corded ropes. Two dozen men behind him added their strength to the line, and the barge groaned and jolted another foot up onto the quay. The rear end was out of the water now, dripping brown mud into the river.

Winter stood with the casualties at the far end of the stone pier. There had been four of these: one ranker who'd taken an unlucky shot through a doorway and lost the top of his head, two men wounded by balls that had punched through their protective walls, and an unfortunate recruit who'd accidentally double-loaded his weapon after failing to notice a misfire. Packed with twice the normal load of powder, the musket had exploded, leaving the side of his face a lacerated ruin.

The dead man was covered by a tarp, while Graff did his best for the three wounded. They hadn't done a precise count of the Khandarai dead, but Winter guessed there'd been more than eighty, plus however many they'd dragged away. For fifty men against two hundred, that was no poor result, militarily speaking, but standing beside the boy with the torn face Winter couldn't help but feel like a failure.

She focused on the river instead. The sun was well up by now, and the morning haze had burned away, but if there were barges on their way back across Winter couldn't see them. Bobby, standing at her shoulder, correctly interpreted her thoughts.

"It'll be at least another hour, sir," the boy said.

Winter nodded and looked away. Her gaze fell on the man who'd taken a ball in the arm. Graff had torn his shirt off and wrapped it round the wound as a makeshift bandage, winding a scrap of wood in the linen to keep it tight. Bobby, following Winter's eyes, gave a little shudder.

"Are you sure you're all right?" Winter said. A flying splinter of clay had given the boy a cut on the shoulder. Winter hadn't noticed the damp patch on his uniform until after the fighting was over.

"It's nothing, sir. Honestly."

Graff stood and came over to them. "Perkins will be all right, but Zeitman will probably lose the arm once we get him back to the cutters. Finn—" He glanced at the boy with the mutilated face. "That needs cleaning out, but he screams if I so much as touch him. He needs a proper surgeon."

"You've done what you could," Winter said. "Go take over loading detail." The weapons they'd gleaned from the Auxiliaries lay in neat rows on the quay, all bright wax and polish. A group of Colonials was methodically cleaning the barrels and loading them, one after another, from a pile of captured ammunition.

There was a great crash from farther up the pier as Folsom's team flipped the barge end over end, so that its flat, dripping bottom was exposed to the sky. Resting lengthwise, it overhung the quay by a few feet on either end. She'd chosen one that was four or five feet high and made of sturdy-looking wood. The sides would probably stop a ball, at least at long range, and it would take a few moments for any attacker who wanted to use his bayonet to scramble over. Combined with the boats tied to the dock on all sides, it would provide a reasonable degree of shelter from fire from the shore. It was the best she could hope for under the circumstances.

Finn touched his face where the metal shards had torn it and gave a little screech. Bobby jumped visibly. Winter laid a hand on his shoulder and conducted him away from the impromptu hospital, back toward the barricade.

"Sir?" Bobby's voice was hesitant. "I don't mean to be . . . that is . . . can I ask you a favor?"

"A favor?"

Bobby stopped. His voice was low enough that only Winter could hear. "If I ever get—hit, you know, and—"

"Stop," Winter said. "Everyone knows that talking like that is the next best thing to asking for it. The Lord Above loves irony."

Bobby winced. "Sorry, sir. But this is important. If—you know—can you promise me something?"

"Maybe," Winter said.

"Don't let them take me to a cutter," Bobby said urgently. "Please. Take care of me yourself."

"I'm not much of a surgeon."

"Then . . . Graff, or someone you trust. But no cutters." He looked up at Winter, and his soft face was full of desperation. "Please?"

Winter would usually have given her word at once, and then broken it just as easily when the need arose. A lot of soldiers had that sort of feeling about surgeons. It was only natural, if you'd spent any time in a hospital or watched the men hobble out short an arm or a leg. Winter wasn't fond of the medical men herself. But when it really came down to it, she suspected she'd rather live as a cripple than die a slow, agonizing death from a festering wound.

Under ordinary circumstances, she would have put this down to pre-battle jitters, the sort of thing Bobby would forget about tomorrow morning. But there was something disturbingly sincere in the corporal's eyes, so Winter chose her words carefully.

"Graff isn't a surgeon, either." She watched the boy's expression. "Let's be clear about this. If it's a choice between going to the cutter or into the ground—"

"I'd rather die," Bobby said immediately. "Promise me."

After a moment of hesitation, Winter nodded. "I promise, then. But you'd better not get yourself hurt, or I'll have a hell of a time explaining myself to Folsom and Graff afterward."

Bobby gave a weak chuckle. Winter tried to think of a way to dispel the grim mood that had descended, but was spared the necessity. There was a shot from the barricade, and a cry of "Auxies!" The quay was suddenly a chaos of rushing men. Winter heard Folsom's voice rising above the din, shouting soldiers into line.

She patted Bobby's shoulder again and pushed her way forward, until she was up against the sloping wall of the upside-down boat. It rose slightly toward the center, forming a shallow keel, but the top was still flat enough to see over. She saw Graff upbraiding a man carrying a smoking musket.

The situation wasn't as bad as she'd feared, then. Looking up the quay, between the wall of boats on each side and into the village, she couldn't see any obvious sign of the enemy. She pulled Graff away and asked for a report.

"Sorry about that, sir. He shouldn't have fired."

"False alarm?" Winter said hopefully. Every minute the Auxiliaries delayed was a minute less they'd have to wait for reinforcements.

"They were there, right enough, but only a couple. I saw three men, but there may have been a few more. Back amidst the houses, sort of skulking, like. Ferstein took a potshot and they all started running."

"Scouts, then." Winter chewed her lip. "He knows we're not in the village, and that we're barricaded in here. Maybe he doesn't know that we're waiting for the rest of the regiment to cross. Could be he's waiting for reinforcements of his own."

"Could be, sir," Graff said.

"Let's assume not."

Winter looked up at the boat Folsom had dragged into place. There was room for only eight or nine men to stand across the quay, shoulder to shoulder. That wasn't a lot of fire, even with a good supply of loaded weapons. On the other hand, the enemy would be similarly restricted, and they wouldn't have anything to hide behind.

"If they come, they're going to get a kicking," Graff said,

echoing her thoughts. "I wouldn't like to try attacking up this way."

"Let's hope they'll be just as reluctant."

As it turned out, they were not.

It was a further half an hour before the enemy commander decided the village was clear and marched his men in. All four companies, or what was left of them, formed up in the town square. They were three or four hundred yards from the edge of the quay, and twenty more from the barricade. Close enough for the Vordanai to shout and make insulting hand gestures, but too far for anything but an extremely lucky shot to carry.

There was one man ahorse just in front of the enemy ranks, who Winter assumed was the commanding officer. She hoped he'd display the same lead-from-the-front mentality that his lieutenant had shown earlier, but no such luck. When the brown-and-tan column lurched into motion, the mounted man stayed well to the rear. Winter signaled for her own men to make ready. Nine of them, chosen by general acclamation to be the best shots in the company, were crouching against the barricade. The rest of the rankers waited nervously behind them, spread out across the quay, sitting or on their knees to avoid showing their heads over the top of the boat.

The Auxiliaries were in a company column, forty men wide and a dozen or so deep. Their drummers quickened the pace as they approached, from the languid march rhythm to the pulse-fast beat of the attack. Winter's men waited, bayonets already fixed on their muskets, until the column was a hundred yards out—still well away from the base of the quay but clear of the last few houses in the village.

At a gesture from Winter, the men on the barricade opened fire. The crash of nine muskets at once, in the echoing confines of the boat-crowded quay, sounded more like a battalion volley. Smoke billowed along the barricade, and here and there in the front rank of the approaching formation men twitched and went down, or dropped out of line and stumbled off to the sides. A hundred yards was still a long shot for a musket, but the target was wide and packed shoulder to shoulder, so some balls inevitably struck home.

As soon as they'd fired, the men on the barricade turned and handed their weapons to soldiers waiting behind them, accepting fresh ones in return. Winter watched the exchange with a touch of pride. For something she'd improvised on the spot, they handled it nicely. Another volley crashed out, more ragged than the first as the individual men fired as quickly as they could mark a target. More Auxiliaries went down. The brown-and-tan column closed up around the casualties, its ranks swallowing the fallen like some amorphous multibodied creature. Winter could hear the shouts of the Khandarai sergeants pushing their men to keep the line straight in spite of the losses.

Another volley, and another, until all cohesion was lost and there was simply a steady rattle of shots. New muskets were handed up as quickly as they were fired, while the balance of the company worked on reloading. The tread of the Auxiliaries' boots was audible under the intermittent cracks of the shots and the fast beat of the drums. Winter watched the remorseless advance of the column with rising dread.

Come on, she thought at them. *You don't like this, do you? Break off—*

The drums stopped, and then the footsteps.

"Down!" Winter shouted.

A moment later, the first two ranks of the column cut loose. The roar of musketry drowned the sound of the balls striking the boat, but Winter could feel the barricade shiver and jump under the impact. More shots zipped and whistled overhead.

"Fire!" she called, and the men who'd ducked behind their makeshift breastwork popped back up and continued their withering barrage. At fifty yards, nearly every ball told. The few that didn't hit the dirt in front of the Auxiliaries, throwing up little fountains of mud.

Another volley from the Khandarai made the boat shake and splinter. Once again, the Vordanai ducked, which rendered the shots mostly ineffective. The Auxiliaries' fire-discipline was breaking under the stress and excitement of battle, as it always did once soldiers were hotly engaged. The next volley was ragged, with shots continuing to sound a considerable time after the main blast, and from that point on the shooting dissolved into a general racket on both sides as men fired, loaded, and fired again as fast as they were able.

One of Winter's nine leapt back from the barricade, cursing and clutching the bloody mess of his left hand. Graff gestured and one of the loaders took his place, taking up the fallen musket and firing into the gathering smoke. It was becoming difficult to see, but judging from the pinkish yellow muzzle flashes the Auxiliaries were still out at fifty yards, some distance from the base of the quay.

Winter could well imagine their commander's consternation. Only his first two ranks could fire, but that still gave him eighty muskets engaged to her nine. On the other hand, Winter's men were getting off three or four shots for every one the Khandarai loosed, and they were protected by the barricade.

Moreover, he had few options for rectifying the situation. The closer he got to the quay, the more the barges lining the sides would restrict his visibility, until he was reduced to the same nine-man front. The only other option was to charge and hope to carry the barricade with bayonets, but the tactics manual said that a bayonet charge would be effective only against an enemy already shaken or routed by fire, and the defenders here were clearly anything but shaken.

Winter hoped like hell the man stuck to the tactics manual. The Auxiliaries had plenty of bodies in the rear ranks to replace those that fell, she knew, but how long would they stand it? No matter how well trained, there was a limit, and no soldier liked to stand in a position where he was obviously getting the worst of it.

One of the men in blue flopped backward from the barricade, thrashing on the quay like a landed fish. Winter glanced in his direction and then looked away with a shudder; the ball had carried away a quarter of his skull, and he'd splashed the stones with blood and bits of slime when he fell. Graff sent another man up the barricade and detailed two more to drag the dead man to the rear and out of view.

She turned back to the battle, only to find it dying away at last. Either panic had triumphed over discipline or the enemy commander had recognized the futility of his position and backed away voluntarily. Whatever the case, there were no more muzzle flashes in the smoke, and no skirl of advancing drums. The men on the barricade fired a few more shots on general principle, then let out a cheer to hurry the Khandarai on their way.

It wasn't until the cheering became general that Winter noticed that one of the soldiers leaning on the boat wasn't joining in. She had a couple of men pull him away, and they found he'd taken a ball in the chest and died in place, painting the woodwork red with gouts of arterial blood. In the confusion of battle, no one had noticed.

That dampened the atmosphere somewhat. Winter stared out into the swirling smoke while Graff conducted the poor dead boy to the end of the pier. Her apprehension increased by degrees, until by the time he returned she was certain something was wrong.

"They're not gone," she told him. "We'd have heard them shouting if they'd really broken." She looked around at her own men. "Quiet! Graff, get them to be quiet."

"Quiet!" said Graff, and Folsom took up the cry at a bellow. One by one the men fell silent, all looking toward the barricade, and hands tightened around weapons. Finally, all that could be heard was the gentle creaks and scrapes of the boats riding against the quay, a little splashing from the river, and—quiet conversations, close at hand. Too low to hear the words, but Winter didn't need to. A horrible picture had sprung full-formed into her mind.

"They're not gone," she said. "They split up and spread out along the shore, behind the boats." While the wall of high-riding barges protected the defenders from enfilading fire from attackers on the riverbank, it also mostly concealed the bank from view. There was only one reason to take up such a position. "They're going to try to storm us."

Graff spat a vile curse and turned to the men. "Fix bayonets! Helgoland, you're on the wall. The rest of you form up—no, stay on your knees! Two ranks, loaded weapons, hold fire until my command!"

"Sir," Bobby said by Winter's elbow, "we'd better move back."

That rankled, but she could see the logic in it. There was no sense in being in the line of fire, where she might prove an impediment to her own men. She and the corporal threaded their way through the double line of kneeling men that Graff was organizing, and took a position beside Folsom and the remaining dozen men of the company, who were still loading muskets as fast as they could ram home powder and ball.

Graff joined them, and just in time. A shout from the men at the barricade warned that the Khandarai were approaching, boiling out of the smoke at a run. There was no careful drum-timed advance this time, just a swarm of brown uniforms and the wicked gleam of fixed bayonets.

The Colonials at the barricade needed no encouragement. They fired at once. At less than twenty yards, the volley had a dreadful impact, bowling men completely off their feet and spraying blood across those who came behind them. The charge had too much momentum to stop, however, and the Auxiliaries came on like maddened hornets, trampling the bodies of their comrades in the narrow confines of the pier.

They reached the boat and started to clamber over, stumbling a little on the still-wet surface. One man lost his footing and crashed back into his fellows, but more made it to the top. For a moment, they were silhouetted against the afternoon sky, brown on blue.

"First rank, *fire*!"

Graff timed it nicely. The men on the barricade had thrown themselves flat after firing their volley, and with the range barely over ten yards the Colonials had a target any game hunter would have envied. The roar of the volley was louder than thunder, and the men standing on the boat jerked or spun away, sliding off the curved wood to land bonelessly on the pier.

There were more behind them, though, pressed forward by the tight confines and the momentum of the rear ranks still pouring onto the quay. Graff waited until a few had gotten their footing before calling for the second rank's volley, which cut them down like wheat. More tried coming over on their bellies, slithering across on the slick undersurface of the upturned boat, but the men who'd crouched in the shadow of the barricade grabbed these brave souls as they emerged and dragged them to the ground to apply their bayonets.

More dangerous were the shots that were starting to come from the Auxiliaries packed against the barricade. Cover worked both ways, after all—now it was Winter's men who were exposed on the naked stones of the quay, while the Khandarai had the boat to hide behind. A man in the second line jerked backward with a screech, toppling against one of the barges. The rest, having retrieved loaded muskets from the fast-diminishing stock, fired back in an effort to force the Auxiliaries to keep their heads down.

That's it, Winter thought. *I'm out of tricks.* Her men wouldn't flee—couldn't, really, with their backs literally against a wall—but at this rate they'd be wiped out. She looked at the tight-packed mob of soldiers on the other side of the boat and wished, absurdly, for a cannon—a single load of canister would have cleared the quay. *Of course, if we could have gotten any guns across the river we wouldn't be having this problem—*

She blinked in disbelief. The mob was breaking up. Auxiliaries were starting to run, first those at the rear, then the men closer to the front as the pressure from behind started to ease. The rest of the Colonials saw it, too. Cheers started to rise again, louder and louder.

But—they finally had us! Why . . .

It wasn't until Graff let out a satisfied sigh that Winter finally turned around. The end of the quay—the only space through which she'd been able to get a view of the river—was now blocked by one of the high-sided grain barges. The front hinged down to make a ramp, and men in blue were pushing past the cheering defenders, weapons at the ready. As the fighting faded, Winter could hear firing elsewhere along the riverbank.

Behind the first wave of fresh troops came a neat figure in dress blues, eagles glittering on his shoulders. His deep gray eyes took in the scene on the quay for a few moments, and then he turned to Winter and smiled. Winter, only partly recovered from her shock, managed a hesitant salute.

"Well done, Lieutenant," said Colonel Vhalnich. "Very well done indeed."

Chapter Eleven

MARCUS

"—Then he'd dragged a boat across the pier, to make a sort of breastwork," Janus said, cheerful as a kid with a new toy. "You really ought to have seen it, Captain, it was a neat piece of work. Brown uniforms lying on the other side as far as the eye could see, and not even two dozen of ours so much as hurt."

"That's why you put them there, wasn't it?" Marcus said.

"I expected them to have to keep off a few raiders. It was pure bad luck there happened to be four companies within an hour's march. Most commanders would have packed their men onto the boats and rowed for it when they saw the odds." He paused. "Most sensible commanders, anyway."

Marcus could have done without the reminder that they'd nearly forfeited the campaign before they'd begun, just because a few hundred Auxiliaries had been in the wrong place at the wrong time. A symptom of inadequate intelligence gathering, of course. The lack of cavalry for reconnaissance had been a handicap from the beginning, but it made Marcus more nervous the closer they got to Ashe-Katarion.

"It may not have the sweep of Noratavelt or the romantic pageantry of Ilstadt, but if you ask me, there's as much artistry in a well-executed skirmish as any proper battle. Or in any painting or sculpture, if it comes to that." He cocked his head. "Another monograph, when I get the free time. 'War as Art.' I think the general's job is harder than the painter's; canvas doesn't fight back, after all."

Art had never been Marcus' strong point. "Have you thought about what you're going to say to the prince?"

"I'm going to tell him to look under his loincloth and figure out if he's a man or a eunuch," Janus said. "And if he does find a pair of balls, I'm going to suggest that he learn to use them."

Marcus stopped in his tracks, so that the colonel walked a few paces farther before turning. Janus sighed at the expression he saw.

"No," Janus said. "Not really. Has anyone ever told you, Captain, that you need to work on your sense of humor?"

"I'm not used to needing one around senior officers," Marcus muttered. Janus, who had very good hearing, chuckled broadly.

The rigors of the march had reduced the prince's ability to keep up his accustomed style, though his entourage made the best effort they could. He had an enormous tent, sewn together from four of the regulation army tents, but the exterior was plain blue canvas and the inside not much better ornamented. Much of what the royal household had been able to carry away from Ashe-Katarion had been loaded onto the fleet at Fort Valor. A few furs and some silk cushions were all the luxury the rightful occupant of the Vermillion Throne could manage.

Razzan-dan-Xopta was on hand to greet the two officers, but much of the rest of the entourage had been left behind, including the Heavenly Guard. Marcus approved—nothing slowed down an army like useless impedimenta—but he doubted the prince shared his reasons. He got the feeling the Khandarai ruler was skeptical about their chances.

Perhaps still stung from his last audience with Janus, the prince dispensed with the formalities. He barked out a question, and Razzan translated, for Marcus' benefit if not the colonel's.

"His Grace is concerned," the minister said. "He wishes to know how you propose to defend him from his enemies when your army is on the other side of the river."

"I must admit that I cannot," Janus said. "Please tell His Grace that I would feel much more assured about his safety if he were to cross with us."

The prince said something petulant. Razzan said, "The Chosen of Heaven points out that, on the other side of the river, escape would be impossible in the event that you are defeated."

Marcus eyed Prince Exopter with distaste. The nobleman had made his preferences clear through an endless stream of "polite" missives, directing Janus to appear before him to "receive guidance on the direction of the campaign." What that amounted to, apparently, was retreat. In spite of the victory over the Redeemer army, the prince wanted to flee to Vordan with his gold. But the fleet would not sail without orders from Janus, and Janus had simply ignored the messages.

And this *is who we're fighting to keep on the throne?* Marcus wondered again who, exactly, would be hurt if they just let Exopter scuttle away, if he wanted to so badly. *The Khandarai certainly don't want him back.* In the end, though, it was the honor of the King of Vordan that was at stake, and implicitly the worthiness of a pledge of support from the House of Orboan. *Not to mention the small matter of the screaming fanatics who want to burn us alive, prince or no prince.*

Among the things that had been left behind was the royal makeup artist. The elaborate red-and-white powder that had been the prince's mask was nowhere in evidence. Underneath it was a rather ordinary face, with sagging jowls and thick, pouting lips. A thin fuzz of hair was just beginning to sprout around the crown of his head, but a patch on top remained bare.

"If we are defeated, Your Grace . . ." Janus paused. "You may tell His Grace that if we are defeated, all hope of regaining his throne falls with us, and so I regard it as my duty to press the campaign to the utmost."

"Your duty to His Grace is to obey," Razzan said, almost before his master had finished speaking.

"My pardon. I mean no offense, but my duty is not to His Grace the Prince of Khandar. Rather, it is to His Majesty the King of Vordan, to whom I have sworn my sacred oath. He has directed me to secure the Vermillion Throne, and I intend to do so or perish in the attempt."

There was a long silence. The prince muttered something that sounded like an insult. Razzan, perhaps remembering that Janus understood well enough without the translation, rendered it after only a slight hesitation.

"You are a most impudent man, His Grace says. He promises that his friend and cousin the king will hear of your conduct."

"I have no doubt of that," Janus said.

Through the Last Duke, if nothing else. He'd seen Miss Alhundt around the camp a few times since the battle, but he'd avoided speaking to her. So far she hadn't pressed the issue. He wondered if he had justified an entry in the reports she sent home.

"His Grace will consider what you have said," Razzan said. "You are dismissed."

"Thank you," Janus said. "The last of the regiment crosses by this evening."

The two Vordanai bowed and retreated from the royal presence. The Chosen of Heaven did not look pleased in the least.

"He'll consider what you have said?" Marcus repeated, once they were outside. "What does that mean?"

"It means he'll cross," Janus said, "but he didn't want to say it, because he'd lose face. The last of the baggage train is over?"

"It should be by now," Marcus said, glancing at the reddening sun. "I'll speak to Fitz."

"Good. Then get the Fourth moving. Save space on the boats for the prince and his retinue when they decide to turn up."

"What if they don't?"

Janus didn't bother to answer that.

The prince turned up, of course. Janus embarked with the second-to-last boatload, and Marcus with the very last. He settled in for the trip among the stacked cargo at the front of the barge. It was well after sundown, and the colors were beginning to fade from the western sky. Ahead, a few stars were already winking. Fortunately the crossing was not hazardous, even in the dark—the broad, flat Tsel was as hospitable a river as could be imagined.

The prince's servants had thrown up a silk curtain around him, cordoning off their lord and his noble attendants from the rest of those on the barge. The boat was only half full in any case, and the Colonials seemed inclined to give the Khandarai a wide berth. They accorded Marcus the same privilege. In the days before the Redemption, the men would have thought nothing about coming over to him to share the latest city gossip or grouse about the duty rosters. Now everyone knew he'd been spending time with the new colonel, and apparently Janus' exalted status was contagious.

He was a little relieved, therefore, to hear the sound of boots on the deck behind him. The greeting froze in his throat when he turned to find Miss Alhundt looking down at him through her spectacles, hands on her hips, wearing a curious little half smile.

I want to know where your loyalties lie. Marcus' eyes darted like a cornered animal, but there was nowhere to run. He stood, instead, and sketched a bow.

"Miss Alhundt."

"Captain." Her smile widened slightly. "I feel like you've been hiding from me."

"Duties, I'm afraid. Colonel Vhalnich keeps me busy."

"I imagine." She gestured at the crate Marcus had been using as a bench. "Do you mind if I sit?"

Yes. "Not at all."

She placed herself delicately on one corner, and after some hesitation Marcus resumed his own seat. Together, they stared for a few moments at the black water of the Tsel, smooth as glass except for the fading scars torn by the other barges. The torches and lanterns of the new camp were tiny specks of light on the distant bank, winking like fireflies.

Miss Alhundt broke the silence. "I heard the colonel had a disagreement with the prince."

"I'm not really in a position to comment," Marcus said.

"No," Miss Alhundt said. "No, I suppose not."

There was something odd in her tone, as though the heart had gone out of her questioning. He waited, expecting another attempt, but when he risked a look at her face she was just staring at the water.

It *was* a pretty face, he noted absently. Soft and round, with a small nose and wide brown eyes. The spectacles and severe hairstyle lent her an air of formality, but it felt like a borrowed thing. *A mask*. He cleared his throat.

"Are you all right, Miss Alhundt?"

"He's really committed now, isn't he?" she said. "The colonel, I mean."

"We all are. With the river behind us . . ."

She nodded. "You don't seem worried."

He almost repeated the line about not being able to comment, but it felt wrong. This wasn't a Concordat agent fishing for information, just a young woman looking for reassurance. He forced himself to relax a little.

"The colonel has been right so far."

"He has." She sighed. "Captain, can you keep a secret?"

"I like to think so." Then, a little unfairly, "I didn't think the Ministry was in the business of sharing secrets."

She nodded, as though the jibe were no more than her due. "Not that sort of secret. This is . . . one of mine."

"Oh." He shrugged. "Go ahead, then."

She turned to face him, swinging her legs over the edge of the crate. "It was at the battle on the road. You remember?"

"I'm not likely to forget."

"I was sitting on my horse, watching the charge come in—it was like watching the sea come in, a wave of screaming faces. And you and your men were out front, such a thin line, and I thought we'd all be pulled under. Just crushed underneath, like a wave lapping over a rock."

Marcus said nothing. He thought back to the same moment, waiting desperately for the order to fire, *this* close to yanking Meadow's head around and applying his spurs.

"I prayed," she said, in a whisper. "I literally, honestly prayed. I can't remember the last time I did that. I said, 'God Almighty, if you get me out of this and take me back to my nice safe desk under the Cobweb, I swear to—to *you* that I will never leave it again.' "

"I think every man in that line had something similar in mind," Marcus said. "I know I did."

She let out a long breath and shook her head. "I asked for this assignment, you know. I was bored. Bored! At my safe little desk in the third sub-basement, where mad priests never came screaming over the ridge to try to roast me alive." She looked up at him, glasses slightly askew. A strand of mouse brown hair had escaped from her bun and hung over her ear. "Do the Redeemers really eat their prisoners?"

"Only on special occasions," Marcus said. At the look on her face, he gave a little shrug. "I expect not. They certainly enjoy setting fire to them, but eating them afterward?" He shook his head. "It's just a rumor. Believe everything you hear in the streets and they'll have you thinking the Steel Ghost is a wizard who can bend space and time, and that the old priestesses on Monument Hill can speak with the dead."

She gave a weak chuckle, then lapsed into silence again. The last of the light had faded from the sky, and the barge rowed by torchlight. The constellation of fires on the far bank spread wider as they approached, as though to engulf them. Miss Alhundt's knee, Marcus noted, had fetched up against his own. He could feel the warmth, even through two layers of fabric, though she didn't seem to notice.

"I wanted to apologize," she said.

"For what?"

"For the way I behaved before." She looked uncomfortable. "I have to write a report—you know that, of course. So when I first met you I thought, 'Aha, here's a good source of information.' "

"I gathered that," he said.

She winced. "Was I that obvious about it?"

"More or less."

"This really isn't my job. I read reports other people write, extract the salient points, and write another report. At first I thought this would be just like that, except I'd have to ask questions instead of reading. But . . ." She paused. "When I saw the barges crossing, it sort of hit me. If we lose—if the colonel makes a mistake—or . . . or *anything*, we're all going to die. *I'm* going to die." She looked up at Marcus again with a brave smile. "I'm afraid I've lost my detachment."

"We won't lose." Marcus wished he felt as confident as he sounded. "The colonel knows what he's doing."

"You really admire him, don't you?"

"Is that going in the report?"

She laughed. "I packed the report away. It doesn't matter much now, does it? Either he wins, or else I won't get the chance to send it."

"Then yes. He's—you have to talk to him to understand. He's *different*. When I was at the War College, I knew plenty of colonels, but no one like Janus."

"Janus?" She smiled again. "You're awfully chummy with him."

Marcus blushed under his beard. "He insists. Usually I can get away with 'sir,' though."

"Better than 'Count Colonel Janus bet Vhalnich Mieran,' I suppose." Her eyes glittered in the torchlight. "Well, if he's Janus, I should be Jen. Can you manage that, Captain?"

"Only if I can be Marcus. 'Captain' sounds strange to me, anyway. Old Colonel Warus always called me Marcus, or just 'Hey, you!' "

She laughed again, and Marcus laughed with her.

"Miss Alhundt . . ."

"Jen," she admonished.

"Jen." In the quiet darkness, that felt oddly intimate. "So what are you going to do now?"

"The same thing as everyone else, I suppose. Hope like hell the colonel knows what he's doing." She sniffed. "I don't even know why I'm here, not really. The Cobweb is that kind of place. You hear rumors, but you never *know* anything."

"Not so different from the army after all, then."

"But with us everyone thinks you know. You can see it in the way they look at you." She glanced up at him again, and he was astonished to see tears in her eyes. "I'm just a clerk, really. It's my job. I write reports and . . . and that's all. Just a clerk."

Without really knowing why, Marcus put a hand on her shoulder and pulled her against his side. She gave a little jerk when he touched her, and her skin pebbled into goose bumps, but she raised no objection. After a moment he felt her head on his shoulder.

"I know," he said. "It's all right."

"I'm sorry," she said again.

"It's all right." He gave her shoulder a squeeze. "It's not your fault."

For the rest of the journey, they didn't speak. Jen soon fell into a doze. For his part, Marcus looked up at the growing ranks of stars and thought about Vordan, and the home that now existed only as a fading memory.

The drums started at sunup, in spite of the moans of exhausted men. Those who'd come over on the last relay of boats had gotten only half a night's sleep, but the drummers were relentless, and bit by bit the encampment came alive. Given that he was one of those who'd been deprived, Marcus found himself sympathetic to the groaners.

"I'm still not happy about the split," Janus said, when they met in the sodden fields outside the little fishing village. "But it's the best we can do."

Marcus nodded. He was taking the Old Colonials with him, and Janus the recruits, rather than splitting by battalion. It made more sense, given the nature of their separate tasks, but administratively it was a headache.

"Figure on four days, at the outside," the colonel went on. "One to locate the enemy, one to destroy him, and two to return. Can you give me that long?"

"I can certainly try, sir."

"Good." His smile again, just a flicker, there and gone. "Good luck, Captain."

Behind the two officers, the First Colonials formed up. The larger column, just over two-thirds of the men, all the cavalry, and half the guns, headed south with Janus toward the upstream ford. The remaining third turned their steps north, toward Ashe-Katarion and the canal that linked the city with the Tsel.

Marcus drove his troops hard, and they made good time, free at last of the cumbersome need to wait for the baggage train. The wagons were strung out on the road behind them, left to straggle in as best they could. Speed, Janus had agreed, was of the essence. By evening the canal was in sight, a winding ribbon of reflected light that looked more like a natural stream than an artificial construct. In spite of protests from the footsore grumblers, Marcus stretched the march until they'd reached the outskirts of the town that was their objective. Then, finally, they were allowed to rest, flopping down wherever they stood without bothering to set a proper camp.

Even then, there was no rest for some.

Marcus looked over his troops by torchlight. They were all First Battalion men, picked soldiers, those whom Marcus knew he could rely on when things got dangerous. At their head was Senior Sergeant Jeffery Argot, a grizzled hulk of a man who was among the longest-serving Colonials. He'd been commander of the First Company as long as Marcus had been in Khandar. What he lacked in imagination, he made up for in solidity. He was as completely unflappable as any man Marcus had ever met. The fact that he could wring a man's neck like a chicken's didn't hurt, either.

By rights, it should have been Fitz leading the sortie. Not having the lieutenant there felt strange, like losing a limb. Marcus kept being surprised to find the vast, pockmarked face of Sergeant Argot watching him instead of Fitz's dark, intelligent eyes. But there was no helping it—six companies of the First Battalion, all the recruits, were away with Janus, and Marcus wouldn't have felt right leaving their command to anyone else.

Val and Mor were there, too, and Give-Em-Hell and the Preacher, leaving Marcus with only Adrecht and a handful of junior officers. It had seemed like a good idea at the time—if Marcus could not be there in person, it was the next best thing—but looking at the silent, brooding town in the flickering darkness he wondered if he should have been quite so quick to send them all away.

Adrecht will do what he needs to do. He had revived considerably since his brush with the colonel's displeasure, attending regular drills and showing a renewed interest in command of his battalion. They hadn't spoken much, but the few words they'd exchanged made it clear they didn't need to, to Marcus' vast relief.

Still. I would feel better if Fitz were here. He pushed the thought away—*too late for that now*—and turned to his picked crew. They numbered only two dozen, which he judged enough for the task at hand.

"I make it just past midnight," he told them. "That means we've got three hours or so before first light. You've got that long to get into position. So be quick, and remember that if they hear a gunshot the game's up. Everyone got that?"

They nodded. He watched their faces and was pleased by what he saw. No fear, just a steady determination. Even a bit of relief, he suspected. These were all Old Colonials, after all. In some ways they were as green as the recruits—marching in line of battle with flags flying and drums beating had been a new experience for all of them, Marcus included—but this sort of nighttime creeping was a familiar exercise.

"Right," Marcus said. "Good luck."

The sergeant doused the torch, and the little column set out. They left the road almost at once, heading due east to swing wide around the borders of the little town. Then, if all went according to plan, they would turn north and cut back west when they came close to the canal.

Marcus had made sure to take a good survey of the ground while there was still light, since he didn't much trust his maps. They'd been drawn by Vordanai cartographers, working on secondhand sketches and descriptions, and were often woefully out of date as well. The town they were approaching was so small it hadn't been granted the honor of a label with a Vordanai name, just a colored dot. From the locals they'd interrogated on the approach, Marcus had gathered its Khandarai name was Weltae-en-Tselika, or "Weltae on the little Tsel."

Seen from above, it was roughly triangular in shape, with the point to the south and one flat side against the canal to the north. The ground rose slightly away from the canal, with a few rocky hillocks looming out of the sodden fields, and it was on one of these that the people of Weltae had constructed their temple. This heavy stone structure formed the point of the triangle. The road ran beside it, cutting through the center of town. The buildings lining the road were mostly clay and thatch houses, with a few wooden structures.

The town's most important feature was at the canal. The "little Tsel" was unbridged outside of Ashe-Katarion, and in most places deep enough that a man trying to cross would have to swim the turgid water. Here, though, a dip in the ground caused the water to spread, and it was shallow enough to wade. Over the years, the Khandarai had made the crossing easier by tipping any stones they extracted from their fields into the ford, until it was very nearly a causeway.

For an army moving parallel to the Tsel, it was the only crossing short of making the long detour through the city streets. When General Khtoba moved to unify his divided forces, as he was surely doing even now, the three battalions at Westbridge would have no choice but to come down this road. By that time Marcus intended to be standing squarely in their way.

The locals had volunteered information readily enough—Redemption or no, the Auxiliaries were not popular—and Marcus had learned that there was a small garrison at the ford. It was hard to hide an army, even a small one, on this floodplain as flat as a billiard table, and they no doubt had seen the Colonials approaching. What they didn't know, and what Khtoba would be eager to learn, was his numbers and intentions.

The southern approach to the village would therefore be watched, even by night. The sergeant's circuitous route would take him as far north as the canal well to the east of the village, however, and hopefully stand a good chance of getting near the garrison undetected.

Any sign that the little party was in place would be tantamount to failure, but Marcus couldn't help staring after them, trying to make his eyes resolve shapes in the darkened village by sheer force of will. Eventually he gave it up and started back to rejoin the Old Colonials, who were camped in the muddy fields up the road far enough to be out of sight of the Auxiliary garrison.

Not much to do now but wait.

Just after first light, with the sun still below the horizon and the sky a deep blue-gray, the Vordanai column began to form up on the outskirts of town. It was an ostentatious display—battalion flags flying, drummers beating for all they were worth, lieutenant and sergeants screaming orders—and by forming in columns of companies the Colonials partially masked the fact that each battalion was only a third the size it was supposed to be. Once these noisy preparations had been completed, the line advanced up the gentle slope toward the point of the triangular town and the stone-built temple that dominated it.

The Auxiliary garrison was not inclined to stay to receive them. They had been deployed to protect the ford against raiding parties, not to try to impede a general Vordanai advance, and clearly here were the "corpses" in considerable force. A few desultory shots rang out from the windows of the temple as the blue line came closer, at far too long a range to find their targets, and then the company of Khandarai retreated in good order through the center of town. Their duty now was to rejoin their main body and report on what they'd seen, and accordingly their lieutenant marched his men hastily up the road and toward the ford.

They were in sight of the canal when shots rang out from all sides, billows of smoke rising from the buildings lining the road and behind the embankment. Argot's men, slipping past the sentries in the darkness, had taken up positions close to the ford from which they could direct a lively fire at the Khandarai column. Men fell, screaming, and in a panic the Auxiliaries spread out, seeking whatever cover they could find. A few shot back, trying to pick out blue-uniformed men crouching in doorways or behind windows, and for a few moments the racket of the firefight drowned out all other sound.

Then, during a brief lull, a voice called in Khandarai for surrender. The Auxiliary lieutenant hesitated—the Redeemers were not kind to those who failed in the line of duty—but the choice was obvious. The way ahead was clearly blocked by an enemy force of unknown strength, and in the sudden quiet the drums of the main Vordanai line were quite audible. In any event, his men made the decision for him. First singly, then in twos and threes, they emerged from hiding with hands raised.

"All in all," Adrecht said, "not a bad morning's work. A dozen enemy dead and a hundred prisoners, in exchange for one man taking a bit of a bump on the noggin."

That had been one of Argot's, slightly injured when a shelf had collapsed on top of him during the firefight. Marcus permitted himself a smile.

"Don't forget the lost night's sleep," he said.

"If we can trade a night's sleep for a company in the bag, I think we'll come out ahead."

Adrecht stretched his arms over his head and yawned. *He'd* been able to put his head down for a few hours. Marcus himself had been too keyed up, thinking about Argot creeping into position and scanning the eastern horizon for signs of the rising sun.

"Are they all accounted for?" Marcus said.

"Yup. Their lieutenant is still doing his fence-post imitation, but a few of the sergeants were more talkative. Looks like we got them clean."

The midnight raid had served its purpose, then. News that the Vordanai had seized the ford had not escaped north of the river.

"Good," he said. "That's good."

He turned his eyes north. The two officers stood outside the front door of the temple, on the low hill that dominated the village and the soggy fields beyond. From here Marcus could see the sludgy brown waters of the canal and a good bit of the land beyond. The horizon was thus far reassuringly empty.

Adrecht followed his gaze. "You think they're coming? Maybe we moved fast enough they won't get the news at all."

"They're coming. That first bunch, where we crossed, sent messengers in both directions as soon as they saw they were in for a scrap." He shrugged. "Besides, we haven't got the men to watch the whole canal line. It'd be easy enough for a single messenger to swim. No, Khtoba knows that we're across, and that means his troops aren't doing any good at Westbridge."

"He still might march them through the city, instead of up the river road."

"If he does, they'll be too late to do any good." *Assuming Janus wins the battle in the south.* The colonel had taken the majority of the Colonials to pounce on the other half of Khtoba's divided army, but even that would only give him roughly even odds. He forced himself not to worry about that. *Concentrate on our own problems.* "Either way, we should assume they'll try to force a crossing."

"Stopping three battalions is going to be a hell of a job." Adrecht looked down at the village with a professional eye. "There's no cover on the bank itself. The shacks are worth something, but if they bring up guns it'll be trouble. Even a four-pounder could probably reach us from the other bank, and anything heavier . . ." He shook his head. "If the damn Khandarai would build their houses out of something a bit more substantial, we'd have more to work with. What I wouldn't give for a proper Vordanai country village."

"I think stone and timber are in shorter supply around here than back home," Marcus said. He glanced at the temple behind them. "We can hold in here, though."

Adrecht grunted. "Hold, sure. But if it comes to that . . ." He trailed off sourly.

Marcus followed the thought. The temple made for a reasonable blockhouse, with thick stone walls and a heavy timber roof. The windows were tall and narrow, and began a considerable distance from the ground. The main doors looked solid, and in any case could be reinforced by a barricade. It was big enough to hold two or three companies, at least, and he wouldn't want to have to take on the task of assaulting it if he were on the other side.

But if it got that desperate—a last-ditch defense that far from the ford—they'd be surrounded for certain. Once the Auxiliaries broke out into the open, their greater numbers would let them circle around and cut off any possible retreat.

"We'll hope it doesn't come to that," Marcus said. "Get the men started loopholing the shacks by the canal, and tell Lieutenant Archer to start setting his guns up at the top of the embankment. We'll have to work on something to camouflage them—" Marcus felt suddenly light-headed. He put out a hand to steady himself on the wall of the temple, missed, and took a few stumbling steps before Adrecht caught his arm.

"I'll take care of it," the other captain said. "Get some sleep."

"You'll wake me if there's trouble?"

Adrecht smiled. "I swear to it. Go."

Marcus lurched away, his feet suddenly feeling like they'd grown thirty-pound weights. Inside the temple, the air was dusty, and the floor tracked with mud and bits of smashed furniture. The crews that Adrecht directed inside, later in the day, were astonished to find their senior captain stretched out on a surviving bench, jacket wadded up as a pillow, snoring loud enough to wake the dead.

Chapter Twelve

WINTER

"*Take the knife—*"

Winter opened her eyes. The light was the familiar blue-gray of the morning sun filtered through the faded canvas of her tent, but her lips still tingled from the kiss. When she blinked, tears spilled from her eyes.

"You were dreaming," said a voice in Khandarai. *Feor.* Winter sat up abruptly, rubbing her eyes with the back of her hand.

"How did you guess?"

"You were speaking to someone," the girl said, propped up on one elbow in her bedroll on the other side of the tent.

Winter cursed silently. If she'd started talking in her sleep, there would be no keeping her secret. "What did I say?"

"Nothing I could understand." Feor raised an eyebrow. "In the cloister, there was a young man who dreamed of the future. Was it that sort of dream?"

"No," Winter said. She could still feel the brush of Jane's hair against her face. "I dreamed about the first time I fell in love."

"Ah." Feor fell silent, and Winter gave her a look.

"I suppose priestesses aren't allowed to fall in love?"

"No," the girl said, serious as always. "We are permitted to take our pleasure with the *eckmahl*, the eunuch servants, but love . . ." She caught Winter's expression. "Is something wrong?"

"Just surprised," Winter muttered. "In Vordan, priests and nuns are expected to be chaste."

"I pity them, then," Feor said. "It seems unnatural."

As opposed to taking little boys and cutting off their balls? But she declined to begin that argument. By the amount of light filtering in through the canvas, she could tell it was past dawn. Before she'd made it across the room to her jacket, the drumroll started, at the double-quick pace that meant "to arms." Winter pulled on her uniform coat, buttoned it, and was working on her socks when there was a rap at the tent pole.

"That you, Bobby?" she said, without looking up.

"Yessir," came the boy's voice from outside.

"I'll be there in a moment." Winter turned to Feor. "We're not breaking camp today, so you should be all right here."

The girl nodded. "You will fight today?"

"Probably."

"Then I wish you luck."

"Even though I'll be killing your countrymen?"

"The men of the Redemption are no countrymen of mine," Feor said, with a rare hint of ire. Then her expression turned worried. "Winter-dan-Ihernglass. If . . ."

She trailed off, lips pressed together. Winter forced a smile.

"It'll be fine. Try not to worry." She finished lacing her boots and got to her feet. "We should be back by evening."

Feor nodded. Winter ducked through the flap and into the gray morning light, where her three corporals were waiting. Around them, the men of the Seventh Company were piling out of their tents like ants from a smashed anthill. Since they were planning to return to camp by evening, they could march light, and the soldiers were taking this opportunity to shed all the kettles, utensils, spare clothing, extra biscuits, and miscellaneous loot that somehow ended up in every ranker's pack.

Bobby was smartly dressed and bright-eyed, as usual. Whatever fit of melancholy had come over him on the pier had apparently passed. He hadn't said anything to Winter about her promise, and she hadn't brought it up. He saluted crisply and handed her a half sheet of flimsy paper.

"Orders from Lieutenant Warus, sir!" he said. "The First will be taking the left center of the line. We've got half an hour to report to the south field."

"Right," Winter said. Then, because it seemed like a sergeant-y thing to do, she shouted, "Hurry it up! You've got fifteen minutes!"

It was in fact more like twenty minutes, but the Seventh was still among the first companies on the field. A thin line of blue stood at attention, thickening by the minute as more troops filed in and were directed to their places. Captain d'Ivoire had taken the Old Colonials with him and even after a week on the march the recruits still presented a nicely uniform appearance. Their uniforms were no longer factory-crisp, but they were still deep Vordanai blue, and the dawning sun gleamed off gunmetal and polished buttons.

To the left of the First Battalion was the Third, whose Captain Kaanos was barking orders to everyone in sight. Fitz Warus stood quietly by his side. Kaanos, with his bushy eyebrows and bushy beard and sideburns, resembled a bear and had a voice and temper to match. Winter hurried her company into position, then took up her place in the center file of the front rank.

Whether she should stand in the ranks was something of a sticky question. The proper position of a senior sergeant was the center of the first of three ranks, while his junior sergeant took a similar position in the rear. The leftmost and rightmost files of the company were supposed to be composed of corporals, while the lieutenant had no place in the ranks at all. He stood in front of the men for inspection and behind them in battle, which as far as Winter was concerned said all that needed to be said about officers. While she had, technically, been brevetted to lieutenant, she couldn't bear the thought of acting that way. Fortunately for her, the Seventh Company was conspicuously under-officered, with only three corporals and no sergeants at all, so there was no one to argue with her choice of position.

Ahead of the forming line, the senior officers gathered. She recognized Captain Solwen of the Second, in charge of the other pair of battalions along with a lieutenant she didn't know. Directly in front of her and ahorse was Colonel Vhalnich himself, talking with Give-Em-Hell and the Preacher. The colonel's mood was foul. The approach march had been plagued with delays, culminating in a loss of nearly six hours' marching time when a supply wagon, attempting to jump its place in line after a rest halt, had broken an axle in a ditch and snarled the guns and rearguard. The recruits had quickly become disorganized, and sorting everyone out had consumed the rest of the day. The colonel had been furious.

The time lost had given General Khtoba the chance to abandon his low-lying position by the Tsel ford and retreat to high ground, a stretch of rocky scrubland that rose from the surrounding fields like the low dome of an overturned rowboat. The Colonial camp was near the base of it, in a miserable patch of watery earth churned to mud by the passage of thousands of boots. There had been talk that Khtoba might retreat from even this position, and fall back all the way to Ashe-Katarion, but the scouts had him still in place on the summit.

The ranks were filling out as company after company trickled in, leaving behind the supply train and a few camp guards to watch for Desoltai raiders. The colonel summoned the two infantry captains and dictated a few orders; these two in turn went back to their assigned positions and conferred with their lieutenants. Winter looked left and right, checking her company's alignment against those on either side. Corporal Folsom stood two ranks directly behind her, in the junior sergeant's position, while Bobby and Graff headed the left- and rightmost files. In between, the rest of the

Seventh—considerably diminished compared to the companies around it—stood in three ranks with shouldered muskets.

Lieutenant Warus, after a few words with Captain Kaanos, walked back to the First and gestured for attention. His immaculate appearance was spoiled somewhat by the mud, which had already coated his boots and splattered his trousers.

When he had the eyes of all six companies, he raised his voice and said, "I've never been one for speeches. The Auxiliaries are up *there*"—he jabbed a finger at the hill—"and we're going to go and get them. There's no time for anything fancy. Just remember that when all's said and done, you are the Vordanai Royal Army and they are a pack of grayskins. All their guns and fancy uniforms were a gift from us. If not for us they'd be out here with clubs and spears! General Khtoba used to say that his men were as good as any troops from the continent. I expect you to prove him wrong!"

Winter, who'd read a bit about Khandarai history, knew that was laying it on a bit thick. She suspected Lieutenant Warus knew it as well, but he was playing to the crowd, and it had the desired effect. A cheer rose from the recruits, and Winter added her voice.

Colonel Vhalnich drew his sword, steel glittering in the sun, and slashed it down in a peremptory gesture.

"Ordinary pace!" Fitz shouted. "Form column of companies, and prepare to advance!"

The first they saw of the Auxiliaries was the flashes from their guns.

There had been a general sigh of relief as the Colonials marched out of the irrigated fields with their clinging mud and onto the good, solid ground of the rock outcrop. The regiment advanced as four columns—not the long, winding column of march but squat columns of battle, with a forty-man front and the companies stacked up one behind the other. The Seventh Company was third in line, and the regulation four-yard gap between its front rank and the rear rank of the Sixth Company ahead meant that Winter had a better view of the action than the men stuck in the second rank behind her.

Each battalion column was separated from the others by a good hundred yards or so, to give them room to maneuver and eventually deploy into line. In those intervals came the single battery of light guns that Colonel Vhalnich had brought along. The guns were still limbered, hitched up and facing backward, and the teams of horses strained to drag the weapons and their caissons up the increasing slope. The gunners in their peaked artillery caps walked alongside, shouting good-natured taunts at the infantry on either side, which the rankers cheerfully returned. Winter caught sight of the Preacher off to her left walking behind a two-gun section, his lips moving in silent prayer.

She couldn't see the cavalry from her position, but when the advance had begun she'd watched them ride off to either side, taking up positions on the outside flanks of the formation. Give-Em-Hell had been the subject of particularly extensive instructions from the colonel, and he'd gone off looking pleased, so presumably he had some important role to play. For the moment, Winter's attention was occupied with searching the crest of the hill for the enemy, occasionally sparing a glance to either side to make sure her company's ranks stayed even.

When guns started to flash ahead, it was a moment before she realized what she was seeing. The *booms*, like the grumble of distant thunder, arrived a moment later, followed by the hair-raising whistle of solid shot. The lines of recruits shivered, like wheat trembling in the breeze, as every man instinctively ducked and shied away.

"Stand up straight, you goddamn cowards!" Folsom roared, battle loosening his tongue. "You think leaning a little is going to get you out of the way of a cannonball?"

Similar admonitions were handed out by sergeants up and down the line. The advance paused only briefly. The drums picked up again, going from the ordinary pace to the quickstep, and the march continued.

The range was still long, even given the advantage of height. Most of the balls went overhead, passing with a whine or a weird warbling trill. Others fell short, raising small explosions of dust and soil where they bounced or plowed into a furrow. She watched one shot jump three or four times off the rocky ground, puffs rising at steadily decreasing intervals, like a stone expertly skipped across the surface of a pond.

Winter saw the first hit, on the Third Battalion. The ball hit the ground just beside the rearmost company, raising a cloud of dust and chips of rock, and skipped off at a low angle. It passed diagonally through the block of marching men as though they were nothing more than a thick mist, leaving nothing but wreckage in its wake. The first screams rose, along with the shouts of the sergeants to close up the ranks. The march went on, leaving the little patch of blue and red behind.

The Preacher's guns were still limbered, pushing forward as fast as their teams could drive them. At least six guns were in action now just below the crest of the ridge, and Winter could see the Auxiliary infantry, too, a solid line of brown and tan waiting behind their artillery at the hill's highest point. They looked solid and unshakable, a dense block of men waiting to receive the fragile Vordanai columns with fire and bayonets, and she felt a sudden thrill of fear. Flags flew above each of the Khandarai battalions, crude white things daubed with the rising-flames symbol of the Redemption.

The Khandarai gunners were firing as fast as they could load their pieces, and as the Colonials closed the range the shots became more accurate. Roundshot screamed overhead, cracked and shivered off the rocky ground, and plunged among the marching blue-coated columns. One shot caught three men from the company ahead of hers, snatching them suddenly out of line as though they'd been grabbed by an invisible giant. Winter fixed her eyes dead ahead as her company marched over the corpses, and tried not to think about what might be underfoot.

The lead companies were taking the brunt of the punishment, and it was some time before the Seventh was hit. Even that was an accident; a ball caromed off a buried rock and came down at a high angle, plunging in among her men before bouncing merrily out again. It was as sudden as a thunderbolt from on high. A blast of dust and splinters of rock, screams and curses, and a gap in the ranks.

"Close up!" Folsom shouted, and the other corporals echoed him. Winter added her own voice, hoping no one could hear the trembling. "Close up! Close up!"

Movement at the edges of the line caught her eye. The Auxiliaries were in motion, and at first she couldn't understand why; then she saw blue-coated figures on horseback around both ends of the line, and she realized they were forming square. They did it with enviable precision, going through the evolutions as neatly as a parade, until two-thirds of the Khandarai line had transformed into diamond shapes bristling with bayonets. Even Give-Em-Hell knew better than to charge home against that with his handful of men, and the cavalry broke off well before contact. Even so, smoke puffed from one face of the square, and Winter saw a few horsemen tumble from their saddles.

A heavy roar, closer to her, returned her attention to more immediate matters. The Vordanai guns had finally unlimbered and turned about, and there were scattered cheers from the infantry as someone hit back at their tormentors. The deep-throated *boom* of friendly guns blended with the more distant rumble of the enemy pieces into a solid wall of noise, like a thunderstorm that never ended. The Preacher's artillerymen, firing uphill, had a harder shot than their Khandarai counterparts, but the Auxiliaries had presented them with a near-perfect target—the squares were combat masses, outlined against the midmorning sky. Soon gaps began to appear in the brown-coated line as well, and to close just as quickly as Khandarai sergeants shoved their men sideways.

The drums changed their tempo again, and Winter recognized the intermittent beats of a command. It was reinforced a moment later by a messenger on horseback, shouting over the tumult. She caught only a piece of what he said, but that was enough.

"Halt!" she shouted. "Form line!"

This, at least, they had practiced on the drill field. The lead company halted in place, while those behind marched sideways, then forward, until they came up alongside their fellows to form a solid three-rank line. That was the theory, in any case. Doing it now, with roundshot whistling overhead and occasionally plowing through the ranks, while the drums were drowned out by the roaring of their own guns, was a bit more difficult. Winter had to leave her place in the ranks when her company came up beside the Fifth, to disentangle Bobby's end of the line where it had accidentally overlapped with the other.

The boy saluted as she hurried over, and between them they managed to get the men pushed sideways into their proper places. Winter was glad to see the corporal was unharmed, for the moment. His face was pale as milk, but his expression seemed determined. She wondered, briefly, about her own complexion. Her stomach churned with acid, and her heart beat faster than the drums.

Bobby opened his mouth to say something, but a blast from one of the Preacher's guns drowned the words. Winter shook her head and clapped the boy on the shoulder, then hurried back to the center of the line. She got there just in time. The drums thrilled again, then settled back into the quickstep, and the whole long formation lurched into motion. At the center of each battalion, the Vordanai colors were unfurled, the golden eagle of Vordan on a blue field and the king's diving falcon. They made for wonderful targets, and Winter sent up a silent prayer of thanks that her company was not expected to carry one.

Occasional rattles of musketry indicated that the Vordanai

cavalry were still playing a deadly game of tag with the ends of the Khandarai line, spurring in close when they gave any sign of weakening their square formation and then turning away when the lines of bayonets firmed up. The Preacher's guns were all in action now, throwing their shot through the gaps in the advancing line of blue. The Auxiliaries seemed to be standing the fire at least as well as the Colonials.

As the Vordanai line drew closer, the rumbles of the guns died away. Winter could see the Khandarai gunners hastily swabbing out their pieces and ramming a new round home, but the next shot didn't come. It felt like a reprieve, until she realized why, and then her breath seemed to freeze in her throat.

Canister. The next round would be the last, unless the gunners planned to load their weapons under fire, and they meant to make it count. That last shot would be a canister load, more effective at close range, and so they were waiting.

It seemed to Winter that one of the guns was pointed directly at her. She could practically look down the barrel, a tiny black hole that seemed to expand until it filled her entire world. She felt as though she could see all the way down it to where the tin of shot waited, balanced atop its load of powder.

She knew, suddenly, that she was going to die. It wasn't fear—she'd gone beyond that, somehow, and come out the other side. Just a cold, icy certainty that one of the balls in that cannon had her name carved on the side, that some invisible string of fate would draw it to her unerringly like iron to a magnet. Her legs moved automatically, one step and then another, matching the pace of the drum. If she tripped, she thought that she'd keep going through the motions, legs pumping stupidly in the dust like a windup toy. There was no room in her world for anything else, just the drums and the ground and the distant, deadly mouth of the cannon.

When the blast finally came, there wasn't even time to flinch. The guns erupted with a flash and a billow of thick gray smoke and a *crump* like a collapsing building. Instead of the whistle of solid shot there was a *pitpitpit* like soft rain, the *zip* of balls passing overhead, and the horrible *thock* when they found flesh.

Winter kept marching. She wanted to run, to hide, to scream. Most of all she wanted to search every inch of her body until she found where the ball had caught her. She hadn't felt it, but that didn't mean anything. She didn't dare look down, for fear of seeing her own guts hanging around her ankles, or one arm shot clean away.

Beside her, a ranker—George, she recalled, and wished she could remember his family name—groaned and collapsed into the dust. The man behind him stepped past without looking down, and the ranks of blue closed around him, like a pond closing over a dropped rock.

The Seventh had been spared the worst of the volley. Two companies down, the main force of one of the blasts had gone through all three ranks and punched a dozen men off their feet, with more limping or rolling away clutching their wounds. Up ahead, in the smoke, the gunners were falling back, leaving their pieces behind to retreat to the safety of the main Khandarai line. That line, visible now through the drifting gunsmoke, stood firm in spite of the Vordanai artillery still slamming away at long range. Bayonets bristled up and down the ranks as the brown-coated soldiers stood at attention. All at once, at an unheard command from their officers, they brought their muskets to their shoulders.

Looking left and right, Winter thought for a moment she could see the battle the way Colonel Vhalnich must see it. Only one battalion of Khandarai was still in line, all its muskets available to deliver a single deadly volley, and that was the one facing the First and Second. On the flanks, the threat of a cavalry charge had forced the Auxiliaries to take shelter in protective squares, and they'd wasted their initial volleys trying to drive Give-Em-Hell and his men away. The Third and Fourth Battalions would face much less fire than they could deliver, and if the Auxiliaries tried to re-form now, there was every chance the Vordanai could charge home in the confusion.

That was small comfort to her, though. The forest of muskets in front of her seemed to stretch on forever. The men of the first rank knelt, allowing the second rank's weapons to sight over their shoulders. It seemed impossible that *anything* would survive, let alone enough men to mount an effective attack, but the drums behind her beat on unconcerned, driving her forward like a clockwork automaton.

The volley exploded around them like a lightning strike, the flash of a thousand muskets going off at once almost immediately obscured by a billow of gunsmoke. Balls twittered and zinged past, and men screamed and cursed all around her. For an instant Winter expected to take her next step forward alone, every other soldier cut to ribbons by the deadly fire, but in fact only a dozen that she could see fell out of place in the front rank. They slumped over silently or with a shout, or fell backward, or dropped to their knees and crawled away. Around them, the march went on, driven by the relentless drums.

Somewhere in the cloud of smoke, the Khandarai were reloading. She wondered how long it would take them. She wondered what would happen when they had marched all the way, when they were so close the Auxiliaries could hardly miss.

"Close up!" Folsom was shouting, and Graff along with him. "Close up!"

Bobby. She couldn't hear him. Winter looked frantically in his direction, but the line was solid now, and she couldn't tell if the boy was still in place or not.

The drums trilled, stopped, and picked out a different rhythm. Winter stumbled onward a half step before she registered the change, and had to shuffle backward to rejoin the line. Her legs burned as though they'd been dipped in oil and set alight.

"Ready!"

She wasn't sure if she gave the shout or not, but it echoed up and down the line, and the men obeyed. Winter knelt in place with the rest of the first rank, though she had no musket to shoulder. A pair of barrels swung into place over her head.

"Level!" This time she was shouting with the rest, in time to the drums.

"Fire!"

The world flashed white, as though lightning had struck a foot from her face, and then boiling gray gunsmoke washed over her. The smell of it, dense and acrid, drilled through her nostrils and into the back of her skull.

"Fix bayonets!"

The drums must have beat that order, too, but she could no longer hear them. The cry passed up and down the line, from one officer to another, and the long triangular blades came out of their sheaths and snapped into place.

Then, at last, the drums broke through, with a heavy fast beat that was the simplest order of all. Winter, throat scraped raw, couldn't hear her own voice.

"Charge!"

The order was drowned by a roar from the men, a growling cry that grew to a scream. They threw themselves into a run, bayonet-tipped muskets leveled at the waist like spears, churning the drifting smoke into boiling vortices as they passed through. Winter ran with them, only belatedly remembering to draw the sword at her belt. They'd given her one from the stores—lieutenants had to carry a sword, after all—and the grip felt slick and uncertain in her hand. The blade still gleamed with factory polish.

Damn stupid thing, she had time to think, *bringing a sword to a musket duel—*

Plunging out of the smoke of their own volley, the Colonials broke momentarily into the open. Ahead loomed the abandoned Khandarai guns, and behind them the vague, menacing shapes of the

Auxiliary line, shrouded in a haze of their own. Muskets started to flash along that line, not as a volley but individually. Winter heard the *zip* and *twang* of balls, and saw men fall, but the impetus of the charge was not so easily stopped. After the long, painful march, the Colonials had the enemy in their grasp, and they would not be denied.

She expected a collision—two lines slamming against each other, bayonets crossed in a vicious scrum—but it never happened. By the time the leading Vordanai were a dozen yards away, the Auxiliaries started to waver. First in ones and twos, then all at once, they turned and ran for the rear. The neat line of brown and tan dissolved into a chaos of running, shoving, shouting men, with here and there an officer trying to restore order.

The Colonials fell on those who were slow, or who'd gotten jammed up with their fellows. Winter stumbled to a halt, sword still raised, and the blue tide washed past her. She watched as brown-coated figures fell, run through from behind, stabbed while trying to crawl away, clubbed down with fists or musket butts. In seconds, there was no one still standing within sight. The rush of men had moved on, chasing the fleeing Khandarai, out the other side of the smoke and across the hill.

Someone grabbed Winter by the shoulder. She spun, sword still in hand, and Graff had to duck to avoid losing an ear.

"Sir!" he said, sounding distant and tinny. "It's me, sir!"

"Sorry," she mumbled. Her mouth felt clotted with grit, and she could taste the salty tang of powder. Mechanically, she tried to sheathe her sword, and managed it on the third attempt.

"Are you all right, sir?" When she only looked at him blankly, he raised his voice and said, "Sergeant! Are you all right?"

Some light was beginning to break through the clouds that had enveloped Winter's brain. She shook her head, trying to clear it, and then at Graff's look of alarm she raised a hand and said, "Fine. I'm fine."

Graff grinned and clapped her on the shoulder. "We did it!"

We did? She looked around, blinking. Brown-uniformed bodies carpeted the ground, broken here and there by a splotch of blue. Out in the smoke, the now-silent guns loomed like distant ruins.

"Grayskins look pretty enough, but they haven't got much of a taste for steel," Graff said, sounding satisfied.

"Bobby," Winter said, suddenly remembering. *The Lord Above loves irony*. "Have you seen Bobby?"

Graff shook his head. "I was at the other end of the line. He'll be up there with the rest, I'd wager. The young ones always get a little hot-blooded."

Winter stared into the smoke, in the direction they'd come. The slope they'd climbed was littered with human wreckage. Graff, following her gaze, shifted uncomfortably.

"Come on," he said. "We've got to re-form. This may not be over."

But it was. The First and Second Battalions, as Winter had guessed, had had by far the hardest climb. On the flanks, the Khandarai had broken at the first volley, trapped as they were in ineffective squares. Give-Em-Hell's pursuing horsemen had reaped a rich harvest, and whole companies had thrown down their weapons and surrendered. The survivors—which, they'd learned from prisoners, included General Khtoba himself—showed no sign of halting anywhere short of the city gates. The colonel sent the cavalry to harry them as best they could, and set the rest of the troops to collecting the wounded and preparing the dead for burial.

The boasting and cheers of the men had died away as they clambered down the slope and began the bloody business. Those of the wounded who could still walk, or even crawl, had already made their way back toward the Vordanai camp, so those that remained were either unconscious, dead, or too badly hurt to move. Pairs of soldiers with stretchers came and went nonstop, carrying the badly wounded toward the growing hospital, while other details dragged or carried the dead to be laid neatly at the base of the hill. Still others collected salvageable detritus—muskets, ammunition, canteens, and spare flints. It was a long way to the nearest Vordanai depot, and the colonel had ordered that nothing was to be wasted.

Winter went straight to the spot where she thought Bobby had fallen, but there were so many bodies in blue. It was Folsom who found the boy in the end, curled up like a baby, hands pressed against his stomach. His face was so pale that Winter thought he must be dead, but when Folsom and Graff rolled him onto his back he gave a low groan and his eyelids fluttered. His hands fell limp to his sides, exposing a gory patch on his midriff, his bloody uniform now caked with sticky dirt.

"Hell," Graff said softly. "Poor kid." He looked up at Winter, then shook his head. "Better call for a stretcher. Get him to a cutter—"

"No." The firmness in Winter's voice surprised herself. "Folsom, help me carry him. We'll take him back to my tent."

"What?" Graff narrowed his eyes. "Sir—"

"I promised him," Winter said. "No cutters. You'll have to do what you can for him yourself."

The corporal lowered his voice. "He's dead, sir. Hit like that, in the bowels, it'll fester certain as sunrise, even if he doesn't bleed out."

Winter watched Bobby's face. His eyes were screwed tightly shut, and if he'd heard what Graff had said he gave no sign.

"Then it won't matter if we take him to the cutters or not, will it?" she said. "Do it, Corporal."

Folsom bent down and picked Bobby up, gentle as a mother handling a babe. Even so, a fresh welling of blood cut through the dirt and washed down the boy's stomach. Winter bit her lip.

"Sir . . . ," Graff said.

"My tent," she told Folsom. "Now."

Chapter Thirteen

MARCUS

It was the evening of the third day before the Auxiliaries turned up, and the Old Colonials made good use of the time. The houses closest to the waterfront had loopholes bashed in their walls, other houses were torn down and converted into barricades in the streets and alleys, and the big twelve-pounder cannon were carefully concealed behind screens of debris and thatch. By the third day, Marcus found that his nervousness had faded and been replaced by a kind of excitement. *Let them walk into this. We're ready.*

When they did come, they were in a hurry. From his vantage point on the hill, Marcus watched their leading battalion approach the ford in a straggly column of march. He'd held out some hope that they were so poorly informed that they would simply push straight across, but obviously some word had leaked out in spite of his precautions. But, with the sun already setting, either the Auxiliary commander was feeling hasty or else he'd underestimated the size of the force opposing him. Either way, no sooner had the enemy battalion arrived than it formed up into a battle column and splashed into the shallows.

What followed must have been a nightmare for the Khandarai. Marcus had briefed his unit commanders for exactly this situation. No shots were fired until the leading enemy company had come ashore on the near bank. Then the screen of debris was dragged aside to reveal the gleaming muzzles of the scripture-inscribed twelve-pounders. The guns belched smoke and canister shot, sweeping away whole swaths of the lead Auxiliary company and turning the river white with froth halfway out into the ford. At the same time, the hidden Vordanai began a steady rain of musketry on the survivors.

The result was everything Marcus had hoped for. The head of the column dissolved in panic, wounded men trying to get to safety while their unhit comrades scrambled for a way out of the killing ground. There was no cover to be had except directly ahead, where the slope of the embankment offered some shelter against the thunder of the guns, and dozens of the enemy chose to throw themselves under that rocky verge. The rest recoiled out into the river, scrambling out of range of the muskets. The *boom* of the guns followed them, flailing the water with canister.

Only when they'd nearly gotten out of canister range did Marcus send a messenger to the other half of the battery, three more guns concealed behind a house on the riverbank. These were quickly dragged into position while the guns in the town switched to roundshot, and soon all six pieces were firing in long arcs over the river and into the milling men pulling themselves out of the water on the other side. Leading elements of the second Khandarai battalion had arrived in the meantime, only adding to the confusion. At that range the artillery fire was more galling than devastating, but the gunners bent to their work with gusto and kept it up until both enemy units finally pulled together enough to retreat out of range.

In the interim, Marcus sent three companies down to the riverbank. The Auxiliaries who'd taken shelter there were in no state to fight, many having abandoned their weapons or gotten their powder wet in the river crossing. They surrendered after a desultory skirmish, and Marcus had another half company of prisoners to add to the hundred or so that were already in his bag. The enemy had lost twice that many killed and wounded, he judged, and he doubted if his own losses numbered a dozen.

"They're not so tough," Adrecht said, reflecting the general mood in the camp. Night had fallen, and campfires were sprouting throughout the village and outside the tents beyond the hill. "If they keep this up, we won't have to trouble the colonel after all."

"If they keep this up, they're not as clever as we've given them credit for," Marcus said. They were still at his vantage point at the front of the temple, from which he could see the whole triangular village, the ford, and a good bit of the country beyond. "They tried to brush past us and got their hand slapped. I doubt they'll try it again."

"What else can they do, though?" Adrecht said. "The ford's not wide enough to send two battalions at once, and if they come one by one they'll just get chewed up the same way."

Marcus shook his head. He was watching more campfires spring to life, like ground stars, on the opposite bank of the river. There were an awful lot of them.

"We'll find out," he said.

They found out the next morning.

The Auxiliary gunners didn't even wait for dawn. As soon as enough gray light had filtered into the sky to outline their targets, the north bank of the river blazed into horrible life, muzzle flashes cutting through the semidarkness. They were followed a moment later by the low, flat booms of the reports echoing across the water, and the drone and crash of incoming roundshot.

The ford was a particularly wide spot in the river, which meant the range had to be at least six or seven hundred yards. Too far to pick out individual men, even if the guns had been capable of such accuracy. The enemy gunners didn't even try. Instead, they went to work on the houses closest to the riverbank, bowling their cannonballs in long arcs that descended screaming into the Colonials' carefully prepared positions. The first few shots were off, either flying wide into the town or splashing in the shallows, but the Khandarai gunners quickly found the range. The clay walls of the village shacks provided no protection at all—worse than nothing, in fact, since the clay had a tendency to splinter and fill the interior of a hut with razor-sharp shards when a cannonball punched through.

Within half an hour, all the houses along the waterfront were piles of broken rubble, and fires had started in a dozen places. That didn't concern Marcus overmuch—there wasn't enough wind to drive a real blaze—but he watched the eastern horizon impatiently. The sun seemed to rise with interminable slowness, the world gradually lightening until it was possible to see the enemy positions. Rising clouds of powder smoke marked each gun. There were four of them directly opposite the ford, arrayed in a neat line right out of the artillery textbook.

"Right," he said to his artillerists, who had been standing by with similar impatience. "Go to it."

The Colonial guns took up the challenge with a roar. During the night Marcus had split them into three divisions, spread out along the riverbank; one directly opposite the ford, for canister work if the Auxiliaries tried a rush, while the other two provided enfilading fire from farther up the bank. Now all six twelve-pounders went to work, probing through the smoke for the enemy cannon.

It was a little like watching a handball match, Marcus reflected. The assembled soldiers of either side had nothing to do but watch and cheer for their own team, as the gunners sweated and struggled with balls, powder bags, and rammers. There was a cheer, audible even on the temple hill, whenever one of their own guns placed a shot near enough to fountain dirt and smoke over the enemy gunners.

Marcus had ordered that the caissons—the big carts that the guns hitched to when marching, which carried the ammunition reserves—be kept well back from the actual firing sites. This meant an inconveniently long haul whenever stores of powder and shot ran low, but he organized details from the infantry to run the supplies up to the front in relays. The men went to it with a will. He suspected that doing *anything* to contribute, however little, felt better than crouching behind broken walls and flinching at the sound of every cannonball.

Under the fire of the Colonials, the Auxiliaries' guns adjusted their aim and tried to reply, but it was an unequal contest. Not only did the Colonials have more pieces, but they were dug in behind barricades of dirt and rubble that shielded the gunners from any but direct hits, while the Auxiliaries were out in the open. The smoke made it impossible to see what effect the duel was having, but it seemed to Marcus that the replies from the enemy pieces were starting to slacken.

That the enemy had not matched his precaution with their caissons became obvious when a fountain of fire blossomed through the fog bank on the opposite shore, lifting and spreading like a great orange flower. A moment later an enormous *boom*, like a single monstrous footstep, drowned out even the sound of the cannon. When the flames faded away, leaving behind a huge mushroom-shaped cloud, the Auxiliaries' guns had stopped firing. The Colonials kept shooting for a few more minutes, then came to a ragged halt. Cheers rose from the waterfront and around the temple.

Lieutenant Archer, the Preacher's second-in-command, arrived at Marcus' impromptu headquarters along with the first of the wounded. With the bombardment halted, details were finally able to get through to the waterfront and start pulling away the rubble. Team after team hurried by with stretchers or improvised travois made from doors, boards, or whatever else was at hand. Other teams, moving more slowly, carried the dead.

Archer himself was unharmed, though the powder blackening his face showed that the young lieutenant had been intimately involved in the artillery duel. He saluted smartly.

"Any losses?" Marcus said. His eyes were still fixed on the other bank, where the smoke was gradually drifting away.

"Two men," Archer said. "One dead, God rest him. The other may live, but he'll lose the arm. One gun's limber damaged. Otherwise, nothing serious. By the grace of the Lord," he added piously. Archer was the Preacher's right-hand man, and shared his spiritual zeal.

"Good," Marcus said. "If that's the best they've got, they're not crossing anytime soon."

"Beg pardon, sir, but that can't be the best they've got. Those were Gesthemel eight-pounders. They've got to be older than I am."

"That's what the Auxies have to work with. For the most part we gave them Royal Army castoffs." Marcus hesitated. "I'm surprised you got such a good look at them."

"I didn't, sir. But you can tell by the report, if you know what you're listening for."

"I'll take your word for it," Marcus said dryly.

"Yessir. But if they were planning on defending the crossing at Westbridge, they must have had more than a few light guns to do it with. My guess is they're still bringing up the heavier pieces."

"Someone over there is in a hell of a hurry," Marcus said. He hoped that was a good thing. *If they wanted to cross so badly, stopping them should be worth something, shouldn't it?* He grimaced as another stretcher team went past. "If you can't keep them suppressed, we're going to have an awful time on the riverbank."

"Yessir," Archer said. "We'll do our best, sir."

There was a lull of a few hours, for which Marcus was duly grateful. It gave him the chance to evacuate the dead and wounded from the wrecked waterfront, and the men took the opportunity to dig in as best they could among the piles of rubble. This was what he'd brought the Old Colonials for. Fighting behind barricades and building field fortifications were not part of the skill set of the average Vordanai soldier, since on the continent wars were simply not fought that way. It was considered impolite to blast an enemy town with siege guns, for example. The Old Colonials, however, had spent years in Khandar—where the bandits and Desoltai raiders thought nothing of commandeering local dwellings as blockhouses—and thus had seen their share of desperate house-to-house fighting. The script was familiar to them.

This is the first time we've been on the receiving end, though. Normally it was the locals holed up in some little speck of a village and the Colonials rousting them out with cannon and bayonet.

He had Corporal Montagne, who reputedly had the sharpest eyes in the regiment, perched on the roof of the temple looking south. Four days, Janus had said, and this was the fourth day. Every time someone shouted, Marcus' heart leapt in the hope that long blue-uniformed columns had been sighted wending their way north.

No such luck. A runner hurried out of the temple, skidded to a halt, and saluted hastily.

"Sir! Enemy movement, sir! Looks like heavy guns, sir!"

Here it comes. He stared north, across the river, where the brown uniforms were boiling into view like angry ants. It was only a few minutes before he caught the first flash of fire, followed by its distant thudding *boom*. He watched to see where the shot would land, and was startled to hear it pass overhead with a shriek like an angry cat as it cleared the roof of the temple to land beyond the village entirely.

"Saints and martyrs," Marcus swore. "What the *hell* was that?" He gestured impatiently at the runner. "Go find Lieutenant Archer and ask him what the hell is going on."

By the time the man returned, though, Marcus had figured it out for himself. Three more of the monstrous guns had opened fire, two overshooting the town and one shot landing well back from the waterfront, plowing through a whole row of houses before it finally came to rest. The runner's breathless report confirmed his suspicions.

"Siege guns, sir," the man said, still winded from running the length of the village twice. "Big ones, twenty-four pounders at least."

"Thirty-six," Marcus said. "Those are thirty-six-pound naval guns."

"Are they?" The runner turned to look at the distant clouds of gunsmoke, impressed. "Well spotted, sir!"

Marcus' lip twisted in a brief smile. "I'm afraid my eyes aren't as good as that. But I used to walk past them at least once a week. The prince had them lined up along the wharf in Ashe-Katarion, remember?"

They'd been a gift from the King of Vordan to his royal friend and cousin. The prince had been very impressed with them, Marcus recalled. He'd been there the day the Colonials manhandled them off the boat, grunting and swearing, twenty men to each gun. If the little Gesthemels were older than Lieutenant Archer, those guns were older than any man in Khandar, relics of an earlier era. No one had told the prince that the enormous weapons he was so proud of were museum pieces, of course.

The runner gaped. "*Those* guns, sir? I always thought they were just for decoration!"

"Apparently General Khtoba has found a use for them." Marcus spared a brief moment of thanks for the foresight Janus had shown in avoiding Westbridge. The thought of trying to charge across a bridge into the face of those monstrous pieces made him shiver. "Does Archer think he can silence them?"

"He said he'll try, sir, but they're well back from the river's edge. Long range, sir."

"Tell him to try. And get the ammunition relay running again." Another shot from one of the monsters landed, closer to the waterfront. The huge projectile tore through the town as if through tissue paper, leaving a neat line of rising dust in its wake. The ranker swallowed hard, saluted again, and ran off.

Archer's guns opened fire a few minutes later. As the lieutenant had predicted, his replies were less effective than before due to the longer range, but the man's skill was evident. It was only a few shots before his pieces were regularly bowling their roundshot into the growing clouds of smoke that surrounded the big naval guns. One mercy was that the ancient pieces would be difficult and time-consuming to aim. If they got into a duel with Archer, it would take ages for them to zero in.

In the event, they didn't even try. The naval guns kept slamming away at the waterfront, blasting through the barriers of wood and clay as though they were made of matchsticks. Instead, a descending scream announced another set of unwelcome arrivals. Marcus watched the first shot fall short, churning up a stretch of riverbank. *Howitzers.*

The king had given those to the prince, too. Marcus wished his sovereign had been a little less generous over the years, even if he was only cleaning obsolete pieces out of his armories. These were midgets compared to the naval guns, stubby weapons that looked vaguely like a washing tub on wheels. They fired shells instead of shot, iron spheres packed with powder and an impact fuse. Like the huge naval guns, they were weapons of a previous age, when wars had been less polite and sieges were common. Unlike the huge thirty-six-pounders, which had been built to defend harbors from enemy ships, the howitzers had been designed for the express purpose of bombarding dug-in enemies and fortifications.

Archer kept trying. It took some time for the howitzers to find the range—they weren't terribly accurate weapons at the best of times, firing as they did in high arcs rather than the shallow trajectories of ordinary cannon. Once they started landing shots close by, however, they made a mockery of all of the gunners' careful preparation. The shells descended from on high, not straight ahead, and they were as likely to land behind the sheltering walls of rubble as in front of them. When they hit, they blew apart into iron fragments as deadly as any musket ball.

The artillerymen kept up the now patently unequal contest for a few minutes, gamely banging away into the cloud of gunsmoke while the shells rained down around them. It wasn't long before they gave it up, however, and one by one the Colonial guns fell silent, leaving only the distant, shuddering *booms* from across the river.

Archer himself turned up not long after, bleeding from a long cut on one shoulder and even more smoke-blackened than before. He saluted, gingerly, and shook his head.

"Sorry, sir. I told my boys to pull out. We've had a dozen men hit already, and one of the new guns is down with a cracked axle—"

Marcus waved him into silence. Once it became clear that the Vordanai guns were no longer replying, the howitzers had turned their attention to the waterfront. Fires were once again burning through the sad little town, and each exploding shell was accompanied by a fountain of debris and burning thatch. Marcus glanced at the sky. The sun had not even reached the meridian, and the southern horizon remained empty.

"Archer," he said, "get your guns back to the temple and start digging in. Get that shoulder seen to while you're at it."

"Yessir. But—"

Marcus was already turning away. "Runner!"

"Here, sir!" said a nearby ranker, a keen-looking young man with a crisp salute.

"Get down to Lieutenant Goldsworth." That was Val's second-in-command, now in charge of the forces along the waterfront. "Tell him he's to grin and bear it until they reach musket range, then give them a volley and *fall back*. I'll be waiting for him with the First, and we'll drive them back into the river. Got all that? Go." He gestured another man forward. "You, find Captain

Roston. Last I saw he was up on the roof here. Tell him he's got the reserve until I get back."

On the other side of the river, the great mass of brown-and-tan infantry was stirring. Neat columns filed between the still-booming naval guns, re-formed, and headed for the ford.

The village wasn't large enough for Marcus' entire command to defend at once. He'd left the Second Battalion—the three companies of it that he had, at any rate—to hold the waterfront, and held the other three units in reserve around the rear of the temple, where they'd be reasonably sheltered from enemy artillery. Of these, his own First Battalion was the largest, more than four hundred men in four companies.

He found the four company commanders waiting for him in a sort of huddle. The sight of them made him wish for Fitz. These were all Old Colonials, which meant they were the dregs of the Royal Army officer corps. Lieutenant Vence was a former cavalryman who'd fallen off his horse and onto his head, which left him with a fragile constitution and recurring bouts of fever. Davis was a fat bully and a blowhard who was rumored to have been sent to Khandar for his part in the fatal beating of a ranker. Lieutenant Thorpe was a man after Adrecht's mold, all lace shirts and fancy living, but with none of the captain's redeeming qualities. And Strache might have been the oldest lieutenant in the service, at close to fifty. His crime, as far as Marcus had been able to make out, had been refusing to retire when he was supposed to.

None of them were the men he would have chosen, but they were what he had to work with. They sprang to attention as he approached. Two of them did, anyway, while Lieutenant Strache moved slowly to spare his back and Davis took his time heaving his bulk into line.

"We're going in," Marcus told them. "Up the hill to the front of the temple. I'll meet you there."

"Yes, sir!" they chorused, and hurried off as best they were able. Marcus spared another glance for the south, but there was still no sign of approaching relief. He looked up at the looming bulk of the temple and caught Adrecht's face peering over the side. Marcus gave the other captain a cheeky wave and trotted back up the hill to meet his men.

By the time the First was in position, the Auxiliaries were nearly over the ford. As Marcus had hoped, their artillery had tailed off. Neither the naval guns nor the howitzers were accurate enough to fire in close support of the infantry without serious risk of friendly casualties. Thatch fires were still burning throughout the town, filling the streets with sweet black smoke that mixed with the acrid gray stuff from the guns and bursting shells. The damage was worst close to the waterfront, where scarcely a building was left standing. Marcus could see a few blue-uniformed bodies lying in the rubble, and other soldiers still working on the improvised barricades.

He turned to his men. They made for a motley picture, uniformed in a catch-as-catch-can mess of army issue and Khandarai fabrics that were only Royal Army blue in broad average. He saw a lot of worried faces, too, which made him uneasy. For all that they'd been through the bloody business before, the Old Colonials had never specialized in fighting opponents on anything like equal terms.

"I've told Goldsworth and the Second to fall back," he told them, "as soon as the Auxies get close. They'll have to break up to come forward, and that's when we'll hit them. Fix bayonets and keep moving, and we'll push the bastards right back into the river. And stay close to them, or else you'll end up wearing a howitzer shell for a hat. Ready?"

They gave a shout. It was less than enthusiastic, but better than nothing. Marcus turned back to the battle. The front ranks of the incoming Auxiliary battalion had reached the near shore, neat lines turned ragged by the challenge of marching through thigh-high water. As they formed up, shots started to issue from the twisted mass of wreckage that was all that remained of the waterfront houses, proving that not all of the Second had been flattened by the howitzers. The bombardment had stopped, and in the relative silence each shot sounded like a distant handclap, accompanied by a puff of smoke. The Auxiliaries ignored the harassing fire, taking a few moments to organize under cover of the embankment and then pushing forward over the top. Marcus could see blue-uniformed figures running in front of them, hunched low and moving from cover to cover.

"Follow me!" He waved down the hill and set off at a trot.

It was not the best-formed advance in the history of military tactics. A body of thirty or forty men came down the road behind Marcus, maintaining a loose order to avoid the broken bits of clay and timber the bombardment had torn loose from the houses. The rest of the rankers had to pick their way around the various obstacles in the town itself as best they could. But the Khandarai were in a similar state—pursuing the retreating men of the Second Battalion, they'd gotten spread out and lost any semblance of formation.

The first brown-uniformed soldier that the advancing First encountered gave a squawk of surprise, fired wildly to no effect, and took to his heels. The next pair, surprised coming around a corner, were the recipients of a dozen musket blasts and dropped in their tracks. Marcus waved the men onward, letting them get up to a run, and they drove the Redeemers back in front of them. Here and there, a few Auxiliaries in a good position put up a determined resistance, but without organization it was easy for the Vordanai to get around behind them and flush them out with muskets or the bayonet.

Marcus kept an eye out for Lieutenant Goldsworth, but never caught sight of him. There were men of the Second all around, though, and some of them decided there was more safety to be had with Marcus than following their own commander. The blue-uniformed mob grew as it advanced, pushing the Auxiliaries into headlong flight, until the Colonials regained their initial position at the top of the embankment.

The rearguard of the enemy battalion was still forming there, two or three companies in good order. The next battalion had just begun its crossing. *If we're going to break them, here's our chance.* He threw himself over the last obstacle, a makeshift wall built by the Second, and waved the men behind him forward. Barely twenty yards ahead, the neat line of brown and tan erupted into flames.

Being part of an attack was a strange thing, Marcus had always thought. It was like being a component in a larger organism, something that could live or die, stand or flee, all on its own and independent of the will of the men who made it up. Sometimes it drove you onward, into the face of what seemed like certain death, in spite of every instinct screaming for flight. Other times, you could *feel* it falling apart, turning at bay like a whipped dog, hunkering down or turning tail to run.

It was apparent almost immediately that this was going to be one of the latter occasions. The Vordanai broke from cover in dribs and drabs, as fast as each man's legs could carry him, with no more order than a rioting mob. The first volley from the Auxiliaries slammed out as they crested the embankment, and men fell backward or tumbled into the ditch. The second round of fire, still aiming high, went over the heads of those who'd made it down the slope and cut down the ones who followed. Scattered fire from the Colonials opened temporary gaps in the brown-coated line, but they closed up neatly, two ranks loading while the third waited with leveled weapons. Bayonets gleamed like a steel-tipped picket fence.

Almost as one man, the advancing Colonials decided they would rather not be at the bottom of the slope when the next volley thundered after them. Those still coming down the hill flopped into the best cover they could find and opened fire, while those who'd cleared the embankment scrambled back up it, vaulting over the bodies of the dead and wounded in their haste to regain some kind of protection.

Marcus couldn't recall the exact moment at which he, personally, had turned around. It hadn't been a conscious decision, any more than any particular cow makes a decision to run when a herd stampedes. The overriding imperative to stay with the group reached down into the base of the brain and flipped all the switches, without consulting any of the higher functions. In his next rational moment, he was huddled behind the wall the Second had built, struggling to load his musket in spite of the protruding spike of the bayonet.

The semicircle of fire and smoke concentrating on the Auxiliaries was getting thicker by the minute, as more men of the First and some of the Second worked their way into range and found positions. The Auxiliaries fired another volley, but with no obvious targets the effect was only to patter musket balls off the barricade like hard rain. Then, at either an officer's urging or an individual soldier's good sense, they broke ranks as well and ran for the cover of the embankment, which provided a natural breastwork. Before long the rattle of musketry had risen to a continuous roar.

"Davis!" Marcus spotted the fat sergeant and gestured him over. "Hold here, you understand? I'm going to find Adrecht and see about getting us some support!"

Davis nodded, looking distinctly pale. Marcus left his musket, got to his feet, and hurried back up the hill, bent double to avoid presenting a neat target to the Khandarai below. Once he'd gone fifty yards, he risked a look back. The second Khandarai battalion was crossing the river now, a thousand fresh troops to oppose the four or five hundred he'd left behind. He broke into a run.

"For Karis' sake," Adrecht swore. "Can't you be a little more gentle? You're not pulling teeth."

"You want me to go and get Rawhide, do you?"

Adrecht sighed and pressed his face into the pillow. "I'll be good."

The sun had set an hour or so past, and with the fading of the last glimmers of light the fighting had finally sputtered to a halt, trailing off as though by mutual consent. As far as Marcus was concerned, darkness had come none too soon.

He'd sent the Third Battalion to the front, just in time to stabilize the line as it bulged under the onslaught of fresh Auxiliaries. The enemy attacks started off strong, while their troops were still formed and in good order, but discipline quickly broke down amidst the narrow alleys and blasted houses of what had been the village of Weltae. The Colonials learned to give ground before the initial rush, then push back hard when the Khandarai lost their momentum, as often as not driving them back to the ground from which they'd started. This seesaw of a battle took its toll in dead and wounded. Brown-uniformed corpses littered the alleys beside the blue, but the Auxiliaries had more men to draw on, and fresh troops to begin each assault.

The worst of it had been just before sunset, when the third Khandarai battalion had gotten across the river and launched a mass assault right up the main street. They'd broken through the thinning cordon of Vordanai and looked set to split the line in two. Fortunately for Marcus, Lieutenant Archer and his remaining gunners had gotten set up at the top of the hill, and the relatively clear slope of the road gave them a wonderful field of fire. A few loads of canister had fractured the leading Auxiliary company, and Marcus had finally turned Adrecht loose with the Fourth in a mad charge that pushed the enemy all the way back to the waterfront.

Adrecht, unlike Marcus, hadn't been quite mad enough to try to get to the river. The narrow strip of clear ground by the shore was now occupied in force, and the Auxiliaries had managed to drag two of their little Gesthemels across the ford and set them to blasting away at the Colonial barricades. Under the circumstances, pressing the enemy back across the ford was out of the question. Instead, Adrecht had hung on like grim death until nightfall, even when the Khandarai commander had once again turned his howitzers loose on the town.

It was during this period that the Fourth Battalion captain had been a little too close to a bursting shell. Fortunately, an intervening wall had absorbed most of the blast, but it had left him with a shredded uniform and a back full of clay splinters. Since Adrecht shared with Marcus a distrust of cutters in general and the aptly nicknamed Fourth Battalion surgeon Rawhide in particular, he'd generously declared that his wound wasn't serious enough to distract a medical man from the more serious cases, and Marcus had agreed to do his best with a needle and tweezers.

There were certainly enough serious cases. Marcus wondered at how quickly he'd become inured to loss and death. He remembered the guilt of looking at the hospital after the battle on the coast road, but now all he could feel was tired. Something like a quarter of the men he'd brought to the village had been hit, to one degree or another. Goldsworth was dead, shot in the leg and bayoneted by Redeemers in the first attack. His replacement in the Second was a sergeant named Toksin whom Marcus hardly knew. Among his own men, Vence had been badly cut by a shell fragment and was confined to the hospital, while Davis was down with a "small" wound Marcus half suspected was imaginary.

He and Adrecht were in one of the little rooms on the second floor of the temple, which had once been quarters for the priests or nuns or whoever had dwelt here. There was little evidence left of them. The Redeemers had thoroughly wrecked the place before the Colonials had even arrived, and what few furnishings remained had been cannibalized by Marcus' men for bandages and firewood. Adrecht lay on his bedroll, stripped of his coat and bloody undershirt, with his face pressed into a thin army-issue pillow. Marcus sat cross-legged beside him, with a damp cloth to wipe away the blood and a pair of tweezers he'd begged off one of the cutters.

"Almost done," Marcus said.

"About damn time. If only they'd have got me from the front I could have done it myself."

Marcus gave one of the remaining fragments a prod, and Adrecht winced. "Quit squirming."

"The hell of it is," Adrecht muttered, "I left all my liquor behind. 'Won't be needing that anymore,' I thought. What I wouldn't give for a bit of that sweet Gherai rum about now."

"Rawhide would probably have commandeered it," Marcus said. "He said he didn't have enough brandy for the ones who were going to make it, let alone the dying."

That silenced Adrecht for a moment. Marcus took the opportunity to get a good hold on the long sliver of clay and yank. It came out in one piece, thankfully, one end dripping blood. Adrecht gave a shudder but didn't cry out, and Marcus went to work on the last splinter.

"There," he said, when he'd dropped it on the little pile of bloody fragments. "Not much left but grit. You'll have some scars, I expect."

"Scars on my back don't worry me," Adrecht said. "Actually, I've always thought I needed one on my face. Not a big one, just a little nick. To give me that air of mystery, you know?"

"On your back is even better. Tell the girl you've been in the wars, and when she asks to see your scars you've got to take off your shirt and you're already halfway there."

Adrecht laughed, sat up, and winced. Marcus wiped up a few new trickles of blood with the cloth, as gently as he could manage.

"It hardly seems fair that *you* come through without a scratch," Adrecht said jovially. As soon as the words had passed his lips, his expression went contrite, as if he wished he could stuff them back in. "Sorry. I meant since you led that attack—that was a damned mad thing to do—not because . . . I mean . . ."

"I know what you meant," Marcus said.

There was a long, awkward silence. Adrecht held up his tattered, bloodstained shirt, cursed softly, and tossed it aside.

"Give that to the bandage pile, I guess." He sighed. "I had those shirts tailored for me in Ashe-Katarion. Only half an eagle for the dozen, would you believe that? The Khandarai were always mad for Vordanai coin."

"Probably because a Vordanai eagle still has more gold in it than lead."

"I always figured they were just fond of King Farus' face." Adrecht smiled, and shrugged into his uniform coat without a shirt. "All right. I think it's time you let me in on the plan."

"What plan?"

"The plan, meaning what the hell we do now." Adrecht grinned crookedly. "It may have escaped your attention, but our relief column hasn't arrived."

"I know." The southern horizon had remained obstinately empty all day. Marcus had left sentries looking in that direction, with orders to report to him as soon as they made contact.

"So we have to fall back," Adrecht continued briskly. "Once the cutters have finished with the wounded, we withdraw out onto the plain. Leave a rear guard to confuse the Auxies, make them deploy for attack, and then run for it before they get here. With any luck we can break contact and head south."

"Leaving them free to maneuver," Marcus said. "If the colonel is still engaged with the enemy, and they take him from behind, it'll be slaughter."

"You want to stay here, don't you?" Adrecht said, his voice flat. "Try to hang on."

"Ja—the colonel said he was coming. If he's been delayed, we've just got to give him a little more time."

"And if he's been defeated? Captured, even?"

Marcus gritted his teeth and said nothing.

"You know it'll be butchery here by morning," Adrecht continued remorselessly. "Right now, at this very moment, those bastards are dragging their guns across the ford. If they get one of those monsters on the near bank, we won't be able to get within two hundred yards of the waterfront."

"We abandon the waterfront," Marcus said. "Dig in around the temple. This place is solid stone. Even thirty-six-pounders are going to take some time to crack it."

"Right. And the hill is good ground, plenty of material for barricades, no problem. Except for one detail—if we fall back, there's nothing stopping them from sending men around the sides of the village and coming at us from behind."

"The walls are just as thick from behind."

"That's not what I'm worried about," Adrecht said patiently. "Once they get there, we've got no way out. When they batter this place down around our ears, they'll have the lot of us on spits."

"Unless the colonel arrives before that happens."

"Unless the colonel arrives," Adrecht said. He paused, then shook his head. "So it comes down to that, does it? You want to bet that Colonel Vhalnich will ride to the rescue."

"More or less," Marcus said. His throat was tight.

"With the lives of every man in this command as the stake."

"The colonel asked me to keep those Khandarai off his back," Marcus said. "I intend to do it. They don't dare march past as long as we're here, and they haven't got enough men to break off a screening force."

"I agree," Adrecht said. "They'll have no choice but to break in here and *kill us all.*"

"Unless—"

"I know!"

Adrecht turned away, pacing once across the room, then again.

Marcus watched in silence while he completed a third circuit. His chest felt tight.

Finally, Adrecht turned to face him, standing at what was very nearly attention.

"I just want to make one thing clear," he said. "The men here are *our* men. The Old Colonials. You know them. You want to risk all their lives for a colonel you've barely met and a bunch of recruits?"

"Val is with them," Marcus said. "And Mor. And Fitz." *And Jen Alhundt.* That thought surprised him, and he squirreled it away for later inspection.

"But you'd stay even if they weren't." It wasn't a question.

Marcus nodded.

Adrecht let out a long breath. "What the hell. I owe you, Marcus. My life, maybe. If you want to throw it away now, who am I to stop you?" He straightened up and snapped a crisp salute. "Give the orders, Senior Captain."

Marcus grinned. Adrecht maintained his serious composure a moment longer, then broke down with a chuckle. The tension drained out of the room like water from a bath.

"They aren't going to like it," Adrecht said. "The men, I mean."

Marcus shrugged. "They always like to have something to grumble about."

Chapter Fourteen

WINTER

Folsom laid Bobby on the floor of Winter's tent, carefully arranging the boy's limbs as though settling him in a casket. The corporal looked half a corpse already, his face pale as milk, but his eyelids flickered and he gave a soft moan when his back touched the ground.

Graff, still powder-blackened and covered with grime, stripped off Bobby's coat and tossed it in a corner. His shirt was shockingly white underneath, with stark gray rings on his cuffs where they'd protruded from his sleeves.

Winter looked down at the boy and bit her lip. Graff, Bobby had said. No one else. "Corporal Folsom?"

The big man was squatting by the boy's side. He looked up.

"I need you to take an inventory of the company. Find out how many we had hit, then go to the cutters and try to track everyone down."

Folsom looked down at Bobby again, then back at Winter. His thick features hardened, but he got to his feet and saluted.

"On your way out," Winter said, "find a couple of men and have them sit outside the tent. No one comes in without my leave, understand?"

Folsom nodded again and ducked out of the tent. It was still broad daylight outside, and a brilliant lance of light from the flaps glowed by the entrance. That felt wrong, somehow. It should have been twilight.

Graff unbuttoned Bobby's jacket, lifting it away carefully where it was soaked with gore. He tried raising the boy's shoulder to get the sleeve off, but Bobby gave another groan, and Graff let him lie and turned to Winter.

"I don't want to move him more than I have to. You got a nice sharp knife somewhere?"

She nodded and pawed through her pack until she found a heavy-hilted skinning knife, which she'd bought in Ashe-Katarion a lifetime ago because she'd liked the embroidery on the leather sheath. She handed it to Graff. "Anything else?"

"Water." Graff looked at the mess on Bobby's stomach and shook his head. "Though I warn you, I don't think—"

"Water," Winter repeated, and ducked out of the tent.

The camp outside was chaos, and it took her a few minutes to track down a brace of full kettles. By the time she returned, Graff had gotten Bobby's jacket off by slicing open the sleeves and spreading them flat, and he was working on the undershirt where it was glued to the boy's skin with sweat and dried blood. It reminded Winter uncomfortably of a hunter skinning a kill, carefully peeling back each layer to reveal the gory interior.

Also uncomfortable was the presence of Feor, who had crawled out of her bedroll and now sat cross-legged beside the sickbed, one arm still in a sling. Winter had forgotten the girl was there.

"Feor . . ." She hesitated, biting her lip. She couldn't very well send the girl outside, not *now*. Even the Khandarai in the army train would no doubt be keeping a very low profile until the excitement of battle had subsided. "You don't have to watch this," Winter finished lamely.

She ignored that. "Will he live?"

Winter glanced at Graff, still picking bits of linen away from the ragged hole in Bobby's skin. "I don't think so," she said in Khandarai.

"Oh." Feor shifted, drew knees to her chest and hugged them tight with her good arm, but she didn't look away.

"Give me some water," Graff said, without looking up. "Right here, where it's bloody. But *gently*. Just trickle it."

Winter hurried over with one of the kettles. Looking closely at the wound made her want to gag, and the smell was beginning to cut through the battle stink of sweat and powder. She forced her hands to remain steady and tipped a shallow stream from the kettle across the boy's skin. Pink rivulets ran down Bobby's sides and soaked into the inside of his jacket.

Graff's mouth worked silently, as though chewing something stubborn.

"Right," he said, not looking up. "Right. Get some clean linen and tear it into strips. I'll get the rest of this shirt off."

Winter nodded and went to her trunk. She sacrificed the cleaner of her two spare shirts, and the fabric tore with a sound like a distant volley of musketry. She'd laid out a half dozen uneven bandages when she heard Graff fall backward, followed by a great deal of swearing.

"Oh, *fucking* Brass Balls of the Beast!"

"What?" Winter's heart clenched. She turned. "What happened?"

"Just look!" Graff said. "Look at—"

At first she thought he meant the wound, around which he'd wiped the skin clean, until there was only a ragged red hole just to the right of the boy's navel. He'd unbuttoned Bobby's shirt to pull away the last bits of clinging linen, and—

"Oh," Winter said quietly. She looked down at Bobby's face—a young, soft, *feminine* face, cheeks unmarred by stubble—and felt a hundred little moments click into place.

"Fuck me," Graff said. "He—"

"She," Winter said.

"She," he repeated dully. "I can't—I mean—"

"Come on," Winter said. "This can't be the first pair of breasts you've seen up close."

"What? But . . ."

"Later," Winter said firmly. "Now. Do what you can."

Graff looked up at her, and she tried to put all the calm she could muster into her gaze. He swallowed, nodded, and bent over his patient.

Some time later, Graff sat back. Sweat trickled across his forehead, and he wiped it away absentmindedly, leaving a smear of red under his bangs.

"It's no good," he said. "The ball's still in there somewhere, but if I go groping around trying to find it I'm just going to make things worse."

Winter looked down at Bobby's face. His—*her*—mouth worked silently, but her eyes were tightly shut, as though in a dream from which she couldn't escape.

"If we were to take her to a cutter . . . ," Graff began.

"Would it make a difference?"

"No," he admitted. "Probably not. There's too much bleeding, and h— She's already running a fever."

"Any idea how . . . long?"

"A few hours at best," he said.

"Will she wake up?"

Graff gave a weary shrug. "I'm no doctor, just a corporal who picked up a little stitching and sawing. Though I doubt even a doctor could tell you."

Winter nodded. "You'd better go, then."

"What?" He looked up at her. "Go where?"

"Someone in the rest of the company must need your help. Folsom, if no one else."

"But—" Graff gestured helplessly at the girl on the floor.

"I'll stay with her," Winter said. "Someone should."

He turned away, but Winter caught a fleeting glimpse of relief in his face. She tried not to hold it against him.

"I'll check back in," he said, retreating. "Later. And you can come and find me if he—I mean, when she—"

"I will." Winter ushered him to the exit. When the tent flap had fallen closed, she stared at it wearily for a few moments, then turned around and sat down beside Bobby.

Graff had covered the wound with makeshift bandages, though the blood was already soaking through. Winter kept her eyes on the girl's face. It was tight and drawn with pain, her boy-short hair clingy and matted with sweat. Winter smoothed it absently with one hand.

"No cutters," she murmured. "Well, of course not."

She hadn't even thought about that possibility herself. *This girl planned better than I ever did.* The breasts that had so disturbed Graff were only slight swells, and Winter wondered how old Bobby really was.

I wish she'd told me. A fantasy, of course. Winter knew as well as anyone that a secret spoken aloud, even once, was a secret lost. *But I would have asked her so many things. How she made it through recruitment. Where she came from. Why she came to Khandar.* It was singularly cruel, she thought, to discover that she wasn't alone just hours before she would be alone again.

Winter was surprised to find that she was crying. She closed her eyes against the tears, but they welled regardless, trickling down her cheeks and pattering onto Bobby's jacket. One drop touched the corner of her mouth, and she licked automatically, tasting the salt and the acrid tang of sweat and powder.

"Winter." Feor was leaning forward, peering at Bobby.

"You don't need to gape at her," Winter said.

"Her," Feor muttered, as though tasting the word. "A girl." And then something else, low and fast, that Winter didn't understand.

"In fact," Winter said, "I should cover her up. Somebody might burst in here, and I'll be damned if—"

"I can help her," Feor blurted.

Winter froze. A spark of hope, the tiniest ember, ignited briefly in her chest, though she felt stupid for encouraging it. But the priestesses of Monument Hill did collect all sorts of esoteric knowledge, didn't they? Was it possible Feor had some strange powder, some recipe, *something*—

She quashed her sudden enthusiasm and said, "You might have said something earlier."

"Earlier I did not know the corporal was a woman," Feor said. "O*bv-scar-iot* will not bind to a man."

Winter hadn't understood the burst of archaic Khandarai. "What is it you want to do?"

"I can bind her to my *naath*," Feor said, so quiet she was almost inaudible.

"Ah." The ember of hope flickered and died. "Magic. You mean you can help her *spiritually*." Winter tried to keep her tone level—Feor looked so serious, and she didn't want to trample on the girl's beliefs—but she couldn't help but a twist on the last word.

"It's not—"

"Look," Winter said, "if you want to . . . to say a prayer, or what have you, I'm not going to object. But I'm not sure Bobby would want you to. She was a Free Church man—woman—like the rest of us."

"It is not a prayer," Feor said patiently. "Prayers are requests to the Heavens and the gods above and around us. A *naath* is an invocation, a *command*. It will be obeyed."

"All right," Winter said. "Go ahead, if you think it will do any good."

Feor sat in silence for a moment, her good hand clenched on her injured arm. She looked—frail, somehow, and Winter felt guilty for her harsh tone. She moved carefully around the sickbed and put a hand on the girl's shoulder in what she hoped was a comforting way.

"I'm sorry," she said. "I didn't mean to . . . it's just hard." She looked down at Bobby and then dragged her eyes away, but too late. The tears returned. She rubbed bitterly at her face with the heel of her palm.

"You don't understand," Feor whispered.

Winter closed her eyes. "You're right. I probably don't."

"It would be heresy," Feor said. Winter was astonished to feel the girl shaking like an autumn leaf under her hand. "The blackest, most wrong kind of heresy. To bind *obv-scar-iot* to her—not a Chosen of Heaven, not even of the true faith! Mother would never forgive me. My whole *life* would be as nothing. Useless."

Feor was crying now, too. She leaned into Winter, who slipped an arm around her automatically. The girl's slim body was convulsed by sobs.

"I'm sorry," Winter repeated. "I didn't understand what you were offering." In Vordan it had been a hundred years since the Priests of the Black had hunted noncomformists with the torturer's knife, and a century of Free Church tolerance had taken the sting out of accusations of heresy. The Redeemer pyres in Ashe-Katarion could attest to the fact that the Khandarai took their religion more seriously.

Feor looked up, eyes still shining, and drew a long breath. She put on a determined expression. "Of course not. How could you?"

"I'm sure that Bobby"—Winter forced herself to look at the corporal's pained, twisted face—"I'm sure she'd appreciate anything you could do."

"She might not. The binding can be unpredictable, even for those who have prepared for it all their lives. She might curse us both afterward."

"Afterward?" Winter looked down into Feor's serious face. "You really think she'd live?"

"Oh, yes." A faint smile crossed the girl's lips. "*Obv-scar-iot* will not be stopped by such a trivial injury."

"What does that mean, *obv-scar-iot*?" From the pained look on Feor's face, Winter knew she'd botched the pronunciation.

"It is the name of my *naath*." This at least Winter understood. *Naath* meant "spell" or "sorcery"—literally "a thing which is read" or "reading." "It means," Feor went on, "something like 'magic for the creation of a Guardian.' Or so I was taught."

"And it will"—Winter hesitated—"heal her?"

Feor nodded. "But . . ."

"But?"

The girl took another long breath and wiped her eyes. "I am *naathem*. It is given to me to bind the *naath*, but once bound it cannot be undone until the bound one's death. Nor can I bind another until that time. I may only be able to perform the binding once in my lifetime." She paused. "You saved my life. You and the others, but it was you who sheltered me when you might have . . ." Feor stopped, swallowed, and went on. "I have no way to repay you other than this."

"Feor," Winter said, "you don't have to—"

"I want to." The girl pursed her lips. "It is only that . . ."

She trailed off, very quietly. Winter stared at her, and after a long pause she spoke aloud.

". . . I meant it for you."

"Me? But—" Tired and befuddled as she was, Winter leapt to the appropriate conclusion very quickly. Obv-scar-iot *will not bind to a man.* She thought about denial, but one look at Feor's face made it clear there was no point. Winter swallowed hard and slowly removed her arm from the girl's shoulders. "How long have you known?"

"For some time."

"And how . . ."

Feor shrugged. "I am *naathem*."

Magic. "But you didn't know about Bobby?"

"I spent only a little time with her. I would have known, eventually."

"Why didn't you say anything?"

"Why should I?" Feor said. "You obviously wished it to be a secret. Knowing that I knew the truth would only have made you uncomfortable. And I worried . . ." Her cheeks went scarlet. "I worried that if you knew I had found out, you might not let me go."

Winter had to smile at that. "Really?"

"Only at first," Feor said. "Before I truly knew you."

Well, it could be worse. The first person to find out doesn't speak any Vordanai. Winter shook her head. "God above. It's been a long time since *anyone* knew."

Feor nodded seriously. "I thought, if you were wounded in battle, I could at least do this for you. Save your life, perhaps, as you saved mine."

"But if you use this *naath* now, on Bobby, you won't be able to help me next time," Winter said.

Feor nodded, looking miserable.

"Do it," Winter said. "I'll just have to survive on my own."

She wasn't quite sure when she'd started taking the whole idea seriously. Something about Feor's quiet faith was infectious. *It's the least I can do to play along, if it helps console her.* It was hard to remember that behind her temple-trained facade of seriousness Feor was still half a child.

"I will," Feor said, and then, "I will!" as though arguing with an invisible presence. The half-light filtering through the blue canvas made her gray skin look like marble. She turned to Winter. "I'll need a bowl of water."

"I'm not sure I've got a bowl," Winter said. "Will a kettle do?"

Feor pried the top off the kettle, peered inside, and nodded. She looked up again appraisingly, and then turned to the tent flap.

"I need you to make absolutely certain I am not interrupted. Do not allow anyone to pull me away from her, you understand? No matter what."

"I don't think anyone's likely to come bursting in here—," Winter began.

"No matter what," Feor insisted. "Even if it's the . . . the King of Vordan himself. It cannot be allowed. It is not just her life at risk, but mine, and . . . other things."

"Right. If His Majesty turns up, I'll tell him to cool his heels." Winter caught the full force of Feor's glare and raised her hands. "I understand!"

"Afterward," Feor said, more calmly, "I will probably sleep. It may be some time before I awaken. Do not fear for me."

"Got it," Winter said. "Anything else?"

Feor shifted uneasily. "This will be like . . . lighting a beacon, in some ways. The sorcerer who rides with your army cannot help but see it. He may investigate."

Winter thought about protesting, but the girl's conviction that the Vordanai were led by a wizard seemed unshakable. She simply nodded, and sat down halfway between Bobby's pallet and the tent flap, ready to intercept any incoming sorcerers or kings. This seemed to placate Feor, who picked up the kettle with some difficulty with her good hand and placed it beside Bobby's head. She closed her eyes, dipped her fingers into the water, and waited.

It was some time before Winter realized she had begun to speak. The girl's lips barely moved, and the sound was just the breathiest whisper on the still, parched air. But it went on and on, a sibilant, muttered litany just below the threshold of understanding. Something in the air shifted, as if in response to the sound. The flimsy canvas walls of the tent still surrounded them, but the *quality* of the space had changed, until Winter had to fight the impression that they were in a vast stone hall. She felt as though any noise she made would echo for hours.

She'd seen the Khandarai at prayer before, and it had seemed ordinary enough. A little exotic, all those gods with fanciful names and painted statues, but fundamentally no different from the services offered by any village priest back in Vordan. "Keep me safe from harm and disease, protect my family, let me live and prosper." The homilies were different, but the lessons were the same, too—respect your superiors, live orderly lives, honor the gods. The only major difference Winter had been able to observe was that the Khandarai had priestesses as well as priests, and they got to wear better costumes.

This was nothing like those services. The archaic form of Khandarai used in religious ritual was grammatically complex and difficult to speak, but still basically comprehensible. As Feor's voice slowly rose, Winter began to catch her words, but they sounded like no language she had ever heard. She wasn't certain if there were words at all. Certainly the girl didn't pause in her recitation, even to breathe. Each syllable flowed into the next in an unbroken stream of gibberish, and yet . . .

And yet, oddly, Winter felt as though she could *almost* understand. That there was meaning there, so clear that it lurked just below the surface, *nearly* comprehensible, slightly out of reach. As though—the thought crept in, ridiculous but still true—it *wanted* to be understood, wanted her to reach out and grasp it, like plunging her hand into an icy stream . . .

Feor raised her hand from the kettle. It ought to have been dripping wet, but the water clung to the surface of her skin, as though she'd dipped her hand in translucent tar. The tent had grown shadowed around her, the full light of day fading into twilight, and in the semidarkness motes of light darted and spun around her fingers.

Without ever halting in her recitation, the girl leaned forward and touched the tip of her index finger to Bobby's eyelids, each in turn. Winter had to stifle a gasp. Where Feor's wet finger had been, Bobby's skin *glowed*, a shifting miasma of color that wavered from brilliant blue to sickly green and back again, like paint swirling in a bucket. She paused, still speaking quietly, and studied the effect. Then, carefully, she started to draw.

Wherever her finger passed, it left those eerie, glowing traceries. The pattern she built up, line by careful line, started from Bobby's eyes and spread across her face, down her neck, out across her shoulders. It was abstract, asymmetric, a complex map that ran over the girl's skin with a geometrical exactitude, as though the design took the contours of her body into account. The lines thickened, thinned, began and ended, but never crossed or touched, no matter how close Feor drew them.

Feor passed her hand along Bobby's arms, the underside of her chin, her collarbone, her slight breasts. Winter wasn't sure if the tent had darkened further or the pattern had gotten brighter, but everything was fading away except for the glow of the lines and the rising sound of Feor's voice. Every syllable echoed as if she were speaking from the pulpit of a grand cathedral. Even Bobby's skin vanished, leaving only the pattern, a glowing web hovering in the void. Once again, Winter had the odd feeling that there was order there, an understanding that beckoned to her beneath the apparent chaos.

Finally, with great solemnity, Feor turned Bobby's right hand over and pressed it to her own. Light bloomed between their palms, and when Feor took her hand away the blaze from Bobby's skin outshone even the rest of the pattern. Her recitation rose to a crescendo, the sound of her voice crashing around them like waves against a rocky shore, and almost lost in the rising roar were a few words that Winter recognized.

"—obv-scar-iot!" Feor's eyes glowed with reflected light from the thing she had drawn. All the sound vanished at once, as though someone had dropped a velvet rug across the tent, and the light on Bobby's skin flared so bright it was painful to look at. Winter tasted blood in her mouth where she'd bitten her lip.

And then, apparently, it was over. The light disappeared, and for the first time since she'd begun to recite Feor was silent. For a moment Winter thought they were still in darkness, but as her eyes adjusted she realized it was only the dim half-light of the tent in daytime. Bobby lay still on her pallet, and Feor sat equally still beside her. For a long while, nothing moved.

Eventually, Winter could no longer restrain herself.

"Saints and *fucking* martyrs!" she exploded, the sound of her own voice alien in her ears. "Brass Balls of the Beast, Karis Almighty on a fucking crutch. Holy . . ." She ran out of breath, and by the time she'd gotten her wind back her composure had at least partially returned. "Feor? What happened? Was that—did it work?"

The girl didn't respond. Winter shuffled forward on hands and knees. "Feor?"

Hesitantly, she prodded Feor's shoulder. The girl toppled over, nerveless and boneless, falling across her broken arm and lying in a tangle on the floor like a discarded puppet.

Winter dragged Feor to her bedroll and laid her out, trying not to jostle her wounded arm. Her eyes were screwed shut, and her breathing was so shallow that Winter had to bend across her face to be certain it hadn't stopped entirely.

As for Bobby, Winter couldn't tell if anything had changed one way or the other. She'd peeked under the bandages, but there was so much blood that she couldn't see much, and she didn't dare investigate. The corporal's face had relaxed a little, at least, and her breathing seemed steadier. Winter covered her with a blanket up to the neck and worried.

The tent suddenly seemed stifling. With a quick glance at her two sleeping companions, Winter slipped out through the flap. She was surprised to find Folsom standing just outside, stiff as a sentry. He saluted grimly and looked at her with questioning eyes. Winter sighed.

"I don't know," she said honestly. "Graff says he's not going to make it." She'd almost said *she.* "I'm hoping he's too stubborn for that. We've done everything we can."

Folsom nodded. He cleared his throat and proffered a folded sheet of paper, which Winter took curiously. Only when she opened it did she remember the errand she'd sent him on to get him out of the tent. In his broad, neat hand was a list of names, most of which Winter barely recognized. Beside each was the notation "dead," "missing," or "wounded," with the last bearing additional notes on whether recovery was expected. Winter folded the paper again and noticed that the list continued onto the back of the page.

"Thank you, Corporal," she said. "You can go. Get some rest."

Folsom nodded and lumbered off. Winter cast about for something to sit on and found an empty hardtack box, which she dragged in front of her tent. She would have liked to sleep herself, but she felt too keyed up for it, full of the nervous, manic energy that comes with the promise of a vicious price the next day. Besides, it was only midafternoon.

Her mind kept going back to what she'd witnessed in the tent, but her thoughts skipped off the surface of it, like a rock bouncing across the thick crust of an icy lake. When she closed her eyes she could still see that tracery of blue-green fire hanging in the darkness like an unfathomably complex equation. It seemed . . . unnatural somehow that after witnessing that she could emerge into the sunlight and see the camp spread out around her as though nothing had changed, stacked arms and hardtack boxes, the distant sounds of horses and shouting men. She would have been less surprised to find that the tent flap had opened onto a fairy-tale kingdom full of dragons and talking animals.

Feor . . . Her mind shied away again, but she forced it back. *She's the real thing. A wizard, or a* naathem, *or whatever you want to call it.* It wasn't that she hadn't believed in such things, exactly. After all, the Wisdoms preached regularly against the evils of wizardry and the vile practice of congress with demons. One whole order of the

Sworn Church, the Priests of the Black, had once dedicated their lives to rooting out the arcane in all its forms, though they hadn't existed for more than a century. Still, everyone knew magic existed, somewhere.

That was the point, really. Wizards and demons were something that happened to someone else, in some faraway country, or else deep in the past where they belonged, with the saints and knights in shining armor.

On the other hand, I suppose that for most people Khandar is *a faraway country*. Most Vordanai would not be at all surprised to hear about magic in such a distant land, so why should she, having gone there, be surprised to find it?

Another thought occurred to her—as far as the Church was concerned, what had happened in the tent was nothing less than the work of a demon, the unholy spawn of the vilest pits of hell. Feor herself had said it was heresy, although presumably judged by different lights. Winter had never been a particularly religious person, but she'd absorbed enough in her years at Mrs. Wilmore's that the idea made her uncomfortable. She quashed that feeling irritably.

If it works . . . She almost didn't dare think about that. *If it works, I don't care if Feor is some fiend from the black pits. If I can talk to Bobby . . .* The need hung in her chest like a painful lump. Something had changed, she realized. Before the revelation of the corporal's gender, he'd been a friend and comrade-in-arms. Now *she* was something else—a co-conspirator, possibly—and the possibility had knocked a scab off a part of Winter's heart that she'd long ago closed off. The thought that there might be someone who *shared* her secret was exhilarating and terrifying, both at once.

"They're leaving the wagons."

Winter almost fell off the box. She'd been so wrapped up in her own thoughts she hadn't noticed that anyone else was nearby. Looking up, she found herself sharing her impromptu bench with a young Vordanai woman in trousers and a loose wool blouse. Her hair was pulled up tight, which gave her a severe air, but she smiled at Winter's obvious discomfiture.

"I'm sorry. I startled you."

"I was just . . ." Winter shook her head, not quite trusting her voice.

"It's understandable," the woman said, and for one mad moment Winter thought she knew everything—her secret, the magic, everything. Then she went on. "The battle seems to take everyone in different ways afterward. Some men want to dance and sing, or go whoring and drinking, whereas some just want to . . . sit." She gave a little sigh. "It was terrifying enough at the bottom of the hill. I can only imagine what it must have been like to actually go up it."

Winter nodded, feeling a bit at sea. She sought for something concrete to focus on. "What did you mean about the wagons?"

"They're leaving them behind. Look."

The woman pointed. The First's tents were near the edge of the camp, and Winter had a view of what had been the regimental drill field the previous day. Men were forming up there now, carrying heavy packs as if for a long march, but the horse lines beyond remained undisturbed and the wagons were still unhitched.

She blinked. "What's going on? Are we marching?"

"The Second and Fourth battalions are. They had the easiest time of it in the battle, the colonel said, so they get to go fight in the next one."

"The next battle?"

"The colonel is all in a lather to go assist Captain d'Ivoire. We're behind schedule, apparently."

Winter could well believe that, given the delays they'd suffered on their approach. "What about us?"

"First Battalion?" the woman said, and when Winter nodded she continued. "Taking a well-earned rest, I should think. First and Third are staying behind with the trains and the wounded." She looked down at herself and smiled ruefully. "And other impedimenta."

Winter put on a vague smile of her own, at a loss how to proceed. The woman regarded her thoughtfully.

"What's your name, Sergeant?" she said after a moment.

"Winter, ma'am," Winter said, feeling suddenly formal. "Winter Ihernglass. And it's lieutenant, actually." She hadn't yet bothered to track down a lieutenant's stripe to replace the pips on her shoulders.

"Lieutenant," the woman said. "Excuse me." She extended her hand, and Winter took it and shook cautiously. "I'm Jennifer Alhundt."

The handshake lasted perhaps an instant longer than it should have. In that instant, Winter got the queerest feeling that there was some *thing* emerging from this woman's skin, some invisible fluid or gas that raced up Winter's arm and wrapped itself around her, sinking by degrees through her uniform and then through her skin to embed itself in her flesh. Goose bumps rose along her arms, and she let go a bit too hastily.

"Is this you?" Jen said, jerking her head.

Winter, suppressing a shiver, forced herself to focus. "What?"

"Your tent," Jen said patiently. "Behind us."

"Oh. Yes. Why?"

Jen shrugged. "Just curious. I'm always amazed at the conditions in which you soldiers manage to survive. Four men to a little tent, for years at a time. I've got one to myself and I'm still not going to regret leaving it behind when this is over, I don't mind telling you."

"It was better when we were in camp by the city," Winter said. "We had time to—spread out a little."

"You're Old Colonials, then?" Jen said.

Winter nodded. "They brought some of us in to teach the recruits a few things."

"Interesting. Is it working?"

Winter thought of the folded paper Folsom had brought her. "No," she said. "Not really."

For some reason that made Jen smile. She stood up, brushing off the seat of her trousers.

"Well, Sergeant Ihernglass—sorry, Lieutenant Ihernglass—I'm sorry to have imposed on your time. I'm sure you have better things to do."

"Not really, ma'am. Except maybe sleep."

"That's awfully important," Jen said. "I'll leave you to it. Thank you for the bit of company."

Winter nodded, and Jen strode off.

I wonder who she is? There had been no Vordanai women among the Old Colonials, so she had to have come over with the colonel. *Some civilian functionary? A mistress?*

Winter shrugged and turned back to her tent. There were more important things to worry about.

Drying blood had stuck the bandages solidly to Bobby's skin, even once Winter had untied the knots.

She really ought to have called Graff back, but he was probably asleep somewhere. And Winter wasn't sure what she'd find, but the fewer people who knew about Feor's—about Feor, the better. She glanced over her shoulder to confirm that the Khandarai girl was still sleeping.

Bobby was sleeping, too, and looking considerably less drawn than she had when Winter had left her. Whatever Feor had done was having *some* positive effect. Winter brought one of the kettles and a supply of fresh bandages to the side of the sickbed and poured a trickle of lukewarm water across the stiff, scarlet-soaked cloth. Once it had loosened a bit, she peeled the ruined linen away, leaving behind a mess of caked-on gore. She soaked a fresh cloth and went to work cleaning the blood away, trying not to touch the wound itself.

Only—something was wrong. With some perplexity, and then increasing excitement, Winter worked the cloth across the spot where the gory hole had been and found nothing but smooth skin under her fingers. She poured another stream from the kettle and wiped it away, then sat staring.

The injury was gone, but not without a trace. An irregular patch of skin, vaguely star-shaped, was *changed*. It was white—not the pale, ugly color of a scar or the sickly white of a fish's belly, but the pure, brilliant white of marble. Winter imagined it even had a bit of sparkle to it, the way some marble did, as if someone had replaced that patch of Bobby's skin with a perfect replica grafted from a statue. Winter touched it, carefully, half expecting to feel the cool hardness of stone, but it gave under her finger just like ordinary skin.

It worked. She sat back, letting out a long breath, her shoulders shaking from released tension. *Whatever Feor did, it worked.* A little patch of oddly-colored skin was a small price to pay. Winter looked from one girl to the other, still half in shock. *It really worked.*

She was suddenly unutterably tired. Leaving the dirty bandages on the floor, she fetched one of her own shirts and pulled it onto Bobby's limp form, struggling with the sleeves and the buttons. Fortunately, the girl's bust was modest even by Winter's standards. The shirt alone would probably be cover enough for the casual eye. *Graff knows, but that doesn't mean everyone has to.*

Winter covered Bobby with a blanket, checked Feor one more time, and then flopped onto her own bedroll. She was asleep in an instant and didn't dream at all, not even of Jane.

Chapter Fifteen

MARCUS

At dawn, the Auxiliaries began a cautious advance, a company in loose order probing the rubble and barricades to their front.

Marcus, determined to buy every minute he could, had sent Adrecht and his Fourth Battalion to man the line while the rest of the Colonials pulled back around the hilltop temple. These soldiers almost immediately began a harassing fire, driving back the initial tentative push. The Auxiliaries formed up, solid blocks of brown and tan parade-ground even, and charged into the tangle of detritus with a yell.

The men of the Fourth did not stand to receive them. They were too few, and in any case their orders were to fall back. Each man fired and then ran for it, finding another covered position farther up the hill to reload. Shots rang out from the spreading Khandarai line, trying to find their attackers, but the men in blue were as elusive as mosquitoes. Marcus watched with satisfaction from his hilltop vantage as the Auxiliary advance fell apart, neat lines breaking down in their zeal to come to grips with a retreating enemy amidst the wreckage.

It would have been an ideal time for a counterattack, as he'd done so many times yesterday, but circumstances had changed.

There were two more Khandarai battalions waiting, well formed and ready, down by the bank of the canal. Worse, there were guns—all four of the Gesthemels and two of the monster naval guns, no doubt loaded with canister in anticipation of just such a move. So the Colonials held their ground, Adrecht's men continuing to deliver harassing fire while the flustered Auxiliary officers reorganized their scattered ranks to continue the advance.

That bought a couple of hours, all told, and left the approach to the hill scattered with brown-and-tan-uniformed bodies. But the ultimate outcome was not in doubt. The Fourth was gradually pushed back through the town and toward the hilltop, until the advancing Auxiliaries finally ran into something solid. The Colonials had constructed a line of barricades, bricks and timber from destroyed houses, with the bulk of the stone-walled temple looming behind them. As soon as the enemy approached, this position exploded into fire, and the startled Auxiliaries reeled back out of range.

A few minutes later, Marcus watched the other two Khandarai battalions start moving up. As Adrecht had predicted, they were veering left and right, respectively, pushing past the now-empty streets of the destroyed village and out onto the plain, where they could get on the flanks and rear of the force on the hill. They would converge, like the pincers of a scorpion, and from the time they came into range of the fortifications the Colonials would be committed. No way out, except for surrender. And everyone knew what the Redeemers did to prisoners.

The two big naval guns each had a cloud of attendants who clustered and fussed around them like priests around an altar. In spite of all the attention, the first shot went wide, whistling past the temple and continuing for quite a long way out across the squelching-wet fields. The next, however, scored a solid hit, and before long both guns were pummeling away. The huge things were a bear to reload, so the shots came at intervals of three or four minutes.

Marcus had never been inside a stone building under bombardment. It wasn't something that had been on the syllabus at the War College because it wasn't supposed to happen, now that big stone castles had gone the way of the crossbow and the trebuchet. A good siege gun would produce an impression on even the strongest stone, no matter how thick or high the walls, so breaking them down was only a matter of time. A *proper* fortification looked more like a burrow thrown up by enormous and geometrically minded moles, with overlapping fields of fire for the defender and sloping berms of dirt to deflect cannonballs or absorb their impact in a harmless spray of soil.

He was unprepared, therefore, for the way that the cannonballs *rang* against the walls, as though the temple were being attacked by a swarm of angry bells. The distant thud of the gun itself arrived only just in advance of the shot, and every hit shook the walls like the entire building was rocking in a gale. Dust sifted down from the ceiling as ancient stones were jostled, and there were periodic alarming cracks and pops. One of the men brought Marcus a cannonball, still warm from its firing, which had ricocheted high and landed amongst the defenders. It was about the size of a child's head, and flattened on one side by the terrific impact at the end of its flight. The iron rippled around that spot, as though it had been briefly liquid.

Marcus called for Archer, who had managed to clean up considerably overnight. A silver Church double circle was prominent on the breast of his uniform.

"How long have we got?" Marcus demanded.

"Well, sir," the lieutenant said, "I'm an artilleryman, not a siege engineer, but—"

"Do your best."

"Yessir. I took a look and there's already a few cracked blocks. On the upside, those guns aren't very accurate, so they're battering away all over the wall. On the downside, this place wasn't designed as a fortress, and as best I can tell there's no bracing or internal supports."

Marcus put two fingers to his head and massaged his temples. "And so?"

"Once part of the wall goes, the whole thing is going to come down in a hurry. A couple of hours, I'd say. It could be longer, of course, if we get lucky, but I wouldn't count on it."

A couple of hours. It couldn't be past eight in the morning. He'd tentatively hoped to hang on until nightfall, but . . .

There was a tremendous *boom* from outside, echoing off the temple walls and shaking more dust from the ceiling. Marcus looked at Archer in a panic. To his surprise, the lieutenant was smiling.

"What the hell was that?"

"Ah. I'd been expecting that, sir. I'll have to go and check, of course, but in my professional opinion one of the thirty-six-pounders has just exploded. Those are old tubes, sir, and they've been working them pretty hard. I'm amazed it took this long."

"I'll give them this," Adrecht said. "They're game little bastards."

He and Marcus stood at a second-floor window, its glass long ago kicked out. The view wasn't as good as it would have been from the front steps, but there was less risk of catching a cannonball.

One team of Khandarai was already dragging the wreckage of the ruined naval gun out of the way, along with the bodies of the gunners who'd been caught by the shrapnel when the overheated tube burst. Across the river, a second team was pushing another of the big guns into the ford, two dozen men hauling on ropes or shoving from behind while four more walked gingerly in front of it, feeling for soft patches of mud that might bog the heavy thing down.

In the meantime, the howitzers had opened up again. They had a harder time of it than the naval guns did, since their fragmenting projectiles were useless against the stone walls of the temple itself. Marcus could hear the steady *ping* of fragments off the facade, but they weren't doing any damage. The big open ground floor of the building had room for only a few hundred men, however, and was currently occupied by the wounded and most of Adrecht's Fourth Battalion, resting up after its rearguard action. Aside from the men at the second-floor windows, all the rest of the Colonials were in a narrow strip of ground surrounding the hilltop on three sides, crouching behind improvised barricades or in shallow ditches they'd scratched in the stony ground. It was into this strip that the howitzers tried to drop their shells, with intermittent but bloody success.

"They're not going to bomb us out, though," Adrecht said. "Not unless they intend to stand a siege."

"No," Marcus agreed. "This is just preparatory stuff. Just wait for a few—ah, here they come."

A brown-and-tan line materialized, rising from the earth as the Khandarai infantry got to their feet and started forward. Amidst the explosion of a few last shells, he could hear their shouting even at this distance. They'd sensibly abandoned any attempt at close order and came forward in a swarm of angry, screaming men. Marcus was forcefully reminded of the battle on the coast road, the thin line of blue standing against the vast horde of peasants. *If only I had a nice, solid line and a dozen guns to back it up . . .*

More shouting indicated that the other two enemy battalions, who had spread left and right to face the sides of the hilltop temple, were attacking as well. *So it's to be a general assault. They must know how few men we've got in here.* A canny commander might focus his attack on the weakest section of the enemy line, but with an overwhelming advantage in numbers there was more value in forcing the defenders to spread themselves thin.

The rattle of musketry rose, first from close by as the defenders opened fire, then more distant shots as the Khandarai started to reply. It was joined shortly by the deeper *boom* of Archer's guns, positioned at intervals along the barricade and loaded with canister, their depleted crews filled out by hastily trained volunteers from the infantry. The smaller Khandarai guns opened fire as well, aiming high to avoid their own troops, and mostly sent their fist-sized balls bouncing gaily off the stone walls of the temple with high, ringing notes.

Marcus was pleased to see the attack had broken down almost as soon as it had gotten started. The Khandarai officers were discovering that most men, given a choice between rushing a fuming, spitting barricade bristling with bayonets and ducking into cover to bang away with their own muskets, would choose the latter. And once so ensconced they were difficult to shift, though Marcus could see a few wildly gesticulating officers and sergeants trying. They were off the tactics manual now. Towns, if they were attacked at all, were invested according to the formal rules of a traditional siege, and expected to capitulate once the proper point had been reached in the proceedings.

"Ha!" Adrecht said, as a Khandarai officer who'd stood up to berate his men suddenly pinwheeled to the ground as though he'd been clubbed. "Good shot. Wonder if that was one of ours or one of theirs."

"I'm going to see how the right is doing," Marcus said. "Check the left, would you?"

He turned without waiting for a reply and hurried through the warren of little rooms that made up the temple's second floor until he found a window that provided a suitable view of the right side of the building. The situation below was not as promising as at the front of the building. There was nothing on the gentle slope of the hill to serve as cover for the Khandarai, which perversely made the attack more fearsome. Deprived of the opportunity to drop into relative safety and exchange fire with the defenders, the Auxiliaries had no choice but to run to the barricade, hunched over as though advancing into a strong wind. Musketry and canister cut them down by the score, and in some places the attack faltered, but in others they had reached the line of barricades and charged into a desperate hand-to-hand struggle.

Marcus cursed and hurried back to the central stair, meeting Adrecht coming the other way.

"We're holding on the left," Adrecht said, "though they got closer than I'd like."

"They need help down there," Marcus said. "That's—" He tried to remember who had charge of the right wing, and then guiltily recalled it was his own men of the First Battalion. With Vence down, Thorpe was the most senior officer, with Davis after him. "Thorpe," he finished. "Come on, let's get them some support."

He detached half a company from the Fourth Battalion and sent them down at the double. The arrival of fresh troops seemed to have an impact out of all proportion to their actual numbers. The Khandarai who'd made it over the barricade fell back or surrendered, leaving a mix of blue- and brown-coated bodies strewn over the debris like broken toys. The other Khandarai battalions were pulling back as well, the men who'd refused to rise from cover to attack only too willing to get up when they were retreating. Marcus returned to his window, where he could see them forming again out of musket range.

In the distance, a puff of smoke was followed by a distant *boom*, and then a much closer blast accompanied by the zip and ping of shell fragments. Then the naval guns opened fire again, and the bombardment resumed in earnest.

That was the pattern all through the morning and into the early afternoon, while the sun climbed overhead to turn the battlefield into a blazing inferno. The Auxiliaries dressed their ranks, listened to speeches and shouts from their officers, while behind them the big guns and the howitzers banged away at the obstinate Colonials in their makeshift fortress. Then, worked to a suitable pitch of enthusiasm, the infantry stormed forward, and the rattling tear of musketry overwhelmed every other sound.

Marcus committed his reserves like a miser spending his last eagle, half a company here and half a company there. It stabilized the line, but in order to keep it stabilized, as often as not the fresh troops had to stay, so the Fourth dwindled from three companies to two and finally to one, barely eighty men strong. As the hale troops trickled out of the temple, meanwhile, the wounded trickled in, faster and faster, until they occupied the entire ground floor and the stretcher details had to haul them painfully up the stairs. The cutters were hard at work, and the inevitable charnel house smell made Marcus grateful for even the bitter reek of gunsmoke. The dead, and the severed, mangled limbs of those who might or might not survive, were piled unceremoniously in one corner to make room for new arrivals.

Two o'clock, Marcus reckoned by the sun. Two o'clock, and the southern horizon was still clear. Another shot from the naval guns rang off the front of the temple, and he could feel something *shift* unpleasantly in the stonework. *How many balls have they got for the damn things?*

One of the sentries on the roof—a dangerous position, given the howitzers' tendency to overshoot—had come down to report that he'd seen something off to the south. Riders, he thought. Marcus had hurried to a south-facing window to check, but either his eyes were not as good or whoever it was had gone. *Or was never there in the first place.* Irritated, he walked back to his usual position. Outside, the big guns fell silent one by one, which could only mean another attack was coming.

Adrecht met him by the window. He did his best to conceal it, but Marcus could see the accusation in his face. *Or is that the imaginings of a guilty conscience?*

"We're not going to make it to nightfall," Adrecht said. "This place is standing up better than we thought it would, but Archer says he doesn't think it will take much more. If it collapses entirely . . ."

He didn't have to finish. Marcus could imagine the stone walls crumbling all too well, enormous blocks coming loose to fall among the tight-packed wounded in the main hall below.

"We might be able to cut our way out," Adrecht went on. "Wait until they start shelling us again, try to pull everyone out of the line before they can get reorganized, make a push across the fields to the south. There's a gap there."

Marcus nodded slowly. Again, the important part went unsaid. Even if it worked, that would mean abandoning everything that couldn't be carried on a soldier's back—the guns, the supplies, the wounded. And breaking contact with the enemy afterward was far from certain.

"Or else," Adrecht continued, "we can surrender. Hope that the Auxies aren't as bad as your common run of Redeemer. We drilled them to do things our way, after all. Maybe they absorbed the bit about the proper treatment of prisoners."

Marcus remembered the pyres in the streets of Ashe-Katarion. "We may not have a choice. If I give the order to punch out, I'm not sure how many men would follow."

"No. They're tired." Adrecht gave a mirthless grin. "It's a good thing the Redeemers have such a fearsome reputation, actually. If they could be sure they'd be treated fairly, I'm certain some of ours would have handed over their muskets some time ago."

Outside, the occasional pop of a musket rose rapidly to a sustained roar. Moments later, an agitated soldier burst into the little cell.

"Sir!" he said. "Captain, it's gone bad on the right. They've taken one of the guns, and they're holding right against the wall. The whole side's cut off, sir!"

"Balls of the Beast!" Marcus hesitated, but only for a moment. The company of the Fourth that remained below was his last reserve, his last card to play. Once they were committed, there would be nothing to do but grit his teeth and fight things out to the finish. *But if they get that gun turned down the line, those men are as good as dead.* His own men, he remembered. The First Battalion, Thorpe and Davis.

Adrecht was already halfway to the door. Marcus hurried after him, pounded down the stairs, and ran across the temple hall, trying not to look at the mounting pile of the dead and the endless ranks of the dying. Instead he focused on the handful of blue-coated soldiers huddled near the front door. Adrecht got there first, and within a few moments the company sergeant was shouting the men to their feet.

There was no time for speeches. Marcus stopped in the doorway, drew his sword, and chopped forward. The company followed, booted feet pounding on the flagstones. A few halfhearted cheers from the men guarding the front accompanied their appearance, but these died away as soon as it became clear the men weren't coming to help them. Instead, Marcus turned right, hugging the wall of the temple. To his left was the barricade, held so thinly it seemed impossible that the Khandarai had not already swarmed over it. Pools and streaks of blood showed where men had been hit and dragged away.

Two of Archer's guns still boomed defiance on either side of the doorway, and Marcus caught sight of the lieutenant himself, face bloodied from yet another wound. He couldn't spare more than a glance, however. The shouts and screams from the melee were audible even above the gunfire. Stumbling a little on the rocky ground, Marcus rounded the corner of the temple with Adrecht and the company hard on his heels and found himself face-to-face with a knot of struggling men.

The Khandarai had swarmed over the gun, and a dozen men were at work on it, turning it to fire down the Vordanai line along the temple wall. The men in blue closest by had recognized the danger, and two dozen men from the right wing and a similar number from the center had already hurled themselves with musket butt and bayonet against the disorganized mass of Auxiliaries around the cannon. There was no order left, no organized charges and countercharges, just a confused brawl where soldiers laid into one another with whatever came to hand.

Marcus didn't need to give a command. He just gestured with his sword, and the men of the Fourth Battalion surged past, shouting with hoarse voices. A few shots rang out from both sides before the masses met, and then the struggle was once again hand to hand.

It was going to work, Marcus saw. His little band, depleted as it was, nonetheless outnumbered the Khandarai survivors, and they were falling back from the captured artillery piece. A few moments more, and they would break. *And then we've bought a few more minutes . . .*

He couldn't hear Adrecht's voice, and it took him a moment to see his frantic gestures. Marcus looked up, toward the Khandarai line, and saw another mass of brown-and-tan uniforms approaching.

At least a company, he had time to register. Obviously the Khandarai commander had seen the same opportunity Marcus had led his men to prevent, and had committed his own reserves. *Damn, damn, damn . . .*

Then the newcomers were on them, a solid line of leveled bayonets that shattered at the last minute as they had to traverse the uneven footing of the barricade. Marcus saw the flash of Adrecht's sword coming out of its sheath. It was a pretty thing, he remembered—gold chasing on the hilt and colored embroidery on the scabbard. He just had time to hope that Adrecht hadn't entirely neglected the edge before the Auxiliaries were on them.

Marcus would never have described himself as a master swordsman. At the War College, there had been students who'd gone in for that sort of thing, studying the ancient forms under the College tutors and staging flashing, glittering contests in the quad while onlookers applauded politely. He remembered the beauty of those bouts, the way the contestants had clashed and spun, almost as though they were dancing instead of sparring.

What experience Marcus had with his blade had come in back alleys and desperate ambushes, and none of it had been beautiful in any sense. He had learned a few important lessons, though, not the least of which was never to discount the efficacy of an unconventional blow. A punch to the stomach or a kick to the groin might not be as elegant as a perfectly executed thrust, but it would put a man on the ground just the same.

In any case, his weapon was not one of the light, elegant rapiers the College swordsmen had favored. It was actually a cavalry saber, begged from the stores after his army-issue officer's sword had broken in a skirmish years ago. The heavy, curved thing was really designed to be wielded from horseback, but Marcus liked the weight of it. The pommel could crack a skull, properly applied, and the blade was a solid three feet of good steel.

He'd also learned, in a rough way, what to do when you were up against more than one opponent. *Keep moving.* Hold still and they'd circle round and skewer you. Thus, as three men clambered over the broken timber that topped the barricade in front of him, he bulled forward, dodging the point of a surprised Auxiliary's bayonet and giving the man a wild slash across the stomach that sent him reeling. Before the man beside him could recover from his surprise and bring his unwieldy weapon to bear, Marcus slammed him in the face with the guard of the saber, which left him stumbling and clutching a broken nose.

There were brown uniforms all around him now. He hacked and slashed at random, grabbed the haft of a musket as it thrust past him and twisted it out of the owner's grasp, blocked another blade by sheer luck and replied with a wild swing that took off most of the Khandarai's face. He expected every moment to feel the sting of a point in the small of his back. Looking around, he saw a knot of blue and struggled toward it, but a hard shove from behind drove him practically into the arms of another Auxiliary. Instinctively, Marcus lowered his blade, and the point went in the man's stomach and came out between his shoulder blades. He sagged, face twisted in a comic surprise, and the deadweight tore the saber from Marcus' grip.

Another bayonet flashed, over his shoulder, and he ducked. Someone kicked him—obviously he wasn't the only one who'd spent time in the back-alley school of swordsmanship—and sent him sprawling. His world was suddenly a mass of dusty, stamping boots. Marcus saw a gap ahead and crawled toward it, grabbing ankles to use as handholds. Someone looked down and a bayonet shivered into the turf by his leg, but the next moment he managed to drag himself into the clear.

He rolled over and looked up, dumbfounded, into the maw of a twelve-pounder. He'd fought his way into the little clear space the Auxiliaries were striving to maintain around their prize. The gun was a few feet away, aimed over his head, but Marcus didn't doubt it would be loaded with canister, which made the precise orientation of the barrel irrelevant. He remembered the fields of fire of the Preacher's guns at the last battle, the men torn to pieces so small they weren't even recognizable as corpses. By the side of the gun, a gawky Khandarai in a brown uniform grinned, showing a mouthful of rotten teeth, and raised a lit match to the side of the cannon—

—and scrabbled at it, mystified. The gun was engraved all over, verses from the Wisdoms crammed in as small as careful hands could manage. A Kravworks '98, Marcus remembered. *Friction primers.*

He jumped to his feet, driven by a sudden, desperate energy, and slammed his fist into the would-be gunner's face. There were four more men beside the piece, though, and these still had their muskets. They surrounded Marcus on three sides, advancing cautiously. He tried to grab a musket by the barrel, but the man pulled back so fast Marcus nearly cut his hands on the bayonet, and one of the others thrust at his head. Marcus avoided being skewered only by falling awkwardly backward, leaving him looking up at four gleaming steel points.

One of which twitched suddenly and fell away. Adrecht broke through the circle of Khandarai, and the other three turned to face him. He raised his sword, and under other circumstances Marcus would have had to laugh at the expression on his fellow captain's face. His blade had snapped off half a foot from the hilt.

Two of the Khandarai thrust simultaneously. The third would have as well, but for the fact that Marcus grabbed his ankle from behind and pulled his foot out from under him, leaving him sprawling in the dust. Adrecht spun away from the pair. One bayonet just missed his back, and the other caught him on the upper arm, ripping a deep, bloody gash through the muscle. Suddenly off balance, Adrecht stumbled against the cannon.

Marcus snatched up the fallen man's weapon, treading on him in the process, and sank it into the small of another man's back. The fourth Auxiliary turned to face him, but Adrecht managed to kick him off balance, and Marcus slammed the butt of the musket into his fingers, then skewered him on the point of the bayonet. He hurried to Adrecht, who was clutching the deep cut just above his elbow.

"Fucking sword," Adrecht moaned. "The damned armorer promised me that was good steel. Remind me to kill him if we ever get to Ashe-Katarion."

"Fair enough," Marcus said. He put his back to the cannon, beside Adrecht, and took a moment to look around. There were fewer brown uniforms in view than he'd expected, and those he could see were retreating rapidly. *Don't tell me we actually stopped them after all?*

There was a *boom*, close at hand. Not the deep-throated roar of a gun going off, but the higher-toned blast of a shell exploding. *Howitzers already?* The Auxiliaries were still engaged all along the perimeter—the inaccurate weapons would be as likely to kill their own men as the Vordanai. He straightened up for a better look.

Another shell exploded with a flash, well back from the temple, down among the wreckage from which the Auxiliaries had launched their attack. Where their reserves, officers, and wounded were presumably still waiting. *That's a hell of an unlucky shot,* Marcus thought, until another one exploded practically on top of the first. Then he understood.

"Marcus?" Adrecht said. His eyes were shut tight against the pain. "What's happening? Are we going to die?"

"No," Marcus said. "Not unless Janus overshoots a bit."

"Janus?" Adrecht cracked one eyelid cautiously.

"The colonel." Marcus waved a hand. "He's captured the guns, which means he's captured the ford. Which means he's captured the whole lot."

All around the temple the Auxiliaries were falling back under the unexpected fire from their own artillery. Most of them were streaming back the way they had come, toward the ford, unaware that they were running straight into the arms of fresh blue-uniformed infantry. The brighter ones scattered, heading east or west or south across the fields, but no doubt there were cavalry waiting to gather them up. The colonel, Marcus knew, did not believe in half measures.

Part Three

GENERAL KHTOBA

Far be it from me, General Khtoba thought, *to tell the Divine Hand that he shouldn't pray.* And, truth be told, a bit of divine intervention would not go amiss. But the man's constant muttering was getting on his nerves.

The general's legs and back ached from hours on his feet and more hours in the saddle, but nervousness would not let him sit. The black felt tent did not offer much room for pacing, and he found himself very nearly turning in place, swatting irritably at the hanging tassels of the pillows with his thin black swagger stick. He'd put on his dress uniform that morning, and the crisply folded brown-and-tan had long ago sagged under his perspiration.

Half the tent was taken up by the Hand and his attendants, a gaggle of black-robed priests that reminded Khtoba a flock of geese in mourning. Most of them had followed their leader's example and settled in for some serious prayer, but one of the older men, with a glance at the Hand's bowed head, scuttled over to Khtoba and spoke in a harsh whisper.

"How dare he keep us waiting!" he said. "These savages need to be taught some respect." But, Khtoba noticed, he didn't raise his voice enough for the two Desoltai lounging by the pinned-open tent flap to hear.

"I'm sure our eminent companion has other things on his mind," Khtoba drawled, his voice dripping sarcasm that the priest completely failed to notice.

"Other things on his mind? What can be more important than a summons from the Divine Radiance himself?"

More of a visit than a summons. He took a certain pleasure in seeing the arrogant pup of a priest brought low, but it was thin recompense for his own disasters. What was left of the Auxiliaries waited outside, in the midst of the Desoltai encampment. Three or four hundred men, all he'd been able to salvage from the debacle atop the hill near Turalin. The remainder, those who'd escaped the sabers of the *raschem* cavalry and hadn't surrendered outright, were probably still running.

As for the other half of his army, reports were still uncertain, but the general did not hold out much hope. What information he could gather said that the Vordanai had captured those three battalions lock, stock, and barrel, and even if that was an exaggeration, he didn't think many of the survivors would be hurrying back to the colors.

It might be possible to rebuild, eventually. He had a disproportionate number of officers remaining. Those with the most to lose by abandoning the uniform had naturally been the most inclined to follow him in the pell-mell retreat to the city. But that would take months, if not years. In the meantime, the fires of the Redemption appeared to be burning low indeed.

"Why doesn't he come?" The priest was pouting. Khtoba recalled that his adopted name was Tzikim-dan-Rahksa, the Angel of Divine Retribution. *Divine Retribution shouldn't pout.*

If that was a prayer, of a sort, it was answered almost immediately. The Steel Ghost strode into the tent, acknowledging the nods of the men on the door and offering the very slightest inclination of his head to the Divine Hand. Khtoba he ignored entirely.

The general's hands tightened, but he said nothing. His

intelligence had reported that the Steel Ghost was with the Desoltai outriders to the south, watching the Vordanai advance to the city. A swift rider on a galloping horse *might* have reached him in time for him to make an equally headlong gallop back to see the Hand, but the Ghost did not have the look of a man who'd just finished a desperate twilight ride. He was wrapped, as always, in neat blacks and grays, with his head covered and his hands gloved so that no hint of flesh showed. The steel mask was thick enough that even his eyes were difficult to see through the small holes.

It was enough to make one believe that he really *did* have strange powers, as the rumors claimed. After whatever wizardry the *raschem* had conjured up to bewilder his Auxiliaries, it wouldn't have surprised Khtoba.

The Divine Hand looked up briefly, then nodded to Tzikim and turned back to his prayer. The older priest confronted the Steel Ghost, but Khtoba noticed he had some trouble meeting the implacable stare of the blank mask. The general also noted he didn't say a word about having been kept waiting.

"My honored friend," the Angel of Divine Retribution said. "You must know of the unfortunate reverses that have overtaken us. The gods require your service, now more than ever. It is time to show your faith!"

Khtoba laughed. He couldn't help it. Tzikim glared daggers in his direction, and the faceless mask turned slowly to regard him. He favored the Ghost with a lazy smile.

"What my *honored friend* means is that his own people have all run away, and he would be most obliged if you would bring your men inside the city to defend him."

The priest gritted his teeth. "As the general says. The walls of Ashe-Katarion are high and strong, but they still require men to defend them. The Swords of Heaven have experienced a few . . . setbacks. We need time to rebuild our ranks. And our companions in the Auxiliaries have proven inadequate to the task of stopping the *raschem*." He flashed a gloating smile in Khtoba's direction. "The Divine Hand therefore requires that you move your men inside the city. He swears that the Heavens will reward you handsomely."

The strength of the walls was questionable, in Khtoba's opinion. They enclosed only the stone heart of the city, including the Palace and the sacred hill, but they were still too long to be defended by less than a few thousand men. Ancient, crumbling in places, they were thick enough, but they hadn't been built to withstand a modern siege. *Especially if the* raschem *have captured our heavy artillery.* He cursed himself, for the hundredth time, for allowing those guns to be removed from the city. It had seemed like such a clever idea at the time.

The Ghost fixed the priest with a steady glare, and under that blank gaze Tzikim crumbled like cheap bricks. His face went waxen and shiny with sweat, and his expression shifted rapidly from imperious command to obsequious supplication. When the Desoltai chieftain looked away, the Angel of Divine Retribution sagged with audible relief.

"No," the Ghost said, in his characteristic growl.

Defiance appeared to revive Tzikim's spirits briefly. "What? You would betray the Redemption?"

"No," the Ghost repeated. "But you ask the impossible. My warriors will not man your walls."

"They're your men, aren't they?" Khtoba put in. "Why wouldn't they follow orders?"

"They are only my men so long as my superior wisdom is evident," the Ghost rasped. "We are not *raschem*, to march to our deaths on the whim of some king. If we are trapped in the city, we will never escape."

Tzikim seemed to shrink back into himself. With a contemptuous glance, Khtoba dismissed the priest and concentrated on the Desoltai.

"Then what course do you suggest?" he said.

"I suggest nothing," the Ghost said. "My people abandon this camp as we speak. We will return to the *Ruskdesol*."

Khtoba had been around the Desoltai long enough to catch that last word, which meant something like "Father Desert" in the nomads' dialect. For the Desoltai, their arid domain was the center of the world. Sometimes they seemed to think of it as a kind of god.

"And then what?" Khtoba said. "Back to raiding towns and ambushing caravans?"

"When the *raschem* follow, we will teach them the true meaning of war."

Khtoba chuckled. "I have no doubt you would, if they were fool enough to pursue you into the Great Desol. But what makes you think this Vordanai captain is such a fool?"

"He is no fool," said the Ghost. "But he will follow nonetheless. We will have a prize that he cannot ignore."

Khtoba glanced over at the Divine Hand, still praying with his eyes tightly shut, and then down at himself. A faint smile played across his lips.

"I take it we're to accompany you, then."

The Ghost inclined his head, flickers of lamplight shifting on the brushed-steel mask.

Khtoba had three hundred men outside, mostly armed and a few ahorse. If he chose to object, they might make a brave show of it. Some might even get away. Then again, that remnant was tired and demoralized after the short, disastrous campaign. They also might put up no fight whatsoever.

Either way, though, it was obvious that Khtoba *personally* wasn't going anywhere. He had a sword at his side, but possessed no illusions about fighting his way out of the tent. And the Hand's gaggle of bootlickers would be worse than useless. The only course, then, was acquiescence.

The Ghost was still watching him. It was strange, speaking to a mask. The thing was like a blank canvas on which the interlocutor could paint whatever he wanted or feared to see. The prospect of that had reduced Tzikim nearly to tears, but Khtoba fancied himself made of sterner stuff. He put on a level expression.

"Very well," he said. "It seems the best plan we have, under the circumstances."

JAFFA

The Justices had come creeping back with the death of Yatchik-dan-Rahksa and the collapse of the Swords of Heaven. For the most part they tried to pretend they'd never left, turning up at the gatehouse in their old uniforms and trying not to meet one another's eyes. Others, who'd deserted to defend their homes or communities, were slower to trickle in. But the city had taken on a deathly calm since the news had gotten out that the Hand had abandoned the Palace. Even the thieves and muggers were hunkered down, hoping to weather the storm. Among those who'd worn the prince's colors before his departure, there was a feeling—at least, a hope—that wearing those colors again to greet their restored monarch might encourage him to some feelings of mercy. Those who'd sewn the red flames of the Redemption to their breasts were rapidly ripping off the patches; those who'd painted the symbol on were working frantically with soap and water.

Jaffa-dan-Iln maintained no illusions about his own position. He'd collaborated with the Council and the Auxiliaries; there were any number of witnesses to that. With the Hand and the general fled, he was the only authority figure remaining in a battered, terrified city, and that seemed to mean that for the moment he was in charge. Unfortunately, once the prince reasserted his authority, that was likely to lead to his execution.

He might have fled, he supposed. The thought had honestly not occurred to him until it was far too late. Jaffa was a man who did his duty. Besides, he was confident in his reward. *After all, am I not acting directly on instructions from Mother?*

Niaph-dan-Yunk, one of the first to march with the Swords and one of the first to return, knocked hesitantly at the open door to Jaffa's office. Jaffa admitted him with a wave, but the younger man stood uncomfortably in the doorway.

"Sir," he said, "our messenger has returned."

"About time," said Jaffa. "And?"

"The *raschem*—" Niaph coughed at Jaffa's look. "The Vordanai colonel has agreed to your request for a meeting. He says he will wait half a mile up the coast road from the gate in one hour."

"Excellent. Tell them to saddle my horse."

"Yes, sir." Niaph hesitated. "Will you be wanting an escort?"

Jaffa could have laughed. The man's thoughts might as well have been printed on his forehead. He didn't think whoever went to meet this demon-commander of the *raschem* had much chance of returning alive. No doubt the feeling was widespread among the Justices.

"No," Jaffa said. "I will go alone." He smiled. "I have his word on my safe conduct. Why would I need an escort?"

The fear in Niaph's eyes instantly turned to pity, with perhaps a hint of admiration. Or maybe Jaffa was deceiving himself.

"Yes, sir. Good luck, sir."

The streets were quieter than Jaffa had ever seen them, especially here, in the direct path of the approaching army. The coast road was lined with tenements, ramshackle multistory buildings assembled from brick, wood, and scraps of stolen stone. For the most part they were empty now, the residents having fled to presumed safety on the other side of the city, but those who couldn't or wouldn't leave were watching from behind rag doors and curtains. Jaffa could feel the questioning eyes.

When he caught sight of the line of soldiers, he dismounted and walked the rest of the way. The Vordanai had drawn up a company across the road, muskets shouldered, their deep blue uniforms covered with the dust of hard marching. Ahead of them waited two officers on foot. Jaffa was relieved to see that the prince was not with them, though he hadn't expected the sovereign to lower himself to this kind of negotiation. His feelings were mixed, though, when he recognized Captain d'Ivoire. He'd known the man slightly before the Redemption. Usually they'd met after the Justices had to pull drunken Colonials out of brawls, and their relationship had been cool at best.

It was the other officer who stepped forward. He wore a colonel's eagles on the shoulders of his immaculate dress uniform and bore himself with an aristocratic mien. When they locked gazes, Jaffa felt the force of his stare as a physical blow. The rest of his features seemed to recede into insignificance around his wide gray eyes, animated by an inner fire. Jaffa approached the last few steps at something resembling a parade-ground march and bowed stiffly.

"Gentlemen," he said, keeping to Khandarai. Jaffa understood a few words of the *raschem* tongue, but not enough for a formal discussion. "I am Grand Justice Jaffa-dan-Iln."

Jaffa wondered if the captain would translate for his superior, but the colonel either didn't require a rendering or didn't care. Captain d'Ivoire stepped forward, offering a slight bow in return, and said, "Welcome, Justice. This is Count Colonel Janus bet Vhalnich Mieran." After the colonel gave a slight nod of recognition, d'Ivoire asked, "How do things stand in the city?"

"The Redeemers have fled," Jaffa said. "General Khtoba and the remnants of the Auxiliaries with them. The Desoltai camp to the east is also gone, though to where I cannot say."

"Then who rules the city?"

Jaffa wondered if he was supposed to say that the prince did, but he decided to stick to practical matters. "At present, no one. I am in charge, to the extent that anyone is. My Justices are trying to keep the peace."

"Do you intend to oppose our entry?" d'Ivoire said, with just a hint of a smile.

"Of course not," Jaffa said. "My men are not soldiers. The gates of Ashe-Katarion are open to you." He hesitated, then added, "I entreat you to be as merciful as you can."

"Some of that will be up to the prince, of course." Jaffa thought he caught a disgusted look in d'Ivoire's eye. "But we will try to keep our men in line. We will camp on the Palace grounds, around the Heavenly Guard barracks. The colonel would like you to prepare a report on conditions in the city, the number of men you have in the Justices, and how many you think you can trust." The captain paused at Jaffa's surprised look. "Is something wrong?"

"No," Jaffa managed. Apparently he was not to be clapped in irons after all.

D'Ivoire lowered his voice. "I told the colonel that you were a man to be trusted. That you'd done your duty under the prince, and done the same under the Redeemers. Can we rely on you to continue to perform it?"

"Yes, of course," Jaffa said. "My loyalty is to the people of Ashe-Katarion."

"Good." The captain straightened up, and seemed on the point of dismissing him, but the colonel broke in unexpectedly. His Khandarai was perfect, even down to his accent.

"Grand Justice, I wonder if you might enlighten me as to conditions on the sacred hill?"

Jaffa blinked. "The hill, my lord? What of it?"

"Did the Redeemers do much damage? Are the priestesses still in their temples?"

"I—" For a single horrifying moment, Jaffa thought that this *raschem* knew about Mother, knew *everything*. But that was impossible, of course. He mastered himself quickly. "Some remain, my lord. There was some looting and vandalism, but the Redeemers believe—believed—that they were returning to the old ways, not overthrowing them entirely. Some priests fled, and those who refused to adopt the new canon were . . . punished. But there has been no wholesale destruction."

"Excellent." The colonel gave a bright smile. "I have read of the magnificence of the temples of Ashe-Katarion. It would be a shame if they had been destroyed before I had a chance to examine them myself."

There was something in Colonel Vhalnich's eyes that Jaffa did not like, but there was nothing he could do about it now. He bowed his head. "I'm sure the priestesses would be honored by your visit, my lord."

CHAPTER SIXTEEN

MARCUS

As the Colonials settled down in Ashe-Katarion, Janus asked Marcus to come up with a detail of twenty men he thought he could trust to keep a secret.

Marcus was tempted to reply that twenty men could keep a secret only if you sank nineteen of them in the river, and even then you'd have to keep an eye on the last one. He was also *strongly* tempted to tell Janus to take a flying leap into the Great Desol. Adrecht was still unconscious in the cutter's tents with a high fever, and the battered Old Colonials had barely finished sorting themselves out and counting the dead. You couldn't say that sort of thing to a colonel, however, so Marcus rounded up Fitz, Senior Sergeant Argot, and a squad he thought he could rely on not to ask too many questions, and followed Janus to Monument Hill.

That was the Vordanai name for it, of course. The center of Ashe-Katarion was a double-humped hillock, tailing off rapidly into the harbor. One crest bore the Palace itself, while the other, surrounded by a second, lower wall, was the traditional domain of the priesthood. It comprised a square mile or so of ancient, rambling sandstone buildings, courtyards adorned with statues, and occasional gardens and orchards. Towering above all of these, their long black shadows cutting over the wall and into the city, were the huge black obelisks that Marcus tended to think of as the Forest of Divine Cocks.

On arriving at the elaborately carved sacred gates, Marcus was surprised to see that the hill's buildings seemed more or less intact. He'd pictured a smoking ruin, Divine Cocks pulled down onto the temples they'd decorated and everything that would burn put to the torch. Apparently, the masters of the Redemption hadn't been certain enough of their support among the populace to make such a visible gesture against tradition. It was midmorning, and the shadows of the obelisks still threw their irregular striped pattern across the streets of the lower city. Past the gate, courtyards that had once bustled stood empty and silent. The massive brazier in front of the Temple of the Eternal Flame was cold and dark, and Marcus could see that the painted sandstone walls of the nearest buildings had been defaced by great cracks and slathered with graffiti, mostly the ubiquitous squat *V* of the Redeemers.

Janus paused at the gateway. He paced, unable to contain his energy, and his deep gray eyes were never still. After a moment he turned to look at Marcus and his soldiers, and apparently reached some sort of decision.

"You want to know what we're doing here," he said, his gaze lingering on Marcus in particular. "I wish I could tell you, but I am enjoined to silence on the matter. I *can* say that I am following an express royal command, and that I am humbled by the trust placed in me by His Majesty. This morning, I am sharing this trust with all of you. I ask only that you follow me, obey orders, and keep silent as to anything you may see." The colonel paused. "Anyone who feels himself unworthy of His Majesty's trust may step away now, and I will forget you were ever here."

There was a long pause. After a moment, Senior Sergeant Jeffery Argot raised a hand like a boy in class. Marcus cringed, but Janus nodded to him, unperturbed.

"Yes, Sergeant?"

"This trust," he said. "Is it likely to involve any fighting?"

There were a few mutters from the rest. The men were armed, but they were all Old Colonials, and they knew the inside of the hill was a nightmare of stone buildings and warren-like alleys.

Janus smiled. "No, Sergeant. At this point the opposition consists of a few elderly women. The worst you'll face today is a bit of manual labor."

Argot nodded. "Fair enough. I guess I can keep my mouth shut."

A few of the others nodded agreement. Marcus gave them an appraising look, but said nothing.

"Follow me, then," Janus said. "Do nothing until I say."

He strode confidently through the gate, and Marcus and the soldiers followed. It was deathly quiet on the hill. The whole city had seemed unnaturally silent, residents cowering and barring the doors against a relative handful of Vordanai, but walking through the streets Marcus had still been able to feel the eyes on him. Here the silence was the quiet of the grave.

The layout of the hill was a haphazard maze, but Janus led the way without hesitation, cutting through narrow passageways and across flagstone courtyards. They passed the base of one of the ubiquitous obelisks, a four-sided spike reaching a hundred feet into the air. A few of the men stared up at it, and under ordinary circumstances Marcus would have expected a rude comment or two, but there was an air about the hill now that weighed against flippancy. Abandoned, it possessed a quiet aura of sanctity that it had never had in bustling life, as though they had walked into a gigantic sepulcher.

They were nearing the center when Janus found what he was looking for. He quickened his steps in the direction of a small building, barely bigger than a farm shed, with sandstone walls and a slate roof. The doorway was tiny, barely big enough for a grown man to fit through, and it was blocked by a sun-bleached wooden door. On each side of it stood a crude statue, worn away by the years to smooth-faced mannequins only just recognizable as human.

It was not a building Marcus had ever seen before. He glanced questioningly at Fitz, who raised one eyebrow and shook his head. The Khandarai had a great many gods, and Marcus certainly wouldn't claim to know them all, but he was familiar with the major divinities. This had the look of a shrine to a minor deity, albeit an ancient one. *What does he expect to find* here?

The colonel went to the door and, to Marcus' surprise, knocked. There was a long moment of silence.

"What do you want?" The voice from inside was a woman's, dusty-dry and ancient-sounding. She spoke in Khandarai. Among the soldiers, Marcus guessed, only he and Fitz understood.

"We would like to come in," Janus said. The colonel used the politest form the language allowed, accent perfect as always. "If you would open the door, I would be grateful."

Another, longer silence. Then the crone said, "There is nothing inside for you."

"Nevertheless," Janus said.

When there was no response, he straightened up.

"If you do not open the door," he said, still pleasant and polite, "these men will break it down."

Marcus could hear mutterings from inside, in at least two voices. The door swung inward.

The inside of the little shrine was a single room. At one end was an altar, a long, flat stone resting on two blocks, adorned with a clay statue of a fat-bellied woman. Lamps burned on either side of the idol. Other than that, there was no furniture, just a few ragged rugs spread across the stone floor. The crone, withered and bent-backed, stood protectively in front of the altar, while off to one side a much younger woman in a plain brown robe knelt as though in prayer.

Janus crossed the room, his step still jaunty, but there was a certain amount of muttering from the rankers. Marcus caught a couple of superstitious double-circle gestures, traditional for warding off evil. There were no windows, and the doorway was shadowed by one of the larger buildings, so the inside of the little shrine flickered yellow in the glow of the two lamps.

"Good day," Janus said to the crone. "I am Count Colonel Janus bet Vhalnich Mieran."

"There is nothing for you here," the old woman repeated. "You can see that now. Go away."

"I would like you to show me the entrance," the colonel said, still smiling.

The old woman glared at him, but said nothing.

"This does not need to be difficult," he said. "I know the *yod-naath* is here. Show me the way in."

"There is no such thing," the woman said stoutly.

"As you like." Janus turned back to his men. "Restrain the women and move the altar."

Marcus snapped a salute and told a pair of soldiers to take hold of the two women, pulling them to the far end of the shrine. Four more men took hold of the altar stone and lifted it with a chorus of grunts. The lamplight flickered as they maneuvered it carefully out of the way and set it down against the wall. At the last moment, one of the men lost his grip, and one corner of the heavy weight crashed against the floor loudly. The fat-woman statue toppled and shattered into ceramic shards, a cloud of fine dust rising from her innards and filling the room with a sweet, pungent smell.

Two more men shifted the blocks that had held the altar up. The young woman had her eyes closed, her mouth moving silently, but the crone watched Janus' every move like a snake. The colonel smiled at her and walked to where the altar had been. He brought one foot down sharply, and the stone underneath gave a hollow *boom*. The soldiers grinned.

"As I suspected," Janus said, stepping aside. "If you would, Sergeant?"

Marcus beckoned Argot forward. The stone was flush with those around it, offering no obvious handholds, so the sergeant shrugged and reversed his musket. Two sharp blows were enough to crack the thin slate, sending fragments of it tumbling into the hollow space underneath.

The young woman let out a long moan, jerking against the guards who held her arms. The old priestess merely redoubled her glare. Janus ignored both, stepping to the edge of the newly revealed hole and peering into the darkness.

"There appears to be only a short drop," he said. "I will proceed alone for the moment. Wait here."

"Sir," Marcus said, "we have no idea what's down there, or how far it may extend. Please wait until we can be sure it's safe."

Janus gave a tight smile. "I have a fairly good idea what's down there, Captain. But if you're worried about my safety, you may accompany me. Is that acceptable?"

It wasn't, by Marcus' lights, but he couldn't back down now. He accepted a musket from the sergeant, checked that it was loaded, and picked up one of the oil lamps from the altar. In passing, he said to Fitz, "If we're not back in an hour, go and get two companies and tear this place apart."

Fitz nodded almost imperceptibly. Marcus tucked the weapon under one arm, set the lamp on the lip of the gap, and dropped into darkness. As Janus had said, it wasn't far, and when he stood from his crouch his eyes were only a foot below the floor of the shrine. Janus handed down the flickering lamp, which illuminated the contours of the underground space, and Marcus was reassured to see that it was more of a basement than a cave. There was a small circular space opening onto the mouth of a corridor, which extended beyond the range of the lamplight.

Janus landed nimbly beside him, raising a puff of ancient dust. Marcus handed him the lamp, to leave his own hands free to hold the musket.

"I doubt you'll be needing that," Janus said.

"I hope not," Marcus said. He was having visions of an underground sanctum, packed with knife-wielding fanatics eager to defend their sacred temples to the death. One musket ball would not be much help, in that case, but the loaded weapon still gave him some comfort.

"As you like." Janus raised the lamp, peered down the corridor, then set off with a confident step. Marcus fell in behind him.

It was a longer walk than he'd anticipated. The faint glow filtering down from the entrance was soon lost to sight behind a gentle curve, and only the narrow circle of lamplight was visible. Ancient stone unrolled in front of them and vanished behind. The air smelled dry, dusty, and dead.

"I don't suppose you'd care to tell me what you expect to find," Marcus said, to break the silence.

"When I first arrived," Janus said, "I told you that I thought Orlanko had some reason to be interested in Khandar. That he's sent his people here looking for something."

Marcus had almost forgotten that conversation. He nodded hesitantly. "What about it? You think it's here?"

"I wasn't certain until we found the tunnel," Janus said. "But now . . . yes."

"What could be down here that's so important?"

Janus stopped, setting the lamp to swinging on its handle. Their shadows danced against the walls.

"You were raised in the Free Church, were you not, Captain?" he said.

Marcus nodded. "Though I was never what you might call religious. I mean—"

Janus held up a hand to stop him. "Did you ever hear the story of the Demon King?"

That rang a very distant bell, but Marcus couldn't bring it to mind. He shook his head.

"It's part of the apocrypha of the early Church," Janus said. "The story goes that back in the days of Saint Ligamenti, during the Holy Wars, there was a sorcerer in the east who had carved himself out a kingdom. He called himself the Demon King, or at least that is the only way he's referred to in surviving records. He used his magic to break every army sent against him, and kept all the surrounding lands in terror. Eventually, the other kings asked the Church to intervene, and the Pontifex of the Black led a Holy War against him."

"I think I remember," Marcus said, poking through ancient, musty memories of sitting beside his parents in a splintery wooden pew. "The evil king was defeated, but he escaped the Black Priests, and fled with all his treasures across the ocean. That's where the Demon Sea gets its name." He stopped. "You're not serious."

Janus only smiled.

"But . . ." Marcus groped for words. "That was a thousand years ago. And, anyway, it's just a fairy tale! Like Gregor and the hundred bandits, or Hugh and the giant."

"There's often more truth in fairy tales than you might think," Janus said. "Not the literal truth, of course. But they represent a sort of folk memory, which at the root sometimes refers to real events. When added to historical evidence . . ." He shrugged. "As to whether there was a Demon King, I couldn't say. But the Pontifex of the Black *did* lead a Holy War in the east in the third century, and there are too many stories of his enemies sailing off over the southern horizon for it to be mere coincidence."

"That doesn't mean they came *here*. Khandar was only discovered two hundred years ago!"

"Two hundred and twenty-four," Janus corrected. "But that's the whole point, really. Cultural studies from those first few expeditions found little coincidences they couldn't explain between the Khandarai culture and ours. Bits of language, symbols—" He caught Marcus' look and shrugged. "Most scholars dismiss the idea, but I've reviewed the evidence for myself. Someone from the continent was here long before Captain Vahkerson 'discovered' the place."

"So *that's* what you think the Last Duke is looking for? Some kind of . . . of treasure?" It sounded like the plot of a bad penny opera—some vast storeroom of ancient loot, dug up by the intrepid hero while he rescued his true love. *What does that make me? The comic sidekick?*

"In a way." Janus started walking again, and Marcus hurried to catch up. "If you're expecting a mountain of gold, however, you may be disappointed."

"Then what's down here?"

"You'll see. Ah." Ahead, the lamplight showed a wooden door set into the rock. "This should be it. We're right underneath the very top of the sacred hill now. Above us is the Temple of the Heavens United."

That was the largest and most impressive of the hill's monuments, a huge sandstone palace covered in grotesque, weathered statues representing hundreds of gods. Marcus had even been inside once, accompanying the prince. There hadn't been much to look at except for more statues and hundreds of supplicating Khandarai, though the sheer size of the pillared hall had been impressive.

"They cut this underneath the temple?"

"It's more likely that they built the temple on top of it." Janus took hold of the ring on the door and gave it a tug. Slowly, groaning with the rust of centuries, it swung outward, revealing a dark space beyond.

Marcus was about to propose a bit of caution, but before he could speak Janus rushed eagerly inside. With his musket ready to hand, Marcus followed. In the light of the oil lamp, the chamber was revealed to be a rough, eight-sided space, with a domed ceiling and crude stone walls. There were no furnishings of any kind, and no decorations. Marcus could see nothing to distinguish this place from the corridor they'd come through to get here. He looked questioningly at Janus.

The colonel stood frozen in the center of the room, his face as slack as if he'd been slapped. His lips worked soundlessly.

"Sir?" Marcus prompted, after a moment.

"It's not here."

"What's not here? What are we looking for?"

"It's *not here*!" Janus' voice rose from a whisper to a shout. He spun on his heel and ran back to the corridor. Marcus hurried after him.

He'd gotten a glimpse, in the flickering lamplight, of his superior's face. So far in their association, Marcus had never seen the colonel lose his temper. He'd started to wonder, in fact, if the man was even capable of anger. Now that question was answered. Janus' delicate features had been twisted into an almost unrecognizable snarl, and his great gray eyes seemed to glow from within with an awful light.

Marcus was out of breath by the time they pounded down the tunnel and reached the little shrine. He called out to the soldiers above to help them up, but before anyone could move the colonel caught the lip of the hole on a jump and hauled himself up. Argot hurriedly leaned down and extended a hand to Marcus, who handed the musket up and levered himself out of the hole, panting.

"What have you done with them?"

Janus' voice was cold and precise again, but there was a dangerous edge to it that Marcus had never heard before, not even in battle. He raised his head and saw the colonel confronting the ancient priestess, who was held from the sides by two nervous-looking soldiers.

"Taken it beyond your reach," the old woman said, her head raised in defiance. *"Raschem."*

There was a frozen, silent moment. Janus' hands tightened into fists, and he turned to the younger priestess, who cowered as best she could in the grip of her captors.

"Tell me where you have taken the Thousand Names," he snapped.

The woman babbled something, her Khandarai too fast for Marcus to parse. It was apparently not what Janus wanted, however, because he stepped closer to her and growled, "Tell me, or—"

"Leave her be," said the old woman. "She knows nothing."

"And you do?"

"Only that Mother will not be found by the likes of you."

Janus pressed his lips together. Then, speaking in Vordanai for the first time since he'd left the tunnel, he said, "Sergeant Argot, give me your knife, please."

The soldiers, unable to follow the Khandarai, had watched this exchange with increasing puzzlement. Now Argot started and said, "My knife?"

"Yes, Sergeant." Janus' eyes never left the old woman.

Argot glanced at Marcus, but the colonel's voice cracked like a whip.

"*Now*, Sergeant."

"Yessir!"

Argot drew a big skinning knife from a sheath at his belt, reversed it, and handed it to Janus. The colonel took it, hefted it thoughtfully, and looked at the old woman.

"Do what you like," the priestess said. "It will not avail you."

Marcus had finally caught his breath.

"Sir," he said. When that drew no response, he added, *"Janus."*

Janus blinked, then looked at Marcus. "Yes, Captain?"

"I just—" Marcus realized he had no idea what he wanted to say, except that he would rather not watch his commanding officer slice an old woman to ribbons. "I don't think she knows, sir. Look at her."

There was a long pause.

"No," Janus said quietly. "I suppose not. If she did, they would not have left her behind." He flipped the knife around deftly and handed it back to Argot. "Still, she may know something useful. Take them back to the Palace, both of them. The prince has people who specialize in this sort of thing."

Marcus swallowed. But an order was an order. And even if he'd wanted to object, the colonel was already stalking toward the door.

WINTER

The big square in front of the barracks of the Heavenly Guard dwarfed the handful of blue-uniformed soldiers drilling in it. It had been built to allow the entire troop to parade at once, back in the days when the Guard had been an actual fighting formation instead of a sinecure for idiot sons of important families and worn-down servants. Sitting on the stone steps leading up from the packed-dirt field to the barracks building, Winter could see a half dozen companies going through their drills, but they filled barely a quarter of the space. It felt oddly disrespectful, like doing jumping jacks in a temple.

The Seventh Company was out there with the rest, going through the *Manual of Arms* and some standard evolutions. Winter would just as soon have let them rest, after everything they'd been through, but Graff had insisted that maintaining at least a bit of daily drill was important to morale. On reflection, Winter could see the point of this; the exercises were a touchstone, and they kept the soldiers from dwelling on those they had lost.

Winter had assigned Bobby to lead the drills today, partly so she herself could sit in the shade but mostly so she could keep an eye on the corporal. To all outward appearances, Bobby had recovered completely from the wound that she—it still felt odd to think of Bobby as "she," even in the privacy of her own skull—had suffered in the charge against the Auxiliaries at Turalin. Close observation, however, revealed that *something* had changed. She didn't seem to be in pain or short of breath, but she would occasionally stare distractedly into space until some sound from the men returned her attention to the here and now.

"Is something wrong with her?"

Winter looked up at the sound of Feor's voice. The Khandarai girl had changed into a fresh wrap and wound a long white cloth around her broken arm, keeping it pinned at her side. Her hair, dark and straight, was tied in a simple tail.

"Be careful what you say, even in Khandarai." Winter glanced around, but just now the two of them were alone on the steps, and none of the Vordanai on the field were close enough to overhear.

"My apologies," Feor said. "You were staring at the corporal. Is something wrong?"

"I'm not sure," Winter said. "*He* seems okay, but he's acting a bit . . . oddly."

"I am not surprised. *Obv-scar-iot* should have been bound to one of the *sahl-irusk*, someone trained to it from girlhood. I did not know if it would accept . . . him." Feor sat down next to Winter on the sun-warmed stone, balancing carefully with her good arm. "*Naath* are unpredictable things. Mother would say that they have a temper."

"Is it . . . are they living things, then?"

"Not as you and I are alive, perhaps, but yes, in their own way."

"If they have tempers, do they *think*?"

Feor shook her head. "Think, no. They have desires. Not quite as a human has desires, but more in the manner a tree desires water and will push a taproot through flagstones to get it. It is a part of their basic nature." She sighed. "Or so we believe. Mother says that we used to understand them better. Much has been lost to time."

Winter's eyes continued to follow Bobby. She leaned back

against the step behind her. "I still can hardly believe I'm having this conversation."

"Why?"

Winter glanced at Feor, wondering if that had been a joke, but the girl's face was entirely serious. She took a couple of moments to compose her reply.

"If I told anyone in Vordan what you did that day," she said eventually, "they wouldn't believe a word of it." Actually, she privately thought they *would* believe it, if she told them it had happened to a friend of a friend of hers in Khandar. People seemed to be willing to swallow any story provided it was thirdhand and a long way off. "They—we, I suppose I should say—don't believe in . . . sorcery, or demons, or whatever you want to call it."

"A *naath* is not a demon," Feor said patiently.

"Regardless." Winter felt a little defensive. "I didn't think most Khandarai believed in *naathem*, either."

"They might not expect to see one," Feor said, "but that is not the same as believing they do not exist. After all, it is the same with the gods." She frowned. "But I do not understand. I thought your holy book spoke of these things. Your Black Priests dedicate their lives to rooting them out. How, then, can you not believe in them?"

Winter thought about starting with the fact that the Priests of the Black had been out of business for a good hundred years now, but decided to start with something more basic. "Do you know the story of Karis the Savior?"

"No. Your Captain Vahkerson gave me a copy of the Wisdoms, but my Vordanai is not yet up to the task." Feor had taken to learning Vordanai with the same quiet determination with which she approached everything, and the sight of her face screwed up in earnest concentration always made Winter grin.

"The story goes," Winter began, adopting the language of half-remembered sermons from her childhood and parsing it inexpertly into Khandarai, "that there was once a time when men were so evil, so prone to consorting with demons and practicing sorcery, that the Lord Almighty decided to destroy them. He sent a great monster, the Beast of Judgment, to scourge mankind from the world. As the destruction began, God heard many prayers to halt it, but the hearts of all of those who begged for mercy were tainted, and He turned a deaf ear. When He heard Karis' prayer, though, He found his heart was pure, and the Lord agreed to give mankind a chance. Karis walked up to the Beast without fear and banished it with a word. He said that the Lord had spared humanity, but only temporarily, unless men could be persuaded to change their ways. The people who listened to him went on to found the Elysian Church, and as you say, they dedicated themselves to hunting down demons and sorcerers."

Feor, somewhat to Winter's surprise, seemed genuinely interested. "But you said they don't believe in those things."

"Karis lived more than a thousand years ago. This is the Year of His Grace twelve hundred and eight, so it's been that long since God agreed to spare mankind." A thought occurred to her. "Maybe the Black Priests got the job done and wiped out all the demons. In any case, by a couple of hundred years ago they were more in the business of putting heretics on trial and interfering in politics. A bit like your Redeemers, really."

"Not so awful, I hope," Feor murmured.

"I wouldn't know. The King of Vordan got fed up with it and threw them out. Ever since, there's been the Sworn Church, ruled from Elysium, and the Free Churches, which don't have to swear fealty to anyone. Vordan is a Free Church country. Maybe they take all the sorcery in the Wisdoms seriously up in Murnsk or Borel, but in Vordan . . ." She shook her head. "Our priest explained to me that it was all a metaphor. The demons stood for the evil that men do to one another, and what the Wisdoms really meant was that we should all be nice to each other." Winter glanced sidelong at Feor. "I thought there was something fishy about that at the time."

"What are 'Borel' and 'Murnsk'?"

"Other kingdoms," Winter said, aware of her acutely limited knowledge. "Well, Murnsk is an empire, I think. There's the Six Cities League, too, and . . ."

She trailed off. Feor was staring out at the drilling troops, but her eyes were sparkling with unshed tears.

"I will need to learn these things, I suppose," the girl said dully, "if I am to live there."

"Live there?" Winter said, confused. "I thought you wanted to find your Mother here in Ashe-Katarion."

"She would not have me," Feor said, very quietly. "Not now. I have bound my *naath* to a´*raschem*. This is heresy."

"You think she'd exile you?"

"I hope she will. She may wish to kill me instead."

"What kind of a mother murders her children?"

"My life is hers to begin with," Feor said. "If she wishes to take it, that is her right."

"Well, you'll always have a place with us." *And,* Winter privately resolved, *if "Mother" decides Feor needs to die, she'll have to go through me.* "What about Bobby?"

"He will be safe, I think. To interfere with a *naath*, once bound, would itself be heresy."

Winter nodded grimly and looked back at the field. The drills were ending, and Bobby was re-forming the troops to march back to the barracks. Her face was drawn with exhaustion, and Winter wondered if she'd been sleeping.

"We have to tell her," she said. "I don't know how much she remembers, but she knows *something* happened." She could scarcely miss the fact that a palm-sized patch of her skin had turned to something closer to marble than flesh.

Feor sighed. "*You* have to tell her." She paused, concentrating, and switched languages. "Me . . . Vordanai . . . not . . . good . . . sufficient."

"You still need to be there," Winter said. "She may have questions I can't answer."

"Are you going to tell her that you know her secret?"

"I think I have to," Winter said. "Graff knows as well, so we can't keep Bobby in the dark that the truth has gotten out. I think we can trust Graff to keep his mouth shut, but . . ."

"And what about yours?"

Now it was Winter's turn to fall silent. That was the real question, and she didn't have a good answer. She was still having a hard time coming to grips with the fact that *Feor* knew, and had known for some time. No matter how many times the Khandarai girl had insisted it was some supernatural *naathem* sense that had told her, Winter couldn't help but feel like there was some flaw in her disguise. *What if they* all *know, and they're just laughing at me behind my back?* That was ridiculous, of course—Davis, for one, would never settle for quiet mockery when there was a chance to push someone in the mud and kick them while they were down.

"You don't trust Bobby?" Feor asked.

"No, not that," Winter said. "God, if there's anyone I *can* trust, it'd be her. And you, of course. It's just . . ."

"Just?"

"It's been two years." Winter drew her knees to her chest. "I feel like I'd nearly convinced *myself*."

Chapter Seventeen

MARCUS

Marcus pushed open the door and found that he was the last to arrive. Val, Mor, and Fitz were all seated in flimsy wicker-and-wood chairs around a lacquered monolith of a table that even the Redeemers had found too heavy to move. Mor was putting a deck of cards through an elaborate shuffle.

"Finally," he said, as Marcus entered. "We were about to start without you."

"Speak for yourself," Val muttered. "If it was just me against you and Fitz, I might as well hand over my purse and be done with it."

"So I'm the other sucker, is that it?" Marcus said.

"Every table needs at least a couple," Mor said.

Fitz coughed. "You saw Adrecht?"

The mood darkened. Marcus nodded, and there was a quiet moment as he pulled out one of the chairs and sat gingerly, lest it collapse.

"And?" Val said gruffly. "How is he?"

"Better," Marcus said shortly. "He's still not awake, but the cutter told me his fever is down and there's no sign of festering at the . . . site."

"I knew he was too irritating to die," Mor said, a little too cheerfully.

"Liar," Val said. "You were practically dividing up his things already."

Marcus looked down at his hands where they lay on the tabletop. He closed his left hand slowly, then shook his head.

"It's a shame," Fitz said unexpectedly. All three captains looked at him, surprised.

"Course it is," said Val.

"That's war," Mor said. "Or at least, it is if you're fool enough to get within sticking range of someone with a bayonet. Getting shot I can understand, but—"

"He saved my life," Marcus said quietly.

That brought another moment of awkward silence, which Marcus felt duty-bound to break. He slapped his palms on the table with a dull thud and put on a grin he didn't feel. "Right!" he said. "Deal the cards already."

Mor started expertly spinning cards across the scarred surface of the ancient table. Marcus was an indifferent cardplayer at the best of times, and this was shaping up to be one of his worse nights. Coins slid back and forth across the table, occasionally catching in a deep rut and bouncing salmon-like into the air. The first of these bounced off the top of Val's head, to general laughter.

In the pause while Fitz collected and shuffled the cards after the first round was over, Val said, "Marcus, you're the colonel's right-hand man these days, aren't you?"

Marcus shrugged uncomfortably. "I'm not sure he has one of those."

"You're the best we've got," Val persisted. "So have you got any idea where we go now?"

"I'm not sure what you mean."

"Oh, come on," Mor said. "Everyone's been talking about it. Are we going to just dig in here, or go after the Divine Hand and his gang of malcontents?"

The Divine Hand's escape had become common knowledge

over the past couple of days. As the initial shock of the Vordanai arrival had worn off, the citizens of Ashe-Katarion had come to see how few of the foreigners there really were, and the continued resistance of the Redeemer leader and the Steel Ghost had caused some dangerous rumblings. Jaffa's Justices were spread thin, and Marcus didn't dare send his men out in groups smaller than a dozen.

"The colonel will have to hunt him down," Val said. "Until we bring that bastard's head back and put it on a spike, they aren't going to believe we're here to stay."

"How many of them even know what he looks like?" Mor retorted. "I don't think spiked heads are going to solve anything."

"Strategically," Fitz said, "going after him would be very dangerous. Until now we've been keeping ourselves fed from local resources, but if we have to leave the valley that will mean a proper supply train, which has to be based here in Ashe-Katarion. And that base would hardly be secure."

"What, then?" said Val. "Sit here in the Palace and wait for the mob to get angry enough to storm it?"

"Yes," Fitz said. "Rebellion has always been a fear of the Khandarai princes, and the inner city is quite defensible. Four battalions can hold it against almost any conceivable force of irregulars."

"It didn't do the prince much good the first time," Marcus put in.

Fitz ducked his head respectfully. "The prince didn't have four battalions the first time. Once General Khtoba threw in with the rebels, the inner city was already compromised."

"There's another bastard I'd like to see on a spike," Val muttered. "Ungrateful son of a bitch."

"If he's still alive," Mor said. "We know he was at Turalin, and the Auxiliaries lost a lot of men there."

"He's alive," Marcus said. He'd known Khtoba, slightly, in the old days. "He's not a man who'd hang around when things went sour."

"Witness him going over to the Redeemers in the first place," Val said. "Like I said—heads, spikes. End of problem."

"Assuming you can lay your hands on the heads," Mor said.

They were interrupted briefly when Fitz began to deal. Mor peeked at his hand, grunted, and dug in his pocket for a few more coins. Val sighed.

I wonder what they would say if I told them it wasn't the Divine Hand the colonel was worried about. Whatever the Thousand Names were, Janus wanted them very badly. *He says he just wants to keep them away from Orlanko, but the look on his face . . .* Marcus shivered at the memory. Janus had been on the point of carving up a helpless old woman to get the information he wanted, and his plan to send her to the prince's torture chambers had been thwarted only by the fact that the torturers had all run away or been burned by the Redeemers. The two priestesses were currently languishing in cells under the Palace.

Marcus played even more poorly in the second round than he had in the first. He'd been dealt a decent hand, for once, but his attention kept wandering. By the time Val collected the cards and shuffled for the third round, Marcus had decided his heart wasn't in the game. He was just preparing his excuse when there was a knock at the door. Fitz, as the lowest-ranking member of the quartet, got up to open it, revealing Jen Alhundt. Marcus stiffened.

"They told me I could find you here," she said. "Gentlemen, I wonder if I might borrow the senior captain for a few minutes."

"Hell," Val swore, looking at Fitz and Mor, then sighed. "I suppose so."

"I'm sorry to take you away from your game," Jen said, when the door had closed behind them.

Marcus waved a hand. "The way things were going, you probably saved me a month's wages."

They walked a while in silence, Marcus awkward, Jen apparently serene. He hadn't spoken to her since that night on the Tsel crossing, which seemed like a thousand years ago. That night, fear and the knowledge of impending battle had closed the distance between them, but here in the Palace it had opened back up into a bottomless pit that threatened to swallow any attempt at small talk.

Jen broke the impasse. "The colonel seems to be a bit . . . distant recently."

Marcus sighed theatrically. "If you ask me what he's planning to do next, I swear I'm going to scream."

"Oh?"

"I just got out of my last interrogation," Marcus said, jerking his head toward the drawing room. "Why everyone seems to think the colonel confides his secret plans to *me* I don't understand."

"You do spend a great deal of time with him," Jen said.

"Yes, but you know what he's like."

"Not really. I've read his file, but we've hardly spoken."

Marcus paused, reflecting. He'd spent so much time in Janus' company it hadn't occurred to him that the rest of the regiment hadn't had similar opportunities, but thinking back he couldn't recall the colonel speaking to Val, Mor, or any of the others outside of a terse order or the acknowledgment of a report. His longest conversations had probably been with the Preacher, with whom he shared an interest in artillery, and Give-Em-Hell, who more and more practically worshipped at Janus' feet.

"He's . . ." Marcus sighed again. "Sometimes I think he just likes being dramatic, like a penny-opera villain. It's always, 'Oh, you'll see, Captain,' or, 'Matters will become clear soon, Captain.' " Marcus managed to produce a reasonable simulation of Janus' erudite accent, and Jen chuckled.

"You must know *something*, even if it's just from standing around behind him," she said.

Marcus shifted awkwardly, and smiled to cover it. "If I did, I couldn't tell you. You're a spy, after all."

"A clerk," she insisted. "Just a clerk. But I do have a report to write." She tipped her head and looked at him slyly. Stray hairs escaping from her bun hung in front of her eyes. "I'm really not going to get any more out of you?"

"I think that's all I can say that's consistent with my duty as an officer," Marcus said, with mock gravity.

"The hell with it, then." She pushed up her spectacles and rubbed her eyes, then reached behind her head and tugged at her hair until it came loose from its bun and flopped free. He'd never seen her let it down before. It fell just to her shoulders, mouse brown and slightly frizzy. "I'm officially off duty. What about you?"

Marcus looked down at his uniform. "We haven't really worked out a duty schedule, to tell the truth. But nothing seems to be going on at the moment."

"Come with me, then. I've got something special I want to show you."

The room she led him to was furnished in the same eclectic mix of ancient and cheap as the rest of the post-Redeemer Palace. Here the ancient included a massive bed with brass poles, big enough to sleep six or seven, with equally ancient faded linen obviously scrounged from the bottom of some dusty closet. Beside it was a little table and chair, and a couple of open trunks.

Whoever was staying in the room was not very organized, and the floor beside the trunk was strewn with clothes. Marcus spotted a few undergarments of a notably feminine nature and felt his cheeks color slightly. He turned to find Jen tugging the thick door closed behind them.

"This is *your* room?" he said.

She grinned wickedly. "Of course. Where better to secretly murder you?" Catching his expression, her smile faded a little. "Is something wrong?"

"No." Marcus cleared his throat. "It's just been a long time since I was in a lady's bedroom."

Jen arched an eyebrow. "Oh, come on. The gallant captain must have had *some* conquests among the impressionable native girls."

"About the only Khandarai women who would have anything to do with us wanted to be paid afterward," Marcus said. He reflected a moment. "Actually, mostly they wanted to be paid in advance."

"Well, I think I can get by without a chaperone just this once," she said. "I don't want to share this."

"Share what?"

She brushed past him, heading for one of the trunks. The casual touch left Marcus feeling even more awkward than before, but Jen didn't appear to notice. She tossed more clothing aside, then a couple of blankets, and finally emerged with a wooden crate the shape of a coffin, a couple of feet long. Words had been burned onto the outside, in such an elaborate script that Marcus couldn't read them, but he recognized the shape immediately.

"Where did you get *that*?" he said.

"It was a gift," she said, setting the little box reverently on the table. "From some of my friends at the Cobweb." She looked up at him. "Looking back on it now, I don't think they ever expected me to come back."

"And you haven't opened it yet?"

"Sort of silly, I know," she said. "If I really *had* been killed at one of the battles, I expect I would have regretted it. But somehow just sitting by myself didn't seem . . . I don't know." She shrugged. "Let me borrow your knife, would you?"

Marcus wordlessly drew his belt knife and handed it across. Jen pried up one of the thin wooden planks, which were nailed only loosely into place, and pulled the top of the box off. Inside, nestled in spun wool like a fresh egg, was a thick-bellied glass bottle that glistened amber all the way up to the wax seal at the neck. Another seal, pressed with a fanciful rendition of the charging-bull standard of Hamvelt, adorned the front.

"It always seemed vaguely unpatriotic to me," Jen said, lifting the bottle gently from its cradle. "I mean, we've got brandy in Vordan. Why does everyone love this Hamveltai stuff?"

"Because it's better," Marcus said fervently. "You've never had any?"

"I could never afford it. Clerking for the secret police doesn't pay as well as you might imagine."

Marcus smiled. Just the sight of the bottle sent him back in time, to his days at the War College. He and Adrecht had had—not friends, not really, but cronies, men they lived, studied, and drank with. Drank with most of all. He'd sometimes thought that the War College was really a thinly disguised royal subsidy to the local tavern industry. Adrecht had once obtained a half-empty bottle of Hamveltai brandy, through some unexplained but presumably nefarious method, and there had been just about enough for everyone to have a sniff. He'd never forgotten the taste, which compared to even the best of the local stuff like pure spring water to sewer sludge.

Jen worked the point of the knife delicately under the wax, split the seal up one side, and peeled it off the top of the bottle. She'd produced a couple of glasses from somewhere, and Marcus watched as she expertly tipped two fingers of the liquid amber into each. She handed him one, held up her own, and met his eyes.

"To Count Colonel Janus bet Vhalnich Mieran," she said. "God grant that he know what the hell he's doing."

"God grant," Marcus said fervently. They both sipped. The bite on his tongue seemed to dissolve into smoke before it reached the back of his mouth. It was better even than he remembered. From the look in Jen's eyes, she was similarly enraptured. She put the glass on the table slowly, and stared at it as though she thought it might move.

"Saints and martyrs," she swore. "Now I *am* glad I didn't get killed in the battle."

"If only we had a bottle for every man in the regiment, they'd all come back alive," Marcus said.

Jen laughed. "If we had that much, we could probably *buy* the throne of Khandar."

"You'd be surprised. You remember those carts, the really heavy ones at the end of the train? The ones that were always getting stuck."

"Vaguely."

"Supposedly the prince packed them full of gold before he fled the city. All the treasures of the Exopterai Dynasty, or at least all the ones he could carry. Now he's probably got them tucked away safe in his dungeons again."

Not every *treasure. These "Thousand Names" weren't in the prince's hoard. But someone else must have had the same idea as Exopter did.* His mood darkened. *Whatever it is, it's clearly more important than a few sacks full of coin. If only he'd* tell *me, I might be able to come up with something.*

Jen, sipping from her glass, watched his face. "Something wrong?"

Marcus shrugged and looked down. "Not really."

"No?" She leaned closer, until they were only inches apart. "You can tell me. I won't even put it in a report. I promise."

Her tone was still light, but there was an undercurrent of real concern. Marcus sighed.

"I was just wishing the colonel *would* take me a bit more into his confidence. Then I might be able to say something when people ask me what happens next."

Jen nodded sympathetically. "It's only natural that they'd want to know, I suppose."

"Of course it is. It's not just the officers, either. Val and Mor are lifers; they're used to this sort of thing. But what about the recruits?" Marcus shook his head. "Most of us Old Colonials got sent to Khandar because we'd pissed off the wrong person, but the recruits just signed up on the wrong day and drew the short straw. How long are they going to stay here? Until we catch the Divine Hand and the Steel Ghost? That could be years—or never."

"Have you asked him about it?"

"Asked who? The colonel?"

She nodded and raised the bottle toward him. He hesitated, then held up his glass, and she poured a generous portion for both of them.

"I've never had the chance," Marcus said. "I barely see him anymore."

"Why not?"

Marcus shrugged. "He spends his time in his room, or in with the prince."

"Has he ordered you to stay away?"

"No," Marcus said, uncomfortably. "But—"

He suddenly wanted to tell Jen about the underground room. The mysterious Names, so important that they warranted a royal command. She might know what Janus had meant. She might be able to help—

Don't be a fool, something whispered at the back of his mind. *She's Concordat. They're killers, spiders, eyes and ears and knives in the dark. She works for the Last Duke, not for the king, and certainly not for the colonel. Tell her anything and God alone knows what she'll do with it.* But looking at her, her head tipped as she studied the glistening brandy through a thin fall of brown hair, he found it hard to picture her in the company of the sinister figures in leather greatcoats that haunted the sets of bad dramas.

He raised his glass abruptly. "To Adrecht."

"Captain Roston, you mean?" she asked.

"He got me my first sniff of this stuff, way back at the dawn of time."

Jen paused. "Is he still . . ."

"He stopped a saber for me at Weltae. It didn't look awful at the time, but it went bad on him. The cutters took his arm off last night. As of this morning, he was looking a little better, but . . ." Marcus closed one hand into a fist and stared at it.

Jen nodded and raised her glass. "To Adrecht, then."

They drank. After a moment's respectful silence, Jen said, "I wanted to ask you about him, after the battle on the road, but . . ."

"But?"

"I figured you'd assume I was fishing for the Ministry and clam up."

"Ah. You might have been right."

"Do you mind if I ask now? I swear it isn't for . . . official purposes. I'm just curious."

Marcus looked at her for a long moment, then shrugged. "Go ahead."

"When the colonel wanted to arrest him, you threatened to resign." It wasn't a question. Marcus wondered if Janus had told her, or if camp rumor knew everything by now.

"I did," he said.

"Why? The colonel could have had you shot."

"He's my friend," Marcus said. "We were at the College together."

"That was a hell of a thing to do for a friend."

Marcus paused, staring into his empty glass. *What the hell?* he thought. *Even if she* does *put this in her report, I can't see how it would matter.* He held out the tumbler, and Jen silently refilled it.

"He saved my life," Marcus said, after a few moments' contemplation.

"Ah. In a battle somewhere?"

Marcus shook his head. "Long before that. You've read my file, I suppose?"

"On the way over."

"How much detail does it go into?"

She shrugged. "Not much. Even the Ministry can't keep track

of everything about everyone. It says you're an orphan, top quarter of your class at the College, requested assignment to Khandar."

"An orphan." Marcus turned the glass on the tabletop, watching the colored light refracted through the liquor. "I suppose I am."

Jen said nothing, sensing that she'd stumbled into dangerous territory. Marcus took a deep breath.

"When I was seventeen," he said, "about a year after I left for my lieutenant's course at the College, there was a fire at home. It had been a dry summer, apparently, and something touched off dry grass on the lawn. It spread to the house before anyone noticed. The whole place burned. Mother was always telling Father it was a rickety old firetrap, but he said it was historic and it would be a crime to renovate." He tapped the brandy glass and watched the patterns of light ripple. "They were both killed. My sister, Ellie—she was four. Most of the servants, too, people I'd grown up with."

Jen touched his arm, very lightly. "God. I'm so sorry."

He nodded. "Adrecht was with me when I got the news. I . . . didn't take it well. I started sneaking out, spending a lot of time in the foreigners' bars, drinking too much, starting fights. I didn't even realize he was keeping track of me, but one night he cornered me in a back garden by one of the passages we used to get past the sentries. He handed me a pistol, and he said . . ."

Marcus smiled slightly, remembering. "He told me that if I wanted to kill myself, I should do it here and now, because the way I was trying was taking too long and causing everyone a lot of trouble. I was furious with him, told him there was no way he could understand, but he kept at me, asked me if I was too scared. Eventually I put the pistol to my head, just to show him. I don't remember if I meant to pull the trigger or if it was just my hands shaking. But I still remember the little click as the hammer came down.

"It wasn't loaded, of course. When my heart started up again, I realized Adrecht was right." Marcus picked up the glass in front of him and drained it. "I went back to class, did well, got my silver stripe. After my tour as lieutenant, Adrecht told me he was going for captain, so I did, too. Then he got himself sent to Khandar, and I told him I would come along. He tried to talk me out of it, but I said, 'What the hell is there for me here?'" He set the glass down with a decisive click. "And here we are."

There was a long silence. Jen took her own glass, refilled it, and held it up.

"To Adrecht," she said.

WINTER

Winter laid her hands flat in front of her and took a deep breath. "All right. We need to talk."

"I know," Bobby said, almost inaudibly. She seemed drawn in on herself, shoulders hunched, staring at the lamp in the center of the table. "I think . . ."

There was a long pause. Then Bobby looked up, and Winter was surprised to see that there were tears in her eyes.

"I think I'm going mad," she finished, all in a rush.

The girl's face was drawn and haggard, and bags under her eyes hinted that she hadn't been sleeping much. Feor sat beside her, resting her splinted arm on a stack of cushions.

They were in the upper room of a Khandarai tavern, the one breed of business that had weathered both the Redemption and the Vordanai reconquest with the equanimity of cockroaches. This one was typical, furnished with only a few threadbare pillows and a low wooden table, but Winter wanted privacy more than comfort. She'd tipped the hostess not to let anyone else up to the tiny second story.

Winter ventured a cautious smile. "Why do you say that?"

"Something happened to me in the battle," Bobby said.

"Getting shot, you mean?"

"I thought so. It certainly felt like it at the time." Bobby shook her head miserably. "I remember thinking, this is it. I'd always wondered what it would feel like, and it didn't seem so bad. Like someone had kicked me. I fell on my ass and watched the rest of you march away, and I tried to get back up to follow you, and *then* it hurt." Her lips quivered. "It hurt like . . . I don't even know how to say it. So I lay back down and thought, 'Oh, okay, I guess I'm dead, then.' And I closed my eyes, and—"

She broke off as the hostess entered carrying a tray with three clay mugs, each half the size of a man's head. Winter had to use both hands to lift her drink. Khandarai beer was thick and dark, and bitter enough to take the uninitiated by surprise. It wasn't her favorite, but she'd gotten used to it. Both Bobby and Feor stared into their mugs as though they weren't sure what to do with them, and Winter took a swallow to provide an example. Neither followed suit, and she gave an inward sigh.

"I don't remember very much after that," Bobby said. "Bits and pieces. I kept waking up and wondering if I was dead yet, and then I'd open my eyes and see the smoke still drifting up and think, 'No, not yet,' and then close them again. Once I remember the pain getting worse, so much worse, and I thought that *had* to be the end. Only I woke up afterward, and I felt . . . okay. Good, even."

Winter, who was watching for it, saw the corporal's hand stray to her side, where the wound had been.

"And ever since then," Bobby went on, "I've been seeing things. Or hearing them. Or . . . something. It's hard to explain."

"Seeing things?" Winter said. That she had not expected.

"It's not quite *seeing*," Bobby said. "Feeling, maybe. Like there's something out there, pressing on me, but I can't quite—I don't know." She stared into the depths of her drink. "Like I said, I'm going mad."

Winter glanced at Feor. The Khandarai girl was regarding Bobby intently.

"She says she's seeing things," Winter translated, and Feor nodded.

"She can sense others who possess power," Feor said. "Me, for example. And perhaps some of Mother's children remain in the city. All who are touched by magic can do this to one degree or another, but . . ." She sighed. "As I told you, *obv-scar-iot* should have been bound to someone who had trained from girlhood to accept its gifts. What it will do to someone so completely unprepared I do not know."

Winter turned back to the corporal, cleared her throat, and realized she had absolutely no idea how to begin. She'd planned for this, but everything she'd practiced in the privacy of her room had flown out of her mind. She took a long swallow of beer to cover it, coughed a bit at the bitter flavor, and cleared her throat again.

Finally, she said, "All right. The thing is . . ." She trailed off again.

"The thing is?" Bobby prompted.

Winter sighed. "You're not going crazy. But I suspect you're going to think *I* am. Just listen, okay?"

The corporal nodded obediently. Winter drew a long breath.

"You got hit on the climb," Winter said. "You know that much. We found you afterward, and it . . . looked bad."

"You promised me," Bobby said in a small voice.

"No cutters," Winter agreed. "Folsom carried you back to my tent, and Graff did what he could."

"Did he—" Bobby's features screwed up as she tried to find a way of asking whether Graff had discovered her secret, without revealing that secret in the process. Winter took pity on her and nodded.

"I know," she said.

"Oh." Bobby's eyes were wide. "Who else?"

"Graff, obviously. And Feor."

"That's why you brought her along," Bobby said. "I was wondering." She hesitated. "And . . . are you . . ."

"We're not going to tell anyone, if that's what you mean."

The relief was plain on Bobby's face. She dropped her eyes and, apparently noticing her drink for the first time, ventured a sip. Her lip curled in disgust as the taste registered.

"It takes everyone that way the first time," Winter said automatically.

"What makes them try it a second time?"

"Stubborn curiosity, I think." Winter shook her head. "Anyway, I'm not finished."

"So Graff patched me up?"

"Graff told me you were dying," Winter said, "and that there was nothing he could do. It was after he left that Feor . . ."

She stopped. This was the sticking point, after all, the bit where any sane, modern, *civilized* person would listen to her story and laugh. She didn't think Bobby would—after all, she could see the evidence for herself—but Winter's cheeks colored anyway.

"Feor healed you," she forced out. "With . . . magic. I don't pretend to really understand it."

"Magic?" Bobby looked at the Khandarai girl, who met her eyes calmly. "She . . . prayed, or something? She is a priestess, I suppose—"

"*Not* like that." Winter closed her eyes. "I know this sounds mad, but I was there. It was real, and . . ." She trailed off, at a loss for words, then shook her head again and glared at Bobby. "That patch of skin. It's still—odd, isn't it?"

Bobby nodded. "But that's just a . . . sort of a scar, right?"

"It's not. You know it's not."

There was a long silence. Both of them turned to look at Feor, who appeared unruffled by the attention.

"So . . . ," Bobby said. "She's a wizard, then?"

"Like I said, I don't understand this any better than you do. She calls herself a *naathem*, which literally means 'one who has read.' The spell she used—she would say *naath*, 'reading'—if I'm getting this right, it's called *obv-scar-iot*. Beyond that . . ." Winter spread her hands. "I don't know if this means anything to you, but she asked me for permission before she did anything. She thought you might not want to live under those circumstances, I guess. I told her to do it. So if you're angry, you can be angry at me."

Bobby just stared. Winter gulped from her beer.

"I brought her along because I thought you might have . . . questions," she said. "I can translate for you."

The corporal nodded slowly. Feor glanced at Winter.

"I told her," Winter said in Khandarai.

"I guessed that from her face," Feor said. "Ask her how she feels, aside from the odd sensations."

"Feor wants to know if you feel all right," Winter translated. "The visions, she says, are a kind of side effect of the spell."

"I feel fine," Bobby said.

Winter rendered this for Feor, who said, "She will be stronger now and require less sleep. Injuries will heal very quickly."

Winter blinked at her. "You didn't tell me any of that."

"There wasn't time," Feor said.

Winter nodded slowly and translated for Bobby. The corporal looked a bit shaken.

"So this thing is . . . still in me?" She looked down at herself. "How long does it last?"

When that question was put to Feor in Khandarai, she shook her head. "It was not merely a healing. *Obv-scar-iot* is bound to her. It will not leave her until her death."

"Forever," Winter said to Bobby. "Or until you die, anyway."

Feor looked uncomfortable, as though there were something she wanted to say but could not. Bobby was staring down at her hands. The silence grew and grew, until it was unbearable, and Winter couldn't help but speak.

"As long as we're sharing secrets," she said, "I feel like you ought to have one of mine. It should balance the scales a bit."

Bobby blinked and looked up. "Secrets?"

Winter nodded. Her throat felt suddenly thick, and she had to force the words out. "Secrets." She took a deep breath. "I am a—"

"Oh!" Bobby interrupted. "A girl. I know."

Winter deflated, feeling an irrational anger rising. "You knew? How? Does *everyone* know?"

Bobby raised her hands defensively. "It was nothing you *did*. I wouldn't have known if I didn't already know. I mean—" She put her head to one side, realizing that last hadn't made much sense. "If I hadn't known, in advance, that you were a woman, then I would never have guessed it just by looking at you."

Winter sat openmouthed, rage replaced by shock. "You knew . . . in *advance*?"

"Not exactly *knew*," Bobby said. "It was more of a rumor. But once I got here and I saw you, I thought, 'Well, that has to be her, doesn't it?' "

"You'd—" Winter broke off and looked sharply at Bobby. "Where did you hear this rumor?"

"I don't remember exactly," Bobby said. "But everyone at Mrs. Wilmore's has heard of Winter the Soldier."

"I," Winter said shakily, after a long silence, "need a drink."

"You have a drink," Bobby pointed out.

"I need a better one."

In the time it took to go into the corridor, find a hostess, and order a bottle, Winter did her best to compose herself. By the time she sat back down at the little table, she felt almost calm, and her voice barely wavered when she said, "You were at Mrs. Wilmore's?"

Bobby nodded. "Since I was ten."

"And they've *heard* of me?"

"Of course," Bobby said. "It's like a school legend. Every new girl hears it eventually."

The hostess stepped in with another tray, this one bearing a fresh set of clay cups and an unlabeled bottle of murky liquid. Winter grabbed the bottle, poured herself a cup, and drank it in one go, feeling the vicious stuff burn its way down her throat and into her stomach.

"What exactly does this legend say?" she ventured.

"I must have heard a dozen versions," Bobby said. "But they all agree that there was an inmate named Winter, and that she escaped from the Prison, which no one had ever done before. I heard stories that she'd gone to Vordan and become a thief, or that she ran off into the country and made herself the concubine of a bandit chieftain, but most people seemed to think that she dressed up as a man and joined the army."

Anna and Leeya must have told someone. Her friends had sworn up and down that they would take the secret of her escape to the grave, along with her tentative plan to be free of Mrs. Wilmore's clutches forever by using the army to get beyond her reach. Looking back, though, Winter could see that was a lot to expect from a couple of teenage girls. *I'm not sure I could have held my tongue, if I were in their place.*

"I never thought about becoming a bandit concubine," Winter said dully. "Maybe I should have."

"When I got here," Bobby said, "and you became our sergeant, I thought it had to be the same Winter. It's not that uncommon a name, but . . . it felt like it was meant to happen." Her young face had regained some of its eagerness.

"But how did *you* escape?"

"I stole a bag of coin from the office," Bobby said proudly. "And I got to know one of the carters who brought in food. After a while I convinced him to smuggle me out."

"Sounds like you had an easier time of it than I did," Winter muttered. Then, catching Bobby's flushed cheeks, she got an idea of the sort of "convincing" the carter had required, and shook her head. "Sorry. I didn't mean that."

"I couldn't believe I'd actually met you," Bobby said, looking as though a weight had been removed from her shoulders. "I thought for the longest time about whether I should tell you, but it seemed like a risk. You had everyone fooled, and I couldn't bear being the one who screwed it up. So I just went along."

"These . . . legends," Winter said. "Do they mention anyone besides me?"

"Not that I recall," Bobby said. "Saints, I wish I could tell the girls at the Prison that I'd met you. Sarah would just about explode."

Winter fought down a looming specter, with green eyes and long red hair. *Can you be haunted by someone who isn't dead?* Her throat was tight as she poured herself another drink. *They don't even remember her.*

"All right," she said again. "Is that enough secrets for one night?"

Bobby looked a bit startled. "I wanted to ask you—"

"Later. Right now I am planning to get very drunk. The two of you are welcome to join me." She repeated this in Khandarai, as a courtesy.

Feor looked down at her beer. "Alcohol was not permitted among the *sahl-irusk* when I was growing up," she said. "The *eckmahl* were fond of it, however, and I was always curious as to what they found so attractive."

"There you go." Winter turned to Bobby. "What about you? Ever been really drunk?"

Bobby shook her head, blushing. "Some of the girls at Mrs. Wilmore's would sneak a little bit, but I never did."

"Can't be a soldier if you've never been really drunk," Winter said. "I'll get us another bottle."

And maybe then, she thought, *I won't dream.*

Chapter Eighteen

MARCUS

After drinking to Adrecht, they'd had to drink toasts to the other captains, to be polite, and then to the king, the Princess Royal, and the Last Duke, and of course to Prince Exopter their royal host. At that point Marcus' memory became a little blurry, though he was fairly certain Jen had suggested getting out the regimental roll and going through every name on the list, amidst a fit of giggles.

While things had not actually come to *that*, they'd made a fair start on the bottle, and it had been all Marcus could do to find his way back to his room at the end of the night. Jen, one arm thrown around his shoulders like an old comrade, had suggested he sleep where he was, but he was fairly certain she was drunk enough that she didn't mean it the way it sounded.

He woke the next morning feeling surprisingly fresh, and moreover suddenly confident of what he had to do. He passed over his usual shabby uniform in favor of his dress blues, which Fitz had carefully laundered. His room included a mirror, miraculously unsmashed during the sack, and he stopped for a moment to regard himself with some satisfaction. If not the spitting image of the young man who'd graduated from the War College, he looked at least like a proper Vordanai officer.

Fitz was waiting in the antechamber, immaculate as usual, bearing a sheaf of paperwork under his arm. He saluted smartly as Marcus emerged. Marcus wondered if the young man's hearing was good enough to tell when his chief was up and about, or if he just stood poised in front of the door all morning, like a guard dog.

"Good morning, sir."

"Good morning." Marcus glanced at the papers. "Anything really important in there?"

"Nothing urgent, sir."

"Good. Put it somewhere and come with me, then."

Fitz saluted again, set the papers on a broken end table that Marcus had been using as a desk, and fell into step behind his superior.

"May I ask," the lieutenant said as Marcus led him through the mazelike corridors of the Palace, "where we're going?"

"We're going to see the colonel," Marcus said.

"Ah." His tone didn't indicate what he thought of the idea.

Marcus struggled to keep hold of the mood he'd had on waking. Jen had been right. Whether the colonel was sulking or not, there were questions that needed to be answered. He tried not to picture Janus' face, gray eyes sharp with irritation, an eyebrow raised in sarcasm. *"Really, Captain? Well, if you're not capable of attending to such matters yourself . . ."*

He shook himself mentally, looked back to make sure that Fitz was still there to provide moral support, and turned down the last corridor that led to the suite of rooms the colonel had claimed for himself. Somewhat to his surprise, the lieutenant stopped in his tracks.

"Something wrong, Fitz?"

Fitz shook his head. "I'm not sure, sir. But the colonel requested a pair of guards for this corridor, and I'm fairly certain I added the post to the duty roster."

"Which company would have it today?" Marcus said. Fitz

seemed to keep the entire schedule of the First Battalion in his head, writing it down only for the benefit of mere mortals.

"Davis', sir."

"That explains it," Marcus said darkly. "Remind me when we get back to have a word with him."

"Yessir."

Marcus continued down the corridor, his good mood draining away. They were deep in the interior of the Palace, and apart from occasional skylights, illumination was provided by braziers of burning candles in discreet alcoves. It was probably his imagination telling him they were getting farther apart as he approached the colonel's door, as though he were descending into a realm of shadows.

Or possibly not. Just up the corridor from the entrance to Janus' suite, one of the braziers had fallen over. The candles had drooled wax all over the flagstones before guttering out, leaving that section of the corridor in semidarkness.

"Sir," Fitz said urgently, "something is definitely wrong. I *know* there should be guards on the colonel's door."

"You're right." Marcus' skin started to crawl, and he let one hand drift to the hilt of his sword. "Maybe he's gone off somewhere and taken the guards with him?"

"Possibly—" Fitz sniffed the air and pointed. "Over there!"

They hurried past the colonel's door. The corridor beyond was disused and mostly in darkness, but the huddled shape Fitz had spotted was wearing Vordanai blue.

"Saints and martyrs," Marcus said, pulling up short. The sentry lay in a boneless heap against the wall, blood leaking from his ear and the back of his skull to pool on the floor underneath him. A spray of dark red stained the wall itself, as though he'd been slammed against it with great force. His musket lay forgotten nearby.

Fitz knelt, but only briefly. "He's dead, sir."

"I can see that," Marcus said, forcing his mind to work. "I want you to run to the barracks and collect as many men as you can round up in five minutes, then come back here. Understand?"

"Yes, sir, but—"

"I'll check on the colonel." Marcus drew his sword. "Go!"

The door to the colonel's rooms was slightly ajar, and something metal glinted in the gap. It took Marcus a moment to recognize it as the bolt, complete with fitting, torn out of the rock wall.

What the hell is going on? Marcus prodded the door with a boot and kept his sword in front of him. The door opened into the suite's anteroom, which Janus used as an office, and more doors let off into a dining room, bedroom, and servant's quarters. The office was dominated by a big, flimsy table, which had been cracked in half by the impact of another body. This sentry's face was contorted and black with the agony of strangulation, and his throat had gone a dark bruised purple.

Marcus took a deep breath, the point of his sword twitching. He considered calling out, but if the assassins—and what else could they be?—were still in the suite, he'd only be warning them. *And if they've done their work and gone?* It seemed unthinkable, but his mouth went dry.

The door to the bedchamber was half open. Marcus padded toward it as quietly as he could, and stopped abruptly at the sound of voices from within. The first, to his relief, was Janus'.

"I had been expecting—something like this," the colonel said in Khandarai. A young man answered, his tone pleasantly menacing.

"You must be a fool, then, to walk so willingly to your death."

"Your mother is the fool, if she thinks that killing me will change anything."

Marcus resumed his quiet advance. Through the gap between door and doorframe, he made out a flash of blue uniform that was probably Janus at the back of the room.

"You understand nothing. The latest fool in a long line of fools who thought us easy plunder, and found out different."

"Times have changed. The Redeemers have—"

"They have changed nothing. They wash in, and wash out again, like waves on a beach. It is of no importance. Mother remains."

"The Last Duke does not agree. Neither, I suspect, does the Pontifex of the Black."

"Gahj-rahksa-ahn." Marcus didn't understand the word, but the Khandarai spat it as though it tasted foul. "If you are the best he can muster, his order has fallen low indeed."

There was a footstep, and Marcus' sliver of vision was eclipsed by someone in brown moving between him and Janus. It was the best chance he was likely to get, and Marcus had not survived five years in Khandar by being chivalrous. He kicked the door out of the way and dropped into a lunge that would have made his old fencing master proud. The sword went in just between the young man's shoulders—

Or should have. As Marcus started to move, the stranger twisted in place, impossibly fast. Marcus got a glimpse of bald head and a thin, mirthless grin. One of the man's hands came up, viper-fast, and the edge of his palm struck the flat of Marcus' sword a moment before impact. There was a sharp, wild ring of steel on stone. The blade had been neatly severed a third of the way down its length, and the shorn-off end slammed against the wall so hard it raised sparks. It bounced like a leaping salmon and pinwheeled across the room while Marcus stared incredulously at the broken fragment protruding from the hilt.

His eyes were still trying desperately not to believe what they'd just seen, but the rest of his body had enough sense to send him reeling backward as the stranger's hand came around again, a lazy backhand blow that whistled through the air with the force of a cannonball. Marcus scrambled away, searching for his balance, and came up against the broken table in the main room. The stranger *blurred* in front of him, and only another wild dive to the side kept Marcus out of his path. With a *crack* like a gunshot, one end of the table exploded in a shower of splinters.

Marcus ended up on the floor, rolling until he bumped into a bedraggled sofa. He'd lost the remnant of his sword, and spent a moment scrabbling for his belt knife, but the Khandarai was on him before he could draw it. Marcus rolled again as the man came at him, but this time the stranger anticipated the move, and Marcus fetched up against his suddenly interposed foot.

"Good-bye, *raschem*," the man mouthed. But before Marcus even had time to flinch, the assassin was gone, twisting away faster than the eye could follow. Marcus saw the glitter of steel overhead, and then heard another tremendous impact, as though a battering ram had crashed home.

Adrenaline drove him to his knees, though he was still desperately fighting for breath. Janus was in the anteroom, a thin-bladed sword in hand, and it was his attack the stranger had been forced to avoid. The Khandarai's riposte had been intended to plaster the colonel against the doorframe, but Janus had ducked away, and the punch had hit home hard enough to crack the ancient sandstone. Janus' sword flicked out as he moved, scoring a line on his opponent's flank that cut through the Khandarai's shirt and left a bright crimson stain.

At least he bleeds. Marcus struggled to his feet as the stranger rounded on Janus, warier now. The Khandarai tried to swat the colonel's blade aside, as he had Marcus', but Janus kept his nimbler weapon just out of reach and circled the tip around to pink his adversary's sleeve. After the third try, this seemed to enrage the Khandarai, who picked up a nearby chair and hurled it like a handball. Janus twisted out of the way, and then had to dive for his life as the assassin came bulling in after the missile.

Marcus cast about, looking for a weapon. The best he could

come up with was an ornamental lamp, and he was just reaching for it when someone whispered in his ear.

"Sir. Perhaps these would serve?"

Marcus glanced over his shoulder to see Augustin, Janus' aged manservant, crouched beside him, a pistol in each hand. They were fancy guns, all oiled wood and silver chasing, but, important to Marcus' mind, they were cocked and loaded. Marcus grabbed them without a word.

"Careful, sir," Augustin said. "Hair trigger."

Marcus was already spinning away, a gun in each hand. Janus had bought himself a few moments by ducking under the damaged table, but the stranger heaved it aside like a cheap toy. Marcus aimed carefully as the Khandarai stalked forward, and even managed a smile.

"Good-bye, demon," he said, but the words were drowned under the blast of the pistol's report, mind-shatteringly loud in the enclosed space.

The Khandarai spun as though he'd been punched in the shoulder and staggered a step. Marcus dropped one pistol and switched the other to his right hand, then let his mouth fall open in naked disbelief. The assassin raised one hand, blood dripping slowly from his palm. When he opened his fingers, Marcus heard the soft *ping* of a pistol ball bouncing off the stone floor.

He caught the thing—

"Get down, sir!" Marcus just had time to recognize Fitz's voice. His instincts threw him to the ground and pressed his hands over his ears. Another roar of gunfire, a dozen times more violent, ripped through the chamber, and Marcus could hear the crazy zing and whine of ricochets. It was followed by a horrible wrenching sound and a shrill scream, then by ringing silence.

Marcus looked up cautiously. A dozen men stood on both sides of the outer doorway, the muskets in their hands still smoking. In the corridor just beyond, another soldier lay in a vividly crimson puddle, one arm and most of his shoulder torn away. Behind him was Fitz, his back pressed tight against the wall, eyes wide as saucers. There was no sign of the assassin.

To Marcus' immense surprise, he himself appeared to be uninjured, or at least in no immediate pain. He found Janus also levering himself to his feet. The colonel fixed Marcus with an almost rueful look.

"Sir," Marcus said, when he'd found his voice. "Are you hurt?"

"I don't believe so, Captain." Janus tossed his sword to the floor and patted himself inquisitively. "No, it appears not."

"Fitz?" Marcus called over his shoulder. "Are you all right?"

"Yessir."

Even the bare few seconds that had passed seemed to have been enough for the normally unflappable lieutenant to regain his composure. *His voice doesn't even tremble,* Marcus thought, a bit enviously.

"Anybody else injured?"

"I'm afraid Corporal Denthrope is dead, sir," Fitz said. "The rest of us seem to be unhurt."

"Right." Marcus almost tossed aside the remaining pistol, checking himself at the last moment when he remembered it was still loaded. He carefully closed the hammer instead and turned to the doorway. "We're going to want runners to every duty company. Close all the gates, start a cordon at the outer wall, and—"

"No," Janus said, behind him.

"What?" Marcus rounded on the colonel. "Sir, with all due respect, that was an assassination attempt. It was nearly successful. We can't just let him go—"

"They won't be able to stop him," Janus said. "And I'd sooner not lose any more men trying."

Marcus wanted to scream. Part of him was still stunned by the impossibility of what he'd just seen, and the fact that Janus obviously knew something he wasn't bothering to share made him want to pick the colonel up by his collar and shake him until he explained what the hell was going on. Half a lifetime of military decorum warred with raw emotion, and his fists clenched until the knuckles went white.

"Sir," Fitz said urgently, "there's more. The lower city is on fire."

"Fire?"

That cut through the budding rage like a bucket of cold water. Marcus had lived in Ashe-Katarion long enough to absorb some of the fear its citizens had for the prospect of fire. Built largely of dry wood and straw-stuffed mud bricks, the city was a perfect tinderbox. Buildings were packed so tightly against one another that a blaze, once started, was almost impossible to stop.

The prohibition on the use of fire as a weapon was the one rule that everyone observed, even the street gangs. For the most part the Khandarai got by without lamps or candles and cooked in stone fire pits, so the risk of accidental flames was small. Nevertheless, large portions of the lower city burned down every twenty or thirty years. Among the upper classes, who lived inside the stone walls that served as a highly effective firebreak, these events were known as the "crimson flowers of Ashe-Katarion," and the citizens often gathered on rooftops to drink and watch the show.

"Where?" Marcus said. "And how bad is it?" There was no such thing as a fire service in Khandar, but the Colonials might be able to accomplish something.

"Bad," Fitz said. "Our sentries on the wall reported that four fires started along the west edge of the city, more or less simultaneously. There's not much wind, but you know how these things spread. I've sent runners to all our patrols outside the walls."

"Good." Marcus turned to Janus. "Sir. Four fires at once has to be enemy action. It could be cover for some kind of insurrection—"

To his astonishment, the colonel was smiling. Not his usual smile, tight-lipped and gone in an instant, but a wild, almost mad grin.

"Go on ahead, Lieutenant. The captain and I will follow presently."

Fitz's eyes flicked from Janus to Marcus, who gave an infinitesimal nod. He saluted and herded the gawking rankers with their smoking muskets out into the corridor. Once they were out of sight, Janus spun to face Marcus.

"Don't you see, Captain? It's *still here*."

"I don't understand. What's still here?"

"The *Names*. When we found the vault empty I thought they must have been removed from the city months ago. With all of the Desol to hide them in, it would have taken years to ferret them out. But this . . ."

Marcus frowned. "What makes you think they weren't?"

"The fire. Enemy action, you said, and very perceptively. But why would the Redeemers burn the city?"

"To try to get us, I would assume . . ." Marcus trailed off as Janus waved his hand.

"No, no. They must know we're camped inside the walls. A fire would be inconvenient, but certainly not devastating. A lone fanatic might try such a thing, but four fires at once? No."

"Then what?"

"*Cover*. You said it yourself. It keeps us penned up inside the walls while they remove the treasure from the city." Janus' mad smile was fading, and his brow furrowed.

"But . . ." Marcus tried to follow this chain of logic, certain that there must be some flaw. "What makes you think this is related to your ancient treasure in the first place?"

Janus raised one eyebrow. "I should think you would have guessed that as well, Captain. After all, it was you who spared my life from their assassin."

"I might have," Marcus said. "But—"

"Tell me, do you think an ordinary man could move so quickly, or strike with such force? Could an ordinary man have caught a pistol ball in flight?" He spun and pointed to the cracked stone doorframe. "Do *you* know of any normal man who could fracture rock with his bare hands?"

"I don't know *what* I saw," Marcus replied, hedging.

"You know," Janus said, with a quick smile, "but you're not prepared to believe the evidence of your senses. I believe mine, Captain, and what they tell me is that the treasure of the Demon King is real. Now we must move quickly to retrieve it, as His Majesty has instructed. And," he added, as an afterthought, "to keep it out of the hands of the Last Duke."

WINTER

Winter woke before dawn with a pounding pain in the back of her head, a mouth that tasted of sewer water, and a need to visit the privy that would brook no delay.

Bobby lay against her, head resting on Winter's shoulder. Feor was in the opposite corner, neatly curled up in a catlike ball on a pile of cushions.

Winter extricated herself from Bobby, who murmured a little and didn't wake, and found that one of her legs had gone to sleep. She quietly slapped the flesh to try to work some life back into it, then limped out into the corridor. The Khandarai practice of large communal chamber pots had caused some serious embarrassment for Winter in the past. Fortunately, at this early hour, no one was about to watch her. Afterward, greatly relieved, she groped her way back through the semidarkness to the little room she'd shared with the two younger girls.

She had dreamed, after all, but her dreams had been strange, disjointed things. Jane had been there, of course, but so had Captain d'Ivoire, and Sergeant Davis, and others she couldn't quite remember. Whatever it had been, it was fading quickly.

Her plan to use her own revelation to distract Bobby from brooding on what had happened to her had worked a bit too well. The younger girls had taken to drink with cautious enthusiasm, and it wasn't long before all talk of magic and Mrs. Wilmore's was forgotten, at least for the moment. Winter had never been a world-class drunkard herself, in spite of her bravado. There was always the danger that, in an inebriated state, she would do something that would compromise her secret. It was oddly liberating to be in the company of people who already *knew*, and after the initial tide of melancholy had receded she found herself enjoying the experience.

It was considerably less enjoyable now, of course. She rubbed vainly at her eyes and wondered if there was anywhere to get a cup of cold water or, more usefully, a pail of it. Pushing back through the rag curtain into the little room, she found that Bobby had slumped the other way, snoring serenely against one wall, while Feor—

Feor was on her feet. Her eyes were open, but queer, as though she were staring at something far beyond the walls of the tavern. She swept her gaze across Winter but didn't seem to see her.

"Feor?" Winter whispered, not wanting to wake Bobby. "Is something wrong?"

Feor's lips worked silently. Winter stepped into the room to take her shoulder, but as soon as the doorway was clear the Khandarai girl bolted, brushing aside Winter's outstretched arm and dashing through the flapping rag curtain into the hallway. Winter stood for a moment in shock, listening to her retreating footsteps, then spat a curse.

"Bobby!" she shouted. "Bobby, wake up!"

The corporal's eyes snapped open and she sat up with a yawn. "Sir? Did I—"

"Come on," Winter snapped. "Feor's gone. We've got to catch up to her before she gets into trouble."

"Yessir!"

Bobby jumped to her feet, military reflex overcoming hangover fuzziness, and followed Winter down the corridor. Winter heard stirring in the other rooms, and a few angry shouts, but paid them no mind. The common room was dark and empty, with no sign of Feor, and Winter dashed across it and out into the predawn street.

Thankfully, the Khandarai girl had not turned off into one of the many twisting alleys that webbed the lower city. Even this early in the morning, a fair number of people were about, mostly tradesmen and porters making deliveries. Among the increasing bustle, Winter caught sight of Feor moving down the street at a jog, heading farther out into the slums and away from the gate to the inner city.

She'd made it three streets before they caught up to her, forcing their way through the early-morning crowd. Winter grabbed Feor's good arm and jerked her to a halt, breathing hard. Spikes of pain lanced through her head with every heartbeat, and her throat felt as though it had been rubbed with sandpaper. *Brass Balls of the Beast. Whose brilliant idea was this, again?*

Feor turned, and after a moment she lost her thousand-yard stare.

"Feor!" Winter said. "Are you all right?"

"She's here," Feor said urgently. "Please let me go."

"Who's here? Where are you going?"

"*Mother* is here. I have to find her." She looked in the direction she'd been running. "I can feel her."

"Mother?" Winter fought for breath. "I thought . . . you said . . ."

"I have to go to her," Feor said. She looked back at Winter, her eyes full of tears. "Please. You don't understand."

"Sir?" Bobby said. "What's going on?"

Winter looked back at the corporal. Remarkably, she didn't even seem to be out of breath, much less suffering the aftereffects of a night's debauchery.

"She thinks she's found her mother," Winter said in Vordanai. "Not literally her mother. The high priestess of her order, or something like that. She wants to go to her."

Feor jerked at Winter's grip again. Winter bit her lip, indecisive.

"We can't stay here," Bobby said.

A quick glance up and down the street confirmed this. The three women were the center of a widening circle of stares, and the cast of the gray-skinned faces was decidedly unfriendly. Winter wasn't sure if they thought they were seeing two Colonials accost a Khandarai girl, or if a general dislike of foreigners was enough, but either way things seemed to be taking an unhealthy turn.

"We can't let her wander off on her own," Winter said. "I'm going with her. You should—"

"I'm coming with you," Bobby said, and smiled. "Besides, I think we'll be safer as a group."

Winter didn't have the strength to argue, and wasn't sure she wanted to in any case. She turned back to Feor.

"We're coming with you," Winter said. "No arguments."

Feor blinked, then shook her head. "Mother will—"

"I said no arguments. Come on—we can't just stand here."

The Khandarai girl hesitated, then gave a quick nod. She set a fast pace down the street, and Winter and Bobby followed close behind.

"Feor, how far do we have to go?" Winter said.

"Not far," Feor said. Her brow was furrowed in deep concentration. "She's moving, I think. And there are others—around this next street—"

She broke off, looking up. Winter followed her gaze. Ahead of them, a faint glow was building over the city. For a moment Winter took it for dawn. Then her slightly befuddled mind reminded her that they were walking basically *west*, away from the inner city. The light grew brighter as she watched, until she could make out coils of smoke rising into the still-darkened sky.

Fire. Shouts of alarm were beginning to rise all around. Fire was the eternal terror of every citizen of the lower city.

"Sir!"

Winter whipped around in time to see Feor take off again, *toward* the flames. There was no time to think. Bobby was already pounding after her, and Winter gritted her teeth against the pain in her head and followed.

For the first few moments they were fighting a sudden tide of people. The beginnings of the blaze brought the lower-city folk out of their buildings like fleeing roaches, carrying their children or bundles of goods. There was no effort to fight the flames, and remarkably little screaming or confusion. This was a moment that these people had expected their whole lives, and they reacted with a silent, deadly determination to escape.

Winter was buffeted from all sides, swept backward a few steps, and torn away from Bobby. She looked about in panic and finally spotted the corporal sheltering in the gap between two wooden buildings. Winter worked her way over, shoving so hard she was practically knocking people over, until she could get out of the main stream of traffic.

"We'll never find her in this," Winter shouted in Bobby's ear. "The roofs, maybe—"

Then she stopped, because the human flood tapered off as quickly as it had begun, leaving the street empty except for a few slower-moving groups or those who'd been knocked down or dazed in the mayhem. Winter got a glimpse of Feor, who had, incredibly, made progress against the tide and was nearly at the end of the street. She pointed, got a nod from Bobby, and started to run again.

No actual flames were visible yet, but the glow was definitely brighter, and Winter could smell woodsmoke. Feor rounded the corner a few yards ahead of them, and Winter nearly collided with two young Khandarai helping an elderly man down the road. She spun out of their way at the last moment, ignoring the vicious looks, and kept after Feor. Bobby was a few steps ahead, but when she came to the corner she suddenly pulled up short, and Winter nearly cannoned into her as well.

The next street was a short one, only twenty or thirty yards before it ended in a T-junction, and judging by the distance they'd run they had to be getting close to the outskirts of the city. The glow was much more intense here, and Winter could see tongues of flame licking up in the brightening sky. None were close, however, and she realized there must be two fires, one to either side of them. Straight ahead, in the direction that led out of the city, the night was still dark.

A dozen men stood in the street. They wore white tunics and grubby white trousers, overlaid with a full-length black hooded cloak that each had tied in a peculiar loop around his waist to leave his arms and legs free. All carried drawn swords, the distinctive heavy-ended falchions of the Desoltai. They were young men, full-bearded, with dark hair and skin a darker shade of gray than the urban Khandarai. One raider had his face concealed behind a blank gray mask, featureless except for a pair of eye holes.

Winter knew him, though she had never seen him personally. Every member of the Colonials had heard the story of Malik-dan-Belial, the Steel Ghost of the Great Desol. He had been causing trouble for the prince and his Vordanai allies since long before the Redemption. Supposedly he was a sorcerer, or had made a pact with demonic powers. She'd always dismissed that kind of campfire story—but now, face-to-face with that blank, glowering mask, she thought about the arcane light that had bloomed under Feor's hands and wondered. He didn't need demonic powers, though. He had ten armed men, and she and Bobby wore only knives. Winter skidded to a halt, her heart pounding, and looked around for Feor.

One of the buildings letting onto the street was an ancient

tumbledown stone place, little more than a wall around a central courtyard with more modern wooden buildings at the back. The makeshift front gates of this relic had been opened, and a small caravan was emerging.

First came a huge, bald man whom Winter recognized as one of the *eckmahl*, eunuch servants like the one who had originally accompanied Feor. Behind the giant walked an old woman, wrapped from head to toe in white linen under a tattered gray robe. She was supported on one side by a boy of fourteen or fifteen, who was also as bald as an egg. Another man walked beside her with the air of a bodyguard.

After these three came a cart, a four-wheeled vehicle with long wooden poles at the front and rear instead of traces. These had crossbars allowing men to haul the load, and there were eight—four ahead and four behind—doing just that. These men were dressed like ordinary Khandarai laborers, but they pushed with a measured, steady tread that spoke of coordination and training. Each of the haulers was trailed by a slowly dissipating wisp of white vapor, as though they were all smoking something in unison, and Winter caught a whiff of the smell of burning sugar.

At the sight of the interlopers, the old woman and her minders stepped out of the way of the cart. It proceeded slowly past the Desoltai and up the street, toward the edge of the city. Leaning on her young companion, the crone stepped carefully toward Feor, while the desert raiders looked at one another uncertainly.

The Steel Ghost said something, too quietly for Winter to catch. When the crone spoke, her Khandarai was dry but intelligible.

"We will attend to them in a moment." Her eyes were fixed on Feor. "First I must welcome my poor wayward lamb."

"Mother!" Feor fell to her knees, sobbing, and prostrated herself full-length on the dirt in front of the old woman. "Mother, I beg forgiveness."

"Shhh," the old woman clucked, in a tone that was not at all reassuring. "All will be well, my child. You have been away for a long time."

Feor, head bowed, said nothing. The old woman looked up at the two Vordanai. Her face was invisible beneath a deep cowl, but the ends of bandages hung limp on her chest and swayed whenever she moved.

"And these are your friends?" she said. "Bring them here."

These words finally broke through Winter's indecision. *Time to run.* She didn't want to leave Feor, but she and Bobby weren't going to be able to rescue the girl from a dozen armed men. *Maybe I can round up a squad or two and intercept them—*

She grabbed Bobby's arm and turned back up the street, then stopped in surprise. Standing in their path was the young man she'd assumed was a bodyguard, bald-headed like the rest but fit and dangerous-looking. She hadn't seen him move. He raised his hands, blood dripping slowly from his palms.

"Don't!" The shout came from Feor. "Mother, please. Leave them be. They *saved* me."

"Did they?"

"Sir?" Bobby said quietly. "I can go left, you go right, and one of us should be able to hit him from behind. He hasn't got a sword."

The young man smiled at them. Winter swallowed hard.

"I don't think that would be . . . wise," she said to Bobby.

"But—"

Footsteps behind them cut the discussion short. Three of the Desoltai arrived unhurriedly, and together with the bodyguard they escorted the two Colonials back up the street. The cart was still grinding away, and the rest of the Desoltai had gone with it, including the Steel Ghost. The old woman remained with Feor, who was speaking rapidly in low tones. Winter caught a few words—she was telling her story, sometimes tripping over her tongue in her effort to get it out quickly.

Something the girl said made the old woman look up sharply at

Bobby. Winter kept one hand on the corporal's arm, and she could feel her stiffen.

"She's . . ." Bobby put one hand to the side of her head. "I can *feel* something. Something's wrong."

Feor had finished, returning to her facedown crouch. The old woman ignored her, focusing on the two Vordanai. When she finally spoke, her tone was even less friendly than it had been.

"I had hoped for better sense from you, my child."

"It seemed the only way. I owed them a debt."

"There are no debts of honor with heretics," the old woman snapped. "No deals with *raschem*."

"I'm sorry, Mother." Feor pressed her forehead to the ground. "Please. I beg for mercy."

"Mercy," the old woman said, almost contemplatively. Then she made a hawking noise, like she wanted to spit. "I cannot. *Obv-scar-iot* must be released to one who is more worthy of it."

"I accept your judgment," Feor said. "But these two—"

"Are *raschem*. If we let them go, they will fall into the grip of the schemer Orlanko. No." She shook her head. "I grant you the mercy of a swift death. Onvidaer, see to it." The hood swung up the street, toward the wagon. "We are falling behind. Akataer, with me."

"Mother!" Feor looked up, anguish in her voice, but the old woman had already turned her back. The young man, Onvidaer, stood in her place, while the three Desoltai gathered closer around Winter and Bobby.

Three. Winter's mind whirled desperately. There had to be a way out, somewhere. *Turn and grab the sword arm of the closest?* She might wrest the weapon away, if he was inattentive, but she was no swordsman. And Bobby would be left unarmed against the other two.

Her chest was tight. Once the old woman had passed out of sight, Feor climbed slowly to her feet and stood in front of Onvidaer. She was a head shorter than the young man, but she looked up at him with a mix of defiance and something Winter couldn't quite place. Something seemed to pass invisibly between them.

Feor reached out and grabbed his hand, guiding it up to her own throat. She raised her chin slightly to let his fingers tighten around her windpipe, and there was a long, frozen moment.

Then Onvidaer let his hand fall away. "I cannot," he said wonderingly.

"You must," Feor said. Her throat was smeared with the blood from his palms. "She will feel my death. She *must* feel it."

He shook his head. "I cannot."

One of the Desoltai stepped forward. "I will take the duty, if it pleases you," he said. His tone was respectful, but Onvidaer glared at him as though he were a poisonous insect.

"Please, Onvi." Feor closed her eyes. "It is Mother's judgment. I accept it."

There were only two Desoltai watching her now. Winter tensed.

Onvidaer pursed his lips briefly, then appeared to reach a decision. The Desoltai who'd stepped forward opened his mouth to speak, but got no further. The young man stepped forward and brought his hand into the side of the desert raider's head. The *crack* of shattering bone was audible, and the Desoltai was lifted off his feet to fall in a crumpled heap on the earthen street.

The other two Desoltai started to shout and raise their swords, but Onvidaer moved so fast he was a blur. He grabbed the sword arm of the first, twisting it easily out of the way with another *crack*, then punched the man in the chest. Something crunched, and the Desoltai staggered backward. Before he could fall, Onvidaer spun behind the third man, grasped his head between his palms, and twisted it one hundred eighty degrees.

The two Desoltai silently collapsed. Feor, still staring at where Onvidaer had been, was trembling.

"Let these two go, then," Feor said. "But she must feel me die."

"No!" Winter said involuntarily.

"She must!" Feor said, turning to face Onvidaer. "Or you will die in my place."

The young man's face was an agony of indecision. He raised one hand halfheartedly, then let it fall. Feor, shaking her head in frustration, bent to snatch up one of the fallen Desoltai's weapons.

"Wait," Winter said, thinking desperately. "Just wait."

Onvidaer turned to her, apparently aware for the first time that she was speaking his language.

"A Vordanai patrol turned up," Winter said. "Ten men. Twenty," she corrected, thinking of the speed at which Onvidaer had moved. "You had to fight your way free."

Feor's eyes glittered with tears. Onvidaer cocked his head, considering.

"A patrol," he said. "Following you."

Winter nodded eagerly, but Feor shook her head. "You will still be punished for failure!"

"Punished, but not killed," said Onvidaer. "I will endure."

"I—"

"Go," he said, gently removing the Desoltai blade from her grip. "Take your friends and go. Leave, and never return."

Feor fell to her knees. "N-never . . ."

Onvidaer looked up at Winter. "You will care for her?"

"Yes," Winter said without hesitation.

"Good. Do not make me regret allowing you to live."

He turned and ran after his mistress, great loping strides carrying him along faster than he had any right to move. Winter, Bobby, and Feor were left alone with the three Desoltai corpses.

Flames were licking ever higher into the sky. Winter fought her instinctive desire to curl into a ball and hide. Instead, she stepped closer to Feor. The Khandarai girl had her head in her hands, her shoulders shaking with silent sobs. Winter touched her tentatively.

"Feor," she said, when this drew no response. "Feor!"

Feor looked up, her normally impassive face flushed gray-red and streaked with soot and tears. Winter grabbed her roughly by the arm and hauled her to her feet.

"We have to go. We can't stay here." She gestured at the flames. "Come on!"

"I . . ." Feor shook her head feebly. "No. Leave me here. Just . . ."

"You heard him," Winter snapped. "I'm supposed to take care of you. Now come on, or Bobby and I will carry you!"

That got Feor moving, at least into a stumbling walk that Winter guided with a hand on her shoulder. Bobby fell in on the other side, having claimed one of the falchions from the dead Desoltai.

"Sir," she said, over Feor's lowered head, "what the *hell* just happened?"

Winter shook her head. Without any knowledge of Khandarai, Bobby was totally in the dark, but Winter didn't feel much better off herself.

"I wish I knew," Winter said. "I'll explain what I can later. For now . . ." She glanced over her shoulder at the growing wall of flame. "I think it's time to run."

Chapter Nineteen

MARCUS

Marcus could see from Razzan-dan-Xopta's expression that the conference had not gone well. He stood hastily as Janus emerged from the august presence of the prince, trailing the Khandarai minister like an overinflated silk balloon.

"Colonel," Razzan said, wringing his hands, "perhaps it was my translations that were at fault here. I urge you—"

"Your translations were adequate," Janus snapped. "Also, as you know, unnecessary. I believe that all that needs to be said has been said. Now, if you'll excuse me, I have a march to organize."

"But . . . the prince has forbidden it!"

"I have informed the prince of my intentions. He is welcome to take whatever steps he feels are necessary."

Janus made a shooing motion, then beckoned to Marcus, who fell into step behind him. They left the bewildered minister gaping like a landed fish.

"I take it he wasn't pleased," Marcus murmured.

"He called me a coward and a traitor," Janus said. "How refusing to sit behind the walls of Ashe-Katarion makes me a coward, I'm not sure I understand, but no doubt the minds of royalty work in mysterious ways."

"You can't blame him," Marcus said. "He's frightened."

"I don't blame him for that. I only wish he would accept the reality of the situation."

The reality of the situation, of course, was that the colonel could do as he liked. The prince had a handful of Heavenly Guards and Jaffa's Justices, and the loyalty of the latter was far from certain. Janus could depose the monarch with a wave of his hand, and they both knew it. Still, old habits died hard, and the Vermillion Throne continued to issue "commands" to its Vordanai allies.

That, in this case, the prince might be *right* made it all the worse from Marcus' point of view. He coughed. Janus turned to look at him, gray eyes glittering.

"You don't approve," the colonel said.

"Of the way you dealt with the prince? Of course I approve. It's about time someone—"

"No," Janus said. "You don't want to march."

"I had wondered whether it is entirely . . . wise," Marcus admitted.

"I've told you before that you may speak your mind to me, as long as we're in private." Janus gestured at the empty corridor. "Speak."

"I follow your logic, as far as it goes," Marcus said. "I agree that the fires and the assassination attempt mean the Desoltai may still be nearby. But if we pursue, they'll fall back into the Desol, and following them seems like it would be playing right into their hands."

"You worry we won't be able to defeat them?"

"I worry that they won't fight at all," Marcus said. "The Desoltai aren't like ordinary soldiers. You can go days without seeing them, and then suddenly they're on top of you like a swarm of angry hornets. They let the desert do their work for them, and trying to strike back is like punching a mist." Marcus had become more fervent than he intended, and he took a moment to regain his decorum. "My concern is that we won't be able to force a decisive action."

"They have towns, I know. Camps. Oases from which they draw their supplies."

"They do, but they're hidden in the depths of the Desol. There are no maps, no roads. Finding them . . ." Marcus shrugged.

Janus looked thoughtful for a moment, then shook his head. "This time is different, Captain. They attempt to bring the Names to a place of safety. If we can keep close enough on their heels, they will eventually lead us to it."

"The Names," Marcus said flatly, and suppressed a sigh. Janus had still refused to explain the exact nature of his mysterious treasure. He tried a new tack. "And you've considered that the prince may be right to worry? Without the Colonials to keep order, Ashe-Katarion may rise against him."

"Unlikely. Whatever standing the Redeemers had left with the people was lost with the fire."

"That doesn't mean they like the prince any better. If they string him up from the walls, we'll have trouble keeping order in all of Khandar."

"It's an acceptable risk," Janus said. "We must have the Names."

"Even if it costs us—"

"Even if it costs us all of Khandar." Janus looked solemnly at Marcus. "I expect this sort of protest from less . . . imaginative minds, Captain. But you were there. You saw what they can do. We cannot leave that sort of power in the hands of a gang of Khandarai witches."

"I . . ."

That awful morning now seemed like the beginning of a nightmare, a day of flame and windblown ash that blacked out the sky and coated the streets with gray. He'd almost forgotten the assassination attempt amidst the chaos that had followed. The fires had been every bit as bad as Khandarai legend said they would be, sweeping unstoppably through the tight-packed tenements and thatch-roofed buildings of the lower city, washing against the thick stone walls of the inner city like waves against a breakwater.

Sparks driven by the wind had overtopped the wall and started dozens of smaller blazes, but the upper city was built largely of stone. Marcus had deployed the Colonials to battle these flames as best they could, and also to assist the Justices at the walls. Mobs of hysterical commoners assaulted the gates, desperate for safety, and against all tradition Marcus decreed that the inner city be opened to these refugees. That meant guards and pickets to protect the property of the aristocrats.

Thousands more Khandarai had run for the other traditional refuge and jumped into the canal or the harbor, until the shallows resembled a gigantic open-air bath. That saved them from the flames, but hundreds drowned in the choking, shoving mobs or were forced out into the deeps and went under when their strength gave out. Thousands were left behind in the city, too, unable or unwilling to run, and had burned along with their homes. The Justices were unable to provide even a partial body count, but burial squads were still working three shifts.

Casualties among the Colonials, fortunately, had been light. Most of the patrols had hurried back to the gates as soon as the fire started. The First Battalion had fewer than a dozen unaccounted for, and Marcus hoped most of those would yet turn up.

And before the ashes were cold, Janus had announced his intention to march.

"I . . . don't know," Marcus said. "I'll admit that *something* supernatural came to attack you that morning, but whether that has anything to do with these Thousand Names . . ."

The gray eyes flashed. "It was a demon, Captain. A creature not of this earth, wearing a human skin."

It caught a pistol ball. Marcus had seen a conjuror do that once in a stage show, but that had only been a trick. This had been a real ball from a real pistol, and he'd pulled the trigger himself. *Which is impossible.* A man might be fast, or strong—*not as fast or strong as that thing was*—but to catch a ball in flight . . .

"Even so," Marcus said. "Even if he was—"

They rounded a corner, and Marcus was relieved to catch sight of Fitz hurrying toward them. The lieutenant stopped in front of them and saluted.

"Your points are noted, Captain," Janus said. "My orders stand. I expect a report by evening."

"Yessir." Marcus stiffened and snapped a salute of his own. The colonel swept past Fitz and on down the corridor, and Marcus didn't let himself relax until Janus had turned a corner.

"Orders, sir?" Fitz said. "Has the colonel finished with the prince already?"

Marcus nodded wearily. "We march," he said. "Tomorrow, at dawn."

"Very good, sir."

His face was impassive. Marcus gave him a penetrating look. "Doesn't that bother you? Just the other day you were telling us how it would be unwise."

"Obviously the colonel does not agree with me," Fitz said mildly. "Besides, circumstances have changed. In some ways, we may be safer outside the city."

"What do you mean?"

"Supplies are already running low among the refugees, sir. I came to tell you that there's been a disturbance. Some farmers were bringing a convoy of food to market—that's the inner-city market, of course—and they were confronted by a mob demanding that they sell it to them at pre-fire prices. When the farmers refused, the mob attacked the wagons and took everything they could carry. There are three dead and a dozen wounded."

"If we leave, that sort of thing is only going to get nastier."

"Certainly our presence contributes to the maintenance of order," Fitz said, in the slow, calm tone he used to explain things to officers and small children. "On the other hand, shortages are only going to grow worse, and it's only a matter of time before the people turn their anger on us."

"Wonderful." Marcus shook his head. "It's all academic, anyway. Unless the prince tries to stop us by force, we leave in the morning. How are the preparations?"

"We've commandeered all the transport we can lay our hands on," Fitz said. "You still mean to take the entire hospital with us?"

"Damn right. If we're marching, that means all of us. I don't want one Vordanai in uniform left behind."

"It's just that the space would be useful to transport more barrels of water, or—"

"Everyone, Fitz."

"Yessir. Food is going to be the issue, sir, at least at first. We've more or less exhausted the supplies that came with the fleet, and there's not much to be had in the city unless we start turning some nobles out onto the street."

"That might make the mob happy," Marcus said, and sighed. "I'll bring it up with the colonel. Is there any good news?"

"Ammunition is holding up nicely, sir. The Auxiliaries left us a substantial supply, and since they use Vordanai weapons the calibers match up perfectly."

"It's a blessing no one thought to torch the magazines," Marcus said. The fire had been bad enough. If one of the big arsenals had gone up as well . . .

"Yessir. Also, Captain Roston appears to have regained consciousness."

"Adrecht? When?"

"Early this morning, I understand."

"You might have told me earlier. I'm going to see him."

"Sir," Fitz said, "about our stock of barrels—"

"Later," Marcus snapped. "Or better yet, whatever it is,

just take care of it. You have full authority to take any necessary steps."

"Yessir!" The lieutenant saluted. "Understood, sir!"

The hospital had been established in a closed-off wing of the Palace. The prince had objected to this use of royal property, but Marcus had insisted and Janus had backed him. The battalion cutters, who handled immediate battlefield triage and most day-to-day complaints, had consolidated the worst of the wounded cases under the regimental surgeons. Marcus had visited a few times to see Adrecht, but until now his fellow captain had never been awake to receive him and the groans of the wounded had quickly driven him away.

Since then, things had quieted down somewhat. The festering infections and bad blood that accompanied battle wounds had reaped their inevitable toll, and the bodies had long since been carried away. Those who were on the road to recovery had left as well, often of their own accord, since no sane soldier wanted to stay under a cutter's care any longer than absolutely necessary. The patients who remained were those who'd contracted something lingering, or who'd been wounded badly enough to require serious surgery and had survived the process.

Marcus was met by a surgeon's assistant, who recognized him, saluted, and led him to the narrow bedroom in which Adrecht had been installed. As Fitz had promised, he was sitting up on the low bed, reading something. The captain was out of uniform, but his blue coat was draped across his shoulders. The left sleeve hung flat against his side, limp and empty.

"Adrecht!" Marcus said. "Sorry I wasn't here earlier. I've been with the colonel all morning. Fitz just told me you'd woken up."

"It's all right," Adrecht said. "I wasn't in a fit state to meet anyone until just now anyway. I finally kicked up enough of a fuss that they brought me a bath and a change of clothes from my room."

Marcus chuckled. Adrecht's smile was strained, and an awkward silence descended as Marcus realized he had absolutely no idea what to say. He owed Adrecht his life, but any kind of "thank you" seemed pitifully inadequate in view of the price his friend had paid. To acknowledge the debt would be unbearable, but to do anything else seemed ridiculous. He opened his mouth, closed it again, and gritted his teeth.

Somewhat to his surprise, Adrecht came to the rescue. He held up the paper he'd been reading. "Have you seen this?"

"What is it?"

"Orders. The colonel wants the Fourth Battalion to get ready to march."

"He sent the orders to *you*?" Marcus had a flash of incredulous rage.

"Not as such. The colonel informs me that the Fourth will be marching with the rest of the regiment, and inquires whether or not I feel competent to take up the command. If not, he quite understands."

Adrecht gave the phrase a nasty spin, but Marcus couldn't help agreeing with his tone. Janus must have written those words while Adrecht still lay unconscious, so he could hardly have expected an answer in the affirmative.

"Have you told him anything?" Marcus said.

"I wanted to talk to you first." A sudden, pained expression crossed Adrecht's face, and he grabbed at the stump of his left arm with his right. The note from Janus fluttered to the floor. "Karis' fucking blood," he growled. "You'd think the goddamned thing would stop hurting once they'd taken it off."

"Should I send for someone?"

"No." Adrecht closed his eyes. Marcus noticed how thin his face had become. His cheeks were sunken hollows, and rings of black circled his eyes. "I'll be all right. Listen, have you talked to Janus about this?"

"About you leading the Fourth?"

"About the march!" Adrecht said. "You know as well as I do that it's madness. Have you explained it to him?"

"I . . ." Marcus hesitated. "I'm not sure I would call it 'madness.' "

"Chasing the Desoltai into the Great Desol? What else would you call it? The Desol eats armies and spits out bleached bones. Damn it, you know what it'll be like. No water, no food, Desoltai raiders snatching up our pickets, night attacks and ambushes—" He broke down into a fit of coughing, violent and disturbingly wet-sounding. Marcus found a basin and cup nearby and poured some water.

"You can't let him do it," Adrecht said weakly when he'd recovered. "Come on, Marcus. Anyone who goes into the Desol isn't coming out again. The Redeemers and 'General' Khtoba are one thing, but this is the Steel Ghost. They say he can't be killed."

Marcus had heard those rumors, too. He'd always discounted them, but in the light of what he'd seen . . . He shook his head.

"The colonel is aware of the difficulties. I've given him my opinion. Fitz is working on the supply problem—"

"The hell with your opinion," Adrecht rasped. "Tell him *no*. Tell him you're not going to do it. The First will follow you, and so will Val and Mor. The Colonials know you. If you just explain it to them—"

There was a sharp intake of breath that Marcus took a moment to recognize as his own. Adrecht halted, aware that he had gone too far.

"I think," Marcus said, "that you may still have a touch of fever."

"I think you're right," Adrecht said dully.

"Shall I inform that colonel that you're not ready to resume command yet?"

"Tell him whatever you like. You can go and die in the Desol if you're so determined, but I'm staying here."

"No," Marcus said. "Everyone comes with the regiment, even the wounded. Relations between the colonel and the prince have . . . deteriorated. Anyone left behind wouldn't be safe."

"Saints and *fucking* martyrs." Adrecht clutched his head with his remaining hand, face contorting as another spasm of pain ripped through him. His breath hissed from between clenched teeth.

"Should I—"

"Get out," Adrecht managed. "Just . . . go, all right?"

Marcus turned a corner of the battered sandstone Palace and found Fitz directing a company of the First hauling the battalion baggage to the edge of the field, where wagons and teams were lined up three-deep. Along with the usual transport for food, ammunition, and guns, Marcus was not surprised to see stack after stack of wine barrels.

"Throwing a dinner party, Lieutenant?"

Fitz saluted. "Sir. I need to report—"

Marcus waved a hand. "I think I get it. For water, right?"

"Yessir. Most of the city coopers practiced their trade in the lower city. It was necessary to obtain a supply quickly, so I took the most expedient route."

"I had a gang of wine merchants waving papers in my face all morning. I take it you handed out promissory notes for compensation, as per regulations?"

"As per regulations, sir." Fitz's face was straight, but his tone held the barest hint of humor. "I'm sure the Ministry will compensate them."

"I'm sure," Marcus said dryly. "How are things progressing?"

"On schedule, sir. We have a slightly longer sick list than usual, but other than that everything is in order."

"Something going around?"

"Mostly hangovers, I suspect, sir."

"Ah." He lowered his voice. "You've been here all morning?"

"Yessir, directing the preparations."

"Do you have a sense of the . . . feeling of the men? About this expedition, I mean."

"Sir?"

Marcus sighed. "I spoke to Adrecht. He's . . ." Marcus paused. "Well, he's not in a good state, but that's to be expected. But he was convinced that the march is going to be a disaster. I was wondering if that was a widespread opinion."

Fitz nodded, considering. He spoke quietly. "I don't believe so, sir. Among the Old Colonials, there may be a few, especially those who've spent time chasing the Desoltai in the past. But the recruits are confident in the colonel, and I have to say many of the Old Colonials have come around as well. Morale seems to be high, sir."

"That's good to know." That meant that Adrecht's complaints—technically treasonous—could safely be dismissed as grumbling. "Do we have our marching orders yet?"

"Yessir. We're to head for a town called Nahiseh. The colonel wants us to reach it by nightfall. I understand that he intends to secure additional supplies there."

At least he's thinking about it. Marcus didn't flatter himself that it was his own harangue that had gotten Janus' mind onto that track, but he hoped it had helped. Looking at the rows of wagons, and the troops forming beyond them in the field, he felt momentarily comforted. It didn't last. Out to the east was the Great Desol, the desert that devoured armies and laughed at mapmakers. And somewhere, hiding amidst the sands, the Steel Ghost.

Once again the long blue snake wound out, flowing through the gate, under the stone walls of Ashe-Katarion, and into the burned-out wasteland that had been the lower city.

The column had changed a great deal since the last time Marcus had watched this scene, back at Fort Valor. For one thing, it had shortened considerably. The battalions themselves had slimmed—the Colonials had lost nearly five hundred fighting men, most of them in the action around Weltae—but the "tail" of wagons was also considerably shorter, shorn of the prince and his entourage as well as the usual gaggle of Khandarai camp followers. Marcus had decreed that nothing that was not absolutely necessary would accompany them into the desert, making the maximum possible use of available wagon space and beasts of burden. Cartload after cartload of barrels rumbled past, weighed down with heavy, precious water.

The men themselves were different, too. It was harder to distinguish between the recruits and the Old Colonials: the new soldiers had lost their fish-belly pallor, and their kit had acquired the patina of dirt and hard wear that marked an army on the march, while the veterans had repaired some of the more obvious shabbiness to make sure they looked better than their younger companions. Strings of cavalry remounts, another thing Marcus had insisted on, walked in riderless lines behind the wagons, while Give-Em-Hell and his troopers were spread in a thin screen around the marching column.

Toward the end came the hospital wagons. Despite his promises to Fitz, Marcus had allowed a few of the very worst stricken to remain behind, those whom the cutters had quietly promised him didn't have long to live in any case. Subjecting dying men to vicious jouncing along rutted roads in unsprung wagons seemed like one cruelty too many, but he hoped that the prince would not inflict some final indignity on them in petty revenge. The rest of the injured, including Adrecht, had been packed into wagon-beds cushioned with commandeered carpets. He could hear the occasional chorus of shrieks and moans when the vehicles hit a bumpy patch in the road.

He'd made all the preparations he could think to make. Probably more usefully, he'd given Fitz a free hand to make all the preparations *he* could think to make, and as usual the young lieutenant had come up with a dozen things his chief had forgotten. In spite of it all, though, Marcus couldn't fight off a dark foreboding. Riding under the walls himself, in the gap between the Second and Third Battalions, he looked at the stout wooden gates and wondered if they would find them closed when they returned.

If we return. He chided himself for the thought.

The fire had left the lower city in ruins, but marching through it reminded Marcus that this sort of clearance was a regular event in Khandar. The scavengers had started in on the rubble before it was cool, and the last of the flames had barely died away before the hunt for building materials was on. New structures were already going up, claiming choice real estate. To Marcus' eyes, they looked ready to topple at any moment, and just as flammable as the last batch, but they were being raised as fast as gangs could haul blackened but serviceable timber from the debris. He'd seen the vast temporary kilns the brickmakers had raised along the waterfront, too. It wouldn't be long until the city sprang from the ashes, like new growth after a forest fire.

A horde of Khandarai had turned out to see the Colonials go. They watched in silence, without open hostility but also without cheers or celebration. Marcus saw a lot of dark, angry faces, and heard a great deal of quiet muttering.

He was glad when they passed beyond the old boundary of the lower city. A few buildings had survived here, better built or simply luckier than their neighbors, and the ramshackle grid of streets dissolved into country lanes that wound their way between ancient, rock-walled fields and irrigation ditches. Unlike their previous march, there was no convenient highway to follow. Roads led west and south from Ashe-Katarion, but not east, since there was nothing in that direction but the wasteland of the Great Desol. Instead, the column followed markers laid down by Give-Em-Hell's scouting horsemen, who rode down any track that looked as though it headed in the right direction and compared what they saw to the vaguely drawn Khandarai maps.

Nahiseh, their initial goal, was a market town twelve miles from

Ashe-Katarion. Marcus had hoped to make it there by midafternoon, but by the time the sun was high he realized they'd be lucky to reach it before dusk. The narrow lanes restricted the column to a long, thin line, and every hesitation or obstacle encountered by the troops in front was transmitted down the length of the snake, forcing those behind to halt while the leaders sorted things out. Worst of all, of course and as usual, were the wagons, which suffered badly on the rocky ground.

Marcus' temper grew shorter each time they had to stop. It was not improved by falling off his horse, which he did just after midday when Meadow shied at a particularly violent outburst. For a terrifying moment he thought the mare was going to trample him, but she stepped daintily aside, leaving him with a long cut on his arm where it had scraped against the stone wall and considerable damage to his dignity.

The colonel, of course, was nowhere to be found. Marcus had seen him go past early in the day, at the head of the column, trotting out as eagerly as if he were off to a fox hunt. Fitz, Val, and Mor were busy corralling their own battalions, so there was nothing for Marcus to do but pick himself up and keep at it, spitting silent curses all the while.

He was just sorting out an altercation between one of the Preacher's gunners and an unfortunate carter who had gotten in a hopeless tangle when Fitz came trotting up, his uniform somehow still spotless in spite of a day of dusty marching. The artilleryman was in the middle of a tirade, threatening to stuff the teamster down the barrel of one of his twelve-pounders and chop off all the bits that didn't fit. Marcus let him go on until he'd exhausted his head of steam, then told the carter to get his equipage out of the way as soon as possible, and never mind the risk to his axles.

Then he turned to Fitz, who'd waited patiently at his shoulder. The young man was blank-faced, as always, but something in his manner made Marcus instantly concerned.

"Something wrong?"

"Could be, sir," Fitz said. "You'd better come and have a look."

"Lead the way," Marcus said, then gave the lieutenant a questioning look when he didn't move.

"Best to ride, sir."

Marcus cursed inwardly, but there was nothing for it. His legs already ached from a long day in the saddle, and his arm hurt abominably. But Fitz knew of his aversion to horses, and if he thought they had to ride, that meant something was very wrong indeed.

An aide brought up Meadow, and the two of them started down the stalled column. "This is a mess," he said, more or less to himself. Fitz answered anyway.

"Yessir. Road's too narrow, sir, and there aren't any good alternative routes. Give-Em-Hell said that we should break out of these stone-walled fields once we get past Nahiseh."

"Just be glad the Desoltai haven't turned on us yet. This would be a hell of a place to be ambushed." The thought of trying to push past those stone walls as they fumed with gunsmoke gave him the shivers. On the other hand, the Desoltai loved their horses almost as much as they hated the Vordanai, so they would find the idea of fighting on such cluttered ground just as uncomfortable. Then Marcus had a nasty thought. "That's not what you're taking me to see, is it?"

"Not exactly, sir. The leading companies of the First have reached Nahiseh, and there was a bit of a fracas."

"A fracas?"

"An altercation, you might call it. The locals are unhappy."

"Wonderful. Where's the colonel?"

"He rode through the town already, sir. Said he saw something on the hill just beyond and took a squadron of cavalry as an escort."

"At least he had that much sense." Marcus wouldn't have put it past Janus to wander off on his own if something really interested him. For a man with his obvious military talent, he could be surprisingly obtuse at times. "Come on. Let's get to this town before someone burns the place down."

It hadn't quite come to that, but it wasn't far from it. Marcus found two companies of the First waiting on the outskirts of the little town, which would barely have qualified as a large village in Vordan. It was a collection of dusty shacks and a few brick-and-timber buildings, not much bigger than Weltae. Its primary purposes were to serve as a way station for farmers carting their produce to the city and to host markets for city merchants to sell goods to the rural folk who never got to make that trip. The main attraction was an underground spring that gave pure, sweet water, which some long-ago ruler of Khandar had built up into a fountain and pool with a statue depicting an unrecognizable god.

It was over this fountain that the "altercation," as Fitz had termed it, had developed. A dozen Vordanai soldiers, looking very nervous, stood with shouldered muskets and fixed bayonets, while another blue-coated man lay in the dust with a corporal leaning over him. In front of the line, Marcus was depressed but unsurprised to find Senior Sergeant Davis, face red and veins bulging, screaming at a square-jawed Khandarai who listened impassively to his tirade. A small crowd of locals stood behind him. They looked more like curious onlookers than an angry mob, but Marcus knew that the line dividing the two could be a thin one.

"You little gray-skinned motherfucker," Davis said. "If you and your little friends don't clear this street right now, I mean *right* fucking now, I am going to order these men to blow the lot of you straight into your fucked-up afterlife. Is that what you want? You want me to take a bayonet and rearrange your insides?"

"Sergeant Davis!" Marcus boomed, in his best parade-ground voice.

Davis whirled, his face still lurid with rage, and for a moment

Marcus thought he was about to receive the benefit of his acid tongue. Then good sense took over, and the fat sergeant quivered to attention and saluted as crisply as he could manage.

"Sir!" he barked. "Request permission to assemble my company and disperse this resistance, *sir*!"

"Are they resisting?" Marcus looked out over the crowd. "They don't appear to be armed."

"They're blocking the road, sir! And one of them decked Peg—that is, one of them struck Ranker Nunenbast, sir!"

"Was that this man here?" Marcus said, indicating the big Khandarai.

"Yessir. I want him punished, sir!"

"Let me talk to him."

Marcus dismounted awkwardly and went over to the man, with Fitz following at his shoulder. He mustered his politest Khandarai and said, "I am Captain d'Ivoire. Whom do I have the honor of addressing?"

The Khandarai blinked, a bit surprised, and said, "I am Dannin-dan-Uluk. I am the headman of this town."

Marcus inclined his head at Peg, who was still groaning theatrically. "And what seems to be the problem?"

"He wished to use the fountain. I explained that he would have to make an offering to the Lord of Waters, but he refused. When he attempted to push his way past, I was forced to do him an injury."

"I see. Did he understand you?"

Dannin shrugged. Marcus sighed inwardly.

"I apologize on his behalf, then," he said. "Many of my men do not speak your language. I wish for them to have free access to your fountain for tonight and tomorrow morning. How large an offering to the Lord of Waters would be appropriate?"

"How many men?"

"A little more than four thousand, and our animals."

The headman shook his head. "Too many. They will deplete

the pool, and it will not refill for many weeks. In the meantime, the town will suffer."

Marcus grimaced. *Here's where I show that I'm no better than the likes of Davis, after all.*

"We must have water," he said quietly, so the crowd behind the headman would not hear. "I am prepared to make a generous donation to your town and your god in exchange for it, and to purchase food and other necessaries besides. If you refuse, however, we can commandeer these things in the name of the prince, and then you will have nothing."

"You have no right to do such things."

I have an army. That's even better. "The prince disagrees. You may apply to him for compensation."

"And if we refuse?"

Marcus glanced over his shoulder at Sergeant Davis, who was still glaring daggers at the Khandarai. Then he shrugged, as though it were a matter of indifference to him.

"You will pay," the headman said, after a moment's contemplation. "And we will bring wine for your soldiers to drink, so only your animals need to use the fountain. You must pay for the wine, too, of course."

"Of course." Marcus' head was starting to pound in time with the ache in his arm. He wondered how he was going to explain this to Janus. *If he even bothers to ask.*

"And did he say where we go next?" Jen said.

"Of course not," Marcus said, pulling off his uniform jacket one-handed and tossing it into a corner. "He just smiles, as though he expects me to enjoy the sense of mystery. I swear to Karis the Savior the man missed his calling as a stage conjuror." He picked up the wineskin—a too-sweet vintage generously provided by the villagers of Nahiseh—and took another long pull.

Jen, sitting on his bed, nodded sympathetically. He hadn't

invited her in, exactly, but she'd been waiting for him outside his newly erected tent, and his anger at Janus' refusal to divulge his plans had come bubbling out almost involuntarily. Now he stood with the skin in one hand, facing her bright, curious eyes behind the thick-lensed spectacles, and wondered if he'd said too much.

She's still Concordat, when all is said and done. And Janus is still my commanding officer. Betraying a confidence went deeply against Marcus' nature. He hadn't mentioned the Thousand Names, or that Janus might have a reason for the march other than to run down the Divine Hand, but he wondered how much Jen might infer from his frustration.

"He doesn't trust me. No surprise, really. I don't think he really trusts anyone." He tried a grin. "No offense intended."

"None taken. His Grace the Duke certainly doesn't trust *him.*" She held out a hand, and Marcus silently handed the wineskin across. "That's why I'm here, after all. Though what I'm supposed to do *now* is beyond me."

"No secret instructions from the Ministry?" Marcus said teasingly.

"No instructions at all. 'Observe and report,' they told me." She shook her head. "I don't think even Orlanko expected the colonel to overthrow the Redeemers so quickly."

"It had to be quickly, or not at all. If we'd settled into a siege, with the whole countryside against us, we wouldn't have lasted a month. Janus was right. Breaking straight through was the only way."

"The men in the camp are saying he's a genius," she said. "Farus the Conqueror come again. Is he?"

Marcus shifted uncomfortably. "That may be going a bit far. But he certainly knows what he's about."

"Then you agree with him about this march into the Desol?"

"I didn't say that." Marcus thought about Adrecht. "It's not my place to agree or disagree. The colonel gives orders, and I execute them as best I can."

"Ever the dutiful soldier."

"Be sure to put that in your report." He reached down to unlace his boots, and winced at a spasm of pain in his arm. "Saints and martyrs. I suppose I'd better see a cutter for this."

"I can take a look, if you like."

Marcus was dubious, but anything was better than a trip to the cutter's tent. He finished with his boots and tugged his shirttails out of his pants, then looked over at Jen, suddenly embarrassed. It must have shown on his face, because she laughed and waved a hand.

"Go ahead, Captain. You can trust to my discretion."

He pulled his shirt and undershirt over his head quickly, to hide the burning in his cheeks, and then gently pulled the bloody part away where it had gummed itself to his flesh, flinching each time it pulled out a hair. When he was done, he worked the arm stiffly, watching fresh blood well up through cracks in the clotted mass. Jen leaned forward and sniffed unhappily.

"That's a mess. Do you have a clean cloth?"

"By the basin."

Jen wet the cloth in the lukewarm water and sat down beside Marcus on the bed. She worked the cloth back and forth across the injury, and he endured the cleansing patiently, trying not to wince as bits of scab tore free. The cloth was streaked with red by the time she was finished.

"Just a little cut," she said, holding the linen against the wound to soak up fresh bleeding. "You'll have a scar."

"It won't be the first."

"I can see that." Her eyes ran across his torso, which was a patchwork of evidence of other minor altercations. Marcus, suddenly uncomfortable again, shifted himself away from her and nodded toward the trunk.

"There should be some fresh bandages in there," he said.

Jen got up and fetched them. When she sat down again, she was right beside him, her knee nearly touching his. She knotted the bandage around his injury with the air of an expert, tested the knot, and let his arm fall. It brushed her thigh on the way down, and the tips of his fingers seemed to tingle.

"You were lucky," she said. "You might have broken your neck."

"I know." Marcus sighed. "Fitz has already lectured me. But I couldn't just let things get out of hand . . ."

There was a long silence, or as close to silence as there ever was in an army camp. Outside, there was the usual buzz of men putting up tents, cooking dinner, and dealing with the thousand other mundane tasks that made up the life of a soldier. But they all slowly seemed to fade away, until Marcus was intensely aware of Jen's breathing. He found himself watching the way her chest moved under the flaps of her coat. When he realized what he was doing, he looked hastily away, blushing again, then caught her gazing at him steadily. He swallowed, hesitated, and opened his mouth, though to say what he had no idea.

"Yes," Jen said.

Marcus blinked. "What?"

"I know what you're going to say. Or what you want to say, anyway. And the answer is yes."

"Yes? I mean—I don't know what you mean. I wasn't—"

"You're very gallant," Jen said. "But if you keep stuttering, I may have to hit you."

He kissed her instead. It wasn't a very good kiss. Marcus was out of practice, and the edge of Jen's spectacles dug into the side of his face so hard they left a mark. But she was smiling when he pulled away, and her cheeks were as flushed as his. She took the glasses off with one hand, snapped them closed, and set them carefully by the side of the bed.

"I didn't mean to be . . . forward," Marcus said. "You don't have to—you know—"

"Please," she said. "*Please* stop talking."

He did. After a while, she snuffed the lamp, leaving them in the warm, dry semidarkness.

It had been a long time for Marcus, and even longer since he hadn't had to hire his company. Adrecht might have been able to get Khandarai women to fawn over him, but Marcus had never had the knack, so his romantic life had been confined to a few of the cleaner establishments in the lower city. Compared to the practiced embraces of those seasoned professionals, Jen was hesitant and awkward, but he found he didn't mind.

Afterward, she lay close beside him, her breast pressed against his shoulder. The camp bed wasn't really big enough for both of them, and Marcus' injured arm dangled over the edge. His other arm was trapped underneath her, but he felt no desire to move. Jen's breathing was so soft he thought she was asleep, but when he turned his head he found her eyes open and watching him.

Marcus raised an eyebrow. "Something wrong?"

"Just thinking." She pursed her lips. "Remember the bottle we opened?"

"Of course."

Jen smiled. "I just thought that if we all die in the desert, at least I won't have to regret not doing this."

"That's not going to happen," Marcus said.

"You didn't sound so confident earlier."

"I was angry." Marcus let out a long breath. "Janus will come through, somehow. He won't say where we're going and he won't explain, but in the end he'll come through, and drag the rest of us with him."

"You sound like you have a lot of faith in him."

For a moment, Marcus was back at Weltae. He saw Adrecht urging him to escape while he had the chance. He struggled to recall the certainty that had blazed in his mind, that Janus would be there. *And he was.* Another, treacherous voice added, *Too late for Adrecht, though. And how many others?*

Marcus shifted, bringing his free hand up to run lightly along Jen's flank. He gave her nipple an idle tweak, and felt it harden under his fingers. A little shiver ran through her body, and she wriggled tighter against him and pressed her lips to his bearded cheek.

She didn't spend the night, of course. Sex on the camp bed was uncomfortable enough. Actually *sleeping* side by side would have been impossible. He must have dozed off at some point, though, because when he woke in the morning, still naked, Jen and her clothes had gone.

There was no question of keeping the liaison a secret—the walls of the tent were just canvas, after all, and there was nothing an army camp liked better than to gossip about its officers. But if the rumors reached Fitz or Janus, neither mentioned them, and the feeling that he was doing something monstrously wrong slowly started to fade from Marcus' mind. Jen shared his bed the next night, when he'd traded the camp bed for a pair of bedrolls, and the night after that as well. The day after that, the Colonials marched into the Great Desol.

They'd been making steady progress through the Khandarai farmland beyond Nahiseh, in spite of the lack of good roads. As Give-Em-Hell had promised, past the town the land flattened out and the fields were marked by rough dirt tracks instead of stone walls, making for a much more comfortable march and easier going for the vehicles. Marcus' spirits had revived somewhat, due both to Jen's ministrations and to the fact that no Desoltai ambushes had materialized.

The second day, the cultivated fields started to give way to patches of rough scrub grass, and the grass in turn to open, sandy wastes strewn with rock. The streams that wound through the low valleys became narrower and farther apart, until they were dust-dry beds more often than not. Huge outcrops of rock, like jagged whales breaching through an ocean of sand and dust, took the place of the gentle hills they had found thus far. There was no definite boundary, but by the morning of the third day Marcus could look back and ahead and see not a hint of green from horizon to horizon.

On the morning of the fourth day out from Nahiseh, Marcus was roused from an uneasy sleep by Fitz, who knocked discreetly but firmly at the tent pole. Marcus had in fact gone to bed alone that night. The camp was abuzz with expectation, of an attack or some other sign of resistance from the Desoltai, and he'd been up half the night waiting for the alarm to sound. Whether she'd sensed this or had just been preoccupied herself, Jen had stayed away, and Marcus had eventually lapsed into a fitful slumber. He woke up, still fully clothed, and struggled groggily to his knees.

"Fitz?" he said. "Is something wrong?" The light outside didn't seem bright enough for it to be much past dawn.

"I'm afraid so, sir," said the lieutenant. "You'd better come and see."

CHAPTER TWENTY

WINTER

"They found them on the rocks?" Winter said.

"Strapped to them, hands and feet," Graff said. He looked a little gray. "Like they were still alive when they put them up there. And that's not the half of it, sir."

"Oh?"

Graff's eyes darted to Bobby. "Not sure the boy should hear, sir."

Winter winced. They were in front of her tent, in the midst of the Seventh Company camp. No one was obviously listening, but she had no doubt a dozen ears were pricked up nearby.

"Corporal Forester is a soldier like the rest of us," Winter said, a bit too loudly. "In spite of his *age*."

"Yessir." Graff swallowed. "Well, begging your pardon, sir, it seems that the grayskins cut the . . . ah . . . equipment off them, stuffed it in their mouths, and left them to bleed out."

"Equipment?" Winter said. She had an image of saddlebags or bandoliers.

"Cocks," Bobby said flatly.

Graff, turning a little red, nodded. "Give-Em-Hell is goddamned furious, I heard. He said he was going to take his whole command to find the bastards that did it and give them the same treatment."

"Which I'm sure is just what they want," Winter said. "Hopefully Captain d'Ivoire or the colonel will have better sense."

"The colonel will," Graff said. "He's a cold bastard, that one. Looked up at those poor men and never said a word. It was the captain who finally got 'em cut down and seen to."

Folsom jogged up, straightened, and saluted Winter, who as usual had to suppress the urge to look over her shoulder for an officer.

"Orders from Captain d'Ivoire," the corporal said. "Break camp and prepare to march."

There was a chorus of groans from the unofficial listeners all around. The recruits had rapidly picked up a bit of the cynicism of the Old Colonials, and they'd been hoping that the brutal murder and mutilation of a half dozen men meant they might get a respite from the day's march. Winter's voice cut through the curses.

"You heard him! Get moving!" As the complaining men got to their feet and the camp started to bustle around her, she leaned close to Folsom. "Can you take care of Feor?"

The big corporal gave a quick nod. Winter had tipped one of the carters to let the Khandarai girl ride with the water barrels, and Folsom delivered her there every morning swathed in a spare army greatcoat. It wasn't the best arrangement, but with the captain's new directives that no surplus baggage or personnel was to accompany the column, it was all that Winter had been able to come up with.

Feor didn't seem to mind. Since the night of the fire, she barely seemed awake. She walked when she was led, ate and drank when food was put in front of her, and when left alone curled into a ball and lay motionless for hours. It was as though something inside her had shattered after her confrontation with Mother, and nothing Winter did could reach her.

Folsom saluted again and went into Winter's tent to fetch the Khandarai girl. Graff followed him with worried eyes, then looked back at Winter.

"You think we'll catch them?" he said.

Winter blinked, distracted. "Catch who?"

"The Desoltai." Graff pitched his voice low. "Only I heard some of the Old Colonials saying that nobody can catch them, not now that we're into the desert. They know every rock and hidden spring, and they've got magic as well. And then there's the Steel Ghost."

"Let me guess," Winter said. "You heard this from Davis?" That sort of malingering sounded like the sergeant's style.

"No, sir. Someone in the Fourth. Apparently Captain Roston shares those opinions."

"The colonel can catch them," Bobby said. "If anyone can."

Graff looked worried. "But what if no one can?"

Winter clapped him on the shoulder. "Then we're in for a long march, aren't we?"

The scouts they'd found without their manhood were the first evidence of the viciousness of the Desoltai, but far from the last.

Every day, Give-Em-Hell took his cavalry out to screen ahead of the column, their sturdy Khandarai-bred mounts struggling over rocks and sand. Every evening, they returned to camp empty-handed, and fewer in number than they'd been when they set out. And every morning, the missing men were discovered just outside the camp, having expired from whatever tortures the endlessly inventive Desoltai raiders had dreamed up for them.

By the fourth day Give-Em-Hell was mad enough to scream at the colonel when he once again turned down the cavalryman's request to ride out in a body after the "cowardly scum." Colonel Vhalnich bore the verbal assault calmly, in full view of half the First Battalion, then told the captain that he and his cavalry were relieved from their scouting duties and would henceforth ride in the center of the column, protecting the baggage.

In their place, Captain d'Ivoire ordered infantrymen to patrol by half companies, in order to prevent any more isolated disappearances. This meant the unlucky troops who'd drawn the job had to wake up hours before dawn and start walking, creating a buffer between the main column and the desert raiders who waited invisibly among the rocks all around them. The Seventh Company made such a patrol on the sixth day, and Winter fully expected a horde of enemy riders to suddenly materialize and massacre the lot of them. It was easy, especially in the predawn darkness, to people every crevice and shadow with watching eyes.

What actually happened was worse, in a way, although it happened on someone else's watch. A company of the Second Battalion, walking a mile in front of the plodding column, surprised a gang of Desoltai watering their horses from a tiny rock spring. Eager for vengeance, the Colonials rushed after them, only to find all the nearby boulders sprouting armed men. Out of forty men, only nine escaped, and the screams of those who'd been unfortunate enough to survive echoed over the camp until well into the night.

The next day, the captain issued orders that the patrols were not to engage the Desoltai under any circumstances, but rather to fall back from any contact until more forces could be brought up. This kept the infantry patrols out of ambushes, but made great sport for the Desoltai, who rode up in twos and threes to fire a few shots and watch the entire column grind to a halt as the lead battalion started deploying for battle. The rate of march slowed to a crawl, which meant that those soldiers in the center and rear of the army spent most of the day standing idle under the blazing sun. April had worn into May, and the days were steadily warming toward the unbearable furnace of the Khandarai summer.

Ten days out from Nahiseh, the Colonials camped in the lee of a massive rock formation. The desert was changing as they marched farther west, Winter had noticed. The rocks were getting bigger, but also farther apart, and the stony ground underfoot was drier and sandier with every passing mile. Dunes had appeared, drifted against the rocks like huge gray snowbanks, and when the wind came up the men had to fasten handkerchiefs across their faces to keep their mouths from filling with flying grit.

Like the rest of the army, the Seventh had dispensed with tents. Setting the pegs was nearly impossible, since the ground was either too hard or too loose, and the effort of erecting the canvas was too much for the increasingly exhausted men. Winter hadn't changed clothes in days, and her undershirt was stiff with dried sweat and chafed her raw where it was tightly bound. Worse, most of the men in the ranks had at least a week's growth of stubble, since there was no water to spare for menial tasks like shaving, and she was starting to worry that her smooth face would be commented on. Bobby, at least, was young enough that she could still pass for a beardless boy.

Even campfires had grown scarce. What wood there was, gleaned from the pitiful local vegetation or carried on the carts, was reserved for cooking fires. For warmth, the troops had to make do with horse and ox dung, which they now collected and hoarded like gold. It burned well enough, but Winter found the smell cut through even the congealed stink of her own unwashed body, and she hadn't bothered to kindle a blaze.

The neat lines of the tent city at Fort Valor, much less the barracks at Ashe-Katarion, seemed like a distant dream. Winter lay on her bedroll, with a thin sheet across her middle and her pack for a pillow, amidst a crowd of increasingly ragged men who'd simply thrown down their things wherever they finished their march. The men of the Seventh gave her a bit of extra room, as a nod to her rank. She wished they wouldn't. It made her feel alone under the great river of stars that blazed overhead. As she stared skyward, the sounds of the camp seemed to fall away around her, leaving only a silence as profound as if she were alone in the world. Her hands clutched the edge of the bedroll to keep from falling *up* into that vast, endless ocean.

She thought about Jane. The dreams had left her, as though they knew that she had enough to deal with. Or, her traitorous mind supplied, perhaps they'd simply *abandoned* her in the end. She tried to call Jane's face to mind, but all she could summon was a pair of green eyes, shining from within like the stars overhead. She remembered the warmth of Jane's body, sweet and soft, pressed against hers, but all that did was make her feel the cold more keenly. She wrapped the sheet tighter around herself and shivered. How it could be so hot by day and still *cold* at night Winter never understood.

The *crunch* of sand beneath a boot made her heart jump wildly in her chest. The colonel had ordered a double line of pickets to defend the encampment, but there were still rumors that the Desoltai could get through, worming their way like shadows across the bare rock or blowing in with the sand. Every morning, they said, men were found dead with a single thin dagger wound to the heart, while all those around them had seen and heard nothing. Winter wasn't sure she believed it, but she wasn't sure she didn't, either.

"Winter?" It was Bobby's voice, a low whisper, as though she didn't really want to be heard. "Are you awake?"

Winter sat up. Bobby was visible only as an outline against the stars.

"Sorry," the corporal said. "I couldn't get to sleep, and I thought . . ."

"It's all right." Winter looked up at Bobby, but she couldn't make out the girl's expression. "Is something wrong?"

"I don't know." Bobby held one arm awkwardly, gripping it with her other hand. "I cut myself earlier today, when we were climbing over those rocks."

"Badly?" Winter said. "Do you want me to have Graff look at it?"

"No," Bobby said. "That's just it. It's . . . gone. When I unwrapped my sleeve to have a look, there was a little blood, but the cut was just gone. It hadn't been five minutes."

"Oh." Winter looked into the darkness toward where Feor was sleeping. The Khandarai girl was invisible, too, huddled miserably under her sheet.

"I looked at it under the lamp," Bobby went on. "The skin is there, but it looks—odd. Like . . ."

"I know," Winter said hurriedly, not sure who was listening. She lowered her voice to a whisper. "In the morning we'll ask Feor. She has to know *something*."

Bobby nodded miserably. Watching her, silhouetted against the carpet of stars, Winter found herself wondering how she could ever have mistaken her for a man. She was so *small*, slender-necked and thin-shouldered. With her head bowed and her shoulders hunched, she looked like a little girl trying to hide her tears. She was shaking, Winter realized.

"Bobby?" Winter ventured.

"It's c-cold," Bobby said, arms wrapped tight against her chest. "During the day it was so hot I thought I was going to die. How can it be cold?"

Winter shook her head. Then, impulsively, she extended her hand and took the girl by the arm, drawing her closer. Bobby looked up, startled.

"Come on," Winter said. "Old soldier's tradition, huddling together for warmth on cold nights. I read that when Farus the Fifth fought the Murnskai, whole companies would pack themselves tight to keep from freezing." Winter smiled. "I always had trouble picturing that. A hundred big sweaty *men*, with the ridiculous mustaches they wore in those days—have you seen the paintings? The smell must have been awful."

Bobby gave a weak chuckle. She folded her legs underneath her and sat on the ground beside Winter's bedroll, and Winter put an arm around her shoulders.

"Mind you," Winter said, "I can't imagine I'm any better off at this point."

"Me, either," Bobby whispered. "I think I'd happily kill for a bath."

"A nice hot bath," Winter agreed. "Did you ever have bath duty at the Prison?"

Bobby made a face. "All the time. We hated it. Scrubbing all those tiles."

"After a while I started looking forward to it." That had been after Jane had initiated her into the joys of not doing as she was told. "I mean, nobody ever *checks* to see that the tiles are scrubbed, and the doors locked from the inside. I would mix up a big batch of soapy water, for the smell, then just fill one of the tubs and soak for hours."

"Really?" Bobby giggled. "Did you ever get caught?"

"Not once. Mistress Dahlgren once complimented me on my attention to detail." Winter squeezed the girl's shoulder. "Come on, I'll shove over."

The bedroll was not really large enough, and Winter let Bobby have most of it, but she didn't mind. And it *was* warmer, especially once Winter had twitched the thin blanket over them. Bobby's body was tense against her, like a taut bowstring, and still shook with occasional shivers. Winter took the girl's hands in her own and found them ice-cold.

For a long time they lay in silence. Bit by bit, she felt Bobby relax, uncurling like a clenched fist as the shared heat warmed her. Winter let her eyes close, and found herself on the point of drifting off.

I wonder what they'll say when they find us in the morning. She couldn't bring herself to care.

"Winter?" Bobby said. "Can I ask you something?"

"Only if I can ask you something, too."

"Fair enough. You go first."

"What's your real name? You know mine."

There was a pause. "I've always been called Bobby," she said finally. "But it's short for Rebecca, not Robert. And Forester was my mother's last name. I never knew my father."

"Oh. That's convenient. At the Prison they called me Farusson, but that's just the family name they give to orphans. I got Ihernglass from a book."

"It's a good name," Bobby said. "Makes you sound soldierly."

There was another pause.

"You wanted to ask me something?" Winter prompted.

"I just . . ." Bobby hesitated. "I wanted to know the truth. About how you escaped. I've heard a hundred stories, but none of them sound *right*."

"Oh." Winter swallowed hard. "That's a bit of a long story."

Bobby wriggled, pressing against Winter a little tighter. "I'm not going anywhere."

"I don't . . ." Winter trailed off, leaving a gaping silence. She felt a little tension return to Bobby's shoulders.

"You don't have to tell me if you don't want to," the girl said.

Winter blew out a long breath. "It's not that. It's just that I've never told anyone."

"Of course not," Bobby said. "Who else would understand?"

That was true, Winter reflected. She was unlikely ever to meet another graduate of Mrs. Wilmore's peculiar institution. She certainly never intended to return there. But forcing herself to speak still took an immense act of will, as though she were stripping off a final layer of armor in the face of enemy fire.

"There was a girl," she said, "named Jane. She was brought to the Prison when I was fourteen, or maybe fifteen, I don't remember. At the time I was—well, not a model prisoner, but not far from it. When I first saw her—"

"How long had you been there?" Bobby interrupted.

"Since before I could remember. I couldn't have been more than six when I arrived."

"How wayward could you have been at *six*?"

"They throw little girls in there when their parents have been bad," Winter said darkly. "I assume my father was a criminal of some sort. Or my mother, I suppose."

"I see." Bobby shifted against Winter's side. "All right. You met a girl named Jane."

"We didn't get along at first." Winter smiled, invisible in the darkness. "She was a hellion. Tried to escape three times in the first month, and the third time she bit one of the mistresses. Mrs. Wilmore whipped half the skin off her back for that. God only knows how I got to be friends with her." Winter could barely remember how it had happened. She and Jane had come together like a pair of magnets, propelled by some strange internal forces. "But I did. We were . . . close."

There was a pause. Winter swallowed.

"Do you know what happens to girls from the Prison when they get too old?" she said, after a moment.

"If they're reformed enough, they get married," Bobby said. "Or else they get sent off to Murnsk to take holy orders."

"Married," Winter said, pronouncing the word with distaste. "That's one way of putting it. Do you know how that actually happens?"

Bobby shook her head, her smooth cheek pressed against Winter's shoulder.

"When some farmer out in the country needs a new wife for himself or one of his sons, and doesn't want to go to all the bother of courting a girl, he sends a letter to Mrs. Wilmore. She writes him back with the . . . the *stockbook*, who's ready for marriage and each girl's disposition, and the farmer chooses the girl he likes as if she were a side of beef in a market stall. Then he comes and picks her up."

"Oh." Bobby was quiet for a moment. "What if the girl says no?"

"She doesn't have a choice. The Prison is a royal institution, which means that we're all nominally wards of the king. Until we're of age he can give away our hands to whoever he likes. Not that most of the girls would think of saying no," Winter added bitterly. "Most of them look forward to it."

Another pause. Winter cleared her throat.

"In any case. Jane was a year older than me, and a man named Ganhide decided she would be ideal. He was a real brute, bigger than Folsom and meaner than Davis. When we heard about it, Jane and I decided we had to run away."

Jane had tried to run away before, of course. It wasn't really very hard to get out, but the problem was *staying* out. Everyone within a hundred miles knew Mrs. Wilmore, and that she paid a bounty on runaways. And even if a girl could get to the city, without a proper identity all she could ever be was a thief or a whore, and that would land her right back at Mrs. Wilmore's, or worse.

Winter took a deep breath. "Jane came up with a plan to run away and stay away. She was always the one with the plans.

"Only Mrs. Wilmore was one step ahead this time. They knew Jane would try something, so they locked her up. It took me ages to find out where they were keeping her, but I managed to get to an outside window. It was behind the old building, you know, with all the brambles?" Winter shook her head. "I tore my dress half to pieces."

"I once chased a fox in there," Bobby said. "I lost a shoe and never did find it again."

"Jane had a plan," Winter went on, "as usual. She told me how to sneak in through the kitchens, and where she thought the proctors would be. And she told me"—Winter's throat grew tight—"to pick up a knife, one of the big ones, while I was there."

"Why?"

"In case I ran into Ganhide. He was due in that evening, you see. There was a rumor going around that Mrs. Wilmore had promised him his 'wedding night.' The other girls were *laughing* about it." Winter's hands clenched into fists. "I told her that if I found him, I'd . . ."

"Take the knife," Jane said, as though instructing a friend in how to carve a roast. "Put the point of it about here"—she raised her head and put a finger on her throat, just under her chin—"and press in, upward, as hard as you can."

"What happened?" Bobby said.

"I found the knives in a locked cabinet, but I broke it open with the back of a ladle. It wasn't hard getting into the main building after dark. There were hardly any lights, just a candle here and there so the proctors wouldn't break their necks when they did their night rounds. Jane had gotten nearly everything right, except—"

"Ganhide was there?" Bobby said in a strangled squeak.

Winter nodded. "Right in front of her room. He must have only just arrived. He was trying to unlock the door. I think he was drunk. When I saw him, I must have made a noise, because he turned around. He was *right there*, right in front of me, stumbling and half-blind in the dark. It was like he was offering me his throat, and all I had to do was reach up . . ."

Winter's fingers had gone very tight on Bobby's arm. It must have been uncomfortable, but the girl made no complaint.

"I couldn't do it," Winter said, after a long silence. Her eyes were closed, but she could feel the tears leaking through. "I just couldn't. I've thought about that moment a thousand times since then. I couldn't bring myself to kill a man, a brute who was going to take my best friend and . . ." She swallowed. "And then I came *here,* and since then I've killed God only knows how many people just because they were fighting on the wrong side, people who probably had families and children who cared more about them than anyone ever did about Ganhide. It doesn't make any goddamned sense."

There was another, longer pause. Bobby, finally stirring from her silence, whispered, "What actually happened?"

"What?" Winter blinked away tears. "Oh. I dropped the knife, and it clattered on the floor and I got scared and ran for it. He didn't get a good look at me, so nobody ever found out. But the next day he took Jane off and I never saw her again. I couldn't even watch when they led her out of the building. I just hid in my bed and cried."

"That's horrible."

"I thought so at the time." Winter closed her eyes again. "But it was nothing out of the ordinary, really. I mean, there are hundreds of girls in the Prison, and most of them go on to marry someone. They probably all have . . . friends who are broken up when they leave." In the darkness behind her eyelids, two points of green light stared at her. *Can you be haunted by someone who isn't dead?*

They lay in silence for another interval. Eventually, Winter cleared her throat. "Sorry. That's not really the story of how I escaped, is it?"

"You don't have to go on if you don't want to."

"To be honest, the rest of it isn't much to tell. Jane and I had planned everything, and a couple of friends of mine helped out. I put together a knapsack, climbed the fence, and spent two very hungry weeks walking through fields and stealing food where I could. Eventually I got to Mielle, where I knew the sergeants recruiting for Khandarai service sometimes came. I made myself up as a boy so I could work on the docks, and made a little money. When the sergeant did come by, I told him I'd run away from my father because he was a drunk, and gave him everything I had to take me on without proper papers. I nearly got caught on the crossing, but—"

"Shh," Bobby hissed.

She rolled over, and suddenly they were face-to-face, only inches apart. For a single frozen moment, Winter thought Bobby was going to kiss her. Her protest froze in her throat.

The corporal sat up, tossing the sheet aside.

"I heard someone moving," she said.

"Someone getting up to take a piss," Winter mumbled, still slightly in shock. "Or have the Desoltai finally come to slit our throats?"

"Feor," Bobby said. "Where's Feor?"

Winter rolled over herself. The other bedroll was empty. She looked up, and just caught sight of a slim figure moving cautiously through the tangle of sleeping men. Winter surged to her feet, kicking the blanket off, and swore viciously. Then, with Bobby just behind her, she set off in pursuit.

"She can't have gone this way," Bobby said. "The sentries would have stopped her."

"We'd have seen her if she doubled back," Winter said. They'd lost sight of the Khandarai girl as they'd approached the edge of the fitfully lit camp. Feor moved easily over the sandy ground and past the sleeping soldiers with more grace than Winter would have given her credit for. "Besides, the sentries will be looking out, not in."

"But there's nowhere to go!" Bobby said. "It's just rocks and sand."

"God only knows what she's thinking, but we'd better find her. The guards will probably shoot her if she tries to get back in."

With more confidence than she felt, Winter walked through the ring of empty ground that separated the camp from the ring of guards. No doubt it would have been possible to slip between the sentries, as Feor apparently had, but she preferred not to risk it. Creeping around outside the sentry ring was a good way to draw a shot in the back. Instead she picked out the closest guard and headed in his direction, calling out when she judged he was in easy earshot.

"Coming out!" she told him. The man, a soldier from Captain Roston's Fourth Battalion, turned around with a belligerent glare. This faded when he got a good look at Winter. After the incident in the barracks at Ashe-Katarion, she'd made a point of having the lieutenant's stripe sewn onto her uniform. The sentry saluted stiffly.

"Sir!" he said. "I'm sorry, sir, but my instructions are that no one is to leave the camp."

"Good man," Winter said, trying to bluster. "That's the problem, in fact. One of mine has gone wandering off this way. Have you seen him?"

"Seen him? No, sir. No one has gone through."

"We'll just be going out to have a look for him," Winter said.

The guard hesitated. By the slump of his shoulders, he was nearing the end of a long shift, and wanted nothing more than to seek a few hours' sleep in his bedroll before morning. Still, orders were orders.

"You must be mistaken, sir. Respectfully. If he'd come this way, I would have seen, and—"

"He might not have come past your patch," Winter said, trying to let the man off the hook.

"But my orders—"

Bobby spoke up. "So you let the lieutenant through, and make sure to note it in your report."

The sentry sagged, apparently satisfied with this compromise. "Yessir. Be careful, sir. Plenty of Desoltai crawling around out there."

"Thank you. We won't be going far." *I hope.*

When they'd passed beyond the ring of sentries, Winter risked a smile at Bobby. "Thanks. Has anyone ever told you that you'd make a good sergeant?"

Bobby patted her stomach. "Haven't got the gut for it, sir. As I understand it, a sergeant's got to be able to drink any man in the company under the table."

Winter laughed. As they hiked on, though, her smile faded. Her eyes were slowly adjusting to the darkness, and the brilliant march of stars overhead provided at least a modicum of light, but the landscape was still a mass of looming rocks and deep shadow.

"We'll never find her in this," she said. "If she's gone to ground somewhere . . ."

Bobby pointed to a rock outcropping a few hundred feet ahead. "Up there. We should be able to get a good view."

"Right." They started walking again. "Do you think there really are Desoltai out here?"

"Could be, sir. We know they watch us pretty closely."

"Are you armed?"

Bobby was silent for a moment, as though she hadn't considered that point until now. "No, sir."

Winter grimaced. She hadn't even thought to snatch up her belt knife. For a moment she wished she'd been a little slower to follow, or had paused to round up Graff and a few reliable men. There was no helping it now, though.

"Best to stay quiet, then," she whispered. Bobby nodded.

By the time they reached the crest of the little mound of rocks, Winter was surprised to find that she could see quite a distance. Away from the torches and low-burning fires of the camp, the cold brilliance of the stars seemed to fill the world, and they drew gleams from the rocks and painted the sand blue-white. She hoisted herself up onto a low boulder and scanned slowly in a circle, looking for movement.

"Anything?" Bobby hissed.

"I'm not sure." Winter blinked as something caught her eye. She scrambled down again and pointed. "Look over there."

Bobby followed her finger. Another hill, a good half mile off, was a looming black shape against the skyline. The corporal started to ask something, but Winter waved her into silence, waiting. Then light blossomed again, very briefly. A flash of orange-yellow, campfire light, looking like a firefly at this distance. It flickered once, twice, then again after a short pause, and then went dark.

"That looked almost like musket fire," Bobby said.

"No," Winter said. "We'd have heard the shots by now. Besides, musket fire is a bit pinker."

"Think it's the Desoltai?"

"It has to be. They've probably got their campfires screened off somehow." It sounded like a desert nomad trick. "They're a long way off, thank God."

"Not that far," Bobby said. She peered into the darkness. "There's a little hill over that way. I bet they're on top of it."

Winter squinted, but she couldn't make anything out through the shadows. "You've got good eyes."

"Not really," Bobby said. "I've always—" She paused, and stiffened. "There's someone out there. Heading for the Desoltai."

"So they really are spying on us at night?"

"I don't think so," Bobby said. "A Desoltai would be mounted, wouldn't he?"

"Probably." Winter glanced at Bobby in alarm. "You don't think—Beast's Balls, of course it's her. Come on."

Bobby fell behind briefly as Winter scrambled down the rocky slope, moving dangerously fast in the dim light, but quickly caught up when she reached the bottom and started running across the sandy ground.

"What the hell does she think she's doing?" the corporal managed, as she drew alongside.

Winter grimaced. "I think I'm getting the idea."

She'd started running on pure instinct, without any kind of a plan other than a vague hope that she might intercept Feor before the girl reached the hill. It quickly became apparent that this was not going to happen. By the time she and Bobby had crossed the flat ground between the two promontories, Feor—even Winter could see her now, a moving shape against the larger darkness—had started clambering up the slope toward the spot where they'd seen the light.

Winter cupped her hands to call out, then thought better of it and kept running.

They were only twenty yards away when a patch of shadow unfolded from the lee of a boulder and took hold of Feor by her still-splinted arm, hauling her off her feet. The Khandarai girl's scream was piercingly loud in the nighttime stillness, and even the Desoltai was momentarily surprised, letting her go and dropping his hands to his weapons.

Winter covered the last few yards at a dead sprint and threw herself at the nomad in a shoulder-first tackle, bowling him off his feet. She'd hoped he'd crack his head on a rock, but no such luck. He grabbed her arms and started to roll her over before they'd stopped moving. Winter slammed her elbows into his ribs, twisting to try to get the leverage to bring her knee up into his crotch. Anything to keep him off balance, so he wouldn't realize he was fighting a girl half his weight. The Desoltai was good, though, squirming out from underneath her and wrenching her into a half crouch with her arms pinioned at her sides. She got a glimpse of a fierce, bearded face, eyes wild in the starlight, before his forehead met hers with a sound like billiard balls colliding at speed. Stars of brilliant pain exploded behind her eyes, and her stomach filled with bile. For a moment her vision narrowed to thin tunnels.

Bobby, coming up behind the nomad, was short on technique but long on momentum. She swung her heavy army-issue boot into the side of his head as though she were punting a handball, and Winter felt his hands spasm and let go of her arms. She collapsed to the side helplessly, her head still throbbing with violent pain. It took all her strength not to vomit. From behind her there was a brief further sound of a scuffle, and then silence.

A timeless interval of agony passed, during which Winter found herself looking forward to the Desoltai coming over to slit her throat. Eventually she heard someone calling her name, as though through thick cotton earplugs. She rolled over, fighting another wave of nausea, and saw Bobby's silhouette against the stars.

"Winter? Sir? Can you hear me?"

"I can hear you," Winter croaked. "I'm . . . I'm okay."

That was a bald-faced lie, but she felt obliged to tell it. Her hands came up to explore her face and found it surprisingly intact. The nomad's head butt had been slightly off target, or else it would surely have broken her nose. Her right eye was already puffy to the touch.

"Where'd he go?" she managed.

"Dead," Bobby said. "And Feor's okay."

Winter sat up.

The Desoltai was indeed sprawled motionless nearby. The hilt of a long knife, presumably his own, stuck up from his throat, just above his collarbone. Nearby sat Feor, huddled protectively around her injured arm.

"We have to get out of here," Winter said. She grabbed Bobby's outstretched hand, and between them they managed to get her to her feet. "Everyone for a mile around heard that scream."

Bobby glanced at Feor. "I'm not sure she'll walk, sir."

"Then we'll fucking carry her." Pain still throbbed in Winter's temples, and she could barely open one eye. "Come on."

The Khandarai girl didn't look up as they approached. Bobby prodded her shoulder cautiously, and got no response.

"What was she thinking, coming all the way out here?" Bobby looked up at Winter. "Was she trying to go over to the Desoltai? I thought they were going to kill her."

"They would. Which, I think, is what she wants." Winter switched to Khandarai. "Stand up."

"No." Feor's voice was tiny. "Leave me."

"I told you to stand up!"

When she didn't obey, Winter nodded to Bobby and they hauled Feor to her feet. She hung between them, limp as a rag doll.

"I don't understand," Bobby said. "You think she wants—"

"To die," Winter spat. "Just as her Mother ordered."

"Oh." Bobby was silent a moment. "If she's going to kill herself . . ."

"She can't kill herself." Winter gave a vicious chuckle. "Suicide is a terrible sin by Khandarai lights. But she can try to get herself killed."

"Just leave me here," Feor whispered. "If the Desoltai do not return, it will not be long before the desert takes me."

"The hell I will," Winter said in Khandarai. "I need you. We need to know what's happening to Bobby." She paused for a moment, then continued in a softer tone. "Besides. Your brother gave you your life back, didn't he? Are you going to throw that away?"

"I . . ." Feor choked back a sob. "He should not have done that. It was not proper."

"Who cares what's proper? You're really ready to roll over and die just because some old woman told you to?"

"She is our Mother," Feor said. "We *sahl-irusk* would not live at all, except by her grace. She provided us with our lives, our purpose. We owe her everything."

"Just because she gave you a place to live doesn't mean she *owns* you."

"It's more than that." Feor shook her head. "You are Vordanai. I do not expect you to understand."

Winter nearly spat at her. "That's right. I'm just a barbarian, and I've given my word I'll take care of you. Now am I going to have to drag you back to camp, or are you going to walk?"

Feor climbed shakily to her feet. "I will walk."

"Good." Winter turned to Bobby, who'd watched uncomprehendingly throughout the argument. "She's coming. Let's—"

She was interrupted by the shattering *bang* of a pistol at close range. Winter ducked, instinctively but uselessly, and heard the whine of the ball going wide. The shot had come from up the slope, but the flash had ruined her night vision, and all she could see against the starlight was two dark shadows charging down the hill. More obvious was the glitter of the faint illumination on drawn steel.

"Die, *raschem*!"

The lead man closed with a shout, headed for Feor. He charged right past Bobby, and Winter realized that the Desoltai must be as near-blind as she was. The corporal bulled into the raider as he passed, pushing him sideways off his feet. She managed to get her hands around his wrist, keeping his sword out of the way, but he grabbed her shoulder and pulled her down to meet a vicious knee to the stomach. Bobby grunted but hung on.

Winter, meanwhile, blinked away the afterimages of the single shot and dove for the spot where the corpse of their first assailant lay. He had a sword at his belt, too, and after a panicked second of scrabbling she wrenched it free. The second Desoltai had closed in on Bobby, his own sword drawn, but he was wary of striking his comrade. He reached out with his free hand and grabbed the corporal by the back of the collar, wrenching her free and tossing her roughly to the ground.

That left the first raider stumbling backward, off balance, and Winter surged to her feet and went after him. He barely saw her coming in time to bring his blade around in a desperate attempt to parry, but Winter threw the whole weight of her body behind the thrust, wielding the curved Desoltai weapon like a lance. It struck the raider high in the chest and sank half a foot of steel in him, and he went down without a sound. His own weapon dropped from nerveless fingers, and Winter abandoned hers and snatched it up.

She looked up in time to see Bobby on her feet again, backing away from the other Desoltai. He advanced cautiously, burdened by some kind of heavy leather pack, but when he finally understood that she was unarmed he charged. Bobby tried a feint to one side, then dove the other way, but the raider followed with a swordsman's grace and intercepted her with a vicious overhand slash. The girl hit the ground with a spray of blood.

Winter wanted to scream, but she didn't have the breath. She came up fast behind the Desoltai. His pack blocked her from a straight thrust into his back, so she went low, swinging two-handed for his legs. The weighted Desoltai blade bit deep, and the force of the blow snapped the bone and took the leg out from under him. He fell on his face with a muffled shriek, sword spinning away. Winter wrenched her blade free and circled him, lining up carefully on the back of his neck, and chopped down hard. The blade bit deep and refused to budge, and so she let go and took a step back while the man's convulsive throes subsided.

"Shit," she said, when she had enough breath to speak aloud. Then, louder, *"Shit."* She skirted the dead man and hurried to where Bobby had fallen.

She lay on her stomach, surrounded by a dark stain on the dusty ground. Winter knelt and rolled her over, already dreading what she would see. The heavy downward cut had opened her from collarbone to navel, and the tattered edges of her torn uniform fluttered loose, already soaked in gore.

But, underneath the blood, there was something else. *Light* was seeping out, a soft white glow tinted with aquamarine, all along the cut. It spread as Winter watched, as though Bobby had starlight in her veins instead of blood. Mild at first, it swelled quickly to an actinic glare almost too bright to look at, then began to fade. Bobby twitched, arching her back, fingers scrabbling in the bloody sand; then she drew a long breath and let it out, and her body went limp. The breath caught in Winter's throat for a moment, but the girl's breathing was slow and regular, and the flow of blood had stopped entirely.

"Obv-scar-iot." Winter hadn't heard Feor approach, but the girl spoke from just behind her shoulder. "She truly has become the Guardian. I did not think . . ."

She trailed off. Winter tore a piece from Bobby's shirt and mopped carefully at the blood, until she could see the flesh beneath. Somehow she knew what she would find. Where the Desoltai weapon had done its vicious work, the flesh was now whole, the skin unbroken, but with the color and glittering black specks of marble.

"She'll be all right?" Winter asked Feor. When the girl nodded, Winter let out a shaky breath. "Will she wake up soon?"

"I do not know." Feor frowned. "She is no servant of our gods. I thought that the spell would reject her, in the end. But now . . ."

Another sound, rolling across the plain, drew Winter's attention away. It was like distant thunder, or the skirl of a company full of drummers barely brushing their instruments. She turned to look back toward the campfires of the Vordanai encampment and found that the night was alive with tiny flashes. They were white, tinged with pink, and she could already see columns of smoke rising against the stars.

"You see?" she said, to no one in particular. "*That* is musket fire."

CHAPTER TWENTY-ONE

MARCUS

Marcus woke to the faint gray light of dawn, the warmth of Jen pressed against his side, and the sound of urgent knocking at his tent pole.

"Come in," he called automatically, already sitting up and groping fruitlessly for his uniform coat. By the time he remembered he wasn't alone, the tent flap was already open. Fortunately, the figure in the gap was Fitz, who could be counted on to be discreet.

"Sir," he said, "you have to get up *now*."

Something in the lieutenant's tone jolted Marcus' mind to full awareness faster than a hot cup of coffee. Fitz never shouted, unless it was to be heard over the noise of battle, but now he gave the strong impression that a lesser man would have been screaming.

"I'm up," Marcus said, rolling off the bedroll. He found that he was naked, and started hunting for his underthings. "What's going on?"

"Desoltai. An ambush."

Marcus paused for a moment, listening. No rattle of musket fire broke the predawn stillness. Fitz, apparently reading his mind, shook his head.

"Not here. About a mile farther on."

"What the hell was anyone doing a mile outside of camp?"

"Captain Roston," Fitz said, "led his battalion—"

"Gods-damned *fucking* Adrecht," Marcus roared. "Is he—? Never mind—fill me in later. Tell the drummers to beat assembly. Have you woken the colonel?"

"The colonel's not here, sir."

Marcus blinked, then remembered his brief conversation with Janus the night before. The colonel was off on another of his wool-gathering expeditions. Of late he'd taken to spending every night outside the camp, perched on one of the rock formations with only a small escort. Marcus had complained, but Janus had been adamant. A few trustworthy men on the colonel's detail had reported that Janus did nothing but stare into the dark and occasionally make notes in a little journal.

He spent much of the day following each of these outings napping in one of the wagons, but even so the colonel had taken on the pallor and hollow eyes of someone who wasn't getting enough sleep. Marcus had undergone a similar transformation, since the responsibility of keeping the column in motion had devolved entirely on his shoulders as supplies tightened and the invisible, ever-present Desoltai raiders grew bolder. What sleep he did manage to grab was plagued by vicious dreams, and he woke sheathed in sweat in spite of the chill of the desert nights.

"Saints and martyrs and fucking Karis," Marcus swore. "Right. Assembly for the First, and find Val, Mor, and Give-Em-Hell. I'll be out in five minutes."

"Yessir!"

Fitz saluted and ducked out, letting the flap close behind him. Once he was gone, Jen sat up, the thin sheet falling away from her bare breasts. She seemed to be naked as well, although as best Marcus could recall they hadn't managed to accomplish anything the night before. His last memory was stripping off his clothes and toppling onto his bedroll, to be instantly drawn under by accumulated exhaustion.

"Stay here," Marcus told her. "I'll send someone back when I've figured out what the hell's going on."

She nodded, half-sleepy and half-alarmed. He tugged savagely at his shirt, fumbled with the buttons, and then pulled his coat on over the top. As an afterthought he grabbed his sword belt, tucked it under his arm, and stepped outside.

The sun was still below the horizon, and the heat of the previous day had long since given way to a sullen, biting chill. Marcus' tent stood alone in the midst of a sea of blue-coated men, most of whom had simply dropped where they'd finished the march without bothering to erect any canvas or undo their bedrolls. The regimental drummer was beating a steady tattoo, and the whole hive was roaring into life. Weary men clambered to their feet, grabbed their weapons, and looked for their sergeants, whose calls rose above the roll of the drums.

Fitz was waiting, his uniform spotless as always. He saluted again as Marcus emerged.

"I've sent runners to captains Solwen and Kaanos," he said. "Captain Stokes will be here in a moment."

"Good. Now tell me what's going on."

"I believe Captain Roston has walked into an ambush, sir." Fitz paused as Marcus swore again, then continued. "Our reports are a little sketchy, but it seems as though a sizable force of Desoltai engaged our pickets on the north side of camp a little more than an hour ago. Captain Roston heard the firing and rounded up as much as he could of the Fourth to 'turn the tables on them.' After that, matters were a little confused, but as best I can tell he put the Desoltai to flight and went after them."

"Whereupon they waited for him to get far enough from camp, then swooped in and cut him off," Marcus said. "Damn Adrecht, he should know better. He couldn't spare anyone to tell me what he was doing?"

He'd heard the firing, or at least it had infiltrated his dreams, but that hadn't been particularly alarming. There were skirmishes every night now, and nervous sentries were always discharging their weapons at moving shadows, desert beasts, and occasionally one another.

"Apparently not, sir. In any case, Captain Stokes sent out a patrol in pursuit. They were engaged by Desoltai horsemen, and only three men returned, but they reported that Captain Roston and his men had taken shelter in a rocky stretch and were holding their own, but that they were pinned by heavy fire from all sides."

"Damn, damn, damn." Marcus' mind whirled. Everything depended on how *many* Desoltai were out there. A small force might pin a larger one at night, but day would expose the bluff and let Adrecht's troops fight their way out. On the other hand, if they were outnumbered, their resistance wouldn't last forever. No matter how good the ground they were defending, eventually they'd run short of ammunition and be forced to either surrender or be slaughtered. *And God forbid the Desoltai have a cannon or two up their sleeves.* "Any more bad news?"

"Just one piece, sir. The cavalry reported that the Steel Ghost himself is leading the attack. Their sergeant claims to have seen him personally."

"Spectacular." If the Ghost was there in person, that meant it wasn't merely a spoiling attack. Which, in turn, meant that any effort at relief would have to go in considerable force.

He turned to find Val trotting up, with Mor close on his heels. The former looked red-faced and out of breath, while the latter, by his expression, was angry enough to spit lead.

"Have you two been apprised?" Marcus said.

"More or less," Mor growled. "Do you ever get sick of pulling Adrecht's chestnuts out of the fire?"

"The thought has occurred to me," Marcus admitted. "But there are at least six hundred men out there with him."

"Right." Mor blew out a long breath. "So what do we do?"

"I'm taking the First and the Third out in support. In the meantime, Val, set up a line here at the camp with the Second and the artillery. Once we break through to Adrecht, we'll fall back on you and see how the Desoltai like the taste of canister."

Val's expression was sour. "Has it occurred to you that this could all be a trap?"

"It was a trap," Mor said, "and Adrecht walked right into it."

"This is the Steel Ghost we're dealing with," Val said. "There may be more to it than that."

Marcus raised a hand to cut off the debate. "I've thought about it, but we haven't got any choice. We can't just leave the Fourth."

"I know, damn it," Val said. He ran his fingers along his pencil mustache, smoothing the ends. "It just feels wrong. I can't put my finger on it."

"This whole damned trek feels wrong," Mor said. "Where the hell is the colonel, anyway?"

"Out doing whatever it is he does at night," Marcus said, without trying to disguise his bitterness. "Which reminds me. Val, find him and bring him in. He's got an escort, but we don't want the Desoltai stumbling across him."

"Right. What about Give-Em-Hell?"

"Keep him here with you, in case they try some sort of wide swing."

Not that the handful of cavalry troopers remaining would help much in that event. Marcus felt a pit yawning open in his gut. There were too many variables, too many things that might go wrong, and far too much he didn't know. He kept picturing Janus, one eyebrow slightly raised, gray eyes impassive.

"And that *was your response, Captain? Interesting . . ."*

Fuck him. Marcus ground his teeth. *He's not here when we need him.*

"Well?" he said to Mor and Val. "What are you waiting for?"

⋆

The spit and crackle of musketry as they approached was comforting, since it meant that the fighting wasn't over. Marcus had fumed and sweated as the First Battalion formed up east of the camp, faster than they ever had at Fort Valor but still far too slow to suit him. They'd marched out in column as the Third mustered behind them, while the Second and the Preacher's guns started creating a defensive line at the edge of the encampment.

There was no road to follow, but it was obvious enough which way Adrecht had gone, even without the reports from the scouts Fitz had interrogated. The sandy ground was marked by the passage of hundreds of pairs of boots, and here and there bodies had been left behind by both pursuers and pursued like a trail of bread crumbs. There were no wounded, though, which Marcus found ominous. It meant Desoltai riders had combed the area after boxing Adrecht in, as far back as the site of the initial ambush.

When the rocks came into view, Marcus could see that the story Fitz had heard from the survivors had left out a few details. He'd pictured a single hill of boulders, with the Desoltai crouched in the rolling badlands beyond it. Instead, three high promontories dominated a sprawling field of jagged, broken rock, forbidding in the shadowy half-light and shrouded by gunsmoke. The shots came in ones and twos, not coordinated volleys, and he could hear the distant shouts and screams of hand-to-hand fighting.

Saints and martyrs. Marcus' heart sank. The rock field was a commander's nightmare, with vision restricted to a few yards in any direction and no chance of maintaining control over his men. He felt a flare of anger. *How the hell did Adrecht let himself get stuck in there?*

He turned to Fitz, who waited at his side as always. "Any thoughts?"

"That's not going to be fun, sir."

"There's an understatement." Marcus looked over his shoulder. He could see the dust cloud raised by the Third, perhaps ten minutes behind him. "Send someone to Mor and have him form up on the edge of this crap to make a rally line. We're going in. Two-company front, reserve companies just behind the leaders."

"Yessir!" Fitz saluted and hurried off.

For once, things went the way the tactics manual said they ought to. It was impossible for Marcus to keep close track of the battle once his men had vanished into the rocks, but he could see the rising smoke and hear the echoing cracks of musketry. One set of flashes marked the progress of the First, while renewed activity from the central hills meant that the Fourth had seen the attackers.

Each pair of companies made a little bit of progress, order dissolving as they closed with the Desoltai among the rocks by a series of rushes. Eventually they would stall as individual soldiers ran out of stamina or courage and sought cover. Then the next pair of companies, still fresh, would rush past them and repeat the process. In the face of determined opposition it was a recipe for a bloodbath on both sides, but judging by the rate of progress, the Desoltai were falling back before the action got too hot.

Mor's Third Battalion was forming up behind Marcus as he fed the last pair of First Battalion companies into the fray. Mor himself clambered down from his big brown gelding and hurried over, eyes on the fuming mess ahead of them. Here and there muzzle flashes were visible, and soldiers in blue flitted like ghosts between the rocks and the drifting smoke.

"Nearly there," Mor said, after a moment.

Marcus nodded. "So far, so—"

Shouts from behind him were quickly drowned out by the boom of the battalion drums calling for square. Marcus turned in time to see Desoltai horsemen, not three hundred yards off, riding hard for the rear of the Vordanai formation. *Where the* hell *did they come from?*

Surprised or not, Mor's men gave a good account of themselves.

The way they formed square, if not parade-ground smooth, was fast enough to get the walls of bayonets up in plenty of time. The Desoltai saw it and sheared off well before contact, but even so a volley of musketry from the nearer face of the square sent a few of them tumbling. There were fewer of them than Marcus had thought, not more than a couple of hundred.

Something's wrong. Val had been encircled by a force big enough to keep him pinned down for hours, but Marcus' men weren't running into anything like that level of opposition.

Mor, evidently thinking along the same lines, said, "Think they saw us coming and ran for it?"

"Maybe." Marcus frowned. "Maybe they're hoping we'll get strung out on the way back."

"Hellfire. That's going to be a long march if they follow us the whole way."

Marcus nodded. Then, catching sight of a familiar figure approaching the square, he hurried over.

Men of the First and Fourth Battalions were emerging from the rocks in small groups, while their officers began the wearying process of sorting them out. Among the first to arrive was Adrecht, with Fitz in tow. The captain of the Fourth was smiling, his uniform ripped by rocks and blackened with powder grime, one empty sleeve folded up and pinned with a silver hair clip. Marcus didn't know whether he wanted to embrace the man or slug him. He settled on a nod, as though they were meeting by chance in a café somewhere.

"Well, this has been a hell of a morning," Adrecht said.

"How many of yours are still with you?"

"All of them, more or less. The bastards were bluffing us. When we went to punch out, they'd thinned the line down to practically nothing."

"That's because they want to try the same trap on a bigger scale." Marcus gestured back to the east. "They've got horsemen in behind us."

"You seem to be holding your own."

"So far. We can't stay here."

"Agreed. Now what?"

Marcus closed his eyes for a moment, thinking, and then shook his head. "We haven't got any cavalry, so this is going to be a slow business. We reorganize under cover of the square and start heading back to camp. Leapfrog-style, if we have to, one battalion in square while the other moves on." That way might take all day to cover the mile or so they had to go, but without screening cavalry of their own or artillery to drive the horsemen off there wasn't much choice.

"Fair enough." Adrecht looked almost pleased at the prospect. Marcus supposed it was better than crouching in a pile of rocks wondering if there was anyone coming to get you. "I'd better get back to my men."

"How are the losses on your side?"

"Light, considering." Adrecht pursed his lips. "A couple of small groups got cut off in the initial dash, when we thought we were chasing a detached force. Once we got to the rocks, we managed to hold them off."

Marcus desperately wanted to ask Adrecht what the *hell* he had been thinking, to go chasing off on his own, but now was emphatically not the time. He gave a curt nod instead and turned away to direct the breakout.

Maybe I won't need to dress him down. After all, assuming we get out of this, he's going to have to answer to Janus. Marcus realized that he'd crossed some boundary, without noticing. He was done with sticking his neck out for Adrecht Roston.

The first booms of the Preacher's guns sent the hovering Desoltai cavalry into full flight, and Marcus gave the order to re-form into column with vast relief. The mile from the rocks to the Colonial camp had seemed to stretch on forever, and the three Vordanai battalions had played a deadly game of cat and mouse with the Desoltai for most of the distance. Riders swooped in whenever they thought they saw an opportunity, whenever one of the three columns looked disordered or strayed too far from the covering fire of the others.

They'd made it, though, and it had been a costly game for the Desoltai. When they saw the squares had formed, too strong to crack, they always turned away, but as often as not they'd strayed into musket range and a volley emptied a few saddles. After several repetitions the desert tribesmen had lost some of their enthusiasm, and they were content to merely escort the Vordanai the rest of the way to the safety of their artillery.

Now they were in full retreat. Marcus caught sight of one party hanging behind the rest. At its head, a tall man pulled back the hood of his robe and offered Marcus a congratulatory wave. The sun, now well overhead, gleamed off a polished metal mask. Marcus stared at the Steel Ghost and suppressed a ridiculous urge to wave back. He wondered briefly if the Preacher could pick him off at this distance, but after his quick gesture the nomad leader was already turning his horse and riding back into the Desol.

Marcus turned away as well, and only then became aware of a commotion behind him. He found Val, uniform grimy with powder smoke, hurrying up with an escort of Second Battalion men. They pulled up short when they found Marcus. The men saluted, but Val was too obviously agitated to bother with formalities. One hand tweaked the end of his mustache with such force Marcus thought he was trying to pull it off.

"Good work," Marcus said. "Looks like the Steel Ghost doesn't have the stomach for charging a line of guns." He paused, feeling a sudden unpleasant premonition. Val wouldn't have gotten so grimy from a few cannon shots unless he'd been standing right next to the gunners. "What's happened?"

"I'm sorry," Val said. "I didn't know what else to do. I didn't—"

Marcus raised his voice, aware of the listeners on all sides. "Captain Solwen!"

"Sir!" Val said automatically, straightening up. His hands snapped to his sides, and his eyes seemed to clear. "You'd better come and see, sir."

"I'm sorry," Val said again, now that they were more or less alone. "They came in so fast, we barely had time to form up."

Marcus nodded slowly, surveying the devastation. Reconstructing what had happened was simple enough. The Second Battalion had formed a line facing east, at the edge of the camp, just as Marcus had ordered. They'd been waiting to intercept a Desoltai pursuit of the retreating First and Third Battalions. When a thousand desert horsemen had descended on them from the *west*, screaming for blood, they'd had only a few minutes' warning from Give-Em-Hell's cavalry scouts.

Under the circumstances, Val had done well. He'd gotten the Second into square in time, and even managed to herd most of the noncombatants and wounded into the safe interior of the formation before the Desoltai had arrived. Walls of bristling bayonets had been ready to see off the riders when they charged, if they were foolish enough to attempt such a thing.

They were not. And, Marcus was coming to understand, they had never intended to, any more than they had intended to press home a costly attack on Adrecht's force or his own. Their real target was spread before him.

Weeks of desert sun had bleached and dried the planks of the carts and wagons that followed the army until they were as dry as driftwood, but the nomads had taken no chances. Bottles of lamp oil had been flung into the bed of each vehicle, followed by blazing brands. Other squads had descended on the lines of penned pack animals, turning them loose to flee in panic from the fires and then slaughtering all they could catch. But the main blow had been delivered by a picked force, armed for the task with hatchets and heavy axes, who had gone straight for the barrels Fitz had extracted from the Khandarai wine merchants.

They'd been thorough. Fire was an uncertain weapon at best, and no doubt a few bits and pieces had escaped destruction, but the vast majority of the Colonials' supply train had been reduced to ruins while a full battalion of blue-coated soldiers stood by and watched.

"Give-Em-Hell wanted to attack," Val said dully. "I almost listened to him, but I knew what would happen. This was the Steel Ghost himself. They'd just ride away while we broke formation, circle around, cut us to pieces from behind. There were so *many* of them." He shook his head. "Maybe you could have thought of something, Marcus. All I could do was watch."

"I wouldn't have had any ideas," Marcus said. He meant it—aside from moving the supplies inside the square, which there hadn't been time for, there was nothing an infantry battalion could do against such a mobile force. He glanced at Val. "You think the Steel Ghost was here personally?"

"I saw him myself," Val said. "Leading the squad that smashed the water barrels, riding a big black stallion."

Maybe he rode around and met up with the other force before I saw him? That seemed like an awful risk to take just to taunt Marcus. Besides, he could have sworn he'd felt the Ghost's guiding hand in the feints and ambushes the Desoltai had executed in the rocks. *They say he can be everywhere at once, and move across miles in an instant . . .*

Smoke was still rising from the burning wagons, forming a thick pillar in the unmoving desert air. Here and there a dying animal thrashed and moaned, but otherwise the scene was quiet. A small escort of Second Battalion soldiers stood at a polite distance, but Marcus could feel their eyes on him. Most of the rest of the Colonials were off to the east, and no doubt Val's troops were spreading news of the disaster. Marcus could almost hear the whispers beginning already.

This is going to be bad. He tasted bile at the back of his throat, swallowed hard, and turned to Val.

"All right. First order of business is to salvage whatever we can. Get squads out looking for any animals that escaped, supplies we can still use, and especially water. We're going to need everything we can get."

Val nodded. His relief at having someone issuing orders was obvious. "Right away."

Speaking of which . . . "What about the colonel? Where is he?"

"He's safe," Val said. "He should be here in a few minutes. I sent some men to escort him back to camp, but when he saw the attack starting they decided it would be safer to wait. I had a runner just now."

Marcus didn't know whether to be relieved or apprehensive. "I'd better go and find him. Do you have a horse I can borrow?" The officers' personal horses had been strung out with the rest of the animals. Poor Meadow was no doubt lying charred on the field with her throat slit.

Val found him a horse from those that had survived the carnage, a big, unpleasant animal that seemed instinctively aware of Marcus' dislike of the equine species. He rode in search of Janus, following the vague directions that Val had given him, and before long he was giving serious consideration to getting off and walking. He was so distracted sawing on the reins to keep the stubborn animal headed in the right direction that he nearly ran over Janus' little party, who were picking their way down a rocky scarp at the bottom of a small hill. The colonel stepped smartly aside as Marcus brought his fractious mount under control and dismounted, handing the reins to a waiting soldier with great relief.

That feeling evaporated instantly as he turned to meet Janus' cool, gray-eyed stare. Marcus stiffened to attention and snapped a crisp salute, which the colonel acknowledged with a nod.

"Sir!" he said. "Have you been brought up to date on the situation?"

"I saw most of it happen," Janus said, holding up his spyglass. "I happened to have a good vantage, though I didn't have any view of the action where you went to rescue Captain Roston. Judging by the returning formations, however, I assume you succeeded?"

"Yessir," Marcus said. "The Desoltai tried to cut in behind us, but we were able to break through."

"I'm glad to see that something came of your blunder, in any case," Janus said. "Although, in the short run, it makes our task more difficult."

The colonel's tone was so pleasant Marcus wasn't certain he'd heard properly. "Sir?"

"Not that you deserve much blame," Janus went on. "Whoever commands the Desoltai clearly has a firm grasp of tactical principles, and obviously knows how to employ the advantages of his mobility and the terrain. It's not surprising that you were overmatched. No, the lion's share of the fault must of course go to Captain Roston, for taking so obvious a bait."

Marcus had thought the same thing at the time, but now he bristled. "I'm sure that Captain Roston made the best decision he could under the circumstances."

"Captain Roston is a cowardly fool," Janus said. There was no rancor in it, just a statement of fact. "I believed I could tolerate him, for your sake, but that was clearly an error, and one that reflects on my own judgment. You see, Captain, none of us escapes censure." Ignoring Marcus' stunned expression, Janus stepped away from him, looking down at the still-smoking camp. "That's something to consider in the future, however. For the present, we must work our way out of this predicament. Fortunately, we have options available to us. Have you completed your survey of the remaining supplies?"

"Ah . . . not yet, sir." Marcus was still trying to digest what he'd heard—Janus apparently blamed *him*, and Adrecht, for the whole disaster, and yet he didn't plan to do anything about it. Not "for the present," anyway. He forcibly redirected his thoughts onto a more practical path. "Captain Solwen's men are still searching the wreckage. At a guess, we'll have quite a bit of food left, but as to water . . ."

"Certainly the more problematic of the two. A man can go a week without food, but a few days without water will kill as certainly as a musket ball. I want you to organize a detail of trustworthy men immediately and collect the canteens and waterskins from the men."

"Sir?"

"We're going to need every drop, Captain, and it's going to have to be rationed. Leaving it in the hands of the rankers only assures that it will be wasted."

"Most of those men have been fighting all day," Marcus said. "They're not going to be happy about this."

"I assume they would prefer to be unhappy and alive to the alternative. Do it. Another detail needs to gather the carcasses from the horse lines and the pack train. Drain the blood and carve as much meat as can be had."

"Drain the *blood*?"

"Horse blood will keep a man alive, Captain. Among the Murnskai, a man on an urgent journey can subsist on nothing but blood and horseflesh for more than a week."

"The men *really* aren't going to like—"

Janus gave a little sigh, as though he were a schoolmaster losing his patience with a particularly slow pupil. "Captain d'Ivoire. I wonder if you fully understand the predicament that you and your *friend* Captain Roston have created."

"I know—"

"We are in the Great Desol," Janus continued, cutting him off.

"We are at least a week's march from the nearest known source of fresh water, even allowing for forced marches, and I estimate we'll have less than two days of half water rations remaining. We are surrounded by hostile forces under an extremely capable commander, who has deliberately created this situation and will certainly be standing ready to exploit our increasing weakness. If we do not act decisively, all that will remain of this army will be a pile of bleaching bones."

Marcus gritted his teeth. "What should I have done?"

"Excuse me?"

"When Adr—when Captain Roston took the Fourth after the Desoltai. What *should* I have done, if going after him was such a mistake?"

Janus blinked, as though the answer was so obvious he was astonished Marcus had to ask the question. "You should have let him go. Kept your men close to the camp, defended the supply train, and carried on with the march."

"Sacrificed the entire Fourth Battalion, in other words," Marcus said.

"Yes," Janus said. "Sacrifices are sometimes necessary to ensure the success of a campaign." His gray eyes glittered. "Besides, if you cared about the welfare of those troops, you would have allowed me to replace Captain Roston with someone more competent."

Marcus had never wanted to hit someone so badly in all his life. Instead, slowly, he saluted.

"Yes, *sir*!"

The gory work of carving and jointing the dead animals went on all through the rest of the day and into the night, with crews of soldier-butchers working by the light of improvised torches cut from the remains of wagons. Barrels that had survived the attack with only minor damage were patched and filled with steaming blood, while other teams carefully extracted the dregs from smashed containers and combined them with the water from the canteens and waterskins collected from the unwilling rankers. They still didn't have a precise accounting, but Marcus could already see it would be a pitifully small collection.

And then this. Marcus stared at the stark white paper, neatly creased, that Fitz had delivered to him under the colonel's seal. One edge was torn where he'd opened it in haste.

"He can't be serious," Marcus said dully.

"In my experience, the colonel is always serious," Fitz said.

"I know." Marcus glared, as though he could force the neat writing to change shape by force of will. *Tomorrow morning, the Colonials will continue the march northeast by north . . .*

He looked up at Fitz. "This is going to be trouble."

"The water situation?"

"Not just that. When the news of this gets out—"

The lieutenant nodded. "I've already received messages from captains Solwen and Kaanos. They want to see you."

"I'll bet they do. Go and tell them to come over, and Adrecht, too. Then . . ." Marcus hesitated, embarrassed.

"Sir?"

"See if you can find Jen," he said. It felt wrong employing Fitz on personal business, but he couldn't help it. She'd been gone from his tent when he'd returned from the ill-fated expedition, and he'd been too busy since then to find her, despite his worry. "I just need to know if she's okay."

"Of course, sir," Fitz said. He saluted and slipped out.

It wasn't long before Val and Mor arrived. The former had changed into a clean uniform and applied fresh wax to his mustache, while the latter was still in the grimy coat he'd worn in the battle. Both clutched their own copies of Janus' orders. Mor waved his in Marcus' face, the creased paper flapping like a broken-winged bird.

"What the hell is this?" he exclaimed.

"Orders," Marcus managed to say. He gestured for the pair to sit. Val took a cushion beside the low table, but Mor remained standing, and so Marcus had to stand awkwardly between them.

"Orders, my ass," Mor said. "'Continue the march'? We're just going on as though nothing has happened?"

"Not exactly," Marcus said. "We're changing direction—"

"We're still going deeper into the Desol! We've got maybe two days of water left, and then we'll be down to drinking blood and horse piss. And when *that* runs out we're all going to end up dead!"

"He's right," Val said. He didn't look up, as though ashamed to be agreeing with Mor. "I know the colonel is determined, but this is madness. He must give up the campaign."

"Even if we turned around now, there's no guarantee we'd make it," Marcus said.

"We can strike toward the coast," Mor said. "There's streams there, and it's only four days' march. We'll be thirsty, but we'll live if we stretch the supplies."

"Some of us," Marcus said.

"Better than none," Mor shot back.

Val smoothed his mustache with one finger. "More important, if we move deeper into the Desol another confrontation with the Desoltai is inevitable. After a few days without water, the men are going to be in no condition to fight. If we retreat, we may be able to regroup and resupply."

"Assuming the Desoltai leave us alone," Marcus said. "Do you really think the Steel Ghost is going to pass up an opportunity to annihilate this army if he has the chance?"

"So the best you can offer is that it's certain death either way, so we might as well march off the cliff?" Mor said. "Is that what the colonel told you?"

"He didn't tell me anything," Marcus said. "He *never* tells me anything, I told you. Except when I've done something wrong."

"Then why are you taking his side?" Mor said.

"I'm not taking his side!" Marcus paused. "Suppose I agreed

with you in every particular. What am I supposed to do about it?" He gestured at the folded paper. "Orders are orders."

"Only if we obey them," Mor said.

Marcus stared at him. "You don't mean that."

Mor's lip curled, but it was Val who spoke. "There are provisions for this sort of thing. In the regulations, I mean. In the event that a commanding officer is deemed to be mad, his senior subordinate can remove him from his post pending an investigation by a court-martial."

"There isn't a court-martial within three thousand miles," Marcus snapped. "Don't mince words. You're talking mutiny."

"I have a duty to the men of this regiment," Mor said stiffly, "not to get them killed to no useful purpose."

"You have a duty to obey orders. An *oath*."

"I have an oath to the *king*, and to defend Vordan. How the hell does leading my men to die in the desert serve either?"

"You don't get to pick and choose," Marcus said. "The colonel gives the orders that he decides are in the interests of the king, and we carry them out. That's *all*."

"Fine," Mor said. "Then let him come and explain to me what he's trying to do."

"He's under no obligation to do that."

"He owes us *something*."

Val cleared his throat. "It doesn't need to go that far, Marcus. What if you just tried to talk to him? He'll listen to you. He has before. Explain it to him—"

"I have a feeling that my stock with the colonel is fairly low at the moment," Marcus said. He sighed. "I'll talk to him. I was going to try that anyway. But I will *not* disobey orders. You understand? No matter how mad you think the man is. And if you try it, I will have you put under arrest for treason."

"Good," Mor said. "Then you can shoot me and spare me a slow death from dehydration."

"Just talk to him," Val said soothingly. "That's all we wanted."

"I'll talk to him." Marcus pursed his lips. "Have you spoken to Adrecht?"

"Not since the fighting," Mor said. "Why?"

"The colonel was not happy with the stunt he pulled this morning," Marcus said. "At this point, it may be better if he resigns after all."

"You really think that matters now?" Mor said.

"It matters to Adrecht. If the colonel has to force him out, and we get out of this, he'll face charges."

"I'll try to talk to him," Val said. "You worry about the colonel."

Marcus promised again that he would, and managed to usher his friends out. Soon after, Fitz arrived to report that Jen was fine and in her own tent, and Adrecht had retreated to the Fourth Battalion camp and was not receiving visitors. Sulking, Marcus decided. He sent the lieutenant off again, this time to Janus to request an audience, and settled down to wait.

"Busy," Marcus deadpanned.

"Busy," Fitz confirmed.

"What the hell is he doing?"

"I couldn't say, sir. Master Augustin said that the colonel was busy and was not to be disturbed."

Marcus shook his head, bewildered. It smelled like panic. Many senior officers in a desperate situation might deliberately shut the door on their subordinates, but it was hard to picture Janus in such a panicked state. Apart from one flash, under Monument Hill, he'd never shown any emotion more vehement than mild disapproval.

Maybe it's a plan? Marcus frowned. *Maybe it's a* test. *Maybe—no.* He would only drive himself mad thinking like that. *Maybe Mor is right after all.*

"I had another note from Captain Roston," Fitz said. "He wants you to come to speak with him."

"I'm the senior captain," Marcus groused. "If he wants to talk, he should come here."

"Yes, sir. I'll inform him—"

"Don't bother."

Marcus stood up from his cushion, legs groaning in protest. His lips were dry and cracked in the desert heat, and his throat was parched. That was nothing new, of course, but thinking of all those smashed, empty barrels brought his thirst inexorably to the front of his mind. He did his best to ignore it.

The table in front of him was covered with hastily scrawled reports, from which he'd been trying to put together some coherent picture of what supplies the regiment had left. A leather-backed map was marked with penciled circles, indicating how far they could march while the water held out and his estimate of what they could make beyond that, but Marcus would be the first to admit it was only guesswork. Mor had been right about one thing, in any event—even making it back to the coast would be difficult. *If we march any farther east . . .*

He put the thought out of his mind as he picked up his coat and emerged from his tent for the first time all day. The encampment outside bore little resemblance to the usual neat army camp town. Most of the tents had gone up in flames with the rest of the supplies, and order had decayed badly in the aftermath of the morning's fighting. Each battalion was sprawled in a rough circle, working to light fires in anticipation of the night's chill. The sun was sliding toward the horizon, and the reddening light turned the rocky ground the color of rust.

Eyes followed Marcus as he picked his way through the First Battalion troops and headed in the direction of Adrecht's Fourth. He studiously ignored the muttering in his wake, but couldn't help but notice that the recruits and the Old Colonials seemed to have separated again, like oil and water. The recruits sat around the fires, but the veterans drifted to the shadowy spaces in between, holding earnest, whispered conversations in small groups. Marcus did his best to convince himself that it didn't mean anything.

It was much the same with the Fourth Battalion. Adrecht's tent was one of the few still standing, and Marcus made his way through the scattered troops to reach it. The stares here were considerably more hostile. The Fourth was obviously aware of the blame Janus had placed on it and its commander for the morning's events, and just as obviously considered Marcus party to that decision. *I wonder if I should tell them that the colonel chewed me out as well.*

Adrecht appeared in response to his rap at the tent pole. He wore his uniform pants and a white silk shirt, one sleeve of which hung loose and empty. When he saw Marcus, he managed a smile, but his eyes were brittle.

"You wanted to see me?" Marcus said.

"Of course. Come in, come in."

Reluctantly, Marcus stepped into the interior of the tent. No candles burned, and not much of the setting sun came through the canvas, leaving the interior in shadow. Adrecht seated himself on a pile of cushions and invited Marcus to do the same. On the low table he saw a copy of Janus' order, and beside it a bottle of Khandarai wine, its wax seal already broken.

Adrecht indicated the bottle. "Help yourself, if you like. We found it while we were gathering undamaged supplies. Some ranker must have been saving it for a special occasion, poor fellow."

"No, thank you." Marcus crossed his arms in his lap and sat stiffly. "What do you want, Adrecht?"

"Just to talk." A grimace of pain flitted across Adrecht's face, and his good hand went to the stump of his arm. "God. It feels like my hand is still there, you know that? Like I've got it clenched into a fist, so tight it hurts my knuckles, but I can't make it relax. It *aches*. Does that make any sense?"

"I'm sorry," Marcus said quietly. "When this is all over, we can send you to the University. I'm sure they'll be able—"

"To grow it back?" Adrecht gave a death's-head grin.

"To do something for the pain," Marcus finished.

"Could be. It makes me wonder what happens to fellows who've had their heads cut off. Does their whole body ache like this?"

Marcus eyed the wine bottle. Adrecht, following his gaze, chuckled weakly.

"I'm not drunk, if that's what you're wondering. Just . . . thoughtful. I'm sorry."

"It's all right."

"In the morning," Adrecht said, "we're to march farther into the Desol."

"Those are the colonel's orders," Marcus said.

"Farther from any source of food or water."

"There are oases in the Desol," Marcus offered. He knew it was a weak response.

"Hidden springs," Adrecht agreed. "Which are, of course, *hidden*. Only the Desoltai know how to find them. I suppose we could always ask."

"What do you want me to say?" Marcus said. "The colonel doesn't consult me when he makes his plans."

"Did you talk to him?"

"Today?" Marcus shook his head. "He wouldn't see me."

"Did he say why not?"

"His man said he was busy." Marcus couldn't disguise a hint of bitterness.

"Busy. Well, I should hope he's busy." Adrecht picked up the bottle of wine, considered it for a moment, then took a swig. "The situation certainly calls for it."

"You've been talking to Mor and Val."

"I have," Adrecht admitted. "And to Give-Em-Hell, and the

Preacher. And the lieutenants and sergeants. To the Old Colonials."

"Performing an assessment of morale?"

"You might say that." Adrecht smiled thinly and set the bottle down. "The opinion of the camp is that the colonel is crazy."

"Mor said the same thing. We'll have to see, won't we?"

"Some of us aren't eager to find out."

Marcus chose his words carefully. "I don't think any of us are *eager*. But I don't see that we have any choice."

"A man with a weapon always has a choice," Adrecht said. "I said from the beginning that we ought never to have come out so far. Are you willing to admit now that I was right?"

"I don't know," Marcus said. "And I don't see that it matters."

Adrecht's lip curled. "What would it take, Marcus? How far does he have to go before you understand?"

"He's the colonel of this regiment," Marcus said. "He has his commission from the king and the Minister of War."

"The infallible Ministry of War," Adrecht said bitterly. "The ones who dumped us here in the first place."

"Get to the point, Adrecht."

Another spasm of pain crossed Adrecht's features. He closed his eyes, breathing deep, until it passed. Then he said, "The regiment will not march tomorrow. Not to the east."

"It's mutiny, then."

"It's common sense. You have to see that."

"Don't do this." Marcus fought to keep the desperation out of his voice. "Please."

"Tell that to the colonel." Adrecht reached for the wine again. "I was hoping you would listen to reason. Mor told me I was wasting my time."

"I'm going back to my tent," Marcus said. "In the morning, I expect the Fourth to be mustered and ready to march. You can still back away from this."

"Go, then." Adrecht swigged from the bottle and gave a crooked smile. "And keep your head down."

Marcus turned and left without another word. The men of the Fourth were still sprawled in their disheveled camp, but he couldn't help but feel an air of menace in their looks as he hurried past them. He wondered how many would follow Adrecht. How many would follow Adrecht and Mor and Val together, against this new colonel who had led them, finally, to the brink of disaster?

Janus has to be told. He'd given Adrecht until morning, but they couldn't afford to wait that long. A real mutiny would tear the regiment apart, and given their precarious position it would as good as sign the death warrant for every one of them. *We have to stop them now,* Marcus realized, and felt a sick weight settle in his gut. Adrecht would have to be arrested, and maybe Mor and Val as well. *And Give-Em-Hell? The Preacher?* That had to be a bluff. He couldn't imagine either of them going along with anything so underhanded.

Lost in thought, Marcus found his way back to the First Battalion's encampment and headed for his own tent. Three men were waiting for him outside it, Old Colonials. They saluted.

"Lieutenant Warus is inside, sir," said one wearing a corporal's stripes. "He had a message for you. Said it was urgent."

Maybe he finally got in to see Janus. Marcus gave another nod and slipped through the tent flap. Only a couple of candles and the light of the failing sun illuminated the interior of the tent, leaving it almost as dark as Adrecht's. A couple of men stood at the other end, both too large to be Fitz. The bigger of the pair stepped forward, and Marcus recognized the rotund form of Sergeant Davis.

"Sir," Davis said, with a lazy salute.

"Sergeant," Marcus acknowledged. "Where's Lieutenant Warus?"

"He's been unavoidably detained, sir," Davis said.

"They told me—"

The sound of canvas and a prickle at the back of his neck made

Marcus turn. Two of the men from outside—men from Davis' company, he now recalled—had entered. Both carried muskets with bayonets fixed, shouldered and trained on Marcus.

From behind him he heard the click of a hammer drawing back. He turned back to Davis. The second figure had stepped up beside the fat sergeant, cocked pistol in his hand.

"Sergeant?" Marcus said, with more calm than he felt. "Care to explain yourself?"

Davis smiled hugely. "I'm afraid you're under arrest, sir. Orders of Senior Captain Roston."

"*Senior* Captain Roston?" Marcus matched the man's stare. "I suggest you take that up with the colonel."

"Regrettably, the colonel has been relieved of his command, on grounds of mental unbalance."

"Don't be stupid, Davis."

"Sorry, sir." The sergeant shrugged. "It's nothing personal. I'm only following orders. Men?"

The men behind Marcus took him by the arms, and the man with the pistol lowered his weapon. Davis sauntered forward. Then, brutally fast, he buried one hamhock fist in Marcus' gut.

"That—" He bent to speak in Marcus' ear as he doubled over in agony. "That, sir, was personal."

Chapter Twenty-Two

WINTER

"Take the knife," Jane said, as though instructing a friend in how to carve a roast. "Put the point of it about here"—she raised her head and put a finger on her throat, just under her chin—"and press in, upward, as hard as you can."

The knife was in Winter's hand. Jane was naked, silken red hair cascading down over her shoulders, green eyes gleaming with mischief.

"I can't," Winter said miserably. "I can't do it."

"You did it then," Jane said. "You can do it now. Come on."

Haltingly, Winter raised her hand. The knife was a long, narrow spike of silvered steel, shining in the pale light. The hilt was cold as ice in her hand.

"Do this one thing for me," Jane said. "Just this once."

The point of the blade seemed to move of its own accord. It pressed against the hollow of Jane's throat, dimpling the skin, then raising a single drop of blood where it pricked through.

"I didn't want to," Winter said, her throat thick. "I never—"

"Shhh."

Jane's hands came up, warm around the icy chill of Winter's fingers. Gently, almost tenderly, she pressed the knife home, until their entwined hands were flush with the skin of her throat. Then she let go, and when Winter opened her fingers the knife was gone.

Blood pulsed from the wound, trickling down Jane's body in a steady stream. It pooled along her collarbone and washed down between her breasts. A crimson rivulet twisted down the smooth skin of her belly and lost itself in the thatch of hair between her legs.

"I'm sorry," Winter, swallowing a rising sob. "I'm sorry."

"Shhh," Jane said. "It's all right."

Wherever the blood had trailed, Jane's skin changed. It went pale and gray, shot through with sparkling dark veins, and shone like polished marble. The transformation spread, accelerating as patches joined together, until it was racing over Jane's body like a tide. Her hair turned to silver in a sparkling wave, and the green in her eyes widened until they were a brilliant emerald from edge to edge.

"Obv-scar-iot," Jane said, her voice resonating with a strange harmonic. "You see?"

Winter gave a weak smile. "You're beautiful."

Jane stepped forward and kissed her. Winter bent eagerly, pressing her body against the shining creature. Jane tasted of dust and centuries, like licking a statue, but her skin was warm and pliant, and her hair fell soft across Winter's bare shoulders. Jane's hand stroked Winter's flank, wandered down across the curve of her thigh, then up again to caress her sex. Winter shivered, pressing herself more tightly into the embrace, even as the cold began.

Her fingers froze first, screaming in protest and then going numb. From there it moved inward, down her arms and up from her toes. Jane nibbled playfully at Winter's neck, and behind her head Winter held up one hand and found her own flesh turning to brilliantly polished stone. Where Jane's was warm and vital, hers was as cold and dead as any statue.

It's all right. She watched the marble spread across her skin, past her elbows, onto her shoulders. Her hair frizzled as it turned to silver. Jane's warm, wet mouth kissed a trail down Winter's neck, past her collarbone, toward her breasts, and in its wake her flesh hardened to lifeless stone. Her vision dimmed as her eyes became sparkling, sightless gemstones.

It's all right. She wanted to say it aloud, but her lips were frozen. The cold pressed inward, until it finally reached her heart.

Winter opened her eyes.

The cold was still in her, colder than the worst winters at the Prison, when the fires went out and the girls shivered and slept three or four to a bed for warmth. It felt as though she were thawing from the outside in as reality gradually reasserted itself, leaving her with pins and needles racing across her skin. She could still feel the ghost of Jane's lips against her breast, and the shivery tingle of deft fingers between her legs.

Saints and fucking *martyrs.* Her heart was beating like a drummer calling the charge. *I think I preferred my old set of nightmares.*

Bobby lay beside her, huddled into the crook of her arm. They'd started out on separate bedrolls, Winter recalled, but the girl must have rolled over in her sleep. Overhead, the fabric of the tent was as dark as pitch. It was still well before dawn.

The recent past was a blur, coming as it did at the end of thirty or forty hours without sleep. From the hillside where they'd fought the three Khandarai, she'd enjoyed a panoramic view of the Vordanai encampment, and she'd watched the first blossom of musketry spread into a general engagement until smoke had shrouded the scene.

It wasn't until late in the day that Winter had dared to venture down, after Bobby had regained a groggy semiconsciousness and the sound of firing had died away. She was relieved to find that there was a camp to return to, although the destruction had obviously been extensive. In the confusion no one seemed to be concerned about her absence.

The returning First Battalion had finally gotten around to erecting those tents that had escaped the conflagration, which included hers. She'd taken Bobby and Feor inside with instructions to Graff that she not be disturbed until at least the Day of Judgment. After that, she recalled nothing but the fading echo of her dream.

She sat up cautiously, worming one arm out from under Bobby. The corporal shifted uneasily, mouth moving as though carrying on a silent argument, but did not wake. Groping past her, Winter located her trunk by feel and after some rummaging managed to find a box of matches and a candle.

Bobby was still in her uniform from the previous day, stained and dampened by sweat and grime. In the opposite corner of the tent, Feor was curled into a miserable ball, huddled around her still-splinted arm.

And what am I going to do with her? Winter sat back against the trunk, chewing her lip. She couldn't help but feel responsible for the girl, as she felt responsible for Bobby, for all that both of them had come of their own free will. In Bobby's case, she had at least the excuse of military duty. Feor she'd adopted willy-nilly, like a little girl taking in a stray cat with no thought of who was going to care for it. *But what else am I supposed to do? Let her get herself killed?*

Beside the trunk was the pack the Khandarai raider had been carrying. Winter had brought it along in the hope there would be food and water inside, but the whole of the bulky thing was taken up with an odd sort of lantern. She'd resolved to turn it over to the captain, in case he saw something important in it that she did not. *Although I imagine he has other concerns right now.*

Bobby shifted again, muttering something inaudible. Her shirt had come loose, and Winter could see a line of pale skin that glittered like polished stone in the candlelight. Winter crawled over to the bedroll to tuck the shirt back in, then hesitated. Carefully, she pulled it up a few inches, exposing the wound that had threatened the girl's life to begin with.

The marble patch was still there, still warm and soft to her hesitant touch but slick and stony to the eye. And, Winter thought, it was bigger. At least it looked bigger to her, in the uncertain light, though she had to admit that her memory of that first night was shaky.

We have to get some answers out of Feor. Was this *change* going to spread over Bobby's body? What would happen when it reached her face? Winter glared at the sleeping form of the Khandarai girl. *She must know.*

There was a knock at the tent pole, and then a harsh, urgent whisper. "Lieutenant? It's Graff."

Hurriedly, Winter fixed Bobby's uniform. Graff knew the truth of Bobby's gender, but not of Winter's, and she imagined that if he found her exploring under the girl's shirt he'd reach an unfortunate conclusion. "Come in."

He slipped through the flap, glanced down at Bobby, and looked instantly embarrassed. Winter rolled her eyes.

"Graff, if you act like *that*, everyone is going to know."

"Yes, sir," he said unhappily. "It's just . . . looking at her like that . . ." He cleared his throat. "It's hard to imagine I was ever fooled."

Winter had thought the same thing. Asleep, there was a softness to Bobby's features that belied her disguise. *Still, I didn't notice, either.* She cleared her throat.

"What's the problem?"

"Right. Sorry, sir, I didn't want to wake you, but when I saw the light—"

"I was up. What's going on?"

"It's Folsom, sir," Graff said. "He and his pickets are gone."

"Gone? What pickets?"

"While you were asleep, sir, Lieutenant Warus asked for a detail to keep watch on the captain's tent. Folsom took a few of the men who needed rest, since everyone else was out working on salvage. He was supposed to be getting off duty around now, so I went to check on him, and he's not there."

"The captain must have taken him somewhere."

"The thing is, sir," Graff said, "there *was* a guard detail on the tent, just not Folsom's."

"Then the captain dismissed him early. Have you looked around the camp?"

"Yessir. No sign of him, sir."

"Odd." Winter yawned. "I could ask the detail commander, I suppose. Did you know any of the new guards?"

"Not by sight, sir. They said they were Second Company."

Winter froze. "Second Company?" That was Davis' men. *The captain would never use* them *to guard his tent.*

"Yessir," Graff said. "As far as I know, the captain and the senior sergeant don't get along. It seemed odd to me, too, sir."

"Maybe it's punishment detail." Winter got to her feet and started pulling her uniform coat on.

"Are you going to talk to Sergeant Davis, sir?"

"No point in that." He'd only heap abuse on her. "I'll go ask the captain if he's sent Folsom somewhere."

"I'll come with you," Graff said.

"No need. Stay here with Bobby. She's had a hard day." Winter paused, then looked over to the other corner. "Make sure Feor doesn't go anywhere. I'll be back soon."

Captain d'Ivoire's tent stood in a wide circle clear of other men and equipment, as though everyone was giving it a wide berth. Winter slowed as she approached, uncertain. *Is the colonel in with him?* She could see only one sentry, a shadowed figure waiting beside the tent flap.

As she got closer, Winter recognized Buck, one of her least favorite among Davis' creatures. She felt her hackles rise. His whole posture was wrong for guard duty. He didn't look like a sentry in the middle of a friendly camp—that is, stiff in the presence of officers and otherwise slouched and bored—but rather kept looking around as though he actually expected something to happen. He looked nervous. There was a certain weasel-like quality to Buck in any case, but it was more pronounced than usual.

She paused for a moment in the shadow of a pile of salvaged ration crates, waited until Buck was looking the other way, then sauntered up to the tent as confidently as she could manage. He didn't turn back until she was only a few yards away, and his wild start was all the confirmation she needed that something was badly wrong. When he recognized her, he relaxed, and his pinched features melted into their habitual sneer.

"Hello, Saint."

"Ranker," Winter returned pointedly. "I need to see Captain d'Ivoire."

"Captain d'Ivoire is busy."

"This is urgent."

Buck's brow furrowed. "What he's busy with is urgent, too. Come back in the morning."

"If I could come back in the morning, it wouldn't be urgent, would it?"

That level of reasoning was beyond the ugly man's capacities. He fell back on a reliable standby. "I'm telling you to fuck off. Nobody goes in. Captain's orders."

"Buck!" a voice hissed from inside the tent.

"Shut up!" Buck said over his shoulder.

He turned back to admonish Winter again, but she was already walking away. She went as far as the crates, then ducked behind them, hoping that the darkness would have swallowed her. When she glanced out, she found that she needn't have worried. Buck was deep in a whispered conversation with someone inside the tent. By his wild gestures, she could tell he wasn't happy.

Now what? Folsom and the others couldn't have just *disappeared.* If the captain was unavailable, she could go to the colonel, but—

A flare of light from the flap of the tent cut her thoughts short.

Two more men emerged, silhouetted against the glow from a lamp. She recognized Lieutenant Warus, the captain's adjutant, but half his face was covered by a massive, purpling bruise. He walked stiffly, hands behind his back, and when he stumbled briefly at the threshold Winter realized he was bound.

The third man was Will, another from Davis' company. He looked as nervous as Buck. After a moment's quiet conversation, the three started moving, heading for the outer edge of the encampment. Behind them, the tent was dark and empty.

By the fucking Beast. Any kind of ordinary explanation had just gone out the window. Winter flattened herself against the crates for a moment, in an agony of indecision, then abandoned the shadows and followed the trio.

Davis' two men walked ahead of and behind the lieutenant, as though escorting a prisoner. Winter kept far enough back that she could plausibly deny she'd been following them, but for all their nerves the pair made poor lookouts, and they never even glanced in her direction.

At the edge of camp, Will stopped for a moment and lit a lamp, which he handed to Buck to lead the way. Winter hesitated as they left the last of the sleeping soldiers behind and headed out into the open Desol. It was foolhardy to go after them on her own, and she wished vainly that she'd taken Graff up on his offer to come with her. If she stopped now, though, she would lose them. She muttered a curse and followed.

They walked for a long way, and without any challenge from the sentries. When they eventually came to a halt, well outside where the sentry line should have been, she waited a long moment before stalking closer.

". . . don't like it," Will was saying.

"I don't like the whole damned thing," Buck said, and spat. "I don't like being out in this goddamned desert, and I sure as hell don't like the idea of drinking horse blood. And what I like *least* is having some fucking Desoltai son of a bitch cut my pecker off. The sooner we get away from here, the better. Getting to pop Smiley here is a side benefit."

"Someone might hear," Will said.

"Nobody out there," Buck growled. "This is our section tonight, remember? And anyway, who gives a shit whether you like it or not. You do it, or else you explain yourself to the sarge."

"I know. I'm just saying I don't like it, is all."

"Oh, by all the fucking saints. Give me the damned thing, then." Winter heard the flat *crack* of flesh on flesh. "On your knees, *sir.*"

By now she was only a few yards away. Buck had set the lantern on a flat rock, and the trio were backlit, throwing long, twisting shadows across the sands. Will stood a pace or two back, closer to Winter, while Buck forced the bound figure to its knees. He had a pistol in his left hand, while his right went for his belt knife.

God above. They're going to kill him. Winter bit her lip, hard enough to draw blood, and groped in the darkness until she found a stone a little larger than her fist. When Will turned his back on her, she charged.

He was barely taller than she was, so she aimed high, bringing the stone against the side of his head in a powerful two-handed swing that met his skull with a sick-making *crunch*. He dropped like a discarded doll, without a sound, and Winter stepped across him toward Buck. He'd taken an automatic step backward in surprise, so her desperate blow whistled a foot from his face. Before she could recover her balance, he hastily shifted the pistol to his right hand and raised it to eye level, backing farther away.

"What in all the hells—*Saint*? Is that you, you little bastard?"

Winter considered throwing the stone at him, but she didn't think she could do it before he pulled the trigger. She nodded slowly.

"What did you go and do that for?" Buck frowned down at

Will. "Will, you all right? Say something if you're all right." After a moment of silence, he cursed softly and glared at Winter. "You've killed him, you son of a bitch."

"Buck—"

"I should leave you for the sarge," he said. "He'd know what to do with a traitorous little shit like you. But we ain't got the time, not tonight. Give the good Lord my regards."

He pulled the trigger. The hammer snapped down, flint striking sparks, but they fizzled and died in the pan without triggering the shot. Buck lowered the weapon, staring at it, then looked up again in time to catch Winter coming in fast. His hand shot up above her head to block the path of the descending stone, but she let her momentum carry her forward and brought her knee up hard between his legs, then gave him a sharp elbow in the back of the head as he doubled over. He groaned and collapsed into the dirt, the pistol falling away.

"Fuck the *goddamned* Savior with a red-hot poker," Winter swore, fighting for breath. When she closed her eyes for a moment, she could still see the tiny glow of the pistol's spark. Her breath came fast and ragged.

Buck groaned again. She turned and kicked him hard in the side, then again, until he got the message and rolled over, eyes still squeezed tightly shut. Winter retrieved the long knife from his belt, then found the pistol where he'd dropped it. She examined the weapon cautiously. There was a cartridge in the barrel, but no powder in the pan; he'd forgotten to prime it.

"You always were a lazy bastard, Buck," she whispered. Setting the pistol aside again, she bent to free Lieutenant Warus.

They'd blindfolded and gagged him, as well as binding his hands, which explained his silence during the fight. When she removed the dirty cloth from his eyes, he looked around curiously, then up at Winter.

"Lieutenant . . . Ihernglass, isn't it?"

"Yessir," Winter said, and nearly saluted before she remembered she didn't have to. "Seventh Company."

"Far be it from me to question good fortune," he said, "but what are you doing here?"

"I followed these bast—these two from Captain d'Ivoire's tent."

"What were you doing there?"

"Looking for the captain. Or for you, I suppose. One of my corporals was detailed to watch the tent, but he seems to have gone missing."

"I see." He looked up at her. "Then you have no knowledge of what's going on?"

She searched his expression. "What's going on, sir?"

"It's mutiny," Lieutenant Warus said. He touched the puffy side of his face and winced. "They've got the captain and the colonel, and probably your men as well."

"Mutiny?" She could believe a lot about Davis, but that? *Not on his own hook. He's not smart enough.* "By whom?"

"Captain Roston, at least. Some of the Fourth appears to be behind him, and apparently some of our men." He looked down at the incapacitated pair. "Do you know these two?"

She nodded. "Will and Buck. From Senior Sergeant Davis' Second Company."

"Davis." Fitz gave a little sigh of disappointment, as though he'd been told he'd be late for the opera. "I suppose I should have known."

"What should we do with them?"

" 'We'?" He looked at her questioningly. "If I recall correctly, you served under Davis."

"Long enough to know that whatever side he's on is the wrong one," Winter muttered.

"I see." Fitz climbed to his feet, rubbing his hands to restore some feeling to them. He knelt to examine Will briefly. "This one is dead. I'd like to take the other with us, but I'm not sure the two of us are up to carrying him. Are there any of your men you trust?"

Dead? Winter looked down at Will. He'd never been one of the worst of Davis' lot. Not that he'd been kind to her, but he'd just gone through the motions of cruelty to fit in with the others. She hadn't meant to kill him.

"Lieutenant?"

She shook herself and took a deep breath. "Yes. I have a few."

Bobby was awake by the time she, Graff, and Fitz returned, carrying the semiconscious Buck between them. Graff told a couple of surprised rankers to sit on the man for a while, and then Winter led the lieutenant and her two corporals back to her own tent. She saw Fitz's eyes flick to Feor, still curled up in her corner, either asleep or pretending to be, but he made no comment.

"This is bad," Graff muttered. "A bad business."

"I'm afraid that's something of an understatement," Fitz said. "We don't know how much support Captain Roston has, but for the moment he seems to have the situation well in hand."

"What happened to Folsom and the others?" Bobby said.

"In the best case, they're captives," Fitz said. "Shortly after the captain left to meet with Captain Roston, Second Company men arrived at the tent with loaded weapons. I believe they took your men into custody and led them away, then left a detail behind to collect Captain d'Ivoire when he returned. From what I overheard, they plan to hold him and the colonel captive while Captain Roston assumes command."

"They were going to kill you," Winter pointed out.

Fitz touched the massive bruise on his cheek again. "I'm not certain, but I believe that Senior Sergeant Davis bears me some personal ill will. He certainly seemed . . . vehement."

"But . . ." Graff spread his hands, frowning under his beard. "Why? What's the point?"

Fitz lowered his voice. "The colonel distributed new orders to the captains this afternoon. We continue the march east, into the Desol. My understanding is that Captain Roston objected, on the grounds that our supplies were insufficient."

Winter remembered the columns of black smoke rising from burning carts, and the daylong labor of the salvage teams. She hadn't thought about their situation in those terms. "Are they? Sufficient, I mean."

"According to my estimates, we have roughly two days of water remaining, given fairly tight rationing. Food will last somewhat longer, assuming we harvest the corpses of the pack animals killed in the attack."

"Two days?" Graff blinked. "With two days left we won't make it back to Nahiseh even if we start now!"

"And the colonel wants to keep going?" Winter shook her head. "That doesn't make any sense."

"I admit that I do not understand his reasoning," Fitz said. "However, it may be that the colonel possesses private information that makes the situation more clear to him."

"Goddamn," Graff said, and whistled through his teeth.

Winter nodded in silent agreement. She'd seen the wreckage and the slaughtered pack animals, but the smoke and confusion had made it hard to assess the extent of the damage. She'd been under the impression that the Desoltai attack had been largely unsuccessful, since most of the Colonials seemed to have fought their way out of the trap.

"It's still no excuse for mutiny," she said, trying to sound more decisive than she felt. "If we lose our discipline now, the Desoltai will slaughter us."

"Of course not," Graff said hastily. "I didn't mean that it was. I just . . . didn't realize how bad things were."

"The colonel must have a plan," Bobby said.

"How many people know about the mutiny?" Winter asked Fitz.

"I'm not certain," the lieutenant said. "It doesn't seem to have become general knowledge in the camp. Davis' men, obviously, and I suspect those of the Fourth Battalion Captain Roston considers reliable."

"What about Captain Solwen and Captain Kaanos? If we go to them, could they put a stop to this?"

Fitz frowned. "It's possible. But Captain Roston must know that he can't proceed without at least their tacit approval."

"Which means there's no knowing whether he's gotten to them already," Graff said. "If we go running to them, they may just add us to the bag."

"We have to do *something*," Bobby said.

Winter grimaced. All the instincts she'd developed in two years under Sergeant Davis were telling her to lie low, let it slip by, join up afterward with whatever side seemed to come out on top. To *not make trouble*, because it would only attract attention.

But that wasn't an option, really. She had a responsibility now to the men of her company, and some of them had been taken prisoner or worse. *More to the point, if we jump the wrong way here, we're all going to die. Who seems more likely to find a way out—the colonel and Captain d'Ivoire, or Roston and Davis?* Put that way, it didn't seem like much of a choice at all.

"They haven't told the camp yet," she said. "They don't want it to look like a mutiny. The Old Colonials might stand for that, but the recruits"—she glanced at Bobby—"I don't think they'd go along. So they're doing it on the quiet instead. Grab Captain d'Ivoire, the colonel, and anyone else who might cause trouble, then make some excuse in the morning and Captain Roston takes command."

"I came to much the same conclusion," Fitz said. "Which, in turn, suggests a course of action, if you're willing."

Graff nodded. "They've got Folsom, haven't they?"

Bobby nodded as well. Her eyes were bright, almost feverish.

Winter wondered if she'd entirely recovered from what had happened on the hill. *Hell, she* ought *to be dead.*

"You think we should break them out," Winter said. "The colonel and Captain d'Ivoire, and hopefully Folsom and the others as well."

The lieutenant agreed. "Captain Roston's actions imply that he is not confident of his ability to persuade the men if the colonel is available to argue against him."

"Right." Winter frowned. "Assuming everyone is still alive."

"Yes. I suspect that depends on the extent to which Sergeant Davis is in charge," Fitz said.

"Goddamned Davis," Winter muttered. "Why did it have to be Davis?" On some level, though, it *had* to be Davis. If there was something nefarious and unpleasant going on, it was virtually guaranteed that he would be mixed up in it.

"Do we know where they're keeping the prisoners?" Graff said.

Fitz shook his head, but Winter smiled slowly.

"I bet I know who does," she said. "Just give me a few minutes alone with him."

The Fourth didn't know, Winter decided. Not for certain, anyway. The encampment seemed on edge, and the number of men awake in spite of the hour and the exhaustion of the day showed that everyone knew *something* was about to happen. But she and Graff were able to walk about in their First Battalion uniforms without being challenged. They found a good vantage point, on the other side of a fire from Adrecht's double-sized tent, and settled down to watch.

Her conversation with Buck had been disappointingly brief. He'd been left to stew while Winter and the others talked, and his bravado had been reduced to a hollow eggshell that cracked under the slightest pressure. Winter told herself that she hadn't *actually* been looking forward to cutting pieces off him, but it certainly would have been satisfying to make him think she was going to. His eyes had been full of the terror of a bully who finds his position suddenly reversed.

Unfortunately, his knowledge had been limited. The prisoners were not in the Fourth Battalion camp, which made sense—keeping them secret among so many men would be impossible—but where they were, Buck couldn't say. Most of the Second Company was still in its encampment, though, with Davis and a few other men staying close to Captain Roston. That led Fitz to propose a new plan. Winter hadn't liked it, and still didn't, but she'd been unable to come up with anything better.

Graff had chosen two dozen men from the Seventh that he thought they could rely on. Armed with muskets, knives, and bayonets, they were approaching Captain Roston's tent from the other side, with Fitz at their head. A ripple of interest in the Fourth Battalion camp, like a ship's wake, marked their path. By the time they reached the tents, Captain Roston had already emerged. From her vantage point, Winter could see him only in outline, lit from behind by lanterns.

Fitz, by contrast, was easily visible. In spite of the bruise on his face that had nearly closed his right eye, he wore his customary smile, and his salute was parade-ground crisp.

"Captain Roston!"

"Lieutenant," Roston said. If he was surprised to see Fitz alive, it wasn't evident from his voice. Winter wondered if killing the lieutenant had been his idea or something Davis had decided on his own initiative. "You seem to have injured yourself."

"Just a bad fall, sir. Nothing to worry about," Fitz said blithely. "I've just come from the colonel. He and Captain d'Ivoire request your presence for a council of war."

Captain Roston paused fractionally too long. Winter smiled in the darkness. *A hit.*

"At this hour?" he said eventually.

"New information has come in, sir," Fitz said. "Or so I understand. The colonel indicated it was urgent."

It didn't take Captain Roston long to regain his composure. "As the colonel wishes. May I have a moment?"

"Of course, sir."

Roston disappeared back into his tent. Winter could only imagine the whispered conversation going on within. So far as Roston and Davis knew, they had the colonel and Captain d'Ivoire tied up somewhere, and they certainly weren't attending any councils of war. On the other hand, Fitz was also supposed to be a prisoner, and possibly dead. Her smile widened as she pictured Davis' fat face going red with anger.

They couldn't just grab Fitz again, not here, with twenty of his own men and half the Fourth watching. It would either have to be open mutiny, here and now, or else Captain Roston would have to keep the charade going a little longer.

Winter let her breath hiss between her teeth when Roston reappeared. She'd been reasonably certain he would play along, but with Davis involved there was always a chance . . .

"Lead the way, Lieutenant," Captain Roston said, with all the appearance of affability.

Fitz saluted again. "Follow me, sir."

Winter tensed as they made their way from the tents back through the encampment toward where the colonel's empty tent stood. It wouldn't be long—Davis had never been a patient man.

"There," Graff whispered.

A bulky shadow had slipped from the unlit rear of Captain Roston's tent and taken off at a run. Winter and Graff gave him a dozen heartbeats to get well ahead, then followed.

A couple of tents, larger than the usual army issue, stood among the detritus of the wrecked, smoking wagons. During the day they'd been used as a clearinghouse for the scavenging teams and a refuge from the sun for the corporals who had to tally and record it all to produce the new supply estimates the colonel had demanded. Now that dark had curtailed these activities, the tents were abandoned, and ideal for quietly keeping prisoners. They were far enough from the rest of the camp that any noise would go unnoticed, and no one was likely to wander casually through the gruesome wreckage of the Desoltai attack.

Davis had headed straight for them, breaking into a jog once he'd left the Fourth's encampment. Winter and Graff had to hurry to keep up. When he reached his goal and ducked inside, they took shelter behind a wrecked cart and waited. After a few minutes, Winter gave a satisfied nod and turned to Graff.

"This has to be it," she said.

The corporal nodded. "It's a clever spot. I have to hand it to Captain Roston."

"Get going, then." Her eyes were still glued to the tents. There were no lights inside.

Graff hesitated. "You're sure you'll be okay?"

"I'll be fine. I'm just going to sit here and watch, in case they get any ideas about moving the prisoners."

"Right." Graff straightened up and brushed dirt from his knees. "Just stay put. I'll be back as soon as I can round up the men."

"Hurry," Winter said. "Fitz will stall Roston as long as he can, but he has to know something's wrong. We need to have things in hand here before he does anything drastic."

Graff nodded and started back the way they'd come, breaking into a run when he was a safe distance away. Winter turned her attention back to the tents, watching for any sign that Davis was bringing the prisoners out.

At least there *were* prisoners, she reflected. Buck had said there weren't to be any killings, aside from Fitz, but Winter hadn't been certain until she'd seen Davis scuttling away from Captain Roston's tents. The fact that he'd immediately gone to confirm that the colonel and Captain d'Ivoire were still in custody implied that both were still alive, which probably boded well for Folsom and the other men from the Seventh. Still, she felt a thrill of tension. *What if Davis decides now is the time to play for keeps?* She imagined an unsheathed knife and blood spilling from slit throats, and tensed herself to move at the sound of a scream. She'd promised Graff and Bobby not to do anything rash, but if Davis was going to murder the prisoners . . .

No sound came. The tents remained dark, without even the faint glow of candlelight leaking through at the flaps.

How long would it take for Graff to make it back with a squad of trustworthy Seventh Company men? How long could Fitz keep Adrecht occupied? Winter shifted uneasily and shuffled a little closer. *What the hell is Davis* doing *in there in the dark?*

A faint sound behind her gave her an instant of warning. She spun, reaching for the knife at her belt, but not fast enough. One big hand grabbed her by the wrist and yanked her forward, off balance. She felt something strike hard in the small of her back, and the stumble turned into a fall. A splinter of wood from the broken cart scraped painfully against her cheek and drew blood before it snapped. Winter struggled to push herself to her feet, but her attacker already had his boot planted between her shoulder blades, and even a fraction of his weight pressed so hard it made her fight for breath.

"Well, well, well," Davis said. "The Saint, as I live and breathe. Oh, that's *Lieutenant* Saint now, isn't it? Forgive me if I don't salute." He pressed down a little harder, and Winter whimpered. "You don't think very highly of ol' Sarge, do you? You think ol' Sarge isn't smart enough to know when he's being followed? Think he isn't smart enough to nip out the back way?"

Davis snorted. The pressure increased again and then, mercifully, relaxed. She felt him take hold of her wrists again.

"Get up," he said. *"Sir."*

Winter was all too aware Davis had muscles like steel bars under his layers of fat. She felt herself shriveling up under the mockery of his voice. For a moment she wanted nothing more than to curl into a ball, hide from him, hope he'd go away.

I can't. She struggled to her feet, then started walking as he shoved her forward. *He'll kill me now. He has to.* Her legs trembled, and not only from pain. She'd faced the Khandarai, walked to the sound of the regimental drum into a storm of fire and lead shot, but this was worse somehow. *This is personal.* She flexed her wrists, searching for an opening, but he was unbending.

Inside the tent, he transferred both her arms to one enormous hand while he struck a match with the other and lit an oil lamp. Piles of scrap wood and discarded, ruined supplies lined the edges of the tent, with only a narrow clear path in the center. Beside the one tent pole, leaning against one of the heaps, was Colonel Vhalnich himself. He was bound hand and foot, and gagged with what looked like a spare shirt. Davis glanced at him and snorted.

"You and him ought to get along famously, Saint. He's a *talker*, just like you. You know, the first time I left him here with Peg to look after him, and by the time I got back he'd nearly talked Peg into letting him out? Mind, Peg always was a bit of a horse's ass. But I like him better quiet."

Winter met the colonel's eyes. They were gray, deep, inscrutable. It shook her. She'd expected rage, or maybe fear, but the only thing she saw there was cold calculation.

"Right." Davis' free hand groped around Winter's midsection. She froze while he patted her down, coming up with the pistol she'd taken from Buck and her belt knife. He tossed both into a corner, then let go of her wrists and pushed her away. "Now, you've got some questions to answer."

Winter turned on him, doing her best to imitate the colonel's nonchalance. "Where's Folsom? And Captain d'Ivoire and the others?"

"I said you were going to answer questions, not ask 'em," Davis said. "Are your friends on their way here?"

"No," Winter said. "It's just me."

He swung for her gut, hard. Winter had expected that, and she lurched to the side enough to take only a glancing blow. It still made her double over in pain.

"Don't fucking lie to me," Davis said. "You were in my company for years, Saint. You know I can smell a lie. Did you kill Buck and Will?"

She managed a breath and straightened up. "Will's dead. Buck we're just sitting on."

"Shit." Davis pursed his lips. "Why in God's name would you do that? I mean, kill Buck and leave Will alone, that I could understand. Buck's an asshole. What did Will ever do to you?"

"It was an accident."

Davis laughed. "Right. It was a good trick, sending Warus back around. The captain scares easy. 'Go and check on everyone,' he says. I told him we had nothin' to worry about, but he wouldn't hear it. Officers." He looked like he wanted to spit. "Hey, you're an officer now, aren't you? Is it true they replace your brains with beef jerky?"

"Give it up, Davis. You and Roston are finished. Lieutenant Warus told us everything. It'll be all over the camp by now."

"Yeah? Did he tell you that this asshole"—he indicated the colonel—"was planning to march us into the desert with no water and no plan? When the boys hear that, which way do you think they'll jump?"

Winter chewed her lip. *The hell of it is, he might be right.*

"The captain figured that if we gave the colonel a chance to talk at 'em, it might confuse things some," Davis said. "So we thought it'd be best to let things take their own course. Natural, like."

"When Graff and the others get here—"

"They won't be coming," Davis said. His fat lips twisted in a smirk. "Reason being, I sent Peg and some of the boys to make sure nobody stirs up any trouble."

Winter shook her head in mock amazement. "Mutiny certainly seems to be your forte."

"Sergeant," Davis growled.

"What?"

He gave her a feral snarl, baring his teeth. "Call me sergeant. Just because they pinned some stripes on your shoulder doesn't make you better than me, you little shit. Get down on your knees and beg, and maybe I won't shove your face through the back of your skull. It's *Sergeant* Davis."

"That's a lie and you know it," Winter said, trying to sound unconcerned. "The way you've been talking, you can't let me out of here alive."

"No." His lips spread wider, into a rictus of a smile. "No, I'm afraid you've got me there. But you can feel free to beg, if you like."

Fuck. Winter looked up at the bulk of him and wanted to shrink into a ball. *Fuck fuck* fuck. He wore a knife, too, but he hardly needed one. The huge scarred fists were weapon enough. The piled debris blocked any way out except through the narrow gap by the tent flap, and Davis stood squarely in the way. *If I can get him out of position, maybe . . .* Outside, she would have a chance. The sergeant was strong as a bull, but he was slow. *I can get away.*

She blew out a breath between her teeth and dropped into a half crouch. Slowly, ridiculously, she raised her fists.

Davis barked a laugh. "Is that how it is, Saint? You and me? Man to man?"

"One of us is a man, anyway." Winter bit back a peal of hysterical laughter.

"You shouldn't try to make me angry. It'll only go harder on you."

"Harder than dead?"

"Well," he said, scratching the side of his nose. "There's dead, and then there's—"

He lashed out in midsentence, a savage jab that snapped

Winter's head back before she could even think about ducking. White light flashed behind her eyes, and the taste of blood exploded in her mouth. She didn't even feel herself falling, only more pain from splinters and nails prodding her from behind as she staggered back into one of the piles of debris.

"Dead," Davis finished, rubbing his knuckles against his uniform coat. "Who are you fucking kidding, Saint?"

He approached, but cautiously. Winter, sucking air through a split lip, tried blearily to gauge the distance. When she thought he was close enough, she brought her knee up in a jerky try for his stomach, but he slammed his palm down on it so hard that she felt something crunch. Tears leaked from her eyes, and she stifled a scream.

"You still don't think much of ol' Sarge, do you?" Davis' smile was brutal. "I may be old and fat, but you don't get to be old and fat without learning your way around a fight or two."

He reached down, batting aside her feebly resisting arm, and took hold of her collar, twisting the fabric of her shirt in sausage-thick fingers. Winter dangled bonelessly from his grip as he raised her to eye level.

"Well, Lieutenant?" he said. "Anything else to say?"

She spit a stream of blood, right in his eye. He reared back, roaring in protest, but retained his grip. Her feet scrabbled, half an inch above the ground, gaining no traction. Over his shoulder she saw one of the tent poles, barely within her reach, and she grabbed it and *pulled*. The unexpected pressure wrenched Davis around, and Winter's feet touched the ground. She pushed off hard, trying desperately to escape from his grasp, her collar twisted tight around her neck.

Something gave way with a *rip*, and suddenly she was free. She dropped on all fours and scrabbled forward, heading for the tent flap, but before she could get there she felt a hand grip her by the ankle, dragging her knees out from under her and leaving her flat in the dirt. A second later a kick exploded into her ribs, rolling her over and onto her back.

Every breath was an agony. Something in her chest felt broken, shifting uneasily with each heartbeat, and there was a line of fire around her throat. She coughed weakly and tried to raise her head.

"I don't believe it," Davis said. "I don't *fucking* believe it. You have got to be *joking*."

Winter managed to push herself up on her elbows. Davis was staring at her, incredulous. In one hand, he held a bloody scrap of fabric that had once been part of her undershirt. The buttons of her coat had given way, and it had fallen open, leaving her exposed from neck to navel.

"Saints and fucking martyrs," Davis swore. "What the *fuck*, Saint? Are you some kind of freak?"

She tried to reply, but her mouth was full of blood. It trickled down her chin and dripped onto her bared breasts. She spit again, weakly, spraying blood all over the sleeve of her coat.

"You mean all those times we were out on patrol, just us boys in those cold tents, there was a nice warm cunt within five feet and I didn't know it? *Fuck*, Saint, you could have told me. I might have been a little nicer to you."

He looked at her, surprise slowly changing to disgust. Winter forced herself to stare back, unblinking.

"No wonder you were always looking down your nose at us. Buttoned-up little bitch. Laughing at dumb ol' Sarge behind his back." His lip twisted. "I ought to fuck you good an' proper, to make up for all those missed chances."

Behind Davis, something moved. Winter looked past the sergeant, and in the lamp's flickering shadows she caught sight of the colonel. His hands were still bound, but he'd somehow freed his legs, and one of his feet rested on the knife Davis had taken from her.

Their gazes met. There was no surprise in his gray eyes, no

disgust or fear, just quiet concentration and, she realized belatedly, a question.

Winter nodded, saw his acknowledgment.

Davis' hands were on his belt, apparently in an agony of indecision. He shook his head.

"Sorry, Saint. I don't think we've got time—"

The colonel moved. He sent the knife skittering over the dirt toward Winter, between Davis' legs. At the same time he twisted, lashing out with a kick that caught the big sergeant precisely in the back of the knee.

Davis bellowed again, one leg folding up involuntarily, and his arms windmilled as he toppled forward. He caught himself before he hit the ground, held up on hands and knees, half over Winter.

She forced herself to move, in spite of the protests from her abused body. Her hand found the knife and ripped off the sheath. It was a short blade, not really a fighting knife at all, but Davis was *right there*, gaping at her, the apple of his throat bobbing stupidly—

"Take the knife," Jane said, as though instructing a friend in how to carve a roast. "Put the point of it about here"—she raised her head and put a finger on her throat, just under her chin—"and press in, upward, as hard as you can."

Winter obeyed.

She didn't recall cutting the colonel free, but she must have. The next thing she remembered was sitting huddled on the floor, arms hugging her knees to her chest, and the colonel was bending solicitously at her side.

"Lieutenant?" When that elicited no response, he bent a little closer. "Winter?"

She blinked, looking up. Colonel Vhalnich gave a quick smile and offered her a canteen.

"Water?"

Winter took it shakily and fumbled with the cap. Once she got it open she took a long pull, wincing at the pain in her jaw, and spat a pink stream into the dirt. Her mouth still tasted of blood, but she downed the rest in a single greedy swallow.

"You look quite a mess," the colonel said. "Are you badly hurt?"

Her brain was slowly starting to function again. "I—" More blood dripped off her upper lip. She wiped her hand across her face and it came away crimson. "Think he broke my nose."

"I'm sorry it took me so long to intervene. As you saw, he had me at something of a disadvantage."

"The others," Winter said, suddenly cold. "What about Folsom and the others?"

"Folsom?" The colonel cocked his head. "Ah, the corporal commanding Captain d'Ivoire's guard. They're in the other tent with the captain, I believe, along with Miss Alhundt. We've really been treated quite well, all things considered. Although the captain was worried about Lieutenant Warus."

"He's all right," Winter said. "They were going to kill him, but I got to him first."

"Remarkable," the colonel said. "You are an officer of considerable resource, I think."

Winter struggled to her feet. The edges of her torn shirt flapped against her skin, where they weren't gummed tight with blood. "We had better let them out."

"They'll keep a few moments longer." There was a hint of amusement in the colonel's gray eyes. "First of all, I suggest that you button your jacket."

Oh. Winter looked down at herself, too numb to feel embarrassment. She closed the buttons slowly, her fingers feeling clumsy and fat. Only when she was finished did she look back up at the colonel. He raised an eyebrow.

"I knew, of course."

"Of course," Winter said, deadpan. "Of course you knew.

Everybody knows." A hysterical giggle escaped, in spite of the pain it brought from her ribs. "You're all just pretending not to notice, for my sake, aren't you? It's a big practical joke. I might as well walk through the camp naked, since *everyone fucking already knows*—"

"I doubt that would be a good idea," the colonel said. "I've been making something of a study of you, Lieutenant, and I don't think I flatter myself too much if I say that I am more observant than the average soldier. As far as I can tell, your secret remains unrevealed."

"Except to the commander of the whole regiment," Winter said bitterly. "Wonderful."

"I'm not planning to mention it to anyone else," the colonel said, "if you were worried on that score."

Winter paused, watching his impassive expression. Her thoughts felt slow and diffuse, and her head throbbed with every heartbeat, but she gritted her teeth and forced herself to focus. *What the hell is he talking about?* Bobby was one thing, but this was the *colonel.*

"I . . ." She shook her head. "Why?"

"Firstly, it would seem to be an ungracious response to your saving my life." He gestured at the facedown body of Davis. "While Captain Roston was concerned with preserving a veneer of legality, I'm certain the senior sergeant would have prevailed on him eventually that his captives were too dangerous to be allowed to live."

"I didn't come here to save you," Winter said. "I came for my men."

"I guessed as much," he said. "It doesn't change the outcome. And, secondly, I've remained silent this long because I feel you show considerable promise as an officer. The army needs more like you, not fewer, the fact of your gender notwithstanding. Your stand on the docks at the river was . . . inspired." Another fleeting smile. "I suspect that few among the army officers are as pragmatic as I am, however. Thus, it is best that your secret remain a secret." He chuckled. "In particular, I suggest you keep it from Captain d'Ivoire.

He has old-fashioned ideas when it comes to gallantry and would feel compelled to hustle you away for your own protection."

"So you're just . . . not going to say anything?" She was having a hard time wrapping her mind around the concept.

"I'm going to thank you for stopping an attempted mutiny," he said. "And probably promote you in the bargain, once we've gotten clear of our current difficulties."

"We haven't stopped anything yet," Winter said. "Captain Roston—"

"Let me worry about Captain Roston," the colonel said. "We'll collect Captain d'Ivoire and your men, and then I think you're due for a rest."

She was too tired to protest, or even ask questions. It felt good to have someone else giving orders for a change. And she had to admit it suited him. She would never have known from the colonel's demeanor that he'd been bound and gagged just minutes before. His thin face was animated, and something in the depths of his eyes made him seem on the edge of a smile that never quite appeared. *He looks happy*. She couldn't imagine why.

He walked to the tent flap, held it open. "After you, Lieutenant."

Winter drew herself up, in spite of the pain, and saluted. "Yes, *sir*!"

Chapter Twenty-Three

MARCUS

Marcus' wrists chafed where he was bound. They'd used ordinary camp rope, thick and rough, and try as he might to hold still, the edges scraped painfully against his skin. At least he hadn't been gagged.

Jen, as a woman, had been spared the indignity; Adrecht remained a gentleman. The same could not be said of the Second Company man Sergeant Davis had left to watch the prisoners, who spent entirely too long staring thoughtfully at the Concordat liaison.

They were in a large tent, empty except for a few makeshift writing desks. Marcus and Jen had a corner to themselves, while the corporal and rankers who'd been taken along with the colonel sat in a huddle on the other side.

Adrecht himself hadn't had the stomach to face to the prisoners, which gave Marcus a little bit of hope to cling to. *He knows he shouldn't be doing this. If I could only* talk *to him, I could make him understand.* Unfortunately, Adrecht seemed to have delegated his captives to Davis, and Marcus harbored no illusions about *his* rationality.

Fucking Davis. I should have had him strung up long ago. He'd known how awful the man was, even in Colonel Warus' day, but back then it hadn't been his problem. Besides, petty cruelty and thuggery were practically a sergeants' tradition. *But not mutiny.*

The Second Company man was leering again. He was a squat, ugly ranker, with a thick black beard and angry red welts on his cheeks. He sat by the tent flap on a biscuit crate, musket by his side, and occupied his time with tuneless whistling and staring hungrily at Jen when he thought no one was looking.

"Marcus," Jen hissed.

He looked across at her, and her eyes flicked to their jailer.

"If he tries anything," Marcus said in a whisper, "I'll—"

"Don't do anything stupid," she said. "Listen. If worse really comes to worst, just keep your head down."

He snorted. "If you think I'm going to sit quietly while he drags you outside and has his way with you—"

"He won't," she said.

"You don't know that."

Her expression grew determined. "I mean, I won't let him."

"But—"

"Just trust me, would you?"

Marcus subsided. With his arms tied behind his back, he didn't fancy his chances in a fight with the hefty ranker, but he didn't see that he had any other options. *No point in arguing, though.* He looked up at a rustle from the tent flap, hoping for Adrecht but expecting Davis. The guard looked up, too, one hand going to his musket.

The pistol shot was shockingly loud at such close range. The Second Company man, eyes blank with surprise, rolled slowly backward with a hole drilled neatly through his forehead. Janus ducked inside the tent and tossed the still-smoking weapon aside.

"Good morning, Captain," he said. "Miss Alhundt, Corporal. I thought we might repair to more congenial surroundings."

He bent, pulled the knife from the dead man's belt, flipped it around, and offered it to Jen. She set to work on the rope binding Marcus' hands. Behind the colonel another man entered, and it took Marcus a moment to recognize young Lieutenant Ihernglass, who looked as though he'd been worked over by a team of men with truncheons. Blood smeared his face and trickled from his nose, his lips were thick and purple, and a bruise was swelling under one eye. He spared Marcus only a glance, then hurried toward where the corporal and the others lay.

"Don't tell me," Marcus said, as his hands came free. "You tricked Davis into slitting his own throat."

"A surprisingly accurate guess," Janus said, "but not quite. The senior sergeant was hardly my intellectual equal, but he proved remarkably resilient to persuasion. I must admit that we have the lieutenant to thank for our liberty."

"Ihernglass? How did he find us?"

"You'll have to get the complete story from him yourself. I understand he stumbled across Lieutenant Warus, and together they concocted a plan."

"Fitz is all right, then?" That had been preying on Marcus' mind.

"I believe so. The lieutenant says he left him with his company."

"Right." Marcus clambered to his feet, massaging his aching wrists. He spared a moment to smile at Jen, then turned back to Janus. "What about Davis? When I get my hands on him—"

"The senior sergeant has, I'm afraid, gone beyond the reach of your retribution."

"He's dead?"

Janus nodded at Ihernglass. "There was an altercation."

Marcus remembered the sheer scarred bulk of Davis, his massive fists, and measured them against Ihernglass' slim, boyish figure. He whistled softly, then shook his head. "Quicker than he deserved. What about Adrecht?"

"According to the lieutenant, Captain Roston is back at the main camp. Lieutenant Warus is endeavoring to keep him distracted."

"Then this isn't over," Marcus said. "We've got to get over there—"

Janus held up a hand. "Indeed. All in good time. Before that, though, I wondered if I might have a word in private?"

Marcus blinked, then looked over his shoulder at Jen. She nodded encouragingly, and Janus gave another of his summer-lightning smiles. He led the way out of the tent and onto the wreckage-strewn plain beyond. The sky in the east was just beginning to lighten, and the air was still heavy with the scent of woodsmoke.

"Jen is . . . ," Marcus began.

"You trust her," Janus said mildly.

"I don't know," Marcus said. "She's Concordat. But she doesn't seem . . ." He trailed off, not sure how to put it.

"It is inevitable that, even among Duke Orlanko's minions, there are good men and women loyal to the king. Since your acquaintance with the young lady is somewhat deeper than mine"—a flash of humor in Janus' eye made Marcus certain he knew exactly how deep that "acquaintance" went—"I am willing to trust your judgment. However, you have mistaken my purpose. My intention was not to keep secrets from Miss Alhundt, but rather to address a matter that concerns only you and me."

Marcus straightened, taken aback. "Sir?"

"To be blunt, Captain, I wish to apologize. I allowed an unfortunate personal habit to get the better of me, and the result was a danger to this entire command as well as an insult to you personally."

"I'm not sure I understand what you mean."

Janus sighed. "It is a failing of mine that when I encounter an intellectual problem of any complexity, I have difficulty in preventing myself from throwing every ounce of my creative energy into its solution, leaving little or nothing over for other pursuits. This has been the case for the last several days, in spite of my best intentions, and the result has been the situation in which we find ourselves."

"I'm not sure there's anything you could have done, sir," Marcus said.

"Nonsense. I should have foreseen Captain Roston's behavior, both during the battle and afterward. And snapping at you on the ridge was inexcusable. If I had left proper instructions, or better yet exercised command in person, you would not have been put in the impossible situation of a choice between rescuing a friend and defending the camp."

Marcus stared at the colonel, searching his impassive face for something to help him respond. He'd almost entirely forgotten his anger at Janus, consumed as he'd been by a much more immediate rage at Adrecht, Davis, and his own stupidity. The colonel's casual rebuke on the hillside seemed a thousand years ago. And yet Janus obviously felt keenly about it, on some level, which made Marcus hesitate from casually dismissing the matter. He finally settled on defensive formality.

"I accept your apology, sir," he said. "Although, of course, you were perfectly within your rights as commanding officer."

Janus nodded. "Nevertheless, I have expressed the wish that you and I have a relationship that is more than simply commander and subordinate, and it is incumbent on me to behave accordingly."

"Well. Thank you, then." Marcus scratched his chin through his beard uncertainly. "What was the problem?"

"The nature of the Desoltai tactical advantage, of course. It has become clear to me, over the course of the march, that our enemies enjoy a considerable edge in terms of information, above and beyond what their natural mobility as a mounted force should provide. Coordinating simultaneous attacks over long distances is a feat beyond the ability of most organized armies with modern timekeeping devices, much less desert raiders reckoning from the sun."

"The Steel Ghost is famous for it," Marcus said, glad for the change of subject. "There's all kinds of stories about him." He broke off, then lowered his voice. "Is it true, do you think? Could he be something . . . supernatural, like the creature we fought in Ashe-Katarion?"

A smile flicked across Janus' face. "Anything is possible, Captain. But in this case I think not. Certainly the coordination of Desoltai attacks is susceptible to a more mundane explanation."

"What is it, then?"

"I'll go through it in a moment." Janus turned away at the rustle of canvas. Lieutenant Iherngl ass emerged from the tent, leaning heavily on the large form of Corporal Folsom, with a few rankers following hesitantly behind. They stopped short at the sight of the colonel.

"No need to salute a fellow captive," Janus said, as Folsom searched for some way to prop up Iherngl ass so he could come to attention. "Lieutenant, I wonder if I might ask you one question before letting you go to a well-deserved rest."

"Yessir," Iherngl ass managed, through puffy lips.

"You told me that you returned to camp after a skirmish with a small group of Desoltai. Among them, was there one bearing an unusually large pack?"

The lieutenant nodded.

"Excellent. If you could indicate where the encounter occurred, Captain d'Ivoire will detail some men to retrieve it."

"Don't need to," Iherngl ass said. "I brought it back with me. We thought there might be food inside, but it was just some . . ." He waved his free hand. "A lantern, or something."

"Indeed." Janus' smile came and went in an instant. "If you don't mind, I'd like to have a look."

The sun was well up by the time they returned to the tents and retrieved the mysterious box, and the encampment was buzzing like an overturned hive. No one knew what was happening, but there was a gradual current of men toward the clear space between the camps of the four battalions, where something interesting was evidently going on. While Janus fiddled with his acquisition, Marcus scraped up two dozen men from the Old Colonials of the First Battalion, made sure they were armed, and brought them back to the colonel to serve as an escort. Whatever Adrecht tried, Marcus didn't intend to be taken so easily again.

That done, their little party headed toward the focus of all the attention. A wide ring of soldiers, craning their necks and standing on their toes to try to get a glimpse, surrounded a small cleared space. Marcus' men had to push their way through at first. Once the men caught sight of Marcus and the colonel, however, the path opened of its own accord, and the beehive roar of thousands of men whispering spread through the crowd like flames leaping across dry tinder.

At the center of the mob were two rings of soldiers, both wearing First Battalion markings. One group, huddled into a tight mass, belonged to Lieutenant Ihernglass' Seventh Company. Around them, muskets at the ready with fixed bayonets, was a circle of men from Davis' Second.

Outside the circle, another kind of standoff was in progress. Adrecht, backed up by a dozen Fourth Battalion soldiers, stood across from Fitz and a pair of corporals from the Seventh Company. Hovering to one side were Mor and Val, the former looking ready to explode and the latter huddled miserably with his arms crossed over his chest.

Everyone looked up as Marcus and Janus passed through the crowd of soldiers. Marcus kept his eyes on Adrecht. A spasm of doubt and fear crossed his face, but he mastered himself almost immediately. Val's eyes lit up at the sight of them, and Marcus caught a knowing glance from Fitz. The lieutenant's face was nearly as badly bruised as Ihernglass' had been.

Janus stepped forward to face Adrecht and waited. Little by little, the susurrus of whispers and conversation died away, as every man in the vast crowd strained to hear. The Fourth Battalion men behind Adrecht shuffled uncertainly, but Adrecht himself stepped forward, came to attention, and saluted stiffly.

"Captain Roston," Janus said.

"Colonel Vhalnich," Adrecht said. "I did not expect to see you here."

"No, I imagine not." Janus looked around. "I must ask these men to stand down at once."

Adrecht glanced over his shoulder. "Lieutenant Gibbons?"

One of the Fourth Battalion men saluted. "Sir!"

"Please place Colonel Vhalnich under arrest."

Gibbons swallowed hard. "Yessir!"

Marcus stepped beside Janus, his own men coming up to stand beside him. Adrecht's men spread out to face them, hands on their weapons. Marcus' hands were clenched so tight that his nails dug painfully into his palms.

If it comes to a fight, this is going to be a riot. Adrecht's people looked nervous, as did the Second Company men. *If any one of them fires a shot . . .*

Janus held up a hand, his voice rising to ring out over the crowd. "Am I permitted to know the charges against me?"

"Being a goddamned lunatic," Mor said. He caught Marcus' eye, winced, and looked away.

"Captain Kaanos is broadly correct," Adrecht said. "Your latest orders indicate your mental unfitness for command."

"Which orders, specifically?"

Adrecht hesitated. Janus' expression was as blank as always, but there was something in his voice. An edge of confidence, the voice of a cardplayer who knows that he holds the last trump.

"Last night, I received an order under your seal to prepare for a march to the northeast," Adrecht said. He looked away from Janus, addressing the crowd. "Given the Desoltai raid and our lack of supplies, further pursuit of the enemy is clearly a serious danger to this regiment. If we don't turn back now, none of us will make it out of the Desol."

There was muttered assent from the assembled soldiers. Those close enough to catch sight of Janus didn't dare voice their opinion openly, but those farther back were less reticent. The words were unintelligible, but their shouts and grumbles conveyed their meaning.

Adrecht seemed to take heart from this backing. "I conveyed my doubts to Captain d'Ivoire, who indicated that he had discussed them with you, to no result. With all other options exhausted, duty to the men under my command forces me reluctantly to take steps to ensure the best chance of our survival."

"It's not relevant, I suppose, that the success of the Desoltai raid was primarily your responsibility?"

Adrecht swayed slightly, as if he'd been slapped. His hand came up and clutched at the stump of his arm.

"No," he said. "Whether true or not, I hardly see the bearing on the current situation."

Janus was silent for a long moment. Bit by bit, the noise of the crowd rose, and shouts and jeers started to come from those safely in the rear. Marcus looked again at Mor and Val, but neither would meet his eyes.

"As you say," Janus began, "our supply situation is critical. Under the circumstances, I thought we ought to make for the nearest source of water."

"The nearest source of water is on the coast," Adrecht snapped. "And we'll be hard-pressed to make it even that far."

"To the contrary. There is an oasis only a day's march to the northeast."

Janus spoke quietly, but the men in the front ranks who heard him repeated what he'd said to their neighbors. Shouts and jeers cut off abruptly as his words spread through the crowd, like a ripple across the surface of a pond. Absolute silence replaced them, the entire regiment holding its collective breath.

"You don't know that," Adrecht said. "How could you?"

"The Desoltai must draw their supplies from somewhere," Janus said. "They can't survive on sand any more than we can."

"Everyone knows they have hidden bases," Adrecht admitted. "But they are *hidden*. Marching into the desert in the hopes of finding one is still a death sentence."

"Fortunately, I know the precise location of this particular base. The fact that it presents an opportunity to destroy the Desoltai force along the way is an additional incentive."

"So you claim," Adrecht said. He sounded rattled. "How could you possibly know for certain?"

Janus turned to one of the men beside him, who handed over the pack Lieutenant Ihernglass had taken from the Desoltai scout. He extracted a wooden box, about a foot to a side, with a small lever protruding from one corner. Adrecht watched, puzzled, and another tide of whispers rose from the crowd. It stopped at once when Janus began to speak.

"This," he said, "was taken from a Desoltai patrol. It's really quite an ingenious creation." He pressed down on the lever with two fingers, and a circular panel at the front of the box opened. Something gleamed bright inside. "The interior is a ring of mirrors, which collect all the light of a candle placed inside and direct it through the aperture. It's similar to the lights used for theatrical productions, though less intense." When he let go of the lever, the covering slid back.

"By manipulating this, one can create a very bright directional beam. In the clear air of the Desol, it can be seen at a great distance." He looked out at the crowd. "I'll hazard that some of you have seen them when you were on sentry duty."

Mutters of assent from the crowd. Adrecht frowned. "A clever trick," he said. "But—"

"Nothing particularly clever so far," Janus said dismissively, handing the box back. "Similar devices are used on many occasions

—aboard ships at night, for instance. Typically, they display a small range of precoded signals. One light for a request to approach, two for approval, four for bad weather sightings, and so on. Our Desoltai friends have gone considerably further than that. They have developed a true language of light, capable of expressing any information they require. Moreover, they have perfected a procedure for repeating these signals from one post to the next, so that this information can cross long distances at fast as light itself."

Marcus nodded slowly. A simple signal might be good enough to start a coordinated attack, but in order to respond to changing conditions, something more was required. *That explains a great deal.*

"This is their secret weapon," Janus went on, "and not surprisingly they are quite reliant on it. They believe that messages passed this way are impervious to interception, because their language of light is a secret they share with no one. They are incorrect. Given a sufficient number of intercepted messages, and with knowledge of the movements that resulted, a sufficiently clever man might be able to learn this language on his own."

Adrecht had gone pale. "And you claim to have done this?"

Janus shrugged modestly. "I am a clever man."

Silence fell by stages. One by one, the men in the crowd stopped talking to their fellows or shouting at one another and went quiet, waiting to see what came next. Janus watched Adrecht, imperturbable, and Adrecht stared back with the desperate eyes of a cornered animal.

Marcus watched the crowd. He doubted one in a hundred had understood Janus' explanation, even among those close enough to hear the colonel's words. But they could see Adrecht giving ground. Marcus could *feel* the balance wobbling around him.

"I don't believe you," Adrecht said. His voice rose to a screech. "You're bluffing."

"I can show you the records," Janus said amiably. "Although I admit I did the final ciphering in my head, while I was confined.

You did me a favor in that respect. Silence concentrates the mind wonderfully."

"Shut up!" Adrecht barked. "You led us out here, and you'd rather let us die than take the blame for it!" He turned away from the colonel and faced the crowd. "Don't you understand? He'll kill us all just so he doesn't have to admit he was wrong!"

Janus looked bemused. Mutters were starting again in the crowd, and the moment was slipping away. Marcus stepped forward.

"We won't make it to the coast," he said, loud enough for everyone to hear. "Not all of us. And for those of us who do, what then? Will the Desoltai just leave us be?"

"It's the best chance we have," Adrecht hissed. "The only chance."

Marcus stared at his friend, his gut churning. At the top of his mind was a black rage that made him want to slam Adrecht's face in, here and now. *After everything I've done for him. After I nearly resigned for him. After I came to Khandar for him!*

Under that, though, was a sick kind of sympathy. Marcus *knew* Adrecht, in a way he knew almost no one else in his life. He could follow along, step by step, through the decisions that had led the Fourth Battalion captain to this decision. Marcus forced himself not to look at Adrecht's empty sleeve. *Would I have done the same, in his position?*

"Why, Marcus?" Adrecht whispered. "I've always been able to count on you."

Marcus gritted his teeth. "I was about to ask you the same thing."

He stepped away and raised his voice to a shout. "If the colonel is willing to give us a shot at the Desoltai in the bargain, I for one am ready to take it!"

Adrecht glared at him in silence. Marcus looked over his shoulder, to where Mor and Val were standing. He sought their eyes, one at a time.

It was Mor who moved first, to Marcus' surprise, stepping forward to stand beside Marcus.

"Hell," he said. "I'd march for a week without water if you told me we'd get to string up this steel bastard at the end of it."

Val was nodding, too. "It seems to me," he said to Adrecht, "that whatever else the colonel is, he is not mad. He's made a reasonable decision in the light of the available information. I think you have no basis for declaring him incompetent."

"But—," Adrecht began.

It was too late. The balance had tipped, and the men were cheering. Even the Second Company men had joined it, lowering their weapons and helping the Seventh Company soldiers to their feet. Whatever Adrecht had to say was lost under the sound, and eventually he fell silent, clutching the stump of his arm and glaring daggers at the colonel.

"Captain," Janus said, nearly inaudible under the roar, "would you please escort Captain Roston to my tent?"

Marcus gave a grim smile. "Gladly, sir."

Paperwork. Marcus would have thought that out in the desert, facing potential annihilation, he would at least be free of his own personal demon. Unfortunately, Janus wanted things done *properly*, and that meant papers for every man.

"Sir?"

Marcus looked up at Fitz and winced. "Have you seen a cutter about that eye?"

Fitz touched the purpling bruise that covered almost half his face. "It looks worse than it feels, sir. I'll be all right. Captain Solwen is here, sir, and would like to speak with you."

Marcus frowned. That was unusually formal for Val. "Send him in, then."

Fitz held the tent flap open, letting Val duck inside. Marcus got up from his writing table with relief, feeling muscles pop all down his legs and back. He'd been at it longer than he'd realized, but the stack didn't seem any smaller.

"Val," Marcus said, then stopped. His friend stood at attention, eyes forward. After weeks in the desert, his uniform was showing signs of wear, but his mustache was newly waxed and perfectly pointed.

"Senior Captain," Val said in a tone as stiff as his posture.

"What's going on?"

"I would like . . . That is . . ." He paused and his shoulders slumped a little. Then he straightened them again and managed, "I would like to consult you on a matter of some urgency."

Marcus looked up for Fitz, but the lieutenant had already slipped outside. *Clever lad.* He waved vaguely at Val. "Of course. Sit down. Would you like a drink? Fitz rescued a couple of bottles."

"No, sir."

Marcus sighed. "Val, we've known each other for five years now. If you're going to start 'no, sir'-ing me, you can damn well keep your urgent matter to yourself."

"Sorry, sir." Val let his shoulders fall again. "Marcus. I just—I don't know what to do."

"Sit down, to start with." Marcus seated himself beside the hated desk, where he could stretch his legs, and gestured Val to the other cushion. "And tell me what the problem is."

"The problem—" Val let out a long breath, making his mustache quiver. Then, all in a rush, he said, "The problem is that I ought to resign."

"Resign?" Marcus blinked. "Why?"

"For not seeing through Adrecht from the start," Val said miserably. "He damn well kidnapped you, and the colonel, and I was ready to follow along and say, 'Yes, sir!' It's a disgrace."

"You didn't know that at the time," Marcus pointed out.

"I ought to have guessed," Val said. "Besides, it was obvious that what he was up to was mutiny. It was my duty to stop him."

Marcus shifted uncomfortably. "With me gone, Adrecht would have been senior captain. You'd have been perfectly within your duties to follow his orders."

"You know what I mean, damn it." Val twisted his mustache anxiously, then smoothed it out again. "I went along with it because I thought he might be right."

"A lot of people went along with it," Marcus said. *Everyone, really, except Fitz and Lieutenant Ihernglass.*

"But they weren't in command of a battalion," Val insisted. "They couldn't have stopped it all."

"What would you have done? Ordered the Second to fire on the Fourth?"

"If necessary," Val said stiffly.

"That would have been worse than anything that actually happened," Marcus said. "Believe me."

"But—" Val hesitated. "After all that, how can the colonel have any confidence in me?"

That was the heart of the matter, Marcus thought. It was one thing to make a wrong decision, and quite another to believe your commander held a grudge against you because of it. He picked his words carefully.

"The colonel hasn't given any indication to me that he's lost confidence in any of the senior officers. If anything, he blames himself." *And isn't that a wonder?*

"You think so?"

Marcus shrugged. "He confides in me as much as he confides in anyone, and he hasn't mentioned anything of the kind. Besides, do you think he would want you to resign *now*? We're going to need every man in the next couple of days."

"I could carry a musket, if necessary."

The images of Val, with his neat uniform and his waxed

mustache, walking in the ranks with the common soldiers was enough to make Marcus chuckle. After a moment, Val managed a weak smile as well.

"You understand what I mean, don't you, Marcus? I just thought I ought to . . . to make amends somehow."

"I know. The best way to do it is to make sure the Second is ready. There'll be action tomorrow."

"You think so?"

"The colonel as good as told me so. And he never tells anyone anything."

Val nodded. "Just as well. Water won't last much longer. The lads are eager for a fair shot at the cowardly bastards, too."

"I think we all are." He gestured at the writing desk. "Anything but this."

"What is all that, anyway?"

"Discharges. For the men of the Second Company who were involved in the mutiny, and a few others in the Fourth as well."

Val frowned. "Discharges? Aren't they being held for court-martial?"

"The colonel said we can't spare the time or the men to keep prisoners. He's going to give them as much food and water as they can carry and turn them loose. Let them make for the coast, if they can."

"Across the Great Desol?" Val sucked in his cheeks. "That's small mercy."

"They'd all hang, if we ever get back to civilization," Marcus said. "The Ministry takes a dim view of mutiny."

"Still . . ." Val looked up. "Is Adrecht going with them?"

Marcus nodded. Val shook his head.

"Poor Adrecht. He ought to have stayed in the city. Losing a limb can have a terrible effect on a man."

"Maybe he'll make it back there."

"Maybe."

They sat for a moment in silence. After a while Val said, "I think Mor feels the same way I do."

"About Adrecht?"

"About resigning. He thinks he's guilty."

"He certainly didn't look it this afternoon."

"You know Mor," Val said. "He's either angry, or pretending to be angry. But underneath—"

"Will you talk to him? Or send him to me, if that's easier."

"I'll talk to him," Val said. "It may take a while to bring him around."

Another silence.

"Well." Val slapped his knees and levered himself to his feet. "I had better get some rest myself. Action tomorrow, you say?"

"Almost certainly."

It was full dark, but sleep eluded him. He lay in the bedroll, thin blanket wadded beside him, and stared at the tent ceiling. Every time he closed his eyes, he saw Adrecht. They hadn't spoken a word to each other while the colonel had pronounced sentence, but Adrecht's eyes hadn't left Marcus for a moment.

How can he tell me I *betrayed* him*? He's the one who raised a goddamned mutiny*. And yet . . .

When he closed his eyes he saw Adrecht, not grim and one-armed but laughing and gambling like he had in their War College days. Sharing a drink, kissing a pretty blond girl with delicate skin and powder-darkened eyes. Offering a pistol in one outstretched hand, his eyes full of pain. *"If you're going to kill yourself, Marcus, at least be a man about it . . ."*

He never belonged here, for all his fancy clothes and Khandarai girls. This was my *post.* Marcus had taken the Khandar posting when Adrecht had been handed his exile, out of solidarity, but he'd fitted into it in a way his friend never had. It had been *away*, about as far away as it was possible to get from Vordan, from the burned wreckage of a house and a family.

The tent flap rustled. Marcus' eyes flicked sideways and he saw a female silhouette against the faint glow of the camp. He relaxed.

Once the flap fell back, the tent was in darkness again. He heard a couple of footsteps, and then the soft cloth sounds of disrobing. A moment later Jen slid across the bedroll and pressed herself against him, bare skin warm against his. Marcus slipped an arm underneath her and turned his head to give her a kiss, but found his nose bumping into something cold and hard.

"Sorry," she said. "Spectacles." She pulled them off and set them carefully aside, then leaned back against him, brushing his lips with hers before settling her head on his shoulder.

A long moment passed quietly. He listened to her breathing, feeling it tickle the hair on his neck, the softness of her body pressed against his side.

"Are you all right?" she said.

"Mmm?"

"Adrecht. He was your friend."

"He was." Marcus let out a long breath. "No. I'm not all right. I just . . . I don't understand."

"People do strange things when the pressure gets too high."

"Is that a professional opinion?"

He meant it as a joke, but by the way she stiffened he realized it was the wrong thing to say. He squeezed her shoulder reassuringly. After a moment, he felt her relax.

"Sorry," she said. "After today . . ."

He was silent. Her hand lay lightly on his chest, fingers tightly curled.

"I was sure they were going to kill me," she whispered. "They'd have to, wouldn't they? If you're staging a mutiny, you don't keep the informer around to write a report. Adrecht might have been too much the gentleman, but not Davis. I kept waiting for them to come back and . . ." She pressed against him a little tighter.

"I wouldn't have let them," Marcus said.

"Then they'd just kill you, too."

"Is that why you told me I should let you handle it?"

He felt her nod. "You have to look at it logically," she said, only the faintest quiver in her voice. "If I'm going to end up raped and dead *anyway*, there's no sense in you getting killed as well if it won't change anything."

"Easy for you to say." He thought about that for a moment, then said, "Well. Not easy. But if I had just sat by while something like that happened, I don't think I could have lived with myself afterward."

"At least you would have had the chance to try."

Another pause. Marcus cleared his throat.

"It's a good thing it didn't come to that, then."

"It's a good thing," Jen agreed.

There was a long silence. With Jen soft and warm beside him, Marcus' eyes finally closed, and sleep beckoned.

"I can't do this anymore." Her voice was so quiet it might have been an incipient dream. "I can't. If it really comes down to it . . ."

Marcus intended to ask her what she meant, but he was asleep before he got the chance.

The sun seemed to have been nailed to the sky. It refused to move, in spite of Marcus' repeated glances and entreaties, and hung a few degrees short of its zenith like the flame in some enormous oven.

If he'd had a watch, he'd have checked it, for the hundredth time. The only watch he knew of in all of Khandar sat in Janus' breast pocket, and Marcus was unwilling to reveal his anxiety by asking the colonel the time.

Trying to conceal that sort of thing from the colonel was a lost cause, however. Janus glanced at him and said, encouragingly, "It's not noon yet, Captain. A few minutes more."

"Yessir," Marcus said. "Besides, I doubt the Desoltai will be completely punctual."

"On the contrary. I expect them to be where we want them at noon on the dot. In fact—" Janus shaded his eyes with one hand. "Yes. I believe that's the vanguard."

Marcus looked, and at first saw nothing. Gradually, though, a patch of the unmitigated brown-on-brown landscape resolved itself into brown-robed riders, on brown or sandy-colored horses, passing across brown rock and rills of windblown sand. With the sun high overhead, there weren't even shadows to give them away. *No wonder we never spot the bastards in time.*

He turned to the two runners, chosen from the hardiest of the young recruits. They saluted and hurried off at his gesture, having memorized in advance the message they were to repeat to Val and Mor if all went according to plan. Marcus satisfied himself that they were scampering down the rear of the hill, then turned back to Janus.

He and the colonel occupied a fissure in a massive boulder, around which sand and smaller rocks had built up until it was nearly covered. The shelf was deep enough for a half dozen men and provided a lip of rock that would screen anyone waiting there from casual observation. It was an excellent vantage point.

"He's getting sloppy," Janus murmured.

"Who is?"

"Our friend the Steel Ghost. Look—they're in a single column. No outriders, no scouts."

Marcus frowned. That didn't sound like the Desoltai. "Do you think they're onto us? This could be a trap."

"Unlikely," Janus said. "I suspect they've simply become a little overreliant on their secret advantage. Remember, the Ghost already knows where the *raschem* army is headed."

They'd been up half the night making sure of that. At Janus' direction, pickets had marked down the locations and patterns of the lights flashing in the darkness around the camp. A detachment of picked men had surrounded one of them, neat and quiet, and dispatched the three-man Desoltai patrol without anyone being the wiser. The messages that followed had been composed by the colonel, an apparently meaningless sequence of flashes and pauses that Janus assured Marcus the Ghost would understand. In the meantime, Give-Em-Hell's cavalry had been noisily unleashed, driving back the other Desoltai observers and guaranteeing there would be no contradictory testimony.

It had all been carried out very smoothly, Marcus had to admit, especially for a regiment that had been on the brink of mutiny the day before. But that was only natural. Every soldier's nightmare was being stuck fighting a foe he couldn't hit back. Offered the chance to strike a blow, the Colonials had jumped at it, and morale had surged. Even the Fourth Battalion troops had shown some spirit.

"They're coming this way," Janus said. "Now it's down to discipline."

Marcus gave a grim nod. He bent his thoughts toward Val and Mor, and every man in their commands, as though he could calm them by mental effort alone. *Hold fire . . . hold fire . . . wait for it . . .*

There were a *lot* of Desoltai. Janus had been right about that, as about so much else. They rode five or six abreast, a rough column snaking along the twisting course between two sandy rills. It went on for what looked like miles. Marcus did a rough mental estimate and came up with two to three thousand horsemen. *That has to be close to everything they have.* He wondered if Janus was right and the Steel Ghost was down there in person. There was no gleam of a metal mask amidst the riders, but those brown robes could hide anything.

"Almost there," Janus said, as calm as if he were watching a tennis match. "Captain Vahkerson has kept his nerve, in any case."

"He always does," Marcus said. The Preacher had a hold over his cannoneers that bordered on the fanatic.

His eyes were glued to the tall blue-and-gray rock that they'd fixed as the starting post, standing out from the dusty landscape like a menhir. It was a few hundred yards from the little hill. The leading horsemen were approaching it, so close that they could have reached out and *touched* it, when one of them reined up. Behind them, the column shuffled to a halt, spreading out across the flat ground and up the sides of the rills.

"Not quite far enough," Janus said. "We'll have to signal from here."

"Now?" Marcus queried.

"Now."

Marcus grabbed the musket that leaned against the lip of rock, aimed it in the general direction of the Desoltai, and pulled the trigger. The familiar mule kick of the gun shocked his shoulder into numbness, and the *crack* of the shot carried out across the desert and echoed off the walls of the valley.

The chance of the ball hitting anything at this distance was nil, but the flash and the sound would be obvious for a long way. Val and Mor would be watching. The single shot from the hill was the signal to open the attack.

For a lingering moment, nothing happened. The Desoltai milled, shouting and pointing. Marcus had a brief fantasy that something had gone horribly wrong, that he and Janus were alone out here with two thousand desert warriors and the Steel Ghost.

Then the flashing tips of bayonets emerged from behind the rills on either side of the long column. Neat rows of dusty blue uniforms double-timed over the crests, far enough to get all three ranks into view, then halted and leveled weapons with practically parade-ground timing. Some of the Desoltai caught sight of them, but they had barely enough time to turn their horses around before sergeants up and down the line yelled the order to fire.

The massed chorus of musketry, at this distance, was a rolling crash like nearby thunder. Neat puffs of off-white smoke rose from every lock and barrel. They were too far away to hear the horrible *zip* of balls and the *smack* of impact in man and horseflesh, but Marcus had heard it often enough that his mind filled it in. Among the Desoltai, all was suddenly pandemonium. Men fell, horses stumbled, lost their footing, rolled over their riders or collapsed in a broken-legged heap. Every one of the riders was suddenly fighting for control of his mount, as even animals trained for battle panicked at the unexpected attack.

Marcus counted heartbeats under his breath. Here and there along the line, flashes and puffs of smoke from the riders' carbines showed they were firing back, but there was no coordinated return volley. A few small groups struggled free of the wreckage of dying horses and tried a charge, fighting to build speed on the rocky slopes. Marcus had reached thirty-five when the men on his left, Mor's Third Battalion, let loose another volley, more ragged than the first but just as effective. The Desoltai closest to the line went down in a single body, as though a giant's hand had swept across them, and the carnage in the valley multiplied. A few heartbeats later Val's troops fired as well, completing the chaos.

"Not a bad rate of fire," Janus mused, "with bayonets fixed. Still, that second shot could have used more discipline. Perhaps a bit of drill is in order."

Marcus didn't bother to reply to that. The Colonials were quickly disappearing inside the smoke from their own discharges, but the Desoltai were still visible. The second volley had convinced them that staying where they were was inadvisable, and the majority seemed to think that safety lay back the way they had come. A few more, either maddened or fanatic, charged the blue lines on either side. The third volley scythed them down, and the handful that made it to the top faced a wall of bayonets. Marcus watched one Desoltai plunge into the bank of smoke, only to have his terrified horse stumble out again dragging its unfortunate rider from the stirrups.

The great mass of the raiders was falling back, hurried along by further fire from the hills, though the shots lost effect as the Desoltai opened the distance. They funneled along the floor of the valley like water in a streambed, keeping to where the going was good. Before long their course curved to the left, taking the head of the panicking horde out of sight.

Marcus gritted his teeth. He understood the necessity, but he couldn't help feeling nervous at this part. *If they press the charge home, it's my boys they'll be riding over.* The First Battalion had double-timed out from cover to draw a line across the riders' route of escape, but unlike the Second and Third they were in the flat, where the Desoltai could easily get up enough speed to attack. *But they aren't alone.*

A deep, hollow *boom* floated over the low hills, then another and another. The crackle of musketry was almost inaudible under the thunder of the guns, first bowling their solid shots through the long, tightly packed mob of riders, then switching to canister as the desperate Desoltai closed. Even the thought of it was fearful, and Marcus was suddenly glad their vantage didn't provide a view.

"A lesson to remember," Janus said. "Use your advantages, but never feel too secure in them. You never know when they're going to be taken away."

Marcus wasn't sure if that was intended for his benefit. He saluted anyway.

"Yes, sir!"

"A couple of hundred got away, all told," said Give-Em-Hell. His diminutive form was practically vibrating with excitement. "Sorry about that, sir."

"Not your fault, Captain," Janus said. "You didn't have enough cavalry to mount a proper pursuit. Did they show any sign of regrouping?"

"No, sir. Pardon the language, sir, but they were running as though all hell was behind 'em, sir."

"Very good. Convey my appreciation to your men, and tell them to get some rest. We'll need you scouting our path in the morning."

"Yes, sir!" Give-Em-Hell saluted and ducked out of the tent, spurs jingling.

"A pity we didn't have a regiment of hussars handy," Janus said. "We'd have rounded up the lot. Still, one does what one can."

"Yes, sir." Marcus waved a scrap of paper. "Captains Solwen and Kaanos have reported in. We have less than a dozen casualties, and only three killed."

"Any prisoners? I'd be interested to see what they had to say."

"Not many, sir, and all of those badly injured. I've had several reports of men running for it when they might have easily surrendered, or turning to fight hand to hand and forcing us to shoot them."

"I see." Janus didn't sound surprised. "I have a notion—"

An excited knocking at the tent pole interrupted him. The colonel looked up. "Yes?"

"Sir," came Fitz's voice. "You'll want to see this."

"Come in, then."

The lieutenant entered and gave a crisp salute. His normally pristine uniform was a little dust-stained, and the bruise on his face was still hideous, but he gave no sign of pain in his bearing. When Marcus caught his eye, he flashed a quick smile. He'd been in command of the First where they'd blocked the valley exit, and according to his initial report none of the enemy had gotten within fifty yards.

"What have you got for us, Lieutenant?" Janus said.

"Take a look at this, sir."

Fitz pulled a heavy object from his pouch and laid it on the colonel's writing desk. It was a blank mask, featureless but for two holes at the eyes. A mangled leather strap dangled from one side, and near the top it was bent, as though someone had struck it a terrific blow. Marcus leaned over and hefted the thing. It had the weight of solid steel.

"Interesting," the colonel said. "Was this taken from a body?"

"No, sir. We found it lying on the ground, amidst the dead, but not on any particular body." He touched the strap. "It's broken, see? Could be it fell off."

"You think he's dead?" Marcus said.

Fitz shrugged. "Only one man in ten got away. If he isn't dead, he's got the saints' own luck."

"Dead," Janus said. "Have you told anyone about this, Lieutenant?"

"No, sir. It's just me and the sergeant who found it, and I trust him to keep his mouth shut."

"Good. Keep it quiet a little while longer." At Marcus' questioning glance, Janus shrugged. "I'd rather not get the men's hopes up. Rumors of the Ghost's supernatural powers have gone quite far enough already."

"You think we'll see him again?"

The colonel gave another summer-lightning smile. "I'm certain of it, Captain. Tomorrow, we attack the oasis."

Chapter Twenty-Four

WINTER

Winter awoke slowly, rising to consciousness like a corpse floating to the surface of a deep, still pond, still wrapped with clinging tendrils of dream. For a moment she tried to grasp them—there had been something, something *important*, and she felt herself losing it. Jane had been there, as always, but she had been different. *Warning. She was warning me about something.*

It was like trying to catch smoke. The dream faded, and she opened her eyes to see the familiar army blue of her tent glowing with the faint light that meant the sun was well overhead.

That can't be right. She tried to reckon the hours. It had been the middle of the night when she'd rescued the colonel and the others, and then . . . her memory was not as clear as she would have liked. She could vaguely recall being helped into the tent, and sometime later being prodded to drink a little water. A concerned face, looking down.

"Bobby?" Her voice was a croak.

"Sir?" Bobby said from nearby. "Winter? Are you awake?"

"I think so." Winter blinked gummy eyes.

"How do you feel?"

She considered that for a moment. Her body was gradually making its protests known. Her nose felt twice its normal size, and every breath brought painful stabs all along her left side. She managed to shift a little, and more bruises announced themselves.

"Lousy," she said, closing her eyes again. "Like some ape used me for a punching bag."

"Do you think you can sit up?"

Winter gave a weak nod, planted her hands, and levered herself off the ground. Halfway there, the world swam sickeningly. She felt Bobby's hands on her shoulders, guiding her the rest of the way. When she opened her eyes again, the corporal was giving her a worried look.

"The colonel had a look at you," Bobby said. "Your nose isn't actually broken, but you took a couple of nasty cracks to the head. He said you might be a little dizzy, but it should pass."

The colonel. The memory of their last conversation came rushing back. *Did he really . . . I mean . . . he* knows, *but he's not going to tell?* She couldn't make that fit in with the world she understood.

"I'll be all right," Winter said, more for her own benefit than for Bobby's. She touched her nose gingerly, and winced again. "Beast's *Balls*. Not broken, he said?"

Bobby nodded. "If you can get out of bed, we ought to get you cleaned up. Graff wanted to look at your ribs, but the colonel said you shouldn't be moved too much." She hesitated. "Does he—did he see—"

"He knows." Winter gave a hollow laugh, which brought a stab of pain from her side. "He's agreed not to tell anyone, what with my saving his life and all."

"Good," Bobby said. "That's . . . good."

Winter looked at her clothes. She still wore the uniform she'd fought Davis in, torn undershirt and all, caked with mud and dried blood. A wide stain across one shoulder marked where the sergeant had slid to the floor. Gripped by a sudden revulsion, she started fumbling with the coat buttons. Her fingers felt thick as sausages, and the buttons slipped away from her twice before Bobby leaned in.

"Let me," the corporal said gently. She deftly got the coat open, then turned away with a blush when Winter shrugged it off as though it was full of spiders. Bobby indicated a bucket and cloth beside the bedroll. "There's not enough for a proper bath, I'm afraid. But we can at least get the blood off. Unless . . ."

Winter blew out a long breath, feeling the ache in her ribs. "It's all right."

It had been more than two years since Winter had been naked in the presence of another human being, and she found the prospect deeply unsettling. Back before the Redemption, when the Colonials had enjoyed unrestricted access to Ashe-Katarion, she had very occasionally scraped together the coin to rent a room at one of the private bathhouses the served the high-rent districts. A big cistern full of blood-warm water, all to herself, seemed like the height of unimaginable luxury, but she'd never been able to bring herself to fully enjoy it. No matter how sincere the attendants' promises of total discretion, no matter how far away from the areas normally frequented by Vordanai the bathhouse was, she could never shake the feeling that someone would take the opportunity to spy on their pale-skinned visitor. Then, somehow, her secret would get back to Davis, and the captain, and the colonel, and then—

She'd never been able to picture what would happen then, but the thought had been horrifying enough that she'd hurried through her ablutions and back into her carefully altered uniform. Now that the worst had actually *happened*, Winter wasn't sure what to think. But the habits of years died hard, and even if Janus was prepared to accept the fact of her gender, she was certain that the men of her company and her fellow officers would not.

Her torn undershirt was so soaked with Davis' blood that the front was as stiff as if it had been starched. Winter tossed it aside with a shudder of disgust and fumbled awkwardly with her belt, trying not to look at Bobby. She stepped out of her trousers and underthings, kicked them aside, and sat back down on the bedroll.

Bobby hissed through clenched teeth. Winter looked down at herself and winced. The bruises had subsided a little from the night before, but they still covered her skin with a mass of blue-and-black blooms, as though she'd contracted some awful plague. Her left side in particular was swollen and tender to the touch where he'd kicked her.

"Son of a bitch," Bobby said. "I wish you hadn't killed the bastard. I'd like to have a turn at him."

Winter gave a weak smile. "You might have to wait in line."

"I should have been there with you."

"You'd already saved my life once that night, and nearly gotten cut in half because of it. I'll live." Winter touched her side and flinched again. "Probably."

"Those cuts need cleaning." Bobby gestured imperiously to the bedroll. "Lie on your stomach."

Winter propped her chin on the pillow, keeping the weight off her bruised face, and waited. The air was warm and dusty on her bare skin. The first touch of the wet cloth made her flinch. Bobby paused.

"Sorry," the corporal said. "I'll be as gentle as I can."

Actually, after a few moments, it became almost relaxing. The bruises hurt in a dull way whenever the wet cloth passed over them, but Bobby had a light touch, letting the rag sit and soak sticky patches of dried blood before wiping them away. Where her skin had been torn up against the rocky ground or Davis' fists, the stinging made Winter chew her lip, but she managed to keep from crying out.

"How long have I been asleep?" she said, in an effort to distract herself.

"More than two days," Bobby said.

"Two *days*?" Winter couldn't help but twitch, and it made Bobby's finger stab hard into her bruised ribs. She pressed her face into the pillow to muffle her shriek.

"Sorry!" Bobby squeaked, dropping the rag. Winter turned her head to look up at the corporal. She wondered again how she'd ever believed Bobby was a boy.

"My fault," Winter said, through gritted teeth. She hissed a few breaths and tried to relax. "But—really two days?"

The corporal nodded. "They had you on one of the carts. Colonel's orders."

Winter didn't remember that at all. Then again, given the tendency of the unsprung carts to bounce over every pebble, maybe it was better to have been unconscious.

"Two days," Winter repeated. "So what's happened?"

She listened while Bobby worked even more tentatively with the rag and explained about the ambush, the near-complete annihilation of the Desoltai fighters, and the subsequent march to the oasis. When the time came for her to roll onto her back, Winter closed her eyes to keep from having to stare up at Bobby's blushing face.

"They tried to make a stand," the corporal went on, "but there wasn't much fight left in them. Most of them broke at the first charge, and we spent the day cleaning out the rest. Give-Em-Hell was all for following the ones that ran, I hear, but the colonel ordered us to stay put. We're camped just by the edge. There's a little town—not much more than a few shacks, really, but there's a spring and a pool, just like the colonel said."

"What about you?" Winter said.

"I'm sorry?"

"You. The—" She drew a line across the front of her body with one finger, where Bobby had been cut, not wanting to say the words aloud. "You know."

"Oh. Fine. The same as always." Bobby gave a weak chuckle. "I don't think I've had so much as a hangnail since . . . the first time."

"That's good." Winter tried not to picture the healed skin

under the corporal's uniform, warm and pliable but glassy as marble. *And spreading* . . . She gritted her teeth again.

Bobby gave the cloth a last swish and sat back. "There. That's better. Do you think we need to bind those cuts?"

Winter opened her eyes and sat up, poking at her torn skin with one finger. "I'll be all right. It doesn't seem to have started bleeding again—"

There was a knock at the tent pole. They both froze. Winter caught Bobby's eye and jerked her head in the direction of the tent flap, and the girl nodded.

"Who's there?" Bobby said.

"Feor."

Winter relaxed. "One moment," she said in Khandarai, and got up to get clothing. She was down to her last clean shirt, and there was no choice but to wear the stained trousers again. She left the jacket in the dirt. It would need a thorough wash before she could even think of putting it back on. Once she was at least decent, she waved at Bobby, who held the tent flap open. Feor ducked inside.

The girl had changed somehow. She'd discarded the splint that had held her arm since they'd first tended her, but it was more than that. The glassy look in her eyes was gone, replaced with a hard sense of purpose. The march from Ashe-Katarion had thinned her, too, hollowing her cheeks and giving her a lean, hungry look.

"Winter," Feor said, looking her over. "You are . . . well?"

"Well enough. Your arm?"

Feor raised it experimentally. "It still feels weak," she said, "but Corporal Graff said the bone has healed true." She cocked her head. "I think that is what he said, at least. My Vordanai is improving, but he still speaks too quickly."

Winter gave an uneasy chuckle. "Good. That's good."

There was an uncomfortable silence. Winter glanced at Bobby, who gave a tiny shrug, reminding her that she understood nothing of the Khandarai conversation.

"I wanted to apologize," Feor said.

Winter blinked. "Apologize?"

"For my behavior the night of the Desoltai raid, and during the time since we left the city."

"Ah." *It's about damn time.* Winter shifted awkwardly and tried to sound conciliatory. Feor was clearly having a hard time getting this out. "I don't know. I mean, it hasn't been easy for you—"

"It's no excuse." Feor swallowed. "Especially for what I . . . tried to do, at the end. I put you and Bobby in danger from my own selfishness."

"But—" Winter shook her head. "All right. Apology accepted. If it means anything to you, I think I understand. After Ashe-Katarion . . ."

"But you had the truth of it all along," Feor said earnestly. "Onvidaer returned my life to me. To waste it now would be to cast away his suffering as well as mine."

Winter *had* said something like that, come to think of it, although at the time she'd just spouted whatever came to mind in order to get Feor moving. She shrugged.

"Well. I'm glad you've worked it out."

"It has become clear to me," Feor said, "that it was the will of the gods that I meet you, and do as I have done. Even Mother's sanction is nothing beside that. Bobby is the proof."

"Proof?" Winter said. "What about her?"

"My *naath* . . ." Feor hesitated. "It is a sacred thing. *Obv-scar-iot.* In Khandarai it means . . ." Her lips worked silently for a moment. " 'Prayer of the Heavenly Guardian,' perhaps. It is the closest I can come. The language of magic is . . . difficult."

"I remember. What about it?"

"It grants the strength and power of Heaven to defend the faithful and the cause of the Heavens in this world. When I used it on a *raschem*, a nonbeliever, I thought it would not achieve its full flowering. The power of the Heavens would not invest one who was not worthy."

"Its full . . . flowering?" Winter said.

"No." Feor hesitated. "Have you examined where she was . . . wounded, the first time?"

"I did." Winter glanced again at Bobby, but spoke in Khandarai. "It's growing, isn't it?"

"I think so."

Winter chewed her lip. "What's happening to her?"

"The Heavens favor her. I do not know why, but they have chosen to grant her their power. She is truly becoming the Heavenly Guardian." Feor blew out a deep breath. "That is how I know that coming to you was their will."

"But what's going to happen to Bobby? Is that stuff going to spread over her whole body?"

"I don't know. There has not been a true Guardian in many generations, and I was not permitted to study the oldest lore." Feor shook her head. "It may be that the process will halt when she has accomplished the purpose the Heavens have set for her."

"'May be'?" Winter tried to squelch her anger. *Without this* naath, *Bobby would be dead twice over, and likely me in the bargain.* "All right. So you don't really know. Is there anyone who does?"

"Mother. Or perhaps not even she. Much of the knowledge of ancient days is lost to us."

"Right." Winter rubbed her forehead with two fingers, trying to fight off an incipient headache. "Right. So when we capture your 'Mother,' I'll just ask the colonel if we can have a moment alone with her."

"She will not be captured." A haunted look passed across Feor's face, and she hugged herself tightly. "She will die instead. They all will."

"They might escape again," Winter said.

"No." Feor looked up. "That is what I came to tell you. Mother is close. I can *feel* her. Onvidaer as well."

"You think they're here? At the oasis?"

"Yes."

"But . . ." Winter turned to Bobby and switched to Vordanai. "You said the oasis was taken, right?"

The corporal nodded. "Why?"

"Feor insists that someone is still there. Those people we saw in Ashe-Katarion the night of the fire. Could they be hiding somewhere?"

Bobby paused. "I know the colonel ordered the place searched for supplies, but I hadn't heard of anybody finding anything like that. They're still at it, though." She shrugged. "Graff and the rest of the company are out there now with Captain d'Ivoire."

Winter went very quiet. Something in her chest had tightened into a knot, and it was a moment before she could speak.

"You stayed behind?" she said.

"We wanted someone to be with you when you woke up," Bobby said. "I thought it would be best if it was me. Because—well, you know."

Winter blew out a breath. Her side ached.

"Well," she said, "now that I'm up, I'd better get back to my post. Let's track down the others."

"That's not really necessary," Bobby said. "Graff can handle things—"

"I'd rather go myself," Winter said, through gritted teeth. The memory of that terrible night in Ashe-Katarion kept playing out behind her eyes, with the young man named Onvidaer dispatching three armed men in the casual way one might kill a chicken for the pot. She turned to Feor and said in Khandarai, "Do you think you can find your way to Onvidaer?"

"Not . . . precisely. I can feel him when he is close, but no more than that."

"If we found him . . ." Winter hesitated. "He disobeyed your Mother once. Do you think he would do it again? If you had the chance to talk to him?"

"I do not know." Something in Feor's expression told Winter that she'd been thinking along the same lines. "But I would like to try."

MARCUS

Up close, a cannon always seemed like a tiny thing compared to the god-awful noise it produced.

Field guns did, anyway. Marcus had seen siege pieces, first at the War College and later on the docks in Ashe-Katarion. Those iron monsters were so enormous it was hard to imagine anyone even being able to load them, much less daring to be nearby when a spark was applied to the touchhole.

The twelve-pounder was tiny by comparison, a six-foot metal tube with a barrel not much larger than Marcus' head at the business end. It was dwarfed by its own wheels, big hoops of iron-banded wood. This was one of the Preacher's original three, carefully engraved from muzzle to axle with scripture from the Wisdoms, and now mottled all over with powder residue.

The Preacher himself was standing beside the gun, talking to Janus. Behind them waited the Seventh Company of the First Battalion. Marcus recognized the big corporal who'd been imprisoned with them in Adrecht's tents, and resisted giving the man a wave.

"You'd get more force if you hit it straight on," Janus was saying. "And those doors can't be solid stone, or they'd be too heavy to move. There's no room for a counterweight."

"No disrespect, sir, but I've seen some clever counterweights," said the Preacher. "Besides, if they are light, it won't matter how we hit them. And if we get a rebound, I sure don't want it coming right back at us." He patted the cannon fondly. "Besides, by the grace of the Lord and the Ministry of War, we've no shortage of roundshot. If we don't break through the first time, we'll just have to try again."

"I suppose you know your business." Janus looked back at Marcus. "You've warned the men?"

"I sent Lieutenant Warus, sir." Unexpected cannon fire had a way of producing unpredictable results, and with the Colonials dispersed through the little oasis town Marcus didn't want to take a chance on someone panicking.

"Excellent." Janus took two long strides back from the gun. "You may fire at your pleasure, Captain Vahkerson."

The Preacher looked at the three cannoneers standing beside the piece, who gave him a thumbs-up. He nodded, and they fell back from the gun, one of them holding the end of a length of lanyard.

Janus retreated as well and, somewhat to Marcus' surprise, jammed his hands over his ears. This undignified but prudent example rippled down the chain of command as first Marcus and then the men of the Seventh standing behind him followed suit. Marcus didn't hear the Preacher give the order to fire, but he saw the cannoneer give a sharp jerk on the lanyard, and a moment later the world went white.

The "oasis" was little more than a spring, in truth, issuing from a crack in the side of a rocky hill that rose out of the endless wastes of the Great Desol like a granite whale. Where the steady trickle of water had once soaked away into the thirsty ground, the Desoltai had built a stone-walled pool, shaded with horsehides to keep off the worst of the sun. Around it was a village, if it could be dignified with the name. It consisted of a wide-open space around the pool, surrounded by a scattering of huts built of stone and scraps of wood and roofed with more hides. Even these must have represented a significant investment for the Desoltai. There were no trees in the Desol, so every piece of timber would have been transported on horseback from the valley of the Tsel.

Whatever noncombatants had inhabited the village had plenty of warning of the Colonials' approach, and the Vordanai had found the buildings stripped of everything a man could carry. A wide corral stank with still-fresh horse droppings, but there were no animals to be seen. Marcus had been frankly glad to hear it. Given the state of their supplies, burdening the column with a few hundred captive civilians would have brought on some choices he didn't like to contemplate.

Beside the spring, where the hill had crumbled into something approaching a sheer cliff, the rock was carved into what must once have been a spectacular bas-relief. That it was ancient was obvious by the weathering. Human figures had eroded to blank-faced mannequins, arms raised in prayer or war or missing entirely. There were dozens of them, stretching for yards on either side of the crack where the spring emerged. Between them the remains of pillars could still be discerned, and in a few spots where a crevice had provided shelter from the wind the original delicate carvings of leaves and foliage were visible.

In the center of the ancient work of art was a pair of doors, twice the height of a man and cut from the same yellow-brown stone as the hillside. They had once been carved as well, but the centuries had weathered them nearly flat. More important, at least to Janus, it was obvious from the wide scrapes in the sandy soil that they had been opened recently. So while the rest of the regiment had been set to hauling water from the pool and searching the town, one company of infantry and one of the Preacher's guns had been quietly commandeered to effect an entry. The men had spent the better part of an hour straining at the door with lines and makeshift crowbars, to no effect, so Janus had decided on more drastic measures.

*

Even with his ears covered, the blast of the cannon filled the world. Close up, it wasn't the bass roar he was used to, but a monstrous crescendo that rattled his teeth and shifted things uncomfortably in his guts. His next breath reeked of powder. When he opened his eyes tentatively, he saw a ragged cloud of smoke drifting upward from the gun's muzzle. Beyond, barely twenty paces away, were the doors of the temple. Marcus couldn't imagine anything resisting the shot at that distance. It seemed as though it would have torn a hole in the mountain itself.

It certainly had done a number on the doors. The Preacher had aimed for the crack between the pair, and his aim had been impeccable, as had Janus' logic. The stone surface was revealed as a thin facade, no more than an inch thick, supported by a wooden frame. The ball had punched clean through, smashing an irregular hole in the stonework and sending a spiderweb of cracks across the rest of the surface. As Marcus watched, a snapped-off section buckled and fell with a sound like someone dropping a tray full of crockery. Other pieces followed, one by one, until only the lower half of the doors and a few scraps around the hinges remained intact. A cloud of dust billowed up from the pile of stone fragments at the base.

"Well laid, Captain," Janus said, when the chorus of destruction had come to an end. "I think no further shots will be required."

"At your service, Colonel," the Preacher said, and saluted. "Shall I send for my teams?"

"Indeed." Janus looked thoughtfully at the dark opening. Sunlight cutting through the dust cloud illuminated only a narrow square of cut-stone floor, the air ablaze with dancing motes. Beyond that, the blackness was complete. He turned to the infantry, who were cautiously lowering their hands from their ears. "Corporal! Clear this mess out of the way, if you would?"

"Yessir!" the corporal snapped, throwing a sharp salute. A team of rankers was soon at work tossing the chunks of rubble aside, while others levered the wrecked wooden structure of the door out of the way. As the Preacher's artillery mounts arrived to drag his gun back to the camp, Janus turned to Marcus.

"You seem like a man with something on his mind, Captain," he said.

"Just thinking, sir," Marcus said. "If there's anyone in there, that just about rang the front bell for them. They'll be ready for us."

"True. But without access to the spring, they couldn't hope to conceal any significant force."

Marcus lowered his voice. "What about that *thing* that came for you in Ashe-Katarion?"

"The demon may try to stop us," Janus acknowledged. "But we demonstrated there that it is not invincible. Formidable as an assassin, certainly, but a full company should see it off."

"And you think you'll find your Thousand Names here?"

"I'm certain of it," Janus said. "We know they moved it this far, and they had no way to take it any farther. We've searched the rest of the town—not that it offers much of a hiding place. There's nowhere else it can be. Ergo, it must be here."

Marcus nodded. Looking into the dark entryway gave him a sour feeling in the pit of his stomach, but he'd had the same feeling in Ashe-Katarion, when the search had led to a dead end. *Nerves,* he told himself. *It's just nerves.*

Saints and martyrs. This place goes on forever.

Once the corporals of the Seventh had managed to round up enough lanterns to light their way, Marcus and Janus had proceeded into the hillside, a squad of infantry in the lead. The doors had opened onto a low-ceilinged tunnel with a gentle curve, laboriously hacked from the native rock. After a few dozen feet, though, it opened out into a much larger space.

"This must have been a natural cavern," Janus mused. "I can't believe anyone would excavate so much stone."

Marcus nodded in agreement. The vaulting cave put him in

mind of a cathedral, high-ceilinged and spreading wide to either side of the entrance. Two great fires burned in the far corners, but they barely served to outline the space and throw leaping shadows. The floor was covered with *shapes*, humanoid figures twisting grotesquely in the bobbing lantern light and the flares of the bonfires, and Marcus had a bad moment before he realized they were statues. He'd seen dozens like them on Monument Hill in Ashe-Katarion, elaborate depictions of the myriad Khandarai gods, each possessing inexplicable animal features and dressed in odd, ceremonial regalia. The closest pair were what looked like a horse-headed man with wings and a snake that walked upright on a pair of grasshopper legs, and had for some reason been provided with an enormous, drooping penis.

"Goddamned priests," Marcus muttered. He wasn't a religious man, but there was something a lot more . . . well, *respectful* about a simple double circle in gold hanging over an altar. He turned to Janus. "You were right. This is a temple."

"There must be a shaft," Janus said to himself. "Otherwise the smoke would be smothering. Unless they only lit the fires as we came in?"

"Either way, they're ready for us."

"As you pointed out, Captain, that was inevitable when we used a cannon as a door knocker." Janus raised his voice. "All right, Corporal. Onward! They're only statues. And ask your men not to touch any of them, please. They are quite old, and some of them seem fragile."

The big corporal barked orders, and the rankers advanced, spreading in a loose formation through the enormous room. The statues were set in a rough pattern, not quite a grid, with ten or twenty feet between them. They seemed to fill the cavern to the walls, giving the impression of an army of shadowy, lantern-lit figures all around them. Marcus heard muttering among their escorts, and more than one man brought his hand to his chest to make the double-circle ward against evil. He couldn't blame them.

Another fire sprang to life, just ahead of them, and men raised their weapons. This one was smaller, just enough to illuminate a small circle of flagstones. On either side of it lay a human figure, spread-eagled, with a wooden box sitting between them. Marcus glanced at Janus, and caught the corner of the colonel's mouth quirked in amusement.

"Sir?" Marcus said.

"Gifts, Captain. Someone is trying to . . . buy us off."

"I'm not sure I understand."

Janus beckoned him forward, and Marcus reluctantly approached the fire. As he got closer, he realized with a start that he recognized both of the men on the floor. The fat body of General Khtoba, still in his stained dress uniform, wore an expression of blank surprise. The young man in black robes who had been the Hand of the Divine seemed more serene. Each corpse had a slim dagger embedded to the hilt in its left eye socket.

The colonel went to the box and flipped the lid open with a boot before Marcus could protest. He stared down at the contents for a moment, then looked up with another brief smile.

"Take a look, Captain. You'll appreciate this."

The firelight glittered across a steel mask, twin to the one they'd found after the ambush. Janus bent and picked it up. Underneath it was another identical copy, and Marcus could see another beneath that.

"What is that?" Marcus said. "The Steel Ghost's spare wardrobe?"

"More like the source of his mysterious powers," Janus said.

"I'm not sure I understand. Was there something special about the masks after all?"

"Only the significance ascribed to them." Janus ran a finger along the smooth metal. "It's inspired, really. I'm amazed they managed to keep the secret for so long."

"The way he could be in two places at once," Marcus said. "The Steel Ghost used doubles."

"In a way. My guess is that there was never any such person as the Steel Ghost to begin with. He was . . . a sort of myth, but one that only outsiders believed in. They must have laughed long and loud around the campfires."

"But someone must have worn the masks!"

"Whoever was convenient. Once you've built up the legend, think of the advantages. Pull a mask out from under your cloak, and suddenly it's not just a Desoltai raid but the Steel Ghost himself out for blood. Take it off when no one's looking, and the Ghost vanishes into the desert like a shadow. Combine that with the intelligence advantage they derived from their lantern codes, and they'd created a shadow puppet that had the whole country running scared."

Marcus looked down at the mask in the colonel's hand. "You knew. That's why you told me not to put it out that we'd killed the Ghost in the ambush—you knew he might turn up here as well."

"Let's say that I strongly suspected. When you have a man whose only distinguishing feature is something that *hides* his identity, why should you assume it's the same man each time? It's like saying the Pontifex of the White has lived for a thousand years because different men keep putting on the hat."

"You might have told me."

"I would have, if it had ever become a serious issue. As it is, it's simply a . . . curiosity." He looked dismissively at the two corpses, then raised his voice to a shout. It echoed off the distant walls. "Very generous! I thank you."

Marcus opened his mouth to speak, but Janus held up one finger for silence. A moment later, another voice filled the cavern, a distant hissing sound that seemed to come from every direction at once.

"You have what you came for, *raschem*. Consider this our surrender."

"Steady," Marcus said, as the rankers looked in all directions. The last thing they needed was a careless shot causing a panic. "Corporal, get the men to close up."

"I am Count Colonel Janus bet Vhalnich Mieran," Janus said in Khandarai. "May I have the honor of knowing to whom I speak?"

"You may call me . . . Mother." The word echoed oddly, repeating over and over through the vaulting hall for longer than it had any right to. "And I know well who you are."

"Then you know that this is not what I came for."

"No?" Mother's voice was a hiss, like windblown sand sliding across stone. The fire lighting the two corpses started to flicker and die. "You have the leaders of the Redemption. Bear them back in triumph to your pet prince. The Desoltai will raise no more rebellions, and the Steel Ghost will vanish into the myths of the Great Desol. What more do you require?"

"I will have the treasure of the Demon King," Janus said. "Give me the Thousand Names."

"Then it is as I feared. You are the minions of Orlanko and the Black Priests."

Marcus glanced at Janus, but the colonel's face was blank. None of the rankers would understand the Khandarai conversation, and Marcus was starting to doubt his own comprehension. *Black Priests? If she means our Priests of the Black, she's about a hundred years too late . . .*

"No," Janus said. "They are my enemies as well."

"You lie," Mother snapped. "Or else you are deceived. It matters not. I offer you this final chance, *raschem*. Take your prizes and go."

"I will have the Names."

The ancient voice trailed off into a fading whisper.

"As you wish . . ."

A new sound filled the cavern. A hiss, rising from the shadows in every direction at once, like the sound of a kettle just before it becomes a shriek. There were a hundred kettles, a thousand, echoing and re-echoing until the whole vast temple seemed to be alive.

Around the edges of the room, where the glare of the bonfires didn't reach, green lights flickered to life. They were eyes, Marcus realized, a swarm of eyes, all glowing a pale, eerie green that put him in mind of lightning bugs. By their faint light he could see ranks of swaying bodies and rows of faces with slack, distant expressions, all framed by wisps of rising white vapor. More white smoke trickled up through the air just in front of him, mixing with the dark woodsmoke of the extinguished fire. Marcus looked down.

General Khtoba had only one eye left, but that was open, filled with green light from edge to edge. His mouth worked, letting out a stream of liquid smoke whenever his fat lips parted. With an arthritic jerk, his corpse rolled on its side and started to fumble its way to its feet. Beside him, the Divine Hand sat up, his burning green gaze fixed on Marcus, and crawled forward on hands and knees.

"Kill them," Mother's voice said, echoing louder and louder until it thundered through the hiss of the smoke. "Kill them all!"

"Saints and *fucking* martyrs," Marcus said. At least he thought he was the one who said it, but the oath had escaped from several mouths simultaneously, along with an assortment of choicer obscenities. At least one of the rankers had a more emphatic response, and the *bang* of his musket going off was loud enough in the echoing cavern to make Marcus duck. It was followed by another, and another, then the whole company, not a single volley but a staccato chorus of shots ripping the air and merging with their own echoes like a never-ending bolt of lightning. The flashes drowned out the bonfires and turned the scene into a flickering montage of light and darkness, men waving and running in jerky stop-motion.

He saw Khtoba rear up, finally managing to lift his fat bulk to his knees. One of the rankers shot him from only a few feet away. In the next flash, Marcus saw the big general jerk, strings of gristle and gore hanging down the back of his uniform where the ball had punched clean through him. No blood ran from the wound, though, only a trickle of white smoke like the trail from a snuffed candle. And Khtoba himself gave no indication of being aware that he'd been hit. He sprinted at the ranker, no more bothered by the hole in his chest than the dagger in his eye. The Colonial screamed, raising his musket in desperate self-defense, but the Khtoba-thing grabbed it with both hands, jerked it out of the way, and bore the man to the ground.

Screams were erupting throughout the cavern. Marcus' night vision had been ruined by the muzzle flashes. All he could see was the distant glow of the fires and the swarms of green eyes closing in. The wave of panicked shouts washed over him.

"Out! Fucking get out of here!"

"Brass Balls of the fucking Beast—"

"Get it off me!"

"Die, you son of a fucking—"

"They're in the door—"

"Form on me!" That was the big corporal, he thought. "Seventh Company, *form square on me*!"

A good idea, Marcus thought half hysterically, but it wouldn't work. Forming emergency square was hard enough in the open, let alone with demons bearing down on you.

Demons . . .

"Captain!"

The colonel's voice snapped Marcus out of his stunned reverie. He looked up to find the Divine Hand nearly on top of him, one arm thrown wide to draw him into a vicious embrace. Marcus jammed his hand into the thing's face and gasped when it bit down hard on the heel of his palm.

The blast of a pistol going off at close range muffled Marcus' scream. The creature's head came apart as the expertly placed ball caught it just above one ear, scattering bits of skull and brain. A torrent of the strange white smoke issued forth, mixing with the pink-gray of powder smoke. It staggered, which was enough for Marcus to yank his hand out of its unhinged jaw and pull himself away. A moment later, the colonel stepped in front of him, his drawn sword a shining line of steel between himself and the still-standing monster.

"Are you all right, Captain?"

"Sir—I think so, sir." He lifted his left hand and winced at the neat half circle of teeth marks. His other hand dropped to the hilt of his own sword.

Before he could draw it, the thing lurched forward again, apparently unimpaired by the lack of the top half of its head. It was clumsy, though, and Janus sidestepped as it came at him. His cut sliced neatly through the back of its leg, which abruptly failed to support the thing's weight, sending it crashing down in a heap. Even so, it scrabbled forward, forcing the colonel to back away.

Marcus had finally gotten his sword free, and he fell in beside Janus. Something brushed his shoulder, and he looked around in panic, but it was only the outstretched hand of one of the ancient statues. Most of the demons had followed the fleeing rankers toward the exit, but there were still two dozen immediately in front of them, closing in a rough semicircle. More clustered around the soldiers wherever they had fallen, tearing at them with fingers and teeth until the screaming finally stopped.

All the creatures Marcus could see were dressed in the brown-and-tan uniforms of the Auxiliaries. Many of them were officers, their uniforms heavy with gold braid and colorful patches, though they'd apparently forgotten the use of their swords. They retained enough sentience to know a touch of caution, however, and even a hint of tactics. Facing a pair of drawn weapons, they halted just out of reach and started to spread to encircle the two officers.

"Sir?" Marcus said, putting his back to the statue and trying to look in all directions at once. "Any ideas?"

"Run," Janus said.

"Run?"

"On count of three." Janus nodded to indicate a direction. "They don't seem so thick that way."

"That's away from the exit," Marcus said.

"One thing at a time," Janus said calmly. "One. Two. Three!"

They spun away from the statue. One of the demons blocked Marcus' path, and he hacked at its outstretched arms, sending one hand spinning off. His second cut went low, cracking its knee out from under it, and the thing toppled. Another came at him from behind, and Marcus whirled around with a desperate swing that caught it in the ribs and slammed it against the statue. He sent up a brief prayer of thanks that he'd retained his heavy cavalry saber in place of a slim officer's blade, and a further offering when the weapon came free without sticking in the bone. Then he was backing away from a pack of green lights, and Janus fell in beside him. Marcus caught the colonel's eye, and they turned their backs on the pack of demons and fled through the maze of statues.

WINTER

"Sir," Bobby said, almost jogging to keep up with Winter's rapid stride, "I really don't think this is a good idea."

"I'm fine, Bobby," Winter lied. She felt better than she'd expected, actually, once she got up and moving. Her nose was still tender, though, and every too-swift movement brought stabs of pain from her side.

"Even if you are," Bobby said, "the colonel gave strict instructions that no one was to go after him."

"That obviously doesn't apply to you and me," Winter said. "He took the Seventh Company with him, and we're part of the Seventh Company. We've got to be allowed."

"What about her?" Bobby said, indicating Feor. The Khandarai girl wore a hooded brown robe, but she was still attracting odd looks from the soldiers they passed.

"She's—got information we might need," Winter said. "I'll explain things to the colonel."

"But—"

"No more objections, Corporal."

"Sir, yes, sir!"

The little town was much as Bobby had described it. The colonel had ordered it searched, but there wasn't really much *to* search. She saw a few men examining the household items and furnishings that had been left behind, following the time-honored soldiers' tradition that anything you could carry off from an enemy camp was fair game, but there wasn't much to loot, either. At least there was water. They passed the cistern, which was at one end of a never-ending bucket chain of sweating men struggling to refill the casks of the regiment and water its thirsty animals.

Bobby had reluctantly pointed out where they were headed, a section of the cliff face at the back of the village that boasted a stretch of ancient carvings. A doorway gaped in the sand-colored wall like a missing tooth, flanked by small mounds of broken stone and smashed wood. A faint smell of gunsmoke hung in the still desert air.

Winter paused just outside, uncertain. The sun was well up by now, and the shadow of the cliff was starting to creep away from the face and down toward the town. After a dozen feet, the tunnel was completely black. Winter glanced at Feor, who had pushed back the hood on her robe and was looking at the carvings with interest.

"Do you know this place?" Winter said.

Feor shook her head. "It is a temple, a very old one. But Mother and the Desoltai have never been on good terms, and they did not share their secrets easily. It took the arrival of you Vordanai and the beginning of the Redemption to bring them together."

"Do you think they're inside?"

"Yes," Feor said. "I can feel them." Her expression turned uncertain. "Something else as well."

"Sir," Bobby said, "something's wrong here."

"How so?"

"The colonel warned everyone off from this place."

"So you said."

Bobby frowned. "Don't you think he would have left a couple of guards outside?"

That made Winter pause. She chewed her lip thoughtfully. "Maybe they're farther in?"

"Could be," Bobby said.

"Come on," Winter said. "Let's find the others."

Winter edged forward, one hand feeling ahead along the dry stone wall. The entrance was a square of brilliant daylight behind them, slipping slowly out of view as the tunnel curved into the cliff face. There was *some* kind of light ahead, something that flickered like an open flame. Just as they'd entered there had been a resounding *crack*, and a rumble like faraway thunder.

"Was that a shot?" Bobby said.

Winter pursed her lips. It was hard to say—the stone made everything echo oddly and changed the timbre of familiar sounds. She kept edging forward, step by careful step. Another *crack*, accompanied by a distant flash, brought her up short.

"That was definitely a shot," Bobby said. "Who the hell are they shooting at?"

They started moving faster. Light gradually started to filter in, a weird, flickering brilliance. It was the red glow of a fire, Winter was sure, shot through now and again by the brighter yellow-white of a muzzle flash. It was enough to make out the bare outline of things, which narrowly prevented Winter from tripping over the first dead man.

She threw out an arm to bring Bobby to a halt. The tunnel

ahead of them was strewn with corpses, a dozen or more, all lying flat or sitting against the walls in attitudes that suggested they'd been propped there like puppets. It was impossible to make out any detail in the firelight, and Winter dug hastily in her pocket for a box of matches.

"Are those—," Bobby said.

Winter struck the match on the tunnel wall. The flickering firelight from up ahead made colors difficult to distinguish, but in the steadier light of the match she recognized the brown-and-tan uniform of the Khandarai Auxiliaries. Bobby let out a long breath of relief.

"What are they doing here?" Winter muttered, half to herself.

"Could Khtoba have followed us across the desert?" Bobby said.

"Or we followed him." Winter looked back at Feor, who was looking down at the bodies with a puzzled expression. "Are you all right?"

"There's no blood," Feor said.

None of the corpses were visibly marked. Winter frowned.

Bobby was already pressing ahead. Feor threaded her way past the Auxiliaries to join her, and Winter followed slowly. Beside the last of the corpses, she paused.

"If they're fighting . . . ," Bobby said in low tones.

"Just a moment."

Winter prodded the facedown man with her boot. He was an officer, judging by the braid on his shoulders and the scabbard at his belt. The corpse rocked slightly when she touched it, and after a moment of hesitation she got down, grabbed his shoulder, and rolled him onto his back. There was no wound on his front, either. The elaborately decorated Auxiliary uniform was unmarred.

Something *hissed.* She watched, fascinated, as a thin wisp of white smoke trickled from the body's slightly parted lips and wafted toward the ceiling.

"Sifatz," Feor said, then repeated it in her half-learned Vordanai. "Run!"

"Wh—"

The corpse's eyes snapped open. They were green from edge to edge and glowed with an inner light that threw Winter's shadow wide across the tunnel ceiling. Its hands came up and locked around her wrist, dragging her off balance. She gave an undignified squeal as she fell across the corpse, her left side lighting up with pain. As she fell, the *thing* shifted its grip, wrapping its arms around her waist in a horrid parody of an embrace. Its mouth opened wide, releasing a gush of white smoke that played across her face and filled her nostrils with a scent like burning sugar.

With sudden horror she realized it was going to *bite* her, rip her throat out like some kind of beast. One of her arms was stuck by her side, but she just barely managed to bring the other up in time, slamming her forearm under its chin and forcing its jaw closed with a *clack* of teeth. She brought her knee up as hard as she could, almost automatically, but it didn't even flinch at the blow to its groin. Its arms merely tightened their grip, holding her as close as a lover. Their faces were inches apart. Winter could see the faint stubble where the man hadn't shaved properly, and the green of his eyes bored into her.

Her left hand groped for purchase and found the handle of the corpse's sword. She didn't have the leverage to draw it, though, and the strength of the creature's arms seemed endless. Her breath came in tiny gasps, and her lungs were starting to burn. She arched her back desperately, trying to break free, but only managed to loosen her grip on the corpse's throat. It bared its teeth again, bathed in white smoke, and tried to force them closer to her face.

Winter gaped, desperate to draw a breath, but the grip around her shoulders pressed her chest too tight. It felt as though her spine was about to snap. Her lungs were on fire. She felt her legs kicking it, distantly, but for all the good it did she might have been pounding on a wall.

Then, all at once, something gave way. One of the creature's arms pulled free, giving Winter a moment to hurl herself away from it with all the strength she could muster. She felt its nails leave long scratches down her back, even through the fabric of her uniform, but it didn't manage to get a grip before she was clear and rolling sideways. She cannoned almost immediately into Feor, who was holding on to one of the monster's wrists with both hands. Winter and the Khandarai girl went down in a heap, accompanied by a metallic clatter.

Breath flooded back into Winter's body, and sight and sound came with it. She heard Bobby's frantic shouts, and saw the corporal struggling with another monster in a brown-and-tan uniform. Behind it, the other corpses were rising, herky-jerky, like puppets on invisible strings. A dozen pairs of eyes bathed the tunnel in their unearthly green glow.

The one that had grabbed her rolled onto its hands and knees and reached for her again. Winter scrambled backward, and felt Feor do likewise. One of her hands brushed something solid—the hilt of the Auxiliary officer's sword, which she'd been holding on to when she'd pulled herself away. Her fingers curled around it, and the next time the corpse reached for her she brought it around in a wild sweep. It was a light, whippy little thing, a dress sword for showing off at parties rather than actual combat, but at least it was sharp. It caught the creature as it went for a grip on her ankle and sheared its hand in half. No blood issued from the wound, only a gout of white smoke. The remaining digits brushed uselessly at Winter's boot as she pushed herself out of range.

Bobby had achieved a sort of stalemate, she saw, by snatching up a musket from beside one of the dead men and using it as a wedge to keep the thing away. More of the creatures were approaching, though. Winter finally managed to get her feet under her and shifted the sword to her good hand. When the thing on the ground reached for her ankle, she stomped down hard on its forearm and heard the bones snap.

"Bobby!" she shouted. "Back here!"

The corporal let go of the musket, jumping backward as her opponent let the weapon fall and stumbled forward. Winter caught the creature in the torso with a textbook thrust, slipping her sword neatly between its ribs, but the wound had no effect at all. She barely managed to yank the blade free in time to avoid its groping hands. Bobby fell in beside her, and she could hear Feor scrambling to her feet behind them.

Winter handed Bobby the Auxiliary's sword and drew her own. It wasn't much better, but at least she knew it was good steel. Three of the things blocked the corridor, with more of them crowding in behind. Now that they faced opponents with steel in their hands, the things seemed almost cautious, though Winter couldn't think why. The one she'd stabbed hadn't even flinched.

"Demons," Winter breathed. "Brass Balls of the Beast, they're fucking demons."

Bobby gave a shaky nod. Winter spared a glance for the corporal. She looked very pale, but the point of her sword never wavered. "What now?"

"Now, I think, we run." Winter slashed at one of the creatures that got too close, leaving another long, unbleeding wound on its arm. "On three. One, two, *three*."

With a final slash, she backpedaled a few steps, then turned and ran for it. On the way, she caught Feor's hand, dragging the Khandarai girl along until she got her feet under her. Soon all three of them were pounding down the tunnel, with the corpse-things shambling in pursuit.

The glowing green eyes had just vanished around the curve of the corridor when it abruptly ended, opening out into a much larger space. Winter had a vague sense of a high-ceilinged cavern, but her attention was absorbed by more immediate details. In the center of the cave, amidst rows of strange Khandarai statues, the Seventh Company had formed a steel-edged square. She could see the gleaming rows of bayonets, and every so often a shot rang out, shatteringly loud in the enclosed space. Surrounding them was a nearly solid ring of brown-and-tan uniforms two or three men deep. The white smoke they leaked mixed with the pink-gray of powder smoke to form a pervasive fog that made the whole cavern smell of saltpeter and burning sugar.

More of the walking corpses were scattered around the perimeter of the standoff, and at least a few of them looked in Winter's direction as she skidded to a halt in the doorway. They started for her immediately, closing in like iron filings drawn to a magnet. The sound of shuffling feet from the corridor behind them grew louder by the second.

She caught Bobby's eye. "Run for the square. I'll go first; you take Feor."

Bobby gave a jerky nod and made no objection. Winter could think of a whole host of objections herself, but there didn't seem to be any other options. She took a deep breath, fighting down the spikes of pain in her side, and charged.

Strong as they were, the demons weren't quick, or terribly bright. She went right at one, and it spread its arms wide like someone accepting a hug. At the last minute she ducked and veered right, slipping past it. From there she pivoted on one foot and brought the pommel of her sword around in a wide arc that ended in the back of its skull. Whether or not the impact pained it, it knocked the thing off balance, and it stumbled helplessly long enough for Bobby and Feor to dodge by.

Then they were in among the statues. Green eyes glowed from all directions, but Winter forced herself to focus on what was directly ahead of her. Another Auxiliary lurched out from behind a snake-headed statue, right into her path, and she barreled into it shoulder first, knocking the creature sprawling. It scrabbled at her as it went down, but Winter danced away, slashing at its hands with her sword. Glancing back, she found Feor right behind her, with Bobby holding off two more of the things with wild horizontal sweeps.

Ahead, the demons were packed tighter. Winter could see blue uniforms through the gaps, but she wasn't certain they could make her out through the crowd. She hoped desperately no one took the opportunity to fire at the commotion. She laid into the first monster with a wide two-handed swing, aiming low, and it toppled with its legs chopped out from under it. Others turned, white smoke gouting all around her, as she pressed toward the line of blue. They shied away from her cuts, though the sword did them little actual damage, and for a moment Winter thought she was actually going to make it.

Then one of the creatures didn't get out of the way in time. Winter's wild swing bit deep into its neck with a puff of white smoke and lodged in its collarbone. Her desperate tug failed to pull the weapon free, and the monster twisted away, ripping the hilt from her hands. They were suddenly all around her, hands scrabbling for a hold wherever they could grab. Winter tried to back away, but one of the things had her by the knee, and it wrenched her leg out from under her with casual strength. The world tilted sickeningly as she was hauled off her feet, and other hands snatched at her arms before she could complete the fall.

Her one free leg kicked until it was grabbed as well, and she felt more hands scrabbling across her, grasping handfuls of fabric and twisting painfully. The things that had hold of her limbs were pulling, all in different directions. She felt something pop in her shoulder, followed by a savage spike of pain. Winter screamed.

A single shot rang out, followed by a roaring voice that she recognized as Folsom at full battlefield volume.

"No, idiots, you'll hit him! Give them steel!"

This was accompanied by a ragged war cry from a dozen throats.

Just when Winter thought her arm would actually tear from its socket, the monster let her go. The others followed, and she slumped awkwardly to the floor, curling into a protective ball. Fighting raged above her. She could hear the shouts and grunts of the Vordanai, and the malign hissing of the demons. Finally there was another voice she recognized, and someone was prodding her tender shoulder.

"Sir! Lieutenant Ihernglass!"

She opened one eye and found herself staring into a bearded face, creased with worry. "Graff?"

"He's alive!" Graff shouted. "Someone help me!"

"Back to the square!" Folsom said, somewhere high above.

Winter found herself being lifted once again. This time she bit back the scream. Ahead was a solid wall of bayonets. It parted as they approached, then formed again behind them as the demons closed in.

Chapter Twenty-Five

WINTER

She never quite lost consciousness, but it was a close-run thing. There was a long stretch when everything was a blur except for the pain—the scrapes and cuts all over, the stabbing agony in her side, the protests from abused joints where the demons had tried to tear her literally limb from limb. It wasn't fair to expect her to get up after all that, she thought. It wasn't reasonable. She ought to be allowed to curl up in a ball, close her eyes, and just wait until it was over.

It lasted until she remembered Bobby and Feor. They'd been with her until she'd hit the wall of demons, and then she'd lost sight of them. Graff and Folsom had come charging to the rescue, but she hadn't seen them find Bobby. Her chest suddenly tight, Winter unfolded herself with an effort and raised her head, blinking back tears.

Bobby was sitting on the flagstones nearby, with Feor beside him. The Khandarai girl had her skirt drawn up, exposing a set of vicious scratches along one leg, and the corporal was helping her with a bandage. That answered that question, anyway, but now that she was in motion Winter couldn't bring herself to just lie down again. She dragged herself up to a sitting position and tried to speak, but managed only a faint croak.

Graff hurried to her side. He handed her a canteen, and she drank greedily, tepid water trickling down her chin and soaking her collar.

"Are you all right?" he said when she was finished.

No, I'm fucking not all right, she wanted to say. *I was nearly torn apart by demons. What do you think?* But Graff looked pretty close to the edge himself, and in any case that would a poor way to repay him for saving her life. So she forced a shaky smile and said, "I think I'll live."

"Thank God. Folsom thought he saw you come in, but we couldn't be sure until you got close. That was goddamned brave of you, charging the lot of them like that." He paused, making it clear by his expression that by "brave" he meant "insane."

"There were more of them coming up behind us," Winter said. "I figured our only chance was to make it to the square."

"Ah," Graff said. "Well."

"Thank you," Winter said.

He looked embarrassed for a moment, and then his expression turned grim. "You may change your mind before long. You're not much better off in here than out there."

Winter took a proper look around for the first time. The company square was tiny, only ten yards to a side, leaving a small patch of flagstones in the center inhabited by the three corporals, herself, Feor, and a few wounded. Beyond that, a double line of rankers held stolidly to their lines, presenting an unbroken fence of bayonet points. She couldn't see past the wall of blue-uniformed backs, but she could hear the hissing of the demons beyond.

"They'd bury us if they really tried a rush," Graff said quietly. "They shy away from steel, thank God, but I don't know why. Sticking them doesn't seem to bother them any. But anytime we weaken the line, even a little, they go for it like we've rung the dinner bell. They nearly had us when Folsom and I went out to bring you back."

"Why aren't we shooting them?"

"For one thing, I can't spare the men to load," Graff said. "For another, it doesn't help much. God be good, I saw one of them keep going with a hole the size of my fist right through him. They don't die like men, so what good is throwing lead at them?"

Winter realized for the first time that Graff was *scared*. She'd never seen him afraid before, at least not in battle. Only a thin veneer of military professionalism held him together. *And he's a veteran.* She looked around at the steady backs of the Seventh Company with a new respect.

"We can't stay here," she said. "They're just waiting us out."

"Looks that way," Graff said. "But that's the trick, isn't it? That last charge was the closest we've gotten to the door, and I lost two men just getting that far. If we try to push all the way to the doorway we'll be crushed."

Two men. Winter's throat closed again for a moment. Two men had died just to rescue her, Bobby, and Feor. She didn't even know *which* two—they were just "men," rankers, expendable assets on the strength report. She fought down an urge to ask Graff for their names. *Later. If we get out of this alive.*

"Bugger all the saints with bloody rolling pins," Winter swore. It didn't make her feel any better. "Give me a minute."

She crawled over to where Bobby sat beside Feor, finishing her bandage. To Winter's surprise, the Khandarai girl's cheeks were wet with tears. Bobby caught Winter's eye and shook her head.

"She seems all right to me, sir," Bobby said. "Maybe she's just scared? When that thing grabbed you I nearly screamed the roof down."

"You weren't the only one," Winter said. "Are you hurt?"

"Just scratches."

Winter nodded and sat down on the other side of Feor. The girl looked up at her, dark eyes blinking away tears.

"Does it hurt very badly?" Winter said in Khandarai.

"No," Feor said. "Bobby is being kind. I will be fine."

"Then—"

"Akataer. My brother." She gestured weakly at the side of the square. "These are his creations, the product of his *naath*. I can feel his agony."

"Forgive me if I don't feel sorry for him," Winter said, more harshly than she intended. "His demons are trying to kill us."

"They are not demons," Feor said. "They are dead spirits, bound to their corpses and forced to serve."

"That sounds like a demon to me," Winter said. "How do we kill them?"

"You cannot. They have died once already. Now the body is just a . . . container. They will keep going, until . . ." She hesitated, then forged on. "Until Akataer releases them, or until he dies."

"Wonderful. Is there anything we can use against them?" Winter tried to remember her fairy tales. *What works on demons?* "Holy water? Silver bullets? Not that we have any. Chanting scripture?"

"You do not understand," Feor said. "They are *not* demons. Not separate entities. They are part of him, part of his *naath*. They *consume* him, little by little. I have seen him tired and weak after binding a half dozen for a day's labor. This many?" She shook her head. "He will not recover."

"Oh," Winter said. Feor's tears had stopped, and she simply looked weary. Winter felt a rising blush in her cheeks, which she tried to ignore. She opened her mouth, found she had nothing to say, and closed it again. Feor lay back against the flagstones and closed her eyes.

Folsom tapped Winter on the shoulder. She turned and clambered awkwardly to her feet, legs screaming protests. He offered her the hilt of her sword.

"One of the men picked this up," he said.

"Thanks." Winter sheathed it. Even her hands seemed to ache. "And thanks for coming to get me."

He shrugged. With the immediate danger gone, the big corporal seemed to have reverted to his normal taciturn persona.

"I don't suppose you have any brilliant ideas on how to get out of here?"

Folsom shook his head. Winter sighed and limped around the inside of the square, searching for inspiration.

The men couldn't salute, and didn't dare take their eyes off the monsters that waited just beyond the wall of bayonets. Nevertheless, she heard their whispers underneath the omnipresent hiss of white smoke. Every second man seemed to be reassuring his fellows now that the lieutenant was here.

"Lieutenant Ihernglass will get us out."

"He came with more troops. Got to be."

"The lieutenant always figures something out . . ."

Whatever reassurance her presence brought the men seemed to drain confidence from Winter in equal measure. She could *feel* the weight of their hope, their faith, stacking higher and higher on her shoulders until she wanted to collapse under the burden and simply die. She wondered briefly if this was how Captain d'Ivoire and Colonel Vhalnich felt every day. *Is there some magic formula they teach you at the War College to deal with it? Or do you just go numb eventually?* This was just a single company. She could hardly imagine what it would be like to have the entire regiment leaning on you for support.

Damn it. Focus! Her head felt like it was filled with cotton. *There's got to be* something. From where she was standing, she could see the doorway, just fifty or sixty feet away. As close as that, and as distant as the moon.

If we can get there, we're safe. The passage was only wide enough for three or four men at a time. The Seventh Company could defend that against these creatures for hours. The problem was that sixty feet. *If we break the square, they'll pull us down. But they're not quick.* She had outrun them easily in the tunnel. *We just need a few seconds, really. Enough time to get past them.*

And what have we got to work with? There wasn't much. Sixty-odd soldiers and no supplies. *The shots in their cartridge pouches, the coats on their backs, the boots on their feet.* Plus three corporals and a Khandarai *naathem* half a step away from tears. *And me.*

Her eye lit on something just inside the edge of the square. It was a metal-framed lantern, scavenged from one of the wrecked carts. *They must have carried it in with them.* Now that she was looking, she could see several more, scattered where the men had dropped them. *So add a half dozen lanterns to that tally. Does that help?*

A few seconds . . .

The hardest part was doing it all without weakening the square so much that the walking corpses would surge through. Orders had to be passed from man to man, since she didn't dare distract them all by shouting. *Plus, who knows how much those things understand?* It was like a giant game of pass-the-story, each man telling his neighbor, with Winter following along behind to straighten out the inevitable misunderstandings.

Eventually, they had a pile of uniform jackets in the center of the square. Winter kept her own, since she was sweating enough that she didn't trust her undershirt to conceal her properly, but everyone else was in shirtsleeves. Beside that they had a smaller pile of cartridge pouches, each a loose leather sack containing the twenty rounds of ammunition that the rankers kept on them. Bobby and Folsom were hard at work on those, while Graff helped her with the lanterns.

It seemed like hours before they were finished. Winter expected a charge the entire time, waiting for the green-eyed corpses to lose patience and simply surge into and over the bayonets to finish what they'd started. But they remained at bay, confident or just uncaring.

Finally, when everything was ready, she stood beside Folsom, facing the doorway. Graff hurried over, carrying an improvised torch in each hand, and Winter lit both with the last of her matches. He touched his torches to Bobby's, and then to one more, which he handed to Winter.

"Okay." Winter blew out a long breath and looked up at Folsom. "If this gets us all killed, let me just say in advance that I'm sorry."

The big corporal grunted and hefted the cartridge pouch he held. A twist of cloth dipped in lamp oil served as a makeshift fuse. Winter gingerly touched her torch to the very end and sent up a silent prayer of thanks when the whole affair didn't go off there and then. Once it was alight, Folsom didn't wait. He gave the thing a heave, and it disappeared over the heads of the men in the square to fall in among the monsters.

They got two more lit and thrown. Then there was a single agonizing second of waiting, in which Winter pictured the pouches bursting when they hit the ground, or the tapers being snuffed out by the wind of their passage—

The sound of the first one going off was disappointing, more of a muffled *thud* than the massive *boom* of a cannon. It was accompanied by the merry *zip* and *zing* of lead balls ricocheting off the stone floor. After tearing open enough cartridges to mostly fill the little sack with powder, she'd stuffed musket balls in until it was nearly bursting. The idea was that it would be something like a load of canister, spraying balls in all directions. Without a musket's barrel to channel the blast, the balls wouldn't go far or hit hard, but she hoped it would still be enough to damage something.

Two more blasts, almost simultaneous, announced the explosion of the other two bags. The wall of green eyes in front of her thinned out as the corpses turned to see what was happening or were knocked down by the blasts. She heard someone cry out, struck by a stray ball. She'd been afraid of that, but it was too late to worry about it now. *A few seconds.*

"First rank, *hold*!" she screamed, tearing her throat raw. "Second rank, past me, *charge*!"

The men had been instructed by the same chain-of-whispers method, and she was frankly surprised when they did what she wanted them to. One face of the square, the one closest to the doorway, erupted with cheers and shouts as men surged forward, leading with their bayonets. Behind them, the second rank of each of the other faces—the innermost line of the square—dropped their weapons, rushed to the center pile, and picked up a uniform jacket in each hand. They rushed past her in a body, into the gap behind the advancing men, where the creatures were just starting to turn back to face their escaping prey.

Just beside her, a ranker tossed one of his jackets. It was a good throw, landing squarely across the face of one of the monsters. The thing plucked at the coat with both hands, but before it could tear the fabric away Winter reached out and touched her torch to the uniform's sleeve. The lamp oil spattered across it caught instantly, and soon the entire jacket was a mass of flames. The sizzle of burning flesh mixed with the ever-present hiss, and black smoke gouted upward to discolor the white.

Bobby, Folsom, and Graff were all wielding torches, touching off the coats the rankers flung whenever they found a target. Those creatures they set aflame staggered away, or were pushed or kicked aside. Once he'd disposed of his burden, each ranker ran for it, sprinting for the doorway behind the vanguard of men still carrying bayonets.

"First rank, *run*!" Winter shouted.

The last of the square backed away a few steps and ran, holding on to their muskets. The monsters following hard on their heels were met by more flung coats, and once afire they blocked the path of their fellows. Winter saw a couple of men go down, tripped or grabbed from behind, but the rest made it past her. She started to backpedal as the wall of corpses approached, then turned to run.

Feor had gone ahead with the first wave, but she'd stopped by the doorway, while the rankers had sprinted out into the passage to press back any of the creatures that were still waiting there. Winter skidded to a halt beside her as the men of her company surged past, a river of tattered blue and white undershirts, carrying muskets or coats or no weapons at all.

"Go!" Winter waved them onward. Folsom had gone with the vanguard. Winter caught sight of Bobby trying to push backward against the tide of rankers, and she waved the corporal onward. Finally, the last few men hurried past, with Graff bringing up the rear.

"Something's wrong with them," Graff said, puffing to a halt. "Look."

The oil-damped coats were going out, throwing the room into relative darkness once again. Winter could see the dead things as vague shapes in the firelight, with green eyes cutting through the smoke here and there. They didn't seem to be pursuing. In fact, they'd all frozen in place, as though some vital force had suddenly been removed.

"Is that everyone?" Winter said. "I saw a couple of men fall."

"We picked 'em back up again," Graff said. "That's every man who wasn't already dead out the door. Except the captain and the colonel, poor bastards."

The captain and the colonel. "Right." Winter waved him on up the corridor. "Go. I'll be right behind."

Graff saluted and hurried after the rest. Winter and Feor remained in the doorway.

The green lights went out all at once. The corpses toppled wherever they stood, sprawling in heaps across the flagstones. Here and there flame still clung to them, filling the air with the smell of burning cloth and flesh.

The captain and the colonel. She'd almost forgotten about them. *But they must be dead. They weren't in the square, so they must be dead.*

"Fuck," Winter said. "Fuck, fuck, fuck."

She chewed her lip for a long moment, then rounded angrily on Feor. "You'd better go after—"

"I'm going with you," Feor said.

"No, you are—" Winter caught Feor's expression and suddenly felt too tired to argue. "All right. But stay close."

Feor stepped up and took her hand again. Winter raised the torch over her head, took a deep breath, and hurried back into the gloom.

MARCUS

Marcus gave a grunt as he wrenched his saber free, stepping away from the demon's still-scrabbling hands. His next carefully aimed stroke split its skull, sending up a torrent of white smoke. Then he retreated to where Janus waited in the shadow of one of the twisted statues. The thing kept thrashing behind him, but without a head it was blind.

"We're almost there," Janus said, tapping the corner of the statue's plinth with the tip of his sword. "Two more, I think."

"Fucking saints," Marcus said. "How many men did Khtoba have left?"

He knew objectively that they'd been lucky. Some of the Seventh Company had managed to form a square after all, and they were attracting the attention of the vast majority of the creatures. Picking their way around the edge of the vast cavern, he and Janus had to deal with only the scattered remnants, and he'd disposed of a dozen or so of those. But it *felt* like they'd been at it forever. He'd opened his jacket, his undershirt was soaked with sweat, and someone seemed to have added several tons of lead to his sword. His shoulder ached abominably from the impact of steel on bone, and the bite on his hand throbbed.

At least the colonel knew where he was going. *Or he says he does, anyway.* They'd been weaving through the statues, cutting down the demons singly or in pairs, but Janus had kept to a relatively constant direction. Marcus hadn't asked where they were going, because he frankly didn't want to know. He just hoped like hell the colonel had some kind of plan.

"Two," Marcus said after a moment. "Okay."

"I'll go right; you go left," Janus said. He didn't even seem winded. "Ready?"

"Ready," Marcus lied.

"Go!"

They spun around opposite sides of the statue. Two of the green-eyed creatures stood in the gap between another pair of idols, as idly as a couple of sentries. They looked up, mouths opening to trickle white smoke, as the two officers charged.

Janus' first instinct had been the correct one. *As usual.* Nothing Marcus had been able to do had put an end to the creatures' scrabbling parody of life, but their bodies could be damaged as easily as any human's. A good hit to the legs would leave them nothing to do but crawl. He ducked and aimed low, swinging the heavy cavalry saber in two hands like a sledgehammer. The demon's outstretched hands brushed past his cheek and over his shoulder, while his blow caught the thing on the knee. Flesh and bone exploded, bloodless as rotten wood, and Marcus spun away from the clutching fingers as the suddenly unbalanced monster toppled.

The colonel had dissected his opponent with typical grace, dodging its clumsy lunge and dancing behind it to neatly sever the muscles in its thighs with his lighter blade. It fell facedown, and Marcus gave it a slash in passing, smashing its face into a ruin. Once they were down and blinded, the demons presented a danger only if you managed to step on one.

"There." Janus pointed with his sword. A small campfire

burned up ahead, banked against the base of one of the statues and invisible from a distance. "Come on—we have to hurry."

He trotted toward it, and Marcus heaved a deep breath and lumbered after him. Janus' reserve of strength seemed boundless, and keeping up with him made Marcus feel like a milk cow trying to race a warhorse.

The little half circle of firelight looked as though it had been someone's camp. A small sack and a waterskin were propped neatly against the statue, and a thick blanket was unrolled over the hard flagstones for use as a bed. Lying on the bed—

At first Marcus thought it was a corpse. It *looked* more like a corpse than the green-eyed demons did. The young man's flesh was withered and shrunken, and his skin hung in loose folds from protruding bones. Ribs and hips were clearly visible, moving slowly under his gray skin like puppies squirming in a sack, and Marcus realized with a start the boy was still breathing in short, sharp gasps. His eyes were closed, but at the sound of the two Vordanai approaching they flickered open.

Janus crossed the flagstones to stand beside the boy in a few quick, sure strides, and flicked the point of his sword to hover just above the throat of the emaciated youth. He spoke in Khandarai, loud and clear enough that even Marcus could follow him.

"Call them off. Now."

A dozen pairs of green eyes turned to stare at them. Marcus raised his sword. The closest of the demons regarded him through the curtain of white smoke rising from its lips.

"Call them off," Janus said. "All of them, or I slit your throat."

The boy's mouth opened slowly. His voice was a thin rasp.

"I am dead already," he said.

A hollow *boom* echoed through the chamber, followed by two more in rapid succession. Marcus tried to see what was happening, but there were too many statues blocking the way. He could hear a tide of shouts rising above the hissing of the demons.

"Call them off," Janus said.

"He won't do it," said a woman's voice, also in Khandarai. "You should know better than to try to reason with fanatics, Colonel."

Jen Alhundt walked between two of the frozen demons, for all the world as if she hadn't noticed them. Her spectacles gleamed white in the light of the campfire. She held a pistol in one hand and had another thrust through her belt.

"Jen." Marcus' sword arm dropped slowly to his side. "Jen? What the hell—"

"Miss Alhundt," Janus interrupted. "I take it you have a suggestion?"

"Only the obvious," Jen said. She leveled the pistol abruptly and pulled the trigger. The boy's body jerked and stiffened for a moment, blood blooming from his chest, and then sagged.

All across the vast cavern, the green lights went out. The corpses dropped into place with a final exhalation of white smoke, staggering drunkenly into one another or sagging against the statues. Silence fell throughout the vast cavern as the inhuman hiss of the demons finally quieted. Marcus couldn't hear the shouts of the Colonials anymore, either. He swallowed hard.

"Jen," Marcus said, trying to keep his voice calm, "what are you doing here?"

"She's doing her job as a member of the Concordat," Janus said. His gray eyes were fixed on Jen. "Completing her assignment from the Last Duke."

"Her assignment was just to observe," Marcus protested. It felt weak, even as he said it.

"It was to observe," Jen said, "unless circumstances warranted other action."

"And they do now?" Janus said.

"I believe so." She tossed the empty pistol aside, drew the other one from her belt, and pulled back the hammer. "Colonel Vhalnich, in the name of the king and the Ministry of Information, I place you under arrest."

"Interesting," Janus said, after a long moment of silence.

"Drop your sword, if you please." Jen raised the pistol to a level with his chest.

The colonel shrugged and let the weapon fall. "May I ask the charge?"

"Heresy," Jen said. "And conspiracy against the Crown."

"I see." His expression was thoughtful. "His Grace may have difficulty making that case to a military court."

"That's not my affair," Jen said. "You're welcome to take it up with him once you return to Vordan."

"*If* I return. Much better for all concerned if I were to suffer a little accident during the crossing. Swept overboard in a storm, say. I'm sure an appropriate storm can be provided. Sea voyages are so dangerous."

She regarded him in stony silence. Janus sighed.

"I suppose it would be uncouth of me to mention that there are close to four thousand men outside who answer to my orders? I assume you have the appropriate paperwork tucked away somewhere, but they may not be inclined to examine it."

"The men will obey their commanders." Jen looked sidelong at Marcus. "Senior Captain d'Ivoire. I have a commission from the king and the Ministry to assume overall command of this expedition if I deem it necessary. As such, I am placing you in command of First Colonials. Your orders are to detain Colonel Vhalnich and return the regiment to Ashe-Katarion, where it will rendezvous with the transport fleet."

The formal language made Marcus draw himself up automatically, his aches and pains forgotten. He gritted his teeth. "Jen, you can't be serious. Heresy?"

"I believe you are aware of the colonel's interest in acquiring

Khandarai relics. If you wish to label yourself an accessory, I am willing to expand the charges. No doubt Captain Kaanos would be willing to assume command."

"Fucking saints." Marcus blew out a long breath. "You said you were a *clerk*. You were lying to me all this time."

"I neglected to tell you everything." Jen gave a slight shrug. "It comes with the job."

"Of course she was," Janus said. "She's Concordat, Captain. This is what she does."

"I'll thank you to be quiet," Jen snapped.

"Do you intend to shoot me?" Janus flashed a quick smile. "I doubt it, now that I think about it. The Last Duke needs to know what I know, doesn't he?"

"I intend to bring you to trial," Jen said, raising the pistol slightly. "If possible."

There was another silence.

"Jen . . . ," Marcus began.

"Don't do anything stupid, Marcus," she said. "Please. You don't know what you're dealing with."

"On the contrary," Janus said. "I think he finally understands."

"I'm not going to let you shoot him," Marcus said. "We'll go back to the camp, talk this over. I'm sure—"

A flicker of motion over Jen's shoulder was the only warning. Marcus dove forward, cannoning into her, and they both slid across the dusty flagstones to fetch up against the base of one of the statues. The pistol clattered and spun to a halt beside them. A silver blur hummed through the space where Jen had been standing, hit one of the nearby statues, and bounced off with a single ringing note, sending stone chips flying. The long, curved dagger bounced twice more, leaping like a fish off the flagstones, before it finally clattered to a halt.

The young assassin Marcus had last seen in the colonel's quarters stepped between two of the statues. He had another dagger, which he tossed idly from hand to hand. Apart from a loose pair of shorts, he was naked, his shaved head gleaming with oil. His chest was striped with bright red welts, as though he'd been whipped.

Marcus didn't spare the time to think. He grabbed for the pistol, brought it up, and fired. The assassin didn't even break his stride, skipping gently to one side as if dancing, and Marcus heard the ball *ping* uselessly somewhere out in the darkness. He was already scrambling to his feet, clawing for the sword where he'd dropped it, as the young man advanced on him and Jen.

"Idiot," Jen said from behind him. "Get out of the way!"

She gave him a sideways shove, sending him stumbling drunkenly against a statue. The assassin whipped the other dagger at her, bright steel blurring into a line too fast to see. Jen brought her left hand up, fingers splayed, and something sparked in front of her like caged lightning. The knife glanced away as though it had struck a stone wall, and went ringing and clattering off into the cavern.

The young man's face clouded.

"You are *abh-naathem*," he said in Khandarai. "A minion of Orlanko. We have expected your coming."

Jen let out a long breath. A grin spread across her face, a savage joy that Marcus had never seen on her before. She let her arms dangle in front of her, fingers working like a violinist limbering up.

"You pestilential goat-fuckers," she said, in perfect Khandarai. "You have no idea who you're dealing with."

"You think you are the first to come in search of the Names? We have held them for four thousand years."

"Until today." Jen brought one hand up and made a double circle over her chest, the traditional ward against evil. *"Ahdon ivahnt vi, ignahta sempria."*

He blurred into motion, covering the distance between them with the horrible, inhuman speed Marcus remembered from Ashe-Katarion. Jen's hand came up, palm out, and the Khandarai crashed into a wall of brilliant silver sparks just before he reached her. He'd been moving so fast he *bounced*, twisting nimbly in midair to land on his feet. His next attack was more circumspect, circling Jen and feinting a few jabs to test the limit of her defense. She faded backward, raising her right hand above her head.

The assassin guessed what was coming, or else had access to some sense that Marcus lacked, and he dove sideways as she brought her hand down. There was an enormous ripping sound, as though the air itself were being torn, and something flashed out from Jen in a vertical wave. It hit a statue behind where the Khandarai had been standing, a snake-headed thing with tree-trunk limbs, and cut it cleanly in half from top to bottom with a billow of dust. The separated pieces fell to the ground in a cacophony of shattering stone.

Demon. There was no doubt in Marcus' mind, not anymore. Janus had warned him the Concordat was after the Thousand Names, but he'd never mentioned anything like *this*.

He levered himself to his feet and looked around for the colonel. Janus was staring after Jen as she followed the retreating creature. He didn't seem surprised so much as in awe. That wasn't quite right, either, though. Marcus was reminded of the very first time he'd seen the man, holding up a venomous scorpion and watching it twist with the same raw admiration a patron of the arts might show for a masterpiece painting or symphony.

"The Panoply Invisible," he muttered. "Borracio said it passed into Church hands, but . . ." He shook his head slowly. "I never thought to see such a thing."

"Sir," Marcus said. When Janus took no notice, he grabbed the colonel's arm. "*Sir!* We have to get out of here."

"What?" The deep gray eyes blinked and seemed to focus once again on the here and now. Another shower of sparks lit up the clouds of dust flowing away from the battle, accompanied by a screech like a glassmaker's knife across a windowpane.

"Come on," Marcus said, tugging the colonel's arm.

Together they stumbled into motion, heading away from the little campsite and toward the center of the room, where the Seventh Company had made their stand. Janus soon recovered enough to set the pace, and before long Marcus was fighting for breath. Another of the tearing sounds sent them both diving for cover, and more statues exploded behind them.

"What *is* she?" Marcus wheezed, rolling over and putting his back to a stone plinth.

"Concordat," Janus said grimly. "But matters have gone further than I thought. I've underestimated Orlanko's allies."

"Is she really a demon?"

"Someone who has summoned and contracted one, yes. *Ignahta sempria*, the Penitent Damned. She works for the Pontifex of the Black."

"There hasn't been a Pontifex of the Black for a hundred years!"

Janus gave him a grim look, but said nothing. Marcus risked a glance around the corner of the plinth. With the dust of ancient statues, the white gas from the corpses, and the powder smoke, the cavern was full of an unpleasant miasma that made it hard to see much. The air reeked of saltpeter and blood, mixed with the gritty taste of blasted masonry. He couldn't see either of the supernatural combatants at first. A curl of smoke off to his left disgorged Jen, peering around with an unsatisfied expression. She caught sight of Marcus at the same moment, before he could duck back, and an ugly smile spread across her face.

"I wondered where you'd gotten to," she said. "Marcus, if you sit down and wait quietly until all this is over, I guarantee things will go well for you afterward. I owe you that much, for everything we had."

"Everything we had?" Marcus used the plinth to pull himself to his feet, breathing hard. "You're not even human!"

"That depends on your point of view," she said. "But I'll spare you the metaphysics. Just step aside, please."

He gritted his teeth. "I won't."

"Idiot," Jen sighed. She raised her right hand—

The assassin emerged from the smoke like a shark from the depths, hurtling horizontally at an incredible speed. Jen turned to meet him barely in time, and the wall of sparks flared between them. His bare feet scraped for purchase on the stone floor as he leaned against her with all his inhuman strength, fingers flexing to try to tear the intangible shield that guarded her.

Marcus grabbed for Janus again, dragging him back to his feet and away from the statue. He was just lumbering into a run when Jen noticed. Her frustrated scream melded weirdly with the nails-on-glass sound of flashing magic.

Her right hand came around in a fast horizontal swipe. Another ripple tore out, and Marcus threw himself to the floor, dragging Janus down with him. He heard shattering rock behind him as the wave hit a statue, and then the ominous groan and crack of shifting stone. On blind instinct, he rolled sideways, and a moment later bits of rock were crashing down all around him, small fragments pattering off his coat and pinging away across the floor.

When it was over, he raised his head. His blue uniform was coated in a thick layer of pale dust, which cascaded off him as he rose. Chips and fragments of stone lay all around. The main body of the statue, an armored figure with the head of a chimpanzee, had fallen near where he and Janus had been lying. Marcus hurried around it to find that the colonel had thrown himself mostly clear. One of the ape's outstretched arms had crashed down on his leg, leaving him pinned under its weight.

"Colonel!"

Marcus knelt and tried to get his fingers under the statue, then gave it his best heave. The mass of stone barely shifted.

"Leave it," Janus said. His voice was still calm, but Marcus could see the strain in those deep gray eyes. "My leg appears to be broken in any case." He pushed himself up on his elbows, shivered, and lay back down. "Yes. Definitely broken. Get out of here, Captain."

"But—"

Janus turned his head, fixing Marcus with an implacable stare. "What are you planning to do? You can't stop her. The whole regiment might not be able to stop her." Janus gave a cough as the clouds of dust swirled past. "I suggest you go along with her. For the sake of your career, not to mention your life."

"I can't just leave you with her!"

"Go, Marcus," the colonel spat. "Now. That is an order."

"Damn it, Marcus!" Jen's voice drifted through the smoke. Sparks flared again, and Marcus turned and ran.

WINTER

Feor collapsed all at once, as though every bone in her body had turned to jelly. One moment she was scurrying along at Winter's side, the next she was dangling from Winter's hand like a corpse.

At the same instant, distant light flared, cutting through the miasma of smoke and dust that choked the ancient temple. The sound that accompanied it set Winter's teeth on edge, a high-pitched scraping whine that seemed to bypass the ears and resonate directly in her gut. She stumbled under Feor's sudden deadweight, then managed to drag the girl a few more feet and prop her against the base of a nearby statue.

"Feor!" Winter bent over her worriedly. Feor's eyes fluttered open, but she seemed to be having difficulty focusing. "Feor? Can you hear me?"

"I . . . can." Feor blinked.

"What happened? Are you all right?"

"I felt . . ." She sucked in a breath, then coughed. "Power. So much power . . ."

"Is it Onvidaer?"

"No," Feor said. "I have felt his *naath* many times. He is here, but this is different." She looked up, fear suddenly showing in her face. "I think it is your leader. The *abh-naathem*, the sorcerer. He has finally shown himself."

"The colonel?" Winter frowned. *Maybe he doesn't need rescuing after all.* "Come on. We've got to see what's going on."

They took a circuitous route, bypassing the mounds of formerly animated corpses where the Seventh's square had been. There were more flashes of light in the distance, and a sound like a giant ripping sailcloth. Feor flinched each time, though she didn't collapse again.

Hurrying around another of the weird, misshapen statues, Winter caught the gleam of distant light on dull metal. Feor pulled up short, dragging Winter to a halt. They had reached one of the walls of the cavern, and leaning against the dressed stone was a long row of enormous steel slabs, each taller than Winter and several inches thick. Their surface was covered with the densely packed curls of strange script incised deeply into the metal.

Feor sucked in her breath. "The Thousand Names," she said, very quietly. "We have guarded it since the time of the kings of Khandar. The *naath* are inscribed there, to be read by the faithful when Mother judges them worthy." There was a touch of awe in her voice. "I have only seen it once before, when I read my own *naath*."

"Where was that?"

"Another cave, in Ashe-Katarion. Even among the priesthood, few knew of it. The Redeemers tried to find it, but could not." She sounded uncertain. "Mother must have brought it here from the city."

Winter remembered a heavy cart rumbling toward the city gate on the day of the great fire, and nodded grimly.

"She warned us that the Church would stop at nothing to gain it," Feor said. "The minions of Orlanko have schemed against us for decades, and the Black Priests for centuries. They would take the power of the Names for themselves."

"I thought there were no more Black Priests," Winter muttered.

"They are hidden," Feor said, with dogmatic certainty. "But still powerful."

Something flashed nearby with another horrible glass-cutting whine. Feor spun.

"Onvi!"

She ran into the smoke, forcing Winter to hurry to keep close behind her. Statues loomed to either side, wraithlike and monstrous. Ahead, light flared, and as the mists parted, Winter grabbed Feor by the collar to keep her from sprinting right into the open.

Onvidaer stood in a fighting crouch, shifting his weight, ready to spring. Opposite him was a young woman it took Winter a moment to recognize—Jen Alhundt, the Ministry of Information liaison. *What the hell is* she *doing here?* Everything she'd heard about Alhundt, in spite of her title, said that she was a nonentity. And that she was sleeping with Captain d'Ivoire, though that hardly seemed relevant. But . . .

She was smiling, a toothy wolf's grin. And Onvidaer seemed wary. He feinted one way, then the other, then jumped almost straight up in a catlike pounce that took him over Alhundt's head. She slashed her right hand vertically, and a wave of distortion fanned out, passing through space like a ripple across the surface of still water but with a sound like it was tearing the air apart. Onvidaer somehow *twisted* in midair, and the surface of the thing missed him by inches. He reached for her, and Alhundt's other hand came up, palm out. A wall of sizzling white sparks crackled into being where the two were almost touching.

Some trick of momentum held them there for an instant, a perfect still life in the wildly shifting light of the effervescent pinpricks. Then Onvidaer was hurled away. He struck one of the statues hard, his momentum tilting the stone giant into a slow but unstoppable fall. Onvidaer bounced away before it hit the ground, vanishing amidst the grinding crunch of stone and clouds of billowing dust.

Alhundt's attention was elsewhere. Following her gaze, Winter caught sight of Captain d'Ivoire peeking out from behind another statue.

"I wondered where you'd gotten to," Alhundt said, turning toward him.

Winter managed to drag Feor back into cover before they were seen. The girl had gone stiff, her hands curled so tightly that her knuckles stood out as white spots under her gray skin.

"It was her," Feor said. "It was always her. Not your colonel. The minion of Orlanko." She screwed her eyes tight. "How could she hide what she is?"

"The Concordat are good at hiding," Winter said. "Listen. I saw the captain down there, and the colonel might be with him. There's got to be something we can do to help. Can Onvidaer beat her?"

"No." There were tears in Feor's eyes. "He is a brave fool to even try. She holds one of the Great Powers. We have not dared such an incantation in centuries. Not even Mother."

"What about . . ." Winter waved a hand, trying to take in Feor, the library of steel tablets, the cavern full of ancient mysteries. "There has to be *something*!"

"I cannot. I—"

The screech of another shower of sparks drew Winter's attention back to the battle. Onvidaer attacked Alhundt again, with as little effect as before, but the captain took advantage of the distraction to make a run for it. Winter could see another blue-uniformed figure with him. *The colonel?*

Alhundt spun. Another rippling wave flashed out, chopping a chimpanzee statue off at the knees. It toppled toward the two men, exploding into fragments somewhere between them and obscuring her view with a roiling cloud of dust.

"Damn it, Marcus!" Jen shouted.

She spun back toward Onvidaer, but he was on her before she could face him, crossing the flagstones separating them so fast he was a blur. His hand grabbed for hers an instant before the field of sparkling light appeared. The incandescent magic washed over him, but he managed to hang on, flapping away from her in the supernatural pull like a flag in a stiff breeze. Alhundt screamed and brought her other hand around in a wild swing. There was a horrible tearing sound, and blood sprayed across the flagstones in a wide arc. Onvidaer shot across the room, to land somewhere in the mists. Alhundt collapsed to her knees, cradling her wounded arm.

This time Winter wasn't fast enough. Feor darted beyond her reach, headed in the direction Onvidaer had flown. Winter spat a curse and followed.

They found him where his flight had intersected with yet another statue. This one had had scorpion pincers, but not much else was apparent, since Onvidaer had hit it hard enough to blow the stone into a spray of a thousand fragments. Winter watched in stunned disbelief as the Khandarai youth struggled to his feet. Any normal man would have been the consistency of gruel after that impact, but Onvidaer didn't even seem bruised.

He wasn't entirely uninjured, however. Alhundt's swing had taken off his left arm, just below the shoulder, with as neat a cut as a surgeon had ever performed. He had his other hand pressed against the stump, but bright red blood was leaking between his fingers and dripping in a steady patter across the floor.

"Onvi!" Feor pulled up short as she realized what had happened. "Heavens above—what are you doing?"

He was getting down off the plinth, stumbling like a drunk, his previous grace gone. Winter stepped up behind Feor, who stared in wide-eyed horror.

"Going . . . to fight her," Onvidaer said. His breath was ragged. Up close, Winter could see he hadn't come through the collision entirely unscathed. His bare skin was covered in tiny lacerations, and a hundred small cuts wept blood. "Mother . . . wants her dead."

"Mother wanted *me* dead," Feor said. "You've done enough, haven't you?"

"You don't understand. She's one of them." He coughed. "The Black Priests. The minions of Orlanko. We can't let her have the Names."

"But you're not going to stop her!" Feor shouted. She was crying freely now. "You're just going to *die*. Onvi, you don't have to!"

He managed a brief smile. "Mother's . . . orders."

"Then why did you spare me?" Feor sobbed. "What was the point of . . . of anything?"

"Didn't have a choice." He shuffled closer, and Winter tensed, but he only bent awkwardly and kissed Feor on the forehead. It left a bloody smear. "Mother was wrong then. But she's . . . right this time."

"But—"

"Feor. Listen." He shifted his grip on the stump of his arm, blood falling like heavy rain. "I can't stop her. Maybe . . . hurt her. Distract her. A little longer. But you can." She met his eyes, and Winter could see something pass between them. "You understand?"

"But . . ." Feor glanced over her shoulder at Winter, then back at Onvidaer. "I understand."

"Good." He coughed again. "Take care. Little sister."

Then he was gone, running back toward Alhundt so fast there were yards between where one drop of blood splashed the floor and the next. Winter stood awkwardly behind Feor, not knowing what to say. The girl had her arms crossed over her stomach, head bowed, as if she wanted to shrink in on herself and disappear entirely. Winter tentatively put one hand on her shoulder, and Feor flinched at the contact. After a moment she relaxed and let her arms drop.

"Feor?" Winter said. "I didn't follow . . . all of that."

"He's gone to buy us some time," Feor said. There was the slightest tremor in her voice, held tightly in check.

"Time for what?"

"I can . . . help. We can." Feor looked up at Winter, her eyes still wet. The tears had cut clean lines through the grime and powder grit on her cheeks. "You wanted to help your colonel, didn't you? You trust him?"

Winter nodded uncertainly. Feor drew in a deep breath.

"Even if it's . . . dangerous?"

Winter nodded again. Feor wiped her eyes with the back of her hand, smudging the grime across her face, and exhaled slowly.

"All right," she said. "Then come with me."

They retraced their steps to the edge of the cavern, where the enormous steel tablets lay against the wall. Before, Feor had been filled with sacred reverence, reluctant to approach the things. Now she ran along the line, periodically stopping to stare at the lines of dense script. She stood on tiptoe, peering up into the gloom, then shook her head and moved on.

Finally, close to the end of the row of metal slabs, she stopped. One finger traced a long line of script, her mouth working silently. When she reached the end, she looked up at Winter.

"There's something here that can stop her. I think. It hasn't been used since long before I was born."

"Can you read it?" Winter said.

"It's not that simple," Feor said. "*Naath* are jealous things. Mine would not tolerate another power in my body, and the conflict would certainly kill me if I tried."

"But—" Then Winter got it. "You can't be serious."

Feor nodded grimly.

"But . . . me?" Winter shook her head. "I'm not a—a wizard, or anything like that. I don't even think I can *read* this!"

"Only those of us who have been trained can read it," Feor agreed. "But you don't have to. You only need to repeat what I say, exactly. Then, when we reach the end . . ." Feor's fingers ran across the marks on the tablet. "The last words of the spell are *viir-en-talet*. You have to remember that. I will guide you up to that point, and then you complete the *naath* yourself."

"And then what?"

"Then you can confront her." Feor looked away. "If you survive."

"Survive?"

"*Naath* are not for the weak. The power coils around your soul like a serpent, and those who are not strong enough may be crushed by its embrace. I think that you will be strong enough, but . . ."

"You're not certain."

Feor nodded, still not meeting Winter's eyes.

There was a long silence. From somewhere out in the mist came the shriek and rip of magic.

"Viir-en-talet," Winter said. "Am I pronouncing that right?"

"Sit down," Feor said, "and close your eyes."

Winter obeyed, resting against the cool surface of the metal. She leaned her head back and tried not to think.

"Repeat what I say. Do not open your eyes. And whatever happens, *do not stop* before you have said the final words. Do you understand?"

"I understand." Winter's mouth was suddenly dry.

"Very well."

Feor paused, then started to intone the odd words of the language of magic. She spoke slowly, emphasizing every syllable. There were no pauses or breaks, just a continuous stream of sound.

Winter repeated each word a moment later. *"Ibh-jal-yat-fen-loth-see—"*

Suddenly she felt monumentally silly. It all seemed like an enormous practical joke, Feor's earnest voice running through volumes of nonsense words carved into steel by some long-ago shyster. Certainly Winter didn't *feel* anything, no more than she had at the Prison, repeating the Church hymns and prayers by rote.

If this doesn't work . . . If it didn't work, she had no idea what she would do. *Hell, I don't know what happens if it* does *work.* There was no kind of a plan. She was running through a fog, one hand waving blindly in front of her, hoping not to crash into anything solid.

Her thoughts had wandered. Winter hesitated, even as Feor went on. *Was that "shii" or "su"?*

Pain lanced through her. Not the dull ache of her bruises or the hot agony from her side, not any of the fuzzy signals that reached her from the pile of meat, bone, and gristle that she called her body. This was sharp, silver pain on a level she'd never known existed, needles tearing into her essential self. It was everywhere at once—ripping at her stomach, clutching around her heart, driving in through the back of her skull—but she knew somehow that it was in none of those places.

She wanted to vomit. It took an enormous effort of will to fight down her gorge and gasp out the next word.

"Shii." The pain abated, a little. Her memory offered up each word only after a fight. *"Nan. Suul. Maw. Rith."*

She heard—a million miles away—the drone of Feor's voice slow down. There was no time to be thankful, no time for *anything* but the next word.

As though the spikes of pain had shocked her into a greater awareness, she could *feel* the *naath* now. It wound around her like a great black chain, drawing tighter and tighter with every link she added. It was *in* her, under her skin, inside her bones, binding itself to an internal essence Winter had never even known she possessed. She realized, in that instant, that she would never be rid of it. How could she be? The chains were tightening until they were as much a part of her as her hands, her feet, her tongue. The thought brought a sudden panic, but this time her voice didn't stumble. She could feel what would happen if she stopped, as well—the chains tearing away, ripping great chunks of her with them. There was no choice, not now. *Finish or die.*

Feor's voice was growing ragged. Winter wondered if she was tiring. She'd been speaking for what felt like centuries. But when the words started to come in gasps, she understood that it was pain she was hearing. The *naath* drew no fine distinctions between teacher and student.

The end was approaching. There was a structure to the words after all, Winter could see that now, and they were building to a crescendo. Every syllable echoed along the fibers of her body, making them hum in unison. The agony had transformed into something else, halfway between pain and pleasure, the chains of the incantation wrapping around her tighter and tighter as her voice drew them together to weld the final link. The pressure of the thing was terrible. When she snapped that last link in place, she wasn't sure if she'd be able to stand it. It felt as though her soul might shatter in a single instant of near-orgasmic relief, leaving the whipping strands of power to thrash like loosed hawsers and demolish whatever was left of her.

It was terrifying, but there was no going back now. Stop, and the thing would rip her to pieces just the same. Winter mouthed the last few words as Feor fell silent. There was a pause that seemed to last forever, like the moment at the apex of shell's trajectory, before it begins its terrible descent. In the roiling tumble of her mind, Winter saw green eyes, red hair, a sly grin.

"Viir. En. Talet," she said.

Feor gave a shocked gasp, as though someone had punched her

in the stomach. Winter felt the last link snap into place, the shivering tension as the thing squirmed across her, searching for a weakness. Little spikes of pain came and went as the energy squirreled around. Then, as it settled, she became aware of her body again. Her heart thumped so fast she thought it might explode, and her legs trembled and threatened to give way beneath her. She tasted blood in her mouth where she'd bitten her lip, and her jaw ached from tight-clenched teeth. She put one hand against the steel plate for support, finding its surface icy cold against her flushed skin.

She opened her eyes.

Feor lay in a crumpled heap at the base of the steel slab, her breathing fast and shallow. Winter automatically knelt beside her, and nearly fell over herself when she tried to move. Her muscles felt as stiff as the morning after a forced march. She sucked at her lip and touched Feor on the shoulder. The girl's eyes fluttered open.

"Are you all right?" Winter said. Feor's skin was far too pale, her normal gray lightening to almost ghostly white.

"You . . . made it."

"I'm alive, anyway. I think it worked." Winter could feel *something* different. The *naath* had worked its way into her, insinuating itself into the core of her being and sinking down like a toad at the bottom of a pond. It lay quiescent, for now, but she could feel it every time she took a breath.

"It worked," Feor said. "You're alive." She grimaced, her back arching, and her breath became ragged.

"What about you?"

"Don't know," Feor said. "Never tried this. Listen. Just . . . touch her. The *abh-naathem*. Call for the power."

"Call for it how?"

"Will. Just . . ." Feor twisted again, her hands spasming. "Just will it to act."

Her breath hissed past clenched teeth, and she went limp. Winter caught her before she slid off the tablet and hit the ground.

Her skin was hot to the touch, and her pulse hummed. Her eyes were screwed tightly shut.

Bloody buggering Beast, Winter thought. *What the hell do I do now?*

Chapter Twenty-Six

MARCUS

Marcus could recognize a tactical stalemate when he saw one.

Jen stood near where the Vordanai had entered, between two of the statues, where she would have a good view of anyone trying to leave. She didn't want him getting outside to rally the Colonials against her, but she didn't dare search for him for fear he might slip past her in the smoke. So she waited, and he waited with her.

Which would be fine with me, under other circumstances. Given enough time, the survivors of the Seventh Company would organize some sort of rescue attempt. *Or Mor and Val will, once the story gets around.* No telling how long that would take, though, and in the meantime the colonel lay among the drifts of Auxiliary corpses, his crushed leg trapped under half a ton of stone. Marcus desperately wanted to wait by his side, but he didn't dare. He couldn't see Jen from there, and if she got too close . . .

Instead he scuttled through the mist, searching the scattered gear for something he could use to try to kill the girl he'd begun to think he was in love with. There were muskets in abundance among the dead Auxiliaries, and he'd filled his pockets with cartridges. Now he was going through the loading drill with one weapon after another, stacking them against one of the statues.

"Come on, Marcus," Jen called. Her voice echoed strangely through the smoke-filled room, coming from every direction at once. "We both know how this has to end. Don't drag things out."

"Why?" he said over his shoulder, trusting to the echoes and the smoke to keep his position hidden. "Are you planning to let me live?"

"If you behave."

"Forgive me for dragging it out, then." He had four weapons ready. Putting two under each arm, he ran over to another pile of corpses and set about gathering more. "If we're just waiting around, would you mind satisfying my curiosity?"

She gave a heartfelt sigh. "Will it make you come out any faster?"

"It might."

"You're stalling. Your precious colonel didn't look healthy, you know."

"Humor me," Marcus growled, ramming another round home. "You said you were a clerk."

"I lied about that," Jen said. The half-playful tone in her voice was so familiar it made him want to vomit. "I lie a lot. It's part of my job."

"What about the rest?"

"The rest of what?"

Marcus tore open another cartridge with his teeth, tasting the salty powder on his lips. He spat the ball down the barrel of yet another musket. "You know. Us. Did you ever really give a damn about me?"

Jen sighed again. "What do you want me to say? 'At first it was just an assignment, but after everything we've been through . . .' " She snorted. "Honestly, you ought to have known better. It wasn't exactly difficult to earn your trust. All I had to do was show a little fear, a little vulnerability, and you came riding over like a white knight in a storybook."

"I believed you," Marcus said.

"Of course you did. I knew you would. It's all in your file. It makes for some interesting reading, actually." She paused. "How about it, Marcus? Would you like to know the truth about the fire?"

"I know the truth," Marcus said, ramming the ball into place and tossing the ramrod aside.

"Are you certain?" He knew exactly the kind of smile that would be on her face. "It does make *very* interesting reading."

He had seven muskets. It was probably enough. *She won't give me time for seven shots.* Marcus picked up the first one, blew out a deep breath, and stepped out from behind the statue. Jen was just barely visible, a shadowy figure in the uneven light of the distant bonfires.

"I thought I was in love with you," Marcus said.

"Poor Marcus," Jen said caustically. "All he wanted—"

Marcus pulled the trigger. The weapon went off with a ear-shattering bang, delivering the usual mule kick to his shoulder. A flood of white sparks exploded around Jen, but Marcus was already moving, snatching up the remaining muskets and hurrying to the cover of another statue.

"What exactly are you trying to accomplish?" Jen said, as another ball ricocheted off her invisible shield and whined into the darkness. "Or is this just one of those doomed last stands you military types are so fond of?" He took another shot, this one missing by yards. She laughed. "I suppose I can oblige you."

Marcus, fighting for breath, threw himself to the ground. There was a sound like the world tearing in two, and the statue he'd just left exploded into flying shards. Jen took a few steps forward unhurriedly, and leaned forward to peer through the smoke and dust. Marcus rolled to his feet, leveled another musket, and fired. This time the shot was dead on target, and for an instant he could *see* the ball, squashed motionless against the field of livid sparks. Then it was hurled outward, almost straight back at him, and he ducked as it pinged off stone behind him. Jen was laughing.

Three shots left. She would be expecting him to move again, so he grabbed one of the still-loaded muskets and fired from where he was. The shot went high, but he didn't wait around to see the result. Last two weapons in hand, he rolled sideways, scrambling to his feet just as Jen blasted out a stone-chipped crater with a lazy wave.

Another statue loomed in front of him. This one was a lobster with two humans in its claws, raising them above its head. Marcus wondered idly if it was exalting them or getting ready to snip them in half. He raised a weapon to his aching shoulder, sighted on the vague silhouette that was all he could make out, and pulled the trigger. The hammer clicked home, and something sizzled, but the shot didn't go off. Bad powder, maybe, or a block below the pan. *We always did give the Auxiliaries junk.* It was too late to regret that particular decision of His Majesty's Ministry of War now. Marcus snatched up the last weapon and charged.

Jen was standing beside one of the statues flanking the entrance, hands spread wide, still smiling. Marcus skidded to a halt at twenty yards and brought the weapon to his shoulder. Her expression was almost pitying as she brought her hand up—

—and turned, at the crunch of stone on stone. The statue beside her, the well-endowed grasshopper, began to topple in a slow, awful arc. At its apex, riding it down, was the young assassin, spattered with blood but still baring his teeth in a rictus of defiance.

Jen raised her left hand, fingers splayed. The wall of sparks sprang into being, its glass-cutter screech climbing to a wail that rose and rose until Marcus could feel it in his teeth. White sparks turned dull red, then crimson, flaring wildly under the strain of holding a ton of stone in midair.

Marcus sighted down the barrel of the musket. Twenty yards. Not an easy shot, not with a worthless Auxiliary musket, loaded in haste, but far from impossible. He was never going to get a better chance, that was certain. He pulled the trigger, and felt the jolt against his shoulder.

He had a sudden vision of Jen—not *this* Jen, this horrible parody, but the woman who'd leaned gently against his shoulder as they crossed the Tsel. His mind's eye watched her gunned down, musket ball taking her in the stomach and blowing out through her back to leave a wound the size of his fist. Blood on her lips, her last, shuddering breaths. Her eyes, staring up at him—

The shot was wide. He saw it spark against the stone wall and hum off into the distance. Jen's grin became an animal snarl, and she brought her other hand around in a vicious swipe. The roar of the rippling wave filled the world, striking the grasshopper statue head-on. For a moment, nothing seemed to happen. Then Jen turned her hand like a man twisting a knife in a wound, and the statue and the assassin exploded together with unbelievable force. Fragments of rock zipped past Marcus, as fast and deadly as any load of canister.

He turned to run, throwing away the useless empty weapon. It was a dozen steps to the nearest statue, but it took a thousand years to cover them, expecting another one of those awful waves to strike him at any moment and smash him to paste. He passed that statue and would have kept going, but something snagged his sleeve. Marcus spun to find a young man holding on with both hands. He blinked slowly.

"Lieutenant . . . Iherngląss?"

Ihernglass nodded. "Captain. I need your help."

WINTER

Leaving Feor had been among the hardest things Winter had ever had to do. The Khandarai girl seemed barely alive, pale and unresponsive, her breath shallow and her pulse humming. Nothing

Winter had tried seemed to make any difference. In the end she'd dribbled a little water across Feor's lips, covered the girl with her uniform coat, and left her among the ancient steel tablets. It felt like a betrayal, but she couldn't see any other option.

She could feel the *naath*, coiled within her. It had settled down somewhat, like a man sinking into a favorite armchair, but every so often it would *shift* unpleasantly and she would feel the world swim around her. She swallowed hard, fighting off nausea, and crept as quietly as she could through the maze of statues.

Ahead, brilliant light cut through the miasma, along with the more familiar yellow-pink flash of a musket. There was another shot, and another, followed by the ripping explosion and the clatter of stone. Winter pulled up short at the sight of the captain raising a musket to his shoulder. He fired into the murk, and a moment later there was another explosion and a rain of stone. Whatever effect he'd been hoping for, that apparently wasn't it, because he turned and ran. Winter caught up with him and grabbed his sleeve. He spun, panicked, then finally recognized her.

"Lieutenant . . . Ihernglass?"

"Captain. I need your help." Winter looked over her shoulder, toward where the light had been. Nothing was visible now except an expanding cloud of dust. "Is that Alhundt?"

"It's her," he said. "Or a demon wearing her skin."

"What about the colonel? Is he—"

"He's trapped under one of the statues," the captain said. "I think he's all right for now, but he won't be if Jen gets a chance at him."

"Saints above," Winter swore. She chewed her lip. *Touch her*, Feor had said. She found herself wishing the girl had been a bit more informative. *Touch her* where*? What do I do then? How long does it take?*

"What are you doing here?" the captain said. "I thought—"

"I'm not sure we have time to get into it." Another thought had been preying on Winter's mind. It wouldn't take Bobby, Folsom, and Graff long to figure out she'd stayed behind. Bobby, at least, would insist on coming back in to look for her. *Brave young idiot that she is.* Graff might be a voice of caution, but he wouldn't wait forever. They'd gather up some kind of a rescue party and come searching. *And when they do, they'll run straight into Alhundt.* "We've got to stop her."

"I'm open to suggestions." The captain sagged against a statue's plinth and ran his hands through grimy hair. "At this point I'm not sure I'd try it with anything short of a siege gun."

"I may have a way," Winter said. "It's . . . hard to explain. I need to get close to her."

"*Close* to her? What, and slit her throat?" The captain frowned. "I think our Khandarai friend has proved pretty conclusively that doesn't work."

"It's not like that." *I hope.* "This is . . ." Winter drew in a long breath. "Magic."

"Magic," the captain said flatly. "You?"

"I know it seems crazy," Winter said. "But—"

He waved a hand. "The things I've seen today, I'm not sure I still believe in crazy. But *you*—you really think you can stop her?"

The *naath* gave a twitch, as though it could feel when it was under discussion. "I do."

The captain leaned back, eyes closed, for a long moment. When he looked up, his expression had hardened. "All right. What do you need me to do?"

"Thank you, Captain."

"Marcus. Call me Marcus. At least until we get out of here."

Winter waited in the shadow of one of the statues, listening for the sound of footsteps.

The statue was some kind of lizard, rendered with a terrifying mouth full of fangs, each impaling a screaming miniature figure. Whatever god it represented seemed like a particularly unpleasant one. *Probably judging the sins of man, or some such. It seems to be a popular theme.* There had been frescoes in the church at Mrs. Wilmore's depicting sinners writhing in the torments of hell, while a cadre of saints looked on. The painter had given the blessed ones a set of rather self-righteous expressions, Winter had always felt.

If tired old Father Jellicoe was to be believed, what Winter had done back among the steel tablets was a sin worse than any murderous rampage or carnal debauchery. What awaited her upon her earthly demise would make her envy the sinners in the fresco. Being whipped and violated with red-hot pokers would seem like a vacation. Or so she assumed, anyway. She'd always dozed during sermons, and in any case the nearsighted priest had been a bit vague on the specifics. But willingly consorting with demons and magic was heresy by any lights, and deserving of divine retribution when the time for judgment came around.

All the more reason to put it off as long as possible. Her mouth was dry. From where she was sitting, she could see one of the statues Alhundt had shattered. Fragments of stone and gravel had sprayed for yards in every direction, as though someone had packed the thing with powder and set it alight. What that would do to flesh and blood she couldn't imagine. Or, more precisely, she could imagine it all too easily.

"Jen?" It was the captain's—Marcus'—voice, somewhere off to her left. "Jen, I'm here. I'm not running anymore."

"Oh, really?"

Alhundt emerged from the smoke some distance away. She'd discarded her spectacles, and singed hair was escaping in wisps and strands from her tight bun. There were burns and scorch marks down her pants and vest, and a few stray splatters of blood. She cradled her left hand in her right, as though it pained her.

"I'm done," Marcus said. He stood between two statues, some distance past the one behind which Winter was hiding. "It's over. Any idiot could see that."

"Any idiot could have seen it right from the start," Alhundt said. "I suppose it took a while for the news to trickle down to *you*."

Marcus raised his empty hands. "As you say. I give up."

The Concordat agent stared at him, eyes narrowed. "I should cut you down right now."

"I can help you. You said it yourself."

"You could." Alhundt started forward again. "If you really meant it. But I don't buy it, Marcus. I *know* you. You missed your place as a knight-errant three hundred years ago. Always defend a lady, always stand by a friend, and never betray your lord." She gave a heavy sigh. "You do a good job of hiding it, though. I admit when I first met you I thought you were a little more . . . pragmatic."

"Then cut me down," Marcus said.

"There's the Marcus I know," Alhundt said. "Always ready to take a bullet for the cause." She stopped, ten paces from Marcus and just short of the statue where Winter was hiding, and gave him a long look. "So what's the plan this time? Got a pistol shoved up your ass?"

Marcus winced. "I don't know what to say."

"It won't work, whatever it is. This isn't a game of cards with the other captains. You're up against the Divine here."

"Jen . . ." Marcus hesitated.

Alhundt started forward again. "Just do it. Get it out of your system. Maybe that will finally convince you."

She passed Winter's statue, barely a yard away. Winter tensed.

Now or never.

When Alhundt took another step, Winter sprang, rounding the plinth with one hand extended. The moment seemed to stretch, as though she were running through molasses. Her fingers were inches away from the Concordat agent's back when Alhundt spun, graceful as a dancer, and brought her left hand up. A wall of scintillating sparks snapped into existence, and Winter felt herself leaving the ground. A moment later she slammed against the belly of the lizard statue, pressed upward against the stone by a force so strong it was a struggle just to draw breath. Through the screeching, fizzing wall of light, she could see Alhundt step closer, hand extended, head cocked to one side as though examining a fascinating insect.

"*This* is your plan? Have some idiot boy try to stick a knife in my back while you keep me talking?" She snorted. "Honestly, Marcus, I would have thought that even *you* could have come up with something better than that." Alhundt peered closer. "Has he even *got* a knife? What were you going to do, boy? Try to strangle me?"

Through the scream of the sparks, Winter could barely hear Marcus' voice. "He's a distraction."

There was the thunderclap of a musket going off in close quarters. The force holding Winter up abruptly vanished as Alhundt turned away, and Winter fell heavily across the stone lizard's taloned feet. The Concordat agent was facing Marcus now, her unearthly reflexes having easily deflected the musket ball. Her other hand came up, ready to unleash a devastating wave of force that would tear the captain to shreds—

Something felt like it had given way in Winter's chest. Pain radiated from her much-abused side, as if she'd been stuck with a knife, and even drawing breath was a painful effort. It took all the energy she could muster to extend her hand a couple of feet. Her fingertips brushed Alhundt's shirt. With a supreme effort, she tugged herself forward and pressed her palm into the woman's back.

Do it, she told the *naath. Come on. Whatever it is you do,* do it*!*

Something flooded out of her. She felt the *naath* rush through her chest, down her arm, through the tenuous contact and into the other woman. At the same time, she could sense Alhundt's power, a spiky, twisted thing coiled around her essence like a wall of thorns. It flared as Winter's *naath* leapt the gap between souls, and pure energy sparked and coiled on a plane far from the merely physical.

Alhundt screamed. Winter would have joined her, but she didn't have the breath.

The two entities slammed together. Or *joined* together, mixed but separate, like oil and water. Wherever they touched, dangerous energy crackled. Winter remembered what Feor had said about *naath*, that they were jealous things, and she suddenly understood the girl's pain. During the recitation, she had had this conflict roaring inside her, as the half-complete incantation warred with her own. *Maybe that's what the* naath *does. Tears people apart with the force of their own magic.* But whatever Alhundt was feeling, Winter also felt, echoing down the link between them. *So does it shred me as well?* The prospect left her curiously ambivalent. She seemed to have passed beyond fear.

Something was changing. On the boundaries, where the magics sparked and warred, one of them was giving way. Winter's *naath* expanded, oil spreading out as the water retreated. It *converted* the other into more of itself, twisted and pummeled and restructured it until it could incorporate the foreign thing into its own fabric. The process began slowly, then accelerated, change running through Alhundt's magic as fast as thought could follow. Then, where there had been two warring powers, there was only one. Winter's *naath* flooded back through the link, diving back into the depths of her soul like a monster returning to its cave, sated with its kill.

The link broke. It felt like hours had passed, but in the real world time had barely moved forward at all. Winter's hand fell away, flopping limply against the plinth. The screech of Alhundt's magic ended abruptly, leaving a tooth-jangling hum echoing in Winter's ears. The Concordat agent herself crumpled on the spot, folding like an empty sack to sprawl bonelessly on the flagstones.

The sound of Marcus running was distant, irrelevant behind the shooting pain that wracked Winter's body. Darkness closed around her. She closed her eyes and surrendered, gratefully, to unconsciousness.

Chapter Twenty-Seven

MARCUS

"*Are you certain?"*

Jen lay on the bedroll, arms at her sides, left hand wound round with bandages. They'd dressed her in whatever could be scrounged from the stores, all much too large. The sleeves of the white shirt overhung her fingers, and the army-blue trousers had the cuffs rolled up like a little boy's. Marcus had retrieved her spectacles, one lens cracked through, and set them beside her head.

He couldn't help staring at her. With her features at peace, she looked like the woman who had cried on his shoulder and shared his bed, rather than the unholy monster she had revealed herself to be. The movement of her chest was so slight, the whisper of air through her lips so faint, that he felt if he looked away they might cease entirely. He rode with her in the carts during the day, and stayed with her in his tent at night. What sleep he did manage was brief and troubled.

No doubt the paperwork was piling up, but Fitz would take care of it. Marcus took his meals alone with his silent patient, and waited. Everyone knew just enough to leave him alone.

"Are you certain?" She'd implied there was more in his file that he knew . . .

The tent flap rustled, and there was a knock at the pole. Marcus looked up.

"Who's there?" His voice was still hoarse from that horrible day at the oasis.

"Janus."

Of course. Marcus sat in silence for a long moment, indecisive.

"May I come in?"

"Go ahead."

The tent flap parted. Janus' left leg was bound up in wood and linen, and he supported himself with a crutch under that arm. He slipped inside with surprising dexterity and hopped over to Marcus' camp chair.

"I hope you don't mind if I sit," he said. Marcus nodded dumbly, and the colonel settled himself down and stretched his splinted leg in front of him. "It could have been much worse, so I suppose I should be thankful. Still a damned nuisance, though."

"Worse?" Marcus said.

"The leg."

"Ah."

Marcus lapsed into silence again. Janus regarded him thoughtfully, gray eyes glittering.

"Another day," the colonel said, "and we'll be at Ashe-Katarion. The fleet should arrive the day after that."

"That's good."

"I'll be going back to Vordan on the next courier run."

"And taking your Thousand Names with you," Marcus said, letting a hint of bitterness into his voice.

"Yes." Janus leaned forward. "Does that bother you, Captain?"

"You never cared about any of this, did you? The campaign, the Redeemers, any of it. It was all . . . a means to an end."

There was a pause. Janus cocked his head.

"I can't deny that it was part of my plans," he said. "But I think you do me an injustice. I was commanded to destroy the rebels and restore the prince, and I have done that to the best of my ability."

"Only because it furthered your private war with the Last Duke." Marcus turned to look down at Jen. "What about the Colonials?"

"The Ministry of War will no doubt find a new commander. I'm sure it won't be long until some colonel disgraces himself badly enough to deserve it."

"Ah."

"On the other hand . . ." Janus paused. "The job is yours, if you want it."

"Mine?" Marcus blinked. "I can't. I'm not—"

"Not nobly born, I know. But conferring a colonelcy on a commoner is not *entirely* without precedent. I'll certainly speak for you, and I suspect my word will carry a great deal of weight on my return. Provided you agree to stay here for the remainder of your career, out of sight of anyone who matters, I believe the Ministry could see its way clear to authorizing the promotion."

"Oh." Marcus paused, not quite able to bring himself to offer any thanks.

"It's the least I can do," Janus said. "Assuming that's really what you want."

"I'm not sure I follow you."

Janus sighed. "May I speak frankly, Captain?"

"Of course, sir."

"You should return to Vordan. You're too good an officer to waste his days in a sinecure. We're going to need men like you." Janus paused. "*I* am going to need men like you."

"What?" Marcus felt a flush of anger rise into his cheeks. "You *need* me? You've spent this whole campaign keeping me in the dark—"

"I told you as much as you would accept." Janus flashed a brief smile. "Honestly, Captain, if I'd told you the truth when I first arrived, you would have thought I was mad."

"I'm half sure you're mad now." Marcus gritted his teeth. "My men *died* chasing that thing across the desert. I had to stand by and watch you sign my best friend's death warrant. What makes you think I want to have anything to do with you ever again?"

"Because I think you are a patriot, Captain. Loyal to your country, and to your king."

Marcus stared at the colonel for a moment in stunned silence.

"You may not like it," Janus went on, "but you cannot deny what we saw. The Penitent Damned, the elite servants of the Pontifex of the Black, working hand in glove with Duke Orlanko's Concordat. Evidently the Last Duke's association with the Sworn Church has gone well beyond a casual alliance. If we do nothing, Orlanko will take power, and Vordan will be as good as ceded to Elysium." He nodded at Jen. "In the hands of people like *her*. We'll have the Priests of the Black back in the cathedral, rooting out heresy with knives and hot pokers. The Great Schism all over again."

Another long pause.

"Even if I believed . . ." Marcus hesitated. "Even if I believed *any* of that, what assurance do I have that you would be any better?"

Janus smiled again. "All the more reason to come with me, Captain. If the day comes when you believe I no longer have the kingdom's best interests at heart, you'll be in a position to do something about it."

Marcus said nothing. His eyes went to Jen. Janus caught the expression and frowned.

"You know what she was," he said. "Is."

"I know," Marcus said. He was quiet for a moment. "The cutters don't know what's wrong with her."

"Unsurprising. It's a bit beyond their area of expertise."

"Is she going to wake up?"

Janus blew out a long breath. "In all honesty, Captain, I don't know. What happened to her was . . . unique. I would not have expected her to survive at all. Given that she has, she might wake up tomorrow, or in a month, or not at all. And if she wakes . . ." He hesitated. "I don't know how much will be left of her."

"You don't know."

"I don't. I'm sorry."

"Did you study my history before you came here?" Marcus said.

Janus nodded. "Of course."

"Then you know what happened to me. To my family."

The colonel ducked his head. "A tragedy."

"They all died. That's what they told me, afterward. I wasn't there, you see. I was still at the College. By the time I got home they'd gone ahead with the funerals. Visiting the cemetery was all I could do. There wouldn't have been anything left to see, anyway. The whole house burned."

Janus nodded.

"All dead," Marcus said. "But Jen . . . when we were in the temple, she said . . ."

"Are you certain?"

There was a long silence.

"I don't want to hold out false hope for you, Captain," Janus said. "Orlanko and his creatures are masters of deceit. There may have been no more truth in it than in her affection for you."

"I know. But—"

"You want to know for certain."

Marcus said nothing.

"If the truth exists anywhere," Janus said, "it's buried under Orlanko's lair in the Cobweb."

"I'll dig it out," Marcus said. The anger in his voice surprised him. "With my bare hands, if I have to."

"Come with me," Janus said. "I swear I'll help you, if I can."

After a long moment, Marcus nodded.

WINTER

Winter pushed the tent flaps open cautiously, and blinked in the full glare of the morning sun. Scrubby grass underneath her feet meant they were no longer deep in the Desol. Ahead, the land fell away in a spectacular cliff. Beyond that, stretching to the horizon, was the sea. The water was deep blue against the cloudless Khandarai sky, and she could see tiny white-tipped waves far below. The air smelled different—salty, and somehow *alive* compared to the baked, dead atmosphere of the Desol. Even the heat was moderated by a cool breeze blowing off the water.

She'd awoken to crisp linen sheets and a surprisingly small amount of pain. Some of her wounds were bandaged, while others had been closed with fine silk stitches that were already sinking under the surface of newly healed skin. Her side still hurt when she touched it, but not nearly so badly as it had. When she lifted the sheet to examine her skin, she saw that the mass of bruises had turned a startling yellow-green.

Waiting at the foot of her bed was her uniform, freshly laundered, the various cuts and abrasions expertly stitched and patched. Beside it was a brand-new coat, with a lieutenant's stripes properly sewn into the shoulders.

Outside, a white fabric awning threw its shadow across a wooden table and a couple of chairs set with pillows. One of them was occupied by Colonel Vhalnich, who was reading a book with his legs stretched out on a cushioned footrest. He looked up at the rustle of the tent flap, then shut the book and flashed her a brief smile.

Winter saluted, heels coming together to straighten her painfully into a parade-ground stance. The colonel winced in sympathy, and gestured to the chair.

"Please, Lieutenant. Sit down and relax."

She unbent cautiously and settled into the chair. His gray eyes regarded her thoughtfully.

"I would get up to greet you, but . . ." He waved a hand at his legs, and she noticed that one of them was bound by a wooden splint. "I've been waiting most anxiously for you to awaken."

"I—"

He held up one finger. "To anticipate your initial questions: We are on the coast, four miles east of Ashe-Katarion. Your corporals and those of the Seventh Company who escaped the caves with them are fine, and have been asking quite urgently after your health. And you have been unconscious for approximately twelve days."

Winter blinked, trying to make room for all that. "Twelve . . . days?"

"Indeed. Our return from the Desol was dusty but uneventful. The same could not be said for your injuries, I'm afraid. For a time you were in serious danger."

Winter remembered feeling as though her lungs were ripping themselves to shreds with every breath. It seemed distant, like something from a past life. "Do I have you to thank for my recovery?"

"You do," he said matter-of-factly. "While I hate to cast aspersions on the humble army cutters, their knowledge tends toward the practical, and their approach is often . . . blunt. If the problem cannot be removed from the patient with a bone saw, they are often at a loss. Fortunately, medicine is among my fields of study."

"Then you saved my life. Again."

He inclined his head. "After you saved mine." The colonel held up his hand again, ticking off more fingers. "To be more precise, you came to save mine, I saved yours, you returned to rescue me once again, and I again managed to be of some service afterward." He raised an eyebrow. "It seemed only polite."

"What about the others who were in there?" Winter drew a sharp breath. "Feor! What happened to Feor?"

"She would be the Khandarai priestess who accompanied you?" At Winter's hesitant nod, Janus gave another fast smile. "She is fully recovered, I believe. Your Corporal Forester claimed her when he led the rescue party into the temple. I was in no condition to give advice at the time, but fortunately it proved to be unnecessary. The wounds magic inflicts on the spirit are painful, and can even be fatal, but they fade quickly compared to the more physical sort."

She's all right. Something unknotted in the pit of Winter's stomach. She'd been convinced that Feor was dying, that the reading of the *naath* had been an effort of grand self-sacrifice on her part. *Hell, maybe she thought it was.*

"I haven't been able to let any of them come and see you," the colonel continued, "as I didn't know which of them were privy to your secret."

"Ah. That was very considerate of you."

"As I said, it seemed only polite."

There was a pause. The clink of glass on glass made Winter look up, and she was startled to see a servant in formal black pouring wine from a carafe. He handed her the glass with a grave expression, and she sipped politely. It was iced, and the chill felt good against her lips.

"Thank you, Augustin. Leave the rest."

"My lord," Augustin murmured. He ghosted away.

"That leaves us," the colonel said, reaching for his own glass, "with the main issue."

"Oh?" Winter did her best to match the man's casual tone.

"How much do you understand of what happened in the temple?"

Winter's cheeks flushed. She drank, to cover her embarrassment, and found the wine surprisingly palatable. "Not much. Alhundt was trying to kill us all, and Captain d'Ivoire and I stopped her."

He glanced at her, his expression unreadable. "I'm not surprised that you'd pretend ignorance. To be knowledgeable is to be involved, after all, and you must know better than anyone how dangerous that can be. However, I believe we are beyond that point. Whatever you know, or don't know, you are involved now, and so I ask not in some attempt to entrap you into revealing your hand but simply so that I do not waste your time with explanations."

"If you say so," Winter said carefully.

"Trust me." He leaned forward. "How much do you know about what has happened to *you*?"

She shrugged. "Only what Feor told me. She recited a *naath*, something that was engraved on those steel plates, and I said it along with her. Then I finished it alone."

The colonel winced. "No wonder she was unconscious. Did she tell you anything about the nature of the . . . *naath*?"

"No. Only that I could use it to stop Alhundt."

"And when you did?"

"It was . . ." She found it hard to put into words. "It was like whatever was inside me reached out, into her. It found the magic inside her and—I'm not sure. It—"

"Devoured it," the colonel said.

"I suppose so."

"Remarkable." He looked at her curiously. "And how do you feel now?"

"All right, I guess." She looked down at herself. "A hell of a lot better than I expected to."

"An expectation I might have shared, had I known what you and Feor had tried." He paused, as though searching for words. "The . . . thing that you have, call it a *naath* for the sake of argument, is one that is known to us, though only distantly. It was discovered in the wild only once, more than a thousand years ago. The Church of the time called it 'Infernivore,' because to them it was a demon that fed on other demons. It resisted every attempt to learn its name, and eventually its host died under the not-very-tender ministrations of the Priests of the Black. In time, however, rumors reached the Church that either the Infernivore or a very similar entity had been discovered in Khandar, among the great store of knowledge we call the Thousand Names."

There was so much that Winter didn't understand in that statement she hardly knew where to begin. She seized on something familiar. "Feor mentioned the Black Priests. I thought they were shut down a century ago."

"Officially, yes," Janus said. "As far as history is concerned, the Priests of the Black expanded their remit from the elimination of the supernatural to meddle in the realm of politics and doctrine, which is true, as far as it goes. In the aftermath of the Great Schism, the Pontifex of the Black lost much of his standing, and the Obsidian Order was eventually disbanded."

"But?" Winter prompted.

"Elysium took the opportunity to purge the rot and return the Priests of the Black to what they had been. They operate in secret, searching out demons and magic in all its forms. Just because they are no longer publicly acknowledged does not make them any less dangerous, however."

"I thought Alhundt worked for the Concordat."

"The interests of His Grace the Last Duke," the colonel said darkly, "align very closely with those of the Pontifex of the Black. It doesn't surprise me in the least to find them working hand in glove."

"But—"

"All of this is a bit beside the point," the colonel said. "At least for the moment, as far as you are concerned."

"So what *is* the point?"

"I also knew the Infernivore was here. I came to Khandar to get it, along with the rest of the Thousand Names."

"*You* did?"

"Of course. I've made a study of magic, you know."

He said it so blandly that Winter nearly choked on her wine. She wiped her mouth with the back of her hand, then said, "So now you've got what you wanted?"

"In a way. Except that you and Feor have taken the greatest prize of the lot."

That made her sit up straight. Winter coughed, then met his level gaze.

"Can't you just . . . recite it yourself? You have the plates, I assume."

"Not without killing you first. Once a Name is spoken, it's bound to the one who speaks it. Another attempt would be pointless."

"So . . ." Winter's eyes flicked down to the wine, then back to the colonel. "Are you planning to kill me?"

To her surprise, he laughed out loud. "You have a truly dour view of authority, Lieutenant. I suppose it suits you."

"It seemed like where you were headed," Winter said. "Kill me, and take this Infernivore for yourself."

"For one thing, reciting the name of the Infernivore is extremely risky. I was planning to undertake it only if there was no alternative. Given the power of the thing, I estimated the chances of survival at no better than one in seven. That you were able to do it with no training at all is frankly astonishing. Given that such a risk has been run, it seems a shame to waste the results."

"Oh." Winter's mouth was suddenly dry. She fumbled with her wineglass.

"Besides, I have taken a liking to you. You are bold and innovative in the field, dedicated to your subordinates, and loyal to those who earn your trust. You also seem to have a habit of saving my life, which is certainly something I would like to encourage. To be frank, Lieutenant, I want to offer you a position."

"A position? On your staff, you mean?"

"Something to that effect, yes. The specifics can be worked out later. I'll be returning to Vordan in a few days, and once I get there I think there will be a great deal of work to be done. I was hoping you could be of some assistance."

"I'm flattered," Winter muttered. "Do I really have a choice?"

"Of course you do. We will be engaged in some extremely delicate maneuvers when we return home, and I don't want anyone by my side whose support is less than wholehearted. If you don't wish to involve yourself, then I will not make an issue of it." His smile came and went within a heartbeat. "I can't promise that the Last Duke and the Church will do the same, of course."

"Of course," Winter said. So there was no real choice after all. *Except* . . . "What's in it for me?"

"Anything reasonable that's within my power to grant," the colonel said immediately. "What is it you want, Lieutenant Ihernglass?"

Winter closed her eyes. She saw a face, as she always did—red hair, green eyes, a bold, sly smile.

"There's someone I want you to find," she said. Her voice rang distantly in her own ears. "An old friend."

"I can't promise success," he said. "But we can certainly make the attempt."

"And my corporals. I want them to come with us."

"Certainly. In fact, I suspect the entire regiment may follow, given the recent news."

"And Feor. There's nothing left for her here."

"As you wish." The colonel cocked his head. "Is there anything else?"

"I'll let you know if I think of anything."

He smiled again. "Of course."

Winter hesitated. "What did you mean, 'the recent news'?"

The colonel raised his eyebrows. "Oh my. I'd forgotten you hadn't heard. There was a courier from Vordan while we were gone."

"Has something happened?"

Janus steepled his fingers. "The king is dying."

EPILOGUE

JAFFA

The Seal of the Grand Justice of Ashe-Katarion was a heavy, unwieldy thing, all carved marble and gold leaf. It spent most of its time in a steel lockbox at the back of Jaffa's office, and he sealed his day-to-day correspondence with an ordinary wooden stamp. Tradition dictated that the official seal be used on a few occasions, however, and one of those was to adorn the Grand Justice's letter of resignation. Jaffa let the gray wax drip onto the paper, waited a few moments, then awkwardly pressed the massive seal home. It left the rearing-scorpion symbol of the prince, with a decorative border of eyes that marked the Justices.

And that was the end. The job to which he'd dedicated his adult life was over. Jaffa-dan-Iln sat back in his padded chair, with the loose, squeaky armrest he'd never gotten around to fixing, and let out a long sigh.

The gatehouse bustled around him with unparalleled activity. The prince's agents had been busy, hiring new men and promoting those who'd remained loyal during the Redemption. Those who had switched sides were being eased out. Not too ostentatiously, of course. The Vordanai commander had expressed his confidence in the Justices, and Jaffa probably had that to thank for the fact that he hadn't been marched to a public execution as soon as the prince felt secure. But the last missive from the Palace had left no doubt as to what was expected of him.

For Jaffa, it hardly mattered. Mother was gone, vanished into the Great Desol, and with her the cause of Heaven that he had come to so late and so fervently. His newfound certainty had vanished with her.

There will be a sign. There must be a sign.

He had decided that he would try to find her. Pointless, of course, given the extent of the Desol, but at least it was a direction. He would take as much food and water as a good horse could carry, and set out into the desert. Either the Heavens would guide him, or he would leave one more set of dusty bones under the dunes.

When he pushed his chair back from the desk and stood, sand crunched under his boots. He frowned, tossed the sealed letter on his desk, and crossed the room. His official sword belt and truncheon hung from a peg behind the door, and his fingers brushed the leather before he realized he wouldn't need them. They belonged to the prince, after all.

Something whispered through the little office. It was in the depths of the gatehouse, far from any openings to the outdoors, but it nonetheless seemed to Jaffa that he felt a faint breath of air. The great logbook of the Justices, lying open on a side table, fluttered its pages slowly, like a lazy bird. Jaffa took a breath and tasted the hot, arid wind of the desert.

There was sand everywhere. Not just on the floor, where someone might have carelessly tracked it, but on his desk and on the bookcases. It was moving, grain by grain, tiny flecks tumbling over and over as though caught in the wind. A patch of gray and brown collected in the center of the room, rose into a little pyramid, and started to grow.

Jaffa fell to his knees and lowered his head. The pile of sand grew larger, accompanied by the keening of the desert wind. As it widened, it took on shape, forming first a rough-hewn mannequin and then a recognizable human form. It was a young woman, naked and beautiful, with skin that turned smooth but remained the mottled colors of the desert. Her eyes were two chips of obsidian, black and so glossy the candles around the room glowed in their depths like distant stars.

"Jaffa," she said. Her voice was a dusty creak, a hiss from the depths of the Desol.

"Mother," Jaffa said, and bowed lower, until his forehead touched the floor.

"They have all failed me," Mother said. "All but you."

"I will never fail you."

"I know. Rise, Jaffa."

He got to his feet. She strode closer, mottled patterns shifting under her skin. He wondered what would happen if he touched her—if her skin would be as smooth as glass, or if his hand would pass through her like an oar through water. Her full lips twitched in what might have been a smile.

"I have a gift for you," she said in her ancient voice. She pressed one hand to her stomach, the flowing sand of her fingers melting into her belly as though she were rummaging in her own innards. She withdrew an object, skittering grains rippling around it like water. Its surface glistened as if it had been oiled.

Jaffa took it from her outstretched hand. It was a blank mask of raw steel with two rectangular holes for eyes. Jaffa hefted it in his hand, feeling the weight of it.

"What would you have me do?"

A ripple passed across Mother's face, like the crest of a dune shifting in the breeze.

"First," she said, "you must find us a ship."

Coming soon from Del Rey:

THE SHADOW THRONE

The next instalment in Django Wexler's incredible Shadow Campaigns series

The King of Vordan is dying, and his daughter, Raesinia, is destined to become the first Queen in centuries – and a ripe target for the ambitious men who seek to control her.

But politics knows no loyalties, especially for Duke Orlanko, spy-master and the most feared man in Vordan. He will bow his knee to no Queen, unless she is firmly under his influence.

Freshly returned from their recent victories abroad, Colonel Janus, Marcus d'Ivoire and Winter Ihernglass must defeat the Duke, using muskets, magic and every weapon at their command.

Also available from Del Rey:

THE CLOWN SERVICE

By Guy Adams

'If the Security Service is The Circus, then Section 37 is where we send the clowns'

Toby Greene has been reassigned.

After one screw up too many, he finds himself at a largely forgotten branch of the British Security Service, working for August Shining, a Cold War relic, and charged with defending the country from paranormal terrorism.

But when an ex-Soviet-era enemy returns with an insidious plan to raise the dead and destroy London, it seems Toby's impossible job is to save Great Britain – whether he believes it or not.

'*The Clown Service* is fun and rips along like the finest episode of the old *Avengers* series'
The Independent on Sunday